WHITE CROW

Also by Mary Gentle in Gollancz:

Ash
Orthe
Ancient Light
1610: A Sundial in a Grave

WHITE CROW

Mary Gentle

First published in Great Britain in 2003 by
Gollancz
An imprint of the Orion Publishing Group
Orion House, 5 Upper St Martin's Lane, London WC2H 9EA

A CIP catalogue record for this book is
available from the British Library

ISBN 0 575 07519 8

Typeset at The Spartan Press Ltd
Lymington, Hants

Printed in Great Britain by
Clays Ltd, St Ives plc

FOREWORD
Gargoyles, Architecture and Devices

I suppose I ought to nail my colours to the mast, here, and announce that these novels and stories are in fact science fiction – apropos of which: in the days of sail, nailing one's colours to the mast meant that you then couldn't pull on those handy ropes and bring your national flag down, signifying your surrender. One wonders how many fearlessly defiant warships in fact went to a watery grave with the crew desperately shinning up the mainmast with bolt-cutters, crying, 'We've changed our minds!'

I feel that ought to be relevant, somehow, if I'm proposing to answer the question of why I'm writing science fiction as if it wasn't.

The sequence of stories and novels that feature Valentine White Crow and Baltazar Casaubon starts with 'Beggars in Satin' and 'The Knot Garden' (fantasy), then moves on to *Rats and Gargoyles* (Hermetic SF) and *The Architecture of Desire* (alternate history) and currently finishes with *Left to His Own Devices* (cyberpunk). So: why do it that way?

The first reason, and not the least, is: for fun.

'Beggars in Satin' and 'The Knot Garden' are written this way for fun. No, really. But what, you whimper, has that got to do with science fiction? Here is a red-headed woman with a sword. Here is a large man in 18th century clothes, with a pork chop in his pocket and a rat on his shoulder. (And sometimes the other way around.) They live in a world of hydraulic engines, magical conspiracies and very big demons. They are both showing more interest in getting their leg over than in the ostensible plot. This has sex and comedy in; it can't be SF!

Especially when, in fact, the two novellas are a love story, *Rats &*

Gargoyles is a political soap opera, *The Architecture of Desire* is a nasty little rape case and a love quadrangle, and *Left to His Own Devices* is a thumbed nose at cyberjunk. So why are they written in a way that makes them look anything else but?

I came across a beautiful quote in *Foundation 64*, in which J. Michael Straczynski, of *Babylon 5* fame, lambasts an endemic mediocrity in the SF field – and, more to the point, the consequences of that mediocrity: 'Cookie-cutter sf novels and worn-out fantasy clichés that pollute the field, diminish reader expectations, and degrade the taste and selectivity of the readership.'

This is why, when I say that there are jokes in *Rats & Gargoyles* that only three people in the world will understand and one of them is dead, this is not an apology.

This is why, in *Left to His Own Devices*, the story of what is really going on is written in iambic pentameter.

This is why, in 'Black Motley', the versifying Music Hall 'Queen's Memory' is interacting with alternate-world versions of Gladstone, Disraeli and a multiplicitous member of the family of Saxe-Coburg-Gotha . . .

And, I hope, these things are pleasurable.

But really – would you rather be told that all you want to read is soggy secondary-world fantasy? Police-identikit characterisation, in engineering SF? Sexist dominatrix versions of cybertrash? Tired-out alternate histories to which there is no alternative? True, there can sometimes appear to be a hundred publishers' editors out there who base their salary on the opinion that all we *can* read is brain-candy: Biker elves; gelded 'mediaeval' fantasy; watered-down mythology and jazzed-up *New Scientist*. Books that do not speak irony. Room-temperature-IQ material, and Centigrade at that.

I know, and I suspect you know, that readers are not like that unless they're made to be like that, unless, as Straczynski says, their expectations are systematically diminished and their taste degraded. And then we stop reading brain-candy for fun, for analgaesia, for something to do on a train journey; and start reading it because it's all we can cope with.

And then, guess what? That becomes the fiction that's published.

And that, I hope, is merely a gargoyle to frighten us. There are plenty of current SF writers who take no prisoners on that front, who believe that multiple layers are valuable in any text, and that anything good enough to be serious in the doing is too good to be solemn about.

Gargoyles, then. Gargoyles are weird-shit architectural jokes: fanciful and grotesque decorations with at least two purposes –

scaring demons, and shifting rainwater off the roof. Jam the physical and the metaphysical together and what you may get (if it's done right) is exhilaration. I started writing 'Beggars in Satin' while I was – for reasons which escape me, but fun was certainly one of them – doing an interdisciplinary MA in 17th Century Studies.

I came home and got off the train at my local station, and Valentine White Crow, Scholar-Soldier and member of the Invisible College, got off a steam train in a fantasy world.

Except it wasn't fantasy, I immediately saw – not big-book, multi-series, mediaeval-Europe-except-for-the-gribblies, capital-F, Fantasy. It was science fiction. No, trust me. It just isn't the science you're probably used to. I was besotted with the early 17th century worldview, especially that part of it called Hermetic science, which says that the world works on magical patterns and resonances, but it works predictably, scientifically. It was never a comfortable ideology: Giordano Bruno, prominent Hermeticist in AD 1600, was burned alive by the Roman Catholic Church for holding forth about this animate universe in which men may become demi-gods by their own efforts, and there are divine spirits in everything, right down to the level of stones and trees.

Valentine went on from her steam-train to find the Lord-Architect Baltazar Casaubon, the oversized love of her life, in a concrete Memory Garden – 'concrete' in the sense that it made material the Renaissance 'Art of Memory', a mental device for remembering words by first memorising visual images. I suppose that building a physical representation of a mental concept could be considered superbly redundant – but then, that's what the story's about.

I like the technique of using the appearance of Fantasy to slide the concepts of SF under the reader's consciousness. It means you get to do all the pyrotechnics and brightly coloured machine parts, but from a rigorous base. And, if the science in question is the model prior to our current one, it means the reader is continually disoriented.

You might not think this is an advantage. True, I could have written the *White Crow* books as historical novels – it's a perfectly possible choice, the Invisible College, for example, being a matter of record. Or I could have written them as current science fiction: time travel, say. But . . . then they're in danger of becoming train-spotter narratives. I have no intention of being followed around by the Reality Police, accused of inaccurate descriptions of the Kings' Memory's total recall . . . or being told that six-foot-tall rats aren't physiologically viable.

On the other hand – or paw, possibly – it matters that I get it *right*: that a sword weighs *this* much, and cuts like *that*, even if it's being handled by a six-foot-tall talking rat. That the logical consequences of there being five points of the compass in the city at the heart of the world, still all 90 degrees apart, are followed through. (Just try drawing the frontispiece map to that!) Naturally our hero keeps getting lost . . .

And it matters that alchemy works like Hermetic alchemy worked, and not like genre fantasy D&D plot-device magic.

And the only way I could get intellectual rigor and flash-bang-WTF-was-*that*? into the same narrative form was to disguise science fiction as fantasy. And, I must confess, sometimes disguise fantasy as science fiction . . . except for *Left to His Own Devices*, which is a Jacobean tragedy disguised as political cyberpunk, but more of this later . . .

The fact that Valentine and Casaubon shift universes, handedness and number of children is another useful technique to keep the reader alert. I owe this one to Joanna Russ's terrific 'Alyx' stories, which I found disturbing in all the right ways when I first read them, in my teens. I think she might be the writer who convinced me one was allowed to put sex and politics in SF as well.

Personally, I have a great appetite for weird stuff, and that kind of straight-faced spoof – like Eco putting Sherlock Holmes into *The Name of the Rose* – which mediaeval scholars would have called a *ludibrum*. However, I also object to losing my footing totally – so *Rats and Gargoyles* uses the technique of one shock at a time: it opens with the judicial hanging of a pig, then brings on young Prince Lucas. Lucas is not too bright, but he doesn't know what's going on either, and at least he's human. Throw in an unknown woman divining the magical 'weather' by a reflection of blood on the moon. Revert to Lucas being flirted at by a young woman: a reader will feel reassured, and comfortable with flirting as a concept. The young woman has a tail. The young woman is a dyke. Now move on to the six-foot-tall talking – or in this case, Machiavellianly plotting – rats.

The reader will keep up.

Trust me. It'll make sense in the end. Would I lie to you?

Not here. Readers can dislike an unreliable narrator. It's the *Richard III* principle: your protagonist can be as devious a bastard as possible to anyone else, provided he is straight with us, the audience. And so there's Johanna Branwen, Valentine's mother in *Left to His Own Devices*, who is completely unapologetic about what she is. After all, who says focal characters in SF/F/H have to be restricted to the emotional development of a first-year college student? Why shouldn't we want to identify with a five-star, solid gold, mid-fifties *bitch* from time to time?

And that brings me to a device, or a piece of architecture – at any rate, to a keystone of all the *White Crow* stories. I adopted it from the Hernandez Bros's wonderful comic, *Love & Rockets*. I could equally well have adopted it from film's camera-eye, or the theatre (Renaissance plays are a constant undertow in these stories, from Casaubon's oblique relationship to the dramatist Ben Jonson, to the jamming together of unmixed raw farce and tragedy). It's a device: it's pure technique. Almost never, in these stories, will you read where a character 'thinks' or 'feels' something. You see what they do, and you hear what they say. How you judge them, thereafter, is up to you. *You do not know what they think.* I couldn't have tried to do justice to these people if I'd had the reader listening to the voices inside their heads.

I've done my best to present the physicality of that snowed-in, not-quite-Puritan London: the smell of stone, and the taste of blood – and, in the same way, the physicality of Valentine and Casaubon's bodies, and the audibility of their speech. If I've done it right, there is more space for the reader to work out why what happened, happened, more than with the writer leaning over your shoulder going *That was immoral!* or *That was heroic!* One should trust the story: one should, similarly, trust the reader.

It's reasonable, I suppose, for writers to be considered ego-maniacs. How else could anyone sit down and think, oh, I guess I'll write a novel on the off-chance that x-thousand people might like to read it? I mean, *what?*

But it's the *story* that comes first, long before any thought of readers or writer.

When I see a story done wrong, I want to do it right. When I see SF and Fantasy novels that insult the intelligence of a weevil, I want to write a novel with an academic reading list in the back of it. Or one that bases a lot of obscure English Civil War jokes on the conceit that Charles Stuart and Oliver Cromwell might, in some other quantum world, be female.

When I get up to *here* with cyber-utopias fronted by dim young men who do not know where their dicks are, Valentine starts making waspish remarks and gets herself a job with the military-industrial complex. When I have seen more gaming fantasy-magic than even *I* can take, I want to write about a magic that works by pictorial association from a vocabulary of Baroque images.

And when I see SF written with a crew from central casting, and a political stance as naïve as the headlines of *The Sun*, then I start writing about trade unions in demon-ruled cities, near-future SF about Valentine and Casaubon's messy personal-political home lives, and Marlowe's take on the information revolution and Fortress Europe.

So here they are, three long stories and three novels, sort-of-sequels to each other; infested with gargoyles that stare at you, grinning, as they contemplate their desires and ours. I leave you with the repertory company – Valentine, Casaubon, their friends, their enemies, their deities – entrusting you to them in the reasonable expectation that, since I could never exercise the slightest control over them when they were infesting my mind, you, the reader will have little better luck.

They may rearrange the furniture, invite in unruly friends, and keep you up of a night-time, but they will be, I hope, pleasant tenants.

Mary Gentle
Hertfordshire
2002

CHRONOLOGY

am not responsible for the order in which these people live their lives. Normal service will be resumed when you close this book.

This book is dedicated to
G. K. Chesterton and James Branch Cabell

ACKNOWLEDGEMENTS

I owe a debt to those investigators who have treated Renaissance Hermetic *magia* as a field for serious scholarly research. The fact that I have treated it as one vast adventure-playground is not intended to detract from this.

Those who helped include Goldsmiths' College, University of London; the albums *I'm Your Man* by Leonard Cohen and *Famous Blue Raincoat* by Jennifer Warnes; Watkins Books in Cecil Court; Rouen; and Alexandre Dumas. I also owe a debt to Sarah Watson for reading the manuscript, and for letting me read her (unpublished) 'The Jaguar King'.

Beggars in Satin

A Scholar-Soldier got down from the steam train, outside the City gate.

Chancellor Scaris called, 'Master-Captain!'

Yellow dust settled down.

She shifted the strap off her shoulder, setting her bundle down at her feet – a satchel holding scrolls. Her sword-hanger was plain. The sword-hilt was wrapped with leather, stained with sweat.

As she bent to adjust the buckles that held scabbard and sword, a braid fell forward. There was grey in her cinnamon-tawny hair, and at her temples it was growing out white. But when she straightened up and squinted against the sun, there were few lines about her eyes: she looked no more than thirty.

Scaris called again. His words were lost in the noise of the train: the steam, the pistons, and the whine of the siren as it pulled away from the city gate in haste. Nevertheless, she looked directly at him.

He walked across the gate-place to where she waited.

'You're the Chancellor?' she said. 'Scaris?'

'And you the Scholar-Soldier Valentine.'

'Why am I not received as that deserves?'

The hard smell of coal and steam was still in his mouth. Sunlight gleamed on the iron rails, and the clanking of the cars faded. The woman's head tilted, listening.

'Why is there no one here?'

Chancellor Scaris looked at the sandstone walls, now unpatrolled; at the gates that stood unguarded. Grass grew in small golden tufts on the street. No market-stalls, no carts from the provinces; no distant fall (felt through the soles of the feet) of the piledrivers on the building-ground.

'Would he send for you,' Scaris said, 'the Lord-Architect Casaubon, would he send for you if he didn't need you?'

Walking the lanes beside the little man, Valentine trod the earth easily. Some few citizens stared out of shutters as they went by, faces hooded. Most of the leaning two- and three-storey buildings were daubed across the windows with silver paint, that glittered in the sun.

The satchel weighed heavier on her back than its load of scrawled paper would seem to justify.

She glanced down at Scaris.

'My business is to know and to fight,' she said. 'The sooner you tell me what you have here, the sooner I'll get rid of it.'

'Master-Captain, wait—'

'Call me Valentine,' she said, 'and tell me why your Lord-Architect needs a Scholar-Soldier?'

He blinked up at her through white hair that the wind blew across his eyes. Dust stained his embroidered black satin robe; heavy in the summer heat. She saw it was cut to disguise a slightly humped shoulder.

'You're very sure of yourself,' he said.

'Oh, see you, I've fought a dozen of these matters out in the last year; I was at Karsethra, with the Master-Captain Lindsay, and at Baynard with Tobias Frith, and I assure you, there's not a Scholar-Soldier better for your contest than Valentine . . .'

Scaris's eyes narrowed.

'And for finding out your causes, first and secondary, your sources and origins, and many methods of discovery—'

'There is none better than your Valentine?' he completed, drily.

The lanes became wider. They had to detour round an abandoned carriage, the ox dead in the shafts and buzzing with flies. Valentine saw a figure scuttle across the road ahead, too far away to tell if it were child or man.

'Master-Captain,' Scaris said.

'Well, sir?'

'Whatever we have,' he said softly, 'it is no shame to be afraid of it.'

Valentine's boots clacked on stone. Cracked paving sprouted goldenrod and wild roses. She sneezed, abruptly, hit by pollen; and then hitched her sword-belt over her shoulder with one hand, and swung the satchel by its strap with the other.

'I don't know the meaning of the word "fear",' she said. 'Terror, yes; blind panic, yes; but fear? Me?'

Scaris laughed. It was an unfamiliar emotion. He looked the woman up and down: her cinnamon hair escaping from its six Scholar's braids; her tanned hands; her rough cotton shirt and breeches. She was still talking:

'—at Mildenhall I was the only one not to run, when Master-Captain Eliade fainted dead away on the spot, and then in Hurot, but you wouldn't know the university barracks there—'

Chuckling, Scaris held up a hand to stem her chatter, and a swiftness passed him, swift as a bird's flight, or a bee, and a bead of blood grew in his palm, drawn out by its passing. He yelled. Pain, bright as metal, stabbed him.

Valentine, ceasing the deliberate flow of inanity, drew her sword left-handed, and swung the bulging satchel into her assailant's stomach. He doubled over with a *Whoof!* and the flat of her sword slammed into his temple.

'Captain!'

Warned, she ducked. Scaris pressed himself back against the wall of the nearest house, feet scrabbling, seeking a doorway to hide in. He yelled again. Valentine parried the other assailant's blow, and – as easily as if the man had consented to it – lifted his blade with hers and spun it away across the street in a great flashing cartwheel of metal and sun. She was caught wrong-footed for a thrust, and by the time she recovered, the man was running.

'Leave him!' Scaris said, as out of breath as if he had been the one fighting.

The Scholar-Soldier lifted her blade in a brief salute. Then she sheathed it, and knelt down to roll over her unconscious assailant. A man, dark haired and with a reddish-dark beard, he was of middle years. There was a smear of some semi-transparent substance across his forehead. She touched it: brought away fingers blotched with silver paint. She looked up at Scaris:

'Now is this a common cut-purse, or sent for you, or sent for me, do you think?'

Scaris's blood hammered in his ears. The man was sprawled on his back on the paving-stones, beard thrust up towards the sky. The silver paint on his brow caught the sunlight.

'My guards have shut themselves away, for fear,' he said. 'And no one knew that you were coming here, Master-Captain.'

Valentine sucked a grazed knuckle. She knelt again, to pack the scattered papers from her satchel. Scaris watched her walk past him and pick up the thrown dart, inspect the tip, and toss it away.

'No venom,' she said. She tugged out her kerchief and took his hand, wrapping the cloth round the cut on his palm. Scaris shuddered. Then, thinking how that must seem, looked up, and met her eyes (that were almost more red than brown) and said:

'Thanks, Valentine.'

She hesitated before she smiled.

'We must *hurry*,' Scaris said.

The Lord-Architect Casaubon saw them arrive.

So deep and so blue a summer's sky shone over the city that it made the marble of the buildings dazzle. The great fretted façades held angular pieces of sky trapped, in their interstices: blue on white.

Floridly carved white columns, and rows of pillars, and covered walks, stretched away around all four sides of the square. Beyond the towering blocks that were the marble-faced palaces of the City, Casaubon saw domes, curtain walls, house façades with niches and statues. But it was the square itself that dwarfed the man and the woman.

They came through the great Sea Gate, whose marble breakers reared up fifty feet, ready to crash down in stony surf. A little man in black robes, his head at this distance no bigger than the head of a pin; and walking with him a figure in brown, equally ant-like . . .

Casaubon shrugged to himself, dug his fingers into the aspic-jar and pulled out another White Gull, ripped the wing from the body, and began to gnaw it. Spots of gelatine spattered his blue coat, unbuttoned to the waist. He stopped chewing for a moment, his eye caught by the proportions of the half-built wall in front of him – he dropped the cooked meat, scrabbled with filthy hands across his plan-table, and began to draw a succession of swift pencil-lines.

A minute of this, and then he ceased. He rubbed thoughtfully at the inadvertent marks of grease on the paper. Suddenly, he ripped it in two, threw it upwards, and let the wind bowl it across the wide acreage of the square, towards the approaching man and woman.

The woman loped five strides out of her way to snare the blowing paper: by that, Casaubon knew that she must be the Scholar-Soldier. He snorted to himself, knocked the neck off a bottle by rapping it on his drawing easel, and began – with delicate care – to drink from it.

And to wonder what he would say.

Valentine scrolled up the torn paper between her calloused hands. She paused, once, to look at a particular mark. Her curiously-coloured eyes blinked. Scaris, out of breath, grabbed her arm for support; and found his triceps caught in the strong fingers.

'No, no – unneccessary—'

White hair was sweat-plastered to his forehead.

'—the Lord-Architect—'

Valentine, amused, pushed the old man towards a low wall,

saying, 'Sit down before you fall down!' Then she dropped her satchel at Scaris's feet, and turned to make her bow to the Lord-Architect Casaubon.

She stood at the foot of a shallow, walled flight of steps. A table and a metal easel stood on the first landing. Above that, the steps went up to end at a rough brick wall, and a stretch of cleared ground, two half-built walls of marble blocks, and a tower smothered in wooden-pole scaffolding.

The Lord-Architect sat on the top step, his belly spreading over his thighs, the top two buttons of his breeches undone. He seemed about to burst the seams of his yellowed shirt and filthy blue satin coat. The sun gleamed on his tarnished brass buttons, and buckles, and on the bottle in his hand. Valentine judged him to be forty, perhaps forty-five. His fair skin was freckled, his red hair straggled down past his collar, and his hands were stained pitch-black with charcoal.

Casaubon ripped a mouthful from the capon in his free hand, half-saluted her with the bottle, and, spitting out fragments of food, said, 'Master-Captain! *Welcome*. Scaris, you fool, who frighted you? You're white as a headstone.'

'Noble Lord—'

'May the Great Architect rot your soul, you piddling little puppy! I've eaten better Chancellors than you for breakfast.'

Casaubon wiped his mouth with a filthy hand. He slammed the bottle down on the step beside him, and beckoned to Valentine.

'You took your time getting here,' he said, suddenly ungracious. 'How much are we paying you? You should have been here a week since!'

'If not for my – I won't say, valour, but take it how you will – neither of us would be here, noble Lord.'

Valentine stood with her fists on her hips, chin raised, staring up the flight of steps. And then she ran lightly up past the noble Lord-Architect, to the cleared building-ground and the half-built walls. She squatted on her haunches, and put a hand to the earth.

Without turning, and in another tone altogether, she said, 'You're building a Miracle Garden. I congratulate you, noble Lord. True, Vitruvius authorises a more westerly aspect, but I think you'll find Palladio differs in that, claims the northerly frontage no less efficient—'

The Lord-Architect Casaubon put his podgy fingers in his mouth and whistled. After a pause (and, by his frown, too long a pause) the square began to fill with running people: officers, guards, cellarers, stewards.

'Very like,' he answered Valentine, and then broke off to gesture to the officers. They set about dismantling the easel, removing the table, and replacing empty wine-bottles.

'Very like,' he repeated, 'if it weren't for this: that I have enemies. Master-Captain, have you heard of the Invisible College?'

Chancellor Scaris limped up the steps, resting every so often on the marble balustrade. He caught Valentine's eye, as she glanced over her shoulder.

'The noble Lord Casaubon has heard of the enmity between the Scholar-Soldiers and the reputed Invisible College. Tell me, Valentine, is there truth in that?'

The woman stood up. She tucked one of her loose braids back behind her ear; and Scaris saw again how white she was at the temples, and how young she was to be so. Behind her, earth and broken marble shimmered in the midday heat. The noise of the people in the square seemed oddly muffled. Where he stood, beside Casaubon, Scaris's nostrils wrinkled at the smell of old grease and cooking, and unwashed linen.

Valentine, with that new seriousness, said, 'Before I tell the noble Lord what I know of the Invisible College, the noble Lord must tell me why he's building a Garden, and what Garden it is, and what this Garden is for.'

'Rot you,' Casaubon said. 'I suppose I must.'

As she walked a few paces to the east, sighting on another half-built structure, Valentine saw the building-ground open up before her, and all but gaped at the extent of it. A tract of earth some two or three miles square had been slashed into the very heart of the City. Part showed traces of formal gardening. Most was overgrown: goldenrod, bramble, vine, and ivy tendrilling up towards the sun. She hid her amazement; stood looking, with condescension, one hand on the sand-abraded hilt of her sword.

'I'll show you the part of the Garden that I've succeeded – for the time being – in building,' Casaubon said. 'Scaris, stay here. You know it. No need to wrack your old bones for this. Master-Captain, this way.'

Scaris eased himself down onto the balustrade. He watched the fat man, and the woman, as they walked out onto the cleared building-ground. Heat made him sweat in his black robes. When they were a distance away, he made a sudden grab for the aspic-jar and, like a cormorant, pulled out a fragment of meat and began to munch it greedily.

Before he'd finished, a voice hailed him. He looked up, hurriedly wiping his mouth. The Scholar-Soldier beckoned, pointing back towards him; and he realised that her satchel still rested at his feet.

He picked it up to carry it to her. And was shocked at how little it weighed – as if the scrolls were friable wafers, for all their bulk.

When he reached them, they had walked back as far as the wide marble cup of a dry fountain. Valentine stood with her back to the sun, her shadow falling across the statue that, holding a vase, should give forth water. The noble Lord-Architect stomped irritably up and down. Valentine said something that Scaris didn't hear.

Casaubon spat into the fountain, and wiped his mouth with a lice-ridden sleeve. 'I know – I don't look the man to be searching for *spiritual* food. Do I? Forty years ago I didn't look like this. It's been a long fight. How old are you?' he demanded.

'Eighteen,' the woman said.

Scaris nearly dropped her pack.

'And how did you come by this?' Casaubon's fat finger touched the silver-white hair at her temple.

'It's been a long fight,' Valentine echoed.

Casaubon grunted. 'Come this way. Down here. I'll show you – a year's work, ruined.'

Valentine walked down wide steps into a sunken garden. A patch of order, surrounded by towering weeds. But now, on the cropped yellow grass, among the shaped dells and hummocks and hedges, the disorder could be forgotten – could it?

She reached behind her, without looking, and felt Chancellor Scaris put the strap of her pack into her hand.

A path was paved with square stones; into each square a pattern of interlocking circles was incised. The sun burned on her head. There was the rank smell of Casaubon's clothes. She squatted down, sorted through her satchel, and took out a bent and thumbed copy of a pamphlet. Then she straightened up, and walked on seven more steps.

The path went through a golden hedge, that was cropped into an arch over it, and on one side of the arch was a bronze statue of a child, and on the other a silver statue of an old man.

Valentine stepped onto an incised paving-stone.

Metal whined. A hollow voice, seeming to come from the bronze child, said, '*All bright youth ends soon in age!*'

She took the next step, onto a plain paving-stone, and a different voice sounded, apparently from the silver-metal statue of the ancient man:

'*All reverend age doth to corruption tend!*'

And as she passed under the hedge's arch, the two voices together said:

'*All things decay to the same end!*'

'Is that how you directed them to speak?' Valentine called back to Casaubon. He shook his head. She walked back, treading carefully, this time avoiding certain paving-stones. But when she was seven steps from the path, a hissing metal voice whispered, '*Hasten, hasten, even now your flesh rots on your bones!*'

'That's an ill trick,' she said, 'and a lesser person might be offended by it, noble Lord-Architect; your good fortune is to have me. How long have these automata been like this?'

'The pneumatic mechanisms were perfect,' Casaubon said soberly. 'I have had executed craftsmen who made me inferior work. These people know, now, to work well. This was to be a device to introduce visitors into the Miracle Garden. They were to speak common pleasantries, *Seize the Hour*, and *Love While Ye May*, to put one in mind of the pleasures of the flesh. Great Architect! Who knows what we're put in mind of now!'

A hiss of steam escaped the child-statue. It was almost like laughter.

'I swear, no hand has altered the mechanisms,' Casaubon added. 'They've been well guarded. And afterwards taken apart, and there is no mechanical reason for them to speak so! It must be the Invisible College. Who else?'

Valentine said nothing. Chancellor Scaris moved to her elbow, with a brief side-glance attempting to see what pamphlet it was that she thumbed through. *Pneumatithmie* and *Menadrie* caught his eye, and *Perspective*, *Stratarithmerie*, and *Zographie*.

'See you,' Valentine invited, offering him the open page. 'There is your art of mechanical devices using air or water, that's your singing fountain or your speaking statue – *pneumatithmie*. And your mathematical art used in moving with weights or pulleys, *menadrie*; and – but you know this, I'm sure.'

Scaris said, 'If you were to come this way, Master-Captain, I would show you what part of the Miracle Garden is of my own devising. Although I fear it is in as great a disarray as the Lord-Architect's statues.'

Valentine followed the noble Lord-Architect, who swore foully under his breath, and Scaris, past the speaking statues and into the hedged garden. Here, many metal and stone figures stood on plinths, or in niches. A slow mutter began to grow in the air around, of mockery, and oaths as foul as Casaubon's. The sun gleamed on the golden hedges, on complex topiary, and on the bindweed and ivy that ran riot across fountain, grotto, and fish-pool.

'It's my design to build a Memory Garden,' Scaris said.

Valentine blinked. 'The same as a memory palace?'

'It would have the same locations, in which to place images,' Scaris said. 'Here.'

Passing under another topiary arch brought Valentine into a maze. The close-leafed hedges were trimmed smooth, with a marble pillar and plinth let into them at intervals of five or so yards, and larger topiary niches at the junctions of each maze-alley. Valentine walked down one alley, turned left and then right, right again, left . . .

Silence clung to the garden.

The tawny-gold leaves breathed out a heavy perfume. She rested a calloused hand on the nearest marble pillar, and the stone was hot in the sun. Then, as she turned her head, she jerked her hand away. On the flat-topped pillar, level with her shoulder, stood the painted stone carving of a lion's paw. From its claws, dripping, hung eyes ripped from their sockets.

Five yards on stood another pillar; on it, something from which Valentine swiftly turned away.

Scaris's voice at her shoulder made her spin round:

'This was to be an image to remind me of canon law; it was a cannon, upon it a shield to mind me of how Law shields the community; on that shield five stars, to call to mind the five branches of civil law. You perceive how it works; the rebus is placed here, immediately I see the image, it calls knowledge out of my memory, that would not have come without the causal image.'

The Chancellor shuddered.

'The images *change*. None of my guards have caught the persons responsible. They . . . change in such ways. I think *that*, now, is *lex tallonis*; the law of—'

'An eye for an eye.'

Valentine abruptly turned and walked back out of the maze (unhesitatingly taking the correct turns), her pace too fast for the old man to keep up with her. Out in the open again, she found the Lord-Architect waiting.

'Turns your guts, don't it?' he observed. 'You should have seen what the Erotic Garden became.'

Valentine said sharply, 'The man's a fool. A memory palace or Memory Garden isn't to be *built*, it's to keep knowledge here, in the mind! If I'd to carry all the written down Scholar-Soldiers' knowledge with me, I'd never walk!'

She rubbed her hand across her eyes as if erasing images. More calmly, she said, 'Pictures are more easily remembered than written words, and carry a whole web of associated knowledge. I've a palace memorised – one of Palladio's – and in every palace room a curious image, that leads me to further volumes of memory, so that I only have to walk through the palace in my mind.'

Casaubon shrugged. 'Some of my marble-pillar-of-rectitude Councillors would say we ought to confine that to images of Justice, in an Interior Temple. But Scaris and I thought it a pleasant conceit, to have a material Memory Garden. You see what becomes of it!'

Valentine pushed the tendrils of white and cinnamon hair back from her face with her palms. She squinted up at the sky. Then she turned her tawny-reddish eyes on the Lord-Architect.

'You ripped out the guts of the City to make this,' she observed.

'Geometry is the culmination of the city. The temple garden must stand in the heart of the city, as the Interior Temple is built in the heart of man.' The Lord-Architect Casaubon broke off, shrugged. 'So, you know this as well as I, Master-Captain. I don't need telling how to construct a building, nor what it's for, nor how to lay out a garden, nor what I may put in it and where. All I need to know is where this corruption comes from!'

Chancellor Scaris appeared at the exit from the hedge-maze. His face was red, sweaty; and he appeared more than somewhat embarrassed. The Lord-Architect broke out into a laugh that sent his reeking breath clear to where Valentine stood:

'Lost in your own Garden, master Chancellor? Great Architect, what next!'

Valentine sat beside the Lord-Architect, on the wide marble rim of a fountain. She put her satchel down between her feet, and rummaged, putting one scroll back, taking out another. Casaubon rested his ham-hands between his fat legs and watched her. The fountain began suddenly to play an ordered, formal tune; but so off-key that Casaubon, Scaris, and Valentine, by common unspoken consent, got up and walked away.

'Now I know what kind of a Garden,' Master-Captain Valentine said, 'I need to know why.'

Scaris said, 'Salomon de Caus built such a Garden, once, four thousand years ago. Why not we, ourselves?'

She nodded. 'But why exactly this, and why now?'

Casaubon's deliberate stomp carried the Lord-Architect at a slow walk; Scaris himself was old enough to move carefully. He saw the young Scholar-Soldier slack her pace. Finally she stopped. Brambles here grew in barbed golden arcs over a disc of polished black stone, laid into the earth, in whose centre was an onyx sundial. Their reflections stared up at them, blinded by weeds.

'It's the oldest Art,' Chancellor Scaris said. 'To build. Our Archemasters laid the City out according to just proportion; therefore Justice exists in us. As above, so below. Our Fathers builded high, according to the principles of universal harmony, therefore we were able to build an Empire.'

Casaubon snorted. He wiped at his nose, leaving a glistening trail on one blue satin sleeve.

'Listen to the orthodox mind! Young Valentine, come here. See that? Past the trees, down the slope – *there*. That's the lower city. There's no more justice in there than in my arsehole. Scaris is an old fool. If we don't do something soon, I wouldn't give you a farting farthing for an Archemaster on the open market! That's what the Garden's for.'

Coming in at the gate, Valentine had only seen a few of the City Lanes. Now, on top of this slope, she could look out over mile after mile of them; brick blockhouses, squat foundry-chimneys spouting steam and dirt. They lay under the midday sun like a scab on the earth. But when Valentine looked over her shoulder, she saw that, even so, the lower city was dwarfed by the extent of the City proper: that dream of white marble.

'What will the Garden do?' She shoved the last pamphlet back under the satchel-flap, and lifted reddish-brown eyes to Casaubon's face. He wiped his sweating forehead and left black charcoal smears across it, over the freckles, and the yellow scurf at the hairline. After some searching in his pockets, he brought out a dubiously-coloured kerchief and wiped his face and hands.

'You're the Scholar, tell me about the first Archemaster,' he invited.

'They write that the first Archemaster builded a Tower, and that when it fell, the One Language fell into babble. And that he retired, and wrote how your Interior Temple of the soul might be builded, which,' Valentine said, 'I suppose if I were such a failure, I might do too.'

Scaris was watching her when she said it; he saw the glint of provocation in her eye.

'Oh, his principles are no failure, witness *that*.' Casaubon's fat arm swung in an arc that took in marble palaces, galleries, temples, domes, and the City wall. 'Don't play the fool, Master-Captain. Where *we* err is in building less than we might. We need to raze the lesser city, burn the warrens down, build again from the ground up.'

Let the paupers live well, as our servants do, not fester down there in those plague-stricken hovels.'

He stuffed the brown kerchief back in an inner pocket.

'Still, that's not to the point. Except that until the Garden's built, I see no way of convincing my Council that we need to rebuild the lower city . . .'

Scaris said, 'It's a Garden in which to learn.'

'Learn?'

It was Casaubon, finally, who answered the Scholar-Soldier.

'It's a Garden that will teach wisdom. The One Language, even. Teach us the knowledge that the ancient rulers of this Earth had, before all fell in fire. When those of the lower city come here, it will teach them temperance – and respect. Great Architect! *Now* do you see why the Invisible College sabotages me at every turn? They're known seditious!'

The Scholar-Soldier said, 'It wasn't the Invisible College that tried to kill your Chancellor, and myself, an hour ago. They're called "invisible" for their secrecy, and that attack was hardly secret!'

Casaubon grinned at her waspishness. 'Well, Master-Captain, what now?'

'I'll do something here,' she said. 'First.'

Scaris, beginning to limp and favour one hip now, followed the Lord-Architect and the young woman back through the corrupted Miracle Garden. At almost every plinth, statue, and dry fountain, the Scholar-Soldier paused to affix a paper strip or scroll, pulled from her bulging satchel. Some she weighted down with rocks. Others she tucked into crevices in the stonework. When they arrived back at the steps leading down to the great square, she unrolled a long thin paper streamer, written over with obscure characters, and fixed it from top to bottom of the stairs.

Then she stood, a hand on her sword-hilt, and absently swung the scabbard up and rested it behind her elbows, and watched the Lord-Architect Casaubon wheeze his way down the steps behind her. She frowned.

Still smarting from her earlier insult, Scaris said, 'I would have thought a Scholar with her own memory palace would have little use for written records.'

'The papers? See you, they're not for me to read. They're for others. Other . . . readers. They're warnings.'

A warm wind blew tendrils of hair, brown and silver, round her plain oval face. Her lashes and brows were reddish-brown. They gave her a look, Scaris thought, like a she-fox.

'Give me the rest of today,' she asked Casaubon, as he stepped heavily down into the square.

He coughed, gobbed on the marble, squinted up at the sun that was passing noon, and then glanced back at the building-ground.

'I can see no way to end the corruption – but pulling down what I've built,' he wheezed. 'And to construct something that won't turn into – abomination – I confess to you, Master-Captain, *I don't know how*! Would I have consented to – you coming here, if I could?'

When she looked enquiringly at Scaris, the Chancellor nodded.

'I suggested a Scholar-Soldier might help us. If not . . . if not, Valentine, we have razed the centre of the City for nothing. We can build nothing new on the site, because nothing is built that does not immediately rot.' Scaris tugged the black satin robe away from his neck, suddenly breathless. 'What do you need?'

She said, 'If you're fool enough to build a material Memory Garden here, Chancellor, then I'd wager that this City has somewhere in it a Library. I'll begin there.'

The Lord-Architect demanded thickly, 'Can you do anything in six hours?'

'That's all the time we have,' Valentine said. 'Noble Lord, I've seen this before – once. You don't have long. See you, *I* don't have long; I must be about it. Something is growing in that Garden that you won't like if it fruits. All you've seen yet are buds and shoots. If you let it come to flower, I think corruption will spread out from here into the City itself.'

The interiors of the Library's domes echoed to a faint whispering, the turning of leaves of parchment. Valentine's boots clicked loudly on the tiles as she walked. Heads lifted. When they saw the swagger in her walk, and the deftly-slung sword-blade, they bent immediately to their parchments again. Valentine grinned.

And then, by a stack so tall that the higher scrolls must be reached by a metal causeway, she stopped, and stared down past the crimson-and-blue painted shelves. She squinted in the hot, gold twilight. Then she walked down and stood behind one of the students.

'I need a book and can't find it.'

The student wore a long dark robe, with a cowl pulled up, half-shadowing her face. She looked up from the scroll she held. Valentine knew the sharp, pale young features, her long lashes, and slightly-snaggled teeth.

'Tell me what theosophist book you need,' the young girl asked ritually.

'*Under the Shadow of Bright Wings*—'

'—*In the Heart of The Womb.*' She finished the recognition-code in a whisper, and laughed.

'Janou, I thought it was you!' Valentine glanced round the vast hall.

'How are things in the Garden?'

'Much as we thought they would be. We must not speak with each other here. Where can we go?'

Janou looked up with clear, irreverent eyes. 'You need to see the other half of it, don't you? Come with me. I know just the place.'

The sky over the city was skimmed with cloud now, and a drizzle fell as they walked, turning the yellow dust to mud that clogged on Valentine's boots and Janou's bare feet. The cowled girl led Valentine a swift way out of the marble avenues, into the lower city.

'I thought I'd have no hard time making contact with you,' Valentine boasted. 'Well, we have a friend in the Garden, although he knows it not; and we have an enemy, also, although he thinks I don't know him. They're a strange pair, and like each other indifferent badly. As for the rest . . . I left warnings. And, to say true, I was never so glad to leave a place in my life. That Garden's deadly.'

Janou pushed the cowl back, and scrubbed her fingers through her baby-short hair. It fluffed up fine-blonde in the warm wind. She strutted beside Valentine, with an occasional skip to keep up with the Scholar-Soldier's longer stride.

'I've not been idle, me. Things are happening here that your Architect-Lords don't credit. Wait,' Janou said, 'and you'll see.'

Now, three-storey buildings pressed close together, leaning over the narrow lane, blocking out the tawny-yellow sky. Valentine's neck prickled. There would be a storm soon. She hefted her satchel on its fraying strap, and plodded on after Janou.

The lane opened into a marketplace.

Dirty straw had been thrown down, to make walking over the yellow mud possible. Market stalls offered bruised fruit, meat stinking in the summer heat, and steaming pies. Further over, beasts squealed in pens. A great crowd of people pushed to and fro. Their voices rang off the plaster-and-daub walls of the inns that surrounded the market square: here a herder, playing Three-Cup with a shabby gallant; there women auctioning for egg-money; a tailor spreading out bales of cotton cloth, and swearing when an end trailed in the mud; a company of players setting up on the back of a baker's cart.

'Down this way!' Janou dug her fists in the pockets of her long robe, hitching up the front of it, walking with a kick-heeled strut that Valentine remembered from way back.

She led the Scholar-Soldier down one of the ranks of stalls. By the time Valentine had pushed through the people to catch up with her, Janou had halted. She stood on bare tiptoes, peering up at a man who, in the shelter of the inn-wall, turned the handle of a hurdy-gurdy.

'*Him*,' Janou said.

He had a trimmed beard, and dark hair growing to his collar; and that was all that was visible – his high-crowned hat had a wide brim, pulled down. A broken feather was tucked into his hatband. His broad hand turned the organ-handle, and a bright tune fell into the air, and two or three of the young children in the crowd jigged up and down at his feet.

Spidering across the ground, in a red velvet jacket, a beast with the gold eyes of a snake, and the spindly limbs of a lizard, danced on its hind legs. Some of the men and women who had turned to look threw coins.

Valentine threw down a silver angel. When the man looked up at her, she said, 'I'll buy you a drink for a song, master.'

There was no trace of the silver paint that had smeared his forehead; there was, however, a purple-and-yellow bruise on his left temple.

Janou said, 'He's my singing-bird, this one. Yes, let's drink.'

Valentine grinned at the man. 'We've met, sir, if you recall; but I'd be glad to know your name.'

Feliche sat with his back to the inn-room's wall. His eyes were never still as he talked to Janou, they sought low door and bottle-paned window and cellar-door in rapid succession. Valentine sat with her satchel between her feet, and her knife unsheathed and held out of sight under the table.

The rest of the conspirators sat round the table – two or three men indistinguishable from the hurdy-gurdy man Feliche except by the colour of their beards; a woman in grey cotton with washer-woman's red hands; two younger women, and a boy. They merged into the market-day crowd drinking in the inn.

'I hold to the original plan.' Feliche's deep voice was pitched not to carry beyond their table. 'Kill the Lord-Architect and the Chancellor, and any other of the Archemasters we can reach.'

Valentine, under the table's edge, picked her nails with her dagger. She watched the lizard-ape squatting on the hurdy-gurdy. From time to time it reached down a scaly hand to touch Feliche's shoulder, and the man put a finger up for it to grasp. He was a big man, a head taller than anyone in the inn-room; with a high gleaming forehead and intense dark eyes. He fixed those eyes on Valentine now:

'I had thought we could take powder from the foundries, and blow their marble Council-chamber to fragments, they with it. Then the City's ours, and can stay as it is. We'll have their riches, besides, then.'

One of the younger women put in, 'Keep the halls. Then we can make our own Council. There's people in my Ward, I'd like them to see me a Councillor, and then wouldn't I make them sweat!'

'I, also!'

'And me!'

Under cover of the general agreement, Feliche bent towards Valentine, laying his big hands flat on the rough wooden table.

'Janou told us a Master-Captain would come here. But why were you with that whoremaster Scaris this morning? And Casaubon – I'm told you spoke for over an hour with the Lord-Architect. What were you telling them?'

Valentine studied the bruise on his forehead, where she had struck him with the flat of her sword.

'At least now you stop to ask questions.'

He coloured. 'Then answer me this, Master-Captain – why is a Scholar-Soldier seen in company with one of the Invisible College?'

Another of the men asked, 'Are you and they allies, or enemies as we've always been told?'

Janou, bouncing up and down on the bench, said, 'Oh, see you, we can trust these people, Valentine! Yes, allies and more than allies. Did you not know, the Scholar-Soldiers are only the College made visible? And we, only they disguised.'

'Janou!'

'We need their help,' the girl said stubbornly. She slicked down her fluffy hair irritably, but the heat made it stick up in cat-fur tufts. She pushed the robe's sleeves up to her elbows. 'Valentine, explain the matter to them; we can never act without allies, and these are mine. Whose are yours? The Chancellor and the Lord-Architect?'

When Valentine turned back to Feliche, she saw him hide a smile. She sighed. She saw him smile at that, too.

'What she says is true, Master Feliche. It's put about that we and the Invisible College are enemies, and opposites, for then, no matter of what faction people be, they are bound to employ either the Scholar-Soldiers or the College in these matters – and so we're safe.'

'Safe?' he echoed.

'Oh, see you, there are matters that only we can deal with.'

Feliche nodded at the inn-room's back window. Through it, Valentine saw a rider in cherry-coloured satin; cursing as he pulled his gelding up, waiting for a butcher's cart to pass through the lane. The noise of his oaths came through the open window, with flies and the stink of slaughtered carcases.

'The Architect-Lords would tear our district down,' the big man said softly. 'In these lanes, even a rider has to stop and wait for a cart or an old man to get out of the way. Up in the City, in their avenues, they force us up onto pavements, and leave us nothing to do but watch them ride by in their carriages. It's fair, Master-Captain, if we seek to bring down their palaces.'

The heat made Valentine sweat. She pushed her braids back and up from her neck, for a moment, leaving her knife in her lap.

The light was an odd colour now, almost saffron. The pressure of the approaching storm made horses shy in the lane, and sparked and crackled on Janou's hand when she stroked the inn's cat.

'Did you tell them about the Garden?' Valentine asked.

'We know about the Garden. It's a teaching garden. We've no great wish to see it completed. What's amiss with it?' the washer-woman asked.

Valentine looked round at their faces. Faded skin, with broken veins in the cheeks; blear eyes and silvering hair; even the young boy seemed a little old man. She put her hands under the table again, sought her knife, and dug the sharp tip of it into her forearm. Pain focused her sight. Their faces regained some life.

Janou said, 'What was *that*?'

Feliche, half up off his bench, sat down again, and stared at Valentine. 'She said it – what *was* that?'

'Something beginning to flower.' Valentine sheathed her knife at her belt. She reached down to her satchel, almost as if that comforted her. 'Now hear what I say to you. Janou's right. We need help. The Architect-Lords of this City have stumbled on something that is found, once in a hundred years, perhaps, and when it's found . . . oh, see you, it was because of the first time this happened that the Invisible College was founded. Our grandsires put an end to it then. Now it's up to us.'

The storm-pressure was building; bad-tempered quarrels broke out in the inn-room. Valentine spoke under their noise:

'*As above, so below*. That's the Archemaster's law, and it's true.

Someone said to me in the Garden that if a city's buildings are built in just proportion, and its streets laid out in the laws of universal harmony, then Justice herself is compelled to come down and dwell on earth, there.'

Feliche laughed sardonically. Valentine continued:

'As for Justice, I don't know. But the Invisible College learned long since, that if a thing is built according to certain laws, then it becomes a dwelling-place, and a thing of its nature is compelled to come and inhabit it.'

Feliche rumbled, 'What thing? Built how?'

'Say, a Miracle Garden. There are patterns in number, universal patterns. The Architect-Lords are building according to those patterns, and,' Valentine said, 'I think, truly, they may not know why corruption is happening. But they've constructed a place in which Corruption is compelled to dwell—'

The young boy protested. 'But houses are for people to live in, and gardens are places for people to go. I don't understand.'

Valentine didn't look at the livid sky outside the inn's window.

'We need your help. We need it now,' she said. 'One man in that Garden has begun to love what it holds. I told you things might be drawn down from the rim of the heavens, to us, but did I say that they would be things that human minds could comprehend? If the Architect-Lords razed the lower city, they could only make a wasteland of it. If what is growing in the Garden spreads here, then you'll think that wasteland would have been paradise!'

In the quiet, they turned each one to look at one another.

'I can't believe it,' one man said.

'It's tales, only tales!' another of the men burst out.

'What does she know?' a woman demanded, 'She's only a mendicant lecturer; what does a beggarly scholar know!'

'She just wants to protect the Architect-Lords!'

Janou shook her head, and vigorously rubbed sweat from her upper lip with the back of her hand. Feliche glanced down at the scarred, carved surface of the table. When he looked up and met the reddish-tawny eyes of the Master-Captain, he smiled wryly.

'I don't doubt you seek to fright us into helping you,' he said. 'That would be easily dismissed, except that I believe, also, you're telling the truth.'

Valentine opened her mouth to reply, and was forestalled by another person entering the inn. A man in a dark robe, who pushed the cowl back from his head as he sighted Janou, shoved his way through the crowd to her, and leaned down between her and the washerwoman to whisper.

Janou's face fell.

'They want you,' she turned to Valentine. 'Someone has died. In the Miracle Garden. The Architect-Lords are turning the City upside down for you.'

The cinnamon-haired woman stood up.

'That doesn't give me long here. Master Feliche, will you come with us? Janou, we'll have to arrange things now, and act at once.'

The body lay on the circle of black marble paving that was set into the lawn, with its arms outstretched, as if to embrace the onyx sundial that stood in the centre. In the livid stormlight, the gnomon cast no shadow. A great streak of drying blood dulled the reflective paving.

'Rot him!' Casaubon said, 'I need the old fool for a while longer. Well, Master-Captain, how did he come by his death?'

Valentine, who knelt by the body of Chancellor Scaris, not touching it yet, said, 'Turn this thing over.'

The Lord-Architect Casaubon grunted in surprise. He scratched at his red hair, inspected the scurf under his fingernails, and then made a shrug with his massive shoulders that strained the blue satin coat almost to bursting, and stepped forward. He planted a heavy foot either side of the Chancellor's head, bent down—

'No!' Valentine grabbed his sleeve. She pulled him back several paces from the sundial.

'I'd give an angel's fart to know what game you're playing!' Casaubon swore. 'Bid a Lord-Architect do your errand, then stop him; I don't understand you! And who in the name of the Great Architect are those two?'

Valentine glanced back at Janou. She was leaning up against the hurdy-gurdy man, a fluffhaired child barely level with his collar-bone, as if his physical nearness comforted her. Feliche himself was staring fixedly at the entrance to the hedge-maze.

'We should leave this Garden before we talk about it, noble Lord. No – leave Scaris. He's not about to walk away. See you, *there*.'

Grunting, Casaubon bent into a half-crouch, looking where the tawny-haired woman pointed. It seemed to him as if the dead Chancellor lay in a pool of black water. Then he saw how that impression came about: the old man's head and shoulder looked half-submerged in the shining onyx. But the body was resting on the surface of the stone. It was glued to the stone by blood, and half the face and shoulder were – missing.

'Great Architect, that's foul!' Casaubon straightened, with an effort, looking pale under the dirt; and turned his head aside to heave. After wiping his mouth, he said, 'You don't cast, Master-Captain? You're used to this?'

'Your fortune to have an iron-stomached Scholar-Soldier,' the woman said greenly, adding, 'We should remove ourselves from here, noble Lord, these people and I would speak with you urgently.'

As they crossed a wide avenue, Casaubon caught his foot on a crack and stumbled. He recovered himself, looked back, and saw that there was a split in the marble paving. A faint, ominous creaking sounded.

'Master-Captain—'

'I see it,' the woman said. She knelt briefly, pulled a strip of character-marked paper from her pack, and gummed it across the split. There was a sense of groaning strain in the air itself. She stood, tossed her sword to Janou (the girl rapidly slipped the hanger over her head and shoulders), and turned, waiting for the hurdy-gurdy man to catch up.

'By the Great Architect's Symmetrical Balls!' Casaubon swore. 'Will you tell me what's happening to my city!'

They were among people now, officers and guards and stewards, who passed them at a jog-trot, urgently on the way to somewhere else. Anywhere else, Casaubon guessed. He panted, breath quite gone, and rested a hand against the balustrade of a palace that fronted the avenue.

There were leprous marks on the marble, blackish and greenish stains. When he dabbed at one with his sleeve, the stone itself liquified and ran down the carved ornamentation.

A crack in the palace façade split, with a noise like a cannon, and opened wide enough to put a hand in. Casaubon heard screams.

'If you're planning something, Master-Captain, now would seem to be a good time to do it.'

'No. We have time yet. Come inside and talk.'

Casaubon limped heavily toward the steps of the Belvedere, with the woman all but treading on his heels. The girl, Janou, picked up the skirts of her cowled robe and ran towards them, sword-blade jouncing on her back.

'Where's Feliche?' Valentine called.

'He has something yet to do. He'll come!'

The last thing the Lord-Architect saw before he went inside was the sky above the City. It hung over the marble avenues, filthy and black, and a grimy rain began to fall, streaking the stone, and eating into it with the ferocity of acid.

*

The Scholar-Soldier Valentine sat on the window-ledge, her back to the City beyond.

'What we must do is destroy the Miracle Garden. If the pattern that it makes no longer exists, then those entities that are . . . growing through into this world . . . will no longer have a guide here. It's the only way. As for how it's to be done—'

Janou hoisted herself up on the sill beside the Master-Captain and leaned out of the window at a dizzy angle.

'Here's Feliche!' she yelled. 'He's brought the wagon!'

'Now see you,' Casaubon scowled thunderously. 'That's five acres, there, in the heart of the City, and—'

'Powder.' Janou slid round, her legs bare to the thighs for a moment, and slipped down to the tesselated marble floor.

'Powder from the foundries,' Master-Captain Valentine confirmed. 'We'll use the cannon you have here; bombard that earth into patternless ruin.'

'*You will not!*'

'Lord-Architect—'

'*That is my Miracle Garden that took me a year to build and by the Great Architect's Womb I will not have it subjected to cannonade!*'

Valentine stood up. 'You will if I say so.'

'I will not!' Casaubon shouted. 'What gives you and your pox-rotted College the right to take my Garden away? Poor dead Scaris and I, we dirtied our hands for a year creating it. Whatever it is now, we made it with love. You and that little girl playing Providence, with the hand of the Invisible College behind you, when did you ever *make* anything?'

She stared at him, wordless.

Janou skipped to the high doorway, and peered down the stairs. 'Feliche! Have you got cannoneers with you?'

'Who fights the Architect-Lords' wars?' the big man asked, rhetorically, taking off his broken-plumed hat as he entered the palatial chamber. 'Every alley in this city has a master-bombardier or cannoneer in it. Greetings, noble Lord.'

'You're all mad,' the Lord-Architect Casaubon said. 'Now hear *me*. I have still men enough and power enough to keep order in this City. Whether it be powder conspiracies (yes, master Feliche, I know you and your plague-sign fraternity), or links between the Scholar-Soldiers and the Invisible College (which I did not know), no matter, there are dungeons deep enough for all of you.

'However,' he added, as another ominous creak sounded, and the storm-light darkened through the grimy rain, 'we stand in some danger, I truly believe it. Master-Captain, you are Scholar as well as

Soldier. Find me some way to save my Miracle Garden. Or else I care not if the City falls, no, not every building in it.'

Valentine opened her mouth to speak, and Feliche interrupted her.

'I think I could ask this, Master-Captain Valentine: how are you different from the noble Lords, who send us out to fight their wars for them? It's we who'll use the cannon. And, if what you say is true, against nothing human.'

He smoothed the broken feather of his hat with one hand, looking remarkably uneasy for a big man. He continued:

'Well then, see you, you cannot tell how Corruption might fight back. And we'll be in the way of it if it does. I hate to speak with the noble Lord's tongue, but I agree with him. Find some way to save the Garden.'

'*It can't be done!*' Valentine shouted. 'I was at Mildenhall, and Karsethra, the first to stand against that enemy and the last to fly from it, and I *know*—'

'That's a pox-rotted shame,' Casaubon said. 'Because I think the slave's right. I've seen the Archemasters' records. What you call Corruption feeds on disorder, and so breaking the Garden-patterns by cannonade will only help it to spread.'

And Valentine shook her head. 'Then . . . I don't know what to do.'

'You're never too old for a new sensation,' the noble Lord-Architect observed. 'Although it may shock you to discover that you're not infallible. I know it would shock me.'

Valentine broke out in a great surprised laugh. Casaubon guffawed. Janou and Feliche looked blankly at both of them.

Janou, puzzling, said, 'See you, there *might* just be a way.'

'We've run out of time.' Valentine pointed outside.

Beyond the window, Casaubon saw the bright disc of the sun bitten into. Over the City spread the crepuscular light of an eclipse.

They ran across the square towards the building ground and the Miracle Garden, dodging the stinging black rain.

Feliche paused, hearing the chittering of the lizard-ape. It danced on the powder-wagon, scarlet coat stark against the black sky. The big man bent down and scooped up the hurdy-gurdy, slung it over his shoulder, and the lizard-ape made a leap and clung to it, gold eyes bright with fear. Valentine heard him call to the men and women who crouched for shelter under the other wagons, before he ran on.

They ran – Janou pulling up her cowl to shield herself from the acid storm, kilting her robe up to sprint; even the Lord-Architect Casaubon managing a jog-trot. He wheezed and panted, and at last fell, belly up against the marble balustrade of the Garden steps, clutching it for support.

It was a while before he realised no rain scalded him.

Casaubon raised his head. He still wheezed. His pulse pounded deafeningly, so that he could see the Scholar-Soldier Valentine speaking, but not hear her. The woman stood on the top step, cinnamon-braids flying loose in the gale. Janou and Feliche stood back to back, staring up at the sky.

Above his head, the Lord-Architect saw a sky of boiling blackness. Spiked lightening walked a circle around the horizon – no, around the *Garden*. Now that he could get his breath, he found the air here was sweet, no rain falling; and when he turned to look up the steps at the building-ground, he saw sunlight.

The mellow light and clear air of a summer afternoon lay over the Miracle Garden.

Casaubon leaned forward on the balustrade and heaved. Only a little bile came up. He spat. He looked up at Valentine, where the Master-Captain gazed into the Garden. 'Great Architect! perhaps you *are* fearless. That turns my guts more than back there.'

He jerked a pudgy thumb at the blackened, decaying marble of the City.

Then he saw that the Scholar-Soldier's face was white; white enough that her freckles appeared dark as moles.

'We must go in,' she said, 'as I think, we can't get out.'

They walked in a close group up the steps and into the half-built Miracle Garden. The Master-Captain Valentine went first, carrying her drawn sword in her left hand, and, with her right, thumbed the scrolls in her pack. Janou, being relieved of the sword, let the lizard-ape ride chittering on her shoulder and pick at her cropped fair hair. She held Feliche's hand. The big man went warily, looking at every bramble-clump and overgrown hedge and statue as if it might bite.

Casaubon brought up the rear. The noble Lord-Architect glared, and muttered under his breath. At one point he stopped, bent down, and picked up an abandoned bottle of wine, and knocked the neck of it off against the marble thigh of a nymph. He drank, and belched.

When they passed the sundial, Chancellor Scaris's body was gone.

'Did you order that moved, noble Lord?'

Casaubon met the Scholar-Soldier's fox-red eyes. 'I did not.'

'No, I thought as much.'

Casaubon snorted. It was much too loud a noise in that silent, sunlit garden. 'Then, if you know so much, tell me what our aim is in coming here!'

Valentine looked to Janou but the girl remained silent.

Feliche spoke. His bass voice had a shake in it.

'Why don't you ask our guide?'

Valentine and Casaubon both turned around. In the topiary arch, between the speaking statues, stood a figure. A fold of its black silk robe cowled its face.

The bronze statue of the child said, '*Time is.*'

The silver statue of the old man said, '*Time was.*'

The cowled figure between them said, 'But, *Time will not be*. Not now. We have taken that for our own.'

The voice was Scaris's, something muffled.

Janou kicked the golden grass with her bare heel. In a high squeak, she said, 'I don't want to see him – not its face.'

It turned away. The fold of black silk fell, as it turned, and Valentine saw fine white hair: the back of Chancellor Scaris's head. When it held up a hand and beckoned them to follow, she stepped forward immediately.

'For fear he should turn round again?' Casaubon needled, but when Valentine didn't answer, only walked on under the topiary arch, he muttered, 'I've had no such nightmares as this since I was breeched,' and followed her.

'I smell spices,' Feliche said wonderingly, as they walked. He looked down at Janou. 'As strong as they were in my mother's shop, when I was a child.'

'Ordure,' Valentine said, overhearing, as they caught up. 'Great Architect knows, I've smelled enough of that since I walked on the highways for the Invisible College!'

'Master-Captain—'

She cut the Lord-Architect's protest off with a gesture.

'If a chance should come, we may only have a minute in which to act. See you, we should not miss it.'

The tufted golden grass gave out a heavy scent. The overgrown garden had no insects, no birds; only the towering masses of bramble and thorn that spidered into the blue sky. Ahead, the clean-cut lines of the topiary maze formed the horizon. Valentine could see the marble niches at the entrance – they were empty.

Janou stumbled. She seized Feliche's arm, rubbing her bruised foot, and the lizard-ape abandoned her shoulder for his. When she looked down, she saw what she had fallen over. Dry bones were half-buried in the golden grass. Skull, femur, vertebrae like a scatter of dice.

The figure of the Chancellor vanished into the maze, without turning round to see if they followed.

'Listen,' Feliche said. He hefted the hurdy-gurdy that weighed down his shoulder. The lizard-ape growled. Feliche said, 'I hear – music?'

It grew stronger as they listened. Valentine shifted uneasily, feeling the vibrations through the ground itself.

'That's – *foul*. It makes me feel dirty just to hear it,' Janou said.

Valentine saw Casaubon, silhouetted in his blue satin against the golden hedge. The fat man had his head cocked, listening. He said, 'You spoke of patterns. I've spent my life in stone, patterning out the order of the universe in City streets. I know others who made that order out of numbers, or out of strings stretched to the just proportion for each note – you follow me, out of music.'

'As above, so below,' Valentine said.

His fingers were wrapped round a bottle, almost hiding the glass from view. Now he lifted the bottle and drank, and added, 'If I were to build a City in *that* pattern, it would be a chancre on the earth.'

Janou said, 'It's a summons.'

'If order and harmony call up Justice,' Casaubon said, over the increasing discordance, 'then what does this music summon? Well and so. Valentine, do we enter the maze?'

Before Valentine could answer him, Janou gave a short choked-off scream. She held her hands out, and Valentine saw that her palms were oozing red; blood dripping down into the grass.

'We're close enough for it to touch us,' Valentine said. She reached out and took the girl's hands, heedless of the stigmata, and hugged Janou close for a minute, and then let her go.

'This will spread out to the city?' Feliche asked. When the Scholar-Soldier nodded, he shrugged broad shoulders, and stepped towards the entrance of the maze. Janou followed; Valentine walked at his side. The Lord-Architect Casaubon drained the wine-bottle and set it neatly upright on the grass before going after them.

As she walked under the topiary entrance, Valentine felt something brush her face.

She put up a hand, and took it away stained black. The close-cut leaves dripped an oily substance onto her rough-cotton shirt. A change in temperature made her stop, stand for a second, while the breath from her mouth clouded the suddenly-frosted air. She couldn't see Scaris, or whatever wore Scaris's shape. This twilight –

Valentine looked up to see the sun a copper disc, edged with fire. The shadow of eclipse lay on the maze.

With a little soft hiss, the hedge in front of her deliquesced. It fell into a black mess of leaves, with a sound like snow thrown onto a fire, and then spread out in sludge over the golden grass. And the grass itself began to blacken like paper held too close to a fire.

She looked, once, at what lay in front of her, and then spun round to face away from it, catching Janou's shoulder as she turned, and pulling the girl with her.

'Filth,' the Lord-Architect whispered, gazing ahead, 'filth, forever. No order, no shape, no *pattern*—'

Feliche rubbed his eyes with his hand, and said, 'It goes down forever – the Pit—'

The discordant sounds grew louder: less music than anti-music. Valentine fumbled with the buckles on her pack. A wind began to gust, seizing each strip of patterned characters and numerals before she could use them, sucking them away into whatever lay behind her. She clutched at them in panic.

Close at her ear, Scaris's voice whispered, *'Time will not be.'*

She felt the earth crumbling under her heels.

A flare of scarlet crossed her vision. Bright in that twilight, glittering with gold embroidery: the lizard-ape's scarlet coat. The beast growled, leaping up and down on the grass, and jumped up at Feliche's hand, where he stood transfixed, gazing ahead. One scaly paw caught the hurdy-gurdy's handle.

A raw, jingling tune jabbed the air, and then died.

Feliche looked down. Almost in spite of himself, he pushed the handle round once more. The cheap tune echoed.

It roused Casaubon: he pulled his gaze away from what had been the maze, and was now patternless Chaos.

'Again!' he said. 'You, beggar, you play for pennies. Now play for silver angels. For our lives!'

'For *you*?' Feliche said.

Janou laughed. 'For us!'

In Valentine's ear, Scaris's voice cried out in pain.

Spurred by the hurdy-gurdy's jangling tune, the lizard-ape began to dance. Valentine slipped to one knee, pushed herself away from the edge – *the edge*? – behind her, and got up from the grass. She seized Janou's hand.

'Dance!' she cried.

'Dance?'

Casaubon suddenly lumbered forward. 'Patterns!' he said. 'Oh, this is not your musico-magic, this is not your high Art, but Great Architect! what does it matter? Old tunes, old patterns – dance!'

Feliche turned a switch. The mechanical hurdy-gurdy began to play a country dance.

'When I was a child—' Valentine began to step, curtsey, step, bow; and Janou, laughing so hard that she could barely stand, began to copy her. With all the airs of a City lady, she took Casaubon's hand and drew him into the figure.

The lizard-ape leaped at their side, bowing, skipping forward, skipping back.

'I cannot—' Casaubon began to wheeze.

'Oh, see you, sir, you must!' Valentine seized his hands. Janou, like a hoyden, waltzed around Feliche where he played. Valentine shouted above the music: 'We're so close to the heart of it now. We can *hurt* it. This is a better way than we could ever have planned. Oh, sir, dance!'

They dance a pavane on the golden grass, to nursery tunes ground out by a hurdy-gurdy.

The crop-haired girl skipping the measure, heels kicking the earth, eyes half-shut, lost in the pleasure of knowing each turn, each move, each step.

The fox-haired woman and the fat man, touch hands and part, turn, touch and part; gliding over the sun-warmed grass, their shadows following them in neat measure.

Ape and player moving also, in gentle steps that go back and forth, back and forth, tapping out the rhythm for the other dancers.

And now there is another shadow on the earth.

The clanking hurdy-gurdy drowns out birdsong and the buzz of insects, playing dances that were old before stone was laid upon stone of the City, playing lullaby rhymes and temple-bell chimes, each note slotting into the next like dovetailed joints or unmortared stone.

The Scholar-Soldier, dancing, pack and sword forgotten, seizes in the dance a stranger's hand, and sees, pink with exertion, the familiar lined face of Scaris.

They dance a pavane, they dance the pattern of the microcosm, number and particle and force; they dance the dance of the world above: stars, suns, galaxies.

The hurdy-gurdy grinds on, tireless, and they dance a pavane on golden grass, circling a sundial that stands at the centre of a maze.

'Rot you!' says the noble Lord-Architect Casaubon, 'Time *will* be!'

The automata have no answer to make.

*

Sun slants in through the clerestory windows of the Belvedere, falling sixty feet to the tesselated marble floor. As the Scholar-Soldier Valentine crossed the Belvedere's presence-chamber, alternate sun and shade made her now a drab brown, now a vixen-red figure. The others turned as she entered.

'He's agreed to see you?' Janou asked.

Janou had abandoned the black robe of the Library. Now she wore a gown of sapphire that shaded in the flowing skirt to rich indigo. The hem, where her bare feet peeped out, was already stained with mud.

Valentine shrugged lithe shoulders. 'Finally, yes.'

Feliche stood with Scaris. At their feet was the hurdy-gurdy, the lizard-ape curled up on top of it, asleep in the sun. Its scarlet coat gleamed.

The big man, having pulled the broken feather from his hatband, picked at his teeth with the quill-end. He said, 'Does he not remember the Garden?'

Scaris fingered the collar of his black satin robe. 'He may remember it too well, I think, for me.'

Valentine smiled at Scaris. 'He'll say *Rot you, I've only just got my Chancellor back, I don't want to lose him again!* But are you determined?'

The white-haired man seemed frailer, and aware, too, of how Janou and Feliche shrank back from him, sometimes, without any conscious intention.

'That evil in the Garden – it took me so easily,' Scaris said, 'that it frightens me still. I cannot be Chancellor, knowing that. What I will do, Master-Captain, is what you mocked me for: I'll care for the Library, and books that are written down.'

He smiled, looking at the lizard-ape asleep on the hurdy-gurdy.

'And on bright days, when I have been too long indoors, I shall shed my satin coat for cotton, and go into the square and play music for pennies.'

The Scholar-Soldier impulsively handed him her satchel, that bulged with scrolls still.

'Choose some of these, to care for in your Library? I can get more when the Invisible College convenes again. They're sovereign against bad dreams. Against things that stray out of bad dreams into waking.'

Scaris took the pack by its worn leather strap, and the weight of it surprised him until he realised it was his, now.

Valentine glanced at Feliche.

'Shall I say, you and yours, in the lower city—'

The big man interrupted her. With a look at Chancellor Scaris, he said, 'When those in satin turn beggars, then beggars take up satin – I plan to travel. Maybe the Invisible College can show me how to solve the City's troubles. For I've seen nothing in the lower city, and, surely, nothing *here* to help us.'

'He's coming with me!' Janou picked up her skirts, strutting back to where they stood. 'Tell the Lord-Architect, the Invisible College will be present in his City from now on – I've had word: they're sending others to replace us, whose faces aren't known.'

Feliche put his hands on Janou's bare shoulders, and the fluff-haired girl leaned back as if he were a wall to support her.

'But tell him, Valentine, there must be something done about the Garden – then we can leave!'

With a brief nod, the Scholar-Soldier Valentine walked on into the marble halls and galleries beyond the ante-chamber.

The same sun shone in through the interior windows of the Belvedere. It gleamed on marble, white and pink and lapis-lazuli-blue, and glinted off ornamental silver taps, and was made hazy by the coils of steam rising up and filling the vast bath-house.

Valentine found Casaubon there.

'Noble Lord,' she said. She put one booted foot up on the rim of the marble bath, rested her arms across her raised knee, and then rested her chin on her arms. She looked down at him.

Casaubon ducked his head for the fifth or sixth time, came up spluttering, and squeezing water out of his copper-red hair. Steam and boiling water made him pink as a new-washed baby; and he rested back in the stepped bath, arms spreading over the wet marble, like some leviathan come to land. Newly clean, he was found to be freckled, and otherwise of pale complexion.

'Well, young Valentine?'

'Nothing's changed in the Garden.' She spoke without moving her chin off her arms. 'That is a fair three days, and so time, I'd think, for anything lingering to show itself. Still, it's an uncanny place. Time will scab over the wound eventually but . . .'

'Oh, see you,' Casaubon said, 'I have my thoughts on that matter also.'

He lowered his head, nestling his chin in three several layers of flesh, and looked up at Valentine with pale-blue eyes. When he rolled over, a wave of hot water splashed the marble surround of the baths. He sat down on the lowest submerged step again, and shook water from his eyes.

'You may hand me the towel,' he said. 'I have master Feliche to see in a short while, which I anticipate to be difficult. I think your colleague will stay here with him for a time. The little Janou.'

'Janou stays nowhere long.' Valentine straightened up, glancing round for the towel.

'As for the Miracle Garden,' the noble Lord-Architect continued, 'it seems to me that it would be dangerous to destroy it, not knowing what patterns we might uncover while so doing.'

'Yes, I'd say that also.'

'And rather than leave it to overgrow, a better manner of proceeding would be to rebuild it as a true Miracle Garden.'

'I agree.'

'You,' the noble Lord Casaubon pronounced, 'are not happy.'

Valentine looked at him in some surprise. She came back to stand by the bath, careful of her boots on the wet marble.

'That has nothing to do with anything, noble Lord.'

He heaved himself up to the next submerged marble step. A lap of water splashed up over Valentine's boots. She didn't move back; only watched his pink, clean bulk.

'Well then,' Casaubon said, 'stay here.'

'Stay here? Why would I do that?'

'Valentine, you're eighteen,' he said as he wiped sweat and hot water from his face, 'eighteen, and you look thirty-five. In a very few years you'll look sixty. Life on the road for the Invisible College I take not to be an easy life. Much better to settle down here in the City and advise me how to build my next garden.'

'Advice?' Valentine said incredulously. '*You?*'

'I would take advice from you,' the Lord-Architect said, 'on that.'

Steam coiled round the woman, shot through with the sun's gold as it fell in through the Belvedere's high windows. It pearled on her tawny-white braids.

'On that. And on much besides,' Casaubon said.

The woman scratched absently at her rough-cotton shirt. There was a scent of bath-oils in the air, sharp herbs and woodsmoke. She opened her mouth, shut it again, looked at Casaubon, and the corner of her mouth twitched up.

He said, 'Stay here. Be my Lady.'

There was silence in the Belvedere's bath-house.

Valentine tucked a braid behind her ear, and began to walk thoughtfully around the sunken marble bath. Casaubon watched, only his head turning. The cinnamon-haired woman absently tugged at one of the buckles of her sword-belt. Then, with a little exclamation, she pounced, and came up with a vast white towel in her hands.

She held it up, outspread.

The Lord-Architect stood up, and water sucked back into the bath with a splash. He trod lightly up the steps and let her wrap the towel around his body.

'*Well?*' he demanded.

'Well enough,' Valentine said, grinning. 'See you, I'll help you build your new garden. Take, oh, four to five years.'

Casaubon clutched the towel round his bulk toga-fashion, with what dignity he could manage. 'And the rest?'

'Why, yes,' Valentine said. 'The rest, too.'

The Knot Garden

don't know why you're so *afraid* of them,' the ex-Scholar-Soldier Valentine protested. 'They'll only be the watchers of the Invisible College, keeping an eye on us.'

She lay on her stomach on the grass and watched him work. Her shaved-off hair was growing back cinnamon-coloured, but still plentifully flecked with white. The short fur made a child of her.

'You're filthy,' she added, throwing a ball of binding-twine at him, 'go and *wash*!'

The Lord-Architect Casaubon straightened up with an effort. All the fat rolls of flesh on his heavy bones settled earthward, answering to gravity. He wiped sweat from his chins, leaving smears of dirt there.

'If it's the pox-rotted Invisible College, they would have contacted *you*,' he said.

'Oh, see you, they maybe would not . . . And if trouble's coming, I'll handle it!'

Sun sank like treacle onto the Miracle Garden. Sweat made vast dark patches on the Lord-Architect Casaubon's shirt, at the neck and in between his flesh-padded shoulderblades. Yellow light drenched the grass, the neat topiary arches, the marble statues from which fountain-waters sang. It made the earth in which he sank his hands warm to the touch.

'They do fright me,' the Lord-Architect admitted. 'Watchers.'

Bags of vari-coloured sand leaned haphazardly together on the lawn. Casaubon stood in a bare octagon enclosed by miniature hedges, with dirty sandalled feet planted apart, tipping out the contents of a sand-bag in a stream. His fat features creased in concentration. As he moved smoothly, he poured out the red sand in curious patterns, figures, sigils, and knots.

'You'll be surprised when you see what I can do—'

He interrupted, 'I want something to drink.'

The skin crinkled around fox-tawny eyes as she grinned. 'Maybe.'

'Dammit, girl—!'

Her gaze went beyond him. 'Here's the Chancellor. You'll have to stop. I'll get you a drink, you baby, wait for me!'

Casaubon straightened up, watching the shaven-headed woman covertly as she limped towards the summerhouse, and the stone bottles left there in the cool. She was only just beginning to recover her strength.

He turned. The white marble façades of the City rose beyond the golden hedges, and the dapper figure of the Chancellor approached from that direction. The Lord-Architect Casaubon wiped his hands on his once-white shirt.

'Chancellor Parry,' he said. 'Have you discovered it yet? Who are they?'

The woman was younger than Casaubon: thirty-five to his forty. Tabitha Parry was debonair, dressed sleekly in blue satin coat and breeches, and as she looked at the Lord-Architect she fastidiously adjusted the clean white ruffles at her wrists.

'That's something strange,' the woman said. 'Lord-Architect, I can find no "they". Only rumours—'

'Oh, Hell's great yellow teeth! What do I keep a Chancellor for? I could have told you myself there were rumours. I want to know who these people *are*!'

Parry reluctantly offered a white cotton-gloved hand. He gripped it as he heaved himself over the low hedge onto the lawn, and nodded thanks. She examined her mud-stained glove dispiritedly. Valentine called a greeting to the Chancellor from the summerhouse.

A shudder went across Casaubon's skin, like a horse troubled with flies. He dismissed it.

'How is she, your Lady Valentine?' Tabitha Parry enquired.

'Well enough. Not one in ten recover from the plague, and not one in fifty so well as she.' Casaubon's blue eyes were troubled with an old, averted grief. Then he admitted, 'She's well enough, finally, to be bored with necessary resting; as a consequence, my life becomes a hell . . .'

'She itches to take up the sword and scroll again.'

Casaubon grunted. 'I'd call in the Scholar-Soldiers myself, if I didn't know them to be the visible branch of the Invisible College, and *she* swears these slinking renegades come from them.'

'Unsubstantiated—'

'Oh, by the Great Architect's Symmetrical Anus!'

Chancellor Parry persisted: 'Merely unsubstantiated rumours of some several unregistered watchers—'

The earth twitched.

Casaubon staggered, lost his balance, sprawled forward on the dry grass, and knocked all the breath from his vast bulk. Tabitha Parry yelped with shock. The dazzling sunlight blinked, once, and then again. Casaubon dragged himself up onto hands and knees, ham-limbs weighing him down, and gasped in the suddenly static-filled air.

Valentine sprinted across the lawn towards him calling, ' 'Quake!'

She cleared the low hedge of the knot garden at a run, bare feet scuffing the sand patterns, silhouetted against the umber and ochre earth.

Suddenly it seemed that she swerved. To Casaubon, it was as if she set her feet on one of the curving sand-lines and ran along it. He caught one glimpse of that fox-narrow face, determined and intent. Then with a twist of her shoulder, and a flick of sand as her heel skidded, she leaped to the side, and faded into the bright air.

A scatter of sand pattered down.

Tabitha Parry covered her mouth with gloved hands.

'Valentine! The roar hurt Casaubon's throat.

He stared at the knot garden. Then he scrambled heavily to his feet and stared around. But the expanse of golden lawn remained empty.

His inner eye kept the image of a tawny-haired woman fading; fading like a lithograph exposed to the light.

'Valentine!'

No footstep, no echo of her voice.

He staggered forward, crossing and re-crossing the knot garden, fat arms outstretched as if he might sweep her into them, until at last he tripped on the hedge-border and fell to his knees.

Chancellor Parry patted his shoulder ineffectively while the noble Lord-Architect Casaubon wept, as noisily as a child.

The wood panelling on the study wall had grown warm in the sun. Casaubon continued to sit and stare at it. From time to time he scratched at his copper-red hair, inspected the scurf under his fingernails, and then went back to staring at the wall.

Chancellor Parry coughed, discreetly.

'Noble Lord . . .'

'It's a pox-ridden trick and I can't see how they did it!'

Tabitha Parry blinked at his vehemence. Casaubon leaned back in his chair. He grabbed another bottle in his pudgy hand, knocked off the neck against the table's edge with practised ease, and drank, and belched. When he slammed the bottle back down a spurt of wine leaped up, soaking his green satin sleeve.

'It's been two *days*!'

Parry smoothed one white-gloved hand with the other, and shot her cuffs nervously. 'She's nowhere in the City. I've searched. I'm sure. As to the lower city, I can't claim to be so certain, but . . . no demands for ransom. Noble Lord, I'm sorry; I swear.'

Casaubon drank from the bottle again. Then he put it down, gripped Tabitha Parry's sleeve with a wet hand, and shook her bracingly. His breath reeked. The Chancellor winced, not quite able to pull away.

'Come with me,' he said. 'Come with me.'

Parry recovered her arm, and trod delicately down the corridors of the Belvedere in the Lord-Architect's wake. Casaubon whistled absently through his teeth. He missed a step, once, and staggered.

'Find me one of these "unsubstantiated" watchers,' he said without looking back at the Chancellor.

'No more available than the Lady Valentine, I fear.'

'She'll survive. She's alive.' Casaubon paused, and spat on the tesselated marble floor. 'She was a Scholar-Soldier before she was an Architect-Lord's Lady – Parry!'

One broad hand shot out and pinned her against the panelled wall. Tabitha Parry pawed ineffectively at her crumpled lace, and the fat, strong hand of the Lord-Architect.

'Don't ever speak to me as if she were lost, Great Architect rot your soul!'

'*Sir—*'

He released the Chancellor and lurched on down the corridor. Parry tugged her ruffle and coat straight, and followed.

Casaubon led her into a small room, where sunlight through the leaded glass windows shone on a bare floor, and a plain wooden table, and on the table, an artefact of metal and glass and wire. Small lights burned like rubies in the heart of it.

'See that?'

The Lord-Architect's warm, alcohol-laden breath hit Tabitha Parry full in the face.

'See that? Janou gave us that. Told me, if ever it stopped transmitting, the Invisible College would come to see why. Well then.'

Casaubon glanced round the room. Nothing presented itself to him. He moved to the table, bent, and wrapped his arms around the artefact's metal casing. Parry watched strain tighten all the muscles buried in his fat. Then he lifted the mechanism, halted for a second, raised it, and flung it down on the marble floor.

It shattered with a stink of sulphur.

Parry stepped back, waving her hand before her nose. When she was certain it would do nothing, she came to look at the smashed mess of metal. The ruby-lights were gone.

'Want to talk to the Invisible College!' the Lord-Architect said pugnaciously. Having squatted down to stare at his handiwork, he now slid down into a sitting position and leaned back against the wall. Before Tabitha Parry could quite collect her thoughts and speak, he began to snore.

'How long will it take the Invisible College to get here?'

The Chancellor realised she was talking to herself.

'Or . . . are they here already?'

Water lapped at the very window-sills of the clapboard houses in the city's River-quarter. The wheels of the cart kicked up spokes of spray, although they went at a slow pace, and the oxen lowed in protest.

'The road's blocked up ahead,' Feliche called back.

Janou sat on top of the loaded cart. She had her heels up, resting on an old leather pack; and across her lap was a plain-scabbarded sword. When Feliche spoke, she shifted round and scrambled on hands and knees across the tarpaulin bundles, to fall on her stomach and stare ahead. The sword jabbed uncomfortably into her belly.

Ahead, the lane went downhill. The floodwaters swirled in and out of windows and doorways. A chair floated past. Some houses had only rooftrees visible, some reared above the flood. All the upper windows were hung with drying blankets and shirts, and children leaned out dangerously and shrieked as they saw the painted carts.

Janou sat round and stood up. She balanced precariously, bare-foot, and gave out with a piercing whistle.

'We'll have to go back – go around! Back up!'

Heads turned on the other wagons. Water, rising up the spiral-painted spokes, lapped at the stars daubed in silver, blue, and emerald on the wagon-sides; and the riders clinging there waved acknowledgement to the girl. A woman in a cape, clinging to the bars of the animal-cage, let go and splashed down into breast-high water, and waded towards the oxen. Two men followed.

While the awkward business of backing and turning the other oxen was underway, Janou slid down to sit beside Feliche. The clouds were breaking. Sunlight shone onto the floodwaters, making the road ahead an unbearable white mirror. A rank smell of fish and rotting vegetables steamed in the air.

Feliche said, 'Well, Scholar-Soldier?'

Janou kicked bare heels against the footboard. Flecks of paint from the old wood starred her skin blue and crimson. She scratched at her cropped spiky hair. 'Call this a disguise? If there's anyone in the City who hasn't seen us this time tomorrow, take my sword and call me witless!'

'The lower city, but not the *City*,' the big man emphasised. 'And in any case, my love, where better to hide than where everybody's looking? Didn't the Invisible College teach you anything?'

'They taught me to stay low, and keep out of the company of seditious anarchists,' Janou said pointedly.

'It's true I have my own business here.'

Feliche tugged his wide-brimmed hat down, so that she saw only his red-brown beard, and a curl or two of his hair. A crimson feather was buckled to his hatband. Shirt and breeches were plain, but he had taken up the travelling fair's habits and wore an orange sash round his waist, and gilded spurs on his high boots.

He said, 'We've got enough material disseminated. I believe the local groups will begin action soon.'

Janou stood up. 'You can back the cart now – I don't think we should wait until we've seen Valentine tomorrow. Let's move today.'

'Are you not anxious to see her, after a year?'

One bare foot went up onto the backboard, and she rested her arms on her knee, and between calling directions to reverse the cart in the flooded street, said, 'I know what Valentine meant when she said a Scholar-Soldier has no friends. Before I come out of hiding, I have to know why we were called here. The College has enemies.'

A voice from below said, 'The Invisible College also has allies.'

'Hell's great gap-toothed gaping maw!' Janou muttered. She leaned precariously off the footboard. 'See you, master, I've not the slightest idea to what you refer.'

Below, a boat wallowed among the refuse of the flood. A man sat in it, dark hands folded. He wore a baggy white tunic and trousers. It was difficult to guess his age: something between thirty and sixty.

Janou met blue eyes made brilliant by his brown skin.

'We're setting up in the market square if you want to see the show.'

Light reflected up from the water. It cast rippling shadows of brightness on the man's face. When Feliche glanced across at Janou, he saw that the girl was frowning. The tip of her scabbard scraped across the headboard as she moved.

'On your way, master,' Feliche rumbled.

Without gripping the sides of the skiff, or even putting down one brown hand, the man stood up in the boat.

It seemed to Feliche as if the mist that the sun called up from the floodwaters muffled sound. The noise of grunting oxen and yelling riders faded. It all became background for the small, dark man who stood in the boat, regardless of the rushing waters, and did not seem even to have to balance. The boat was as steady as dry land.

The man held up his hands, open and empty, to Janou.

'Master-Captain, I mean nothing but peace.'

Feliche was about to protest, but the girl flopped down on her stomach on the cart and reached for the man's hand, turning it over, studying something that had sparked sunlight.

'That's one of the rings mentioned in *Ghâya*. Oh, say you, I meant no offence! What brings one of you to the City?'

Bewildered, Feliche said, 'You trust him?'

Both of them ignored the big man.

'Well?' Janou persisted.

'They have already taken your colleague Valentine,' the brown-skinned man said. 'I thought it might be as well if they failed to take you. I come with that warning. And, it might be, if the Invisible College will accept it, an offer of help.'

Janou asked, 'What is it we face here?'

'My name is Al-Iskandariya,' he said, 'and I will tell you.'

They came from diverse places, each one alone. Some lost, some lame, some full of knowledge; dark and twisted from what had happened to them on the way.

But the stars were turning, returning to their ancient configuration.

And as the constellations returned, so did they, the Circle drawing together again, not one of its long-dead members lost to this new life and ancient purpose.

They met secret from all the world.

And as the Circle joined again, their power grew.

'But, rot you,' Casaubon said, 'all I need to know is whether she can be alive or not!'

His voice echoed in the vast Library. Some of the students raised their heads, saw the Lord-Architect, and went back to their scrolls and parchments. A final echo whispered off distant stacks, and the blue-and-gold constellations painted on the interior of the dome.

'What's so difficult? You're versed in those Arts, more than any man I know. Tell me if I can hope or not!'

Scaris, the Librarian, blinked watery eyes. 'Noble Lord, I don't know. Nothing like this has ever happened before in the City.'

'Not the City,' Tabitha Parry (in unaware echo) said, 'but, perhaps, the lower city?'

'Oh, see you, that's good! That's it!' Casaubon's meaty hand smacked her on the back. The Chancellor staggered.

'*Sir,*' she protested.

The Lord-Architect seemed to sag where he stood, all the weight of flesh pulling him earthward. There were new wine-stains on his green satin coat, and his shirt was rimmed with black; a stench of unwashed linen came from him. He looked at Parry, rubbing a hand through his slick copper-red hair.

'I'll have the man or woman who robs me of hope into the oubliettes beneath the Belvedere, so fast—'

Scaris interrupted.

'Noble Lord, has it occurred to you to think this might be voluntary on the Lady Valentine's part?'

'Oh, what!'

'No, hear me out.' Scaris collected his thoughts. It was hot in the Library, and he pushed sweat-soaked white hair out of his eyes, and adjusted the neck of his black satin robe. Age made him wish for somewhere to sit down; caution, thinking of what he was about to say, made him wish himself younger and faster.

'Think about it,' he said, slightly breathless. 'You still do not know, I think, where she was born. You know she was a Scholar-Soldier, which means (we now find) she was *aide* to the supposed Invisible College. Into what grey areas of Art that may have taken her . . . well. She had mercenaries for close friends, and agitators, and—'

Casaubon said, 'True, you were my Chancellor before Parry here. That doesn't give you licence to slander.'

The old man threw up his blue-veined hands.

'I should have said this before! She was nothing but a mendicant lecturer before she came here and enspelled you. She had no fortune, no beauty, and not enough wit to – and you were three times her age!'

Chancellor Parry stepped in front of Casaubon as he lumbered forward.

'*That woman saved your life!*' Casaubon roared.

'It isn't myself I'm concerned with!' Scaris pushed the dapper Chancellor out of the way, and glared up at Casaubon. 'This is the only opportunity I've had in a year to say this. The girl was young, and lively, and she loved the sword and the scroll; and yet she gave

it up to be your Lady? It was *obvious* she would do this – choose a
way to leave you that absolves her of blame. Why would she stay
with you?'

Tabitha Parry glanced from the breathless old man, his rheumy
eyes brilliant with anger, to the Lord-Architect. Casaubon's ham-
like hands were clenched into fists. There was something terrible in
the deliberation with which he relaxed them.

He said mildly, 'You could ask why, since Valentine was the most
cross-tempered and curst woman I've ever met, *I* stayed with her?
Truth, I don't know. We laughed at one and the same things. Scaris,
you would say none of this if you'd seen her face when – when it
happened.'

'I don't doubt she could *feign* well enough.'

Tabitha Parry smoothed her embroidered lapels into place, and
continued the gesture easily into taking the Lord-Architect's arm as
he stepped forward. For a second it was as if she had taken hold of a
rolling ox-cart.

'One of my clerks.' She pointed with one white-gloved hand.
'*Lord Casaubon!*'

The clerk's boots clicked across the floor as he approached.
Tabitha Parry beckoned him across to her, glad beyond words for
the interruption, and then gaped as he was pushed aside by the two
people who trod at his heels.

The first was a slight, dark man. Parry thought him unremarkable
until she caught his gaze, and felt a literal physical jolt at the
intensity of his blue eyes. The second, energetically kicking out the
trailing hem of her robe as she walked, was a young woman.

'Lord-Architect or not, you'll get no help here!' The Librarian
turned his back on Casaubon and limped off across the wide floor.

'Whoreson ungrateful bastard!' Casaubon yelled at Scaris's
departing back. He swung round, ungainly. His copper hair was
disordered, and his skin flushed red. His chins shook with anger.
'What do *you* want?'

Al-Iskandariya, in quiet amusement, said, 'I came to tell the
noble Lord-Architect there is a power abroad in his City. It has
begun to act. If you wish to know how, noble Lord, I suggest . . .'

'Janou!'

Casaubon's loud yelp made Chancellor Parry jump. The fat man
lumbered across the marble floor and enfolded the second person in
a cushioning embrace.

'Oh, see you, do you want me suffocated? Put me down!'

'Where's Valentine? Is she with you?'

'If I knew what happened to Valentine, I wouldn't be coming to *you.*' The girl shook out the folds of her long, black gown, and adjusted the straps of her backpack. She looked up from this, and made the somewhat embarrassed admission: 'See you, I didn't mean that as it sounded.'

A laugh growled in Casaubon's chest. He looked at the dark man. 'Who's this? Another of your beggarly College?'

With something between asperity and wounded dignity, the man said, 'I am Al-Iskandariya of the Brotherhood. The stars have led me across half the world, to this place. Noble Lord, if you want to know why, then come outside, and look at your city!'

A clot of dung, thrown accurately and hard, smacked into the back of Casaubon's head. Someone laughed. The noble Lord-Architect dragged out a large dirty kerchief and wiped at the rolls of fat at his neck.

'I don't like to disappoint you,' he said to Al-Iskandariya, 'but the Architect-Lords have *never* been popular in the lower city. Dissent hardly counts as a supernatural omen!'

Chancellor Parry picked her way along the lane beside Casaubon. Her nose wrinkled in helpless disgust. Here, the floodwaters had recently receded, leaving a thin skin of slime over the cobbles. Steam went up in the hot sun. There was a stink from fishheads in the gutter, and ordure. Many windows were marked with a smear of silver paint.

Al-Iskandariya said, 'There are a group of people coming to the City, or it may be that they are here now. Either they have a power, or they are proxies for people who have. You will not find them easily. But we may see signs of their power growing.'

'You'll see,' Janou said. 'You'll see. This way. Down here.'

The sight of satin coats in the lower city attracted a crowd. Thin urchins hung lovingly at Tabitha Parry's heels, holding up filthy hands for pennies. Her gloved hand went automatically to the pocket of her blue satin coat, and found that her purse was already missing. She muttered something obscene, and then blushed in case she should have been heard.

'I always said we should have burned this lot to the ground,' Casaubon rumbled. 'House this rabble up in the City, clean 'em, give 'em honest work, they'd be far better off.'

'You're a whoreson ignorant pig,' Janou said. Before the noble Lord-Architect could reply she led them into the market square.

'There.' Al-Iskandariya pointed.

The Lord-Architect stared. He had a supreme unconsciousness that he also was an object of regard, that the men and women in the marketplace stopped their business to gape at Lord-Architect, Chancellor, and two strangers. The noble Lord-Architect only looked where the dark man pointed, at a canvas-covered structure set up against the corner of Blind Lane and Bone Alley.

'It's a fortune-teller's booth,' Casaubon said blankly. 'You dragged me down into the lower city, on the hottest day in the year, to see a charlatan fortune-teller?'

'Wait,' Al-Iskandariya said. 'Watch. See the pattern.'

The sun shone on the marketplace. Wet straw, trodden underfoot, steamed. To begin with there was no pattern, only people. There might have been fewer children squatting under the edges of stalls, playing, or sitting up on the rails of beast-pens; fewer men and women in conversational knots outside each of the three inns.

Fully half the stalls were bare.

The weatherbeaten wood, marked with a slash of silver, spoke *plague*. There was a shrillness about the customers at remaining stalls, where they argued or bought or talked while they waited for purchases to be boxed. People moved quickly: carters driving oxen carelessly down the gaps between the tables. A scorching yellow sky hung over the gables, beneath it were arguments.

Gradually Casaubon began to see the others. Two drunken rapier-wielding boys attempting a show-duel for pennies and falling over each other. Bundles against the walls that might be sleeping men, or dead.

A woman with black-grimed skin and ratty hair shoved a few blown wild roses into Chancellor Parry's face, mumbling something, other hand outstretched. Parry sidestepped her. There were two small, silent children clinging to the woman's dress.

Strangers soon ceased to be a novelty. Only the occasional glance was spared now for the satin-coated.

'If it's sedition being spread under cover of a debased Art, that's not new,' Chancellor Parry protested.

'Oh, what! You think these people have to be *told* when they should complain?' Janou glared up at Parry. She jerked her thin shoulders, hitching up her gown, and scowled. 'You don't even know the River-quarter's flooded – you can't see what's in front of you!'

A man came out of the fortune-teller's canvas booth. He was fair, bearded, young. He stood for a moment, blinking, and it seemed to the Lord-Architect Casaubon that the man stared over the roofs of the leaning tenements, towards that dream of white marble that is the City.

A sense of strain made itself felt in the air. Casaubon felt his skin twitch.

He grunted, opened his mouth to say that he recognised this, that they should run, flee, and then he bent and retched. He spat on the filthy straw.

He saw the fairhaired man take a step forward and fade. Fade into the air, as dust sifted down. Fade: with a look not of surprise but of recognition on his face.

A child ran off, crying.

Casaubon wiped his mouth on his wine-stained sleeve. No man or woman turned to see what had happened. And, now he looked, it seemed that no one in the marketplace willingly turned towards Blind Lane or Bone Alley. As if there was a conspiracy against seeing the canvas booth . . .

The woman selling wild roses met Casaubon's eyes. She had something in her hand, some small object that she caressed with her grimy thumb. She smiled. It was an odd, self-conscious smile; it had regret in it, and a rueful admission. She stepped away from her flower-stall. Her two silent toddlers wandered away, hand-in-hand.

He was not surprised when she, also, merged into the air and vanished. It seemed as sweetly natural as a bird flying to its nest.

'Pox rot it! It's no more *natural* than the plague—'

Al-Iskandariya's voice at his ear said, 'But for a moment you felt it was.'

In a voice of concern and paternal outrage, Casaubon said, 'They're taking my people!'

Janou leaned up against the side of the inn, standing on one leg, kicking a bare heel against the lath-and-plaster wall.

'Oh, that's horse-dung! Nobody's being *taken*. They're going because they want to. Because the lower city's a plague-ridden slum. Because they'd rather take the unknown than stay here!'

The Lord-Architect looked round the marketplace and counted the number of empty stalls.

'They go of their own wish,' Al-Iskandariya said, 'or, most of them do. But the Brotherhood is not certain that where they go is where they wish to go. I have tracked this across continents. Noble Lord, it could empty cities.'

The fat man did not reply. He stared at the dirty canvas booth that stood in the marketplace.

'Perhaps she did leave me,' Casaubon said; and, in a lower tone, 'Perhaps I am not the man that she would choose to stay with.'

Janou shifted off the wall, and swiped him across the arm with a swift hand. 'Dolt!'

'Does it matter?' he asked. 'I am not such a fool, to think because she means so much to me, it has any other importance.'

Al-Iskandariya's sapphire eyes sought Casaubon's face.

'Lord-Architect, the first thing the Circle did, before they acted openly, was to rid themselves of the Scholar-Soldier Valentine. *That* tells me she is important.'

The air quivered.

Tabitha Parry jumped. She felt as if some appallingly loud noise had just ceased to sound. When she looked at the Lord-Architect and the dark man, their faces showed something of the same disquiet.

The crop-haired girl shivered, and thumbed the strap of her backpack; scabbarded sword bound in with scrolls and parchments.

Parry said, 'Noble Lord—'

The air sung like struck glass, shattered, just for a second.

A large drop of dark red blood fell onto the straw at Tabitha Parry's feet.

'—And stay out.'

Casaubon hurled a pewter pot for emphasis. It smacked into the closing door, behind the landlord's departing back.

Janou picked at her slightly-snaggled teeth with the quill end of a duck feather. '*Someone* has to go into that fortune-teller's booth. I'll go.'

Al-Iskandariya, who had not eaten, remained standing at the window, looking out into the square. The abandoned market stalls now outnumbered the occupied ones.

'That, or one of the dozen others.' He shrugged. 'There will be a hundred before the week is out.'

Sun tumbled into the inn's main room through leaded panes.

Tabitha Parry shook out a white silk kerchief and placed it on the inn bench, before sitting down carefully, with her knees pressed together. She fiddled with her hair, tied formally at the nape of her neck.

'Here.' The Lord-Architect pushed the pewter ale jug across to his Chancellor. 'You look as if you need it.'

Casaubon sat in a stout-armed chair. He wore a brown satin coat, with deep cuffs and pockets, unbuttoned; and his belly hung out and rested on his spread thighs. As Tabitha Parry watched, the Lord-Architect dug in one pocket and produced a rat, which he sat on his wide white-breeched thigh, and proceeded to feed scraps of cooked duck from his fingers. The rat was a dirty yellow, with spiky fur, mad red eyes, and a bald and scaly tail.

After the blood-fall, perhaps nothing could have retrieved Parry's scattered wits but this. She watched, fascinated and appalled, as the rat sat on its haunches and took titbits from its master. It had enough, finally, and scuttled up Casaubon's mountainous belly, and vanished into an inside coat pocket, with a last flash of carious fangs.

The Lord-Architect, not pausing to wipe his hands, dug into the pan for another slice of meat. He chewed thoughtfully, licked grease from his fingers, and then, through a fine spray of food-fragments, said, 'Now that I've seen others go, I'm convinced Valentine's alive.'

'If I might,' Al-Iskandariya began. Janou interrupted him:

'We don't know what it is she knows.'

'Her friends—' Casaubon frowned. 'Master-Captain, that hurdy-gurdy man that we knew last year, Feliche, was it?'

Janou said, 'Who?'

'It may be something she learned while she was a wanderer, before she came to the City, that made them choose first to be rid of her?' Tabitha Parry made the suggestion with diffidence.

Al-Iskandariya said, 'I—'

'She'd never have kept it quiet!' Janou crossed her heels, and rested them up on her pack on the bench. 'She was the most braggart Master-Captain we had!'

Casaubon frowned. Janou waved an airy hand:

'Valentine could never have taken to the *covert* side of the College. She could never keep her mouth shut about how wonderful she was. And she was good. Best for fighting, and for finding out your causes, first and secondary . . . If she discovered anything, she'd have let everybody know!'

The Lord-Architect pushed himself up out of the chair. The wood groaned. Yellow sunlight stained his dirty shirt, shot copper lights from his hair. 'The other possibility is that she was not taken, that she chose to go.'

Chancellor Parry looked up from smoothing her blue satin knee-breeches, and her compulsive search for blood-marks. 'Noble Lord, she wanted to shine in your eyes. She would have told you anything to her credit. And . . . her illness may have made her think, for the first time, of the future.'

Then she smiled, slightly. 'Valentine would give me advice, being new, on how not to offend ex-Chancellor Scaris's faction. It was well-meant; I thought well of her for it.'

'Didn't need it, did you?' Casaubon grunted.

'She had a good heart, noble Lord.'

Al-Iskandariya said, 'If her illness were near-mortal, that would make her sensitive to occult influences. I, myself—'

'I'll go after her,' the Lord-Architect announced.

The dark man said, 'Noble Lord—'

'Whatever the reason for her kidnapping,' Tabitha Parry put in, 'would it not be better if we first knew something about those supposedly responsible? This "Circle"?'

'*That is what I am trying to tell you!*'

Casaubon looked at Al-Iskandariya with great kindness and said, 'Please. Proceed.'

Sounds came in through the inn-door, now ajar; the shrill voices of the diners in the next room and the drinkers out in the yard; the bellowing of oxen, and the squealing of pigs in market pens. Smells of stale cooking lingered. The dark man clasped his hands, and looked down at them as if they (or his rings) were a source of strength.

'The mathematico-magical treatise *Ghâya* speaks of those whose powers derive from the star-daemons,' he said. 'I believe the Circle to be of that nature.'

He raised his head. The sapphire eyes met Casaubon's.

'I do not know who they are. Or what they are. Lord-Architect, listen to me. Whatever they are now, they *were* alive, last, six-and-twenty thousand years ago. It was they who brought the Sardicinien Empire down. The *Ghâya* speaks of them. There are covert references in the *Hieroglyphika*. It was they who made dust from the City of Bright Waters.'

Now they were silent, even Janou. Chancellor Parry began obsessively to smooth down every crease in her knee-breeches. The Lord-Architect nodded for Al-Iskandariya to continue.

'The Brotherhood of which I am one is old. The Invisible College knows us. To us, the infallible signs by which to recognise the Circle were passed down – how wandering stars return at last to certain constellations, and the sun rises in ill-fated Houses, and the Great Conjunction comes. That Great Conjunction will occur soon now. We must find the Circle before the Circle is complete, and they can call on all their power. Find them, and we will find the Art of compelling the star-daemons to serve us —'

Janou sat up. 'Oh, see you, what happened to how you'd save the City? You just want their knowledge!'

'No, no, no.' Al-Iskandariya shook his head. 'But if we have not their Art, we have nothing to fight them with. They will corrupt the City. Until it pleases the City to serve them.'

Casaubon snorted. 'Not after last year! Master Al-Iskandariya, I am still an Architect-Lord. This City is laid out according to the principles of harmony and hierarchy. My Miracle Garden is a

microcosm of the great cosmic harmony. There's nowhere for
Corruption to gain a foothold.'

'We also study the stars,' Chancellor Parry said quietly.

'*But I tell you—*'

Casaubon interrupted Al-Iskandariya for the last time. 'The
answer in all cases is my Valentine. Find her, find what she does or
doesn't know; find out, so, what the future holds for the City. Parry,
I'll leave you to alert the City Councillors. I myself will go after
Master-Captain Valentine.'

Pewter pots scattered from the table as he pushed past. He strode
from the inn, out into the plague-hot marketplace, heading for the
fortune-tellers's booth.

*The hot darkness of the canvas booth is empty, no one is there. A rickety
table occupies the space, covered with a dirty grey cloth, and on it a scatter of
gemstones: carved in minute detail with the faces of old gods, the symbols of
decans, and the hieroglyphics of a language long forgotten.*

Amber, tiger's-eye, black pearl, and diamond.

Beautiful enough to attract the eye, and the hand.

Casaubon thrust under the flap and into the tent. A rip in the
canvas let a hot fragment of sun in.

By that gold light he saw the stones. An agate with an intaglio
of a man carrying a cornsheaf and leading a bull. A black pearl
layered to the silhouette of a barbaric city gate. A carnelian with
twin androgynes carved on it. Carved with a glyptic Art lost long
ago.

'Master-Captain!' He would not touch these for his life.

On the last stone, a striped gold tiger's eye, was carved a fox-faced
woman, hardly more than a child, the face Valentine's.

'Noble Lord!'

They staggered in after him: Al-Iskandariya running, Janou
tripping over the hem of her black robe. The young Scholar-Soldier
cannoned into the back of Tabitha Parry, who fell forward onto the
straw floor of the booth.

'*Don't touch that—*'

'It's her face!' Casaubon seized and held up the carved tiger's-eye
stone.

There was an ominous creak. Janou recovered her balance
and looked up. Over their heads, the canvas of the tent was
sagging.

'We'd better leave!'

The Chancellor knelt up and pointed at Janou. Janou couldn't make out what brought fear to the woman's white face. She grabbed Parry's arm and pulled her towards the exit.

A sharp *crack!* and one corner of the tent came down. As if some great weight pressed on it – Janou picked up her skirts and followed the Chancellor out through the booth's loose flap. Her feet burned with pain. White light dazzled her. Another *crack!* and then she turned to see the old canvas shred and fall in on itself under a weight of white.

Under snow.

Janou spat, 'Casaubon, you great fool—!'

Tabitha Parry pointed again at clouds of frosty breath issuing from the girl's mouth.

They stood in the great City square, knee deep in snow.

It stretched away from them, acres of unbroken whiteness, merging with the distant marble façades so that Tabitha Parry was uncertain whether she saw a city of stone or ice. She looked across to the Belvedere, and then to where steps went up to the Miracle Garden. All the same: all transmuted to winter.

'How . . . ?'

The shadows of buildings cast on the snow were lilac, almost purple. The sky burned deep blue. Air snagged in Janou's throat, cold and electric, and the sun on the snow hurt her eyes. There was a scent on the wind of nothing ever encountered before.

'He's still in there!' Tabitha Parry swung round and began to tug at the heavy folds of the collapsed canvas. Janou scrambled to help her.

It was not until some minutes later that it became apparent: neither the Lord-Architect nor Al-Iskandariya were trapped under the fallen tent. There was nothing but snow. They were not there.

'What *is* this place?' Tabitha Parry whispered.

A slow, rhythmic sound echoed. Far off, but heard clearly across the winter City. Something in its timbre and slowness made Parry uncomfortable.

Thin particles began to appear. They didn't fall from the sky. Silver metallic flakes appeared in mid-air, dusting the crusted snow. The snow-dunes shimmered, edged with a purple light. Janou felt the icy wind again blow in her face. This time it cut deep, and smelled of wild roses.

'Wait!' She swung her pack off her back, and fell to her knees beside it in the crusted snow. Blowing on her fingers, she ripped open the leather flap, strewed scrolls out of her way, and flipped up the top of a metal box.

The crop-haired girl paused, held up a hand, muttered something, and made a sequence of signs, tracing geometries on the cold air. A faint purple luminosity clung to her fingers. She reached down into the box and began to tap.

Tabitha Parry leaned closer. She saw ruby-lights in the heart of the machine. The girl was tapping out a sequence, pausing, repeating it, waiting again for an answer.

'The College?' Parry asked.

Janou continued to code into the transmitter for long minutes. When she peered in at the tracer-light, she swore.

'Whoreson stupid object! Great gaping Hell's *teeth*!'

Janou picked the backpack up by its straps and swung it, two-handed. It curved in a short are and smacked into the stone wall of the nearest palace façade. Metal smashed.

'Whore! Pimp! Bawd! *Stupid!*'

Red-faced, she glared at Tabitha Parry.

'Whoreson College told me it would work anywhere!'

Tabitha Parry shivered.

'It appears that this is . . . not the lower city.' She stared at the girl suddenly. 'You're not wearing *shoes*.'

Janou scratched at her fluffgold hair. She picked up one foot and studied the sole, that was still black with the warm mud of the lower city. Her skin was beginning to redden with cold.

'Here.' Tabitha Parry pulled off a buckled shoe. She unrolled her thick stocking and passed it to the girl, put her shoe back on her bare foot, and repeated the process.

As she was pulling on the woollen stockings, Janou paused, reached up to her backstrap, and pulled free a scabbarded sword.

'The winged watchers!'

Parry raised her head.

A chasm gaped across the square.

Bemused, she stared at the raw gash of earth and rock. The marble paving was split in a jagged line that ran between them and the steps of the Miracle Garden. There were other gulfs, further off. She sniffed back ice-tears, and caught a scent from the depths. Something rank, with roses. Parry sank to her knees in the snow.

'I thought – it was a *building*—'

Tabitha Parry, melted snow soaking the knees of her breeches, craned her neck.

The winged watcher crouched at the chasm, front paws on the edge of emptiness. The leonine body shone a dazzling blue-black against the snow. It rose up like a cliff, twenty feet high: paw, shoulder, massive bull-neck and bearded human face . . . and the blue-black pinions, closed against its flanks, rose at their tips thirty feet above the snow in the square.

Janou's hand closed on Parry's shoulder, painfully.

'That . . .'

The winged watcher crouched, barbed tail wrapped round its hindquarters. Its beard hung in tight shiny coils. Its hair, tight-curled, was held back by a basalt fillet. Tabitha Parry stared at its sensual, full lips; at the tip-tilted, closed eyes. Shining blue and ebony under the sun.

'It's a statue,' she said. She did not know, until she gasped air, that she had stopped breathing. 'Look. There's snow on its back. It's *stone*.'

Their breath smoked on the cold air.

Janou leaned against the kneeling Chancellor, and stood on one leg to brush snow off her makeshift stocking. She seemed to be sorting images in her head.

'They're the Lords of the Shining Paths,' she said. 'So *that's* Al-Iskandariya's star-daemons. Turd! Won't I have words with the College when I get back!'

Tabitha Parry heard a soft sound . . . It came again: a distant, implosive noise.

Snow sliding and hitting ice.

She looked at Janou. The girl whisked her sword from its scabbard.

The woman pushed her dishevelled hair back into its clasp with gloved filthy hands, and stared across the chasm. She pointed, mutely. Janou followed the direction of her finger.

The winged watcher opened stone eyelids and fixed them with a yellow gaze.

The winter city sang.

As if every stone vibrated to the frost working inward to its heart, every marble statue and step and balustrade; as if each ice-spear hanging from palace façades chimed; as if the automata in the distant Miracle Garden began to strike; as if the sky itself thrummed with electricity.

The winged watcher lifted its front paws from the lip of the chasm. The remaining snow slid from its back and wings.

It drew back, muscles bunching in the massive shoulders, wing-tips rising. Its hindquarters rose from the snow. The barbed tail flicked once. Then in one movement the winged watcher sprang upwards. Black wings darkened the sky.

The ground shook with its landing, on their side of the chasm. Janou fell to the snow. She clutched the Chancellor, who stared, open-mouthed.

The watcher settled, couchant, folding blue-black pinions down its flanks. The curling blue-black beard touched massive paws. Snow settled. It shifted a hind paw, leaving a mark that an ox-cart would have vanished into, and the full, closed lips curved. A glint of citrine light showed under the eyelids.

Chancellor and Master-Captain pressed close together. They stared up at that vast face. Janou felt a feather of warm breath touch her skin.

Parry whispered, 'Did – is that what's responsible for us being here?'

'Being lured here? Oh, what else!'

Chancellor Tabitha Parry stood. She kicked snow aside as she walked forward, and stopped after a few yards.

'*Send us back!*'

Parry's voice sounded shrill in her ears.

There was a bass rumble that shook snow off the palace roofs. Particles of air began to tingle and glow and dazzle in Janou's vision. She turned her head and spat into the feathery snow. A shadow cut the bright sunlight, and it was suddenly arctic cold.

Janou trudged back to her broken pack, saying over her shoulder, 'It can't hurt us. Not materially. Not yet.'

The Chancellor stared up at the crouching bulk between her and the sun.

'This wants our City?'

A thin sound grew out of nowhere. It sang into loudness, ceased; and the marble paving under the snow split with a *crack!* The chasm gaped another foot. Loose earth tumbled down into the gulf. Parry heard no sound of it landing.

The winged watcher opened yellow eyes, and the curving full lips parted. The rumbling sound modulated into a higher tone. There were separate, distinct sounds in it.

Janou kicked her way through the snow, sword resting back on her shoulder. She was shivering in the thin black robe, but she walked with a swagger, and her eyes were bright. 'Oh, see you, I know that language!'

'Then ask it: where's Master-Captain Valentine? Ask it: where are the lower city people?' Tabitha Parry stripped off soaking gloves and blew on cold-mottled fingers. 'Ask it: how do we get home?'

Janou drew a deep breath, and forced it out again in a chthonic, guttural chant.

The winged watcher stretched a paw. It bent one elbow, raked; claws as long as a human being was tall pulled ice into splinters. As it rose on all four paws, it stretched its wings. Black pinions rustled over their heads; then folded.

The bass tone boomed.

As the winged watcher moved in feline strides over the snow, Janou said:

'That means, *follow*.'

There had been nothing there before, but it was there now, almost daring them to deny it: an unmortared stone bridge that arced up over the chasm. Janou ran to its foot, and then hesitated as she stared down into the gulf.

The winged watcher paced past the Belvedere, across the square, across that great expanse, to the marble steps that led up to the heart of the City: the newly constructed Miracle Garden. Its shadow darkened the snow, with a stain that remained for some seconds after it had passed.

Ahead, voices rang out joyfully across the snow.

Casaubon thrashed free of the entangling tent-folds. An oblong of light appeared. The Lord-Architect staggered through it, and yelped as he cracked his head on the stone lintel. He touched his hair, and looked at his red-stained fingers in injured affront. Then he licked his fingers.

'Janou? Parry, rot your guts—'

A green and gold light shimmered.

'Noble Lord. Speak softly: there may be strange inhabitants of this plane.' Al-Iskandariya brushed tendrils of green from his baggy sleeves, and trod down spear-bladed grass.

Gold sun slanted through a tangle of vines, creepers, and fern-trees. It was impossible to see the sky. Pink flowers grew knee high. When Casaubon glanced over his shoulder, he saw a stone pyramid, some twelve feet high. Set into one triangular side was a dark oblong: a doorway.

He took his other hand out of his pocket and opened it. The carved tiger's eye glinted. The intaglio face was still that of Valentine.

Casaubon reached inside his coat, drew out a metal flask, twisted the top off, and drank. The alcohol caught in his throat. He coughed, sniffed back tears, and offered the flask to Al-Iskandariya. The small man refused. The rat peered out of Casaubon's coat, twitched its whiskers, and vanished back into his inner pocket.

'Is this where she went?'

Al-Iskandariya frowned, studying the hieroglyphs cut into the pyramid's sides. He glanced inside the doorway, shrugged; and then looked up at Casaubon. 'For each of certain Lords of the Shining

Paths – the Power of Strife and Abundance; the Power of the Night
of Time; the Power of the Wild Land; the Power of the Throne of
Lights and Dominions – for each, there is a realm mirroring our
earth. Whether Lady Valentine came to this realm, or another . . .'

'Pox rot your guts! don't you *know*? What use is your "Brotherhood" if you can't answer a simple question!'

'Hardly simple.' Al-Iskandariya bristled.

The moist heat made the Lord-Architect sweat. There were scents
on the air that seemed incongruous – dry air and frost?

Casaubon began now to pick out shapes under the covering ivy,
vines, and flowering creepers. Here, a pointed gable; there, a glint of
light off window-glass. A vine spiralled up and hung lumps of
grapes, not from a fallen tree, but from the jutting shaft of an ox-
cart. They stood at the bottom of a well, the sides formed by
decaying walls, so thickly grown over that the lath-and-plaster
could not be seen.

Abandoned, grown over, lost: but still just recognisable as River-
quarter.

Casaubon reached into his coat for his flask, and took a deep
swallow. He choked, wiped streaming nostrils, leaving a trail on his
satin sleeve, and sniffed. 'If Valentine's here, I know where she'll
be. The Miracle Garden.'

Fern-trees and vines tangled in baroque complexity.

'Here' said the noble Lord-Architect Casaubon, 'I *know* you. I had
you on trial for sedition in the Moon-hall last year!'

The woman looked up lazily from where she lay in her vine-
hammock, a child curled under each arm. She paused in feeding the
younger one milk. Light fell green and gold on her emaciated
features.

'We were promised freedom from the Architect-Lords—!' She
lifted her pointed chin and grunted: a guttural, choking call. Then
she looked back at Casaubon, and with the air of one waiting, said,
'I hope he takes you to a world where you fry!'

Al-Iskandariya peered around the Lord-Architect's massive
shoulder. ' "He"?'

The woman chuckled. The hammock-bower smelt of milk, and
nectarines. She stretched one bruised calf and ankle, turned her
face up to the shaded forest heat, and smiled. The baby made small
sounds of pleasure. The woman opened eyes that were darkest blue,
staring directly at Casaubon.

'Noble Lord, have you been down to those dungeons lately, that
you're so proud of? Have you ever spent a night in those oubliettes?

Where it's too cramped to lie, and too short to stand, and too cold to sleep? Have you? No – of course not. Noble Lord, you condemned me to *weeks* of that. I was carrying Gillan here at the time. If I don't greatly care what becomes of you, don't be surprised.'

Al-Iskandariya wiped at the sweat that poured down his face. He squinted, trying to see what lay ahead of the woman. Through the crushed grass and fungi underfoot, he began to feel a rhythmic, slow vibration.

'Lord Casaubon, we should leave. There is something approaching that my Art warns me—'

Casaubon waved a meaty hand dismissively. His eyes almost vanished into his cheeks as he screwed up his face in concentration.

'Barbary Axtell,' he remembered. 'You had a printing press.'

Axtell said, 'Yes.'

The Lord-Architect tugged at the black-stained neck of his shirt. The arms and back of his brown satin coat were soaked with sweat, and he had tugged his carefully tied ruffle open. Sweat glinted in the copper hairs on his chest.

'Oh, see you, how could you expect to print what you did and be allowed to get away with it! You'd have had all River-quarter up in arms!'

'*Yes. Rightly so.*' She shut her eyes. The lids were shaded lilac, sepia. 'But now I've to care for Gillan and Romiley. They're safe here. Someone else will have to carry on the fight. Noble Lord, there were scum and petty tyrants that we scorned to use against you – remember that, now we're gone.'

A skein of flower-vines snapped and fell from a fern-tree.

Al-Iskandariya seized the Lord-Architect's coat sleeve and pulled him onwards. Casaubon stumbled as he went. He looked back over his shoulder at the woman, opened his mouth as if to make some reply, and then closed it again, and plunged on through the vegetation beside Al-Iskandariya.

They had struggled perhaps five yards when they came to an open space.

A dozen or so people were eating a feast, spread out in the vine-cloaked ruins of a brick dome – green and gold light fell on them, their laughter echoing. The Lord-Architect recognised most of them from the jails. He paid them no attention. The domed building was different in all else but its contours . . . his Belvedere. He turned to point this mirror-image out to Al-Iskandariya.

The dark man hit his own temple with the flat of his hand. 'I am a fool! An ignorant fool! There was nothing to say that any member of the Circle had to be human!'

Casaubon scowled. 'Oh, what?'

'Noble Lord, here is what made that woman promises.'

Casaubon looked. Where the square should be, that here was golden grass and thick tree-ferns, a basalt statue stood. The light slid down its carved flanks like honey, shining on massive wings, and curled beard, and open yellow eyes. The ground shook to its tread. A great cloud of bees rose up and swarmed joyously round its glistening ringlets, with a hum that deafened Casaubon.

The dark man moved to stand in front of Casaubon.

'O Thou, greatest among the Great, Thou whose name is written in the ragged stars, Thou who hast for Thy province all fruitfulness, all strength, all sweetness; O Thou for whom the silt-rivers flood their blessing to the fields, Thou of majesty and power—'

The Lord-Architect saw how his pale blue eyes glittered.

'O Thou to Whom of old my prayers have been addressed, Thou journey and destination; O Thou Who Standeth at the crossroads; Thou Who art my desire and my joy and my subject of praise; hear Thy servant and forbear to take that life which we owe Thee!'

Tree-ferns tumbled, lashed aside. The swarms of bees rose up into the gold air like mica-flakes. One paw lifted. It came down, crushing tree-ferns and vines. The full lips opened a fraction. Casaubon scented something, a warm breath that had a ripe tang in it, like carrion left in the midday heat.

'Great Architect! Is *that* what she was calling?' Casaubon jerked his head, indicating the woman they had left in the hammock.

A young man stood and left the feast. He held up honey-sticky hands. The great winged being halted, one forepaw raised, and the stone-crowned head bowed until the yellow eyes perceived the small figure before it.

The air shimmered and sang.

It was as if the young man became invisible to the feasters; they turned away, laughing; and suddenly the temperature soared so that sweat sprang out on the Lord-Architect's face, and he saw Al-Iskandariya's intense gaze falter as the winged watcher reared up and back, wings furling out, knocking aside vines and flowers, to rustle closed again about itself and the young man.

The air sang like cracked glass. A drop of blood fell to the rich grass.

Its wings unfurled. It was alone.

Al-Iskandariya gripped Casaubon's arm. 'It is a star-daemon, a *power*, it has a Name visible in the celestial sphere these six-and-twenty thousand years! Lord Casaubon, *this* is what makes promises to your citizens and lures them onto this plane. Think what we might do now! If we compel it with incantations and diagrams—'

'Compel my great hairy black arsehole! Let these pox-rotted fools stay and be prey to it,' Casaubon advised. 'I'm going to get to the Garden if it kills both of us.'

A few minutes later, red-faced, panting in the forest heat and still running, the Lord-Architect realised that they could not begin to outdistance the winged watcher's slow pacing.

Al-Iskandariya gasped, 'It is – herding us – where it wants us to go.'

'The Lords of the Shining Paths,' Tabitha Parry said, her eyes screwed up against the brilliance of sun on snow. She shook her head. 'The Lord of Winter . . . is there a Summer Lord, too, and a Moon Lord, and an Ocean Lord, as history says?'

'Wouldn't be at all surprised,' Janou grunted.

Voices shouted, louder now, as Janou and Chancellor Parry picked a way up the ice-covered steps.

Before them, the winged watcher paced on.

The Miracle Garden lay under a cover of white. Snow choked the sundials, froze up the fountains, silenced the automata.

A young man and a woman ran past, kicking up scuffs of snow with their bare feet as casually as if it were grass-cuttings. One tagged the other; they collapsed, laughing and rolling in the snow. The girl's eyes were purple-dark with malnutrition. The boy was thin, and the flower-scabs of the plague dotted his face. They were laughing too hard now to run.

'You!' Tabitha Parry snapped. Neither looked at her.

Two women and a child sat by a snow-cloaked sundial. They were cramming their mouths with fruit, fruit as transparent as glass; that when Janou bent to touch it, was cold and ice. The women fed each other quarters of ice-apples and ice-tangerines. One gave the baby an ice-cherry.

Parry shivered.

'Can't you almost hear it?' she appealed to Janou.

An old woman played a pipe. Her mean, thin face transformed, she played music they could only guess at.

Janou's foot tapped on the snow, seeking that silent rhythm and failing. She moved to stand directly in front of the old woman, and was rewarded with a halt in the silent music and an absent-minded smile.

'Don't speak to them,' Parry begged. 'We might . . . join them?'

Janou grabbed the Chancellor's arm and tucked it under her

own. 'Not us! It'll have different lures for us. See you, we'll follow it, and plan according to what we see.'

Men broke off from drinking when the winged watcher padded towards them. They took up a kind of running game, with snow-vines and snow-flowers, that ended when they threw the vines over the winged watcher's back in pale festoons. Laughing, they desisted. The watcher shook blue-black wings, and paced on, snow-crowned.

When the men looked at the Chancellor, their gaze never altered.

The winged watcher led them past topiary mazes, marble pools and waterfalls thick with ice. Janou began to limp. She halted with Tabitha Parry at the top of a small rise.

Below, the Garden stretched on forever. White, blue-shadowed, filled with dancers whose feet never printed the snow. Crowds moved there in silent festival. There were men and women marked with plague-flower who now harvested cold fruit, and ate ice as if it dripped all the honey of summer.

'They don't feel the cold.' Janou sheathed her sword, and slapped her mottled hands together as if they were a badge of humanity. 'Do we try to bring them back?'

The Chancellor looked at her in complete incomprehension. 'Of course! They're our citizens.'

The winged watcher led them on, down the far side of the slope. Tabitha Parry recognised the place. Here, a snow-covered hedge rimmed an octagon of ground. The patterns of the knot garden showed silver on white, in ice on the snow.

This knot garden was complete. Its pattern wove in, out, under, through . . .

A bird fluttered past Janou's face. She swatted at it automatically, and then gaped when she found herself with it clasped in her hand.

Tabitha Parry took it from the amazed girl's fingers. Light wood, carved into fluted feathers, and inside a ticking mechanism of gut and watchsprings. She raised it, let it go. It fluttered up into the frosty azure sky.

The winged watcher stepped forward.

Its vast bulk could not have been contained in the space of the knot garden: still, it seemed that the great paws trod the silver pattern, until with a flick of a wingtip and a skirl of ice, the winged watcher walked out of the world.

Janou caught her skirt up with one hand. The other held her unsheathed sword. She kicked one wool-stockinged heel against the ice, and jumped the low hedge into the knot garden.

She called back, '—a gateway between *their* planes of existence—', and was gone.

Tabitha Parry gazed around the snow-shrouded Miracle Garden.
The dapper woman's face was red with exertion; her blue satin was
ice- and sweat-stained. She gazed, tempted, at those who trod
the ice and never felt it. Then she followed the Master-Captain
Janou.

*Buildings line the wide, dusty streets. Yellow grit lies heavily piled
on triangular pediments, and flat roofs; and on the sides of squat pyramids,
into which time has worn cracks and ridges. All the square windows are
empty, dark.*

Dust skirls on the humid air.

*Great buildings, that stand with hieroglyph-covered frontages towering a
hundred feet high, now shimmer in the heat-haze. It seems that a radiance
clings to lintel and pediment and frieze, honey-coloured and expectant.
Dark arches that gaped for long-dead inhabitants now, within their depths,
shed sparks of static light.*

*Now the constellations returning to their ancient positions bring walkers
into the streets. By pattern and by patience they return. They spread dark
wings in their slow pacing, they turn ancient heavy-lidded eyes to the sun.*

Almost unnoticed in the wide streets, four people are reunited.

They followed a winged watcher.

Janou swaggered as she walked the wide street, kicking the hem
of her gown out so as not to tread on it. She slicked her hair down,
but the heat made it stand up in spiky tufts. Yellow dust crusted on
her lips. She grinned at the Lord-Architect.

'Got your flask? I'm thirsty!'

'This won't cure it.' He put a protective hand on the breast of his
brown satin coat, that was stained with vegetable green.

Chancellor Parry complained, 'Where's the *real* City?'

The Chancellor seemed unsurprised to see Casaubon and Al-
Iskandariya. Casaubon, studying her ravaged face, judged that
nothing would affect the woman now, short of an apocalypse.

'And we may get that yet,' he muttered to himself.

The rat scuttled up onto his broad shoulder, and nestled against
the rolls of fat at his chin. It fell to washing its spiky yellow fur with
a pink tongue. The Lord-Architect gave it his finger to chew.

'We were wrong, I think, to fear a material hurt,' Al-Iskandariya
said. His brilliant blue eyes were a little glazed. 'If they were
material enough yet to harm us, they would have no hesitation in
doing it.'

Janou skipped a step as they walked, to catch up. 'They'll *become*
material. The Great Conjunction will happen. Well then. What can
we do about stars? Nothing! But there must be something we can
do about *them.*'

Casaubon's tree-trunk legs pounded the hard-packed earth of the
street. He saw the watcher some hundred yards ahead, where
streets intersected. It seemed to be the one from the summer forest.

'They've got their worlds. Why do they have to come scratching
after mine?'

Each street that they passed opened up a perspective view. Lined
by vast pyramids, sarcophagi, and mausoleums; carved over with
the hieroglyphics of a language aeons dead. The sun glared from a
humid yellow sky.

'Even star-daemons can become corrupted, longing for the
material plane of existence.' Al-Iskandariya's pace slowed at each
inscription that they passed; he spelled out formulae under his
breath.

'*Look!*'

Casaubon, who had taken his hand out of his pocket, held it
open. The carved tiger's-eye stone rested on his fleshy palm. A
purple luminosity edged it. Janou touched a finger to it. A blue-
white spark singed her. Light limned the edges of the carved face:
Valentine's face.

'Even in this dream-world,' the Lord-Architect demanded, 'could
I find something – someone – real?'

Janou lifted one thin shoulder.

'They brought us here. Ask them what they want with us!'

They reached the junction of avenues. The winged watcher paced
on, stately and slow, in company with another. This one seemed, if
anything, slightly younger: the curved lips fuller and more cruel.

A little way on and, pacing the dusty avenues, came another,
sleek and sinuous, whose face was beardless, and whose almond
eyes were full of a slow, sweet, lazy wickedness.

'One for each sphere,' Janou said.

They came at last to a Square where great winged watchers lay,
barbed tails curled around their flanks, blue-black pinions whispering in the still air. They lay in a vast circle. Between their paws, and
facing the great Patriarch of the watchers, a thin, shaven-haired
figure sat, cross-legged, studying something that lay on the earth.

Cuneiform clay tablets. Al-Iskandariya took a step forward, as if
he ached to run and read them.

But it was Casaubon who cried, 'Valentine!' and lumbered into
the circle, between the great haunches and shoulders and forepaws

that made him a midget, and without looking at any of the lazy-eyed smiles, seized Valentine in a crushing embrace.

The thin woman stood on her toes to throw her arms about Casaubon's neck; one foot hooking behind his leg, her face pressed into his shoulder. Janou grinned broadly at Tabitha Parry. Then, getting no response, she looked more closely at the Chancellor's face, and frowned to herself. Parry's eyes were fixed: the shining lenses reflecting nothing but the towering figures of the winged watchers.

'Al-Iskandariya,' she said softly, 'have you any medical skills?'

The dark man started. He took his gaze from Casaubon and Valentine.

'Are you hurt, Master-Captain?'

Janou pulled Tabitha Parry forward. 'See you, what can you do for her?'

While the girl supported her, Al-Iskandariya fixed his intense pale eyes on Parry's face. He murmured under his breath. Janou felt the rock-hardness of the woman's muscles begin to shift.

'*How did you get here?*' the Lord-Architect was demanding.

Valentine scratched at her cropped red hair. She seemed no different from that moment in the knot garden, when she had fled into thin air. She shrugged, and said:

'I saw the way through, and I took it. They teach that a near-mortal illness can give you vision. I'd been having true-dreams for days. I saw that some danger threatened you, and the City. When I saw a chance, I had to jump at it.'

Casaubon dragged out a brown kerchief and dabbed at his forehead and chins.

'*What* chance?'

The thin woman put her hands on her hips, and gazed up at the Lord-Architect. Although she was only two years older than Janou, her hair was growing out white at the temples. She stood there as if the great waiting watchers were no more than cliffs or buildings or statues.

'With the celestial conjunction that was coming up, there was *bound* to be some disaster. I had dreams of ancient ages. Too long ago for the College to know.' She caught sight of Al-Iskandariya, by Tabitha Parry, and casually saluted him. 'Or the Brotherhood. So, if the only way to avert the danger was to know how it was averted *before*, and if that knowledge was on this plane, then obviously when I saw the chance—'

'You shouldn't have done it!' Casaubon was reduced to sounding petulant.

'Why shouldn't I?' Valentine protested. 'There was a danger, I came here—'

'—to confront the watchers of the world in the city where they sleep out the ages,' Al-Iskandariya completed. 'Fool!'

'Oh, see you, they can't hurt you.' The ex-Master-Captain kicked the vast paw that rested in front of her. She grinned up at the idol's wicked smile. 'Takes all their energy now to hold a material form. Janou, I think I have it. You want to check my translation?'

'Show me.'

Valentine knelt by the spike-haired girl to point at cuneiform tablets. The Lord-Architect reached down, grabbed the scruff of her shirt, and pulled her to her feet.

He said, 'You scrofulous, pox-scabbed, dung-brained, irresponsible—!'

Valentine distastefully picked his pudgy hand off her shoulder. She looked at it thoughtfully, and then wrapped it in both of hers, and hugged it to her sharp-ribbed chest. She was still painfully thin.

'You didn't have to come after me,' she said. 'I can handle it.'

The noble Lord-Architect threw down the metal flask that he was holding, stamped it flat, and fetched it a kick that had it skittering off the basalt elbow of the beardless watcher.

'*Women!*'

Janou lay on her belly sorting through clay tablets. She kicked one raised foot against the other, and hummed absently. Her bare sword lay a few yards off, forgotten. She flinched at Casaubon's bellow.

'She *has* got something,' Janou protested. 'Here!'

She rolled over and tossed a clay tablet to Al-Iskandariya. He gasped, all but dropped it, and abruptly sat down on the earth and put it in front of him.

'What is it?' the Lord-Architect snapped. 'Does it help us?'

'Ah.' Valentine scratched her fox-tawny hair. She put her fists in her breeches pockets. 'As to that – you might say, they win, and we win.'

Al-Iskandariya demanded, 'Explain.'

Valentine, slightly pink, said, 'Until the Great Conjunction, more or less all they could do is lure people away – people who might have opposed them for one reason or another, when they broke through and took the City. Agitators, rabble-rousers. Architect-Lords. Chancellors.'

'Master-Captains?' Casaubon suggested pointedly.

'Oh, see you, when all the celestial spheres move into conjunction, what do *you* expect to be able to do about it? The Circle would take the City now, even if you and I had done nothing but sit in the knot garden!' Valentine threw up her dusty hands, gesturing. 'Yes, I was tricked into coming here. Yes, they lured you away after me. But they had to use genuine bait – and I know something now that *they* don't.'

Al-Iskandariya snorted. 'You claim to know how to stop a star-daemon in the fullness of its power?'

The flanks and haunches and wingtips rose up, shining ebony and blue, into the hot yellow sky. Occasionally, heavy lids blinked. The ancient smiles might have been carved in stone.

'It's to do with the influence of the stars . . .' Valentine flopped down on hands and knees, sorting through clay tablets which she pushed at Al-Iskandariya. 'The fifth Sphere affects the heart, the sixth the limbs, the eighth the brain, the tenth the liver—'

'Yes, yes,' the dark man said.

'A Sphere affecting melancholy; and one for the sanguine of us, and those who are choleric—' Here she grinned at Janou and Casaubon in turn. 'So for each quality of the human, there is a Shining Path of influence from each celestial sphere. But, *non cogunt*, the stars don't *compel* us. And Paracelsus argues that the influence of the Lords of the Shining Paths isn't binding, or even one-sided ah!'

Valentine seized on one tablet, the surface cracked and flaked.

'You're familiar enough with medico-magical theory, master. To even the humours in a body that suffers ill-health, talismans may be used to draw down the stars' influence.'

'And to draw bodies *into* the celestial spheres?' the Lord-Architect Casaubon tossed the tiger's-eye intaglio to Valentine. She, seeing it, was silenced. He added, 'I am not so ignorant of these matters either. It seems to me that the influence might work both ways!'

Janou jumped up. The front of her black gown was printed with dust, and she shook it vigorously. 'Let's go back. I won't speak of answers. I don't trust these watchers. They could pick it out of your head.'

Casaubon blinked. 'We can go back? So easily?'

'It's near the Great Conjunction.' Valentine nudged a cuneiform clay tablet with her boot. 'I learn fast.'

She squatted down, and drew the pattern of the knot garden in miniature in the dust. It was a different pattern, Casaubon thought.

As he bent forward to study it, the rat slid from his inner pocket, dropped to the earth, picked itself up and sneezed, and trotted, bald tail cocked high, into the dust-drawn pattern. Every yellowish spike of fur bristled. It sprang forward – and faded into the humid air.

They waited, but no blood-drop fell.

Valentine seized Casaubon's hand. Janou sheathed her abandoned sword, linked her arm through Tabitha Parry's, and reached out to the dark man. Al-Iskandariya stepped back, shaking his head.

'It'll work,' Valentine protested.

'It will,' he said. His eyes were on the discarded clay tablets, and not at all on the winged watchers. 'And if I need it, I'll find it, but I wouldn't be part of the Brotherhood if I could pass by an opportunity like this!'

One wing stretched a little, and the sun became shade.

The Lord-Architect Casaubon took Janou's free hand. And then the young Master-Captains dragged him out of the square, and out of the city where watchers wait, and out of the celestial Spheres, and into the world.

Red sand lay across the square, in knotted patterns as Valentine had drawn them.

'We're here!' Tabitha Parry threw her head back, hair flying loose from its clip, and slapped the Lord-Architect's padded shoulder. 'The City!'

Casaubon knelt down, huffing, and snapped his fat fingers. The rat scuttled back across the red sand and up his sleeve, into an inner coat pocket. He grabbed Valentine's hand and got to his feet again.

'How long before they follow us?'

'Hell!' Janou pointed.

Casaubon raised his head, expecting to see the shadow of dark wings.

Late morning sweltered. Wine and blood were splashed on the marble paving of the square, staining it black. A great crowd of people jammed the place, thick as a market-day crowd. But they were not Architect-Lords.

Casaubon kicked a litter of bottles and papers aside, and glared at the men and women who snored drunkenly under the hot sun; at children shrieking and running; at people talking or dancing or sorting through piles of goods.

'What in Hell—'

A sharp cry interrupted him.

'Another whoreson Lord!'

They had meat and drink clasped in their bare, dirty hands: priceless foodstuffs, and bottles from cellars laid down a hundred years past. A woman not far away pointed. She was tall, fair, in her fifties; and wrapped in torn silver-thread draperies. A musket rested back across her shoulder. An emaciated older man beside her yelled and pointed. Heads turned. Gangs of drunken youths began to run across the square.

Tabitha Parry, appalled, cried, 'Where are the Council Lords?'

Valentine grabbed for her sword-hilt; Janou's hand was already over it.

'Are you mad? They'll tear us to pieces!'

A crystal glass arced past Casaubon's head and shattered on the paving. The stench of wine and blood and vomit was strong. Men and women ran towards them. One shrieked Casaubon's name.

Tabitha Parry stepped forward, holding up a peremptory hand, ignoring Janou's grab at the back of her coat. A young man threw himself forward and grabbed Parry's knees, bringing both of them crashing down; and men and women in rags and torn finery piled on top, until the Chancellor was lost from sight.

Casaubon pushed Valentine and Janou behind him, in cover of his bulk. Janou brushed him off and plunged forward into the scrum, bright-eyed, screeching something that made the nearest man leap back; and Valentine struggled first to draw her sword and then to get her breath.

'Hell's red and rotten gullet!' Casaubon snarled. People came running from all directions. The screeching and yelling deafened him. '*Parry—*'

Several men grabbed Casaubon, pinioning his arms.

A hiss of steel: Valentine drew her blade.

'Lay a hand on him and lose it!' the Scholar-Soldier advised as she stepped closer to the Lord-Architect. Four ragged children flung themselves onto her, mobbing her; she struck uselessly with her bare hand.

Casaubon thrust people aside in sheer astonishment. A weight hit his back. As he went down, he saw Janou with one arm around the Chancellor; heard Valentine yell; and then the marble paving cracked across his knees. The noble Lord-Architect batted away fists that struck him.

'Hang him!'

Above, the sun rode up a tawny sky toward the meridian.

Casaubon, brown satin coat filthy and split at the seams, was dragged upright by six of his captors. His copper hair was disordered, there was a bruise under one eye, and his pudgy knuckles were skinned. Hats flew up into the warm air, faces turned to each other, grinning; and a great yell of approval split the morning.

'Make the bastard suffer!'

'*Lynch him!*'

Casaubon fixed first one and then the other of his persistent attackers with an arrogant stare.

'Master Gamaliel' he greeted one. 'How's the pimping trade? Are you still having to cut your whores to get them to work for you? Or is he feeding them your happy-dust, Mistress Weston?'

He saw Janou staggering beside Valentine in the crowd, Tabitha Parry's arm pulled across her shoulder, holding the battered woman up on her feet. From somewhere a voice yelled:

'*And* the Chancellor!'

'Put her with the other Lords!'

Janou swung around, kicking out the hem of her black dress.

''Ware the Invisible College—!'

A snarl of contempt answered her, but no one moved to challenge the Scholar-Soldiers.

All the silk banners of the Moon-hall had been dragged out to make cloaks for the people, trodden underfoot and filthy. Silver-thread embroidery and seed-pearl decoration glinted in the sun. Bottles went from hand to hand. The great City square was packed full, people jammed together in the stink of sweat and alcohol and sun.

'We'll hold a *trial*!' a young man yelled.

'Trial?' Casaubon yelped. The men and women who constituted themselves his impromptu jury yelled insults at the Lord-Architect. 'This is frivolous! You expect to try *me*?'

The crowd parted and he saw a group of battered men and women standing with their wrists tied and ankles hobbled, and he recognised the faces and satin coats of the Council of Architect-Lords.

'Is that serious enough for you?' a ragged woman asked.

Under the plague-hot and yellow sky, between the white marble façades of palaces, people stood or sat or stamped or yelled. One or two heaved up cobble-stones to throw. Dust swirled in the hot air. Makeshift galleries had been built up from benches, thrown out of palace windows; and men and women clung to precarious balances on slender mahogany and oak posts.

Casaubon sniffed, and thrust his hands into his deep pockets, and nodded casually to the bruised and filthy assembled Lords.

'See what happens,' he grunted, 'when I leave you alone for five minutes?'

In the centre of the makeshift amphitheatre, backed by the great white marble crest of the Sea Gate, twelve figures stood waiting. Robed in torn, richly embroidered draperies; scarlet and gold and azure in the noon sunlight. Casaubon could make out nothing of their faces.

The twelfth figure turned to face the Lord-Architect. The nearby people fell silent.

It slid the cloth back from its body.

A sudden stench made the Lord-Architect gag. He gasped, tears running, and leaned forward to vomit; and when he straightened up there was utter silence. Casaubon stared, not wiping his dripping chins.

A ragged, naked figure stood before him.

It had the rotten fragments of skin or cerements still clinging to its bones. It dripped, and stank. White bone shone out through the liquid corruption of its body. Tufts of black hair clung to its skull. It was putrifying, crawling with white grubs that fell from its eye-sockets. And resting around its skeletal neck, the metal sinking into the dead-living flesh, was a collar of iron, from which hung a cuneiform-marked tablet.

All the Lord-Architect Casaubon could think of was what Al-Iskandariya had said: *I do not know who they are. Or what they are. Whatever they are now, they were alive, last, six-and-twenty thousand years ago.*

Lost in the crowd, Valentine's voice came clearly:

'We're too late – the Circle have already come together.'

A man and a woman came forward from the crowd, eyes glittering, lifting the torn length of richly-embroidered scarlet cloth. What had once been a woman or a man lifted its rotting head to receive it as cowl and robe. The stench did not abate.

'*He is not yours to have. He is a sacrifice that will ease the accession to this earth of the Lords of the Shining Paths.*'

A chill went across the square. Some quality of the light altered. Those people nearest – the ones who neither drank nor celebrated nor rioted – murmured, almost with approval, as the edge of the sun's white disc was bitten into. As a solar eclipse began.

'*Hurry. It is almost noon.*'

An anonymous voice protested, 'But he was ours!'

The cowled figure raised its head. '*Bring him.*'

Four of the heavier River-quarter men hustled the Lord-Architect towards the centre of the makeshift amphitheatre.

Most of the crowd – men and women drunk, asleep, love-making, or deep in their own talk – simply did not see. But Casaubon saw an eddy of movement, heard one choked-off scream, and knew that within a few moments he and this abomination would be the focus of noon and the eclipse.

They thrust him, staggering a few paces, towards the circle of Twelve.

'Damn you!' Casaubon yelled. 'You shouldn't even be able to enter the City! I've spent thirty years constructing orders and harmonies and just proportions—'

'Not in the lower city,' several voices shouted.

He glanced round. Valentine, white with exhaustion, had sunk to one knee, swordpoint resting on the marble paving, supporting herself on the sword-hilt. He saw Janou slip away into the mass of people. She didn't return. The Chancellor was being thrust in with the other Architect-Lords.

Casaubon turned belligerently back to the hooded figures. 'Those are my citizens you've been luring off into your private kingdoms, and I want them back – and I want them back *now*.'

One figure spoke, so softly that Casaubon found himself almost bending nearer to hear it.

'We are they who once ruled, in aeons past; we have tarried,' the figure said, 'until the stars returned again. Now will we summon our ancient Masters—'

'Ancient dog-turds,' Casaubon muttered.

The other eleven figures began to cross and re-cross the square before the great Sea Gate. Where they passed, their skeletal feet tracked a pattern in the dust.

The eclipse moved to the full. A white corona sprang out in fire around the ebony disc of the sun, the eye of the sky. The stars of the Great Conjunction began to become visible in the darkened noon sky. Great shapes became implicit in the air; imminent in the shapes of the wind.

'We will give you one chance,' it went on. 'If these try you they will tear you to pieces. We will save you, if you worship us.'

'Worship you?' the Lord-Architect Casaubon said. 'I wouldn't wipe my arse with you!'

'It will not be easy, when our Masters return. They will wreak bloody havoc with their panic terror. Will you have half your citizens crushed, maimed, even killed?'

The figure leaned closer. The air that came off it was chill as a mausoleum.

'It may make the panic a little less dangerous if they see you worship us. It will prepare them. Give your citizens an example, noble Lord. Calm them before they trample each other to death.'

Light crept like honey down the frozen marble breakers of the Sea Gate. Within its Palladian columns the air shivered in a probability of shapes. Stars burned in the gold-brown sky. There came the rustle of vast wings.

The Lord-Architect felt silence lapping out into the square like ripples from a stone. Faces whitened. A dropped bottle smashed, glass skittering across the marble; and with it rose voices, protesting, vehement, tense to breaking.

Casaubon took his ham-hands out of his pockets. He spread his arms in appeal, half-turning to face the people, and raised his own voice over theirs:

'You can't expect a Lord-Architect to bow down to this filth!'

'*Thief in satin!*' The old cry came from somewhere high up on the rickety, makeshift galleries.

Someone laughed. To the Lord-Architect's strained ears, the voice was Janou's.

Casaubon scratched at his copper hair, tugged his dirty satin coat straight, and flung out one arm to the men and women clinging to the upturned benches.

'My noble citizens, I appeal to you—'

'Now it's *noble*!'

'Get down and beg for your life, *noble* Lord!'

A ripple of laughter went across the galleries. Those people nearest the Lord-Architect did not smile. One went to speak urgently with the unrobed figure, and Casaubon saw the woman point back at him in unmistakable warning, and then smack her fist emphatically into her palm.

He took a pace towards the crowd, and then made an undignified skip to one side as a lump of dung shied past his head. The yellowing ruffle at his neck had come untied again. Jeers sounded louder now: people's attention not on the livid sky or the Sea Gate, but on the Lord-Architect.

'Would you have me to beg?'

A roar went up. Two or three youths collapsed a lower bench, and came up laughing from the wreckage; a whole gang of children in River-quarter's rags began to jump up and down and jeer. By the Sea Gate, the hooded figures moved in their minuet, tracing a pattern that was almost complete.

The noble Lord-Architect lumbered round to face the half-robed skeletal figure. He threw out his fat arms, palms upturned; and then fell down on his knees, so heavily that the ground shook. He clasped his hands together. '*Mercy!*'

The men and women nearest to the Sea Gate roared. Crowds were pressing in now, as the news spread. They yelled as they ran, and caught the sides of makeshift benches and galleries, and hauled themselves up to stare at this spectacle.

Casaubon threw himself prostrate in front of the hooded figure, full length, arms outstretched. Keeping his head down, he wriggled awkwardly forward a few inches.

'Mercy!' he yelped, into the cold marble on which his bulk rested; and then hid his face in his pillowy arms. Something solid bounced off his left buttock, and he muttered; and tried to keep the tension out of his prone body.

The woman wrapped in silver draperies yelled, 'Oh, see you, that's our noble Lord-Architect – dignified to the last!'

Casaubon grinned into his muffling arms.

'Let's keep him as a clown—'

The scarlet-robed figure paced forward. In that crepuscular light, it seemed a blackness on the earth, putrid and shifting. It spoke, a hissing sound that cut through the crowd's laughter:

'*Casaubon is condemned to death. You others, and his whore, and his Chancellor, may live and think yourselves fortunate to serve our Masters.*'

The arctic silence chilled. Only the summer wind blew, and it did not warm: it carried the scent of carrion.

'*Execute the Lord Casaubon.*'

It took all of the Lord-Architect Casaubon's willpower to stay prostrate.

The Scholar-Soldier Valentine stood up, at the front edge of the crowd. She glanced round in the strange eclipse-light. Then, she abruptly reversed her grip on her sword-hilt, and handed the blade to the man nearest her.

Valentine walked out into the open space before the Sea Gate. Once, she hesitated between step and step. Then the narrow shoulders straightened, and she walked forward to stand beside the prone body of the Lord-Architect, and fix her gaze on the glistening faces of the Circle.

'If you kill him, you'll have to kill me too.'

The men and women on the galleries murmured. One voice yelled approval, was abruptly silenced. Another shouted, 'Kill him then!' There was a confused surge in the space before the Sea Gate.

A scuffle broke out near the captive Council Lords. A woman kicked and gouged her way out of the crowd and ran forward.

Tabitha Parry, one sleeve missing from her satin coat, hair falling in rat-tails, clenched gloveless fists and planted her feet either side of the prone legs of the Lord-Architect.

'Come on, then!' she yelled, 'come on, then, try it, why don't you!'

The emaciated man with the musket laughed so hard that he fell over. He sat sprawled on the marble, pointing, robbed of speech and breath.

The marble columns and statues of the Sea Gate grew stark, livid white. A sky of brown shadows clustered over it. Thunderously, in the blood, came the beat of wings. The Circle ceased their pacing. They stood in their ragged, bright finery; in the shadow of the eclipse.

At the laughter, one turned a glistening face to the people of the City. Valentine and Tabitha Parry stood, tiny defiant figures at the front of the crowd.

From somewhere far back, a young woman's voice called across the silence.

'Who gave *you* the right to kill him? He's ours!'

'Ours!'

'*It is noon!*'

Casaubon attempted to get to his feet, but his knee bent, suddenly, unable to take any weight, and he sat down again on the marble paving.

Because there was time for nothing else, he reached up and enfolded Valentine's narrow hand in his immense one, and pulled her down beside him. She threw an arm round his neck, the other across his mountain-belly.

Mouth to his ear, she said, 'It may have worked—'

The marble paving-stones of the square shook. A man fell, sprawling across Casaubon's legs, with a girl on top of him, pushing the Lord-Architect over; and the light shifted from brown to yellow to brilliance.

As if they were doors and sockets sliding into place, the interlocking Spheres reach conjunction. All shining paths lead now to the material plane of existence. As carefully, as delicately, as most fragile as if they created spun glass, the Lords of Celestial Power begin to make their selves upon the material Earth.

Sunlight shone out of the Sea Gate.

They came in slow procession, greater here than in their own spheres, towering so high that it was not clear how they passed through the Gate, great wings raised up and blotting the stars from the sky. The vast leonine bodies trod the earth, leaving with each step of hind- and forepaws a deeper imprint. They came, the Lords of the Shining Paths: the Power of the Wild Land, the Power of the Thrones of Light, the Power of the Night of Time . . .

Valentine stared up at vast human faces, at hooded eyes that opened with new appetites, at full lips that slid into lazy, sweet, wicked smiles, to see what they now saw.

'*It is noon!*'

On her knees beside Casaubon, she looked back from that split-second vision. The River-quarter crowd were shouting. Some protested, one fired a musket; children shrieked. Then the front of the crowd surged forward.

'He's ours!'

Valentine put up her hands instinctively, buffeted from side to side. An elbow knocked her, she braced herself, and someone's hand grabbed her arm and hauled her upright. The man, a stranger, grinned. The men and women of the lower city shoved and pushed round Valentine and Tabitha Parry and Casaubon in a tight, protective group.

'*It is noon . . . !*'

'Who gave you the right to tell us what to do?' a woman yelled.

'We had enough of that with the Architect-Lords!'

As if this were the hinge upon which they turned, all things seemed to wait.

Valentine, heart hammering, held fear and awe in effortless check, as if she balanced in some realm where control and abandon were identical. She rested one foot back so that it touched Casaubon; where he lay. 'As above, so below. They influence us, *and we influence them.*'

Tabitha Parry's mouth hung open. She shoved the filthy hair back from her face as she looked up. In an instant of stricken terror, she backed up against the close-pressed bodies of the city people. One man instinctively gripped her shoulder; a child clung to her ripped coat. Tabitha Parry stared up from amongst their awed, ambiguous, quixotic protection – and then she smiled. Gazing over the heads of the people in the square, Architect-Lords and citizens, only staring up at the Powers as they paced into the world.

She said, in wonder and joy, 'But why didn't I realise—!'

Layers of shadow lifted from the world.

The unstained sun, first crescent, then half, then fully itself, the star-eye of the heavens, spread a hot summer light over the square and the city.

Something cold that had been growing in Valentine's blood winked out like an extinguished fuse. She began to laugh.

Some of the people behind her moved, and Janou reappeared, dragging behind her a bearded man who wore one of River-quarter's green arm-bands. He, with sharp gestures, ordered men and women away from the prostrate Lord-Architect.

Casaubon pushed himself up onto his elbows, and rested his chins in his hands.

Standing in front of the Sea Gate, still wrapped in the stained, foetid remnants of banners, twelve rather ordinary-looking men and women stared at each other in bewilderment. A hot, healing, ocean-scented breath touched them again as it passed.

One of the Lords of the Shining Paths lay, wings furled, massive head lowered, the tip-tilted eyes fixed on a dirty child that sat between its front paws. The child reached up and tugged the curled black ringlets of its beard.

The Lord-Architect Casaubon rolled over with all the grace and gravity of a rhino, and grinned up at the Scholar-Soldier Valentine. 'What would you do without me?'

And slowly, by ones and twos; healed, hidden, and now returning, the refugees of the celestial spheres came walking back through the Sea Gate and into the city.

They are the Lords of the Shining Paths. As they become of earth, Her waters flow back from the tenements and lanes; as they become of earth, His plague and scourge passes from the city; as they become of earth, Their power is a tide moving with Moon and Sun, with Summer and Winter.

They are the Lords of the Shining Paths; they have not the desires and ambitions of men

All empires fallen, all cities dust that once they knew, they are content now: content to bask under this new sun, in the city of mud and marble, and to watch (with old amusement) the scurrying of humanity about their feet.

Sunlight poured down on the Miracle Garden. Valentine walked with Janou and Feliche, through the holiday crowds.

'The Lord Casaubon may be a little distressed,' Feliche warned. He took off his plumed hat and fanned his face, eyes scanning the crowd. The big man still wore River-quarter's colours, but now in a sash of office.

'Distressed?'

'I couldn't talk them out of throwing him into the Belvedere's dungeons for the night.'

Janou grinned. She had shed pack and sword for the day, and strutted all the lighter for it.

Somewhere a consort of music was playing, something with rebecks and trumpets in it. A spangle-canopied hot air balloon tugged at its moorings. The travelling fair people let a few more passengers climb on, and then released it into the summer sky. Valentine craned her neck to watch it pass over her head.

When she looked down again, dazzled and dizzy, the Lord-Architect Casaubon was standing in front of her.

His hair shone like copper wire, and every freckle was visible on his scrubbed pink skin. He wore white breeches – the top three buttons unbuttoned – and a satin coat of royal blue, embroidered with gold, left open across his ursine bulk. Insouciantly, he tugged the snowy lace at his wrists into place with be-ringed fingers.

'I thought you . . . no, never mind.' Valentine hooked her arm through his.

'Public bath-house,' the Lord-Architect explained, with an expression of distaste. 'The sooner I return to my Belvedere, the happier I'll be.'

As they left the Miracle Garden, they passed by the couchant figures of winged watchers – closed eyelids raised to the sun, sable wings a little stretched, inhaling the material scents of dust and summer. Young men and women particularly, under Janou's age, congregated in the watchers' shadows to argue and drink and debate over the occasional gnomic answer that a Lord of the Shining Paths might give.

'I begin to understand,' Feliche said. 'I think. If there is so intimate a connection between us and the Spheres, that even flesh and blood is affected, it was wittily concluded to suppose that we equally affect *their* nature. But – if you'd not been able to change the temper of the people in the square?'

'Received with terror, they'd have been malevolent, as they were six-and-twenty thousand years ago.' Valentine glanced at Janou for confirmation. 'The clay tablets – what was written there was in a language much too young for the Lords of the Shining Paths to understand. It said, *as they are received, so will their nature be*. From that, I guessed.'

'From that,' the Lord-Architect Casaubon announced, '*I* improvised.'

Janou whooped. 'Oh, see you, as if you know anything about it!'

'A man who is unacquainted with the workings of celestial Spheres could not begin to build a Miracle Garden, which,' Casaubon added, 'you seem to be making remarkably free with.'

'They're public gardens now.' Feliche paused on the marble steps going down into the square, looking back up at the Lord-Architect's massive frame, in gold and blue against the summer clouds. The fat man offered a ringed hand to the Scholar-Soldier Valentine. Janou walked down the marble balustrade, balancing barefoot.

'Given your services to the republic,' Feliche said, 'we thought we might omit your sentence of execution.'

Casaubon's face crimsoned.

'*What* republic?'

'This one,' the Scholar-Soldier Janou advised him. She jumped down from the balustrade into the square.

'This is ludicrous!' Casaubon grunted. 'See you, where's my Chancellor Parry?'

'You mean Senator Parry.'

'*I do not!*' He came to a halt, chins quivering with what Janou took to be outrage. 'Tabitha *Parry's* one of your anarchist council now? Great Architect! what next—'

He stopped, staring at the Belvedere as they came up to that building.

The great doors were flung wide: people walking in unhindered. The palace's many ornamented windows and columned galleries now had mattresses and sheets hanging out over their ledges, airing in the sun.

Casaubon looked up at the patched cloth, bright and faded colours; and heard voices drifting down. Snatches of conversation came from each of the large halls. A sackbut was being played, rather badly, in an upper chamber; and somewhere someone was cooking cabbage.

He sat down heavily on the Belvedere's entrance-steps.

'This is unfair!'

A woman going into the building heard him, and paused to squint at his face. She had rough, reddened hands, and brown hair with violet ribbons threaded through it.

After a moment she approached him, almost curtseyed, and then stopped herself.

'Did it ever occur to you, noble Lord, to wonder who does your washing?'

Casaubon lifted his head and looked at her in bewilderment. 'My *washing*?'

'I do. Did. My name is Tybba,' she said, folding her arms. 'If I'd ever had the price of that coat – even of the *lace* on it – then my Corran would be alive today to see all this.'

Casaubon put one fat hand down, and heaved himself up onto his feet. He opened his mouth to reply, and then said nothing. He took her hand and turned it palm-upwards. As if he could read a past in her rough skin.

Valentine turned away from watching Casaubon when Janou spoke:

'Thought it would be so easy. Giving up the sword and scroll.'

She was looking across at Feliche, and his Senate's sash of office
that now replaced the embroidered cloth of the travelling fair.

Valentine looked down at her hands, that had on the right middle
finger the callous that comes from holding a pen, and on the left
palm the hardened pads of the long-time duellist. 'Yes. So did I.'

'Oh but the road – you miss the road?' Janou smoothed down her
spiked hair. 'He actually asked me why Al-Iskandariya stayed
behind!'

Valentine lifted narrow, bony shoulders in a shrug. 'I know why.
You know it. But do they?'

Janou had her eyes still on Feliche's bearded face as the big man
stooped, seriously, to talk to Tabitha Parry. The dapper woman was
neat, now, in ruffled shirt and breeches, with a green sash round
her waist. She was pointing at Casaubon, seeming to protest
violently something Feliche had said.

'Oh, see you, Valentine, if I go, I'll be back soon enough! Who
knows how long these watchers will stay, or what will come of it?
They're not *tame*. The City won't do without Scholar-Soldiers for
long.'

'But she is an Architect-Lord's Lady,' Feliche spoke to Janou as he
rejoined them. 'Valentine, you'd better get him out of the City
before they forget his part in saving it, and remember the sedition-
trials in the Moon-hall.'

'You think he'll go, being Lord here all his life, and the Miracle
Garden being here besides?'

Valentine drew a deep breath. The sun was hot on her close-
cropped hair, and she felt the shade of the Belvedere welcome on
her skin as she walked into it. The Lord-Architect was sitting on the
marble steps, outside what had once been his home. She turned to
look back across the thronged square, and the white stone under
the summer sky.

As if it stood sentinel on the unbroken paving, a Lord of the
Shining Paths lay under the carved crest of the Sea Gate.

Casaubon raised his head. 'I spoke to the Lord – the ex-Lord –
Lindley, when I went this morning to borrow a shirt and coat. It
isn't everyone can lend me clothes . . .'

Valentine sat down on the steps behind him, just able to lean
forward and loop her arms around his neck. She made a warning
noise in her throat.

'However – to omit detail – he told me something of note.'
Casaubon paused. 'I think I've decided to travel.'

He felt her arms tighten slightly round his shoulders but all she said, in a sardonic tone, was, 'That's remarkably wise. Prudent, even.'

The Lord-Architect looked down at his ringed, plump fingers, where tiny copper hairs caught the light.

'Lindley told me there have been *no* new incidences of plague in the City – and that those sick are already recovering. He attributes it to the Lords of the Shining Paths being here, and, who knows, if we and they are so closely connected, that may be so.'

Valentine made a prompting murmur.

Casaubon continued: 'Al-Iskandariya's Brotherhood – they know something of this medical branch of the Art. I had thought . . . you see, these watchers will go, someday, and then the plague may return. If I were to go and learn that branch of the Art to do with healing, the city might have me back – that is, it might be some use my returning here. If,' he said, 'you could bear to travel with me?'

The thin woman vaulted down the steps to stand in front of him. He gazed up at her flushed face, and the greying hair that travelling for the Invisible College had already put at her temples.

'I should not ask—'

'*Travel*, and with us not left a copper penny by this new Senate, and likely they'll be hunting us for jail when they remember who you are, and never mind that it's cold season in two months, and no one between here and the coast to give us refuge, because the Invisible College won't favour an Architect-Lord's Lady, and no idea in the world where to find this Brotherhood? I wouldn't,' Valentine said, 'miss it for the worlds, and you know it!'

Janou heard Casaubon's shout, but by the time she spun round, they were walking decorously across the square towards her: Master-Captain Valentine with hands deep in pockets, and the ex-Lord-Architect reaching up to feed a scrap of something dubious to the white rat that rode his satin shoulder.

Black Motley

A hand rapped the rickety dressing-room door.

'Ashar! *Two minutes!*'

In no apparent haste, Ashar-hakku-ezrian leaned forward to the mirror and applied greasepaint. The fly-spotted silver reflected his dusty yellow hair, guileless blue eyes, and a baby-fat face marked with kohl – lines that it wouldn't acquire in flesh for ten years or more. He preened a wispy almost-beard.

'*Ashar!*'

He straightened, easing the sash around the middle of his black robe to conceal his plump waist, and twisted himself to check right profile, left profile . . . His thin tail coiled about his ankles. Its plush fur dappled brown and a darker blond than his hair. As he pulled on his gloves, he flicked dust from his hem with the whisk-end of his tail.

'I'm here.'

He pushed past the tumbling act, trotting through the dark and cluttered backstage area, and halted in the wings as the compère's voice rang out.

'And now, ladies and gentlemen! All the way from the world's end, and brought here at great expense – for your delection and delight: the Katayan with the marvellous mind, the master of prose and genius of rhyme – *Ashar-hakku-ezrian!*'

Saturday night, all the week for a reputation to build . . . In the dazzling space beyond the naphtha footlights, applause roared.

'Good introduction,' the small female engineer-conjurer remarked, waiting in the wings beside him.

'It ought to be. I composed it.' Ashar flashed her a grin, tightened his sash, and walked out on to the music-hall stage. Applause hollowed the high spaces of the auditorium; the stalls crammed full of workers in worn doublets and patched knee-breeches.

'Ladies and gentlemen, you see me *honoured* to appear before you!' He swept a deep bow. Beyond the row of naphtha footlights, bottles and pewter cutlery shone. Smoke-haloed and dazzled, easily five hundred men and women stared up at him; those there from earlier in the week banging their fists enthusiastically on the scarred tables.

'This evening my poor talents are at your disposal, entirely at *your* command—'

Close to the front of the stage, one woman wiped her mouth with her doublet-sleeve; a man bent across to whisper to a friend. Beaming, Ashar advanced downstage.

'—I will rhyme for you, I will compose for you; each monologue of mine is, as you know, *completely* extempore – no one like another, no night like the last!'

He swung his gaze up from the smoke-filled stalls to the circle. Merchant families slumming in factory-new finery; frock-coats and periwigs; one man laughing loud enough to drown him out. He fetched voice-projection from the pit of his belly:

'And to prove it, sir, to *prove* what I say, you may give me any subject and I'll begin – *any* subject that you please! Yes, you, sir! And *you*. Anyone!'

He backpedalled, hand ostentatiously to his ear. Raucous voices prompted from the stalls. Ashar crossed upstage, light glittering from the silver braid on his black robe, pointing randomly and encouragingly into the auditorium: waiting for his previously rehearsed subjects to arise. He backed far enough to get the boxes into his line of sight – unprofitable, most evenings; and sure enough, either side of the stage, both empty.

No. *Not empty*. One box occupied.

'Do us a monologue about the Queen!'

'Naw, make it Lord William, the bastard!'

'—one on pretty girls!'

'As you command! Wait, now.' He held up both hands until silence fell, then stood straight under the spotlight. Piano accompaniment rose from the orchestra pit:

> *'Lord William treats her Majesty*
> *Like a meeting in Hyde Park:*
> *Harangues and preaches, talks and teaches,*
> *Not a word of cheeks like peaches,*
> *Shining eyes or love's bright spark.*
> *Lord Benjamin with trembling lip*
> *Speaks soft and low of legislation:*
> *Handsomely sighs, bats his eyes,*
> *Compliments, flatters – I can't say, lies—*
> *And governs the whole nation!'*

Under cover of the loud applause, Ashar slid a swift glance left into the Garrick Box. Naphtha flares dazzled his sight. Jewelled sword-hilts glinted in the interior of the box.

'Want one on *love*!'

'What about the pawnshop?'

'What about my missus here!'

A tall black Rat leaned up against the carved pillar at the back of the Garrick Box. Some five foot ten or eleven inches tall, with a lean-muzzled face, black fur scarred with old sword-cuts; and a plume jutting from his silver headband and curving back over translucent, scarred ears. The Rat wore the plain harness of a swordfighter.

Devilment spurred him. Ashar clapped his hands together. 'Lord Benjamin *again*, did I hear? Yes! yes, *and*—?'

Other Rats had crowded into the box. Not unusual to see a drunken Rat lord sprawled there some evenings, slumming, but this . . . They wore the sleeveless blue jackets that are the livery of the Queens' Guard.

Ashar hooked his tail up over his arm, bowed to the stalls, and held up both hands for quiet.

The music-hall auditorium hushed.

'In honour of our esteemed visitors.' His hand swept out grandly to indicate the box. The black Rats faded back into further shadows. He grinned. 'I give you a completely new monologue, concerning our noble Lord Benjamin, minister to our Queen—'

'Gawd bless er!'

Ashar bowed expansively to the stalls at the interruption.

'—Lord Benjamin, together with that most delicate of sweet-meats, that most rare *candy*—'

'*Ashar-hakku-ezrian!*'

A female Rat's voice cut him off. He drew himself up, mouth opening for his usual response to hecklers; then shaded his eyes as he stared down into the stalls.

A Rat pushed between the dining-tables, her sword already drawn and in her long-fingered hand. Her white fur gleamed in the reflected footlights. Leather sword-harness crossed her silver-furred breast, and she wore a sleeveless, belted black jacket. She stood lightly on clawed hind feet, scaled tail out for balance, staring up at Ashar challengingly.

He glared back, uncharacteristically bad-tempered. 'Damn you, Varagnac, I warned you! Wait and see what you'll get for inter-rupting me.'

'I'll give you a subject for a monologue,' she shouted. 'A renegade Kings' Memory! *Take him!*'

Long-clawed feet scrabbled as the Guards leaped the low wall
from the box to the stage. Steel grated from scabbard. Ashar swung
round, open-handed, weaponless. A brown police Rat blocked the
nearest wing, sword drawn; others blocked the far side. He turned.
Varagnac shoved two tables aside and grabbed for the edge of the
stage.

A black Rat Guard walked tentatively out on to the exposed
boards towards Ashar, one slender-fingered hand up to keep the
spotlights from his eyes.

'You're under arrest!' Varagnac shouted over the growing noise.
A bottle crashed past from behind her and shattered on the stage.
Feet stamped. Men and women hung over the edge of the circle,
screeching abuse. Those in the stalls backed away, unwilling to
confront Rat Lords. A child shrieked.

Ashar halted, dead centre-stage. 'I—'

He put his fists on his hips, sucking in his plump belly, and glared
at the chaotic auditorium. Noise defeated his attempt to speak. He
scowled, and stamped his left heel twice on the boards.

The stage trapdoor fell open.

He plummeted through, robes flying, arms and tail upraised;
knees already bent for the mattress-landing below.

'Stop him!' Varagnac heaved herself up on to the stage and
leaped forward. One of the Rat Guards threw himself down into
the gap. She stopped on the very edge and stared down into
darkness. 'Have you got him?'

A chop-bone from the auditorium clipped her shoulder, smearing
grease on her white fur. She straightened, speaking to the other
Rats. 'Keep this lot quiet. Clear the building if you have to. You
down there! *Well?*'

From the open darkness of the trapdoor, the black Rat's voice
drifted up.

'Nothing, ma'am. There's nobody down here.'

The woman sprawled back in her chair at the crate serving for a
desk, one booted heel up on the heaped cash-books; her fingers
steepled. Dawn air nipped her chin and nose. Through the open
warehouse doors the river air gusted in, loud with the shouts of
dock workers unloading clipper ships.

She tucked her hands up into the warm armpits of the black
redingote, slightly too large, that swathed her.

'Have you found him yet, Master Athanasius?'

Her husky voice penetrated above the efforts of men wheeling
trolleys, women shifting crates; shouts and grunts; all the bustle of

the warehouse being stacked full. Athanasius Godwin spared a glance at the high brick interior, the stacked wooden shelves, and bit back his resentment at being summoned to a warehouse.

'I regret to say – not yet. Madam.'

'I've heard *not yet* until I'm very tired of it. For the best part of ten days.' Jocelyn de Flores sat up. Grey streaked her shining black hair, that curled to her collar; and she looked up with a confident and capable smile.

'Now walk with me, sir, and I'll explain something to you, and *you* can explain it to the Academy of Memory.'

Athanasius Godwin pulled his cloak more tightly around his thin shoulders. The damp morning spiked rheumatic pains in his hip. Leaning on his silver-headed cane, he followed the woman through the crowded warehouse – she calling directions to left and right, not pausing in her stride – and came up with her out on the quayside. She stepped back against the warehouse wall, out of the way of a carter and his team. A Percheron huffed warm, equine breath

'Madam, I also was a Kings' Memory, before I retired to teach. I remember what you said at our last meeting. *There is a contract at stake here, Master Athanasius. The way that the world is going, you may wake up one fine morning, and find yourselves more* Merchants' *Memories than Kings' Memories. Remember it. Though I mean no disrespect to our Queen, God rest them.* The Academy of Memory is not unaware of that.'

She nodded at his word-for-word recollection.

'Perfect as ever, Master Athanasius. I believe you don't have to tell me you're good. We wouldn't use the Academy of Memory if it failed us, too much—' Her bare hand swept out, taking in the dock, the forests of sail-hung masts, and the tarpaulin-shrouded cargoes. 'Too much depends on it.'

'You have no choice about using us. We are all there is.'

'I would to God I was allowed to write down words, as I'm licensed to set down figures in my account-books! But the world isn't made as I like it.'

'Written words have too much power.'

The early sun brought out crow's-feet around her eyes. Light gilded her sallow skin. Her shadow, and the masts' shadows, fell all toward the west. She thumbed a silver watch from her waistcoat pocket, flicked it open with a fingernail.

'I can't spare you much time. I'll be square with you. You Kings' Memories set yourselves up to be the records of this country. You set yourselves up as trained and perfect memories, to hear all agreements and contracts and recall them at demand. Now, when one of your people goes renegade, and runs off, and takes with him the only proof of *my* contract—'

A call interrupted: 'Madam de Flores!'

Opalescent light shifted on the river, the east all one lemon-brilliant blaze. Athanasius Godwin narrowed his eyes and squinted. A fat black Rat strode along the quay, cloak flying. Dock workers got out of his way without his noticing.

'Ah. The *nouveau* poor.' The woman gave a slight smile, partly self-satisfaction, partly contempt. 'You've met my business partner, haven't you. Master Athanasius Godwin, of the Academy of Memory. Messire Sebastien.'

'I know you.' The Rat nodded absently at the old man while plucking darned silk gloves from dark-fingered hands. His embroidered cloak hung from his broad furred shoulders, swirling about his clawed hind feet and his scaled tail, that shifted from side to side. Lace clustered at the throat and wrists of his brocade jacket. A silver headband looped over one ear, under the other; and carried in its clip a dyed-scarlet ostrich plume.

'The 'Change is busy this morning.'

'Have you seen the Queen?'

Sebastien shrugged. 'With what in view? The Queen is as displeased as we are.'

He tucked his gloves under his sword-belt. A swept-hilted rapier dangled at his left haunch, and a matching dagger at the other. Plain, cheap weapons. the sword's velvet-covered scabbard had once had gems set into it, now the metal clasps stood levered open and empty.

'I say we should see their Majesties.' De Flores folded her arms. 'It's in the Queen's interest that we have this contract back in our hands immediately, before someone else finds him. Surely even you can see that!'

The Rat looked sourly at her. 'Madam partner, when they permit such as you into the audience chamber, then do *you* go to see the Queen. Until such time as that, permit me my own judgement as to what is wise.'

He lifted a lace-wristed hand, pointing. Athanasius Godwin winced back from the accusing gesture.

'Master Athanasius, *find* this young man. Quickly. This is the height of foolishness. This Ashar-hakku-ezrian – he should never even have been acting as Kings' Memory to *begin* with!'

Nathaniel Marston ran up the cobbled hill from the docks. Towards the brow of the hill he stopped, breathing heavily, and leaned up against a wall, unlacing his doublet.

Indubitably, Madam de Flores, you don't know all your employees by sight, even if you claim you do!

He reversed his jacket, so that the plain hemp-coloured lining was replaced by rich blue velvet; wiped disguising dirt from his face, and rubbed a thumb over the calluses on his palm that shifting crates had given him.

But unless I miss my guess, the Academy of Memory didn't have good news for you. They haven't found Ashar-hakku-ezrian yet. And no wonder.

The sun, risen higher now, brought moisture to his fair-skinned face. He scrubbed his sleeve across his mouth. Sweat tangled stickily in his close-cropped beard.

A few men walked past, coming or going from early factory shifts; a coach with Rat Lords' heraldry on the door jolted down the hill. The city fell away in oak-and-white-plaster houses and spiked blue-tiled roofs, to the docks. Sun burned off all the spring's dawn cold. Haze clung to apple-blossom, white in gardens.

He moved off again, this time less hurriedly.

Narrow streets closed him in between barred doors and shuttered windows: a scarecrow-thin man in rich blue jacket and breeches, his hands heavy now with gold rings; and his dark red hair tangled down to his collar. Shadow slanted down. A quick turn into an alley – beyond that, he stepped from congested streets into an enclosed square.

Dust skirled across the great courtyard between sandstone walls. Thin ogee-arched windows flashed back the light. Wisteria, some eighty or ninety years old, spidered purple blossom all across the carved and decorated façade of the east wing. Students clustered on the steps leading up to the great arched entrance, talking; or ran, late for seminars.

'Nathan!'

A lead-paned window creaked open on the first floor and the Reverend Principal Cragmire leaned his elbow on the sandstone sill. The tall man beckoned. 'Get yourself up here, man! I want to know what's happening.'

Conscious of curious student eyes on him, Marston nodded acknowledgement, straightened his back, and strode up the steps and into the building.

This early, the corridors were full. Anglers and curbers waited to be led out for practicals in the city. A false beggar sat in a window embrasure painting on a scar. Two graduate nips and foists stood discussing the finer points of dipping pockets with a research professor.

'Excuse me.' Marston eased between a doxy and a mort, answering the latter's practised smile with a pinch on her buttock; and slid thankfully through into Cragmire's room.

'Come in, Nathan, come in. You look as though you've had a busy night.'

Sun gleamed on the panelled walls. He caught a wing-armed chair, pulled it up to the Principal's desk, and sank back into it with a grunt. 'Damn busy. What *I'm* worried about is my teaching load. Who's taking care of that while I'm watching Ashar-hakku-ezrian?'

The tall bearded man grunted. 'Sulis is taking your class in knife-fighting. Chadderton can handle the sessions on dangerous drugs and poisoning; and I've given first-level card-sharping and basic disguise to young Dermot. Ah . . . the administrative work you'll have to clear up yourself when you get back.'

Nathaniel Marston grunted. 'I thought as much.'

'So what's happened?'

'I really *don't* know what that young man thinks he's doing. If I were Ashar-hakku-ezrian I'd stay under cover and pray to ship out of the city. *He's* making himself a career on the stage! Last night he didn't even bother to use a false name.'

'He's still at the Empire?'

Marston scratched the hair at the back of his neck and chuckled.

'Not after last night! We were right – they've put Varagnac on to the boy. A misjudgement, I'd say; but then, we know Varagnac better than they do . . .'

'She found him?'

'Even she couldn't miss him. I'd have stepped in, but there wasn't any need. If Ashar-hakku-ezrian wasn't a Kings' Memory, I'd sign him up for us tomorrow. I'll swear he was about to spill the whole thing on-stage, Lord Benjamin and all – at any rate, Varagnac thought he was. She all but pissed herself.'

Cragmire frowned. 'To go renegade is one thing. I could almost understand that, with the particular contract that he's carrying in his head. But then, Nathan, wouldn't you hide, if it were you? And what does he do?'

'He goes on the stage. Under his own name.' Nathan shook his head, marvelling, amused. 'He's quite good. No, I do him a dis-service. He's very good.'

There was a pause.

'If Varagnac's people found him yesterday, then they'll find him again. Ten days ago I would have said it was to keep him alive. Now . . . Lord Benjamin may be having second thoughts.'

'It may be.' Marston shrugged.

'What about the commercial cartel?'

'De Flores has no idea where her missing contract is, and neither does the Academy of Memory. But they will, of course, if he goes on like this. The question is, what are *we* going to do about it?'

'There is the question of what the Queen . . .' Cragmire scratched at his dark beard. 'I think you'd better keep a friendly eye on Ashar-hakku-ezrian. Protectively friendly. While you're doing it . . .'

He stood.

'I'll call an emergency governors' meeting of the University of Crime.'

Far beneath the advancing morning, Ashar-hakku-ezrian stripped the black stage robe off over his head. His hands scraped the top of the brickwork tunnel.

'Shit!' He disentangled himself and sucked grazed knuckles. Cobwebs trailed lace-like across his plump belly and chest. He squatted down, sorting through the heap of stolen clothing at his feet, and hooked out a pair of black knee-breeches.

Unseen outside the circle of his dim lantern, a black Rat continued to follow him softly down the disused sewer tunnel. Blue livery caught no light. She paused, translucent ears and whiskers trembling like taut wire.

One thin, strong-fingered hand went to her belt, drawing a loaded pocket-pistol. She raised it and sighted.

In the lantern-light, the Katayan knelt, ripping out part of the breeches' hind seam with a pen-knife. He sat back on bare buttocks, lifting his feet and drawing on the breeches, and reaching in to adjust himself: close-furred tail hooked out through the slit seam. The watching Rat grinned.

A scent bitter as ammonia stabbed her nostrils.

Copper blood in her mouth, brickwork slamming her face and body as she fell; hands that caught and made her descent soundless – all this before she could recognise the scent and taste of pain.

A man lowered the Rat's unconscious body to the tunnel floor. He tucked his lead-weighted cudgel away under his belt.

After a minute's thought, he dragged the dead-weight back into the tunnel's darkness.

Ashar-hakku-ezrian stood, belted his breeches, and shrugged into an over-large shirt. He flicked his cuffs down over his callused fingers. The lantern cast his shadow on the wall. He turned,

checking silhouettes, and combed his hair back with the whisk-end
of his tail.

Whistling softly, he picked up the hurricane lamp and walked on
through the disused sewer.

'Any mask put on will, after long enough, grow into the skin.'

Lord Benjamin, Prime Minister and Home Secretary both, stood
looking down into Whitehall. A lone carriage and pair clattered
past, rattling over the cobbles. Parliament Clock struck one.

He added, 'A surprisingly short time elapses before one cannot
tell which is which.'

The silver-furred Rat standing beside his desk grunted. Benjamin
turned to face her. One of his pale hands played with the scarlet and
orange cravat at his neck. His other thumb hooked into the pocket
of his embroidered waistcoat, pushing back his sober black frock-
coat. Where one trouser-cuff pulled up an inch, a red sock was
visible.

'But this isn't to the purpose. What happened to the young man?'

Varagnac leaned one furred haunch up on the desk, reached
across, and struck a match on the casing of the ornate desk-lamp.
Her slender, longer-than-human fingers manipulated flame and a
thin black cigar. She blew out smoke. Her scabbard scraped the side
of the desk, scarring the veneer.

'You don't intimidate me. You never have.' Her lean-muzzled
face was sullen. 'You're an outsider, and you play the fool – the
Queen's fool. And you play it well. But you forget one thing. You're
human. You'll always be here on sufferance.'

A springy dark curl fell across Benjamin's forehead. He flicked it
back. Some glance passed between himself and the female Rat, and
he put his hands behind him, clasped at the back of his frock-coat,
and let the smile surface.

'For now, you take my orders, Madam Varagnac.'

'For now, I do, yes.'

'And so – our young Katayan friend.'

The Rat stubbed out her partly smoked cigar on the polished desk.
She straightened up: something close on five foot ten or eleven, all
whipcord muscle: her silver fur shining. 'Do you know, he's making
songs in the music-halls? If I hadn't stepped in last night, I swear
he'd have put the whole contract into rhyme, and let the scum hear
it!'

Impassively unimpressed, Lord Benjamin said, 'And?'

The Home Secretary and the officer of the secret police looked at
each other for a while.

'Well,' Varagnac said at last, 'he slipped away. We had to step in before everything was ready. My people are already paying for that one. I give it three or four days before he surfaces again. Then—'

She stopped. Benjamin schooled his features to order. In his luminous and large eyes, devilment shifted.

'Then?' he prompted, demurely.

Varagnac scowled. 'Do you want him dead? It could happen, resisting arrest.'

'There is the difficulty, you see, of needing to control the proof of contractual agreement, while needing *not* to have it made public . . . I think you had better take him into our private custody. I'll give you my own authorisation. But if that seems too difficult, and time is short, then it may be better if he dies.'

Varagnac's lean face altered, in some way not readily decipherable. She bit at one claw nail. 'If you told me the details of this contract, I could tell you if it's worth keeping him alive?'

'No.'

Thoughtful, the middle-aged man turned again to look down from the baroque-façaded building into Whitehall.

'Whatever I may be, madam, I'm trusted. I endeavour to continue to deserve it.'

The theatre manager sorted through a cluttered desk, fidgeting among painted picture-playbills, seat-tokens, account-books, and a laddered silk stocking. Ashar-hakku-ezrian waited.

'Sixth on the bill,' the plump woman offered.

'Not good enough.' He stroked his wispy beard with his thumb. 'You know I'll get seats filled. I should have at least third billing.'

The fair-haired woman sat back and tugged at her bodice, sweating in the afternoon heat. Her lined eyebrows dipped. 'Yes, my chick, and I've heard of you from Tom Ellis down at the Empire. Half the Guard you had turning his place upsidedown. Oh, you'll put bums on seats all right . . . but if you do it here, you'll do it under a stage name.'

Ashar, sublimely ignoring dignity, hitched up his over-large breeches. The late afternoon sun slanted in through the high garret window and into his eyes, only partly blocked by the rear of the man-high letters spelling out ALHAMBRA MUSIC HALL outside the glass.

He protested, 'Who'll come to see an unknown?'

'Oh, word'll get round, my pigeon, don't you worry. I'll risk *that*, for the few nights that'll make it worth it. After that, you're on your own.'

Ashar-hakku-ezrian grinned. 'I want more than a twentieth of the door-take. I'm *good*.'

'No one's as good as you think you are, dearie.'

'No one except me.'

'I'll start you Thursday matinée. Don't come back here before then. In fact, if I were you, I'd keep out of sight entirely for the next three days.'

At the door, her voice made him pause.

'Ambitious little bastard, aren't you?'

'Of course. What I can't understand—' Ashar-hakku-ezrian looked at the woman over his shoulder. '—is why they won't all leave me alone to get on with it.'

Athanasius Godwin walked along the colonnade, drawing his robes about him in the evening chill. The shadows of pillars fell in regular stripes across the paving. His feet scuffed the worn stone.

The feet of the man walking with him made no noise.

'He's one of you. A Kings' Memory. Damnation, man, what's happened to him?'

Godwin didn't choose to answer immediately. Outside the colonnade, students of the Academy of Memory walked the courtyard. Most young, all with preoccupied faces and intense vision: all memorising, as Athanasius remembered doing in his youth, the *loci* of the place as a structure for meaning.

One brown-faced girl paused, placing in the palaces of her interior vision the words of a speech given by her older companion. She squinted, eyes shutting, mentally walking the memorised rooms; recalling placed images and their associated words. She repeated exactly what he had dictated.

A low mutter filled the air, other students repeating back complicated sequences of random numbers; long speeches; random snatches of conversation.

Athanasius, through shrewd and rheumy eyes, looked up at the bearded, bald man. 'Master Cragmire, you have all the University at your disposal. If your sturdy beggars can't find him, being on every street-corner, nor your doxies who hear all bed-gossip, nor all your secret assassins – how am I to be expected to find one young man?'

Without detectable change of expression, Cragmire said, 'I lied, he is found. Rather, we know where he is *going* to be. That may be too late. Tell me about him, Master Athanasius.'

'So you can predict his actions? Oh, I think not.'

Irritation grated in his voice. Athanasius Godwin gripped his hands together behind him as he walked, turning his face up to what was visible above the Academy roofs of the orange western sky. Slanting sun showed up the peeling plaster on the walls; the water-stained, cracked pillar-bases. He picked words with a desperate, concealed care.

'Young Ashar . . . what can I say to you about him? A phenomenal memory. Very little application . . . No application. He became Cecily Emmett's pet. Cecily – but of course, you were there when that happened. Sad.' Godwin sighed over-heavily. 'The young man was on his last warning here. His very last. Another few weeks would have seen him sent back to South Katay in disgrace. Which disgrace, to my mind, would have no effect on Ashar-hakku-ezrian whatsoever. Of all the irresponsible – *this* is characteristic, this going into hiding in the city! You wait, Master Cragmire. A week or so and he'll surface, charm his way out of trouble, smile sweetly, and begin to cause trouble all over again!'

A genuine anger made him breathless. He glared at the Principal of the University of Crime.

'You sound reluctant to have him back.' Cragmire shrugged. 'What will happen to our young Katayan friend when you throw him out of here? Do Kings' Memories resign, Master Athanasius?'

'We have techniques to dim the memory. Drugs.'

Godwin brushed his hand against a pillar. Sun-warmed limestone was rough against the pads of his fingers.

'It is untrue, and cruel, to accuse us of turning failed students into idiots and fools. Young Ashar would lose nothing but a certain ability to concentrate.'

One set of footsteps echoed back softly from the colonnade. Godwin stopped. Silence fell. He did not look at Cragmire. Above, the sky glowed blue; all the motes of the air coloured gold.

'Do you have any idea,' the man's voice said, 'how badly we could hurt the Academy of Memory?'

'Or vice versa?'

Aware that tears leaked from the corners of his eyes, Athanasius Godwin reached out and grabbed the man's doublet, gripping the soft leather with age-spotted fingers.

'Ashar is a stupid child. Remember that.' His ability to hide desperation vanished. 'Cragmire, he's *not* to be hurt. If you want your University of Crime to continue visible with impunity – he is a boy, he is not to be hurt in any way, he is to come back here to me where he's safe: understand that!'

Cragmire reached down and detached his grip. Athanasius Godwin stared at his own hand, flesh cramped and white; and not at the forgettable face of the other man. Breath rushed hot and hollow in his chest.

Principal Cragmire said, 'If you can do anything, do it now. Your "stupid child" is in intense danger. I think we don't even have another day.'

The crowd outside The Fur & Feathers thinned now. A distant church clock struck midnight. Ashar-hakku-ezrian leaned both forearms on the bollard, and his chin on his arms, and flirted his eyebrows at the fair-haired human girl. 'But *when* do you get off work? They can't keep you here all night.'

The human girl bundled her skirts back between her knees, shifting the bucket; scrubbing brush in her other hand. The wet tavern step gleamed, the slate clean now of spilled beer and vomit. 'Can't they, though?'

He squatted, sliding down with his back against the metal pillar, twitching his tail out of the way of the road.

'Leave this. Come with me. I'm going to be famous.' The plush-furred tail slid across the air between them, nestled gently at the nape of her neck, between her caught-up hair and shabby dress.

'Oh, Ash . . . I don't know you hardly.' She rubbed the back of her wrist across her forehead. 'You better get gone before the old man comes out. Get along now!'

'I'll see you back there.' Ashar-hakku-ezrian nodded in the direction of the cobbled alley opposite the public house.

'Well, I don't . . .'

'Yes you do. You will. You *must*. For me.' He kissed her as he stood, grinned, and loped across the road. The noise of music, and quarrelling voices quieted as he entered the alley.

A slight thud sounded.

Curious, he turned. Several other alleyways split off from the main one, none lit, all now quiet. One of his eyebrows flicked up in momentary puzzlement.

He shoved both hands in his stolen breeches pockets and walked on, tail switching from side to side; debating whether the fair-haired girl was a sure enough bet to wait for, or if The Pig & Whistle would repay a visit.

Six yards up a side alley, an unconscious brown Rat's heels jolted over the pavement as Nathaniel Marston dragged him into concealment.

'Her Majesty is receiving the Katayan Ambassador,' the brown Rat major-domo said. 'If my Lord Benjamin would care to wait.'

Benjamin inclined his head to her. 'I shall always have time at her Majesty's disposal, I hope.'

He walked across the corridor to the arched window, tapping his folded gloves against his trouser leg, whistling softly under his breath. Light slanted down from above. Red, blue, gold, white: rich colours falling through a black tracery of stone.

The brown Rat appeared again, opening the antechamber's high door as a portly black Rat in lace and leather arrived. Benjamin moved smoothly forward, stepping through on the heels of the visitor with a nod to the doorkeeper, calling ahead:

'Messire Sebastien!'

The pudgy Rat turned, unlacing his cloak and dropping it for the anteroom servants to pick up. 'Benjamin. I – you – that is, my duty to her Majesty—'

Benjamin met the gaze of bead-black eyes and smiled only slightly. 'How interesting to find you here, Messire Sebastien. Perhaps we arrive on the same business, hum?'

'I don't think so. I'm sure not.'

'How prescient of you, messire. I don't believe that I mentioned what my own business might be . . .'

The black Rat's eyes gleamed, set deep in his fat and furry cheeks. He folded his arms across his broad, velvet-doubleted chest; scaled tail sweeping the stone-flagged floor. 'Now you take good notice of one thing, *boy*. When all this scheming comes out, and has to be denied by certain highly placed people, no one of *us* is going to stand the damage of it. For that, they'll pick a human. I'll let you speculate about which human it might be.'

'"Speculation" is not a word you should be using at the moment,' Benjamin said.

Squat white columns held up the anteroom's vaulted ceiling. Two men in Court livery scuttled away with coats and cloaks. Benjamin glimpsed through the square window the finials and carved façade of the palace courtyard.

Sebastien tugged his doublet down, pulling the lace at the wrists forward over his ringless fingers. 'I'll use what words I please, boy, and you'll have to show me a much better return on my investment before I stop. Damme, I don't believe you ever intended to go through with this mad scheme, it's all just to line your own pockets!'

'I think you should carefully consider what you're saying.'

'We've suffered you too long, in any case; and it's the last straw to be *cheated* by—'

Benjamin raised his hand and struck the Rat a stinging blow across the face.

'I will not be insulted by some down-at-heel has-been with a grudge and the brains of a mayfly! Will you complain? Do so. Do so! And the next time I see you I'll carry a horsewhip, and give you the thrashing you deserve, public scandal or not!'

The black Rat waddled back a step, long jaw dropping; made as if to speak; abruptly turned and flung out of the exit, pushing the doorkeeper aside with a furious oath.

Lord Benjamin stared, fabricated anger subsiding; sucked his skinned knuckles, and broke into a coarse laugh.

'Do you think the Prime Minister is going to fight with you in the streets like a barrow-boy? Such *stupidity*. Ah, but it has its uses. It does. I can well do without your company here today.'

The further anteroom doors stood shut, great black iron hinges spiking across the oak-wood. They slid at his slight touch, gliding open, and he walked through. He stood a moment while his eyes accustomed themselves to the gloom.

The great arched throne room opened up before him. Traceries of white webs snarled the walls, spindles of spider-thread curtaining off other doors and the lower, blacked-out windows. Webs dripped from the arched ceiling. One torch burned low in a wall-cresset, soot staining the already black masonry.

Kneeling priests flanked the walls, each at a low mausoleum-altar. Benjamin crossed himself thoughtfully, walking past them towards the high end of the hall. The Ambassador was gone. Perpendicular windows slotted down a little light. Upon the dais at the end, where all windows had been bricked up, a great mass of stonework stood. Close up, this could be seen to be an immense baroquely-carved and decorated tomb, Latin inscriptions incised in silver below the legend SAXE-COBERG-GOTHA.

'Your Majesty!' Lord Benjamin beamed effusively. 'To see you in such health is a privilege – to see your beauty, a delight given to few men in any age of the world.'

Below the tomb, on the granite platform, a profusion of black silk cushions lay scattered. Small stools had been set amongst them. Nine slender black Rats lay asleep, or sat sewing, or with folded hands and melancholy eyes gazed up at the tomb. They wore black silk robes.

On a larger cushion in the centre, attended by a brown Rat page, the nine Rats' tails rested, coiled into an inextricable and fifty-years grown-together knot.

Some of the Rat-Queen looked at Lord Benjamin.

A slender Rat who sat sewing at a sampler left off, extending one long-fingered dark hand. Benjamin bowed over it, kissing the narrow silver rings.

'We welcome your presence, Lord Benjamin. We were thinking of our departed Consort, and I fear falling into a sad melancholy.'

'Your Majesty might marry again. Such beauty will never lack admirers.'

'We could not be unfaithful to the memory of our dear husbands, Lord Benjamin. No, we—' She bit off a thread between front incisors. A more bony and angular Rat seated at her feet raised her lean-jawed muzzle:

'—could not think of it. What news have you for us, dear Lord Benjamin?'

Benjamin pondered *Only that the world misses you who are its sunlight* and decided to leave that one for another occasion. A third Rat-Queen shifted around so that she sat facing him, this one with something of a sardonic gleam in her eyes. He bowed again, floridly.

'I should ask news of you, dear lady, you having most recently spoken to the Katayan Ambassador, or so I hear.'

The third Rat-Queen frowned. 'They came to protest the siting of another garrison on their north coast, even though we are only there to protect them. Really, it is—'

She reached out to the tray of tea being offered by the brown Rat page. The Rat-Queen who had resumed her sewing completed:

'—most provoking. Do not make that the subject of your visit, I pray you. Dear Lord Benjamin, we have been giving serious consideration to your suggestion for our Accession Day Festival.'

'And your Majesty desires?'

'We think that we will indeed have a theatrical performance in the palace—'

'—by our command, this performance—'

'—because it will please the dear children,' another, more bony and angular Rat-Queen, cut in. 'And therefore we should have theatricals, songs, tricks, jugglers; all drawn from our great capital's theatres and places of entertainment. What—'

'—do you say to that, Lord Benjamin?'

'Admirable. Stunning! Quite the best notion I have ever heard.' His large and liquid eyes shone.

'So you should say, when it was your own.' The sardonic Rat-Queen smiled. 'We see through you, dear Lord Benjamin. But we know—'

'—that you have our best interests at heart.'

A tiny echo came back from each word, the Queen's high voices reverberating from the Gothick stonework. Further down the hall a torch guttered, and the scent of incense came from where the priests constantly prayed.

'A celebration would be much in order.' Benjamin said.

'We have drawn out a list—'

'—of those performers we hear are suitable. Our noble friend the Ambassador of South Katay recommended one young person, who sounds most amusing.'

He reached out to take a paper from one of the Rats lying amid the silk cushions, bowing as he did so; casting a rapid eye down the list until the name *Ashar-hakku-ezrian* leaped out at him.

'Yes, your Majesty.'

He rubbed an ungloved hand across his forehead, slick with a cool sweat, and smiled.

'And something else most intriguing came from our meeting with the Ambassador.' The Rat-Queen lowered her sleek muzzle over her sewing. 'We hear—'

'—interesting things of this most new discovery of the lands about the East Pole. We wonder—'

This black Rat fell to grooming the fur of her arm. The bony black Rat beside her opened onyx eyes:

'—whether we might receive ambassadors from them, as we do from South Katay. A peaceable treaty might lead to much trade, Lord Benjamin—'

'—do you not think so?' the first Rat concluded.

'Indubitably, madam. I'll be only too pleased to discover, for you, how this may be brought about.' Lord Benjamin, flourishing his yellow gloves, bowed himself out of the throne room.

A horse-drawn carriage took him back to Whitehall. He sat with his chin on his breast, slumped down in the seat, no expression at all on his face. Not until he stood again in the office overlooking Whitehall did he break silence.

He picked the telephone-mouthpiece off its stand, dialling a confidential and automatically connected number.

A click, the phone picked up and answered. 'Varagnac.'

He nodded once to himself, silently, said 'Kill the contract. Immediately.' And put the telephone back on its rest.

'I tell you, Benjamin will sell us out!'

The fat black Rat slammed his fist down on the makeshift crate accounts desk, his voice cutting through the noise of work in the warehouse.

'Every penny I have is tied up in this, and as for every penny I *don't* have – I'll be ruined.'

Jocelyn de Flores sank her chin lower in her greatcoat collar.

Slumped in the chair, so low as to be almost horizontal, she moved only her eyes to look up at Sebastien. 'So?'

'So we ought to destroy all trace of our ever having been involved in this scheme. Especially the contract. Gods, woman, even a sniff of the *candy* trade and we'll end up in Newgate!' The Rat moved from clawed hind foot to foot, rolls of fur-covered flesh shifting. He pulled out a darned lace kerchief to dab at his mouth.

'I trust our friend Benjamin as you do.' Jocelyn remained still. 'That's to say, not at all. Master Sebastien, do try not to be stupid – please, listen. I think we ought to have that contract safe. Very safe. Remember, it isn't only we two that it implicates.'

The black Rat began shakily to smile. 'Benjamin.'

Jocelyn de Flores came to her feet in one movement, coat swirling, striding out towards the quay and the chilly evening.

Ashar-hakku-ezrian passed the clock shop's window, paused, stepped back, and stared into the dark glass. After a moment's thought he brushed his blond hair further back behind his ears, preened his beard, and tried a left and then a right profile, gleaming his eyes at himself in the reflection with a grin.

'You could lose a little weight but you'll do.'

The glass reflected plane trees behind him, planted in a triangle of earth at the junction of two streets, their leaves rustling in a spring gust. He turned away, towards the main road further down, seeing noon and horse-drawn carriages and the corner of the Alhambra, and a man shifted out of the next doorway.

The man gnawed absently at a knuckle, among gold-ringed fingers. His greasy dark-red hair and beard straggled down over the collar of his royal-blue coat.

Ashar smiled very pleasantly, side-stepping. 'Can I help you?'

'A word with you, master. I've got a message from your sister.'

Coldness stabbed him just in the pit of the belly. Ashar shrugged. 'Which one? My father has ten wives, that gives me a number of sisters to choose from—'

'Not half-sisters, Master Ashar. Full sister. Ishnanna-hakku-ezrian.'

'How do you know about her?' Ashar stopped. The spring wind blew through the thin weave of his stolen shirt. He clutched his arms across his chest. 'Who are you? Have you seen her? Where is she? Is she all right? What does she say?'

'Don't listen to him,' a woman's voice cut in. 'All Katayans look the same to him anyway. He hasn't got any message. Have you, Nathan?'

Ashar looked away from the red-haired man. A woman walked up the cobbled road from the direction of the Alhambra, her black coat open, its hem swinging about her calves. She stopped, hooking one thumb in her waistcoat pocket, and inclined her sleek head momentarily to him.

'Nathan?' she needled the man.

'I find your presence, madam, entirely superfluous.'

'On the other hand.' Grey eyes shifted, caught Ashar's gaze, and he blinked at that impact. 'The University of Crime has a way of finding out most information, even that the elusive Ashar-hakku-ezrian had a sister.'

Ashar made a jerky bow. 'Madam de Flores.'

'You remember me. For a moment I was worried about your memory – not that it isn't much on my mind in any case.' She smiled mordantly.

Her remark barely irritated him. He stared at the man. A lean, pale face; not to be read easily. Words cascaded through his mind, all of them drying up before they reached his mouth. He shook his head, shivering.

The thin sun showed up grey where it shone on de Flores' hair. She thrust her hands into her greatcoat pockets. 'How old are you, young man?'

Ashar swallowed. 'Sixteen. Ishnanna's – she was twelve.'

'You're old enough to make judgements. I want you. I want what you have in your head, and I want it safe.' Jocelyn de Flores shrugged. 'I can't say the same about Marston here. He's been hanging around my warehouse for the past fortnight. One of Cragmire's men – that ought to give you some idea. Come with me now.'

The man Marston shook his head. 'He goes with me.'

'*Do* you know anything about Ishnanna?' Ashar shuddered. 'I don't think so. I really don't want anything to do with this contract. It's boring. I don't know what you're all making a fuss about.'

Uncharacteristically abrupt, he shouldered between the two of them and walked on down the street, feet knocking clumsily against the cobbles and making him stagger. The wind smelled of dust and horse-droppings. He sensed rather than heard them stride after him.

He wanted – momentarily wanted so hard that he could not breathe – the dusty rehearsal rooms of the Alhambra: the piano with one key missing, the dancers' discarded stockings, sunlight through the brick-arched windows; sweat, effort, repetition.

The two called his name behind him. He broke into a run, swinging towards the corner stage-door; dodging between two passers-by, jigging a yard left to avoid the matinée coaches pulling up at the kerb.

Movement and mass in the corner of his eye made him stumble, shy away.

Neatly, hands went under his armpits from behind.

'*Hey—!*'

Two thick-set brown Rats in blue livery bundled him towards the nearest carriage's open door, his heels skidding across the cobbles, head ringing from a shocking blow. Steps, seat, and floor scraped his hands as he thudded across the carriage's interior. Cloth muffled his head. A horsewhip cracked. The carriage jolted into immediate motion.

A red-headed man and a woman in a black coat walked moderately rapidly in the opposite direction to the carriage, heads bent concealingly against the cold spring wind.

The theatre manager stared down from her office window at the carriage pulling away and resignedly tore up the sticker to be stripped across the night's billboard:

SPECIAL ATTRACTION!!! WORLD-FAMOUS KATAYAN MONOLOGUIST – ONE NIGHT ONLY!!!

A Rat's voice said, 'You're dead.'

The copper taste of blood soured his mouth. Ashar rolled over, the shackles that hobbled his feet to an eighteen-inch stride clinking. Metal cut his bare ankles.

'Should I feel unwell, do you think?' he said lazily, pressing up against her haunch. 'Being dead, I mean.'

Varagnac, leaning against the bed's headboard, reached out with one sinewy arm and slid it under his, gripping his body, pulling him up closer. Ashar kneaded his hand in the sleek fur of her shoulder, feeling her muscles bunch and shift.

She said, 'Dead as far as anyone else is concerned. You're mine now.'

Ashar-hakku-ezrian smiled. It cracked his split lip open again, and a thin thread of blood seeped down his chin. He wriggled his hips deeper into the rumpled bed sheets. Outside the inn window, a vixen shrieked.

'Well, boy?'

Candlelight gleamed golden on the timbers and beams of the room, on the bare floor and the bed. Shadows danced in cobwebs in the corners of the blackened ceiling. A cold draught shivered his bare spine. He pressed closer in to her warm pelt.

'Damn you, say something!'

'Rubbish. And you know it.'

Livery coat, sword-belt, and feather plume lay strewn across the floor, discarded. Ashar-hakku-ezrian eased the silver-furred Rat a little over on to her side and began to manipulate and knead the tense muscles of her back. She grunted deep in her throat.

'You know something about my sister.' He read the giveaway message of stress through his fingertips. 'You do! I always thought so. From the very first time I came asking!'

Her arm pushed him flat. Long grey-skinned fingers traced a line down his chest, claws leaving the thinnest trail of reddened skin. It patterned across other scored lines, raised and swollen.Her bead-black eyes shone, reflecting candlelight.

'You won't keep me,' he said softly. 'Even now you're thinking: *it was a moment's mistake, how can I get back to the city without being spotted, how can I put it right?'*

He smiled. It had no malice in it. His fingers plunged into the softness of her fur: throat, chest, belly. He curled up and lay his head across her chest.

'Which is not impossible. If it finishes all this, and it means I can get on with doing what *I* want to do, then yes! I'll tell you what to do to get out of it.' His breath pearled on her fur. He sensed her lean forward: sharp incisors just dinted his bare, scarred shoulder.

Ashar knotted fists in soft fur. 'What just happened was fun; but why did you think you had to go to all *this* trouble?'

Varagnac sat back and laughed.

Her chest vibrated. Ashar straightened up into a sitting position, shackles chinking. The Rat, head thrown back, wheezed for breath between paroxysms of laughter; at last reaching out and putting her hands on his two shoulders and shaking him, a half-dozen times, hard.

'Damn you! Well, and what do *you* suggest, if you know so much?'

'Ishnanna-hakku-ezrian.'

'Yes, I know what happened to her.'

Toneless, no hint in the voice; no clue in the language of her lean body. Ashar sat back on his heels, his tail coiling about hers.

'Tell me that and I'll tell you . . . what the contract was.' He grinned. 'You were there. Well, almost there. Present, shall we say; even if you didn't know what went on—'

Her claw-nailed finger touched his lips, silencing him momentarily.

'Fast talker.'

The long-fingered hand straightened, patting his cheek hard
enough to redden the skin. Her lean, long body shone in the yellow
light; shadows lining jaw, eye, and translucent ears.

'At least I had you.' Varagnac chuckled in her throat. 'For a short
enough time. It may be just as well. You bid fair to be unbearable.'

Ashar grinned. 'And then I'll tell you how we go back to town.'

The wind guttered the candle. Below, horses stamped in the
stables. The silver-furred Rat grunted, rolled over, and retrieved her
livery jacket from the floor, diving into the pocket for a thin black
cigar. She tilted the candle to light it.

'So.'

'So . . . it was hot.' Ashar rubbed his bare arms. 'You may not
remember. I, obviously, do. Two weeks ago, at the official opening
of the Royal Botanical gardens . . .'

. . . The ribbon being cut, now, the assembled dignitaries wandered
between tall lines of palms and ferns in the main body of the
Palm House, few climbing the spiral iron staircases to the higher
balconies.

Ashar stared at the thermometer in a pained manner. Spring
sunlight through several thousand panes of glass added to the
underfloor heating. The thin silver line topped out at 95 degrees
Fahrenheit. Humidity quickened his breathing, put black sparkles
across his vision.

'Ashar!'

He flicked his tail down to push aside a palm-frond. Wetness
sprinkled his shoulders. Five or six people walked on this high-
railed balcony. The elderly Kings' Memory Cecily Emmett, at the
rear of the group, beckoned furiously. 'Come here!'

He smiled as he approached her. 'I'm listening. You don't really
need me for this, you know. I could just slip away and not be
bored—'

Cecily Emmett stepped back and grabbed his arm. Her weight
startled Ashar momentarily. He braced himself as the large woman's support.

'I'll be bored, then.'

'You'll pay attention!'

A short, slender man in a black frock-coat stood with one hand
on the balcony rail, the other gesturing. Curling black hair fell
across his sallow forehead. His cravat was wide, striped candy-pink

and white; and his top hat sat rakishly cocked to one side. Ashar, fascinated, caught the man's eye across the intervening yards.

'Two Kings' Memories?' the human queried.

'Ashar-hakku-ezrian, your lordship. My apprentice.'

The man signalled acceptance with a hand in which he held sweat-stained white gloves. 'I understand. Very well.'

A slight wheeze hissed in Cecily's undertone. 'That . . . is Lord Benjamin himself. Sebastien you know. De Flores you know.'

Lord Benjamin's light, penetrating voice cut through the humid air. 'Forgive me if I take advantage of this official opening for us to meet. It seems secure, and opportune.'

Ashar saw, over Lord Benjamin's shoulder, the hard jaw-line of a familiar face. Jocelyn de Flores. The fat black Rat Sebastien stood beside de Flores, talking across the trader to one well-dressed black Rat, and two brown Rats.

Ashar leaned his elbows on the balcony.

Below, out of earshot, stood a silver-furred Rat in plain leather harness and the indefinable air of covert authority that argued security police.

The Rat lifted her head. Varagnac.

Varagnac and he stared at each other.

Cecily's voice hissed in his ear. 'Listen to me, boy. You're on parole already. I want this meeting repeated back word-perfect from you; as perfect as my official record, *is that clear*?'

He beamed. Varagnac turned away.

'Of course,' he said.

A brass band played on the lawns outside the Palm House. Music came muffled through the arching glass walls. Here, the fronds of giant ferns swept down to shield the balcony from sight of the main part of the hall. Isolated by height and occasion, the group halted.

'Master Cragmire.' Cecily introduced a tall, bearded man; balding, dressed in a plain frock-coat; whose image would not stay in the memory for more than seconds. 'From the University of Crime. And not an ornament to any of these discussions, Ashar, at least as far as we're concerned.'

The dark-bearded man laughed. 'I'm not prolix. A little verbose, perhaps. Veritably, that's the worst criminal infringement you can accuse me of, Cecily.'

'Will you *listen* to him.' Amused, the fat woman shook her head.

Ashar stared between his booted feet, through the open iron-work floor of the balcony, looking directly down on water and the wide leaves of water-lilies. He lifted his head. White-painted iron chairs and tables stood on this wider part of the balcony, and the sallow-skinned Lord Benjamin already sat at one table, pouring out tea from a silver service.

'Gentlemen. Ladies.'

The trader, de Flores, fell into the chair beside Lord Benjamin, pulling at her high collar to loosen it. Sweat pearled on her face, and her grey-streaked hair plastered to her forehead.

'*Damn* stupid place for a meeting, my lord.'

'It has its advantages. Messire Sebastien?' The Home Secretary passed a fragile china cup up to the fat black Rat. Messire Sebastien shook lace ruffles back, and took the cup in fat, ringless fingers.

Cragmire drew out a chair for Cecily Emmett to sit; then seated himself beside her. The three Rat lords took chairs. Ashar hitched himself up to sit on the balcony rail.

Lord Benjamin lifted an eyebrow, then sipped cautiously at the hot tea. 'Well, now . . .'

Prompted, Cecily Emmett looked up from arranging her long skirts and surreptitiously loosening her bodice. She blinked against the refracted sunlight. 'I speak now, officially, as the Academy of Memory directs. *You are heard.* What is said now, will be remembered. What is recalled by Kings' Memories is valid in law, in custom, and in the eyes of the gods. You are so warned.'

'I believe that is what we are met for. If someone would like to outline the proposition . . . ?' Benjamin set his cup down on the white-painted iron table, and leaned back with his arms resting along the spiral chair-arms. His large eyes moved from the Kings' Memory to the rest of the group.

Ashar hooked one ankle about the balcony strut he sat on and, balanced, leaned back into open space. Sword-bladed palms shone dully green around him, trunks rooting a dozen yards below.

Jocelyn de Flores said, 'For my part, it's simple. I want to open up trade with the newly discovered East Pole. Since one of my skippers came back from there a month since, I've realised it isn't as simple as sending a clipper-ship and a cargo.'

'Your ship?' Cragmire queried.

'The *Pangolin*. The master is a man I trust.'

A Rat in a red jacket with gold epaulettes bowed, frigidly, to Jocelyn de Flores. 'You have described this new territory to us. Savages, ruled by theocrats.'

Inattention; a sudden quarter-inch shift of balance – his every muscle from ankle to thigh locked. Heart hammering, Ashar leaned forward and slid back down on to the balcony floor. His tail coiled about one strut. Across the group, he locked eyes with Cecily

Emmett as the elderly woman wiped her sweating face with a handkerchief. Paleness blotched her skin.

'And the Queen?' another Rat asked. 'Lord Benjamin, it is common knowledge that you – make yourself agreeable – to her Majesty . . .'

The sallow-skinned man smiled. He waved one hand expansively. 'Messire, I flatter the Queen, and I lay it on with a trowel. The Queen is not fool enough to believe me.'

'So why do it?' Ashar asked. Cecily Emmett glared at his daring to open his mouth.

'The Queen's pride is to see through me. I am quite transparent about it, you see. A rogue may get away with much, when making no pretence to be anything else but a rogue.' Lord Benjamin turned to the brown Rat. 'Have no fear of her Majesty. The Queen is always interested in new territory.'

'The lands that lie about the East Pole are *rich*.' A raw edge scraped in Sebastien's voice. The sun through the glass shone on his plump-jawed muzzle, glinting from his bead-black eyes. The light showed scuff-marks on his sword-belt and scabbard inexpertly concealed with polish.

'Rich,' Sebastien repeated. He tugged at the faded lace at his throat. 'Benjamin, you know all this: we can import enough in herbs, spices, and exotics from the East Pole to make all our fortunes ten times over. We'll never do it. Not while their Church of the White Rose is in power. The Heptarch wants nothing to do with foreign lands: *he* says, they need nothing from us, and will give us nothing.'

'And bribery?' Lord Benjamin looked to Jocelyn de Flores.

'Tried and failed, my lord. Their peasants have done nothing for centuries but toil and worship; and the Church nothing but *be* worshipped. Money doesn't mean anything to either.'

Here she shifted down in her chair, the collar of her shirt rucked up around her neck with the movement.

'Let me hear your suggestion again,' Benjamin asked mildly. 'For the record.'

'The question is, what do we have that they don't? And the answer's simple, if not obvious. We have this.'

Jocelyn de Flores took her hand out of her breeches pocket and stood a small phial upright on the table. Her black eyes gleamed, looking around the circle.

'I see you gentlemen don't frequent the docklands. This is called *kgandara*. More commonly, *candy*. I always have trouble with my deckhands using it. It comes from Candover,' the woman said thoughtfully, 'and it is an extremely addictive drug.'

Lord Benjamin stretched out an ungloved hand and took it back without touching the phial of yellow powder.

'What does it do?' one of the nameless Rat lords asked.

'To your people, my lord? I don't know. It gives us dreams.' Again, that smile. Ashar blinked. Jocelyn said, 'Dreams are always better. I don't use *candy* myself. I have known men kill for half a gram of it. Once introduced into the new territories, we have a market that will *always* exist. After that, I think trade might move very briskly, and we might set our own prices for what we please to sell and buy.'

Cragmire sat forward, his heavy hands dangling between his knees. 'Part of the price being that the White Rose, also, sell *candy* as middlemen.'

'Oh, yes.'

The bearded man sat back. One of the anonymous Rat lords asked, 'Are you serious?'

Lord Benjamin shrugged. 'It is no worse, I dare say, than introducing muskets into Candover; which as I recall my predecessor undertook to do. With some success. Cragmire, you can supply what is necessary?'

'Indubitably, my lord. The University has connections with the *candy* trade.'

Ashar reached across Cecily Emmett's fat shoulder and helped himself to a cup of tea, now pleasantly cold. Sweat trickled down between his shoulder-blades, and he scratched at it with the tip of his tail. The several unnamed but unmistakably influential Rat lords bent their heads together in conversation. De Flores whispered to Sebastien.

Ashar squatted briefly beside the elder Kings' Memory. 'What a bitch of an idea.'

Cecily Emmett coughed. 'It's your business to remember. Not judge.'

'Not even admire?'

'More trade means more employment, of course.' Lord Benjamin nodded approvingly to de Flores. 'Now, as to my own part—'

Cecily Emmett's elbow slammed across Ashar's hands.

The china cup flew, splintered on the iron balcony floor. He put a foot back, tail hooked out on the air for balance; and caught her arm as she slumped across him. Her chair tilted and fell. The fat woman's body fell, pressing him against sharp angles of chair, table and balcony as the group sprang to their feet.

'Madam Cecily!' Ashar got his shoulder under her back.

The weight lifted suddenly as Jocelyn de Flores and Cragmire cradled the Kings' Memory and eased her down against them.

'Fetch a doctor!' De Flores thumbed up Cecily Emmett's half-closed eyelids, and rested a hand against her throat. 'Quickly. My lord, if you call—'

Cragmire said tersely, 'A stroke.'

Lord Benjamin stepped back from the balcony. Beneath, the clatter of running footsteps already sounded; Varagnac's voice yelling orders. He held up one hand.

'Messires, my people will see the woman to hospital, and notify the Academy of Memory.' His wide-nailed hand shifted to point at Ashar. 'This meeting should not be interrupted, being so hard to bring about. Messire Ashar-hakku-ezrian, you will act as sole Kings' Memory now. I'm sorry you have to end your apprenticeship in this abrupt manner.'

'I – yes.' He stepped back, not remembering standing up; watching in horrified interest as men and women from Lord Benjamin's staff stripped off frock coats and, in their shirtsleeves, began to lift and manoeuvre the woman down the spiral iron staircase to the exit.

'Kings' Memory!'

Ashar-hakku-ezrian turned, hands thrust deep in his breeches pockets. 'I'm listening.'

'My last words?'

He met Lord Benjamin's gaze. ' "More trade means more employment, of course. Now, as to my own part—" '

'Excellent.' The flamboyantly dressed man took a last look over the balcony, and reseated himself beside Jocelyn de Flores. 'You need have no fear of her Majesty's disapproval. Let them wink and say they saw nothing. When "Empress of the East Pole" is added to the Queen's other titles, I think you'll find yourself rewarded well enough.'

He steepled his fingers. 'My notion is to float a somewhat larger company than you at present can, Madam de Flores; invite investment, and then further investment when the market proves itself open. The initial capital will come from these gentlemen here—'

He nodded at the Rat lords. One sniffed, adjusting an epaulette.

'—and the returns will be, I imagine, quite magnificent. It wouldn't do for her Majesty's approval of the *first* part of this scheme to become widely known; therefore, I think, we make secrecy one of our prime concerns.'

'It'll take cash to finance the introduction of *candy*.' Jocelyn de Flores glanced at Cragmire. 'I won't enquire into the University's methods, but you'll want funds.'

'Among other things.'

'Government resources.' De Flores looked back at Lord Benjamin, who spread his hands.

'As you say, dear lady, government resources. Which you will have. The House will approve it as part of the confidential budget, my colleagues here assure me.'

Jocelyn de Flores looked at the shabby black Rat, and Sebastien inclined his plump head. 'Well then. The University of Crime will undertake to supply *kgandara*, for a substantial share in the East Pole Trading Company. We'll handle transportation and trade. Lord Benjamin will—'

'—as I have said, expedite matters,' the flamboyant, sallow-skinned man cut in. 'Kings' Memory, do you hear?'

Outside, the brass band shifted into a martial tune played in three-quarter time. Under a blue sky, the sun blazed down on crimson and blue flowers in ranked beds. Ashar-hakku-ezrian slitted his eyes. Light shattered in through glass and ironwork. A fragile fern brushed damp against the skin of his sweat-damp upper arm. 'I hear.'

'I set my word to this as a binding contract: Benjamin.'

The black-haired woman licked the corners of her mouth. 'I also set my word to this as a binding contract: Jocelyn de Flores.'

'And I, Sebastien.'

'My word is given for the University: Cragmire. This binds me.'

Ashar cocked his head, gazing at the Rat lords.

'Seznec: this binds me.'

'Ammarion: this binds me.'

'De L'Isle: this binds me.'

The Lord Benjamin nodded once, sharply. 'So. It is remembered.'

'. . . and that's all.' The Katayan leaned his elbows back on the thwarts.

Varagnac shipped oars and held up long fingers for silence. The stolen wherry grated on shingle. She stared up at the underside of the river bridge. The estuary tide being out, they beached some thirty feet from the bank.

'You did it. We're home.' She heard the admiration a little too ungrudged in her own voice, and chuckled throatily. 'I don't have to ask if you remember what I told you – the procedure in case we become separated?'

Ashar leaned over the edge of the boat.

'I'm going to get my feet wet. You couldn't get this thing further inland?'

'No!' Varagnac swore. She vaulted over the side, landing lightly on mud-slick shingle. 'Move.'

The wind, bitter cold from the river, blew in her face. Her ears twitched. She loped across the shingle to the shelter of a pillar, tail out for balance. Her sword-belt bounced against her haunch.

'Now.'

Only pale hands and face visible, the black-clothed young man slid out of the boat and ran towards the bank. A soft noise triggered her reflexes in the same second as Ashar-hakku-ezrian swore and sat down heavily in the mud.

'*Damnation*—!' A scream sounded over his whisper.

Varagnac sucked her fingers, where the tip of her throwing-knife had caught on leaving her hand, and widened her eyes. Night sight showed her a slumped body at the foot of the embankment. She caught the Katayan's wrist and threw him into the shelter of the pillar behind her.

A voice rang out above. '*Ashar-hakku-ezrian!*'

'Nearly home,' Varagnac amended.

The male voice came again. 'Ashar! I want to talk. We *must* talk.'

The young man shrugged easily. 'I can talk to him. Why not?'

Varagnac drew her oiled blade soundlessly from its sheath. She pressed up against the wet masonry, every knob of her spine grating on the stone, back protected. A glance showed her Ashar-hakku-ezrian on the river side of the pillar, watching the other direction.

From the bridge above, the male voice sounded. 'You know she'll kill you, don't you? She has her orders.'

Tidal water lapped the shingle. The stolen wherry lifted, rocked, settled. Moonlight strengthened as clouds dissolved. She met Ashar's gaze.

'Ask her!' The voice rang out above, some yards differently positioned. 'Benjamin ordered it. Yesterday. At five-and-twenty to six.'

A blink: Ashar's lashes covered dark, glowing eyes. 'That's a man called Nathaniel Marston. De Flores calls him that, anyway.'

Varagnac's mouth quirked. 'So the University of Crime are tapping departmental telephone lines.'

Varagnac reached out a hand to the Katayan, steered him running, miraculously sure-footed in the river slime, to the shelter of the next bank-ward pillar.

Another voice came from further down the bridge. 'Ashar! You know we don't mean you any harm. We want the contract preserved. We've got every reason to keep you safe.'

'Cragmire,' the Katayan muttered. 'I told you he was at that meeting.'

Moonlight shattered on the river. A bitter wind ruffled her fur.

'If I go with them, will they let you alone?'

It was said with a serious, pragmatic curiosity. Varagnac didn't smile. She said, 'All the University wants . . . They want you – no, they want the contract – so they can extend their *candy* trade. That's all. You don't want that.'

'What the hell do I care about whoever these East Pole people are!'

'Your conscience does you credit,' she remarked acerbically.

'They're a long way away, and my friends are here and now. Mistress Varagnac, I'm going with Cragmire. If you wait until we're gone—'

'You'll do as I damn well tell you.' Varagnac stepped out from under the bridge support, left hand going up to her shoulder-sheath and forward in one movement. A high shriek echoed across the city, ripping at the bitter cold air, ringing from warehouse walls.

She caught Ashar's hand and ran five yards, pulling him towards the steps rising up through one arch to the road.

'Because . . .' At road-level she pushed him down beside her where she knelt, in a wall's shelter, peering out. Every sense alert for sound or movement, she murmured, 'Because I can tell you about Ishnanna.'

'Tell me!'

'You must go *now*. When I say.'

'Varagnac . . .'

Varagnac ruffled his brown-blond hair. It stuck to the drying blood on her hand. She winced, laughing. 'You know how to get there?'

'Yes.'

'Go in the way I told you and you'll miss the security systems. Once you're in, ask for that name: "William".'

He reached up one hand from where he crouched at her side, running his fingers down the long line of her jaw. She pushed him: he stumbled into a run, fleeing towards the warehouses, bare feet soundless on the cobbles.

She stood up from the stairs' concealment. The full moon flattened itself against a blue and silver sky, drowning stars, chilling the air, spidering the pavement with shadows. The lean Rat turned, silver fur shiningly visible. She hitched up her sword-belt and wiped mud from her doublet. There was no sound.

Varagnac bent down, scraped a match along the pavement, lit a

cigar that made a minute red ember in the night, and let them come
to her.

'A command *performance*?' Jocelyn de Flores sat up at her warehouse desk, incredulous.

Sebastien nodded, halfway between satisfaction and hysteria.
'Ashar-hakku-ezrian performing monologues in front of her Majesty themselves. Madam, you think I'm a fool. Well, even this fool
can guess what we'll hear from that stage!'

He had the satisfaction of seeing her quiet for a second.

'This is certain? He's alive?'

'The young man was found this morning by Lord William, in the
grounds of the palace. He's keeping him as her Majesty's guest until
tonight. The only place in the dominion where none of us can reach
him!' Sebastien slumped down on the desk, tail shoving account
books on to the warehouse floor. He pulled his headband off and
scratched at his sweaty fur, looked at the broken plume, and threw
it down vehemently. 'I'm ruined. I'll get nothing back from that
bastard Benjamin. When this blows, we all go bankrupt, if not to
prison!'

'You must shift for yourself,' the woman said coolly.

'*We're* ruined!' He hardly noticed the woman leaving until she
was a dozen yards away. He looked up, opened his mouth to call,
and, too dispirited, made no sound.

Outside the river lapped at the dock. He wondered to what
distant port the *Pangolin* might be sailing next.

Staring across the crowded palace anteroom, Jocelyn spotted very
few human faces among the assembled Rat lords. She pushed her
way through towards a young man in a half-unlaced black leather
doublet, leaning casually with one arm across a sofa-back, the other
hand moving in rapid gestures. Several Rats leaned up against the
back of the sofa – a sharp brown Rat in linen and leather, fidgeting
with the point of her dagger; a slender black Rat in mauve satin; two
of her sisters in black sword-harness – debating across his head,
fiercely, on subjects of his devising.

'What do you think?' He and a buxom black Rat had their heads
together over sheets of paper that, Jocelyn saw, bore line-sketches.

'Well, I don't know, Master Kit; I think it comes perilously close
to the forbidden art of writing.'

'Oh, no. No. Not at all. It's graphic art. Wordless graphic art –
silent comics.' He riffled through the pages. 'I don't know about
this, though . . . I had the artist do my signature-portrait three-

quarter profile, but it makes my nose look big. Do I really look like that?'

Leaning over the drawing, comparing it with the original, the buxom Rat traced a jaw-line and nose with a slender claw; then raised her hand to touch the young man's face, presented for her inspection with a certain complacent vanity.

'Kit!'

He excused himself politely and turned, with a ready sweet smile. 'Yes, sweetheart?'

Jocelyn de Flores folded her arms, hands in the sleeves of her overcoat. 'Who's got the ear of the Queen right now? Who are they listening to?'

The young man reached up and took off darkened spectacles, blinking thoughtfully. His smile flashed. 'Well, let's see. Yes. There's the very person. Imogen!'

A striking and statuesque woman in black leather stood in the centre of another group, one finger raised, halfway through the conclusion of a reported conversation:

'. . . completely evocative: but I said to him, a battle of wits, yes; but why should I fight an unarmed man?' She halted, turning to the young man and speaking in a slightly breathless, husky voice: 'Yes, Kit?'

'Imogen, this is Jocelyn de Flores; she runs the East Pole Trading Company; Jocelyn, this is Imogen, wit, truly wonderful person, and . . . well.' Kit smiled and put his darkened-glass spectacles back on. 'What can I tell you? She'll know what you want to know.'

'I need,' Jocelyn said with a degree of determination, 'to see the Queen. Today.'

'Now let me see, who would do . . .' Imogen lifted her chin, lively eyes searching the assembly. Poised, questing, she mentally sorted through faces and names. 'She won't be giving an audience, as such: I was just saying to Vexin and Quesnoy.'

Jocelyn looked blank.

'Oh, you don't *know* them.' Rapidly, apologetic, breathless. 'Vexin is the woman who's owned by Seznec.'

'Seznec?'

'Seznec left Barbier for Chaptal.'

Jocelyn gave it up. She glanced back at the young man.

'Look, I have to go.' His gaze moved to the group of Rats at the sofa, the dynamics of which had shifted towards dissolution without him. 'Imogen will look after you. Call me if you need me; I'll be right there.'

Imogen, who had looked enthusiastically ready to continue the conversation, spotted a face across the audience chamber.

'*Ah.*'

She turned and swept off, Jocelyn stepping rapidly to keep up, and bore down on a small red-headed woman dressed in black. The woman stood talking to a brown Rat:

'. . . I said to him, *Why, this is the Invisible College, nor am I out of it* . . . Hello, Imogen.'

'Æmilia, you can do this for me, can't you? Jocelyn needs to see her Majesty. Sorry, I *must* rush. Hope it goes well for you, Jocelyn.' Smiling, breathless, a little hurried; she moved with utter confidence into the crowd.

Æmelia lifted a dark eyebrow. She wore black breeches, boots, and a shirt embroidered in baroque death's-heads. For a second she stood with her weight back on one heel, surveying the far end of the hall. The glass of red wine in her hand wavered slightly. 'Right . . . See that door there? In about three minutes you'll see the guard leave it. Go through. Got that?'

'He'll leave?'

The woman grinned. 'You watch. Have a little trust. Honestly, the things I *do* for people . . .'

Jocelyn stared after her, losing her among the crowd of tall black and brown Rats. The background noise rose. She sniffed, smelling sweat and fur and scent, not the spices and tar of the docks; and stared the Rat lords up and down with some contempt.

The Rat Guard turned his head as the door behind him opened a fraction. He nodded and strode away, businesslike, towards the entrance. Jocelyn walked without any hesitation up to and through the door.

The heights of the Feasting Hall opened around her.

Brown stone arched up into Gothick vaults, by way of carved niches full of figures of Rat saints, statesmen, monarchs, and lords of antiquity. Blue velvet drapes curtained the draught from the hall doors. A spiky-branched candelabra hung down from the peak of the ceiling, candles as yet unlit.

The Rat-Queen in their close group stood, some directing servants in their cleaning operations, some supervising the erection of the makeshift stage, one reading in a prompt-book. Brown Rat servants made rows of chairs, and two velvet-lined boxes: a theatre set up in miniature.

Jocelyn swept a bow that left her greatcoat brushing dust from the hall floor. Some of the Rat-Queen turned. A sleek-faced one gestured to the page nursing their knotted tails; he set down the velvet cushion.

'Ah. One of our merchant-venturers, we believe. We hear that you wish to see us, Madam de Flores.'

'Mercy!' Jocelyn de Flores, with a mental and ironic acknowledgement to Lord Benjamin, theatrically fell on one knee.

Another sleek black royal head turned, wearing an expression of bemusement. 'Whatever for, Madam de Flores?'

'I know something that I must tell to your Majesty,' Jocelyn said. 'A crime. Of which I myself am not entirely innocent.'

Ashar-hakku-ezrian looked down with an expression somewhere between embarrassment and searing relief. The girl's arms locked about his waist, her face buried in his chest: only the top of her head and buttercup-yellow hair visible.

'Varagnac told me where you were.' He tentatively stroked her back. Her plush-furred tail looped up and coiled snake-tight about his forearm. 'But I'd have got round to looking here pretty soon.'

He brought his free hand round and shifted her embrace, getting fingers to her pointed chin and forcing it up. The twelve-year-old leaned back slightly and fixed him with impossibly large eyes.

'*Sure* you would.' A head and a half shorter than her brother, with cropped blonde hair, brown skin dotted with a hundred thousand pale and minute freckles, a body whipcord-thin: Ish-nanna-hakku-ezrian.

Malice flicked her inflected speech: the dialect of South Katay. 'Oh, and if you think that, tell me what I'm *doing* here. *If* you can.'

The midday sun shone with a new warmth on the formal gardens of the palace. Topiary yews cast shade over grass walks, and, where the two of them stood at the edge of the grand canal, the water reflected hedges, the palace's Gothick heights, and the blue sky of spring becoming early summer.

Ashar-hakku-ezrian ruffled her cropped hair. 'So what did you run away to be, shorty?'

The Katayan girl stepped back and held up her hands. Black gum smeared her fingers, palms, wrists, and one elbow. Ashar began tetchily to examine his shirt where she had hugged him. 'What the hell is that?'

'Cartographic ink.' Ishnanna's white-blonde tail whisked dew from the flagstones, dipped into the canal, and brought up water for her to dabble on her stained hands. Her big eyes gleamed. 'I'm nearly trained, Ash. The Queen's Mapmaker has five apprentices, but *I'm* the one he's going to send on the *Hawthorne* when it sails to look for the West Pole. Oh, can't you just think of it!'

'Miles of empty ocean, ship's biscuits, storms, uneducated ship-masters, no destination, *seasickness* – yes, I can think of it.'

'*Ash* . . .'

'Did I *say* I wouldn't come with you?'

The girl smiled, short upper lip pulling back from white teeth. She squinted up at him, against the sun. 'Well . . . it's not for a year or more yet. Ash, what are you doing here? Did you just come looking for me? How's Mother? Did she say anything about me? Why didn't you get here sooner? Why did Lord William bring you in this morning? Are you in trouble?'

'Who, me?'

Ashar-hakku-ezrian grinned and looked up past her, at the sprawling bulk of the palace that squatted black and spiked and perpendicular in the sunlight.

'We are *most* displeased.'

The Rat-Queen's tone was icy. Benjamin bowed deeply. 'Your Majesty.'

'An attempt to undermine the ruler of these East Pole lands – why, the man is a monarch! As we are. How dare you even contemplate such an action?'

Lord Benjamin put his hands behind his back, gripping his folded yellow gloves. Just to his right, the stout and sober figure of Lord William waited.

'I had thought to make your Majesty's dominions wealthy with trade.'

Nine pairs of eyes fixed on him. Some of the Rat-Queen folded their hands in their laps. Lean-jawed faces stiffened, stern.

'And what example will you give the mob, Benjamin, if you begin by bringing a monarch down from his god-given station in life? How will the rabble out there think of *us*? Would you have us condescend to explain—'

'—our actions for their good, that they, being the common herd, cannot understand?'

High Rat voices reverberated from the white-cobwebbed walls.

'Or excuse ourselves—'

'—when our responsibility is solely to ourselves and the god that gave us this land to rule?'

'You may not do this thing! We are angry with you, Lord Benjamin. We think it best—'

'—that you conclude this sorry affair now. End it. Never more speak of it.'

One of the Rat-Queen laid a gloved hand on the edge of the baroque marble tomb, her face thoughtful.

'Lord William is to be our first minister in your place. We are sorry you should bring such disgrace upon yourself, my lord. Be thankful the punishment is no worse.'

Lord Benjamin swept a bow, turned, and, as he passed Lord William on the way out, murmured to those impassive, craggy features, 'Make the most of your turn in favour my lord. While you have it.'

Ten thousand candles illuminated the Feasting Hall. The naphtha jets stood unlit. A heavy scent of wax and warm flame filled the air.

Varagnac eased at the sling cradling her fractured arm, buttoned into her livery jacket; one sleeve hanging empty. She undid another button. Analgesic drugs buzzed in her head. She grinned lopsidedly, standing at the head of the steps and surveying the crowd.

Stage and royal box faced each other across thirty feet of hall space, the wooden framework bright with purple velvet coverings and the royal crest. Stage-curtains hung closed as yet. Some fifty plush chairs occupied the intermediate space, and between them Rat lords in evening dress and satins stood drinking green wine and talking. Varagnac eye-checked the positions of her plain-clothes guard.

'Madam Varagnac.'

'Sir.' She walked down to join Lord William at the foot of the steps. Stout and stolid, he gazed across the hall.

Beyond the rows of seats, in front of the stage, Ashar-hakku-ezrian stood talking with Athanasius Godwin. The old man frowned. Ashar spoke, tail cocked, head to one side; and Godwin chuckled. Ears shifting, Varagnac caught a fragment of their conversation:

'. . . accept hospitality . . . Academy . . .'

The Katayan took the offered glass from Godwin, drained it, and wiped his wispy beard. Varagnac saw him grin, and vault up on to the stage and peer through the closed curtains.

She gazed up at Ashar-hakku-ezrian on the platform. In black evening dress, and with a silver sash slightly disguising his plump waist, the young man raised arched blond brows at Varagnac, and tipped her a twitch of his groomed tail.

'Isn't he something?' She shook her head and looked down at the stout man beside her. 'Sir.'

'Undoubtedly.' Lord William's tone was dry. 'However, he still carries dangerous knowledge. He knows more about certain people's business than is entirely wise for any of us.'

Varagnac rubbed lightly at her splinted arm. Through the crowd she glimpsed a red-bearded man leaning up against the empty royal box. His blue doublet had been abandoned in favour of formal dress; he moved stiffly.

'So Marston survives? Hrrmm.'

'Exactly. Watch the young man. I believe that that is all we can do. And I fear it will hardly be enough.'

Lord William bowed formally and continued to plough through the assembled dignitaries, towards the doors by which the Queen would enter. Varagnac circulated, checking more guard-points. She impressed in her mind the positions of Athanasius Godwin, and a small troop from the Academy of Memory; and Jocelyn de Flores and two other ship-owners. She searched keenly for signs of the visible Nathaniel Marston's invisible associates.

A voice some yards away said, 'I'm surprised that you're still here. After the fall of your patron.'

'Sebastien . . .' She gave it a toothy emphasis.

'That's Messire Sebastien to you.' Fat and sweating in leather and lace, the black Rat narrowed his eyes in her direction. Varagnac chuckled.

'The security services are always here . . . If you're looking for Madam de Flores, she's over with Lord Oudin. Or do you think that even a human won't welcome your company now?'

'Don't be insolent!'

'Don't be ridiculous.' She dropped humour and spoke concisely. 'My department has sufficient proof of your involvement. I know how deep in debt this puts you. If you're thinking of repairing your fortunes, go overseas to do it. You won't take a step here that I don't know about.'

The black Rat brushed her elbow as he strode off, sending pain up her arm and shoulder. She swore. Wax dripped down from the spiky chandelier, spotting the silver fur of her haunches. Her tail whipped back and forth a few irritated inches either way.

'Fool!' She clapped hand to her sword-hilt, avoiding spearing two black Rats in identical cerise silk, and took a few paces closer to the stage. Ashar-hakku-ezrian slid in between the closed curtains. She halted.

'Good god.' She failed to keep the amazement out of her voice. 'Lord Benjamin?'

Benjamin acknowledged her with a wave of his free hand.

Resplendent in evening dress with a pink tie and cummerbund, curly hair shining with oil, he walked with a very young woman on his arm. Varagnac blinked.

'Varagnac, I don't believe you know my acquaintance of this evening. This is Mistress Ishnanna-hakku-ezrian. Queens' Mapmaker.'

Enormous dark eyes looked up from a level somewhat below Varagnac's collarbone. Freckled, darker, and with dandelion-fluff hair: the girl stood with all her older brother's aplomb.

'Apprentice Queens' Mapmaker.' Her tiny voice was husky, accented. 'You're the one Ash tells me about? *Mmmm* . . .'

Hackles ruffled up Varagnac's spine. 'One of your family patronising me is quite enough. Benjamin, are you mad? You shouldn't be here. She certainly shouldn't.'

'And for his own safety, nor should the lady's brother. I hold him no ill-will; what's happened has happened—' The ex-minister broke off. 'Speak to me after this. Ishnanna, look, there: her Majesty.'

'Oh, I've met her Majesty; they like me.'

A fanfare of silver trumpets interrupted, slicing the air like ripped silk; notes dropping a silence over the fifty or so Rat lords and humans.

Heels clicked across the tiled floors: the uniformed trumpeters retired. The great doors swung open. A line of three Rat priests padded in. Varagnac automatically crossed herself. Censers spilled perfumes. With a rustle of cloth, the crowd sank formally down on their knees.

'God save the Queen!'

Slender, pacing slowly in a close group, the Rat-Queen entered. Open-fronted black silk robes rustled. Diamonds flashed back the candlelight from rings, pectoral plates, and headbands bearing slender black ostrich plumes. Onyx mourning jewellery weighed down their slim bodies.

They spoke no words, only looking with black bright eyes at each other, and sometimes smiling as if in response. Some of the Rat-Queen walked arm-in-arm, some with hands demurely folded before them. The royal pages carried the knot of their intertwined tails on a purple silk cushion.

'Regina!'

Varagnac narrowed her eyes. Nathaniel Marston knelt with only his dark-red hair showing, head bent. Two of Varagnac's officers flanked him, with another cater-wise two yards away. Lord Benjamin, kneeling next to Lord William, was muttering in the sober man's ear; Ishnanna-hakku-ezrian, peering everywhere but at the royal entrance, waved to someone—

To Ashar, looking out from backstage.

Guards unobtrusively shadowed the Rat-Queen down the hall and up into the royal box. Individuals approached to be presented by the major-domo.

Varagnac sighed with relief, surprised at the strength of her feelings. She got up, dusting the fur of her knees, and slipped between the crowd as they took their seats. She ducked around the curtained edge of the stage and into the backstage area.

A tall Rat faced her: blue livery half-unbuttoned, sword slung for left-hand draw; silver fur spiky with exhaustion. Lean, lithe; clawed hind feet braced widely apart, tail out for balance . . .

Varagnac moved around the conjuror's mirror.

Rails of costumes, trestle tables, standing mirrors, and a confusion of people crowded this blocked-off corridor. Varagnac stepped back as musicians piled past her, a furious argument in progress that stopped instantly as they emerged onstage.

'Ashar.'

'I'm here.' The Katayan drew the edge of a finger along his eyebrows, darkening them, and met her eyes in the make-up mirror. He grinned. 'House full?'

'Full of people who are dangerous.' The Rat ticked off points on long, claw-nailed fingers. 'I don't count de Flores, she's only lost one opportunity. Sebastien may hate the person responsible for his ruin, but *Sebastien* . . . Benjamin will merely wait his turn out until he's in again. But you're a witness against the University, and I see Marston out there; and no doubt there are more of them here that I don't know.'

The Katayan stood and put his hands in his evening dress pockets.

Varagnac's left hand strayed absently to her splinted arm. 'Lord William's spoken to the Katayan Ambassador. You're going back next week.'

Music and song resonated through from the Feasting Hall. In a sphere of silence, she watched him.

'There are things even *you* can't do anything about, Ashar-hakku-ezrian. In a year or two it won't matter – some other company will have contracted to supply *candy* to the natives, and her Majesty will have been persuaded into turning a blind eye. For now, you're a serious embarrassment, and a high risk.'

He stepped closer to her, raising his chin so that he could look her in the eye. Varagnac stroked the side of his face. Cosmetic dust adhered to her long grey fingers.

'Rough night.' Without quite touching, his hand sketched the shape of her bandaged arm.

'Don't you hear what I'm saying!'

Head cocked to one side, he flirted eyelashes at her in a deliberate parody; she laughed; and he, soberly and easily, said, 'I've got it under control. Don't worry. Trust me.'

With the air of a respectable grandfather, he bent over her hand and kissed it. His fingers caressed the sensitive short fur under her wrist.

Varagnac remained staring after him until minutes after the young man had walked through on to the stage. She moved back through the side exit into the hall and positioned herself unobtrusively. Decorous requests for monologues were already being called out to Ashar-hakku-ezrian, poised on stage in the full light of two thousand candles.

He shone.

'Master Katayan.' The Rat-Queen's silvery voice cut across the theatre. 'Oblige us, please—'

Ashar-hakku-ezrian flourished a deep bow, tail cocked behind him. His eyes were brightly expectant. The candlelight dazzled on his black clothes and blond hair. Varagnac watched him spread his hands a little.

'I am entirely at your Majesty's disposal: command me!'

Two of the Rat-Queen looked at each other, relaxed, laughing; with the unconscious condescension of royal enjoyment. A slim Rat-Queen spoke. 'We know your skills are in spontaneous verse—'

'—but we find a great desire to hear a poem of yours which is somewhat famous.'

Ashar-hakku-ezrian bowed again.

'We would hear your rhyme of—'

One of the Rat-Queen unfolded a fan and hid her face. A bolder one continued, '—of the flea.'

Ashar snapped his fingers at the instrumentalists without even looking at them. He put his hands behind his back.

Varagnac's gaze shifted across the assembled company. Ammarion, Seznec, and De L'Isle. Commander-general. Speaker of the House. And First Lord of the Treasury. A cluster of judges, one with her pectoral badge showing four capital verdicts handed down. And merchants, businessmen, one theatre-owner; and Jocelyn de Flores with the literary mafia: Kit, Imogen, Æmilia.

For this second, all their eyes were on Ashar-hakku-ezrian. Obsessively she checked that her security officers were in their places . . . Athanasius Godwin of the Academy of Memory had

Nathaniel Marston seated next to him. She scowled, moving in their direction.

The drum beat: Ashar's voice filled the hall.

> *'Young Frederick, a famous flea,*
> *Ambitions had to climb, you see,*
> *Be bettered in the social scale,*
> *And buy a better-class female.*
> *He found a King whose mighty itch*
> *Was for a—'*

A silence fell. Varagnac glanced up at the stage.

Ashar smoothed back his hair with both hands. He glanced down at the leader of the musicians, nodded, and began again:

'A king whose mighty itch—'

He hesitated, stopped.

One of the Rat-Queen frowned, ready to pardon satire wittily expressed, but not ineptitude.

Varagnac's hand went to her sword, her eyes fixed on Marston.

The red-bearded man's mouth opened in a momentary, amazed O.

She looked rapidly back at the stage – Ashar-hakku-ezrian stood, red under his cosmetics, one hand still outstretched as if he could summon up the words: a royal Fool become a plain fool, evening dress become motley.

'—and so to scratch—' He wiped the back of his hand across his wet forehead. A shiver constricted Varagnac's spine. She dropped her gaze, not able for sympathy to look at him.

'I . . .' Ashar's voice faltered. His eyes narrowed, dazzled by candles. He stared into the fallen silence. 'I don't . . . don't remember it.'

From a mutter, the buzz of voices grew louder, masking his. One unidentified woman laughed, loud and coarsely. 'Nothing but a child with stage-fright!'

Varagnac's hand clenched. A movement in the row of seats beside her caught her attention.

Athanasius Godwin put his hand into his lap and then took it away. A cut-glass phial rested on the brown velvet folds of his robe. A tiny glass: empty.

Nathaniel Marston threw back his head and added to the laughter. Varagnac moved soundlessly to stand behind his chair, and overheard:

'Your Academy believes in precautions, doesn't it? Just as well,

Master Godwin. Trying to hold him as a threat over us would have been dangerously stupid.'

The red-bearded man pushed his chair back and, under cover of the noise of people talking, changing seats, calling for drinks, and flocking around the royal box, walked past Varagnac towards the exit.

The heat of a myriad candles and gnawing pain from her arm dizzied her. She smiled, the expression turning sour. Weariness hit every muscle. Left-handed, Varagnac buttoned one more jacket button and straightened up.

Ashar-hakku-ezrian stood in front of the purple silk curtains. Sweat plastered his brown-blond hair to his face. He ignored a persistent hiss from the wings to come off, hardly seeming to notice.

'How can they?' Ishnanna's tiny gruff voice sounded beside her. Varagnac looked down. The pallor of anger showed up the girl's thick robin's-egg freckles. Tears stood in her eyes. Varagnac rested a sinewy furred arm across Ishnanna's shoulders. 'It's for the best—'

And then she saw it.

A split-second exchange. Ashar's head lifted slightly, his face red and sweating, and his gaze searched out and found Athanasius Godwin. The old man from the Academy of Memory sat serenely. And the slightest movement curved Ashar-hakku-ezrian's mouth into a momentary smile. He gave an almost imperceptible nod of recognition and thanks.

'Damn me.' Varagnac re-checked, glimpsing between Godwin's age-spotted fingers the glass stained with an unmistakable residue. *And people have ways of testing that.* She looked up again with something approaching respect.

Ashar-hakku-ezrian very quietly walked off-stage.

'It's for the best – trust me,' Varagnac finished.

Rats and Gargoyles

CHAPTER 1

In the cathedral square, the crowd were hanging a pig.

A young man slowed his pace, staring.

The yellow wood of the gallows wept sap; hastily nailed together; the scent of pine reached him. Stronger: the stench of animal dung. Lucas reached for a kerchief to wipe his sweating face. Finding none, he distastefully used a corner of his sleeve. He thrust a way between the spectators, head ringing with their noise.

A man and a woman stood up on the platform. Between them, a great white sow snuffled, wrapped in a scarlet robe that her split feet fouled, jaws frothing. She shook her snout and head, troubled by the loose hemp rope around her neck. It went up white against the sky, to the knot on the gallows-tree.

Sun burned the moisture from the flagstones, leaving dust that took the imprint of the young man's booted feet. The steps and entrances and columns of the cathedral towered over the square: a filigree of brown granite against a blazing early sky; carved leaves and round towers still wet with the night's dew.

'This beast has been duly tried in a court of law.' The priest's voice carried from the platform to the small crowd. 'This she-pig belongs to Messire de Castries of Banning Lane, and has been found guilty of infanticide, most filthily and bestially consuming the child of the said Messire de Castries' daughter. Sentence is passed. The animal must be hanged, according to the law and justice. Do your duty!'

The priest lumbered down the rickety steps from the gallows-platform, her leaf-embroidered robe tangling at her ankles. She elbowed Lucas aside just as he realised he should move, and he bristled despite himself.

The man remaining on the platform knelt down beside the sow. Lucas heard him say: 'Forgive me that I am your executioner.'

'Hang the monster!' one fat woman in a velvet dress screeched beside his ear, and Lucas winced; a tall weather-beaten man cupped his hands and shouted through them: 'Child-killer!'

The executioner stood up and kicked back the bolt holding up the trap.

The trapdoor banged down, gunshot-loud. The sow plunged, a *crack!* cut off the squealing, screeching – the groan of stretched rope sang in the air. In the silence, Lucas heard bone splintering. The sow's legs kicked once, all four feet splayed. The scarlet robe ('I' for *infanticide* stitched roughly into the back) rode up as she struggled, baring rows of flopping dugs.

'Baby-killer!'

'May your soul rot!'

Lucas wrenched his way free of their rejoicing. He strode across the square, dizzy, sweating. The ammoniac stink of pig dung followed him. He stopped where a public fountain and basin stood against the cathedral wall, tugging at the buttons of his high collar, pulling his jacket open at the neck. Sweat slicked his skin. He bent and scooped a double handful of water to splash his face, uncertain at the novelty of it. Burning cold water soaked his hair, his neck; he shook it away.

Then he leaned both hands on the brown granite, head down. Sun burned the back of his neck. The water, feather-stirred by the fountain's trickle, mirrored a face up at him: half-man and half-boy, against a blue sky. Springy black hair, expensively cropped; eyes deep-set under meeting brows. For all that his skin was tanned, it was not the chapped skin of an apprentice.

He shifted his padded black jacket that strained across his muscled shoulders; moved to go – and stopped.

The moon gleamed in the early morning sky. He saw it clearly reflected beside his face, bone-white; seas the same pale blue as the sky.

Across the moon's reflected face, a line of blood appeared, thin as a cat's scratch. Another scraped across it, curved; dotted and scored a third bloody weal across the almost-globe. A symbol, glistening red.

He spun round and jerked his head up to look at the western sky. The moon hung there, sinking over the city's roofs. Pale as powder, flour-dust white. No unknown symbols . . .

A pink flush suffused the gibbous moon, now almost at its full; and the seas flooded a rich crimson.

He turned, grabbed the edges of the basin, staring at the clear water. The reflected moon bore a different symbol now. As he watched, that faded, and a third set of blood-lines curved across that pitted surface.

Men and women passed him, dispersing now that the pig's

execution was done. He searched their faces frantically for some sign they saw his bloody moon; they – in spruce city livery, open to the heat – talked one with another and didn't glance above the rooftops.

When he looked back, and again to the sky, the moon was clean.

' 'Prentice, where's your workshop?'

The man had obviously asked twice. Lucas came to himself and, seeing the man wearing the silk overalls of a carpenter, assumed the extreme politeness of one unfamiliar with such people.

'I have no workshop, messire,' he said. 'I'm a student, and new to your city. Can you tell me, please, where I might find the University of Crime?'

Not far away, a gashed palm bleeds. The hand is cupped. Blood collects, trickles away into life-line and heart-line and between fingers, but enough pools to be used.

The moon's face is reflected into a circular mirror, twelve hand-spans in width. This mirror, set on a spindle and in a half-hoop wooden frame, can be turned to face the room's ceiling, or its east, or (as now) its west window.

Through the open window comes the scent of dust, heat, fur, and boiled cabbage. Through the open window comes in the last fading image of the morning moon.

With the tip of a white bird's feather, dipped into the blood, she draws with rapid calligraphic strokes. She draws on the mirror glass: on the reflected image of the moon's sea-spotted face.

She draws, urgently, a message that will be understood by those others who watch the moon with knowledge.

White sun fell into the great court, on to sandstone walls as brown as old wax. Sweeping staircases went up at cater-corners of the yard to the university's interior, and Lucas thought of eyes behind the glazed, sharply pointed windows, and straightened. He stood with two dozen other cadets under the sun that would, by noon, be killing, and now was a test of endurance.

'*My* name,' said the bearded man pacing slowly along the lines of young men and women, 'is *Candia*.'

He spoke normally, but his voice carried to bounce off the sandstone masonry walls. His hair was ragged blond, tied back with a strip of scarlet cloth; he wore boots and loose buff-coloured breeches, and a jerkin slashed with scarlet. Lucas put him at thirty; upped the estimate when the man passed him.

'Candia,' the man repeated. Under the lank hair, his face was pale and his eyes dark; he had an air of permanent injured surprise. 'I'm one of your tutors. You've each been invited to attend the University of Crime; I don't expect you to be stupid. Since you've been in the university buildings for an hour, I don't expect any one of you to have purses left.'

Candia paused, then pointed at three cadets in rapid succession. 'You, you and *you* – fall out. You've just told a pickpocket where you keep your purse.'

Lucas blinked.

'Right.' The man put his fists on his hips. 'How many of you now don't know whether you have your purses or not? Tell the truth . . . Right. You four go and stand with them. *You—*'

He pointed back without looking; Lucas found himself targeted.

'—Lucas.' Candia turned. 'You've got your purse? And you know that without feeling for it, and giving it away, like these sad cases? Tell me how.'

Surprised at how naturally he could answer the impertinent question, Lucas said: 'Muscle-tension. It's on a calf-strap.'

'Good. Good.' The blond man paused a calculated moment, and added: 'As long as, now, you change it.'

He barely waited for the ripple of laughter; flicked his head so that hair and rag-band flopped back, and spoke to them all.

'You'll learn how to take a purse from a calf-strap so that the owner *doesn't* know it's gone missing. You'll learn about marked cards, barred cater-trey dice, the mirror-trick, and the several ways of stopping someone without quite killing them.'

Candia's gaze travelled along the rows of faces. 'You'll learn to conjure with coins – get them, breed them, lend them out and steal them back. There are no rules in the university. If you have anything still your own at the end of the first term, then well done. *I* didn't.'

He allowed himself a brief, tailored grin; most of the cadets grinned back.

'You'll learn about scaling walls and breaking windows, about tunnels and fire-powder, and when to bribe a magistrate and when to stage a last-minute gallows-step confession. *If you live to learn, you'll learn it.* Now . . .'

Heat shimmered the air over the flagstones. Lucas felt it beat up on his cheeks, dazzle his water-rimmed eyes. His new cotton shirt was rubbing his neck raw, and when the shadow crossed him he was conscious only of relief. He glanced up casually.

The blond man raised his head. Then he took his hands from his hips, and went down on one knee on the hot stone, his head still raised.

Lucas gazed upwards into the dazzling sky.

He glimpsed the lichen-covered brick chimneys, wondered why a bole of black ivy was allowed to twine around one stack, followed it up as it thickened – no, it should grow thicker *downwards*, towards the root – and then saw the clawed feet gripping the chimney's cope, where that tail joined a body.

The sky ran like water, curdling a yellowish brown. Lucas felt flagstones crack against his knees as he fell forward, and a coldness that was somehow thick began to force its way down his throat. He gagged. The air rustled with dryness, potent and electric as the swarming of locusts.

Wings cracked like ship's sails, leathery brown against the shadowed noon.

It clung to the brickwork, bristle-tail wrapped firmly round the chimney-stack, wings half-unfolded and flicked out for balance. The great haunches rose up to its shoulders as it crouched, and it brought the peaks of great ribbed wings together at its flaking breast, and Lucas saw that the bat-wings had fingers and thumb at their central joint.

All this was in a split second, reconstructed in later memory. Lucas clung to the other cadets, they to him, no shame amongst them: each of them having looked up once into the great scaled and toothed face of the daemon poised above them.

A fair-haired girl of no more than fifteen stood up from the group. She began to walk towards the iron gates. Candia's gaze flicked from her to the roof-tops; when he saw no movement there, he relaxed. The girl paused, turned her thin face up to the sky and, as if she saw something in the gargoyle-face, slipped out of the side-gate and ran off into the city streets. Her footsteps echoed in the quiet.

The sky curdled.

That same gagging chill silenced Lucas's voice. He coughed, spat; and then the heat of the sun took him like a slap. He winced with the feeling that something too vast had just passed above him.

The blond man rose to his feet, dusting the knees of his buff breeches.

'Why did you let her go?' Lucas demanded.

Candia's chin went up. He looked down his nose at Lucas. 'She was commanded. The city proverb is: *We have strange masters.*'

His gaze lingered on the gate. Then, with a final flick at buff-coloured cloth, Candia said: 'You'll all attend lectures, you'll attend seminars; most of all you'll attend the practical classes. Punishments for absence vary from stocks to whipping. We're not here to waste your time. Don't waste mine.'

Lucas rubbed his bare arms, shuddering despite the morning heat.

'First class is at matins. That's now, so *move* . . . You four,' the blond man said, as an afterthought. 'Garin, Sophonisba, Rafi and Lucas. Accommodation can't fit you in. Here's addresses for lodgings.'

Lucas paused over his slip of paper. The other three cadets wandered away slowly, comparing notes.

As Candia was about to go, Lucas said amiably: 'I don't care to live out of the university. Fetch the Proctor.'

Candia shot a glance over Lucas's shoulder, Lucas turned his head, and the man cuffed him hard enough across the face to send him cannoning into the sandstone wall.

'You address tutors as "Reverend Master,"' the man said loudly, bent to grab his arm and pull him up; winked at Lucas, and added: 'Do you want everyone to know who you are?'

Lucas watched him walk away, the cat-spring step of the man; opened his mouth to call – and thought better of it. He read the printed slip of paper:

Mstrss. Evelian by the signe of the Clock upon Carver streete neare Clocke-mill. Students warned, never to leave the Nineteenth District between the University and the Cathedral. And then, after the print, in a scrawling hand: *Unless commanded by those greater than they.*

Candia pushed the cathedral door open and moved rapidly inside, shutting the heavy wood smoothly behind him. He stopped to quieten his breathing, and to adjust to the dimness. Light the colour of honey and new leaves fell on to the smooth flagstones, from the green-and-gold stained-glass windows.

The blond man's nostrils flared at the incense-smell: musky as leaf-mould and fungus. He padded slowly down between the pillars towards the altar, and his boots, practised, made no sound. He saw no one in all that towering interior space. The pillars that were carved of a silver-grey stone to resemble tall beeches concealed no novices.

Once he froze, reached out to a pillar to catch his balance and remain utterly still. The stone was carved into a semblance of roots, with here and there a carved beetle or caterpillar, as above where the carved branches met together there were stone birds. The sound (if there had been a sound) was not repeated.

Coming to the altar, Candia settled one hip up on it, resting against the great polished and swirl-veined block of oak. He listened. Then he drew out his dagger, and began to clean casually and delicately under his fingernails.

He swore; stuck his finger in his mouth and sucked it.

'Master Candia?'

A man stood up in the shadow of a pillar. White hair caught a dapple of green-gold light. He dropped a scrubbing-brush back into a galvanised-iron bucket; the noise echoed through all the cathedral's arches.

Candia straightened up off the altar. 'My lord Bishop,' he acknowledged.

The Bishop of the Trees came forward, wringing water from one sleeve of his robe. The robe was full-length, dark green, embroidered with a golden tree whose roots circled the hem and whose branches reached out along each arm. The embroidery showed threadbare; the cloth much worn and darned.

'The most recent intake – is there *anyone*?' He paused to touch the wooden altar with thin strong fingers, mutter a word.

'No. No one. Four from Nineteenth District, nine from docklands and the factories; the rest from Third, Eighth and Thirty-First Districts. Three princes from the eastern continent incognito – two of whom have the nerve to assume I won't know that.'

'None disguised? Scholar-Soldiers travel disguised; one might be waiting to test you.'

Now Candia laughed. 'One of the acolytes came and took a girl. Just an acolyte terrified *all* of them. No, there's no Scholar-Soldier amongst them.'

'And this was our last hope of it. We can't wait for the Invisible College's help indefinitely.'

White hair curled down over the Bishop's collar. Seven decades left his face not so much lined as creased, folds of skin running from his beaked nose to the corners of his mouth. His eyes were clear as a younger man's, grey and mobile, catching the cathedral's dim light.

'Are you willing to risk waiting now, young Candia, with no assurance our messages have even reached them?'

Candia glanced at the washed flagstones (where the traces of scrawled graffiti were visible despite the Bishop's work) and then back at the man. 'So events force us.'

'To go to The Spagyrus.'

'Yes. I think we must.' Candia put the knife back into its sheath at his belt, fumbling it. He drew a breath, looked at his shaking hands, half-smiled. 'Go before me and I'll join you – if the faculty see me with a Tree-priest, that's my lectureship lost.'

He followed the Bishop back down the central aisle, through green light and stone. Dust drifted. The man picked up a broad-brimmed hat from a pew. Then he opened the great arched doors to the noon sun, which had been triple-locked before Candia chose to pass through.

'You and your students,' he said, 'make a deal too free with us—'

'I send them here, Theo. It's good practice.'

'I was a fool ever to advise you to apprentice yourself to that place!'

'So my family say to this day.'

The Bishop snorted. He wiped a lock of white hair back with the sleeve of his robe, and clapped the hat onto his head. 'I had word from the Night Council.'

'And there was a waste of words and breath!'

'Oh, truly; but what would you?' The Bishop shrugged.

Candia smelt the dank cellar-smell of the cathedral's incense, all the fine hairs on his neck hackling. He shook himself, scratched, and moved to stand where he would not be visible when the door opened.

'You take underground ways. I'll follow above. We're late, if we're to get there by noon.'

Lucas put the address-slip in his pocket and strode across the yard, the side of his cuffed face burning.

A last student waited, leaning up against the flaking iron gate, hands thrust deep into the pockets of a brown greatcoat two sizes too large, and too heavy for the heat.

Either a young man or a young woman: the student had straight black hair falling to the coat's upturned collar and flopping into dark eyes. A Katayan, the student's thin wiry tail curved under the flap of the brown coat, tufted tip sketching circles in the dust.

'I can take you to Carver Street.' The voice was light and sharp.

'And take my purse on the way?' Lucas came up to the gate.

The student shifted herself upright with a push of one shoulder, and the coat fell open to show a bony young woman's body in a black dress. Patches of sweat darkened the underarms. Her thin fine-furred tail was mostly black, but dappled with white. Her feet were bare.

'I lodge there, too. By Clock-mill. The woman in charge – um.' The young woman kissed the tip of a dirty finger and sketched on the air. 'Beautiful! Forty if she's a day. Those little wrinkles at the corners of her eyes?'

The smell of boiled cabbage and newly laundered cloth permeated the narrow street; voices through open windows sounded from midday meals. Lucas fell into step beside the young woman. She had an erratic loping stride. He judged her seventeen or eighteen; a year or so younger than his calendar age.

'That's Mistress Evelian?'

'I've been there a week and I'm in *love*.' She kept her hands in her pockets as she walked, and threw her head back as she laughed, short fine hair flopping about her ears.

'And you're a student?'

At that she stopped, swung round, head cocked a little to one side as she looked him up and down.

'No, you don't. I'm not to be *collected* – not a specimen. You take your superior amusement and shove it up your anus sideways!'

'Watch who you're speaking to!' Lucas snarled.

'Now, that's a question: who *am* I speaking to?'

Lucas shrugged. 'You heard the Reverend Master read the roll. Lucas is the name.'

'Yes, and I heard him afterwards.'

'That's my business—'

'This is a short-cut,' the student said. She dived down a narrow passage, between high stone houses. Lucas put one boot in the kennel's filth as he followed. He called ahead. Her coat and tail were just visible, whipping round the far corner of the alley.

The light voice came back: 'Down here!'

As Lucas left the alley she stopped, halfway over a low brick wall, to beckon him, and then slid down the far side. Lucas heard her grunt. He leaned his arms on the wall. The young woman was sitting in the dust, legs sprawled, coat spread around her, wiry tail twitching.

'Damn coat.' She stood up, beating at the dust. 'It's the only thing that makes this filthy climate bearable, but it gets in my *way*!'

'You're cold?'

'Where I come from, this is midwinter.' She offered him her hand to shake, across the wall. 'Zar-bettu-zekigal, of South Katay. No one here seems to manage a civilised language. I'll consent to Zaribet; not *Zari*. That's vomitable.'

Lucas grinned evilly. 'Honoured, Zari.'

Zar-bettu-zekigal gave a huff of exasperation that sent her fine hair flying. She crossed the small yard to a building and pushed open a studded iron door. It was cold inside, and dank. Wide steps wound down, illuminated by brass lamps. The gas-jets hissed in yellow glass casings, giving a warm light.

The side-walls were packed with bones.

Niches and galleries had been left in the masonry – and cut into natural stone, Lucas saw as they descended. The gas-jet light shone on walls spidered white with nitre, and on black-brown bones packed in close together: thigh and femur and rib-bones woven into a mass, and skulls set solidly into the gaps. Shadows danced in the ragged circles of their eyes.

When the steps opened out into a vast low-vaulted gallery, Lucas saw that all the walls were stacked with human bones; each partition wall had its own brick-built niche. The gas-lights hissed in the silence.

'Takes us under Nineteenth District's Aust quarter. Too far, going round.' Zar-bettu-zekigal's voice rang, no quieter than before. The tuft of her black tail whisked at her bare ankles. She pushed the fine hair out of her eyes. 'I like it here.'

Lucas reached out and brushed her black hair. It felt surprisingly coarse under his fingers. His knuckles rubbed her cheek, close to her long fine lashes. Her skin was warmly white. Practised, he let his hand slide along her jaw-line to cup the back of her neck and tilt her head up; his other hand slid into her coat and cupped one of her small breasts.

She linked both hands over his wrist, so that she was resting her chin on her hands and looking up at him. One side of her mouth quirked up. 'What I like, *you* haven't got.'

Lucas stood back, and ruffled the young woman's hair as if she had been a child. 'Really?'

'Really.' Her solemnity danced.

'This really is a short-cut?'

'Oh, *right*.' She stepped back, hands in pockets again, swirling the coat round herself, breath misting the cold air. 'Oh, right. You're a king's son. Used to stable-girls and servants; poor tykes!'

Lucas opened his mouth to put her in her place, remembered his chosen anonymity, and then jumped as the black-tipped tail curved up to tap his bare arm.

'I recognise it,' Zar-bettu-zekigal said ruefully. 'I'm a king's daughter. The King of South Katay. Last time we were counted, there were nine hundred and seventy-three of us. Mother is Autumn Wife Eighty-One. I don't believe I've ever seen Father close to. They sent me here,' she added, 'to train as a Kings' Memory.'

Lucas took her chin between his thumb and finger, tipping her face up to his, and his facetious remark was never spoken, seeing those brown eyes turned sepia with an intensity of concentration. He took his hand away quickly.

'Damn,' Lucas said, ears burning, 'damn, so you are; you are a Memory. We brought one in, once, for the Great Treaty. Damn. Honour and respect to you, lady.'

'Ah, will you look at him! He's pissing his britches at the very thought. Do you wonder why I don't shout about it—?'

Her ringing voice cut off; the silence startled Lucas. Zar-bettu-zekigal's eyes widened.

Lucas, turning, saw a cloaked figure at one of the wall-niches, and a beast's hand halted midway in reaching to pick up a femur.

Zar-bettu-zekigal's last words echoed, breaking the stranger's concentration. A hood was pushed back from a sharp black-furred muzzle. Gleaming black eyes summed up the young man and woman, and one of the delicate ears twitched.

The Rat was lean-bodied and sleek, standing taller than Lucas by several inches. He wore a plain sword-belt and rapier, and his free hand (bony, clawed; longer-fingered than a human's) rested on the hilt. In the other hand he carried a small sack.

'What are you doing here?' he demanded.

Steam and bitter coal-dust fouled the air. The slatted wooden floor of the carriage let in the chill as well as the stink, city air cold at this depth; and the Bishop of the Trees gathered the taste on his tongue and spat.

Spittle shot between his booted feet, hit the tunnel-floor that dazzled under the carriage's passing brilliance.

The wooden seat was hard, polished by years of use, and he slipped from side to side as the carriage jolted, rocking uphill after the engine, straining at the incline. The Bishop of the Trees stared out through the window. Up ahead, light from another carriage danced in the vaulted tunnel. Coal-sparks spat.

The window-glass shone black with the darkness of the tunnel beyond it; and silver-paint graffiti curlicued across the surface. Theodoret's gaze was sardonic, unsacramental.

A handful of young men banged their feet on the benches at the far end of the carriage. The Bishop of the Trees caught one youth's gaze. He heard another of them yell.

First two, then all of them clattered down the length of the empty carriage.

'Ahhh . . .' A long exhale of disgust. A short-haired boy in expensive linen overalls, the carpenters' Rule embroidered in gold thread on the front. He grinned. Over his shoulder, to a boy enough like him to be his brother, he said: 'It's only a Tree-priest. Ei, priest, cleaned up the shit in your place yet?'

'No, fuck, won't do him no good,' the other boy put in. 'The other guilds'll come calling, do more of the same.'

Theodoret loosened the buckle of his thick leather belt, prepared to slide it free and whip the metal across the boy's hands; but neither youth drew their belt-knives – they just leaned heavily over the back of his seat to either side of him.

'Ei, you learned yet?'

'Tear your fuckin' place down round you!'

'*Tear it down!*' Spittle flew from the lips of the short-haired boy, spotting his silk overalls. 'You didn't build it. Fuck, when did any of you parasite Tree-priests *build*? You too good to work for our masters!'

'You make our quarter look *sick*,' a brown-skinned boy said. The last of the four, a gangling youth in overalls and silk shirt, grinned aimlessly, and hacked his heel against the wooden slats. The rocking car sent him flying against the dark boy; both sparred and collapsed in raucous laughter.

'Fuck, don't bother him. Ei! He's *praying*!'

The Bishop of the Trees looked steadily past each of the youths, focusing on a spot some indeterminate space away. Anger flicked him. Theodoret stretched hand and fingers in an automatic sign of the Branches.

'If you knew,' he said, 'what I pray for—'

He tensed, having broken the cardinal rule, having admitted his existence; but the gangling youth laughed, with a hollow hooting that made the other three stagger.

'Aw, say you, he's not worth bothering – fuck, we're *here*, aren't we?'

The four of them scrambled for the carriage-door, shoving, deliberately blocking each other; the youngest and the gangling one leaping between the slowing car and the platform. The door slammed closed in Theodoret's face. He opened it and stepped down after them on to the cobbled platform.

He grunted, head down, bullish. Briefly, he centred the anger in himself: let it coalesce, and then flow out through the branching channels of vital energy . . . His breathing slowed and came under control. The colours of his inner vision returned to green and gold.

He walked through the great vaulted cavern. Sound thundered from stationary engines, pistons driving. The hiss of steam shattered the air. Vast walls went up to either side: millions of small bricks stained black with soot, and overgrown here and there with white lichen.

Water dripped from the walls, and the air was sweatily warm.

Somewhere at the end of the platform, voices yelped; and he quickened his steps, but saw nothing at the exit. He stomped up the stairs to ground-level. A vaulted roof arched, scaled and glittering, that might once have been steel and glass but now was too soot-darkened to let in light. Torches burned smokily in wall-cressets.

'Lord Bishop?'

Candia leaned indolently up against the iron stair-rail.

'I was delayed. The lower lines are closed off,' Theodoret said.

'*Already?*'

'I've always said that would be the first signal. Have you asked to see . . . ?'

Candia flashed him a knowingly insouciant grin. 'As we agreed. The Twelfth Decan – The Spagyrus. I've had dealings with him.'

Theodoret grunted.

As the Bishop of the Trees followed Candia out of the station hall, he passed the group of young men. Three crowded round the fourth, the youngest, whose nose streamed blood. The gangling youth swore at the blond man. Candia smiled serenely.

Outside the brick-and-glass cupola heat streamed down. Theodoret sweated. Pilings stood up out of the tepid sluggish water all along the canal-bank. The tide was far out, and the mud stank. Blue and grey, all hardly touched by the sun's rise to noon.

The Bishop knelt, resting his hand on the canal-path.

'It remembers the footprints of daemons.'

He reached, caught Candia's proffered hand, pulled himself upright.

'*They*' – Candia's head jerked towards the city – 'they're like children teasing a jaguar with a stick. When it claws their faces off, *then* they remember to be afraid.'

'Still, this will be a difficult medicine for them to swallow. For them and for us.'

The Bishop turned away from the canal, treading carefully across a long plank that crossed a ditch. Half-dug foundations pitted the earth, and the teams of diggers crouched in the meagre shadows in the ditches, eating the midday meal.

Broken obelisks towered on the skyline.

Candia picked his way fastidiously across the mud. His gaze went to the structures ahead. He thumbed hair back under his ragged scarlet headband. 'The Decans don't care. What's another millennium to them?'

Blocks of half-dressed masonry lay on the earth. Jutting up among them were narrow pyramids of black brick. Theodoret and Candia followed a well-trodden path. Half-built halls rose at either side, festooned with wooden scaffolding. The place was loud with shouts of builders, carpenters, bricklayers, carvers, site-foremen.

With every step the sunlight weakens, the sky turns ashen.

Theodoret favoured his weak leg as he strode, passing teams of men and women who (ropes taut across chests and shoulders, straining; silk and satin work-clothes filthy) heaved carts loaded with masonry towards the area of new building. All were dwarfed by what rose around them.

Staining the air, blocking every city horizon to east, west, north, south and aust; heart of the world: the temple-fortress called the Fane.

Sacrilege tasted bitter in Theodoret's mouth. The granite buildings, the marble, porphyry and black onyx; it grew as a tree grows, out in rings from the heart of divinity. Accumulating over centuries, this receding mountain of roofs, towers, battlements, domes and pyramids. The nearest and most massive outcrop drew his eyes skyward with perpendicular arches.

'Candia . . .'

Black as sepulchres, windowless as monuments. It flung storey upon storey, spire upon tower, straining towards the heavens. Walkways and balconies hung from slanting walls. Finials and carved pinnacles jutted dark against the noon sky.

The nearer they drew, the quieter it became. Silence sang in the dust that tanged on the Bishop's tongue. The paving that he trod on now was old. The flights of steps that went up to the entrances, wide enough to ride a horse up, were hoary with age and lichen.

Theodoret smoothed down his worn green robe. He and Candia stood out now, among the servants all in tightly buttoned black, lost in the silent crowds at the arched entrances.

Candia snapped his fingers at the nearest man.

'Tell The Spagyrus I am here.'

The Bishop glanced back once. The city sprawled out like a multicoloured patchwork to the five quarters of the earth.

Noon is midnight: midnight noon.

The two pivots of the day meet and lock, and in that moment men are enabled to pass over this threshold. There is a tension in the filth-starred stone, receiving their footprints.

There are guides. They do not speak. They climb narrow flights of stairs

*that wind up and around. The stairways are not lit. Their fingers against
the slick stone guide them.*

*Theodoret and Candia climb, ensnared in that mirrored moment of
midnight and midday.*

'What are you doing here?' the black Rat demanded.

'My lord.' Zar-bettu-zekigal bowed, the dignity of this impaired
by her hands being tucked up into her armpits for warmth. 'We're
students, passing through to the other side of the Nineteenth's Aust
quarter.'

Lucas noted the black Rat's plain cloak and sword-belt, without
distinguishing marks. A plain metal circlet ringed above one ear
and under the other; from it depended a black feather plume. The
black Rat, despite being unattended, had an air that Lucas associated with rank, if not necessarily military rank.

'You're out of your lawful quarter.'

The Rat swept the last fragments of bone from the niche into
the sack, and pulled the drawstrings tight. His muzzle went up:
that lean wolfish face regarding Lucas first, and then the young
Katayan.

'A trainee Kings' Memory?' he recalled her last words. 'How good
are you, child?'

The young woman lifted her chin slightly, screwed up her eyes,
and paused with tail hooked onto empty air. 'Me: *What I like, you
haven't got*; Lucas: *Really?* Me: *Really*; Lucas: *This really is a short-cut?*
Me: *Oh, right. Oh, right. You're a king's son. Used to stable-girls and
servants—*'

The Rat cut her off with a wave of one be-ringed hand. 'Either
you're new and excellent, or near the end of your training.'

'New this summer.' Zar-bettu-zekigal shrugged. 'Got three months
in the university now, learning practical self-protection.'

'I'll speak further with you. Come with me.'

'Messire—'

The Rat cut off Lucas's belated attempt at servility. 'Follow.'

They walked on into vaulted cellars, where the loudest noise was
the hissing of the gas-lamps. Soft echoes ran back from Lucas's
footsteps; Zar-bettu-zekigal and the Rat walked silently.

A distant thrumming grew to a rumble, which vibrated in the
stone walls and floor. Bone-dust sifted down. The Rat carried his
ringed tail higher, cleaning it with a fastidious flick. His hand fell to
the small sack at his belt.

'Zari.' Lucas dropped back a step to whisper. 'Do they practise
necromancy here?'

'I'm a stranger here myself!' The young woman's waspishness faded. 'The only good use for bones is fertiliser. Who cares about fringe heresies anyway?'

'But it's blasphemy!'

The Rat's almost-transparent ears moved. He stopped abruptly, and swung round. 'Necromancy?'

Lucas said: 'Not a fit subject for the location, messire, true. Does it disturb you?'

The black Rat's snout lifted, sniffing the air. Lucas saw it register the sweat of fear, and cursed himself.

'Even were it a fit subject for our discussion, necromancy – using the basest materials, as it does – is the least and most feeble of the disciplines of *magia,* and so no cause for concern at all.'

The Rat drew himself up, balanced on clawed hind feet, and the tip of his naked tail twitched thoughtfully. Metal clashed: sword-harness and rapier.

'Who sent you here to spy?'

'No one,' Zar-bettu-zekigal said.

'And that is, one supposes, possible. However—'

'*Plessiez?*'

The black Rat's mouth twitched. He lifted his head and called: 'Down here, Charnay.'

Lucas and Zar-bettu-zekigal halted with the black Rat, where steps came down from street-level. The bone-packed vaults stretched away into the distance. In far corners there was shadow, where the gas-lighting failed. Dry bone-dust caught in the back of Lucas's throat; and there was a scent, sweet and subtle, of decay.

Zar-bettu-zekigal huffed on her hands to warm them. The Katayan student appeared sanguine, but her tail coiled limply about her feet.

A heavily built Rat swept down the steps and ducked under the stone archway. Lucas stared. She was a brown Rat, easily six and a half feet tall; and the leather straps of her sword-harness stretched between furred dugs across a broad chest. She carried a rapier and dagger at her belt, both had jewelled hilts; her headband was gold, the feather-plume scarlet, and her cloak was azure.

'Messire Plessiez.' She sketched a bow to the black Rat. 'I became worried; you were so long. *Who are they?*'

She half-drew the long rapier; the black Rat put his hand over hers.

'Students, Charnay; but of a particular talent. The young woman is a Kings' Memory.'

The brown Rat looked Zar-bettu-zekigal up and down, and her

blunt snout twitched. 'Plessiez, man, if you don't have all the luck, just when you need it!'

'The young man is also from' – the black Rat looked up from tucking the canvas bag more securely under his sword-belt – 'the University of Crime?'

'Yes,' Lucas muttered.

The Rat swung back, as he was about to mount the stairs, and looked for a long moment at Zar-bettu-zekigal.

'You're young,' he said, 'all but trained, as I take it, and without a patron? My name is Plessiez. In the next few hours I – we – will badly need a trusted record of events. Trusted by both parties. If I put that proposition to you?'

Zari's face lit up. Impulsive, joyous; cocky as the flirt of her tail-tuft, brushing dust from her sleeves. She nodded. 'Oh, say you, yes!'

'*Zari* . . .' Lucas warned.

The black Rat sleeked down a whisker with one ruby-ringed hand. His left hand did not leave the hilt of his sword; and his black eyes were brightly alert.

'Messire,' Plessiez said, 'since when was youth cautious?'

Lucas saw the silver collar almost buried under the black Rat's neck-fur, and at last recognised the *ankh* dependant from it. A priest, then; not a soldier.

Unconsciously he straightened, looked the Rat in the face; speaking as to an equal. 'You have no right to make her do this – *yeep!*'

His legs clamped together, automatic and undignified, just too late to trap the Katayan's stinging tail. Zari grinned, flicking her tail back, and slid one hand inside her coat to cup her breast.

'I'll be your Kings' Memory. I've wanted a genuine chance to practise for *months* now,' she said. 'Lucas here could practise his university training for you!'

'*Me?*' Her humour sparked outrage in him.

'You heard Reverend Master Candia. There *are* no rules in the University of Crime. Think of it as research. Think of it as a thesis!'

Frustration broke Lucas's reserve. 'Girl, do you know who my father is? All the Candovers have been Masters of the Interior Temple. The Emperor of the East and the Emperor of the West come to meet in his court! I came here to learn, not to get involved in petty intrigues!'

'Thank you, messire.' Plessiez hid a smile. He murmured an aside to the brown Rat, and Charnay nodded her head seriously, scarlet plume bobbing against her brown-grey pelt.

'You'll guest at the palace for two or three days,' Plessiez went on. 'I regret that it could not be under better circumstances, heir of

Candover. Oh – your uncle the Ambassador is an old acquaintance. Present my regards to him, when you see him.'

Zar-bettu-zekigal nodded to Lucas, thrust her hands deep in her greatcoat pockets and walked jauntily up the steps at the side of the black Rat.

'When you're ready, messire.'

Charnay's heavy hand fell on Lucas's shoulder.

As always, the height of the enclosed space jolted him. Candia reached to grip the brass rail as they were ushered out onto a balcony. The sheer walls curved away and around. Twilight rustled, shifted. The darkness behind his eyelids turned scarlet, gold, black. A stink of hot oil and rotten flesh caught in the back of his throat.

One of the servants clapped his hands together twice, slowly. Sharp echoes skittered across the distant walls.

A kind of unlight began to grow, shadowless, peripheral. Candia's eyes smarted. In a sight that was not sight, he began to see darkness: the midnight tracery of black marble, pillars and arches and domes. Vaulting hung like dark stalactites. A rustling and a movement haunted the interiors of the ceiling-vaults. The gazes of the acolytes that roosted there prickled across his skin.

Pain flushed and faded along nerve-endings as a greater gaze opened and took him in.

Hulking to engage all space between the down-distant floor and the arcing vaults, the god-daemon lay. Black basalt flanks and shoulders embodied darkness. Behind the Decan the halls opened to vaster spaces, themselves only the beginning of the way into the true heart of the Fane, and the basalt-feathered wings of the god-daemon soared up to shade mortal sight from any vision of that interior.

Between the Decan's outstretched paws, and on platforms and balconies and loggias, servants worked to His orders: sifting, firing, tending liquids in glass bains-marie, alembics and stills; hauling trolleys between the glowing mouths of ovens. Molten metal ran between vats.

'My honour to you, Divine One.' Candia's voice fell flatly into the air.

'Little Candia . . .' A sound from huge delicate lips: deep enough to vibrate the tiled floor of the balcony, carried on carrion breath.

Lids of living rock slid up. Eyes molten-black with the unlight of the Fane shone, in chthonic humour, upon Candia and the Bishop. The grotesque head lifted slightly.

'Purification, sublimation, calcination, conjunction . . . and no nearer the prima materia . . .' Reconstructed from an illustration in *Apocrypha Mundus Subterranus* by Miriam Sophia, pub. Maximillian of Prague, 1589 (now lost)

A bulging pointed muzzle overhung The Spagyrus' lower jaw. Pointed tusks jutted up, nestling against the muzzle beside nostrils that were crusted yellow and twitched continually. Jagged tusks hung down from the upper jaw, half-hidden by flowing bristles.

'Purification, sublimation, calcination, conjunction . . . and no nearer the *prima materia*, the First Matter.'

Down at cell-level, the voice vibrated in Candia's head. He stared up into the face of the god-daemon.

The narrow muzzle flared to a wide head. Cheek-bones glinted, scale-covered; and bristle-tendrils swept back, surrounding the eyes, to two small pointed and naked ears.

Theodoret leaned his head back. 'Decans practising the Great Art? Dangerous, my lord, dangerous. What if you should discover the true alchemical Elixir that, being perfect in itself, induces perfection in all it touches? Perhaps, being gods, it would transmute you to a perfect evil. Or perfect virtue.'

The great head lowered. Candia saw his image and the Bishop's as absences of unlight on the obsidian surfaces of those eyes.

'We are such incarnations of perfection already.' Amusement in the Decan's resonant tones. 'It is not that alchemical transformation that I seek, but something quite other. Candia, whom have you brought me?'

'Theodoret, my lord, Bishop of the Trees.'

'A Tree-priest?'

The unlight blazed, and imprinted like a magnesium flare on Candia's eyes the gargoyle-conclave of the Decan's acolytes: bristle-spined tails lashed around pillars and arches and fine stone tracery; claws gripping, great wings beating. Their scaled and furred bodies crowded together, and their prick-eared and tendrilled heads rose to bay in a conclave of sound, and the unlight died to fireglow.

'I will see to you in a moment. This is a most crucial stage . . .'

On the filthy floor below, servants worked ceaselessly.

The platform jutted out fifteen yards, overhanging a section of the floor (man-deep in filth) where abandoned furnaces and shattered glass lay. Here, the heat of the ovens built into the wall was pungent.

'Take that from the furnace,' the low voice rumbled.

One of the black-doubleted servants on the balcony called another, and both between them began to lift, with tongs, a glowing-hot metal casing from the furnace. Sweat ran down their faces.

'Set it there.'

Chittering echoed in the vaults. A darkness of firelight shaded the great head, limning with black the foothill-immensity of flanks and arching wings. One vast paw flexed.

'We reach the Head of the Crow, but not the Dragon. As for the Phoenix' – unlight-filled eyes dipped to stare into the alembic – 'nothing!'

Candia said: 'My lord, this business is important—'

'The projection continues,' the bass voice rumbled. 'Matter refined into spirit, spirit distilled into base matter, and yet . . . nothing. Why are you here?'

Candia planted his fists on his hips and craned his neck, looking through the vast spaces to The Spagyrus. The bruised darkness of his eyes was accentuated by the pallor of fear, but determination held him there, taut, before the god-daemon.

'It happens,' he said, 'that we're traitors. The Bishop here, and I. We've come to betray our own kind to you.'

A shifting of movement, tenuous as the first tremors of earth-quake, folded His wings of darkness. The body of the god-daemon moved, elbow-joints above shoulders, until He threatened emergence from unlight-shadows. Lids slid up to narrow His eyes to slits.

'Master Candia, you always amuse me,' He rumbled. 'I welcome that. It's a relief from my failures here.'

Candia made a gesture of exasperation. He paced back and forth, a few strides each way, as if movement could keep him from seeing where he stood. He directed no more looks at The Spagyrus, his stamina for that exhausted.

The Bishop of the Trees reached to rest a hand on Candia's shoulder, stilling him. 'Even the worst shepherd looks to his flock. Doesn't the Lord Decan know what's happening in our part of the city?'

'Do the stock in the farmyard murmur?' A bifurcated tongue licked out and stroked a lower fang. The Spagyrus gazed down at Candia and Theodoret. 'What I do here leaves me no time for such petty concerns. The great work must be finished, and I am no nearer to completion. If it comes to rioting in the city, I shall put it down with severity – I, my Kin, or your lesser masters the Rat-Lords. You know this. Why bother me?'

Theodoret walked forward. His lined creased face, under the shock of dusty-white hair, showed sternness.

'Lord Spagyrus!'

'Harrhummm?'

'Our *lesser masters* are what you should look to.' Theodoret's grey eyes swam with light; mobile, blinking. 'The Rat-Lords are meeting now with the Guildmasters – the human Guildmasters, that is.

Meeting in secrecy, as I thought.' Incredulity sharpened his voice. 'And I see we're right, Lord Spagyrus. *You don't know of it.*'

The Decan roared.

Candia slid to one knee, head bowed, ragged hair falling forward; and his white-knuckled fist gripped the Bishop's robe. A thin green-gold radiance limned him. He smelt the blossom of hawthorn and meadowsweet. The tiles beneath his knee gave slightly, as if with the texture of moss.

The Bishop of the Trees said softly: 'We were here before you ever were, Lord Spagyrus.'

The tendrilled muzzle rose, gaped, fangs shining in unlight and the furnace's red darkness, and a great cry echoed down through the chambers and galleries and crypts of the Fane.

Candia raised his head to see the acolytes already dropping from the ceiling vaults, soaring on black ribbed wings.

In a room that has more books than furniture, the magus stares out at a blinding blue sky.

Her mirror is shrouded with a patchwork cloth.

The day's air smells sleepy, smells sweet, and she sniffs for the scent of rain or thunder and there is nothing.

Suddenly there is a tickle that runs the length of her forearm. She holds up her hand. The gashed palm, half-healed by her arts, is aching now; and, as she watches, another bead of blood trickles down her arms. She frowns.

She waits.

Charnay paused on the landing, examining herself in the full-length mirror there. She took a small brush and sleeked down the fur on her jaw; tugged her headband into place, and tweaked the crimson feather to a more jaunty angle.

'Messire Plessiez has a superlative mind,' she said. 'I conjecture that, by the time you leave us, in a day or two, he'll have found some advantage even in you.'

Lucas, aware of tension making him petty, needled her. '*Big* words. Been taking lessons from your priest friend?'

'In!'

She leaned over and pushed open a heavy iron-studded door. Lucas walked into the cell. Afternoon sunlight fell through the bars, striping the walls. Dirt and cobwebs starred the floor, and the remnants of previous occupations – tin dishes, a bucket, two ragged blankets – lay on a horsehair mattress in one corner.

'You have no right to put me here!'

Charnay laughed. 'And who are you going to complain to?'

She swung the door to effortlessly. It clanged. Lucas heard locks click, and then her departing footsteps, padding away down the corridor. In the distance men and Rats shouted, hoofs clattered: the palace garrison.

Lucas remained standing quite still. The sky beyond the bars shone brilliantly blue; and light reflected off the white walls and the four storeys of windows on the opposite side of the inner courtyard, mirror to his.

He slammed the flat of his hand against the door. '*Bitch!*'

Four floors below, the brown Rat Charnay had stopped in the courtyard to talk and to preen herself in the company of other Rats. Her ears moved, and she glanced up, grinning, as she left.

The shadows on the wall slid slowly eastwards.

'Rot you!'

Lucas moved decisively. He unbuttoned his shirt, folding it up into a neat pad. Goosepimples starred his chest, feeling the stone cell's chill. He rubbed his arms. With one eye on the door, he unbuttoned his knee-breeches, slid them down, and turned them so that the grey lining was outermost.

'If you're going to study at the university, start acting like it!'

His fingers worked at the stitching. A thin metal strip protruded from the knee-seam, and he tugged it free; and then stood up rapidly and hopped about on one foot, thrusting the other into his breeches-leg, listening to check if that *had* been a noise in the corridor . . . No. Nothing.

His dark-brown meeting brows dipped in concentration. The metal prong plumbed the depths of the lock, and then his mouth quirked: there was a click, and he tested the handle, and the heavy door swung open.

Clearer: the noise of the garrison below.

Lucas buttoned his breeches. He took a step towards the open door. One hand made a fist, and there was a faint pink flush to his cheeks. Caught between reluctance and fear of recognition, he stood still for several minutes.

Coming in, they had passed no human above the rank of servant.

He bent to remove stockings and shoes, wrapping them in his shirt. Then he knelt, shivering, to rub his hands in the dirt; washing arms, face and chest in the cobwebs and dust.

A black Rat passed him on the second floor. She didn't spare a glance for this kitchen-servant. With the bundle under his arm, and an old leather bucket balanced on his shoulder, Lucas of Candover walked free of the palace.

*

Zar-bettu-zekigal leaned out of the carriage window, regardless of the dust and flying clots of dung the team's hoofs threw up.

'See you, we're out of Nineteenth District's Aust quarter already – oof!'

Plessiez's hand grabbed her coat between the shoulder-blades and yanked her back on to the carriage seat. 'Is it necessary to advertise your presence to the entire city?'

'Oh, we're not even out of a Mixed District, messire, what's to worry?'

She leaned her arms on the jolting sill, and her chin on her arms, and grinned out at the street. The carriage rattled through squares where washing hung like pale flags and fountains dripped. The sun beat down from a blazing afternoon sky. Humans and Rats crowded the cobbled streets – a dozen or so of the palace guard, in silks and satins and polished rapiers, drank raucously outside a tavern, and sketched salutes of varying sobriety as Plessiez's coach and horses passed them.

Zar-bettu-zekigal drew a deep breath, contentedly sniffing as they passed a may-hedge and a city garden.

'You have no Katayan accent,' the black Rat said. The dimness inside the coach hid all but the glitter of his black eyes, and the jet embellishment of his rapier's pommel.

'Messire' – reproach in her tone, and humour – 'Kings' Memories remember inflections exactly – we have to. What would I be doing with an *accent*?'

'I beg your pardon, lady,' Plessiez said, sardonically humble, and the Katayan grinned companionably at him.

The coachman called from above, sparks showered as the brakes cut the metal wheel-rims, and the carriage rattled down a steep lane. Plessiez caught hold of the door-strap with a ring-fingered hand.

'Mistress Zekegial . . . Zare-bethu . . .' He stumbled over the syllables.

'Oh, "Zari" will do, messire, to you.' She waved an airy gesture. Then, leaning out of the window again as the carriage squealed to a halt, she said: 'You're holding this important meeting in a *builders' yard*?'

Plessiez hid what might have been a smile. The black Rat said smoothly: 'That is one of the Masons' Halls, little one. Show the proper respect.'

Zari pushed the carriage door open and sprang down into the yard. Two other coaches were already drawn up in the entrance, horses standing with creamed flanks and drooping heads. Plessiez stepped down into the sunlight. It became apparent that the black Rat had changed uniform: he now wore a sleeveless crimson jacket, with the neat silver neck-band of a priest. His crimson cloak was also edged with silver.

He paused to adjust rapier and belt, and Zari saw him straighten a richly gemmed pectoral *ankh*. A flurry of black and brown Rats from the other coaches rushed to meet him, those with priests' collars particularly obsequious.

'Mauriac, make sure the guards are placed unobtrusively; Brennan, you – and *you* – get these carriages taken away.' The black Rat's snout twitched.

A heavily built brown Rat swaggered out from the back of the group. Pulling her aside by a corner of her cloak, Plessiez said sharply: '*My* idea of a secret meeting does not consist merely of arriving in a coach without a crest on it! Yours does, apparently. Get rid of this crowd. I'll take you only in with me.'

Charnay laughed and slapped Plessiez on the back. The black Rat staggered slightly.

'Don't worry, messire! They'll just think you've come for a plan for the new wing.'

'Perhaps. But do it.'

Zar-bettu-zekigal's bare feet printed the yellow yard-dust. The air shimmered in the heat. She wrapped her greatcoat firmly round her, and squinted up at the stacked clay bricks, timber put out to weather, and piles of wooden scaffolding that surrounded this Masons' Hall. Tiles and wooden crates blocked the view to the nearer houses.

She cocked her head, and her dappled black-and-white tail coiled around her ankles. With a nod at the weathered-plank structure – half hall, half warehouse – she said over the noise of departing coaches: 'Well, messire, have I begun yet?'

'As soon as we enter the hall.'

Leisurely, hands folded at his breast, the black Rat paced forward. Charnay fell in beside him. Two men pushed the hall doors open from the inside, and Zari gave a half-skip up the steps, catching up, as they went in.

'Messire Falke!' Plessiez called.

In a patch of sunlight from the clerestory windows, a man raised his bandaged face. His short silver-white hair caught the light, pressed down by the strips of cotton.

'Honour to you, priest.' The man faced Plessiez with a wry, somewhat perfunctory grin. His black silk overalls shone at collar, cuffs and seams; sewn with silver thread. A heavy silver pin in the shape of compasses fastened the black lace at his throat. Diamond and onyx rings shone on his left hand.

'Oh, what . . . ?'

The merest whisper. Charnay nudged the Katayan heavily in her ribs, and Zari bowed. She continued to stare at the fine linen bandaging the man's eyes.

The men and women with Falke drew back, bowing respectfully to the black Rat, and the sleek priest strode down the passage that opened in the crowd and seated himself on a chair at the head of a trestle table. This gave signs – like the eight or nine others in the room – of having been rapidly cleared of site- and ground-plans, measurements, calculations and scale models.

Charnay ostentatiously drew her long rapier and laid it down on the plank table before her.

'Zari,' the black Rat prompted.

The young woman was standing on tiptoe, and leaning over to stare into a tank-model of a sewer system. She straightened. Hands in pockets, she marched across the bright room and hitched herself up to sit on the trestle table.

'Kings' Memory,' she announced. 'You have an auditor, messires: you are heard: this is the warning.'

Some of the expensively dressed men and women began to speak. Falke held up a hand, and they ceased.

'What is your oath?'

She took her hands out of her greatcoat pockets. 'To speak what I hear, as I heard it, whenever asked; to add nothing, to omit nothing, to alter nothing.'

Falke passed her on his way to sit down, close enough for her to see dark brows and lashes behind the cloth shield. A lined face, and silver-fine hair: a man on the down side of thirty-five.

'And the penalty.' he said, 'if otherwise?'

'Death, of course.' She slid down on to a collapsible chair, positioning herself exactly halfway between Falke's people and the Rats.

The light of late noon fell in through clerestory windows, shining on the plans, diagrams and calculations pinned around the walls. Falke, without apparent difficulty, indicated the half-dozen men and women who abandoned compasses, straight-edge and fine quill pens for the cleared trestle table, as they sat down. Silk and satins rustled; white lace blazed at cuffs and collars.

'The master stonemason. Master bricklayer. Foreman of the carriage teams. Master tiler.'

Plessiez, who sat with his lean black muzzle resting on his steepled fingers, said: 'You may give them their proper titles, Master Falke. If we're to talk honestly, we must have no secrecy.'

' "Honestly"? You forget I've dealt with Rat-Lords before.' Falke sat, pointing with economical gestures. 'Very well, have your way. Shanna is a Fellowcraft, so is Jenebret.' He indicated an older man. 'Thomas is an Apprentice. Awdrey is the Mistress Royal of the Children of the Widow. I'm Master of the Hall.'

Zar-bettu-zekigal leaned forward on the wooden table, brushing the black hair from her eyes.

' "Children of the Widow" . . . "Master of the Hall" . . .' she murmured happily. She caught Plessiez's warning stare and grinned, professional, her own eyes enthusiastic with Memory.

Falke began. 'We—'

The doors at the end of the hall slammed open. Plessiez stood up, his chair scraping back.

Two Rats and three or four men struggled to hold back a middle-aged man, himself in the forefront of a group. '*Falke!*'

Falke peered towards the bright end of the hall through his cloth bandage.

Charnay glanced to the black Rat for a cue, one hand reaching for her sword. Plessiez shook his head. 'I know the man, I think. East quarter. East quarter's Mayor?'

'Certainly I am!'

The man shook himself free of the brown Rats' restraining grip. He was in his fifties, and stout; raggedly cut yellow hair framing a moon-face. Confronting Falke, he tugged his greasy breeches up about his belly, and straightened a verdigris-stained chain of copper links that hung across his frayed jerkin.

'*Mayor* Tannakin Spatchet,' he rumbled, and pointed a beefy finger at Master Falke. 'What do you mean by holding this meeting without me? At the very least, some of the East quarter Council should be here!'

'Tan, get out of here.' Falke waved a dismissive hand. 'You'll bring the dregs in with you. A rabble of bureaucrats, shopkeepers, lawyers and teachers!'

The five or six men who had come in with Tannakin Spatchet shuffled and looked embarrassed.

'We have every right to be represented! If you're talking to the Rat-Lords, that concerns everyone in the quarter.'

Falke shook his head. 'No. You're not admitted to the mysteries here, not even to the outer hall. Thomas, take these people outside.'

'Damn your hall! Just because you won't admit us . . .'

Plessiez pushed Charnay in the direction of the hall door, and turned to Falke. 'Pardon me, messire, but it might not be amiss if other trades were represented here.'

A fair-haired woman leaned forward, looking down the table to the black Rat. 'Then we can't speak freely. Craft mysteries aren't to be disclosed to outsiders. You *know* that.'

Plessiez shrugged. 'Then, I must go. I don't belong to any Craft hall.'

'We can't have this scum here!' The Fellowcraft, Shanna, pointed at the Mayor, who bridled. 'You'll have us inviting *councillors* next.'

Falke's cupped palms slammed down on the table. The *crack!* echoed. In sudden silence, his bandaged head cocked to one side, he spoke.

'Our quarrels are meat and drink to our masters. Aren't they, messire priest?'

'I don't understand you, Master Falke.'

'You do. You think no more of using us than of saddling a horse to ride. You'd no more think of a man's name than a dog's name in the street if you kick it!'

His hand went up behind his head, pulling the knotted cloth bandage down. Prematurely white hair slid free. His fingers immediately clamped across his eyes, features blasted by the sudden light. Zari glimpsed wide eyes: no injury, no scar; only immensely dilated black pupils.

He said: 'Because *my* name is on file, you can find and use me.'

As if prompted, the Fellowcraft Shanna spread her hands, turning to the other men and women around the table. 'The Rat-Lord's obliged to tell us nothing more than pleases him. We must tell him all. For all his alliance with us, he can sell us out any time that it should please him, and walk away unharmed. Remember that, when we come to trust him!'

Zar-bettu-zekigal's gaze darted from Falke to Plessiez. Her tail coiled up, lying across her arm, tense and twitching. Hearing and all senses acute – her smile widened suddenly.

Charnay marched back from the hall door, whisking her cloak past the seated Fellows, and leaned over to speak in the black Rat's ear. The Katayan heard: 'Desaguliers is coming!'

Falke froze.

The black Rat's whiskers quivered. His bright eyes fixed on Charnay, and the brown Rat stumbled back a pace.

'This was your idea of secrecy, was it, Charnay!'

Before she could do more than mumble, voices were raised, and the group of men at the door were pushed aside. Five sleek black

Rats, with black-plumed headbands and drawn rapiers, shoved them aside; and a taller black Rat stepped in from the sunny yard to the white hall.

'Was it necessary,' Plessiez murmured silkily, 'to bring the Cadets in such strength, Messire Desaguliers?'

The watermills turned slowly, dripping water catching the sun. Lucas gazed at the water running past the building's stone wall (some part of a concealed stream uncovered?), and then up at the watermills' tower.

A twelve-foot gold-and-blue dial gleamed in the sun. The clock's hands twitched once, to a metallic click inside the tower, and a bell chimed the quarter. Lucas stood watching as a silver knight, some two feet tall, slid out on rails from one side of the tower, to meet an approaching bronze knight on a similar curve. Their swords lifted jerkily; they struck a *clang!* that echoed the length of the cobbled street. A pause, and both began to retreat.

Lucas rubbed his sweating neck, took his hand away filthy, and glanced speculatively at the running water. He still carried shirt and stockings. His bare feet were chafing in his boots, and his filthy chest and arms were beginning to sting from the sun.

A first floor window opened further down the street, and a woman shook out a quilt and laid it on the sill.

'Lady,' Lucas called, 'is this Clock-mill?'

She leaned one bare forearm on the sill, her other hand supporting her as she leaned out, so that her elbow jutted up and her thick yellow hair fell about her shoulders. She wore a blue-and-yellow satin dress slashed with white, with puffed sleeves and a low full bodice. Lucas moved a few steps down the street towards her.

'Clock-mill and Carver Street,' she called.

Lucas gazed up at the window. The quilt hung down, half-covering a frieze carved in the black wood: hour-glasses, scythes, spades and skulls. Seen closer, the woman's face was lined. Lucas judged her forty at least. Some twinge of memory caught him.

'Is there . . . are you Mistress Evelian?'

'You're not one of my lodgers?' The woman's china-blue eyes narrowed, studying the filthy ragged young man. 'Good God. What does Candia think he's sending me these days? Come in: don't *stand* there. Third door down will take you through into the courtyard. I'll let you in.'

Lucas had only taken a few steps before she stuck her head out of the window again.

'Have you met the other students yet? Have you seen anything of that Katayan child, Zaribeth?'

Zar-bettu-zekigal sat with her grubby hands in front of her on the table. Her dappled tail flicked sawdust on the hall floor. A smell of cut wood, pitch, and long-boiled tea filled the heavy afternoon air.

Her eyes moved from the white-haired Falke, poised at rest in his chair, to Tannakin Spatchet (stiffly upright), and the well-dressed builders and ill-dressed councillors; to Plessiez and Charnay, and to the black Rat Desaguliers, standing and glaring at each other across the table.

'I think the King might be interested in this meeting,' Desaguliers challenged. He was a lean black Rat, tall, with the plain leather harness and silver cuirass of a soldier; the hairs on his thin snout grizzled.

'The Captain-General is aware, of course, that the King has full knowledge of—'

Desaguliers bluntly interrupted Plessiez: 'Horse-dung! I'm aware of nothing of the sort.'

'How very remiss of you.'

'Gentle lords. Please.' Falke spoke with a sardonic gravity. He sat with his hand shading his uncovered eyes against the hall's white-washed brilliance. Tears ran down his cheeks; he rapidly blinked. 'You know how your honour suffers, to be seen quarrelling by we underlings.'

'Master Falke!' Plessiez snapped.

'I apologise. Most humbly. I hazard my guess, also, that this terminates our discussion. And that we shall be the ones to suffer for your plotting.' He smoothed the cloth bandage between his fingers, and bent his head to tie it back over his eyes.

Zari's gaze darted back to Plessiez and the black Rat Desaguliers.

'No.' Plessiez, sleek in scarlet. 'I put this hall under Guiry's protection. Let Messire Desaguliers hear our talk. Since I perceive his spies will have it sooner or later, let it be now. I have nothing to hide.'

Desaguliers snorted. 'A miracle, that!'

Welcome heat touched her with the room's shifting patches of sun. Zari coughed, and stuck her tail up above head-height, twitching it. 'If you talk through me, messires, it'll be easier for the record.'

Desaguliers peered down the table. 'What is *that*?'

Plessiez, seating himself, and draping his scarlet cloak over the back of the chair, murmured: 'Zari, of South Katay. A Kings' Memory.'

'A Kings' Memory.' The taller Rat shook his head in reluctant admiration, and slumped back into a chair on his side of the table. The sun glinted off his cuirass. He kicked his rapier-scabbard back with a bare heel. 'Plessiez, you miss few tricks. Let's hear what you have to say, then.'

Plessiez rested one slender clawed finger across his mouth for a few seconds, leaning back, thin whiskers still. His eyes narrowed to obsidian slits. The hand fell to caress his pectoral *ankh*.

'I don't think I need to do more than say what I said when we last met. Master Falke, we, your masters, confine humans to certain ghetto areas within the city—'

'As you are yourselves confined, by those Divine ones who are masters of us all.' The white-haired man sat back with his arms along the arms of the chair, cloth-blinded eyes accurately finding Plessiez's face. 'It may gall you, Messire Plessiez, but there are Human Districts forbidden even to you. The Decans decree it.'

'If I spoke sharply, Master Mason, you must pardon me. There is much at stake here.'

'You apologise to *this* scum?' Desaguliers guffawed loudly; broke off as Zari glared at him. He glanced around at black Rat cadets positioned on guard about the hall. She resumed the concentration of listening, head cocked bird-like to one side.

'We need your help, Falke,' the black Rat Plessiez said, in a tone of plain-dealing, 'and you, you say, need ours. Both of us for the same reason: that one can go where the other cannot.'

Falke inclined his head.

'If, therefore, we agree an exchange of mutual help—'

Tannakin Spatchet rose to his feet. He mopped his face, reddened by the airless heat. 'We don't enter into blank contracts. As local Mayor, I *must* know what you intend, messire priest.'

'You "must" nothing.' Plessiez's rapier-hilt knocked against the chair as he shifted position. 'However, I am prepared to discuss a little of the situation.'

The black Rat glanced towards Zari. She grinned and tapped her freckled ear-lobe with one finger.

Plessiez said: 'There are a number of locations within the city, at which, for purposes of our own, we intend to place certain . . . "articles". Packages. Three of them are within quarters humans may enter and we may not. Therefore—'

Desaguliers snorted. 'Purposes of your own, yes, messire, surely!'

'I see no need to discuss it with you.'

'It may endanger the King.'

'It will not. But if his Majesty is ever to be King in more than name only, then some of us must act; and you and your cadets will oblige me by keeping silent while we do!'

'Is this treason, messire!'

Zar-bettu-zekigal reached, sprawling halfway across the wooden table, and slapped her hand down over the hilt of Charnay's discarded sword as the Captain-General grabbed for it. Plessiez slowly relaxed his hands that gripped the arms of his chair.

Still sprawled across the sun-warmed wood, the Katayan said: 'You wouldn't be here if you didn't want to know what was going on, Messire Desaguliers, so why don't you shut up and listen?'

Plessiez threw his head back and laughed.

Zar-bettu-zekigal slid back into her chair. 'I don't have all day. If I miss this afternoon's lectures, I'm dead. So could we get on, please?'

The white-haired Mason, Falke, watched the armed Rat-Lords. 'Our part of the bargain is this. There are ancient buildings of this city that we may not enter, because of where they are situated. There are records and inscriptions in those buildings that we need. If Messire Plessiez and his people can gain us that, we'll run his errands.'

'No!' Tannakin Spatchet's fist hit the table. 'Who knows what retribution we'd bring into our quarter if we did? As Mayor—'

'Tan, be quiet,' Falke ordered.

Desaguliers leaned forward. 'The peasant's right. I want to know what and why, messire priest. Some scheme to open up every district to us, is it? That would be foolhardy, but of use. But, if you say to me certain "articles" needing to be put in certain places, that sounds like *magia*. Which one might expect from the damned Order of Guiry priests!'

Falke, head sunk to his chest, seemed by the turning of his chin to direct quick glances at both armed Rat-Lords. The corners of his mouth moved. 'Will you tell him, Messire Plessiez?'

The black Rat's eyes darted to Desaguliers and back to Falke. 'Would *you* speak of what it is you need, and why?'

Zar-bettu-zekigal held out her hand to Falke. Prompting.

'If I must. If it will make you speak, after.' Falke reached up with grazed and cut fingers. A few strands of black still ran from his temples into his curling white hair. He pulled the cloth bandage free of his eyes again.

'You and I,' he said, 'are ruled by the Thirty-Six.'

His long fine lashes blinked over eyes without irises. Midnight-black pupils, vastly expanded, unnaturally dilated, swallowed all the colour that might have been.

He rubbed water from his left eye, blinking again, and shot a glance at Desaguliers.

'I don't want to make a display of this, but I will. I hide my eyes, because all light's too strong for me now, and because I don't want to think about them, being like this, what they are.'

'How . . . ?' Zari clapped her hand over her mouth.

Falke wound the cloth around his knuckles; his hand lifted to shade his eyes.

'You come to me, a Master Mason. I, and my hall brethren, all of us are builders for our strange masters. We build still, as we have built for generations uncounted. What we build – the Fane – is a cold stone shell. Nothing human has been into the heart of the Fane since building finished there.'

Sun and silence filled the hall.

'Except, once, myself. I *saw* . . .

'I was fool enough to find my way in. In to the centre. There's a cold cancer eating away, spreading out, stone by stone, year by year. We build it for them, and then they make it theirs. We build for God and They transform it. We only see shadows of what They seem. Inside, in the heart of the Fane, you see what They really are.'

His strong fingers began to smooth out the bandage; shifted to knuckle the sepia lids of his eyes.

'Only, having once seen that, you never truly cease to see it.'

The lean Rat, Desaguliers, grunted. 'All of which is no doubt true, and was true in our fathers' fathers' time, so why should we concern ourselves with it?'

Falke, very quietly, said: 'Because we are still building. We are compelled. Not even their servants – their slaves.'

'I can't see the importance of that. It's always been so. You . . .' The Captain-General's gesture took in the men and women who sat around the trestle table. Scepticism was plain on his wolfish face. 'You think you'll do what, exactly, against the Decans our masters?'

The fair-haired woman next to Zari sighed. 'Tell them, Falke.'

Falke stared at his hands.

'This hall is searching for the lost Word. The Word that the Builder died to conceal when this city was invaded, and the Temple of Salomon abandoned. The Word of Seshat – that has been lost for millennia. And for that long our own Temple has remained unfinished, while we're forced to build in slavery for strange masters.'

Tannakin Spatchet slowly sat down, pale blue eyes dazed.

'Yes, I'm speaking of Craft mysteries.' Falke's wide-set eyes met Zari's gaze, dark lashes blinking rapidly over pupils clear as polished black glass. 'We search for the lost Degree, and the lost Mark. And the lost Mystery: we know who built the South side of our Temple, and what their wages were; but until we know the secrets of the Aust side, and what the black-and-white pillars support, we remain as we are – slaves. When we know, when our New Temple can be begun—'

'We'll build it and make the heart of the world the New Jerusalem,' the fair-haired woman completed.

Falke lifted his shoulders in a weary shrug. 'We must have our own power, you see. Build for ourselves again, and not for our masters.'

The Captain-General stood, scaly tail lashing. 'And this is what you've got yourself mixed up in? Plessiez, you fool! Will you listen to him talk against the Thirty-Six and not protest? They'll eat him alive, man!'

Plessiez smiled. 'If I were afraid of the Decans our masters, I would not have begun this.'

Tannakin Spatchet stared at the *ankh* on the black Rat's breast. 'You're a priest, my lord! How can you talk against Them? They're the very breath and soul of your Church—'

Plessiez reached down and ran a thumb along the *ankh*'s heavy emeralds. Whimsical, he said: 'It is a little oppressive for any church, you must admit, to have God incarnate on earth; and not only on earth, but also, as it were, down the next street, and the next . . .'

Scandalised, the plump Mayor protested. 'Messire!'

'That They are god is true, that They are with us on this earth is true; and some say, also,' Plessiez added, 'that we would be better off were They to abandon Their incarnations here and resume Their Celestial habitations.'

Desaguliers' tone of incredulity cut the hot white hall like acid: 'And *you* hope to affect the Thirty-Six?'

The black Rat smoothed down his scarlet jacket, a slightly dazed expression on his face. 'Ah, perhaps my ambitions are not so high. Perhaps I only seek to move Them by affecting Their creations. I will say no more on this, messire; it is not part of our bargain.'

Desaguliers swore, and Zari motioned him to silence. She swung round in her chair, drawing one leg up under her, staring at Plessiez.

'Then, I'll speak for you.' Falke stood, both empty hands resting palm-down on the table. 'Knowledge was the price of my consent to the bargain. If our plans are betrayed to the King, then so will yours be!'

He faced Desaguliers. 'As to *magia* – yes. What Messire Plessiez will do might be called necromancy, being that sort of poor *magia* that can be done using the cast-off shells of souls, that is, mortal bodies.

'I know that Messire Plessiez plans the invoking of a plague-*magia*. A great plague indeed, but not a contamination that will kill my kind, or yours, Messire Desaguliers; instead a plague of such dimensions that it will touch the Decans Themselves.'

Desaguliers stroked the grizzled fur at his jaw-line. His slender fingers moved unsteadily. 'Plessiez, man, you are mad. The Fane knows all the pox-rotted arts of *magia*. This is lunacy.'

Plessiez rose from his chair. 'I will see his Majesty made a true King, Desaguliers, and that can't be done while there are masters ruling over us!'

Desaguliers snapped his fingers. Metal scraped as three more of the lithe black Rat Cadets drew their swords.

'Lunacy – and treason. I'm having you arrested—'

Zari felt the wood of the table shake under her spread palms.

The fat Mayor sprang back, swatting an armed Cadet aside like a child; seized the arm of one of his companions and pulled her towards the door. 'What did I tell you? I told them so!'

A copper taste invaded her tongue, familiar from that morning in the university courtyard.

'*Run!*'

She got one foot on the chair, launched herself off it as dust and splintered wood thundered down across the table, blinded by sudden hot brilliance; missed her footing and sprawled into the warm brown fur of Charnay. She sat up, head ringing.

Falke stared up and flung an arm across his lined worn face.

The Katayan grabbed, missed, then got her hands to Plessiez's ankle where he gazed up, transfixed, and brought him crashing down on top of her; coiled her tail around Falke's leg and pulled. The man fell to his knees.

A searing chill passed overhead.

Zari gazed up at the open sky: brown now, and blackening, like paper in a fire.

Dust skirled up from the hall's collapsed roof. The far wall teetered, groaned, and with a wrench and scream of tearing wood fell into the yard.

Feet trampled her, human and Rat, running in all directions. She saw some men, fleeing, almost at the yard-gate, duck as they ran; and something chill and shadowed passed above her.

'*Look—*'

She caught Falke's arm, but the man was too busy scrabbling at the planks they sprawled on for his eye-bandage. Charnay grabbed her discarded rapier and pushed Plessiez down, half-crouching over him, snarling up at the sky.

A woman in red satin overalls threw up her arms and screamed. Coils of black bristle-tail lapped her body, biting deep into her stomach, blood dulling the satin. Ribbed wings beat, closing about her as tooth and beak dipped for her face.

Fire burst from the wooden hall walls in hollow concussive plops, burning blue and green in the noon-twilight. Rapidly spreading, consuming even the earth and the yard's timber outside, it formed a circling wall of flames. One of Desaguliers' Cadets thrust at it with his sword. A thin scream pierced the air: the Rat fell back on to the hall floor, fur blazing.

The sun burned with a searing storm-light.

Out of that sky, stinking of wildfire and blood, wings beating the stench of carrion earthwards, by dozens and hundreds, the Fane's acolytes fell down to feed.

CHAPTER 2

Evelian bent over the washtub in the courtyard. The young man locked his apartment door and began walking towards the exit-passage. She looked up, red-faced, wiped her forehead with a soapy wrist, and called to him.

'Lucas, wait. Is Zaribeth there?'

The dark-haired young man shook his head. Despite the misty heat he was buttoned to the throat, in a black doublet with a small neck-ruff, and his breeches and stockings were spotless.

'Her bed hasn't been slept in.'

'*Her* bed!' Evelian snorted. Lucas paused.

A granular mist fogged the air, blurring the roofs of the two-storey timber-framed apartments overlooking the yard. Intermittent watery sun shone down on washing, limp on the cherry trees, and the scent of drying linen filled the air.

Evelian slapped a shirt against the washboard. She wore her yellow hair pinned up in a tangle, and an apron over the blue-and-yellow satin dress. 'Brass nerve, that child! Do you know, one night, I found her in *my* bed? Yesterday. No; night before last.'

She put a hand in the small of her back and stretched. 'I came up to my room and there she was, under the sheet in my bed, naked as an egg! Looked at me with those big brown eyes, and asked did I really want her to go, and didn't I need keeping warm of nights?'

Lucas coloured. Outside the yard, Clock-mill struck the half-hour.

'I told her we're in the middle of a heatwave as it is,' Evelian added, 'and up she got, all pale and freckled, little tits and fanny, with that fool tail of hers whisking up the dust. I turned her round and smacked her one that'll have left a mark! Told her not to be an idiot; I don't sleep with my lodgers. Oh, now, see you; I've made you blush.'

'Not at all.' Lucas shifted awkwardly. 'It's just a warm morning.'

'I *wish*' – a vicious slap at wet cloth – 'that I knew where she *was*.'

Lucas felt the mist prickle warmly against his face. Looking at the cloud that clung to the roof-trees put the black timber frieze in his line of vision; bas-relief spades, crossed femurs, hour-glasses, money-sacks sacks and skulls.

He snapped: 'I don't know where she is. I don't care! If you knew what I had to go through yesterday, to get out of what that little bitch got me into . . .'

Evelian flipped shirts into the soapy water, and plunged her arms in, scrubbing hard. The shadowless light eased lines from her face. She could have been twenty rather than forty.

'I'm not getting mixed up in whatever's biting you, boy. I swore last time that I'd have nothing to do with organising against the Rat-Lords. The only good thing I ever got out of that was my Sharlevian. But, there, I live in the city; there isn't any escape from it.' Evelian stepped into the cherry tree, into cool green leaves and damp linen. 'The little Katayan's hardly older than Sharlevian. I like the girl. I worry about her.'

Another door opened across the yard, and a student scuttled towards the exit-passage, calling: 'Luke, see you there. Don't be late!' Evelian saw him bristle at *Luke*.

On the point of going, he turned back.

'Yesterday afternoon. I tasted . . . could taste blood. Coppery.' He went on quickly. 'Others, here, they did, too. Like yesterday morning, when one of the . . . one of them came to the university. As if something watched . . .'

She wiped her hands on her apron, and her blue eyes went vague for a long minute.

'Mistress Evelian?'

'Get someone to read the cards or dice for you,' she said.

'Yes! But is there anyone, here?'

Evelian nodded. A coil of fair hair escaped a clip and fell down across her full bodice.

'The White Crow. That's who you want. Do you dice, cards, palms – anything you can think of. The only practising Hermetic philosopher in this quarter, as far as I can make out.'

'I can't be late; it's my first day—' Lucas shut his mouth with a snap. 'Yes, I can. To quote Reverend Master Candia, there are no rules at the University of Crime. Where is this White Crow?'

'Right across the yard here. Those top two apartments on the left-hand side.' Evelian pointed to the rickety wooden steps leading to the first floor. 'Just knock and go in. All my lodgers are . . . *unique* in some way.'

He took a few steps, and her voice came back from behind him: 'Ask about Zaribeth!'

The wooden hand-rail felt hot, damp in the swirling mist. Lucas glanced up at the windows and open skylight as he mounted the steps. The diamond-panes fractured thin sunlight into splinters. Children yelped in the street beyond the passage; somewhere there was a smell of boiled cabbage.

He rapped on the door, and it swung open, outwards. Calling loudly, 'Hello in there!' Lucas walked in.

The first room was light, airy, and piled high with volumes of leather-bound books. Books stood on chairs, shelves, leaned on the window-sill, slid off a couch. Only the round table, with its patchwork cloth, was clear.

'Mistress White Crow?'

'Here.' The far door opened. A woman in a white cotton shirt and cut-off brown knee-breeches came in. A white dog followed at her bare heels.

Her hair was a tumbling mass of dark red-brown, almost a cinnamon colour; and, where she had pinned the sides back from her face, bright silver streaked her temples. She stood a few inches shorter than Lucas, wiry, with something languid in her movements. He thought her about thirty years old.

She nodded to him, and crossed to the window, leaning on the sill and sniffing at the heat of the morning. Her smile was melancholy. Lucas caught a flash of white; noticed that she wore a fingerless cotton glove on her left hand. The palm was dotted with red.

'Don't touch Lazarus,' she warned. 'He isn't a pet.'

Lucas turned his head. The dog was no dog. Large, with a shaggy white coat that faded into a silver ruff; the muzzle sharp and thinly pointed. It turned its head, staring at him with blue eyes. Sweat prickled between his shoulder-blades as the silver-grey timber wolf padded past him and lay down across the doorway.

The door swung back open, on creaking hinges. The White Crow raised red-brown eyebrows, and smiled at Lucas. 'Disconcerting, isn't it? Tell me about yourself.'

'Aren't *you* meant to do that?'

'You want me to read dice or cards,' the woman remarked, lifting several volumes of Paracelsus from an armchair, 'and you act like a damned aristo. You're studying at the university, but all of that I could have heard where I heard your name, Lucas. From gossip. I don't do party tricks. Sit down.'

Lucas stiffened. The cinnamon-haired woman dusted her hands together, and winced.

She pulled the patchwork cloth from the round table. Mirror-glass glimmered. Businesslike, she bent down, undid a catch, and spun the mirror on its spindle until the wooden backing was uppermost. A click of the catch and the table was firm.

Reaching up to a cupboard, the White Crow remarked, 'Dice, I think,' and pulled a brown silk scarf out and floated it down across the table.

Lucas picked the empty chair up and put it by the table. Something brushed his hair, buzzed sharply; he shook his head, and a honey-bee wavered off across the room. The woman put up a finger. The bee clung there for a moment while she brought it up close to eyes that, Lucas saw, glowed tawny amber; her lips pursed, and she blew gently. The bee hummed, flying drunkenly through the open window.

'Why "White Crow"?' Lucas sat, lounging back in the chair and crossing his legs.

She smiled. Under the white cotton shirt, her breasts were small and firm. Crow's-feet starred the corners of her eyes, and the slightest fat was beginning to blur the line of her jaw.

'Because it's not in the slightest like my own name – Quiet, Lazarus.'

The wolf snapped, snarled a quick high whine, as two more bees flew in at the door. The White Crow held out a hand absently. As the bees alighted there, she transferred them to her red-brown hair, where they crawled sluggishly, buzzing. Lucas's skin crawled.

'If you have a silver shilling,' she said, 'it would speed matters up considerably. Now where did I . . . ? Oh, yes.'

She pushed books off the window-sill left-handed, regardless of where they fell. The sill opened. From the compartment, she took a handful of dice. She looked about for a moment for somewhere to sit, and then pulled a tall stool out from a corner.

Lucas sat up. The White Crow threw the dice loosely onto the brown silk covering the table. There were eight or nine of them: cubes of bone. And laid into each die-face, in brilliant enamel, was a picture or image.

'Just handle those for a minute, will you, and then cast them?'

Mist cleared and clouded, visible through the open skylight, and the room seemed to swell or darken as the sun shone or diminished. The woman reached up to a high shelf. Her shirt pulled taut across her breasts and pulled out of her breeches waistband, so that he saw tanned flesh in the gap. Lucas shuffled the dice in both hands, leaning forward to the table to conceal his arousal.

She took down a stole and slung it about her neck. The white satin shone, embroidered with dozens of tiny black characters.

'Now,' she said, and Lucas cast the handful of dice on the table.

He drew in a sharp breath. Of the nine die-faces, four were showing a white enamelled skull with blue periwinkle eyes, the other five a tiny knotted cord – the knot with which a shroud is tied.

The White Crow leaned over, squinting, and her dark red eyebrows went up.

'Damn things are on the blink again. Here, we'll try the cards. How old are you?'

'Nineteen.' Lucas slid a hand down between himself and the table, and tugged surreptitiously at the seam of his breeches. His eyes followed the woman as she padded about the room, turning up books and piles of paper, obviously searching.

Something about her made him want to drop all pretence. 'Actually,' Lucas said, 'I'm the heir to the throne of Candover. Prince Lucas. Eldest son of King Ordono.'

She trod on the end of the satin stole, and swore.

'Incognito?'

'That was my idea.' He pushed his fingers through his thick springy hair. 'I thought it would be good. To not be a king's son. I suppose I thought people would treat me the same; that it would show through, naturally, somehow – what I really am.'

The White Crow said drily, 'Perhaps it does,' and straightened up with a much-thumbed pack of cards. She gave them to Lucas and slumped down on the stool, puffing.

'But there's no advantage to it, I can see that.' Lucas shuffled the cards. 'I'll give it up, I think.'

'Oh, to be nineteen and romantic!' The woman smiled, sardonic. She took the cards back and began to lay them out on the brown silk cover. When she had put twelve in a diamond-pattern, she stopped.

As she bent forward, squinting down at the table, Lucas saw that she had faint golden freckles on her cheek-bones. Her hair was coming down on one side, the silver flowing.

The White Crow fumbled in her shirt pocket for a pair of gold-rimmed rimmed spectacles, shoved them firmly on, and announced: '*Now* . . .'

Lucas saw a mess of deuces and knaves.

'What's a king's son doing studying at the University of Crime anyway?'

'My father said it would be the best-possible training for the crown. I already had an aptitude for it. What can you see?'

The spice-haired woman sat back and whipped off her glasses.

'Nothing. Oh, I can see pointers . . . You should go to the docks, soon.'

She peered at the cards again.

'Or the main station.'

She turned up another card: the Page of Sceptres.

'Or the airfield.' Disgusted, she swept the cards together. 'This is ridiculous! I've been doing this more years than you've been alive, and now I'm getting nothing here, nothing at all.'

Silence filled the room. The White Crow stood, moving to the window, replacing dice and cards in the sill-compartment. Mist frayed, admitting light. and the sun caught the silver in her hair; and Lucas stood up and walked to the window.

'It reminds me of the White Mountains,' he said, sniffing deeply.

The woman folded her satin stole. She put it down on the sill, rested her fists on it, and leaned out to look at the heat and droplets of fog. Sheets and linen draped the trees in the yard. There was a lingering scent of soap and drains.

'There comes a time,' the White Crow said, 'when you can't smell the air of *any* kind of a day without it bringing some other past day to mind. When that happens, you're not old, but you're no longer young.'

Lucas leaned his arm across the window-frame behind her back, close enough that the hairs on his bare skin prickled.

'You're not old.'

The timber wolf whined, half-rose, and sank down again across the doorstep.

'Telling you you'll meet someone at an airfield, or a station, it's kitchen-teacup magic!' She picked up a heavy octavo volume from a chair. 'Birthdate?'

Lucas took his arm away, not certain it had even been noticed.

'Midwinter Eve, the seven hundred and fiftieth year from the founding of Candover.'

'That corresponds to . . .' She flicked pages, resting the book on the sill, searching for the relevant page. A whisk of dust caught in Lucas's throat. Midway, she glanced up, thin shoulders sagging.

'Why lie? I can't do this. Yesterday – there was such a use of power in the city yesterday that it's deafened and blinded me. I could no more read for you than fly.'

'Evelian told me some people were injured, over in one of the other quarters.'

'Injured and killed. That's twice the acolytes have been sent out to feed since the spring.'

The White Crow held out a hand into open air, and another bee alighted, crawling across her unbandaged palm.

'Maybe I can do something for you, all the same.'

She nudged at her temple. One of the bees that crawled in her hair flew off. She abruptly closed her hand over the remaining one, blew a *ftt!* into her fist and opened it in front of Lucas's nose.

A solid gold bee lay on her palm.

'*Take* it. Think of it as a hair-grip.' The White Crow's humour was exasperated. 'Go to your meeting, whoever it turns out to be. This may be some protection. You won't have heard of it, but a while back it was a recognised sign. If you need to convince anyone that you know a magus, then show them this.'

Lucas picked it up gingerly, between thumb and forefinger. It was cold, heavy, hard metal.

'But I'd be obliged,' the woman added, 'if you didn't show it to anyone unnecessarily.'

He opened his mouth to voice discontent, and the wolf raised its head and gazed at him with pale blue eyes. It did not look away. Lucas broke the contact first.

'One more thing,' he insisted. 'Evelian will be worried if I don't ask. The South Katayan student who lodges here. Zari. Can you find out where she is now?'

Desaguliers paused outside the audience chamber, removing his plumed headband. A blowfly buzzed round his ears, and he swatted it irritably away. He pulled his cloak up about his lean shoulders, concealing the worst patches of charred fur, and took a deep breath.

'Enter!'

The Captain-General hesitated. His wolfish face was lost for a moment in calculation. Then he shrugged and pushed his way through the double doors.

Watery sunlight shafted from full-length windows into the audience chamber, glowing on the blue drapes and gold-starred canopy. Desaguliers approached the bed.

'Your Majesty,' he said.

Eight Rats lay on the great circular bed on the dais. Three were being fed and groomed by servants. Another lay asleep. One black Rat had a secretary seated on the carpeted dais steps, reading a report to him in a low voice, and two Rats (fur so pale it was almost silver) dictated letters. The eighth Rat beckoned Desaguliers.

The Captain-General climbed the steps to kneel before the bed. The Rats lay with their bodies pointing outwards, their tails in the centre of the bed's silks and pillows. Each scaly tail wound in and out of the others, tangled, tied, fixed in a fleshy knot; and Desaguliers could see (as a brown Rat page carefully cleaned) where the eight tails had inextricably grown together.

'A serious matter.' The Rats-King brushed crumbs from his gold-and-white jacket. He reclined on his side, facing Desaguliers: a bony black Rat in late middle age.

'One of my Cadets lost his life. Three others are so badly injured that it will be months before they return to military service.' Desaguliers paused. 'Has your Majesty received word from the Fane this morning?'

'No word—'

The bony Rat picked a sweetmeat from a dish, bit into it, and the half-sleeping black Rat on his left opened his mouth to murmur: '—from the Fane at all,' while the first Rat chewed.

Desaguliers suppressed a shiver. He straightened his shoulders, wincing where his leather harness galled burned flesh.

'I discovered what I could, your Majesty. There were Rats present at this hall meeting, a priest called Plessiez, and one of your Majesty's guard, by name Charnay; both of whom were killed. There were also a number of humans that died in the attack, most but not all of hall rank.'

The first Rat bowed his head, while a page brushed the fur along his jaw and behind his translucent ears. His shining black eyes met Desaguliers'.

'And you have no idea of the purpose of the meeting?'

Desaguliers' gaze did not alter. 'None at all, your Majesty. I continue to investigate. The attack came very shortly after I entered the Masons' Hall, and I had no chance to question anyone.'

The bony Rat nodded. A fly buzzed thickly past. The sleeping Rat, eyes still half-shut, said: 'You were lucky, messire, to live.'

'The hall turned out to have a small cellar underneath. I and my Cadets took shelter there.' Desaguliers halted at the black Rat's glare, and qualified: 'Truthfully, your Majesty, we fell through when the floor collapsed, and emerged after the Fane's acolytes had gone. I had the cellar and the rubble searched for bodies – rather, remains of bodies.'

Another brown Rat secretary came to read reports; and Desaguliers overheard the twin silver Rats say, in perfect unison: 'Send in the ambassador first; then the Second District Aust quarter delegation—'

'—afterwards,' the bony black Rat finished, smiling. 'Very well, Desaguliers. We're pleased that we still have our Captain-General.'

'Luck,' Desaguliers said, relaxing, and with a genuine regret in his tone. 'We were lucky to come out of that. No one else who was caught in the building survived.'

No through-draught moved in the room under the rafters. A fly skewed right-angles across the air, sounding distant in the heat, although it was only a few feet above his head. Lucas bent over the paper, imprinting neat cuneiform characters with an ink-stylus.

I like the University well enough, sister; you'd like it, too. Tell our father that I will stay here for the three years. It will please him.

Candover seems very far away now.

He put the stylus down on the table. His jacket already lay over the back of his chair; now he unbuttoned his shirt and pulled it out of his belt. Scratching in the dark curls of his chest, he wrote:

I consulted a philosopher (which is what they call a seer here) earlier this morning, but she could tell me nothing. She says she will draw a natal chart for one of the other students, but it will take her a few hours. I've said I'll go back at noon.

Footsteps crossed the courtyard below. Lucas leaped from his chair and leaned over the window-sill.

Mistress Evelian waved a greeting, gestured that she would speak but couldn't: mouth full of clothes-pegs. Last remnants of mist blurred the tiled roofs. A smell of boiled cabbage drifted in. On the street side of the room, the noise of a street-player's lazy horn wound up into the late-morning air.

Hugging himself, sweaty, Lucas crossed back to the table.

Gerima, perhaps I won't come back to Candover at all. I might not go to the university. I might just stay here in the city.

The skylight screeched, dropping rust-flakes into his eyes as he wedged it further open. The air up on the slanting roof hit him like warm water, and he drew his head back inside. A bird cried.

The seer is a woman who calls herself the White Crow. I said I would call back for the birthstar chart myself, although the person it concerns is no friend of mine. The White Crow—

The slow horn milked heat from the day, drowsing all the morning's actions away into dreams.

He scratched at the hair of his chest, fingers scrabbling down to the thin line of back-growing hair on his belly. Sweat slicked his fingers. The narrow room (only bed, table and cast-iron basin in it) stifled him. Dizzy, dazed, drunk on nothing at all, Lucas threw himself down on his back on the bed and stared up through the open window at the sky.

Imaging in his mind how her hair, that strange dark red, is

streaked with a pure silver and white, flowing from her temples. How her eyes, when they smile, seem physically to radiate warmth: an impossibility of fiction, but striking home now to some raw new centre inside him.

Gerima, so much of her life has gone past and I don't know what it is. I would like to go back and make it turn out right for her. If she laughs at me, I'll kill myself.

The slow heat stroked his body as he stripped, lying back on the white linen. Imaging in his mind how sweat darkens her shirt under the arms, and in half-moons under each breast, and the contrast between her so-fine-textured skin and her rough cloth breeches. His fingers pushed through the curly hair of his genitals, cupped his balls for a moment; and then slid up to squeeze in slow strokes. His breathing quickened.

A faint breeze rose above the window-sill and blew the unfinished letter on to the floor.

On the far side of the courtyard Clock-mill struck eleven. An authoritative knocking came on the street-door. The White Crow swore, threw down her celestial charts and padded barefoot down the narrow stairway to the street.

'*Yes?*'

A man gazed nervously up and down the cobbled lane. A dirty grey cloak swathed him from head to heels, the hood pulled far forward to hide his face.

'Are you the White Crow?'

The White Crow leaned one elbow on the door-frame, and her head on her hand. She looked across at the hooded face (standing on the last step, she was just as tall as he) and raised an eyebrow.

'Aren't you a little warm in that?'

The air over the cobbles shimmered with heat, now that the early mist had burned away. The man pushed his hood far enough back for her to see a fleshy sweat-reddened face.

'My name is Tannakin Spatchet,' he announced. 'Mayor of the District's East quarter. Lady, I was afraid you wouldn't want to be seen receiving such an unrespectable visitor.'

The White Crow blinked.

'What do you want?'

'Talismans.' He leaned forward, whispering. 'Charms that warn you when the Decans' acolytes are coming.'

'No such thing. Go away. That's not possible.'

His fleshy arm halted the door as she slammed it. 'It is possible! A girl saved six people's lives yesterday with such a warning. She's dead now. For the safety of my quarter's citizens, I want some talisman or hieroglyph that will give us warning if it happens again!'

The White Crow gestured with spread palms, pushing the air down, as if physically to lower the man's voice. She frowned. Lines at the corners of her eyes radiated faintly down on to her cheek-bones, visible in the sunlight.

He said: *'Is* it possible?'

'Mmm . . . Bruno the Nolan incontrovertibly proves how *magia* runs in a great chain from the smallest particle, the smallest stone, up to microbes, bacteria; roses, beasts and men; daemonic and angelic powers – and to those Thirty-Six who create all in Their divinity. And how *magia*-power may be heard and used up and down the Great Chain of Being . . .'

The White Crow tapped her thumb against her teeth.

'I use the Celestial world. Yes . . . Master Mayor, you realise talismans can be traced to the people who made them? People who make them, here, they don't live long. Who sent you to me?' she temporised.

'A friend, an old friend of mine. Mistress Evelian. She mentioned a Hermetic philosopher lodging with her . . .'

The White Crow shoved a hand through her massy hair, and leaned out to look up and down the street. 'That woman is perilously close to becoming a philosopher's pimp. Oh, come in, come in. Mind the – Never mind.'

Tannakin Spatchet rubbed his forehead where the low doorway caught him, and followed her up the dark stairs.

She led him through a room with an iron stove to one side and a scarcely less rigid bed to the other, and through into an airy room smelling of paper and leather bindings. She held out a hand for his cloak.

'Can you help, lady?'

The White Crow folded the cloak, studying the bulky fair-haired man. He seemed in his fifties, too pallid for health. She dropped the cloak randomly across a stack of black-letter pamphlets.

'Mayor of the Nineteenth District,' she repeated.

'Of its East quarter. I regret coming to you in this unceremonious manner. I brought no clerks or recorders, thinking the whole matter best kept quiet.' He cleared his throat. 'Yesterday . . .'

Tannakin Spatchet touched a finger to the cleared chair, looked distastefully at the book-dust, and seated himself gingerly. Then he met the White Crow's gaze, his fussiness gone.

'Yesterday I saw Decans' acolytes,' the Mayor said, 'closer than I ever hope to see them again. Five of my people are missing – dead, I should say. I need someone to advise me.'

A beast yipped. The White Crow's preoccupied gaze snapped back into focus. She crossed the room and squatted down, picking up from a padded box a young fox-cub and reaching for a glass bottle. As she seated herself on the window-sill, the reddish lump of fur in her lap stinking of vixen, and bent her head to feed it, she said: 'At a Masons' Hall, in the East quarter.'

'You know of it?'

'Evelian told me this morning. I think she knew someone in the hall. I knew that *something* had been destroyed.' She held out a free hand, the bandages on the palm newly bloodstained. 'We respond, some of us, to such disturbances.'

The warm wind blew in at the window, easing the fox-stink.

'What I say must go no further.'

She jerked her head at the room: the books, charts, orreries and globes. 'I am what I am, messire. If you want my help, tell me why.'

'I . . . know so little,' Tannakin Spatchet confessed. 'We're not admitted to the mysteries of the halls. I heard of the meeting only at the last moment. I and my councillors thought fit to force an entrance. Would to god we never . . . Master Falke spoke there. Of ways to free us from those who rule the city.'

Pain ached in her palm. The fox-cub whined, nipping sleepily at her wrist.

'Stupid! *Stupid*. What were you going to fight Decans with, messire – your bare hands?'

'Lady, I have no proof, but I believed Master Falke to be a secret officer in the Society of the House of Salomon – they having their secret officers infiltrated into almost every hall.'

He glanced over his shoulder at the open window.

'The House of Salomon say that since we build stone on stone to increase the Fane's power, then we could raze stone *from* stone, so raze the Fane and the power of the Thirty-Six with it. Could that be so, lady?'

'In all the greater and the lesser *magias*, patterns compel.'

The White Crow rubbed her knuckles along the fox-cub's rough coat. It opened tiny amber eyes. She yipped under her breath, very softly, and reached down to tap a heavily bound copy of Vitruvius' *The Ten Books on Architecture* resting on the sill.

'This House of Salomon seems to follow orthodox teaching. Vitruvius writes that the measurements of a truly constructed building mirror both the proportions of the human body and the shape of the universal Order. Microcosm mirrors macrocosm; the Fane mirrors the Divine within. Theoretically, break Their mirror and you remove Their channels of power. But we speak of the Thirty-Six.'

Tannakin Spatchet shivered. The White Crow shrugged.

'It's foolhardy. The Decans aren't so easily challenged.' She spoke with the contempt of long knowledge. 'They loosed the *least* of their servants on you, and—'

Tannakin Spatchet rose. 'Do I look so much of a fool? Falke called the meeting; I heard of it only by chance. Falke called in Fellow-crafts from half the halls in the quarter; *Falke* brought in the Rat-Lords, and a Kings' Memory!'

'This is the Master of the Hall? And you couldn't stop it, Master Mayor?'

'A builder listen to any one of us! Very likely.' Deep sarcasm sounded in the Mayor's voice. He looked down at the White Crow. 'Someone betrayed the meeting to those at the Fane. Falke's dead. So are those others who didn't get out in time. If they knew who betrayed them, I don't.'

He wiped his forehead. 'I'm sorry, lady. I've spent the morning with widows and children. It isn't easy explaining to them how I am still alive and the others dead.'

The White Crow put the fox-cub back into its box. She brushed orange hairs from her shirt and knee-breeches, sniffed her fingers, and wrinkled her nose. She raised her head and stared through the open window. No dark in her vision, no taste in her mouth but sour wine.

'Decans. As if,' she said, 'you or I were to pour boiling water into an ants' nest. Does it matter if a few escape? With only a little more effort they could cauterise the city itself, humans and Rats together.'

Tannakin Spatchet sat down slowly. He absently began to straighten the edges of the stacked papers on the table. 'What are we? Their hands. Their *builders*. Of no more significance than a trowel, a hod, a pair of compasses. The least we need is warning, when they exercise their power. Lady, can you help me?'

'If I can, I will.'

The determination in that seemed to surprise even her. She stood and briskly began sorting through books on a low shelf.

'You tell me other halls were involved? And so there'll be more meetings . . . ?' The White Crow straightened, a hand in the small of her back.

Tannakin Spatchet said: 'Is a scrying spell possible?'

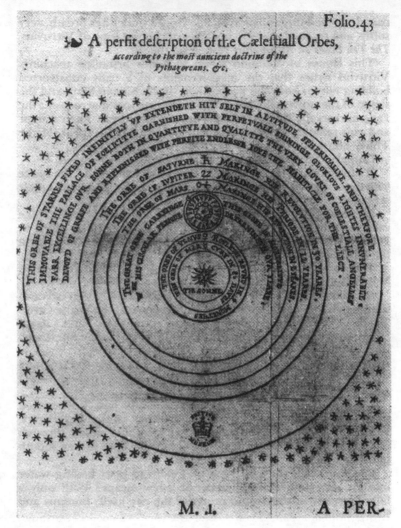

'In all the greater and the lesser magias, patterns compel.' From *A Perfit Description of the Cælestiall Orbes*, Thomas Digges, London, 1576

She looked questioningly at him.

'To discover who betrayed them to the Decans,' the Mayor amplified. 'And why.'

'More difficult. I can try. Tell me, first, who was there. Who was in the hall when it was destroyed.'

The White Crow looked out into the courtyard, and saw Mistress Evelian, golden hair shining in the sun, pegging out washing; and holding a shouted conversation with the dark-haired student, Lucas, at his attic window.

'The Master of the Hall, Falke; and his sister, Awdrey, who was Mistress Royal to the Children of the Widow. Two Apprentices from out of the quarter. A man and two women I didn't recognise. The Captain-General of the King's Guard, Desaguliers.'

Tannakin Spatchet paused. The White Crow scratched at rough parchment with a quill pen, noting names.

'". . . Captain-General." I'll have to ask questions carefully in *that* quarter. Who else?'

He watched her handwriting: stark and sloping across the page.

'A brown Rat. I believe she was a soldier. A priest: a black Rat that the Captain-General called by the name of Plessiez. And the girl who gave the warning, the Kings' Memory. Lady, she was very young. I don't know her name. She is the one who died – a Katayan.'

On the highest pinnacle yet built, among scaffolding lashed with hemp rope and net-cradled blocks of masonry, men are talking in whispers. Any sun is absorbed by the black stone. Acres of stone fall away below them, in crevasses and coigns.

Distance hides the ground below.

'They know!'

The hooks dangle from the derricks, empty, ropes creaking. All the cranes are abandoned.

'I tell you, they know what we're doing!'

They are in working clothes, silk and satin, each with the mark of his own particular Craft.

'We must act as if we were innocent. They need us to build for them.'

This ziggurat will rise between two pyramidical obelisks that are equal in thickness to the building itself. A mile away an identical pair of obelisks rises, completed two generations ago. Great hieroglyphs are burned into their stone sides. This burning of stone happened during an eclipse of the sun that lasted four days.

'No. We don't wait.' This speaker is the most assured. 'You're right: they need us to build, because they can't. So—'

'*If we stop work, they'll kill enough of us that the rest will go back to work. We're tried that before.*'

To north and east and aust of the ziggurat, more of the Fane's perpendicular frontages cut the sky. Here, the sky itself is the colour of ashes.

'*They can force us to work,*' the first speaker says, '*but who can force a man to eat or to sleep?*'

The ceiling-fan's eight-foot blades circled a slow *wck* . . . *wck* . . . *wck* . . . The only other noise came from the clerk's quill pen. Afternoon heat slanted in through pale-green shutters, drawn closed on the large room's south-austern side.

A breath of air came in from the opposite full-length shutters, open to the terrace, and touched the forehead of the man sleeping in the chair behind the desk. His eyelashes flickered. The Candovard Ambassador saw through sleep-watered vision the whitewashed walls, the pale-green fretworked wood that decorated doors and shutters and terrace balustrade.

A fist rapped the shutters. The thin young clerk stood up.

'Mhrumhh?' Andaluz raised his head alertly.

A young man held one shutter open, slatted shadow barring his body: bare feet and knee-breeches, and a doublet carried slung over one shoulder. Chest and shoulders and arms were rounded with muscle. He looked at Andaluz from under meeting brows.

'My dear Lucas!' Andaluz sprang up, waved the clerk back and came round the desk. 'My dear boy! I've been waiting for you to call.'

The younger man dropped his doublet over a chair, and the smaller man embraced him, kissing him on both cheeks. He put Lucas back to arm's length, studying him.

'I hear that you came in on the *Viper* yesterday morning. You should have called. Do I take it from this dress that you're still determined on disguise? Your mother wrote to me some months ago about that. Most censoriously, I might add.'

The young man laughed, holding up both hands. 'I'll tell you, Uncle, if you'll let me speak.'

'Tea.' Andaluz snapped his fingers. The clerk left silently. Andaluz tugged at the hem of his sleep-creased white jacket, not bothering to do up the neck buttons. He scratched at his curled, grizzled hair.

'And how is my dear Pereluz?'

'Mother's fine.'

The youth looked up at a portrait hanging above the mahogany filing-cabinets. A patch of light picked out the woman who sat beside a sun-haired man. She wore a coronet, as her husband did, on hair as dark as Lucas's; and her fine brows came within a hair of meeting.

Andaluz saw, reflected in the glass covering, his and the young man's same features: forty years between them. Andaluz's hair was grizzled sharply black and white, with little grey in it.

'She told me to tell you she misses her favourite brother at court.'

'Ah, Pereluz.' The Ambassador patted Lucas's shoulder as he bustled back behind his desk. He picked up gold-rimmed spectacles and put them on. 'What can I arrange for you, Prince?'

He saw the dark gaze glint out from under heavy brows. Lucas moved in the heat-shadowed room like a breath of the outside world: sweet-tempered, smelling of sweat and sunshine.

'Yes, I do want you to do something for me. I want it made clear to the university that I start there tomorrow, not today.' The young man paused, as the clerk returned with iced tea.

Andaluz scribbled a short note, handed it to the clerk and sent her off with whispered instructions.

'Done, I think. What else?'

Lucas smiled. 'Does it show so clearly?'

'My dear Lucas, if this were a social visit, you would have called yesterday. Besides, I'm told that your stay here, short as it is, hasn't been uneventful.' Andaluz broke off, rubbing the bridge of his nose. 'Tell me about it. I can cease to be official for a few minutes.'

The young man shook his head decisively.

'I want you to investigate a death. A girl. She was a student, a Katayan; I can give you her full name.'

Andaluz's bushy eyebrows rose. 'A friend?'

'No. No . . .' The young man looked away. 'I didn't like her, and I haven't changed my opinion because she died. I suppose I feel guilty about – *De mortuis nil nisi bonum*. But I want the full story. There are friends of hers who need to know. Her name was Zarbettu-zekigal.'

Andaluz copied down the carefully enunciated syllables.

'Assume that I know something of this,' he said. 'The Embassy keeps an eye on you. What else?'

The young man paced across the faded carpet. He stopped for a time, looking out on to the wooden terrace, and across the stretch of yellow earth that, if not for the heat, would be a garden.

'I had another message for you, Uncle, but the person who sent it probably died when Zari did.' Lucas turned. 'A priest, a black Rat by the name of Plessiez. He said he knows . . . *knew* you. He sent his regards.'

Andaluz took off his spectacles, laying them on the papers on the desk. The ceiling-fan's *wck-wck* sounded loudly.

'The little priest is dead?'

'It's almost certain. Sorry.'

'I always *told* Plessiez that he'd go too far. Tell me all of it,' Andaluz directed and, when he had heard the boy out, shook his head slowly. 'The Embassy Compound's been quiet. I don't think we've had to deal with more than the Fane's intermediaries in five years. Now three secretaries and two ambassadors summoned by the Decans in half a day . . .'

Lucas said: 'I also need to know if you have a file on a woman. A natural philosopher: she calls herself the White Crow. Most of what I've heard about the hall, I've heard through her. I want to know how reliable she is.'

Andaluz picked up a bell on his desk and rang it. After a few seconds, another clerk appeared; and the Candovard Ambassador handed him a slip of paper with two names on it. He sipped at his iced tea while he waited, studying the Prince's face.

'You're no longer incognito,' he said. 'Will you be moving in here? I've plenty of room.'

A chessboard occupied one corner of the large desk. Lucas leaned on his forearms, studying the game in progress, and reached to move a jet-carved pawn with dirty fingers. Andaluz all but saw images in the boy's mind: of the odd house off Carver Street to which the university had sent him. He restrained himself from comment.

'I'll stay where I am, Uncle, for the moment.'

The second clerk returned, putting a thick file of papers down in front of Andaluz. The Ambassador began to skim over the notes. When he spoke, it was without looking up.

'Your "White Crow" is easily identifiable. There aren't too many foreign natural philosophers in the city. Even though this one appears to change her name and move around – six months here, eight months there . . .'

Andaluz sat back. 'We have records for her going back five years. No reason in particular, except that, as a philosopher, she's kept under observation. She practises a little natural magic in order to make a living, it would seem.'

The boy had leaned forward. Now he bent his head, rubbing with both hands at the back of his neck. When he straightened, that might have been the reason for his heat-reddened cheeks.

Andaluz said gently: 'I hope you'll come here often, Lucas. I miss my countrymen, and family.'

The young man nodded, shifting awkwardly. 'Of course.'

'Sending you to the university was your father's idea. Of course, the Ortiz have always had a strain of eccentricity in the blood—'

'And the Luz haven't?'

'My *dear* Lucas.'

A pair of blowflies buzzed around the tea-bowl, and Andaluz carefully fitted the weighted net cover over the ceramic. The flies settled on the cracked plaster ceiling, crawling there, beyond the fan-blades, with several dozen other insects.

'I intended to say, only, that this is not the summer I would choose to have the heir of Candover here.'

Lucas shrugged. 'I'm staying.'

'So I perceive.' Patience stayed Andaluz's tongue, long assumed and long practised. He looked up as the first clerk returned, handing him a written note in return for his message.

'Is there going to be trouble with the university?'

Andaluz read, and then looked up.

'I think not. All today's lectures were cancelled,' the Ambassador said. 'Term starts tomorrow. It seems that one of the lecturers has gone missing. A Reverend Master Candia?'

Lucas stared, startled. 'He was there yesterday with us. With the new intake.'

Andaluz shrugged. 'And now, apparently, drunk or dead or whatever the reason might be, completely vanished.'

Voices sound in the dark. The tones echo, as if from an immense space: bouncing back from hard surfaces. Mixed with those echoes is the sound of dripping water.

No light; no slightest peripheral gleam.

'Will you wait for me!' A scuffle and thud. 'You bastards can see in the dark and I can't!'

'Are you hurt, little one?'

An inaudible mumble.

Further off, another voice demands: 'What's she doing here?'

'She blundered in, Charnay, rather as you have a habit of doing. Don't complain. You have her to thank for your life.'

'Where the hell are we?'

'Not, I hope, in hell, although I confess to some doubt on the subject.'

Another voice speaks: 'Listen!'

The silence resumes. Far off, there is a noise that might be water, or wind, or some element of flux peculiar to darkness.

CHAPTER 3

'The use,' Reverend Mistress Heurodis announced, 'of the knife. You. Lucas. Come here.'

Light shone from perpendicular windows down into the university's training-hall. Lucas rubbed the sleep of his second night in the city from his eyes and walked out of the group of students.

'The knife can kill quickly, efficiently and, above all, *silently*.'

Heurodis's smoky blue eyes moved to Lucas. He hunched his shoulders unconsciously: her head only came up to the level of his collar-bone.

'Here.' She offered him the bone hilt of a knife, with a hand upon which the veins stood up, skin brown-spotted with age.

'Stab him,' she directed.

Lucas closed his hand on the knife. The blued-steel blade flashed, ugly; and he looked up from it to meet the glazed stare of the bound man beside Heurodis.

A smell of grease and old sweat came off the man; his ribs were visible under his shirt, and his yellow-grey hair marked him as only a few years younger than Heurodis.

'What are you waiting for?' the old lady demanded. 'A killing stroke – you would aim where?'

Lucas heard someone gasp behind him; refused to look back at the half-dozen other students. He nipped lower lip between tooth and incisor, frowning. The knife-blade chilled his thumb. A trickle of sweat ran down between his shoulder-blades.

'In cold blood?'

'This isn't a *game*, boy. If you think that it is, you have no business at the university!'

'I . . .'

He moved forward, boots loud on the scrubbed wooden floor. The bound man didn't move: drugged, dazed; the pulse beating steadily at the base of his corded throat. Heurodis leaned on her cane.

'I would cut the carotid artery *there*' – Lucas's free hand tapped the side of the man's throat – 'from the rear for preference, Reverend Mistress.'

He flipped the steel knife, caught it by the tip, held it out to her.

'But first I would make sure not to get into the situation. Or, if I had, that there was another way out of it. Or, if not, that I could stun rather than kill.'

Someone behind him muttered. A shadow flicked across the floor, from a bird passing the high windows; and far off a clock struck nine.

'Are you disobeying me, boy?' Her wrinkled face puckered into a smile. 'Good! The time will come when you have to kill to stay alive. But life is precious; you should always have a better reason for taking it than someone else's order.'

A tall girl stepped forward from the group. 'But we're here to learn, aren't we?'

Heurodis reached to take the knife from Lucas's outstretched hand. 'Certainly. And Reverend tutors musn't be disobeyed, which is why Master Lucas will be scrubbing out the latrines this morning, as a punishment.'

Lucas wiped his wet palm on his shirt.

'As a point of reference,' the elderly lady said, 'we usually don't do any killing – knives, poisons, traps – until well into the second term.'

She gave the drugged man's tether to one of the hall-assistants, and as she passed Lucas he smelt frangipani and the scent of lilac. The old woman smoothed down her cotton dress.

'Pair off now. I want to see your techniques for disarming someone who has a knife. Master Lucas, a word with you.'

The other new students began unrolling practice-mats. Lucas walked a few paces aside with the white-haired woman.

'I hear that you used some family influence yesterday to avoid the punishment for not attending.' She placed the top of her cane against Lucas's chest. 'Don't do that again. You could spend the rest of this term cleaning latrines.'

'I—' *was led astray by a dead girl*, Lucas finished the thought; and shut his mouth, and met Heurodis's smoky gaze. 'Sorry, Reverend Mistress.'

The cane rapped him familiarly under the fifth rib. She smiled, displaying long regular teeth. 'Good man.'

'When I've finished . . . *cleaning*' – Lucas's nostrils flared slightly – 'do I rejoin the class?'

'Yes.' Heurodis raised her voice inclusively. 'This afternoon you

all have a session with Reverend Master Pharamond – and your first
practice-session, out in the city itself.'

In the darkness, water dripped. Echoes ran off into the unseen
distance. Cold moist air blew steadily now; and the stench of ordure
was interrupted by scents of unbearable sweetness.

Rubble skittered across a hard surface. A grunt and an oath were
succeeded by a splash.

'Zari?'

'My *foot*! My bare foot!'

The Katayan sprawled face-down across brick paving, half in and
half out of a pool of water. She raised her head, pushing a chopped-
off fringe of black hair out of her eyes, and then held up her hands,
spread-fingered.

'Ei! I can *see*. It's light. Where's it coming from?'

She knelt up, wringing out the hem of her greatcoat. Her dappled
tail cracked like a whip, and a fine spray of water flew into the
darkness.

'Where are we? Can we get out of here?'

'I think it unlikely.'

Dim illumination shone on Plessiez, where the black Rat, drawn
rapier in his hand, stood staring up a brick shaft that opened above
his head. A cone of silvery light fell from it, on to a floor cluttered
with broken bricks, stones, heaps of dried ordure, ossified branches
and yellowing bones.

'Charnay, see if it's possible to climb here.'

The brown Rat emerged from the gloom. She put her fists on her
furry haunches, craning her neck. The arched brick roof passed five
or six feet above her head, and the shaft in it (easily thirty feet in
diameter) opened without lip or ledge.

'It's smooth,' Charnay reported.

'I see that. Try if you can get a grip. *Climb*.'

Zar-bettu-zekigal stood up, shaking her dripping foot, and
padded towards the light. The skeleton of a snake curved across
the brick paving in front of her, entire, the delicate-branched
vertebrae all intact; and she stooped to peer at the wedge-shaped
skull.

It rose an inch, empty eye-sockets turning towards her; and
glided smoothly under an abandoned heap of brushwood.

Zari took one step after the loose-rattling tail, hesitated, and
limped over to the two Rats.

'Where's . . . ? We've lost Falke again,' she said.

Charnay's leap for the edge of the shaft connected briefly, and

Plessiez stepped back as the brown Rat's wildly scrabbling hind foot swung past his head. Her tail whipped in wild circles.

'Damn the man.'

The brown Rat lost her tenuous grip, tangled a foot in her scabbard and tail on landing, and fell heavily on her rump. Plessiez side-stepped.

'I'm not his nurse!'

'Where *is* he?'

The shaft's dim light showed little around them but the walls. The scent of sweetness was stronger here. The Katayan narrowed her eyes, discerning a phosphorescence patterning the brick vaulting. A paleness of brambles, toothed leaves, petals . . .

Zari stepped forward and stared up the shaft, hands shoved deep into her pockets. Dizzied by the receding circle of brickwork and the sweet stench, she stumbled back against Plessiez, grabbing the black Rat's arm.

'It goes way up, messire. I think it's elbow-jointed. What are the flowers?'

The priest fingered his pectoral *ankh*. 'A haunting of roses. One rarely sees such things above ground. I'd advise you to leave them alone.'

Her shivering communicated itself through his arm. Plessiez chose a dry area of paving, in the shaft's light, and pushed the Katayan woman to sit down.

'We're taking a rest now. Charnay, find Falke.'

The black Rat sheathed his rapier and reached up to untie his scarlet cloak. He swung it free, knelt down, and took the Katayan woman's freckled foot in his hands; drying it with the cloth, and examining it.

'Bruised. Can you walk?'

She withered him with a glare. 'Messire, of *course* I can walk.'

The black Rat dug thumbs into the ball of her foot, with hands upon which the rings were chill. His obsidian eyes glinted in the twilight.

'Honest assessment of your capabilities would be more useful than bravado, I think.'

Her calves ached with an infinitude of steps, passages, iron-rung ladders, and tunnels. 'I can walk.'

Plessiez swathed her feet temporarily in the warm lined cloak and sat down at her side. His lean wolfish face was thoughtful. In the twilight she could see how his scarlet jacket was mud-stained, and the plumed headband bedraggled. Only a twitching of his scaly tail showed his reined-in temper.

'Damn the man! This is his escape-route; he should know where it leads.'

Zari turned her greatcoat collar up, and sat hugging her knees. 'Messire, be honest. Did *you* stop to ask where this went, when it went away from those . . . things?'

'I did not.'

Plessiez removed his headband, scratching at the fur between his ears; and smoothed the broken black feathers. Two of the yellow nails on his right hand were broken. Scuffs and dishevelled patches showed in his sleek fur. He looked sideways at the young woman.

'I don't forget that your prompt action saved us.'

The Katayan shoved pale fingers through her hair, head bowed; and shook the black hair back from her face as she looked up. 'Falke did that, with his traps and false cellars.'

She knelt up, feet still swathed in Plessiez's cloak. She reached across, put her hands on the black Rat's shoulders, and absently began to knead the muscles that were tense under the sleek fur. Some of his rigidity dissolved. 'If this is a sewer system, then it's been here for *ever*—'

A sound thrilled through the dark.

Plessiez grabbed his rapier, scrambling upright. Zar-bettu-zekigal half got to her feet, tangled herself in the cloak and sat down. Charnay's voice, nearby, said: 'So it's salt. Then you ought to be glad that I pulled you out, instead of bitching about it, messire!'

The brown Rat staggered into the circle of twilight, a man's body over her shoulder. With a grunt of effort, she knelt and eased him down on to the terracotta paving. Black overalls streamed water on to the brick.

'We've got to get out of here! If we don't, we'll starve!' Falke caught the harness of Charnay's rapier in a white fist. His translucent hair dripped, sleeked dark with oil and water, and his eyes, uncovered, stared wildly: velvet pits.

Plessiez sheathed his rapier, watching the pale fire of spectral roses.

'The last of our worries is starvation, messire.'

The brown Rat clapped Falke roughly on the back. 'No need for hysterics.'

Zari kicked her bare feet free of the cloak and scrambled upright. She seized Charnay's arm, as the brown Rat began to scrub water from her fur with a silk kerchief.

'It's wet!'

'So it's wet.' Charnay's tail whip-cracked, flicking water-drops off with an audible *spuk!* 'So what?'

Plessiez put his hand on the Katayan's shoulder, restraining her. 'Water?'

'Oh, yes, messire.' The brown Rat began cleaning dampness from her rapier.

'Where?'

Surprised, she said: 'Up ahead. Not far. Falke here found it the hard way, I don't know why; there was light enough that even a Ratling needn't have fallen in—'

Plessiez shoved Zar-bettu-zekigal back. The Katayan danced from foot to bare foot, hardly bothering to avoid the shivering Falke where he huddled, dripping.

'Light? Light from *what*, you dim-witted idiot!' the black Rat demanded.

Charnay sheathed her cleaned rapier, adjusted the hang of her cloak and looked down at Plessiez with a puzzled expression.

'The canal has lamps,' she explained.

Sun from the hard yellow sand dazzled him. Lucas sat on the lagoon wall, dealing cards on to the smooth stone surface.

White marble palaces shone under the luminous blue sky, rising up in terraces from the lagoon. Pink and blue banners hung from balustrades, from walls, from arches and domes. People on the streets made pin-pricks of bright colour. The thin thump of drums came down from a procession, up on a higher street, and the brass tang of cymbals. On the promenade, several black Rats in litters stopped to talk, blocking the way. The sun glinted off the cuirasses of their bodyguards.

'Play you at Shilling-the-Trump?' a voice offered.

Lucas nodded to the woman in sailor's breeches and shirt, identifying her as a transient worker, and so allowed to carry coin. She set down her kitbag and sat on the carved balustrade beside him. He dealt, businesslike now.

'You're too good,' she said at last. Her yellow eyes narrowed suspiciously. 'You're not a student, are you?'

Lucas, lying only by implication, said deprecatingly: 'Only came in on the *Viper* two days ago.'

'I've been warned about students . . .'

The calm lagoon waters mirrored marble-white terraces and a clear sky. Gilding glinted from temple columns and dome-friezes. Far off, where the lagoon opened to the sea, masts were visible, and sailors loading ships, and merchants outside warehouses.

Here, on the flat-packed sand, immense oval shadows dappled the ground: airships tugging at mooring-ropes.

'Five shillings you owe me.'

The woman paid, and Lucas watched her walk away. Barely three o'clock, a dozen other students scattered across the promenades, and already five impromptu cardsharp games since his arrival . . .

None of them the meeting *she* foretold me. Still, she did say the station, and the docks, as well as here.

He dealt idly: Page of Sceptres, Ten of Coins, Three of Grails. A breeze whipped the pasteboard off the marble. He made a sprawling grab for the cards.

A hand the size of a ham slapped down on the stone balustrade, trapping the Page of Sceptres and smearing both card and stone with heavy streaks of machine-oil.

'Here.' A resonant good-natured voice.

'Of all the *filthy*—'

Lucas straightened up, the sun burning the back of his neck. On the sand-flats, crews were scurrying about a moored helium-airship; trolleys and small carriages scored ruts in the sand. Lucas's voice trailed off as he realised that all his view was blotted out.

The man wiped the Page of Sceptres on the lapel of his pink satin coat. Black oil smeared the satin. He peered at the card with china-blue eyes, and dropped a kitbag from his other ham-sized fist. It thudded on to the sand.

'Nothing wrong with that,' he remarked encouragingly, and handed the pasteboard back to Lucas.

'Just wait a damn minute—!'

'Yes?'

Cropped hair glinted the colour of copper wire. As he looked down over his mountainous stomach at the seated young man, his several chins creased up into sweaty folds. He beamed. The smell of the distant surf was overlaid by oil and sweat and garlic.

Lucas opened and shut his mouth several times.

The big man moved and sat down companionably on the balustrade. The marble shook as his weight hit it. He tugged his oil-stained silk breeches up, loosened his cravat and belched; and then gazed around at the surrounding city with immense pleasure.

'Architectonic,' he murmured. He scratched vigorously in his copper hair and examined his fingernails, flicking scurf away. 'Wonderful. Is all the city like this?'

'Uhhrh. No.'

'Pity.'

The man offered a plump fat-creased hand. His sleeve was coated in some yellow substance, almost to the elbow. Wet patches darkened under his arm.

'Casaubon,' he said.

Lucas managed to swallow, saliva wetting his dry mouth. Half-lost in thoughts, he muttered: 'You can't possibly be . . . *No!*'

'I assure you, my name *is* Baltazar Casaubon.' The big man enquired with gravity, over the noise of engines, voices and distant bells, 'Who ought I to be?'

'I'm not sure. I don't know.' Lucas closed his fist over the pack of cards. Badly startled, he began again. 'A seer foretold a meeting for me, here . . . Somehow I hardly think that you're the person in question.'

'Foretelling interests me.' Casaubon dug into the capacious pockets of his full-skirted coat and brought out a handful of roasted chicken-wings. Picking what remained of the meat from the bones, he said: 'I'll give you a shilling to help carry my gear, and we'll talk about it.'

Lucas stood up off the balustrade. Patience exhausted, the afternoon sun fraying his temper, he said: 'Oh, really! There are limits to what a prince will do!'

The big man looked down at the cards, and at the heap of small coins at Lucas's elbow. Through a fine spray of chewed chicken and spittle, he remarked: 'Are there? What are they?'

Lucas stared, silenced.

'Sir?'

A thin brown-haired woman in a frock-coat walked across the sand. Behind her, silver highlights slid across an airship's bulging hull. She snapped her fingers for a porter to follow: the man staggered under the weight of a brass-bound trunk. Two other men followed, carrying a larger trunk between the two of them, their boots digging deep into the sand. The woman made a deep formal bow.

'Ah – *Parry*! Here.' The stentorian bellow beside him deafened Lucas.

'I've summoned a carriage, Lord-Architect. Now, are you sure that—?'

Casaubon stood. He bulked large above Lucas, easily six foot four or five inches tall. He waved a dismissive hand at the woman.

'Parry, don't fuss. Go back, as arranged. And *try* to keep the Senate from bankrupting me while I'm gone, won't you?'

The woman, sweating in woollen frock-coat and breeches, gave a long-suffering sigh. 'Yes, Lord-Architect.'

One carriage rolled up, and the porters began to load it from the luggage piled up around the airship's steps. Case followed case, trunk followed trunk, until the metal-rimmed wheels sank inches deep into the sand. The precise woman snapped her fingers and beckoned another of the nearby carriages.

Casaubon strode over to supervise the loading, mopping at the rolls of fat at the back of his neck with a brownish kerchief. Two of the men struggled to raise a square chest. He motioned them aside, squatted, and straightened up with it in his grip. He heaved it up on to the cart.

'Oof! We'll need another cart. Parry, you're about to miss your ship.'

The thin woman glanced over to where crews were loosening the anchor-ropes of the nearest airship.

'I'll manage,' the big man forestalled her. 'My friend here will call another carriage.'

The woman made a hurried bow, looked as though she would say more, heard a hail from the airship, and turned and strode away. Casaubon stared after her. Ponderously regretful, he shook his head, and then turned back to Lucas.

'Won't you?'

Lucas, a step away, hesitated. He scratched at his thick springy hair, and tugged the linen shirt away from his neck. The heat of the afternoon sun cleared promenade, sand-flats and streets; litters vanishing into cool courtyards, and men and women into cafés and bars. No one now to be inveigled into a game of Shilling-the-Trump, and risk sunstroke.

He put a hand into his breeches pocket, and brought it out closed. 'I can only think of one way to tell if this is a waste of time.'

Lucas opened his hand. On his palm, heavy and intricate, glittering with sharp sun-sparks, lay a golden bee.

Falke shuddered as he walked through humid heat, arms tight about his body. One hand clenched, frustrated, lacking the sword that a Rat-Lord would kill him for owning. He flinched as wet petals brushed his face. Great single-petalled roses shone ebony in the gloom, each bramble and leaf and bud outlined in mirror-silver.

Their touch glided through his skin: substanceless.

'Here!' the brown Rat called from ahead.

Falke pushed sopping hair out of his eyes, staring into the sewer-tunnel. Every noise – brushwood shoved aside, a stone kicked, the sharp sound of water dripping from the brick roof – thrilled through him. The reflexes of his illegal weapons-training made him twitch and start.

Stinking sweetness filled his nostrils, throat and lungs.

'Messire.' The young Katayan woman appeared at his side. Her pale skin glimmered in the tunnel's gloom. His dilated vision saw her face clearly.

She shrugged the heavy greatcoat back off her shoulders and swung it up to shroud him. 'You're shivering. Take it. Down here's the first time I've been warm since I came to your damn city!'

Hot humid air brushed his skin, leaving him clay-cold. He reached up, tugging the coat about his shoulders. The taste of copper lingered in his mouth.

The young woman, walking with a kick-heeled stride, plunged her hands into the pockets of her plain black dress. 'I thought it would get colder, the further down we went.'

The black Rat, outlined briefly at the mouth of the tunnel, stepped down to the left and vanished. Falke heard his voice, with Charnay's; and then Zar-bettu-zekigal slipped her arm under his, and steered him down two steps and out on to a sewer-quay.

The first oil-lamp, searing blue-white, hung in a niche in the tunnel wall. Above it, the ceiling soared thirty feet. Below, the brick went down in steps to the quay. Glass splinters of light pierced his eyes from the ripples. Other lamps shone, further off; gleaming on the filth-choked black quay and the massive tunnel that curved off to either side into the distance.

Oily water glistened and shifted. The Katayan woman coughed. 'The *stink* – it's like dead fish. Like the sea.'

Falke's heel skidded on the wet paving. He gripped her arm.

'Too much light. I can't see.' His clothes clung wetly to him, and he huddled down on the top step, the greatcoat wrapped round him, hands over his dilated eyes.

'Interesting.' Plessiez's voice came clearly. 'The oil has some way to burn yet. I wonder if these lamps are replaced at regular intervals?'

Zar-bettu-zekigal's voice said: 'If it's tidal, we're near the sea. Nearly outside.'

Falke raised his head, shading his eyes.

'No. Sea-water comes in a long way. There are hundreds of miles of sewer-system back of docklands.'

The black Rat paced back, lightly alert, drawn rapier shining in the lamp-light. His scarlet jacket, unbuttoned, gave him the raffish air of a duellist; little trace of the priest now. Only Falke saw how he shied away from black and silver phantoms.

'Charnay, you go two hundred paces up the tunnel, I'll go two hundred paces the other way; then come back and report.'

'Yes, messire.'

The brown Rat leaped down on to the lower quay and walked off.

Falke heard her humming under her breath. He looked up to meet
Plessiez's puzzled expression.

'Stay here, messire, with the little one. *No*, Zari, you're not
coming. Stay where you are.'

The young woman brushed dirt from her dress with the tuft of
her tail. 'Of course, messire.'

The black Rat padded soundlessly away. Falke watched the lithe
figure merge into the wall's shadows; loping easily towards the
bend in the tunnel. From the opposite direction, a loud curse was
followed by the splash of some obstacle kicked into the water.

'Stay *quiet*!' He pushed his fist against his mouth, muffling his
outburst.

Zar-bettu-zekigal flopped down on the step beside him. 'If someone hears her, that's a good thing. We want to get out of here.'

His laugh caught in his throat. He put both hands over his face,
drew in a shaky breath; then took his hands away and clenched
them, staring at his trembling fists.

Her voice came quietly. 'The acolytes frightened me, too.'

'It's . . . more than that. More than cowardice.' He chuckled,
painfully, back in his throat. 'I am a coward, of course, but . . .'

The young woman's sepia eyes darkened now, with the concentration of a Memory. She put black hair behind her ears with
both hands, and shifted her hip so that she sat close to him. Falke
drew unadmitted comfort from the proximity.

'*Only, having once seen that, you never truly cease to see it.* Inside the
Fane. But why here?' she asked.

Now the black Rat was out of sight, around the curve in the
tunnel. Falke leaned forward to peer after Charnay, but she also
was gone.

'When I made escape-routes from my hall, I only ever meant to
get into the upper levels. Down here, do you know how old this is?
These sewers – if you go deep enough, they're part of the catacombs
under the Fane.'

Moisture trickled down from somewhere into the sluggish
channel and, with the ripples, new stenches arose from the disturbed sewer-water. Saliva filled his mouth, prelude to nausea. He
clenched his hand as if that could put one of the House of Salomon's
illegal blades into it, and turned his dilated eyes on the Katayan.

'Once, six or seven years back, I was an architect on the Fane.
Only a small addition to one wing, but I was proud of it – the tallest
perpendicular arches yet, a hundred and eighty feet high, and flying
buttresses as thin as lace . . .'

The Katayan bent forward and skimmed a stone across the quay.

It struck a scorpion, that plopped into the water, threshing, and sank.

'I couldn't bear never to see it again after it was finished.' He pushed his fine white hair out of his face. 'How stupid . . . I was too old to be that stupid. I thought that I would conceal myself in it, as they came to take occupation, and see, and then I would know.'

Words tumbled out of him now, falling into the sepia gaze of her Memory.

'All the grimoires along Magus' Row couldn't hide a human soul from them. They dragged me out into the open. And took me in, into the heart of the Fane. Where nothing human had been since it was built, millennia past.'

He drew in a rough breath.

'Decans like The Spagyrus, that deal with humankind from time to time, become corrupt, become a little like us.'

Hot moist air pressed close. Muffled echoes came from some unidentifiable direction. Bones rattled and scuffled in the storm-flood piles of brushwood. Zar-bettu-zekigal's head rose with a jerk as the bright oil-lamp flickered.

'What else?'

'The noise. The *noise*. Agony. Torn flesh. Torn souls. Yes, the soul can be hurt.' He laughed: painful, embarrassed. 'Don't listen to me. I was afraid of nothing before that, and now I'm afraid of almost everything. The powers that are in there aren't corrupt with humanity. They're the Thirty-Six Decans, the Celestial Powers of hell, and they live on this earth, and we *build* for them!'

Zari turned towards him, cocked her head to one side, and stared into his eyes.

Flake said: 'Eyes that have seen the heart of the Fane are afterwards changed.'

Something in her body's stiffness cautioned him. He braced himself for her next words.

'See you, if it was me, I wouldn't make up stories about having been in the Fane to account for it.'

His heart beat once, with a white pain. Very still, he said: 'Stories?'

'Aw, Messire Falke! Go into the *heart* of the Fane? No one ever has. You'd be squished like a bug.' Her dark eyes momentarily reflected storm-light. 'Or else you'd be lunch.'

Zar-bettu-zekigal stood up. The hem of her dress brushed his face, and Falke caught a scent of dry grass and sweat; and he reached up and knotted a corner of the cloth in his fist.

'I don't like to be called a liar, girl!'

'Or a coward?' One freckle-backed hand ruffled his hair. He raised his head. Her white face and black hair stood out against black and silver roses. The brambles that trailed down across the air passed harmlessly through her arm and shoulder; and she stretched up, as if she would grasp them, arcing her back and tail.

'If I've worked it out, then messire will have, too. He probably even knows why you tell stories. If it isn't just vanity.'

She dropped down to squat on her haunches before him.

'Ei! I bet it impresses people, though. If they're gullible enough. Hello, messire, find anything?'

Plessiez stepped silently out of the gloom.

'More of the same. The lamps in that direction have less oil. Where's Charnay?'

'Fallen into the canal?' the Katayan suggested.

'Oh, I hardly think so. Strategy and tactics may be beyond her, but at feats of strength she's . . .' Plessiez's voice trailed away.

Falke stood. A pounding fear filled his head, discovery and shock mingling; and his fingers fumbled as he began to fit his arms into the sleeves of the young woman's greatcoat, cold despite the moist heat. Grunts and snarls came from the far darkness of the quay.

Zar-bettu-zekigal hopped from one bare foot to the other.

'Oh, see you, *look* at that!'

Falke's dilated eyes searched the darkness beyond the lamps, first to find the approaching figure of Charnay.

For the first time, he smiled.

The brown Rat leaned forward as she walked, gripping a rope that ran taut over her shoulder, muscles straining under her brown fur. Ripples spread out from the water at the edge of the quay, following her, slopping thickly onto the brickwork. The Rat grunted. She planted both her feet squarely on the slippery quay, and heaved at the rope and the heavy object to which it was attached.

'Hell damn it!' Falke said. 'It's a boat.'

Lucas swung around as the carriage rattled under the arch, into the palace courtyard. He slid back on to his seat. The Rats in guard uniform took as little notice of him as they had when he had walked past them the day before, filthy with disguise.

He looked up at the white walls, the windows and the blue-tiled turrets and spires, an odd smile appearing on his face.

'So this is their idea of a palace . . . You're a stubborn man, Lucas.' Casaubon rested his bolster-arms across the back of the facing seat, turning his face up to the white sunlight.

His pink frock-coat fell open across his immense chest. Yellow sweat-rings marked his unlaced linen shirt, under the arms; and he scratched at the fine copper hairs on his chest with pudgy fingers. He leaned forward as the carriages halted in the courtyard, resting a forearm on his spreading thigh.

'Have you ever heard of the Invisible College?'

Lucas shook his head. 'Nothing to do with the University of Crime?'

'Oh, hardly, hardly.'

At the far side of the yard, another archway opened through to two successive courtyards, each surrounded by four- or five-storey blocks. The afternoon sun blazed back from white walls. Lithe black Rats in blue uniform jackets and plumes stood by every door opening into the yard, some carrying pikes and some rapiers. Heads turned as Casaubon's carriage drew up in a spray of gravel, followed by three loaded-down baggage-carts.

'I must go. I'm wasting your time and mine,' Lucas observed. 'I'll go back to the airfield. I might be missing the person I *am* meant to meet.'

The copper-haired man's head came down, chin resting in rolls of fat. His bright blue eyes met Lucas's. Lucas judged him somewhere in his late thirties or early forties.

'Time was when everyone recognised the golden bee,' Casaubon said, 'which, I suppose, is why they stopped using it.'

He reached out an imperious palm. Lucas reluctantly dropped the metal bee onto it. Gold sparked in the sun, almost lost in the folds of Casaubon's hand.

The big man closed his palm. His eyes squeezed shut in immense concentration, vanishing into palely freckled cheeks. Lucas leaned forward anxiously, pointing at the approaching guards.

'They—'

'There!'

Casaubon opened his hand. A live bee, wings translucent and body black-and-brown-furred, flicked into the air and flew drunkenly off across the crowded yard.

'How did you . . . ? Then, you *are*—?'

'Can I help you, messire?' a uniformed black Rat enquired, strolling to stand beside the open carriage. Her hand was not far from her rapier-hilt.

'Yes. Find me whoever's in charge.'

The big man reached across with one ham-hand to push open the carriage door. He eased one thigh forward, then the other, and dropped to the ground with a grunt. The carriage rocked on its

'Time was when everyone recognised the golden bee.' From *Summum Bonum*, Part IV,
Robert Fludd, 1629. The inscription translates: 'The rose gives honey to the bees.'

springs. Casaubon picked thoughtfully at his nose, gazing up at the windows.

'What the hell am I supposed to do now?' Lucas slid down to stand on the gravel beside him. 'I was in a dungeon here yesterday.'

'You do lead an eventful life, young Lucas.'

Casaubon hitched up his white silk breeches, fumbling to do up the top two buttons and abandoning the unequal struggle.

'But—'

A black Rat emerged from an arched stone doorway close by, slitting his eyes against the sunlight. His clawed hind feet scraped the stone steps as he strode down into the courtyard.

'Are you the architect?' he called.

He stood a head taller than Lucas: lean, heavy-shouldered and scarred. A blue sleeveless doublet came down to his haunches, so that it looked as though he wore black breeches; and a blue plume jutted from his headband. A basket-hilted rapier swung at his side.

'Are *all* these carriages yours?'

The copper-haired man felt inside his satin coat, dipping into voluminous pockets. A waft of garlic and dirty linen hit Lucas. Casaubon frowned, and turned down one of his great embroidered cuffs. He beamed, taking out a heavy black wax seal on a ribbon; and grunted with effort as he put it around his neck.

'Casaubon,' he announced, as the black Rat's tail began to twitch. 'Baltazar Casaubon, Lord-Architect, Knight of the Rose Castle, Archemaster, Garden-Surveyor—'

'You *are* the architect,' the black Rat interrupted. 'Good. My name is Desaguliers. Come with me. I'll show you what you have to do. How soon can you start work?'

Casaubon frowned, and looked as though he might be about to recite further titles in spite of the interruption. Instead he broke into a smile, clapped Lucas firmly on the back, and added: 'Master Desaguliers, this is Lucas – my page.'

The courtyard was crowded despite the heat, Rats and some humans passing through on business; and two or three of the guards stopped to exchange a word with Desaguliers. The black Rat turned back to Casaubon, and said briefly: 'Follow me.'

Lucas, rubbing his bruised shoulder, fell in behind the immense expanse of pink satin that was Casaubon's back. He glared at it as they walked into a cool white entrance-hall, neatly stacked on either side with firewood, and continued to fume as they followed the Rat into the spiral stone staircase jutting up through the centre of the building.

The big man slowed on the stairs, stomping up step by step,

pausing to peer through the slot-windows cut in either wall. One side looked out into rooms; the other on to the other side of the stone double-spiral. Lucas dropped back a pace.

'I'm not your page!'

Casaubon said tranquilly: 'I know that.'

'Tell me how you did that, with the bee.'

'Tell me who gave it to you.'

The lean black Rat waited for them on the third floor. He strode across the tiles, between gilded-plaster walls, to where leaded casements blurred the afternoon sunlight. Reaching to swing one window fully open, he said: 'His Majesty wishes you to design him a garden. Here.'

Casaubon paused at the exit from the stairs. His cheeks and neck glowed pink, and he pulled out a filthy brown square of cloth and wiped sweat from his face and neck.

'I trust there is some challenge involved.'

Lucas followed him across to the window. It overlooked the eastern side of the palace. Black shadows of roofs, gables, oriel windows and tiled turrets fell on acres of rubble. Broken masonry, splintered glass and white dust ran out as far as the curtain-wall, two hundred yards distant.

'A wing of the palace has been demolished for the purpose,' Desaguliers observed.

The Lord-Architect said weakly: 'What *sort* of a garden does his Majesty want, exactly?'

The black Rat leaned up against the window-frame, arms folded. Sardonic, he said: 'Does it matter? You'll be paid.'

'It does matter! For one thing, I must know the intended function. Is it a Memory Garden, or merely illustrative of certain mythological and philosophical devices? Should it invigorate or relax? Does his Majesty wish to be entertained or spiritually instructed?'

Casaubon rested plump hands on the window-sill. Lucas, behind him, noted how one scuff-shoed foot scratched at his opposite calf, leaving marks on the silk stocking.

'I must know,' the Lord-Architect persisted.

Smoothly diplomatic, Lucas ventured to say: 'That can be discussed at the proper time, surely . . . my lord?'

Desaguliers spoke over him. 'You're familiar with garden machinery, Lord-Architect? Automata, water-organs, mechanical dials? His Majesty especially requires facility with machines.'

'Of course.' The big man sounded hurt. 'I think I should speak to the King, Master Desaguliers.'

He turned away from the window, resting his hand on Lucas's shoulder. 'My boy here will find me lodgings in the city. I prefer not to live where I work. Lucas, see to the unloading of the carts. Any box or chest marked with red chalk stays here; anything marked with blue chalk goes to my lodgings; anything unmarked you may return to the airfield, on the grounds that it isn't mine. Pay the men off.'

The black Rat seemed to notice Lucas for the first time. As he strode off, beckoning Casaubon to follow, he remarked: 'Boy, you do *know* where to find his Majesty's guest lodgings?'

'Yes, messire.'

Lucas looked up at the big man, meeting shrewd blue eyes. The Lord-Architect's mouth twitched, and a smile creased its way across his features.

'I do know where there's a room to let,' Lucas said hurriedly. 'I wish I didn't know why. The girl who lives there won't be coming back. I'll speak to Mistress Evelian and return here. There's one thing you ought to know.'

Casaubon, complicit in the necessity of their further meeting, raised a copper-coloured eyebrow. 'And that is?'

'I've heard of Desaguliers. Most people here have. He's a strange person to have developed a taste for gardening. Desaguliers is Captain of the King's Guard.'

A boat wallowed under vaulting brick roofs.

One oil-lantern, tied at the stern, shed illumination on a seated black Rat. His ringed right hand grasped the tiller. The other lay at rest on his stained scarlet jacket. Beside him, curled up with her spine against the warm fur of his flank, a young woman slept.

The other lantern, in the prow, reflected light back from oily water. A brown Rat drove a pole into the pitch blackness, strongly thrusting the boat forward; matched by the pale-haired man in black, poling on the boat's other side.

Zar-bettu-zekigal stretched, eyes still shut. Her pale nostrils flared. She opened her eyes, sat up, and leaned over the side of the boat to spit.

'Pah! The *stink*!'

'It fails to improve,' the black Rat observed gravely.

Zari grinned. One hand and dappled tail extended for balance, she stood up in the boat. She scratched at her dishevelled hair. 'Is it tomorrow yet, messire?'

Falke, as the sweep of the pole brought him round to face her, said: 'Your friend Charnay thinks it's night outside. I say it must be day again.'

Zari leaned over the stern, peering down into clotted liquid. 'We can eat fish. If we can catch them. If there are any.'

'If we have no objecton to poisoning ourselves.' Plessiez called towards the prow: 'Are we still following the lamps? Is there any other sign of occupation?'

Charnay wiped a hand over her translucent ears, and straightened up from the pole. 'You mean there are people down here?'

'I see no reason why there shouldn't be.' Plessiez leaned over, searching for some trace of the salty current. He sat back, remarking: 'After all, as our great poet once said, "There be land thieves and sea thieves, that is, land Rats and Py-Rats" . . .'

Charnay looked blank.

'Py-rates,' Plessiez enunciated clearly. 'Pirates. Pi . . . Charnay, education is wasted on you.'

'You're probably right, messire,' she said humbly. 'I think it's getting lighter up ahead, messire.'

'Where?'

'Ei! It *is*!' Zari scrambled over the planks, dipping a hand to catch the wildly rocking side of the boat, and flung herself down on her knees in the prow. Leaning out over the stinking water, she stared ahead.

'Falke – come *here*! Is that light? There?'

The black-clad man squatted down, following her gaze; shading his dilated eyes from the oil-lamps. He stood up. Charnay took her wooden pole and drove it into the mud simultaneously with his. The boat began to wallow forward.

Zari stuffed one sleeve of her greatcoat across her mouth and nose. She knelt up in the prow, intense gaze fixed on reflections in black water.

'*Ei, shit!*'

Light blazed. Zari fell back against Charnay. The brown Rat cursed. Eyes watering in an actinic glare, she took in one image of a vast brick cavern, quays on three sides ahead, tunnel-entrances; all weltering in sludge and nitre, and people; crowds of men and women.

With a noise like hail on corrugated iron, a metal-mesh net winched up out of the canal behind the boat. It rose rapidly, blocking the only exit.

'Shit!' Zar-bettu-zekigal pitched forward as the boat rammed, head-first over the side on to the quay.

Feet rushed towards her. A hand thrust her down. The torn-silk sound of a rapier drawn from its scabbard sounded above her. She sat up. Falke leaped for the dock. He swung the iron-tipped boathook up two-handed in a broadsword grip.

Tatterdemalion men and women ran down the quay, yelling. She saw ragged banners, raised sticks, swords; a woman screaming, a man leaping to avoid fallen rubble, and the white blaze of light began to fade. Yellow torchlight leaped.

'Stop—'

Zari ignored the voice, pushing herself upright, brick cobbles hard first under her knees and then under her bare feet.

'Guard yourself, messire!'

Charnay thrust coolly, sending her rapier into the shoulder of a man in ragged blue. Her brown fur shone in the torchlight. Bright-eyed, showing yellow teeth in a grin, she vaulted the quay steps and drove a group of men down the dock.

'*Stop—*'

Falke's iron-hooked staff cracked down on the cobbles. Zari swung round. The boat drifted, empty, three paces out into filthy water. The boathook darted out, struck: a woman's face twisted in pain and a sword hit the ground.

'*Messire?*'

Zari fell forward. Something splashed into the canal behind her. A tall man in green met her eyes, grinned, swung up an axe into a two-handed grip. She crouched, snapping her left hand and tail, circling left, watching his stubbled face for distraction; scooped up a stone right-handed and skimmed it.

The man dropped the axe and clapped both hands to his face. Blood blossomed from his eye.

Her heel caught the shallow step leading up from the quay. She sat down abruptly. Plessiez shouted. The black Rat's rapier darted, his left arm wrapped in the scarlet cloak, feinting; he backed up against the edge of the quay, driven by three or four men.

'*Stop!*'

Yellow torches wavered.

Zar-bettu-zekigal put both hands over her mouth, muffling her suddenly audible breathing.

Slowly, eyes on the tattered men and women, she got to her feet. The sump (one canal and six tunnels opening into this great chamber) breathed a fetid quiet.

Heaps of black ash along the quays marked where flares had burned out. Men and women stood around the canal-end, tar-burning torches raised, the light falling on to black brick vaults, on to oily water and the metal net swaying from its winches. Most of the crowds carried swords, staves, banners. She let her eyes travel across them, tense, searching for whoever had shouted.

'Stop fighting and we won't kill you,' a man in red called from a tunnel-entrance. Five or six voices immediately added, '*Yet*,' and there was a rumble of amusement.

Zar-bettu-zekigal, slowly, hands held out from her sides, walked down to rejoin Falke and the Rats at the canal's edge. The white-haired man rested on his staff, free hand shading his eyes that ran with tears in the torch-glare. Plessiez muttered to Charnay. She reluctantly lowered her rapier-point to the ground. The crowd grew minute by minute, pressing closer around them.

Abruptly banners at the back of the crowd jerked and moved aside. The tattered men and women fell back as a litter came through the crowd, carried by six men in ragged back clothing and remnants of unpolished armour.

'They're all human,' Zari muttered, not taking her eyes off the approaching litter.

'They are all pale,' the black Rat said, his tone thoughtful, although his chest heaved under the sword-harness. 'I think it some time since any one of them saw sunlight. Honour to you!'

The partly armoured men set down the litter on its stilts, jolting on the brick quay. It was large, swathed in water-stained red curtains; and from an elongated corner-pole a banner painted with a sun hung in rags.

Plessiez bowed elegantly to the invisible occupant.

Zari stepped back as two men pushed forward with a carved oak chair. They set it down on the cobbles. A woman in armour shoved herself out of the litter, inch by strenuous inch, thumping the scabbard of a long sword down on the quayside, and using it as a support.

'Next person who doesn't *stop* I'll gut. That goes for you, Clovis. What have you found me?'

She stumbled in three great strides to the chair, sitting with a clash of armour, and waved away all offer of assistance. As she slumped back into the cushioned chair, two men came to kneel at either side of it.

The thin blond man at her left said: 'They came so close that we had to decoy them in.'

Her torn shirt and breeches were dark red, blood-red in torch-light; and vambraces gleamed on her forearms, greaves on her calves. Plate armour covered her torso; and she reached up and pulled off a horned laminated helmet, and shook her head, short greasy hair flying.

'Find out how they got here and then kill them.'

Zar-bettu-zekigal, hands in pockets, swirled the skirts of her greatcoat about her, and stepped forward. Eyes glowing, she stood and gazed – at the woman's dirty sardonic face: the high cheek-bones, nondescript hair, the beginnings of crow's-feet.

Speaking over Plessiez's protest, and the armoured woman's next words, the Katayan said: 'Who *are* you?'

Silence. Two women with raised swords hesitated, looking to the armoured woman, whose slanting red-brown eyes narrowed. A frown indented lines on her forehead. She hitched herself forward in the chair, and Zar-bettu-zekigal smiled, dazed, dizzy with the fear that never touched her in the preceding quarter-hour.

'Who-are-you yourself,' the woman said laconically. 'I'm called The Hyena. I rule the human Imperial dynasty – what there is left of it.'

Dust rose up, yellowing the sills and steps all down Carver Street. Two carts rumbled past men and women (some in satin, some in rough cloth) who swore at the coating of flour-thin dust. Casaubon leaned back mountainously in the first carriage-seat and beamed at Lucas.

'Comfortable lodgings, I hope . . . ?'

Three harsh clangs drowned out his voice. Clock-mill struck the hour, its gold-and-blue dials revolving a notch; sun, moon and stars shifting to new configurations.

A great-maned lion rolled jerkily round on one set of rails, gilt flashing in the afternoon sun; passing a sleek silver hound on the other rail. From somewhere deep in the tower's mechanism, a mechanical *vox animalis* roared.

Casaubon sat up. 'An early Salomon de Caus—'

Lucas, muscles aching from getting from the palace to Carver Street and back again (by way of the Embassy Compound) to pick up the Lord-Architect, wiped his forehead and loosened the lacing of his thin shirt.

'Mistress Evelian should have the rooms cleared out,' he announced.

Casaubon winced as the carriage jolted to a halt. One of the drivers dismounted to see to the oxen, the second stepped down to put blocks under the wheels. Lucas beckoned one of the men.

'This load goes up to the first floor – through the street-door, there.' He slid down to the street, and glanced back up at the fat man. 'The person I mentioned, the White Crow . . . may not necessarily want to see you.'

Casaubon scratched at his crotch with plump fingers, still gazing up at the great dial of Clock-mill.

'Who knows?'

'Well . . . I'll make enquiries first.'

He left the big man gazing up at the clock, while the crates and chests and boxes were dumped on the cobbles beside him. The passage into the courtyard felt cool after the sun's heat, and he came out of the shadow blinking at the light beyond.

White sun warmed the wood-friezes: skulls, shovels and bones. He began to walk across to the far steps, towards the White Crow's rooms. Out of the tail of his eye, he caught a glint of red under the trees.

'Have . . . ?'

Lucas's voice dried up. A small square of brown grass under the cherry trees was the courtyard's only garden. Cinnamon-red hair tangled the sun in spidersilk fineness. The woman rested her head on her bare arms, gold lashes closed; and her white almost-freckled back and hips and thighs shone in the dappled shade. Her feet were a little apart, the cleft of her buttocks shadowed.

'Mmhhrm?'

The White Crow rolled lazily on to her back, one hand reaching for the spectacles that lay beside her, on the open pages of a handwritten grimoire. As she turned on to her back, Lucas saw her flattened breasts stippled with the imprint of grass, her dark aureoles, and the curled red-gold of her pubic hair. She pushed the spectacles on to her nose and raised her head without lifting her shoulders, momentarily double-chinned.

'You're not Mistress Evelian.'

'No.' Lucas shut his mouth on a croak.

Without any haste, the White Crow began to feel about for her cotton shirt, after some moments tugging it down from a cherry-branch and sliding the sun-warm fabric over her shoulders.

'Who were you looking for?' She eased her hips up to pull on thin cotton knee-breeches.

Her tawny eyes met his, and Lucas blushed sweaty red. He glanced up at the black-and-white half-timbered frontages and the blue sky beyond; and then couldn't help but drop his gaze back to her. The White Crow knelt up, tucking her shirt into her knee-breeches.

'I hear we have a new tenant. Know anything about that?'

'Very little.' He forced self-possession. 'And it isn't for want of looking in my uncle's confidential files, either. Have you ever heard of something called the Invisible College?'

The cinnamon-haired woman froze, one hand at her breeches waistband: her lips parted. Simultaneously Lucas heard Casaubon's heavy tread in the passage.

'I haven't said anything about you,' Lucas added hurriedly.

Casaubon stepped out into the sunlight. It glinted off his greasy copper hair, showed every stain and sweat-mark on his linen and satin coat.

Lucas turned back to the White Crow, one reassuring hand held out. 'He—'

'*Valentine!*'

Lucas spun round, deafened by the stentorian bellow.

The big man crossed the courtyard in half a dozen rapid strides, the cobbles shaking to his tread. The skirts of his pink coat flew wide. His shirt had fallen open, copper hairs glinting across the fleshy bulk of his chest; one silk stocking hung out of its garter. A great beam spread across his face.

'Valentine!' he cried happily.

The woman stood frozen, white-faced. His massive arms went forward, his hands seized her under the ribs; he grunted with joy and swung her up, lifting her, tossing her up as if she were a small child. In a flurry of hair and shirt-tail and flailing arms, she soared skyward, six or seven feet above the cobbles – fell back and was swept into a massive hug, bare feet never brushing the ground.

'Valentine!'

'*Put me down!*'

Lucas snapped out of his astonishment and strode forward. 'Put her down – you heard her!'

Casaubon's grip loosened. The woman slid down, tiptoe on the cobbles; and he flung his arms round her again, pressing her nose into his sternum, grinning generously, laughing with unbelief. Looking down over the mountainous chins and the swell of his belly, he gripped her chin in his hand and bent down and kissed her, smackingly enthusiastic.

'*Will* you' – she elbowed room, and punched him smartly in the stomach – 'put me *down*?'

'It's you.' Amazement blazoned itself across his face. 'It's wonderful!'

'Casaubon!'

He loosened his embrace, still smiling happily. Lucas halted. Poised on the edge of violence or violent embarrassment, he looked to the White Crow for help.

She put tumbled red hair back from her face with hands that shook. Frowning disbelief, she shook her head, eyes for no one but the big man; and suddenly clenched her fists and rested them against her lips, still staring at him.

Lucas, bewildered, said: 'But this is the White Crow . . .'

Casaubon's china-blue eyes filled with water. Tears overflowed, runnelling the dirt down his fat cheeks. He laughed, shook his head, laughed again.

'This is Master-Captain Valentine. This is a Scholar-Soldier, Valentine of the Invisible College.'

'*Not any more!*'

As if suddenly aware that she still stood within his embrace, the woman stepped back. A bare heel skidded on the dry grass; she caught her balance, one protesting hand stretched out against the fat man's movement to help.

'Don't!'

Casaubon clapped vast hands together, and then spread his arms expansively. 'Wonderful!'

Lucas reached out and closed, first, his right and (since it could not enclose the girth) then his left hand around Casaubon's wrist. Tensing muscles that had heaved the Lord-Architect's crates from an ox-cart, digging in his heels, he pulled the big man around in his tracks.

'Leave her alone.'

Casaubon blinked, blue eyes bright in his big, faintly freckled face. He scratched at his copper hair with his free hand, and looked down at Lucas; and suddenly swung his other hand around and clapped him on the shoulder, knocking Lucas six inches sideways.

'I've *found* her,' he beamed. 'It's wonderful.'

'She doesn't think so.'

Lucas felt muscles tense under his hands, in the hard fat that sleeved the man's wrist. He gripped more tightly, but the girth forced his fingers open. Lucas stepped back, seeing the red mark of his grip on the man's fair skin.

Casaubon, with no apparent resentment, remarked: 'Wonderful!'

'*Will you stop saying that?*'

Blind exasperation edged the White Crow's tone. Her arms fell to her sides, hands still clenched into fists. The sun through the leaves stippled her face with gold and shadow, and as she stepped out into the exposed courtyard her hair and linen blazed copper and white.

'I don't want you here!'

A stale scent of cooking wafted across the courtyard. Lucas heard Evelian's voice, singing, from one of the open casements; and panic stabbed through him, thinking that she or anyone might come outside.

' "Valentine" isn't a name on your file,' he protested.

The woman squinted at him briefly, lines webbing the corners of her eyes; her gaze hard now with a professional calculation. Lucas's heart thudded into his throat, and without any pride he said: '*Don't.*'

She took another step forward, glaring up at the fat man.

'Get out!'

Casaubon still smiled. He shrugged, massive weights of flesh shifting with his shoulders.

'I'll go.'

The gold-braid-edged skirts of his satin coat swirled as he turned. Lucas, bile and jealousy burning his gut, stared after the man as he strode ponderously towards the passage's archway.

The White Crow stared irresolutely at his retreating back. One hand went up to smooth her tumbled hair, straighten her spectacles – as Lucas was about to open his mouth, protest support and loyalty, she snatched off her gold-wire spectacles, gripping them in a fist.

'Where have you come from?' She raised her voice. 'Where have you been?'

Casaubon continued to walk away. The courtyard's quiet, born of sun and distant voices and the scent of dry grass, sifted down like dust.

'What the hell do you mean by just turning up!'

Lucas saw her fist tighten: gold-wire frames twisted. She stamped past him, flinched, reached out a hand to grip his shoulder and brush a stone from her bare sole.

'Damn you! Do *you* know what's gone wrong in this city?'

Lucas's dry mouth silenced him. He felt her warm hand; gazed at her profile, fine-textured skin, and darker freckles on her ears. Her long-lashed eyes fixed on Casaubon's departing back.

'And what *about* the College?'

Almost gone now, his scuffed shoe entering the shadow of the passageway that ran under Evelian's rooms.

'I used blood on the moon—'

She stepped past Lucas, ignoring his exclamation.

'—Are you the answer to my message?'

The shadow-line of the building slid down Casaubon's back, pink satin turning strawberry in the archway's dimness.

'*Casaubon!*'

The big man stopped and looked over his shoulder, a profile of forehead, nose, delicate lips; chins; belly swelling like a ship's sail.

'You want me to stay, then?'

'*Shit!*'

The White Crow stomped back past Lucas, stooped to pick up the grimoire from the grass, shut it with a clap that echoed flatly back from the courtyard walls, and stalked across the yard and up the wooden steps.

The outer door slammed violently behind her: a second later the inner room's door crashed to.

Lucas started as Casaubon's arm fell across his shoulders, greasy, massive, delicately light. He looked up. Orange-gold hair glinted, falling over a forehead where freckles were hardly visible under dirt.

The fat man glanced down at Lucas, beaming beatifically.

'She wants me to stay.'

Spiritual corruption crackled in the air. It tanged dry as fear in Plessiez's mouth. The black Rat priest's hand moved to the looped cross at his breast.

'I'll take that.'

The Hyena snatched the silver *ankh* from Plessiez's neck. He spun round, slender dark fingers reaching for the rapier that was no longer at his side; wincing as the chain cut fur and flesh.

The woman threw the jewelled chain carelessly away. 'A rich priest! How unusual . . .'

Plessiez shuddered, hardly aware of her sarcasm. Chains clanked above his head. All around the vast walls of the cavern, broken metal beams jutted out. From each beam hung chains, and in the chains hung corpses. Some showed bone and dried sinew only. The one above him was fresher.

'Messire,' Charnay leaned down to mutter. 'You're not afraid?'

Plessiez suppressed a shiver, fur hackling with horror and satisfaction.

Here, raw brick edges showed how a dozen sewer-chambers had been knocked into one, many-ledged and on multiple levels. Ragged sun-banners hung everywhere. Flames licked the soot-stained walls. They burned in apparently empty ram's-horns and wide dishes. Niches and ledges higher up gleamed with the spectral light of roses.

'The sheer power . . .' Plessiez breathed, for once unguarded. 'Digging bones from crypts is well enough, but *this* . . . The Order should – I should have discovered this before now!'

Ragged men and women crouched around individual fires, between heaps of rubbish. Sullen, they watched. Ordure stank underfoot; the smells of decay and cooked meat choked the air.

Plessiez, unarmed, black eyes bright, took busy steps back and forth, peering at how woodlice and centipedes swarmed over the heaps of rubbish, active in the humidity. The delicate skulls of herons, mounted on poles, rustled with a ghost of feathers and air.

'Now, messire,' Charnay warned, 'your Order's plans are very pleasant in a tavern of a summer evening, but this is serious. Let me break some heads. We don't need swords to get out of here; they're a poor lot!'

'No!' Plessiez shook his head violently. 'Do nothing before I tell you. Think, for once in your life! What better place to raise plague-*magia* than *here*? Let the Cardinal-General weep; I'll be head of the Order before I'm much older.'

The walls sweated a dark nitre that stank of blood.

The brown Rat put her hand on his arm. 'Plessiez, we're old friends. Sometimes you're an ambitious *fool*.'

Furious, he swung round, and then lost his balance on the filth-choked earth as the young Katayan woman pushed him to one side. The thick light that swam in metal bowls shone on her dirty face and on her fever-bright eyes.

'Feed us!' She gazed up at the Hyena, hands still in greatcoat pockets, with a grin that might have been confidence or agony. 'Two days we've been lost. You brought us here. *Feed* us!'

The armoured woman leaned weight on her scabbarded long sword, all the metal glistering dully in the light. She spat. A globule of spittle hit the earth-choked brick paving by Plessiez's feet. It moved. It scuttled, and he set his heel on it, grinding the aborted by-product of *magia* into the earth.

She said: 'Won't waste food on you. You wouldn't have time to shit it out again before we killed you. *Clovis!*'

The blond man ran to kneel before her. She spoke rapidly to him.

Plessiez watched the men and women of the Imperial dynasty sleeping, eating and arguing in the shadows of gallows; never glancing up.

Wiry arms flung themselves around him. He swore, bit the words back. Zar-bettu-zekigal hugged, pressing the sword-harness painfully into his fur, resting the top of her head against his chest.

'Eeee!' The Katayan kicked a bare foot against the ground, and looked up with glowing eyes. 'She's *won*derful!'

'Damn you, Zaribet!' Plessiez's pulse jolted. 'Hell damn you, you little idiot!'

The Katayan beamed uncomprehendingly. 'I must be mad. She isn't a day over twenty-five; she's a *baby*. Mistress Evelian's all woman. This one's flat as a yard of tap-water . . .'

Exasperation sharpened his voice as Plessiez gathered his shaken self-possession. 'I grant you, if she were about to kill us, she would have done it immediately. *However—*'

The Hyena's voice cut across his.

'How long is it since we last caught someone down here?'

She reached up with her free hand, skin filthy in the yellow light, and jangled the gallows chains high above Plessiez's head. The stink of rot drenched the air. He coughed.

Something unidentifiable in the shadows fell from the gallows, hitting the earth with a squashy thud.

'About a month,' she judged.

Plessiez swallowed hard. Falke's shoulder shoved him back as the white-haired man pushed forward. He snarled at the armoured woman: 'Scare *me*, "Lady" Hyena. Try. These eyes have seen the heart of the Fane. Nothing *human* is going to make me afraid.' He dropped the hand that shaded his eyes, staring at the woman with pit-velvet pupils.

'Clovis!'

The armoured woman snapped her fingers. Two men in half-armour heaved a wooden block across and slammed it down at the Hyena's feet. The taller of the two drew a thin curved sword; light dripped along the edge of the blade. The other grabbed Falke's arms, twisting them up behind his back, and dragged him sprawling half across the block.

Plessiez narrowed his eyes to furry slits. He met the Hyena's gaze, and said softly and clearly:

'Honour to you.'

She stared, shook her head and made a bitter sound. 'To me? Messire priest, if I had any honour left, why would we be down here?'

Men and women mostly between the years of fifteen and forty watched, faces sullen. Plessiez ignored them, ignored Falke.

'These are offal, and you know it,' he said clearly. 'Since you're not blind or deaf, you can hardly mistake them for anything else. I'm not concerned with them.'

She limped, armour clashing, until her face came within an inch of his. He smelled blood; ghostly in the air about her. 'What can we humans *be* but your servants or your whores? You starve us and use us. What can we do? Leave the city? *No.* Carry a sword, and defend ourselves when you kick us in the streets? *No.* Carry *money*, even? No!'

She scowled, black brows dipping; and a strand of lank hair lodged across her cheek, as her head moved with passionate anger.

'Work our guts out and then die while you sleep on silk; and even when we die we're not free of the city!'

Plessiez smoothed his fur with fingers that trembled.

' "We"?' he said delicately.

The Hyena struck backhanded without looking, and the nearer man let Falke pull free of his grip. The white-haired man stared up from under tear-dazzled lashes at the gallows.

'We,' she said, wiping the hair away from her face. Her hectoring tone gave way to puzzled suspicion. 'Yes, and you, too – the Decans are your masters.'

Plessiez nodded.

'Honour to you,' he repeated. 'People who are going to kill do it quite utilitarianly. A knife between two neck-vertebrae is efficient. Charnay will not admit it, I think, but I believe that humans may have a soldier's honour.'

Charnay straightened, tail lashing. 'Imperial horseshit! I don't care if they have stolen swords from somewhere; they're a rabble.'

Plessiez very carefully caught the armoured woman's eye, letting a little humorous resignation show. After a long moment, the Hyena's mouth moved in a smile.

'A priest, a King's Guard, a Master Builder and' – her red-brown eyes moved to Zar-bettu-zekigal – 'something from half the world away . . . It would be a shame to lose a ransom. I'll kill you after I've let you prove to your masters that you're alive. Then you won't tell them where to find us.'

Plessiez smoothed down his fur again, shooting a brief humorous glance at her; sure of himself now, and ebullient.

'I'll pay you more than a ransom,' he said. 'I'll pay you a King's ransom that his Majesty is far too mean to give. Your people go under the city, don't they? Under the whole city? Let's talk. You can do something for me, and I can do much for you.'

'If you Rat-Lords kill each other, that's good, but it doesn't help us.'

'I belong to an Order within the Church,' Plessiez enunciated carefully, aware of knife-edge balance, 'and I fear, madam, that we have too short a time for me to retell thirty years of their history; but suffice it that we're not interested in factions at the court of his Majesty the King. Shall I say we're concerned with the city's strange masters?'

'The *Decans*?'

The woman glanced round, gripped the litter's pole with a gauntleted hand and slumped down to sit. She looked up at Plessiez from among ordure-stained drapes and cushions.

'A mad priest. We've found ourselves a mad priest. You'd fight god, would you? *Stupid* – and more fool me for listening.'

Plessiez let the chill humidity of the cavern sink in; the devil-light and the little hauntings. He took the risk quite deliberately.

'Fifty years ago the plague wiped out a third of the population. It didn't touch the Fane. Why should it? It only killed bodies. Since then the organisation within the Church to which I belong has been studying *magia*.'

Falke hauled himself up by Charnay's helping hand, shading his eyes that were intent on Plessiez.

'Plagues may exist in flesh, in base matter, and bring bodies to death. And, we discover, there are other pestilences that may be achieved, plagues of the spirit and the soul.' His long fingers searched the fur of his breast for the missing *ankh*. 'And there are plagues that can be brought into existence only by acts of *magia*. They bring their own analogue of death – to such as our masters, the Thirty-Six Lords of Heaven and Hell: the Decans.'

The woman took hold of the ragged sun-banner hanging from the litter-pole. '*Death?* Theirs?'

'To the Divine? No. Naturally not. Lady, what we can and must do is make Them sicken, so that They abandon Their incarnations in flesh and remove to that Celestial sphere that is Their proper habitation, leaving' – his tone sharpened – 'the world to us.'

The Hyena, without any sign of hearing Plessiez, looked past him to the young Katayan woman. 'You – what are you?'

Zar-bettu-zekigal scratched her ear with the tip of her tail.

'A Kings' Memory?' she offered.

The woman stood, tossed her lobster-tail helmet underarm: Zari caught it in both hands, and the Hyena took firm hold of her shoulder and drew the Katayan aside.

'You've been with the priest; you tell me what you've heard.'

Plessiez straightened his shoulders, sanguine in the haunting-light for all his ruffled fur. His brilliant eyes darted, missing nothing: the two women, dark-haired and dirty, almost twins, standing by poles decorated with the shifting-eyed skulls of cranes.

The older and taller bent her head, listening. The younger stood with eyes half-shut, in the concentration of Memory, the speech of Masons' Hall unrolling in smooth sequence. Plessiez narrowed his eyes, translucent ears swivelling; stood still, and listened.

'Vitruvius writes . . .'

Casaubon sprawled back in the sagging armchair, legs planted widely apart, a book held at a distance in his free hand. He bit into a

gravy-soaked hunk of bread, chewed, and put the remainder of the
bread down on the expanse of his spread thigh. Dark liquid blotted
the silk.

'In *The Ten Books of Architecture*, writes of . . .' He squinted, licked
a gravy-stained digit and thumbed ponderously through the pages.
' *"Hegetor's Tortoise: A Siege-Engine."* *"The Ballista."* Catapults, crossbows; *"The Automata of Warfare"* . . . Military engineering. Hardly
what I'm *used* to, but I can do it.'

'Casaubon!'

The White Crow smacked the side of his head. Lucas seethed as
she pulled out the tail of her shirt, grabbed first one and then the
other of the Lord-Architect's plump hands, and wiped each relat-
ively clean.

'Master Desaguliers has put a factory production-line at my
disposal.' He sucked a finger clean. 'And the King offers me ample
funds.'

'The King's as interested in military engineering as Desaguliers?'
The White Crow picked up her glass of red wine again. She left her
shirt-tail hanging out.

'His Majesty are interesting people,' Casaubon remarked.

'Why don't you go back to your rooms and your books,' she
enquired pointedly, 'instead of making a mess of mine?'

Casaubon's head turned as he surveyed the book-strewn, map-
and chart-walled room. One eyebrow quirked up.

'Mess?'

Lucas took a deep swallow of wine, slid down in his chair and
continued to glare at the Lord-Architect. Blue-grey storm-light
blurred the window. The heavy air and wine made his temples
throb.

The remains of a meal were spread across the round table. White
Crow – or Valentine – walked restlessly about the room, glass in
hand.

'In any case,' Casaubon added, in tones of injured reasonable-
ness, 'the porters are still moving my belongings into *my* room.'

His fat arm reached up to the table. He grabbed two tomatoes
from a dish and bit into both at once. Through a handful of red pulp
and seeds, he added: 'Who does Master Desaguliers wish to attack,
or defend?'

'Who cares?' Valentine paced back across the book-cluttered
floor. She hitched a hip up to sit on the window-sill. 'Lucas will
know. Won't you, Lucas? Tell us about the politics, Prince.'

He struggled to sit up, meeting her tawny eyes.

'Any news I had at my father's court will be eighteen months out of date. I'll have to speak with my uncle. He might be able to tell you something.'

'You do that, Prince.'

Her grin blurred; and she reached over to pick up the wine-bottle, nursing it on her lap before refilling her glass. Her eyes moved to the Lord-Architect, and Lucas could not read her expression.

'Why are you here—? Lazarus, no!'

Lucas shifted his legs as the timber wolf trotted in from the further room. Its ice-pale eyes fixed on the Lord-Architect, and it began to whine: a nail scratched down glass. Casaubon reached down and shoved his fingers through the animal's hackle-raised ruff, gripped the wolf's muzzle and shook it.

'There was blood on the moon,' he reminded the White Crow.

The timber wolf made an explosive *huff!* sound and curled up beside the armchair.

Lucas scratched through his springy hair and stood up, striving for calm or authority or anything but confusion.

'I saw,' he insisted. 'I saw that when I hadn't been in the city an hour.'

The White Crow nodded her head several times. She lifted one shoulder; the cotton slid across the curve of it and her breast. 'You're talented, Prince—'

Footsteps sounded on the outer stairs. Evelian put her head around the door. She knocked on the open door lintel. 'Messire Casaubon?'

'—He's here,' the White Crow finished.

'The porters can't get everything up to your room.' Evelian wiped a thick coil of yellow hair back with her wrist. Her smile showed pale; flesh bagged under her eyes. 'If you're not over in two minutes to sort it out, I'm telling them to leave the rest in the street!'

Her blue-and-yellow satin skirt flashed as she turned, and her footsteps clattered down the steps.

Casaubon tossed a handful of tomato-skins to the timber wolf. It snapped them out of mid-air, chewed – and immediately hacked the fruit back up, onto the carpet. The Lord-Architect stood, agile. He drew the skirts of his coat about him, bent to peer out of the casement, and held a fat palm out to test the air.

Heat-lightning whitened the rooftops, erratic as artillery. Spots of rain darkened the blistered paint on the window-sill.

'Brandy is good for aposthumes and influenzas,' he remarked hopefully. 'I'll return shortly, Lady Valentine. *Ah.* Excuse me.'

He bent ponderously and picked up an object from a corner of the room.

Lucas slammed his glass down, slopping wine; staggered across the room, and made it to the window at the same time as the cinnamon-haired woman grabbed the frame and leaned dangerously far out. He leaned out beside her, rain cool on his face.

Casaubon strode across the yard, coat flying, one massive hand gripping the stem of a lace parasol.

His head was high. He did not look up. As he disappeared into the passage Lucas heard his voice rumble, baritone, and the noise of a dropped crate.

'Oh!' The White Crow's arms clamped tight across her ribs. Mouth a rictus, she leaned against the casement and wheezed for air. Lucas opened his mouth to speak and caught the infectious laughter.

'Shit!' he said. 'Oh, shit, what a sight!'

The woman rubbed her eye with the heel of her hand. Stormlight gave a warmth to her fine skin, her dark-red curls; and from the open neck of her shirt Lucas breathed a scent of sun and grass and flesh.

He sat down on the opposite side of the sill. Laughter slowly stopped shaking her.

Finding words from nowhere, he explained: 'I thought that you were on your own in the city.'

'So did I.'

Relaxed, her mouth curved; and the terrible warmth of her eyes hit him in the pit of his stomach.

'I am,' she contradicted herself softly. 'Sometimes I look ahead, and I can see the days, each one a little cell. He knows me, you see, The clown. He thinks that if he entertains me I'll . . .'

Lucas picked up her hand and rubbed it against his face, feeling the warmth; the calluses on her middle finger.

'No.' The woman shook her head. 'The easiest thing in the world to say to you: stay. Don't listen to *la belle dame sans merci*. I won't listen to her, either.'

Lucas marvelled.

'I didn't think you knew I was here at all.'

She took her hand back, slid one cotton sleeve of her shirt to show the curve of her shoulder, and winked at him. Her breath was soft with wine.

'Ah, but now it wouldn't be because of you.'

'Valentine—'

'No. Not "Valentine",' she said. 'Not ever again.'

Not ever again beat in his pulse with the wine. Thinking how a Lord-Architect would not be here for ever, and how a student might be three years in the city, Lucas grinned crookedly.

Wood creaked with the returning tread of the fat man. The banisters protested his grip. The Lord-Architect and Knight of the Rose Castle stooped, still cracking his head lightly on the door-lintel.

'There was too little space,' he confided sunnily. 'I told the porters to store certain items in another room. The Lady Evelian suggested yours, young Lucas. I thought that particularly apt, since you're my page.'

The light is green, the colour of sunlight through hazel leaves in April. It shines on the frost-cracked masonry of a tiny cell. It shines on a thick rusty iron spike.

The air curls with vapours.

His hair is the same, gentle silver-white waves, and it is an untidy thatch above the same creased labile features. Vulnerably swimming eyes blink, would turn away if they could. Instead the mouth stumbles to form words, responds to insistent questioning.

The iron spike is slippery, clotted with blood, plasma, mucus; stringy with sinews. Knobbed bone shows a gleaming red and white.

His head ends raggedly at the stump of a neck . . . torn muscle, wrenched vertebrae, split skin upon which age-freckles are still brown. His head is impaled on the iron spike.

Time has ceased in the stone labyrinths of the Fane. He is lost in a moment of butchery, endlessly prolonged; still balancing his endurance against the endless, endless demands for his knowledge.

The grey eyes brim with tears: not because of the moment's pain, but because the Bishop of the Trees has discovered that the tortures of the gods are infinitely diverse, and eternally prolonged.

'I *am not* your page!'

The White Crow rolled wine in her mouth, the numbness of alcohol pricking her tongue. The muscular young man stiffened, spine straightening; his black brows scowled: turning in a second from relaxed adult to tightly buttoned boy.

'He's a prince.' She sighed, the last vestiges of humorous teasing falling away from her. 'Princes can't be servants, you see.'

Casaubon placed one hand on his massive chest, and inclined his head in a bow to Lucas of Candover. His heel struck the door, and knocked it to.

'Page of Sceptres,' he said.

She walked to the reversed-mirror table, concentrating on the lifting and pouring of a bottle. Cool damp storm-air rustled the star-charts pinned to the walls.

'I know. Yes. Lucas is concerned in this somehow,' the White Crow admitted, clunking the bottle of straw-coloured wine down on the wood.

The Prince sank into the cleared chair at the table, his dark eyes not leaving her face.

'So.'

Casaubon grabbed a cold chicken-wing from the table as he passed, eased himself down into the creaking armchair, bit into the oily flesh and, in an indistinct but inviting tone, echoed: 'So?'

The White Crow walked to the street-side window. She leaned up against the jamb, banging her shoulder, and pushed the casement open. Rain spattered her face.

A yellow storm-light coloured the streets, and the roofs of the houses beyond. Past them, on the swell of the hill and horizon, running in a south-austerly direction to mark the quarter's boundary, a toothed line of obelisks and pyramids made a stark skyline.

Chitinous wings whir, too distant for human hearing. Like distant fly-swarms, acolytes darken the air over the distant stone.

She tasted rain on her lips.

'I know exactly what this is about.'

She heard the armchair creak, knew Casaubon's vast bulk must have shifted. The thinning rain glistened on the tiled roofs opposite; and an odour of straw and oil drifted up to her. She fisted one hand and stretched that arm, feeling the wine unlock the muscles.

'Here at the heart of the world . . . it's lazy, don't you feel it?'

Cloud-cover tore in the high wind. She tasted in her mouth how the skyline runs true on Evelian's side of the building: another black chain of courts and wings and outyards, the Fane cutting across aust-easterly to divide the Nineteenth District from the Thirtieth and Dockland.

From behind her Lucas's voice volunteered, 'We're souls fixed on the Great Wheel.'

The White Crow spluttered, wiped her hand across her nose and mouth, and turned around and sat down on the damp window-sill in one unwise movement.

'Now gods defend us from the orthodox!' She shook her head. The room shifted. She set her empty glass down clumsily. 'Next you'll think you have to tell me that everything that is is alive, and held in the constant creation of the Thirty-Six. From stones, bees and roses, to worlds that in their orbits move, singing with their own life that moves them . . .'

'Unquote.' The Lord-Architect belched. He settled back down into the armchair. 'Valentine, you've grown regrettably long-winded since we last met.'

The White Crow stood. Anger moved her precisely across the room, avoiding piles of books and the table.

'*Four times.*' Her index finger stabbed at him. 'The first time it happened was the first year I came here. It's why I stayed. Then another, three years later. And then *two* in this year alone: one in winter and one a month ago. Now, don't tell me the College can't read the stars as clearly as I can. Don't tell me that's not why you're here!'

Casaubon watched her with guileless china-blue eyes.

'*What* happened four times?' Prince Lucas asked.

She swayed, and reached out to steady herself on empty air. The stale smell of an eaten meal roiled her stomach.

'I'll show you.'

The White Crow walked unsteadily to where a chest stood against the wall. Leather-bound volumes weighed down the lid. A chair scraped: Lucas was beside her, suddenly, lifting the books and setting them down on the carpet. The smell of leather and dust made her nostrils flare.

She pushed up the lid of the chest, and took out, first, an old backpack, the straps cracked from lack of polish; and then a basket-hilted rapier, oiled and wrapped in silk.

'Scholar-Soldier!'

The White Crow ignored the Lord-Architect's muttered exclamation. She let herself grip the hilt, lifting the sword; and the memory of that action in her flesh made her eyes sting.

'You'll make me maudlin,' she snarled. 'Here, look at these.'

She flung the rolled-up star-charts at Casaubon. Lucas moved to stare over the Lord-Architect's shoulder as he unrolled them. The White Crow rose cautiously to her feet, and sat down in Lucas's vacated chair.

'The Invisible College must know,' she said, 'that The Spagyrus practises Alchemy. Yes? Up there, in the heart of the Fane. While we turn with the Great Wheel, and return on this earth, *he* practises sublimation and distillation and exaltation, to discover the elixir of life – or so I thought, until this year.'

'Mmmhmrm.' The Lord-Architect swivelled a star-chart with surprisingly precise movements.

'And since there's no eternal life but the life of the soul, that would have been harmless enough. He is a Decan, eternal, divine. He'd be playing. You see?'

'Oh, yes. Certainly.'

She was aware of the dark-browed young man frowning. The White Crow leaned back, struts of the chair hard against her spine. A half-inch of wine remained in the bottle. She held the bottle, tilting it gently from one side to the other.

'Oh, Lucas . . .'

His body brushed her hair as he passed. 'Tell me.'

'There is a thing that men search for.'

She spoke into the rain-scented air, not attempting to watch him as he paced about the room.

'Although the Decans found it long since; or, being gods, never needed it. I mean the Philosopher's Stone: that same elixir that, being perfect in itself, cannot help but induce perfection in all that it touches.'

The after-effect of wine dizzied her, and she laughed softly.

'Including the human body. And a perfect body couldn't be corrupted. Couldn't die. Hence it's sometimes called the elixir of eternal life.'

The parchment star-charts crumpled in Casaubon's fist as the Lord-Architect heaved himself out of his chair. He knelt down beside the chest. The thud vibrated through the floorboards. He lifted the leather satchel and the sword, laying them carefully in the trunk.

'You can still clean a sword,' he said, 'but I fear for your scholarship, if that's how you interpret these charts.'

She reached across to ruffle his orange-copper hair, and feel the massive shoulder straining under the linen shirt.

'No. *No*. I was just explaining to Lucas that . . .'

Light shifted from storm-cloud yellow to sun: the evening clearing. A cold air touched her. She sat at table, among the remains of the meal, still tilting the wine-bottle. A deep sky shone through the street-window. She looked at the black-obelisked horizon.

'Lazy, this heart of the world . . . I came here when I thought I would do nothing but listen to it beat, hear the Great Wheel turn; forget I had ever studied *magia*, wait to die and be reborn.'

She thumbed the cork out of the bottle with a hollow sound. The glass was cold at her lips.

'And then, a month after I got here, I saw it. Written in the sky, clear for anyone who could read the stars. A fracture of nature. I didn't know what it was; I hardly believed I saw it. So – ah.'

She laughed deprecatingly, and waved both hands as if she

swatted something away from her; meeting Casaubon's gaze as he got to his feet.

'So just what you'd expect to happen, happened. I'd thought I'd done with study. But I paid with labour for a room, and worked in kitchens and bars for what else I needed – optic glass and books mainly – and stayed here searching the *De occulta philosophia*, the *Hieroglyphika*, the *Corpus Hermeticum*, the *Thirty Statues* . . . Everything and anything. So much for Valentine's history, hiding out in case the College should find her.'

The Lord-Architect still held one chart in his ham-hand. The most recent, she saw.

'Four is too many to be accidental,' he remarked.

'Now, I believe that. I thought it might just be an accident, and the second time coincidence. There are god-daemons on earth here in the heart of the world – is it so surprising if miracles happen? Black miracles,' she said. 'Black miracles.'

Lucas, tracing a finger down the annotated line of the star-chart the Lord-Architect held, frowned in concentration.

'It's a death-hour, isn't it? The heavens at the moment of somebody's death?'

The White Crow reached up to take the parchment and unroll it among the dishes and plates on the table. She weighed one corner down with the wine-bottle.

'Not some *body*. Bodies die all the time, young Lucas. The Great Wheel turns. We're weighed against a feather, *ka*-spirit and shadow-soul both; and then the Boat sails us through the Night, and back to birth.'

The last after-effects of the wine tanged melancholy on her tongue. Workaday evening light glowed in through the window.

'It's a chart of the heavens at a moment I've only seen these four times. When the Great Circle itself has been broken.'

'It's not possible,' Lucas denied.

'It is possible. Black alchemy, and an elixir not of life but of death, true death . . . Four times the Great Circle has been broken by a death that was not merely the body's death.'

Her callused finger touched at the alignment on paper of Arcturus, Spica, the Corona, the *sphera barbarica*. The constellations of animal-headed god-daemons marched across a sky of black ink on yellow parchment.

'In this city the soul can die, too.'

CHAPTER 4

'But I must keep hostages,' the Hyena concluded. She turned her slanting red-brown eyes on Falke and Charnay and Zar-bettu-zekigal.

Plessiez's slender dark fingers moved to his neck, feeling in his black fur for the missing *ankh*. His piercing black eyes narrowed.

'I need Charnay; the Lieutenant's familiar with the plan. And the Katayan. Keep Master Builder Falke.'

The man did not stir. He sat with his back to the sewer wall, head resting down on his arms. Zari sprang up from where she sat beside him. Her dappled tail coiled around her leg, whisk-end wrapped tight about her ankle.

'I could stay!' she volunteered.

Plessiez hid an icy amusement. 'You will come with me, Kings' Memory, to repeat your record to his Majesty, and to the General of my Order; I will then send you *back* here, to tell your Memory to the Lady Hyena.'

'So long as I get to come back.' Unrepentant, the Katayan grinned.

The Hyena glanced up at Charnay. 'The Lieutenant stays here. You won't be concerned if I kill a man, even a Master Builder. If I kill a Rat, you will. She stays, with him.'

'Lieutenant Charnay—'

The brown Rat chuckled, and hitched up her sword-belt on her furry haunches, the empty scabbard dangling. She flexed massive shoulders.

'No problem, messire. I'll even keep your pet human alive for you.'

'How very thoughtful,' Plessiez murmured.

His eyes moved to the crowd of ragged men and women who pressed in close now. Sun-banners and skeletons' shadows danced on the walls, above their heads, in the flickering torchlight. The stench of unwashed flesh and old cooking made his mobile snout quiver.

'I can give no guarantees that I will achieve your demands.'

The Hyena swung round, one fist clenched. A babble of voices echoed off the sewer-chamber's walls.

'Our freedom—'

'To walk in the streets—'

'—To carry weapons—'

'Carry swords without being arrested, gaoled—'

'—Defend ourselves—'

'Trade—'

One of the raggedly dressed men drew his sword, holding it up so that it glinted in the light; a rust-spotted épée. Two or three other men and women copied him, then another; then, awkwardly, most of the assembled crowd.

'*Freedom!*'

'Ye-ess . . .' Plessiez straightened, one slender hand at his side, head high. He gazed around at human faces. Each one's eyes fell as he met them: subservient, angry, afraid. 'I'm not impressed by third-rate histrionics.'

He turned back to the Hyena, adding: 'If only because I know how effective they are with the General of my Order, and with his Majesty the King . . . Lady, you could kill me now. You could let me work to gain you the concession of returning to the world above, carrying arms, and then do nothing of what I've asked.'

Her dark face glinted with humour.

'That may happen, Plessiez. Or we may let you try to work your necromancy. Let me warn you: we go above ground secretly, and we know the city. If you don't get the truce for us, we'll stop you dead in your tracks.'

Sweetness made saliva run in his mouth. The stench of roses leaked down from the sewer walls, gleaming with a phantom sunlight.

'Come here.'

As Zar-bettu-zekigal came to his side, Plessiez rested clawed fingers lightly on the shoulder of her black cotton dress.

'Memory, witness. The Lady Hyena's people to carry arms, to walk the streets above ground, to be free of the outstanding penalties against them as rebels and traitors.'

The Katayan nodded once.

The woman folded her arms, metal clicking. 'We do nothing until that happens. Very well. Memory, witness. Certain articles of corpse-relic necromancy to be placed at septagon points under the heart of the world, for the summoning of a pestilence . . .'

'Which will happen before very long,' Plessiez added smoothly. 'I have already placed two; the rest are yours. And if no plague-symptoms appear soon, Desaguliers' police will have words with your people, lady.'

Her slanting eyes met his. 'If your Order's *magia* does work, messire priest, then it's everyone for themselves.'

The hunger on her dirty face made hackles rise down Plessiez's spine. He abruptly turned, snapped fingers for Charnay's attention, brushing aside humans who sought to stop him. He waved Zarbettu-zekigal away.

'Charnay and I are old friends. She may have messages for her family . . .'

He caught the scepticism in the Hyena's expression, and the last inches of his scaly tail tapped a rhythm of tension.

'Lieutenant, give me as many days as you can before you escape from here.'

The brown Rat matched his undertone. 'I'll stay, messire. To tell you the truth, I'd sooner duel Desaguliers' Cadets any day of the week. These scum are amateurs. Just as likely to stab you in the back as fight . . .'

She dropped her resonant voice a tone softer. 'Give it a couple of weeks, let the plague get a grip down here, and I'll come out in the confusion. Don't worry, messire! I'll do it.'

His hand closed on her brawny arm, dark against the glossy brown fur. 'If it's from you that they discover they're not immune to this plague, I swear I'll have you gutted at the square and chasing your own entrails round a stake!'

She nodded, good-humoured, still smiling. 'Plessiez, man, give me credit for sense! I want to die as little as you do. The only way they'll find out is when they start burying each other.'

Plessiez looked up at her. 'See that's so.'

He stepped back, adding in a louder tone: 'We'll leave you now.'

The blond man, Clovis, squinted at the woman in ragged armour. 'Lady, who'll lead him out?'

'I will.' The Hyena pointed. 'Take those others and give them food.'

A man in the tatters of a satin suit jeered. Youths scrambled to follow Falke and Charnay as they were led off, scooping handfuls of ordure to throw, screeching insults. Plessiez bristled, tail cocked high.

As she turned away, he spoke unpremeditatedly:

'*And give me back my sword.*'

The armoured woman beckoned, not turning to see if she was obeyed. The great silence of the sewers pressed against his ears. The substanceless brambles of roses brushed his fur.

'No,' she said. 'Feel how it is to go unarmed, messire, in the presence of your enemies.'

Above, in the city, clocks strike four in the morning.

Footsteps echoed down the main aisle of the Cathedral of the Trees.

'You!'

The novice sleeping on the oak altar started awake. Bright starlight showed his patched water-stained robe. He rubbed his eyes. 'The cathedral's closed.'

The brusque voice said: 'We don't close the cathedral.'

She moved into the starlight, monochrome through night-stained windows. The novice saw a black-skinned woman in her twenties. Her tree-embroidered robe had a wide belt, cinched tightly, so that she seemed an hour-glass: round hips and buttocks, round shoulders and breasts. Her short hair tangled darkness in loops and curls.

'Archdeachon Regnault, I beg your pardon!'

He slid down from the altar, an awkward bony young man.

'I didn't know you were back from the Aust quarter.'

Regnault smiled briefly. 'We remain a church, in despite of all they can do to us. Are you the only one here?'

'The others are out looking for Bishop Theodoret.'

'So am I,' the Archdeacon said. 'The old man's put his head in the Decan's mouth once too often. We'll have to do what we can to get it out.'

'You think . . . you think he's alive, then?'

The Archdeacon tugged at the waist of her robe. Her dark hand brushed the hawthorn spray pinned on her breast. Her fingers splayed in a Sign of the Branches.

'Where's your faith?' she asked.

'Ei!'

Feathers swooped down and flung into an upward curve. Zari crooked up an arm. Wings splayed like spread hands in front of her face. She flinched away as the bird skirred past, burring up to the unseen roof.

'Little one?'

'Oh, see you, it's nothing.'

Her voice died. The black Rat stopped, and she cannoned into his elbow. Humidity had slicked his fur up into tufts. She pressed close to his side.

A few yards ahead, the Hyena swivelled, pivoting on the scabbard she used as a crutch. 'Keep moving! I told you that we'd have to cross the bridge.'

Cloud and blue vapour drifted across the stonework. Here, in older tunnels, the brickwork had given way to masonry. Zar-bettu-zekigal reached out to trail her fingers across one immense pale-blue block of Portland stone. Chill wetness took the print. A wind gusted into her face, lifting strands of black hair.

'Messire, where are we?'

The black Rat limped now, weary with four hours' walking, and his tail dragged in the stone-dust. Thrown ordure marked his scarlet jacket. His dark fingers continually reached for his empty scabbard.

'In Hell. I—' His arctic calm shattered. *'What's that?'*

Zar-bettu-zekigal scurried three steps to the Hyena's side. She pushed past the woman in red cloth and armour, skidded, slipped to one knee, tail crooked out for balance; pointed ahead.

'That—!'

Great wings beat, a thirty-foot wing-span: dipping down so slowly that the up-curve of flight-feathers clearly showed at their tips. Zari fell to hands and knees. The sharp beak and amber eyes soared towards her. Gleaming black, only wing-tips and head feathered white, the condor rose on a column of air that blew in her face, scattering the white clouds and blue vapour.

It scored the air towards her, rising, too large for the narrow tunnel. Wing-tips thirty feet apart brushed through the blue stone walls and ceiling. As the feathers passed through the substance of the stone, the stone crumbled away, falling on the downsweep into newly created void.

Zar-bettu-zekigal craned her neck to follow as the condor soared over her head. The great bird vanished into mist. She looked down again, to see in its wake – sky.

'Messire Plessiez!'

She knelt up, tail tucking around her knees.

Ahead, voids of empty air opened up. The walls and roof of the tunnel crumbled, blue stone falling into blue air.

Zar-bettu-zekigal stared at the masonry of the floor, momentarily solid and spanning the gulf. Emptiness began to eat into it, stone melting like frost in sunlight.

'But we're underground,' she protested.

Slender strong fingers grasped her shoulder. She looked up to see Plessiez gazing ahead, black eyes narrowed.

'*What is this?*'

'You're under the city,' the Hyena said. 'You're under the heart of the world.'

Zar-bettu-zekigal stood, brushing dust from her black dress. She pulled the greatcoat firmly around her. The vast gulfs of air pressed in on her, swelling her skull with emptiness; until she swayed, and caught hold of the woman's arm, steel vambrace cold under her hand.

Miles below, a plain stretched out into blue mists. She gazed at a middle region of cloud, eyes squinting against a cold wind. The breath she took smelt of burning.

A steel-gauntleted hand pushed Zari in the flat of her back.

'Move, or you'll never cross.'

Zar-bettu-zekigal stepped forward, bare feet testing the Portland stone. Chill water slicked the surface. The stone bridge diminished into distance and perspective before her. She lifted her head and saw, where vapours shifted, the ragged ends of arches and stone groynes hanging down into the void.

'*Look*,' she breathed.

Masonry towers ended above her, hanging their sealed cellars down from the underside of the city into the gulf. Blended with brick, and with steel girders; and structures the shape of building-foundations. And random jammed-together masses of stone and mortar and wood. Further off, raw rock jutted down into the sky: the undersides of hills.

Zar-bettu-zekigal strained her vision, searching the vapour.

Between the underside of the city and the plain, a waning moon stood flat and white in a blue sky. A second half-globe hung behind it, larger and more pale. Within the larger moon's curve, Zar-bettu-zekigal saw the fingernail-paring of a smaller satellite.

She looked down, off the slender span of stone.

Her stomach wrenched. Six miles below, the plain burned with visible flames. Licking orange-and-yellow fires, hearth-fire welcoming; until she made out how condors and eagles soared in the depths under the bridge.

Plessiez's fur brushed her shoulder. Water pearled on the Rat's glossy black coat. The priest walked steadily beside Zar-bettu-zekigal, hand gripping her arm. She looked up and saw that his eyes were clamped shut.

Behind them, the woman laughed.

The masonry floor of the tunnel shifted, etched away piecemeal by the air. Zar-bettu-zekigal peered over the edge again as she walked, heels kicking the slick stone, and stopped.

'How much time do we have?'

A whisk of metal and leather sounded, yards behind. She spun round as Plessiez did. The woman leaned now on a naked sword, some yard and a half long, that spangled light from its outside curve. She rubbed a hand across her filthy face.

'Not long,' she said, 'and we can't turn back. Now let's *move*.'

Clock-mill strikes four-thirty.

Stars hieroglyphed the night sky, blotted by rain-clouds.

A large figure trod stealthily across the dark courtyard, smelling of fresh soap. The Lord-Architect padded towards the steps in the far corner, the silken tail of his night-robe flapping in the wind.

He rubbed thumb and middle finger softly together. Faint gold light glimmered, died. His shoulders straightened. Invisible in the night, he smiled. No natural magic tripwires guarding the steps to Valentine's rooms . . .

He put one foot on the bottom step, hesitated as the wood creaked. Her window showed dark. He climbed another step, and another.

The Lord-Architect's foot caught a metal rim. The handle of the saucepan flew up, cracking his shin. His other foot came down firmly inside a pot and, as he stumbled, two cans rattled and clanged down the wooden steps.

The Lord-Architect exclaimed, '*Helldammit!*' arms wheeling, flailing massively. Another pan clattered from stairs to cobbles.

Upstairs, a woman rubbed cinnamon hair from her mouth with one wrist, rolling over in bed on to her stomach; eyes glued shut, smiling in her sleep.

Lights came on in several windows round Evelian's courtyard: flints struck, copper lamps groped for and lit; fingers burned, swearwords muttered.

With immense dignity, and his left foot jammed tightly into an enamelled chamberpot, the Lord-Architect Casaubon clanked back to his own rooms.

'I'll be back!'

Zar-bettu-zekigal clung with both hands to the iron ladder's rails. Looking between her feet, she shouted down the narrow shaft again:

'Don't forget me!'

Far below, a woman laughed.

'Come, little one.' The black Rat leaned over, standing above her where the ladder hooped over to the head of the shaft. Light shining up from the depths illuminated his snout and brilliant eyes.

Hunger dizzied her as he reached down. Her foot slipped. She whipped her tail around the ladder, grabbed the Rat's sword-belt, and felt her greatcoat ride up over her shoulders as Plessiez grabbed her under the arms, hauling her up on to a flat brick floor.

Far, far below, the laugh modulated out of the sound a human voice makes: raked up into higher, yelping registers; echoed away in whoops, giggles, vixen-yawps.

The light that shone up the shaft began to fade. Zari raised her head, peering at the surrounding dark.

'I've seen places I liked better.' She stepped out of the Rat's inadvertent embrace, pushing lank hair out of her eyes.

This shaft opened into a brick chamber some twenty by thirty feet, empty in the fading illumination. The black Rat reached up to the ceiling, eighteen inches above his head, testing each of the interlocked metal plates.

'She was laughing at where we'll come out,' Zari guessed. 'It *has* to be in the city still. When I came in on the ship it took five days just to sail up the estuary, and the city all around us all the way.'

Fading light showed her his face, lean and drawn with hunger, with the weariness of climbing shaft upon shaft of the endless sewers.

'Ah!'

One plate swung up and over, vanished with a *clang!* and Plessiez sprang to hoist himself up through the now-open trapdoor. Zari danced from one foot to the other beneath.

'What is it? What's there? Where are we?'

Plessiez began to laugh.

Zari leaped up, hands gripping the sides of the trap; got one bare foot up for leverage. She heard him laugh again, a loud uninhibited guffaw: part awe, part admiration. Metal clanged. Rapid footsteps went back and forth.

'*What?*' Huffing, she pulled herself up through the trapdoor.

'But this is wonderful!'

Plessiez's expression changed from enjoyment to second thoughts. He stood in a passageway lined either side with barred rooms, and had been banging on the iron-studded door at the far end of the passage.

'Amazing. Little one, these are the oubliettes of the Abbey of Guiry.'

Zar-bettu-zekigal rubbed at green stains on the sleeves of her greatcoat. 'The Abbey what?'

A last gust of laughter shook Plessiez.

'My Order is the Order of Guiry, the Guiresites,' he explained gravely; and swung round and struck the door an echoing blow. 'Guards! What, *guards ho*!'

There were green stains on the soles of her feet, Zari discovered, as she balanced precariously on one leg. And stains on her black dress.

Over the clatter of approaching feet, the black Rat said: 'Listen to me, Kings' Memory – you stay with me, now, and only with me. Above all, you say nothing except when I direct you to.'

'I'm a Kings' Memory; I speak to whoever asks me.' She buttoned the great overcoat, covering the worst of the stains. 'Messire, can we have something to *eat*?'

The rattle of the door unlocking was followed by a rush of black and brown Rats into the corridor. Zari gazed at their sober black dress. The first Rat, plumed and wearing a black jacket, came to a skidding halt when she saw Plessiez; grabbed the *ankh* at her neck, and exclaimed: 'Plessiez! Cardinal-General Ignatia told us you were dead—'

His glance crossed hers. Zar-bettu-zekigal saw the black Rat grin, showing sharp incisors. Amusement, triumph, and a febrile excitement gleamed in his eyes.

'There's much that Cardinal-General Ignatia doesn't know, I assure you.'

A brown Rat pushed to the forefront of the guards and priests, looked Plessiez up and down, and with an air of triumph concluded: 'You're not dead, are you?'

Plessiez smoothed down his torn scarlet jacket. '*No*, Mornay – and nor is your sister Charnay. Hilaire, order my coach brought to the front of the palace. Lucien, ride immediately to his Majesty and say that I must have an immediate audience. *Now*. I want no argument. I must see the King.'

Zari grinned at the startled faces. Plessiez's slender-fingered hand swept her along, trotting beside him while he fired orders to left and right. Her calves ached sharp protests at the steps up from the oubliette to the guardroom.

'Fetch Reverend Captains Fenelon and Fleury. They'll be accompanying me to the King. Lay out my best clothes in my rooms. Also my sword. Sauval, come with me; I'll want you to take down a dictated report as we go—'

'Food!' Zari yelled succinctly above the confusion.

'—and have the kitchens bring something to eat.'

A black Rat some years older than Plessiez pushed through the crowd, past Zar-bettu-zekigal. She had little enough of the priest about her: her plumed headband was gold and white, and her jacket white with gold piping. 'I'll have to inform Cardinal-General Ignatia, Plessiez. You can't ask to see the King if she doesn't know why.'

Plessiez hesitated at the guardroom door, head cocked, translucent ears tensing. Zari saw him listen to some interior voice urging caution and discard it.

'The Cardinal-General Ignatia,' Plessiez said, 'is a useless old bitch.'

'What?'

Zar-bettu-zekigal put both hands on separate Rats' shoulders and shoved them aside. Sunlight dimmed the candles in the corridor outside, patched with colour the coats and embroidered scabbards of the priest Rats. She blinked water from her eyes. Pushed, shoved, ignored by the quarrel rapidly forming, she thrust a way out of the group and padded across the white-walled corridor to the nearest window.

The sun hung a hand's breadth above the horizon. Sharp-edged clouds glowed, indigo above, translucent pink below. She pushed the casement open. Cold air flooded her lungs – the chill of evening or the dew-damp of dawn? She scrunched her fingers through her hair, and twitched the kinks from her black-and-white furred tail.

'Morning or evening?' She caught a passing Rat's arm. He stared at her, and she jerked her head at the window. Light as cold and clear as water covered the city, that stretched out unbroken to the horizon.

'Dawn. Messire—'

Plessiez's voice ripped the air. 'Silence! Captain Auverne, you may make yourself useful by taking a squad of guardsmen and investigating the sewer-shaft that opens into our cellars. But use all possible caution. I want a day-and-night guard kept down there from now on.'

The white-and-gold-clad Rat snarled something under her breath, reluctantly turning away to summon guards.

'And I am most disturbed to discover that you knew nothing of this entrance, Captain Auverne. Kindly report to me later with the explanation. Zari.' Plessiez turned his back on the indignant captain.

'I'm here, messire.'

'Come with me.'

She followed the priest as he strode off through the whitewashed stone corridors. A faintness of hunger sang in her head, cramped her guts; and at every sunlit window they passed she grinned and skipped a half-step. Each window gave her a wider view of the dawn: the pale sky deepening to azure.

Inside the doors of extensive apartments, the small group grew to a crowd, augmented as other Rats came running. Plessiez's voice rose over the noise, his rapid-fire orders sending junior priests off on errands. Zari flopped down on a satin-covered couch, her attention taken up with a tray of bread and goat-cheese, and a flagon of cold water.

'Steady, little one.'

She looked up, jaws clamped on a crust; tore and swallowed and nodded, all in one movement.

'I know, I know . . .' Cramps from too-rapid eating griped in her gut.

The outer doors swung closed. Sunlight blazed in the white low-roofed rooms; on carpets, tapestries, desks, globes and icons. Plessiez dictated to his secretary as Rats sponged and brushed his filthy fur. Zari switched to sitting cross-legged on the couch, gazing round at the royal-blue drapes, the silver goblets and plates.

'It isn't,' she said into a gap in Plessiez's dictation, 'an austere Order, the Order of Guiry.'

Plessiez chuckled. He slipped his arms into a crimson Jacket slashed with gold and, as a brown Rat servant buttoned it up to his throat, remarked: 'An academic Order, little one; and austere as – ah, as all academics are.'

The silver rim of the water-jug chilled her mouth. She drank, colicky; and belched.

'*Plessiez!*'

'Here.' The black Rat acknowledged the yelp of joy, raising his arms while a servant buckled and adjusted his sword-belt and basket-hilted rapier. He shrugged himself back into it, hand going at once to rest there. The junior priests and servants fell back before two newcomers.

Zari switched round to kneel upright on the couch. She put both hands over her mouth, muffling a giggle. A short plump black Rat slitted her eyes, her gaze passing over the Katayan silhouetted against the rising sun.

'You're going to see the King?' she asked Plessiez.

'Fleury, of course he is!' A tall and very thin Rat, with raffish black fur and a cheerfully unworldly look, slapped Plessiez's shoulder. 'Must have worked out, eh? When do we give the word to move?'

With a start, he noticed the Katayan.

'Zar-bettu-zekigal,' she said gravely, scratching her ear with her tail. The Rat bowed.

'Fenelon,' he said.

'Fleury, Fenelon, you'll come with me to the King.' Plessiez beckoned. 'Little one.'

Zar-bettu-zekigal got off the couch, and bent to rub her calves with both hands. 'I'm dead beat!'

'Rest in the coach. Come.'

'Messire Plessiez!'

An elderly black Rat stood in the doorway, the white-and-gold-clad captain beside her. Her ears showed ragged, her muzzle grey. The sleeveless open robe over her jacket glowed emerald. Lace foamed at her wrists and at her throat. A gemmed pectoral *ankh* hung between her rows of dugs.

'I regret I cannot stay to serve the Cardinal-General,' Plessiez said, picking up his scarlet cloak and plumed headband. 'The Cardinal-General will excuse me.'

'What are you doing?' Cardinal-General Ignatia frowned, bewildered. 'Captain Auverne reports you asked for an audience with the King. You must, of course, first report to myself anything concerning the use of *magia*—'

'Is my coach there?' Plessiez asked Zar-bettu-zekigal. She padded across to the window.

'There's a coach waiting in the courtyard, messire.'

'Good.'

'Messire Plessiez, you will explain yourself!'

Zari saw the black Rat's tail sweep into a jaunty curve. With a studied recklessness, Plessiez faced the Rat in the doorway.

'The explanation would be a little too complex for you, Ignatia. Short of force, you won't stop me seeing the King. And you won't use force.'

The black Rat that Zari identified as Auverne stepped forward. Fleury's sword scraped out of the scabbard: a ragged raw noise. The Cardinal-General held up her hand.

'Really, Messire Plessiez, the haste, if nothing else, is most unseemly; and, even without that rashness, protocol demands that your superior in the Order first hears whatever information you may possess.'

Zar-bettu-zekigal rubbed her eyes, planting her bare feet four-square on the floorboards; dazzled by whitewashed walls and day-light. The sun-warmed wood thrummed, once, and she winced: the tensile memory of the skin on the soles of her feet still tingling with the dissolution of stone.

'That child has seen *magia*!' the Cardinal-General protested. Zari opened her eyes to find the elderly Rat peering at her.

'Yes, *magia*. Thirty years' study should at least enable you to recognise it when you see it!'

Plessiez snarled, not slowing as he approached the Cardinal-General.

'Or has it been something in books for too long, Ignatia? Don't you care for it raw? Now, while you've been poring over the Library for decades, I've *acted*.'

The elderly Rat involuntarily stepped back.

'This is your old talk of power under the heart of the world? Plessiez, you demean yourself, you behave no better than a Tree-priest. We have our God at hand, their *gaia* is nowhere to be seen, and as for beneath the city—'

'Messire Plessiez,' a guard interrupted, as he pushed his way through the crowd at the door. 'That sewer-shaft. We've investigated. It goes down about six feet. Then it's completely choked by new rubble.'

Zari's feet tingled, remembering the floorboards' tremor. She tried to catch Plessiez's eye, but the black Rat only beckoned her and Fleury and Fenelon.

As they passed the Cardinal-General, Zar-bettu-zekigal glanced first at her and then sympathetically up at the raffish Fenelon.

'End of a long fight?'

'About six years' worth,' he agreed. He put himself between Zar-bettu-zekigal and Auverne's novice-guards.

Plessiez carried his slim body taut, swinging cloak and headband from his free hand. As Zari caught up, he called back over his shoulder: 'Make the most of your time, Ignatia. I'll be asking the King to appoint a new Cardinal-General of the Order of Guiry.'

Far into the Fane, day and night are lost memories. The light that shines on the stonework is cool green. There is no slightest hint of decay in the air.

—Why did you betray your people?—

He hears no audible voice. It writes, instead, in lines of blood forming behind his shut eyelids. The Bishop can croak air through ripped vocal cords. But he will not speak.

His wrinkled lids, blue-veined, open to disclose rheumy eyes. No matter how he tries to look down (head held immobile by the iron spike upon which it is impaled) he cannot see the peripheral obstructions of chest or shoulders. They no longer exist.

—Why did you betray the Builders' conspiracy?—

Lines of blood, forming in the empty air.

His creased lower jaw works. Drying blood and sinews constrict his throat.

—How did they think to threaten god-daemons?—

'I . . . don't . . . know . . .'

—Answer and it will count well in your favour. Those are coming who need to ask no questions, all-knowing and all-seeing. The Decans will be less kind than we who are only their servants—

'Lady . . . of . . . the . . . Woods . . .'

Unable to see his interrogators, unable to move anything but that once-eloquent mouth, the Bishop of the Trees begins to pray.

The heat of the early sun drew vapour from the black wooden sill. Earth and cobbles in the courtyard below steamed, the previous night's rain drying. The young man on the truckle-bed rolled over. Half-asleep, sweating, he got up on one elbow. The vibrations of Clock-mill striking eight jarred his brown eyes open.

'Awshit,' Lucas of Candover muttered. 'Awshitshit . . .'

A long *cre-eak* disorientated him. He kicked free of the sheet and sat up. Something large, pink and swathed in wet towels loomed over the bed. Lucas swallowed the foul taste in his mouth.

'Wh—?'

The Lord-Architect Casaubon said: 'Step across the landing for a moment, Prince. I need help.'

'Mmhrm – *What?*'

The door to Lucas's room creaked shut. He rubbed granules of sleep from his eyes, staring around the tiny room. Only the smell of steam spoke of recent occupation. He groped for his breeches.

'*Shit!*' Struggling into his clothes, he barged out and across the tiny landing to the Lord-Architect's door. 'What is it? What's wrong? Is it her – White Crow?'

The Lord-Architect sat on his creaking truckle-bed, towelling his hair vigorously. A claw-footed iron bathtub in one corner was surrounded by sopping-wet towels. Crates and brass-bound trunks occupied what space that left. Through the leaded window, a blue summer sky grew pale and hotter by the second.

'*Is she in danger?*'

'What?' The Lord-Architect emerged from his towel, wet hair standing up in red-gold spikes. He beamed at Lucas. 'Some ridiculous ordinance in the city – a human being can't hire *servants*! Of all the pox-rotted pig's-tripe. Hand me my vest, will you?'

'Servants?'

'Body-servants,' Casaubon amplified. He pushed himself up from the bed, and the wooden frame creaked a protest. The wet towel joined the others on the floorboards. Pulling a vest over his head, he repeated from the depths of the folds of cloth: 'Hand me *that*, there.'

Lucas glared. 'I'm a Prince of Candover and no man's servant!'

'Hmm?' The Lord-Architect thrust his head out of the muffling cloth. 'Hurry it up, will you? There's a good lad.'

Something in the Lord-Architect's tone convicted Lucas of dubious manners at best. Lucas picked up the canvas garment hanging over the back of a chair and passed it across. He caught a jaw-cracking yawn, stifled it, and combed his sleep-tangled curls with his fingers.

'This is what you woke me up for? Of all the *insolence*—'

He stopped, and stared at Casaubon's back. The fat man's vest rode up over slabs of thigh and buttock as he fitted the canvas garment over his head, tugging it down over the full-moon swell of his belly.

'Poxrotted-damned-cretinous—' One elbow jammed in the air, the other caught in the laced-up garment. 'Lend a hand, can't you, boy!'

The court of Candover requires tact and diplomacy from a prince. Lucas sniffed hard. 'Is that a corset?'

'Damned poxrotted full-dress *audience*—'

Lucas looked at canvas, bone-ribs and thick cord lacings, almost as bewildered as the older man. He bristled, caught between the insult to his dignity and the sneaking suspicion that his lack of knowledge was about to make a fool of him.

'The Princes of Candover don't dress themselves!'

He reached out and tugged tentatively at the bottom hem. Casaubon's elbow slid free. The fat man pulled the garment lower, huffing, until it girdled his stomach.

'Can't hire a damned servant, can't get a decent meal.' He turned, glaring down at Lucas. 'Does your poxrotted landlady ever serve anything without boiled cabbage in the meal?'

'I don't know,' Lucas shot back with satisfaction. 'I've only been here a week!'

The Lord-Architect chuckled resonantly. His companionable beam took in Lucas, the summer morning, the bell-notes of birds in the courtyard.

'Pull,' he ordered, presenting the Prince of Candover with his back and the lacings of the corset.

Lucas stepped closer, staring up at the fat-sheathed muscles of the Lord-Architect's shoulders and arms. He tugged the two flaps of the corset towards each other across the broad back.

'Right,' he said. *'Right.'*

He grabbed the two cords and pulled, sharply. The Lord-Architect grunted and braced his massive legs apart.

'She doesn't want you here.' Lucas emphasised his speech with a hard pull on the lacings. 'She's only talking to you because you won't answer her questions!'

The top of the corset, under the fat man's arms, began to pull together. Lucas, sweating, poked at the lacings further down; hooked his fingers under a point where they crossed over, and heaved.

'What's more, you're bothering her, and I don't like it.'

Casaubon grunted. He scratched at his newly washed hair, spiking it in tufts. Craning to look back over his cushioned shoulder, the Lord-Architect said mildly: 'Now, if I'd answered her questions when I arrived, what would she have done?'

'Told you to—' Lucas trapped his finger between tight lacings. He swore under his breath. 'To go away.'

'Precisely.' The Lord-Architect sucked in his breath and belly. The two edges of the corset creaked closer together. 'Now, how else could I get a bad-tempered impatient woman like Valentine to stand still and hear my message?'

Lucas glowered at the Lord-Architect's back. He wrapped the cords around his fist, put a knee at the cleft of the fat man's buttocks and pulled.

'What message?'

'Valentine will be asking herself that.'

Lucas whipped the cords into a secure knot, and sat down heavily on the Lord-Architect's bed, panting. Casaubon picked up a ruffled shirt and slid his arms into it, the bone-ribs of the corset gently creaking.

'I said . . . you're bothering her . . . and I don't like it.' Lucas rested his arms back, propping himself up, chin on his chest. Outside, the heat whitened city roofs, turned the air dusty. He sweated. The sour smell of bathwater and wet cloth filled his nostrils.

'You're right,' Casaubon said contritely. 'It was too sudden.'

He fastened the toggles on his shirt. The tails hung down almost to his massive calves. Lucas shook his head, and handed up the bright-blue silk breeches laid out on the bottom of the bed.

'Much too sudden!' The Lord-Architect stopped, one foot in his breeches, the other wavering in mid-air. He beamed widely at Lucas.

'I shall woo her,' he announced.

His foot hit the floorboards with an audible thump. As he fastened his silk breeches, he added: 'Do you think she likes poetry? I'll write her a sonnet. Two sonnets. How many lines would that be, exactly?'

Lucas fell back across the bed, wheezing, water leaking out of the corners of his eyes.

'Have that hay-fever treated,' the Lord-Architect advised. He cumbrously hooked his braces to his breeches, and over them eased an embroidered waistcoat on to his massive torso.

The attic-room's airless heat increased. Lucas rolled across the bed and pushed the casement window open.

Mud patched the courtyard, remnant of the storm. The White Crow stood up, two battered saucepans under her arm, and waved as she saw Lucas. He stared after her as she climbed her steps, picking up another can on the way. He realised he hadn't waved back.

'*What* message? If you're getting her involved in anything dangerous . . .'

The sun tangled in her hair that, he saw now, shone red without a gleam of gold or orange in it. Her white shirt hung out of the back of her brown knee-breeches.

The door swung to behind her.

Casaubon came to the window, shrugging into a royal-blue satin coat, deep-pocketed, with turned-back embroidered cuffs. It fitted across his corseted stomach like a second skin. The full skirts swirled. Lucas, momentarily petty, enjoyed a thought of how hot and uncomfortable the Lord-Architect was going to be at a formal audience.

'Valentine has faced danger for the College since she was fifteen,' Casaubon said soberly. 'The woman enjoys it. Foolish child.'

Lucas stood. The Lord-Architect still topped him by six or eight inches.

'My uncle the Ambassador has a fairly efficient intelligence service. If I want to find out what's going on here, I can. Suppose you tell me.'

Casaubon lifted the corner of the bedsheet, peering under the bed. He padded to the other side of the room in stockinged feet.

'Can you see a shoe?'

Lucas scratched his chest. Muscles slid under sweaty skin. Almost despairing, he burst out: 'If you care about her so much, why won't you take help when it's offered? I'm a prince. I can command my people who are here. I could help!'

'It was here somewhere . . .'

Lucas picked up an extremely large black shoe from behind a crate. Acting on nothing but impulse, he walked around the bottom of the bed, put his hand on Casaubon's chest and pushed. The Lord-Architect sat down heavily. Wood screeched. Lucas squatted down on his haunches in front of the fat man.

'You won't get rid of me.' He grabbed one stockinged foot, shoving the shoe on to it. Casaubon grunted. Lucas snared the other high-heeled court shoe from under the bed and fitted it on. 'So you might as – uh – might as *well* get used to me. There.'

Casaubon rested his elbows on his massive thighs, and rested his chins in his hands. China-blue eyes met Lucas's.

'I am about to go and give Valentine her message,' he said gravely. 'Would you care to come with me, before you leave for the university?'

Lucas stood. 'Yes! Yes . . .'

'Good.'

Hazarding a blind guess, Lucas said: 'You'll take her with you, to your audience with the King?'

'I have an audience,' the Lord-Architect Casaubon agreed, 'but not with the King. I have an audience at eleven, at the Fane.'

'No, true, my eyes are a natural condition. Permanently dilated pupils. My grandmother suffered them, too.'

Falke pulled down the sleeves of a slightly overlarge grey leather doublet, shrugging his shoulders into the new garment.

'Do you blame me for impressing the gullible? You must know what it's like to grub for every scrap of influence, the dynasty being powerless these many centuries . . . I tell them: every guttersnipe in the city walks into the Fane to talk to God; but I don't mean antechambers or building-sites, I mean the infinite interior of what we build . . . I say: *I've seen*. It works.'

Silver buckles clinked at his wrists, and he fastened them; thumbing back the dove-grey silk that protruded through the slashing on the leather sleeves. Pinpoints of brilliance reflected back from the metal into his vision. His eyes watered.

'And, gullible or not, I have a large number of people who listen to what the House of Salomon says. You need support. Your numbers are comparatively small – compared to our masters the Rat-Lords, that is.'

A last movement, tucking grey breeches into new boots (the leather a little bloodstained still at the toes), and he straightened; dry and clothed, now; gambling; meeting her red-brown eyes where she sprawled across the carved chair, under the torches and banners and bones.

'I've listened to you.' She snapped her fingers, not looking at the blond man who ran to her side. 'Clovis, feed him. I'll speak to him again later.'

'What about the Lieutenant?' Clovis asked.

'Nothing. I must think. Go.'

Falke followed the man through the makeshift camp in the vast chamber, walking easily across shadowed broken earth. A warm wind blew in his face, with a stench of carrion and sweetness on it; nevertheless he expanded his chest, drawing in the air.

'There.'

Clovis jerked his head towards a wide brick ledge. Falke leaped up lightly as the man walked away towards cooking-pots on tripods.

Charnay opened shining dark eyes. She lounged back against the brick wall with something of a disappointed air, furry body half-supported against sacks and barrels, her long-fingered hands clasped comfortably across her belly. 'Didn't expect to see you again. Who gave you the new kit?'

'The Lady Hyena.'

Falke reached up to tie his silver-grey hair back into a pony-tail with a length of leather thong. Fingers busy, facing into the great cavern, arms up and so unprotected. 'There's always a way, and I found it!'

The Rat rolled over on to one massive brown-furred flank. 'I wouldn't trust one of you peasants to find your backside with both hands and a map.'

A pottery dish clunked on the edge of the brickwork. Clovis walked away without a word. Falke watched him stumble over rocks plainly visible in the somber torchlight that mimicked night.

He chuckled quietly, back in his throat.

Squatting, he scooped up the stew-bowl and prodded the mess of cooked weeds with his forefinger. Warm, greasy; the smell made his stomach contract. He shoved a messy fistful into his mouth, spilling fronds down the front of the leather doublet, and spoke between chewing.

'She knows, now, that I've been inside the Fane. Something your messire Plessiez can't claim.'

'What use is that to her? You fill your breeches at the mention of daemons.'

Falke stopped chewing. 'True, but that's not to the point now. A *magia* plague, a plague to send into the Fane. Very good. I like that.

House of Salomon will approve. *I understand the Fane*. Listen, and try to understand me, Lieutenant. Messire Plessiez would want you to support me in making an alliance with this woman. She has a number of people down here; she can be useful.'

Shining black eyes shifted. The Rat lumbered to her hind feet and stood over him, looking down. 'Too late. He has his bargain with her already, boy. He doesn't need you now.'

Warm shivers walked across his skin, raising the small hairs. Cramps twisted his gut. Falke turned his back on her momentarily. Shadows shifted. Hauntings whispered at the edges of light. A jealousy shifted in his breast. Across the vast brick chamber, under a ragged sun-banner, two men circled each other, sparring: light sliding down the blades of broadswords.

'You think so? It isn't the first time Rat-Lords have used me. I may surprise them yet.'

The anvil-clang of weapons-practice echoed in the sewer chamber. Stenches drifted up from the distant canal. Falke, hands tucked up under his armpits, stared across the expanse of camp-fires, brushwood heaps, gallows, and men and women. Each speck of light pricked at his unbandaged eyes.

'I shall live to thank Messire Plessiez for abandoning me here.'

He missed what she rumbled in reply, still staring out at the armed camp.

At human men and women carrying swords, pikes, flails, daggers. Carrying weapons and practised in their use.

The fox-cub nipped at the White Crow's wrist. She swore, put the feeding-bottle down on the mirror-table, and the cub back in its box. She reached up to the herb shelf for witch-hazel to put on the blood-bruise.

'Where did I . . . ?'

The silver wolf padded across the room, pushing over two precarious piles of books. They slid to rest in the sunlight slanting whitely in at the street-side and courtyard windows, and at the roof-trap. Light fell on opened books, star-charts propped up with ivory rods, wax discs scattered in three heaps, and discarded hieroglyphed scrolls.

'Here.'

She tapped the wolf's muzzle. Pale eyes met hers. It gaped, letting her finger the socket where a rotten tooth had been removed. Its head twitched irritably.

'Lazarus, you only come to me to get your teeth fixed,' she accused. 'I'd wait a day or two yet—'

She heard footsteps, and raised her voice without looking up: 'We're shut! Go away!'

The door swung open. She raised her head to see the dark young man open it with a mocking flourish, and bow most formally. The Lord-Architect Casaubon strode in past Lucas without a blink of acknowledgment.

'Valentine!'

The White Crow looked down at the timber wolf. 'No. *I* don't know how he does it.'

'I must say,' Casaubon remarked, 'that you could keep this place a good deal tidier.'

She put her fists on her hips.

'I've been up since dawn working on the last batch of Mayor Spatchet's talismans, which aren't finished, which *won't* be finished today unless we're all very lucky, and so I advise you not to make critical comments of any sort, because my temper is not of the best, is that clear?'

The Lord-Architect tugged at the turned-up cuffs of his blue satin coat. 'I had something of a disturbed night myself.'

'Aw—' The White Crow sat down heavily at the table, sinking her chin in her hands. Bright eyes brimmed with laughter, fixing on Casaubon; she snuffled helplessly for several seconds.

Lucas's dark brows met in a scowl.

'Good morning . . . Prince,' the White Crow said.

Lucas picked up one of the discarded wax tablets. 'Talismans?'

'Oh . . .' She took it out of his hand. 'Easy enough making something to warn when Decans exercise their power. The difficulty is making one the god-daemons' acolytes won't immediately feel being used and flock to.'

A light wind lifted papers as it brushed past her. She anchored one heap on the table with the handful of talismans. A number of crates stood open under the table, carved wood and incised wax talismans nesting in oakum. Her hand went to the small of her back, rubbing. She looked past the young man's earnest face to Casaubon.

'Now I suppose you'll tell me why you're here?'

The Lord-Architect stood by the open street-side window, face intent. He whistled through chiselled lips. The White Crow stood and walked across to sit on the sill, drawing her feet up, bracketed by the frame.

'There have been three other Scholar-Soldiers come to the heart of the world,' Casaubon said, 'since you disappeared.'

Feathers rustled by her head. She flinched at the fluttering.

Bright chaffinches flew to perch on the Lord-Architect's extended plump fingers. A thrush's claws scored his head, pricking sharp through his hair; and a humming-bird the same brilliant blue as his satin coat hung so close before his face that his eyes crossed watching it. He whistled again.

She met his gaze through vibrating wings.

'None of them survived a half-year,' he concluded.

'I didn't know. This place is scaring me shitless.' The White Crow lifted her chin. 'You're not helping.'

'I have a message from the Invisible College.'

She reached forward, past her raised knees, touching the wooden window-frame. Sun-warmed, barely damp now. She breathed the acrid smell of street-dust. Heat already soaked the sky: people hurrying past kept to the buildings' shadows. Clock-mill's half-hour chime came from the far side of the building.

'I haven't written on the moon in ten years. Believe that I wouldn't have sent out any warning unless I had to. If I'd known it would bring *you*—'

His cushioned arms pushed between her back and the window-frame, and under the arch of her knees. She grabbed wildly, balance gone; blindly lurching back from the one-storey drop. His arms tightened. The White Crow knotted fists in his shirt as the fat man lifted her, holding her across the swell of his stomach.

'I am not in the habit of being a messenger-boy! Sit down, sit still, shut up and *listen*!'

Her bare feet hit the floor stingingly hard.

'Get the hell out of here!'

Lucas's voice came from the corner of the room: 'How does an invisible college find itself, to send messages?'

'Oh, what!' Exasperated, the White Crow swung round. She met his dark gaze, seeing both amusement and calculation. She nodded once. As she tucked her white shirt into her breeches, she said: 'Well done, Prince. But you won't stop the two of us quarrelling. As to your question, the College is wherever two or three Scholar-Soldiers happen to meet. Often you never *do* find out just who suggested what.'

A last sparrow flew out of the street-side window. The Lord-Architect rubbed absently at his sleeves, smearing guano across the blue satin. Wet patches of sweat already showed under his arms.

'You're promoted,' he announced, 'from Master-Captain to Master-Physician Valentine.'

She felt an amazed grin start, and touched clasped fists to her mouth to hide the joy. 'You're joking. No, really.'

'I'm telling the truth,' Casaubon said.

'I never thought they'd ever – But I've left the damned College!' She sat down at the table and looked at Lucas. 'Yes, and your next question is *How do you find the College to leave it?*'

The Lord-Architect rested his hand on Lucas's shoulder as he walked around to face her. 'The Invisible College's rules are strict. We travel incognito, Prince, and never more than two or three together.'

'Oh, this is quite ridiculous.' The White Crow pressed the heels of her hands into her eyes, lost in a sparkling darkness. Evelian's voice sounded out in the courtyard, talking to her daughter Sharlevian. It came no nearer. A bee hummed in through one window, out through the other.

'Stupid.' She took her sweat-damp hands away from her face. 'I did leave. You knew it; so did Master-Captain Janou. You can't make me a Master-Physician, because I won't let you.'

The young man squatted down, fiddling with one of the chests against the wall.

'You know what's truly stupid?' She turned her head towards Casaubon. 'What's stupid is that it comforted me, sometimes, to think that I might be part of the College still – whoever we are, and however many there may be of us. I had to leave you, but I lost something when I left.'

'And so did I.'

The White Crow felt her cheeks heat. She rubbed her flat palms against her face.

'And so did you . . . And now I don't want anything to do with this. I sent that warning because I want nothing to do with this; I wanted someone wiser to come here and *do* something about it!'

Casaubon *tsk*-ed ironically. 'Poor Valentine.'

Lucas's hand passed over her shoulder, and she sat up as a long bundle clattered on to the mirror-table.

'I asked the Lord-Architect about Scholar-Soldiers,' the young man said. 'You should be carrying this.'

She ignored Casaubon's startled look. Her fingers undid the wrappings, sliding scabbard and sword onto the table. The sweat-darkened leather grip on the hilt fitted her fingers, ridged to their exact shape. The weight on her wrist when she lifted it, familiar and strange now, made her throat ache.

'Why does the College need a Master-Physician here?'

'I would like to know that,' Casaubon said.

She rubbed her finger along the oiled flat of the blade. Cold metal, cold as mornings walking the road, or evenings coming to an inn. The smell of the oil mixed with the smell of the ink on the table, drying on the hieroglyphed parchments.

'What could possibly need *healing?'*

In one flawless movement she clicked the rapier home in its scabbard. The straps and buckles of the sword-belt tumbled across the table.

'I'm frightened.'

The Lord-Architect's voice rumbled above her head. 'That makes me afraid.'

'Well, that's sense enough.' Hands still on the scabbard, she looked across at Lucas. 'Oh, and if I wear this in the street I'll be in the palace dungeons before you can say *his Majesty.'*

'You need to wear it,' he insisted. 'You need to. Not for protection.'

She looked down at hands tanned and with a fine grain to the skin, the blue veins showing faintly under the surface. She flexed her fingers.

'A wise child. My lord, you have a wise child with you.' She took Casaubon's cuff between thumb and forefinger. The sweat-damp satin smelt of an expensive scent. 'Something formal, is it?'

'The Fane. An audience, at the eleventh hour.'

'*What?* Who with? The Spagyrus?'

The Lord-Architect spread padded hands. 'How can I tell you that? You've left the College.'

The White Crow drew in a breath, saliva tasting metallic. Gaining time, she stood, her practised fingers unbuckling the straps of the sword-hanger and belt. She muttered irritably, waving away Lucas's offered help; and busied herself for almost two minutes in slinging straps over her shoulders and around her hips, buckling the scabbard so that it hung comfortably across her back, hilt jutting above her right shoulder.

'If I accept Master-Physician?' she queried.

Casaubon pushed the piles of paper from the table onto the floor, spun the table to its mirror side, and began to comb his copper hair into a neat Brutus style. Before she could get breath to swear he straightened, and pulled white cotton gloves from his capacious pockets.

'I am told' – Casaubon tugged glove-fingers snugly down – 'that I shall be seeing the Thirty-Sixth Decan, whose sign is the Ten Degrees of High Summer.'

The White Crow worked the belt around her waist, made an alteration of one notch to a buckle. Then she reached across and brushed the Lord-Architect's fingers away, and buttoned his gloves at the wrist.

'Lucas . . .'

She crossed the room and hugged the young man, having to stand up on the balls of her feet and stretch her arms around his muscled back. His eyes shone. She stepped back, reaching up to touch the hilt of her sword, where it hung ready for a down-draw over the shoulder.

'Thank you,' she said, and to Casaubon: 'I'll come to the Fane with you. Lucas, can I ask you a favour? I need you to go and see your uncle, the Ambassador.'

Blinding and imperceptible, the sun rose higher.

Pools of rain in Evelian's courtyard shrank fraction by fraction. The heat of the sun drew mosquito nymphs to the water's surface. The wooden frieze of skulls and spades grew warm, and hosted colonies of insects swarmed out of cracks.

Wings skirred: one of the Lord-Architect's sparrows fluttering to the eaves.

Beyond Clock-mill, lizards sunned themselves in corners of streets left drowsy and deserted. White dust and white blossom snowed the streets of the city.

The sparrow flicked from eaves to tiles to roof-ridge, crossing the quarter. Where the Fane's obelisks cut the sky, the bird scurried for height, lost in the milk-blue heavens; flying swiftly south-aust.

Down between marble wharfs, heat-swollen helium airships tugged at mooring-ropes. Crews rushed to the gas-vents. The bird's bead-black eyes registered movement. A dusty-brown mop of feathers, it fell towards an airship's underslung cabin.

Aust, north, south, east and west: the city stretches away below, reflected in the sparrow's uncomprehending vision.

A day later, one woman crewing an airship will find the bird, half-frozen, and feed it drops of warm milk and millet. Thinking to keep it as a pet, when the airship's long overseas voyage is done.

The Lord-Architect's sparrow rests, cushioned under her shirt, between her breasts. The bead-black eyes hold a message that is simple enough for those with the power to read it.

'Carrying a sword?' the Candovard Ambassador exclaimed.

'It was wonderful. *She* was wonderful!' Lucas sobered. 'At first . . . I don't know what she's seen to cause her so much fear. But she's going to the Fane at eleven this morning.'

'A sword,' Andaluz repeated.

'Well, yes, technically she shouldn't, but . . .'

Andaluz scratched his salt-and-pepper hair. One stubby finger pointed at his Prince.

'This is the heart of the world, not the White Mountain. Cand-over sees its Rat-Lord Governor only once or twice a year, and you're let carry weapons there because who else could? Here, every Rat with pretensions to gentle blood carries a sword. Gods preserve men or women who trespass on their privileges!'

Dust drifted in from the compound. Flies haunted the ceiling, undeterred by the *wck-wck-wck* of the fan.

'I . . . didn't realise.' Lucas, who had carried his shirt in his hand, slung it about his neck like a towel, and tugged it back and forth to mop up sweat.

'Your father could never bear it. I discourage him from travelling here.' Andaluz pushed his chair back from the big desk. 'Lucas, dear boy, here I'm the ambassador from savages – yes, *savages* – who are suffered to live with only minor supervision, because we're far away and beneath the Rat-Lords' notice.'

'And I told her to carry a sword.' Lucas's eyes showed dark in a face gone greenish-white. 'I'll have to warn her!'

'If this White Crow woman has been five years in the heart of the world, I assure you that she knows.'

'She *needs* it. To be what she should be.' Lucas looked up from the dusty patterned carpet. 'She asked if you would attend at court today. I told her that you would. I told her that you'll use all of Candover's influence with the King, Uncle, if she's troubled or arrested.'

'Yes, Prince.' Andaluz made a face. 'What there is of it. Ah . . . the university?'

'I'll take care of that. Reverend Mistress Heurodis has her own way with students,' the young man said. 'I'm coming with you to court. A prince's word may carry weight.'

'Aww, this sun's too bright. Hold on a minute.' The cinnamon-haired woman clattered back up the stairs from the street-door.

The Lord-Architect Casaubon waited by the carriage, easing his shirt away from the rolls of flesh at his neck. Sweat trickled down his back.

She re-emerged holding a white felt hat, wide-brimmed and with a dented crown. It had a black band, and small black characters printed into the felt. She clapped it on to her head and tilted it, shading her eyes.

'And you say *I* have no dress sense.'

She smiled. 'No sense of any kind, as far as I could ever make out . . . You know what this hat needs?'

'Euthanasia?'

'A black feather. Tell me if you spot one.'

She leaned automatically up against his arm, sparking backchat off his deadpan replies with the ease of habit and practice. Now he saw her frown. She moved away.

'Master-Physician.' The Lord-Architect very formally offered a glove, handing her into the carriage.

He settled himself opposite her, with his back to the driver, the carriage sinking on its springs. The oxen lowed and pulled away. The red-haired woman tilted her hat further down towards her nose, and rested one heel up on his seat.

'The Decans,' she said, 'won't swallow any story about your being a travelling horologer or garden-architect, or whatever nonsense you gave Captain-General Desaguliers. Who have you said you are?'

'A Scholar-Soldier of the Invisible College.'

He beamed, seeing Valentine reduced to complete speechlessness. 'They'll know, in any case,' he added.

'And you think they're going to let us out of there after that!'

He smiled.

'Casaubon!'

Casaubon dug in one pocket, thumbed ponderously through a very small notebook, extracted a pencil from the spine, and began to write, with many hesitations and crossings-out. The carriage jolted into wider streets.

The White Crow stood it for all of three minutes. 'What are you writing?'

His blue eyes all but vanished into his padded cheeks as he squinted in concentration.

'Poetry,' said the Lord-Architect, 'but I can't think of a rhyme for "Valentine".'

His formally buttoned black doublet left Lucas dizzy with the heat. He fingered the short ruff, moving a step closer to Andaluz. Loud talk resounded from almost two hundred and fifty Rats and humans crowding the main audience chamber.

The clover-leaf-domed hall soared, and Lucas lifted his head, gaping up at the four bright domes. Andaluz's pepper-and-salt brows dipped in the family frown.

'Two of the – no, *three* of the Lords Magi are here,' he said, looking through the crowd at black Rats in sleeveless gold robes.

'And most of the noble Houses . . . And all seven Cardinals-General of the Church . . .'

Rows of paired guards in Cadet uniform lined the interlocking circular walls, black fur gleaming. At regular intervals ceiling-length curtains were drawn across windows that, none the less, admitted chinks of sunlight.

'Whatever this is, it's blown up fast as a summer storm.'

'What . . . ?' Lucas moved away from the main entrance's staircase. He began walking towards the point where two of the four semi-circular floor areas intersected.

A treadmill stood a little out from the blue-draped wall, on the spindle of some panelled and bolted metal machine. Blue-white sparks shot out of the metal casing.

The treadmill itself stood eight feet tall. In its cage, two men and a woman, stripped to breech-clouts, trod the steps down in never-ending repetition. Lucas, shoved by the press of assembled bodies, turned away. He saw two more treadmills over the heads of the crowd.

Thick cables wound up from the machines to the ceilings. In the four hollow domes, a stalactite-forest of chandeliers hung down. Lucas saw clusters of glass, wires burning blue-white and blue-purple, and lowered his gaze, blinking away water.

'Impressive,' Andaluz said. 'If they didn't have to close the curtains to show it off, and stifle all of us.'

The actinic light wavered down on Rats in the sleeveless robes of Lords Magi, on the jewelled collars and swords of nobles and soldiers, the red and purple of priests.

'Uncle . . .' Lucas turned. Startled, he met the gaze of a youth much his own age. The young man smiled. Fair-haired, stripped to breeches and barefoot, he wore a studded collar round his throat. From it hung a metal leash. A middle-aged black Rat robed in yards of orange taffeta held the end of the leash casually in her hand.

'Bred from the finest stock,' Lucas heard her say to another female black Rat, 'and trained fully in all skills.'

She trailed the chain-leash over one furry shoulder, and tugged the metal links. The fair-haired young man squatted down on his haunches at her side.

'A pretty little thing, yes.' The second black Rat, slender in linen shirt and breeches enclosing furry haunches, her rapier slung at her side, turned to eye the treadmills. Two men and a woman in the wheel plodded, heads down, gripping the central bar with sweat-stained hands.

'Don't stare,' Andaluz murmured. 'You're being provincial.'

The Rat in linen and leather swaggered a little, by the treadmill, hand on her sword, ears twitching. The other Rat tugged the leash, walking away with the young man trotting at her heels.

'I must confess,' Lucas heard his uncle saying to a robed man as he rejoined them, 'that I feared an incident of some magnitude. For one of your King's daughters to be killed here . . .'

The South Katayan Ambassador shrugged.

'I knew Zari briefly.' Lucas met the man's pale amber eyes. His white robe had been slit at the back, and a sleek black tail caressed the tiled floor.

'King's daughter is hardly a unique position. South Katay's full of them.' The Ambassador, off-hand, reached to pick up a wine glass from a passing brown Rat servant's tray. 'The King will naturally be grieved to hear that Zar-bettu-zekigal could not complete her training as a Memory.'

'She—'

The Katayan Ambassador caught a tall Rat's glance across the crowd and murmured: 'Excuse me. I must speak to Captain-General Desaguliers.'

Lucas slid a court shoe across the gold-and-blue tiles. Black and brown Rats surrounded him, in formal silks and jewelled collars and cloaks; he stood lost in the noise of their voices. A few inches shorter than most, he could not, from this corner by the full-length windows, see over heads and feather-plumes to the throne.

'She made me laugh,' he said. 'She didn't give a damn for anyone. Maybe I would have liked her, if I'd had time.'

Andaluz nodded gravely.

'Keep your eye on Desaguliers,' the older man directed. 'If there are any arrests, Desaguliers' police will be making them. He'll be notified. If we can see when that happens, I can try to bring it to his Majesty's attention.'

'Right.'

Casually keeping the South Katayan Ambassador and Desaguliers in sight, Lucas threaded his way through the crowd. A word here and there to other ambassadors, as his training inculcated in him; pitching his voice above the chatter, side-stepping the jutting scabbards of rapiers, the trailing silk-lined edges of cloaks.

'Mind out!' A brown Rat pushed him aside, jerking his tail out of the way. 'Why they let these peasants in, I'll never know . . .'

Lucas bowed formally, one hand clenching in a fist.

Brass horns shattered conversation. A uniformed brown Rat at the head of the stairs announced lords whose names Lucas didn't catch. Satin and lace flurried as the Rats walked forward to make their brief bows to the Rat-King. Conversation resumed.

Desaguliers, shedding the South Katayan Ambassador, pushed his way towards the centre of the hall. High above, the clover-leaf of domes intersected in a fantasia of vaulting. Lucas fell in a few paces behind, taking a glass from a passing tray; all training in unobtrusive crowd-movement coming to him without thought.

'—let the Kings' Memory speak—'

He cannoned into the back of a tall Rat in grey silk. The Rat's hand cuffed his ear, jewelled rings stinging, and a drop of blood fell onto his ruff. Lucas only continued to stare. Using elbows, he shoved two brown Rat servants aside and forced his way to the front edge of the central crowd.

Drapes soared tent-like from a central golden boss to hang down the intersecting walls. Where the lights struck, they glowed sea-deep in shadow purple as evening. Framed by this canopy, the white silk of a great circular bed gleamed.

Sweet incense reached Lucas's nostrils.

Dais steps went up to the bed-throne, where the Rat-King lay among cushions and pillows of silk. Eight scaly tails showed dark in the middle of the Rats' groomed fur and silk jackets: gnarled and knotted, grown together.

Lucas ignored the dozen Rats of various rank and dress who knelt on the dais steps, talking to the Rat-King. Tense, he willed the long-coated figure to turn around . . .

Black hair fell lank to either side of a sharp face. The skinny young woman stood barefoot, scuffing her toes down on the tiled floor below the dais, head about on a level with one of the silver-furred Rats-King. One hand stayed thrust in the pocket of a stained and torn brown greatcoat. The other gestured fluidly.

'*Zari?*'

He stood some four yards from her, but names draw attention: the Katayan's head turned, and she nodded once in his direction.

'*. . . the Lady Hyena's people to carry arms, to walk the streets above ground, to be free of the outstanding penalties against them as rebels and traitors,*' she concluded, the concentration of Memory leaving her voice.

The silver-furred and the bony black Rats-King spoke in tandem to a kneeling Rat priest. Lucas made covert frantic signals which Zar-bettu-zekigal ignored.

He looked again at the priest. A black Rat, down on one knee on the dais steps, his scarlet jacket blazing against the white silk of the bed. He held his plumed headband clasped in one slender-fingered ringed hand. His mobile furry snout quivered, speaking to the silver Rats-King in a rapid monologue.

'It is her. *She's alive!* And the priest is Plessiez,' he muttered to Andaluz as the older man reached him. 'The one we met in the crypt. I'm certain of it.'

He read hunger and exhaustion in her face – high on tension, high on hardship – and glanced again at Plessiez. The same, better-concealed, showed in the black Rat.

'We can't speak to her now . . .'

Lucas caught the approach of Desaguliers out of the corner of his eye. He nudged the Candovard Ambassador's arm, and faded back a rank or two into the crowd. Practised, he lost the Captain-General's attention, thinking furiously. He ducked past a fat female Rat in mauve satin and came out by the wall and the edge of the drapes. A brawny Rat edged backwards into him, muttered an apology without turning to see she had apologised to a man. Lucas became aware that most of the front rank of the crowd tensed, eavesdropping; and he slid his black-clad form behind the brawny Rat, and strained to listen.

'Your Majesty will appreciate the necessity,' the black Rat, Plessiez, said.

The silver-furred Rat rolled on to his left side, scratching idly at one furry haunch. 'Indeed we do, messire. Messire Plessiez, in view of what you say, we have decided to grant your request. For a preliminary trial period.'

Lucas saw Zar-bettu-zekigal straighten, enthusiasm in the line of her narrow shoulders. Plessiez rose to his feet, bowing, and backing unerring down the dais steps.

'Then, with your Majesty's permission, I'll send the delegation and the Memory to inform the Lady Hyena of your decision.'

Lucas scowled, bemused.

'Go. We do so order.'

In the gap between Plessiez's snout and Zari's head, Lucas glimpsed the South Katayan Ambassador clutching Desaguliers' arm, muttering rapidly at the Captain-General. A short plump Rat blocked his view. She and a raffish black Rat flanked Zar-bettu-zekigal as Plessiez directed the Katayan to leave.

Zar-bettu-zekigal passed close enough for her greatcoat to brush Lucas's leg. The briefest glance of helplessness and humour darted in Lucas's direction. She left a scent on the air of water, stagnant and stale. Lucas pondered the nature of the stains on her coat, scowling to himself.

'Her ambassador didn't seem pleased,' he said as Andaluz reappeared through the crush.

'Ger-zarru-huk's a bastard at the best of times. Strictly off the record.'

'I have to talk with Zari.' Lucas put a hand against his side, still expecting to find a sword there. He scowled.

'You resemble your mother greatly when you do that,' Andaluz remarked, 'and gods know she's a stubborn enough woman. This student romance of yours—'

'No. By no means that.' Lucas stopped the older man. 'Uncle, what have you got on file for the Invisible College?'

Andaluz blinked, matching his nephew step for ratiocinative step. 'Mendicant scholars and mercenaries spread rumours that there is such a thing. All mythical, of course. It's been quite fully investigated.'

The buzz of conversation rose by several levels. Lucas, pressed between two black Rats, side-stepped a dagger-hilt at one's belt and slid back to the Candovard Ambassador. Doubt jolted him, as sudden and shocking as stepping off a stair in the dark.

'But—'

Brazen horns blared. This time the sound echoed from the high vaulted ceilings, bright sound in artificial brilliance; muffled itself in drapes and hangings; and blew again, redoubled, in a shriek that cut through every Rat and human voice. It sounded a final time and fell silent.

A black Rat in major-domo's robes rapped her garnet-studded ivory staff on the tiles.

'*Hear his Majesty the King!* The hall is to be cleared of all below the rank of noble. All servants, ambassadors and other humans will leave immediately. *Hear the word of the King!*'

The mounts spooked as the carriage jolted under the fifth arch on Austroad. The driver swore. The White Crow gazed up at the shaking roof of the carriage and the unseen coachman, and lifted her black-and-white hat in salute.

Through open shadowed windows, the chitinous hum of insects echoed in the canyon between wall and high wall.

She saw Casaubon lean back in his seat, rummaging through an inside pocket. He brought his hand out, ink-stained fingers all but concealing a silver hip-flask.

'Give me that,' the White Crow said, reaching across. She tilted her head back, drank, coughed, and wiped her nose. 'You're *still* drinking this stuff?'

The Lord-Architect took the hip-flask back. He made to replace it in his capacious pocket, shook it close to one freckled ear, listened – and up-ended it down his throat.

'*Casaubon* . . .'

He raised it to drink again, spilling the sticky metheglin down his embroidered blue-and-gold waistcoat and blue silk breeches. He cracked a phenomenally loud belch.

'You can't leave me to do this on my own,' the White Crow protested.

The Lord-Architect stowed his empty flask away, and looked down owlishly at the small notebook lying open on his spreading thigh.

' "Valentine".' he mused. ' "Eglantine" . . . ? "Porcupine" . . . ?'

The White Crow ran her tongue over the back of her teeth, wincing at the aftertaste.

' "Turpentine"? ' she suggested.

The strokes of ten clashed across Nineteenth District's tiny south quarter. Reverend Master Candia took his hand away from his face. The unfamiliar open sky shocked him. He looked at the blood on his palms.

'Did They brand me?' His voice croaked. 'I should be marked.'

Pigeons scuttered up into the air, their shadows and guano falling into the alley at the back of the deserted Cathedral of the Trees. Slumped into the corner of wall and door, masonry bruised Candia's shoulders and buttocks.

'Bastard!'

'Down him again!'

'Here, Sordio, let me—'

'He's *mine*. No one else's!'

A hand grabbed his collar. His loose lacy shirt ripped. Candia pitched forward on to hands and knees, groaning; and yelled with pain as a boot slammed into his ribs. He scrabbled and caught the iron drainpipe stapled to the wall, pulling himself up on to his knees.

A familiar voice rasped: 'I might have known we'd find you slumming around this place. Thirty-Six! Why did you *do* it?'

Candia rubbed the back of his wrist across his mouth. Stale food crusted his straggling beard. His own breath came back to him, stinking; and he coughed, tears running from the corners of his eyes. A spurt of fear pushed him to his feet, eyes wide.

He staggered forward, other hands grabbing him before he fell.

'*Why?*'

'Mendicant scholars and mercenaries spread rumours that there is such a thing. All mythical, of course.' From the tomb of Christian Rosenkreuz

A taste of copper in his mouth faded to the taste of old vomit. Candia smiled shakily. He reached out and stroked the face of the man who held him by the shoulders: a crop-haired man with his own sandy colouring; a man with dust-sore eyes; large, furious, utterly familiar.

'Sordio.' He patted the older man's cheek. 'And Ercole here, too. Is all the family—?'

Out of nowhere, a fist slammed into his face. Agony blinded him. Vision cleared, and through pain's water he saw a dozen men in silk overalls, some with sticks, all much of an age with Sordio; and he brushed uselessly at his own filthy clothes. Bruises purpled his fingers.

'Brother—'

'You're no brother of mine.' Sordio's hands flexed. 'We should have drowned you at birth.'

'*Damn you, do you know what I had to do?*'

He stared down silenced faces. Sun beat into the alley. He shifted scuffed boots, tucking his ripped shirt back into his breeches, fastening his thick leather belt on the third attempt. All the university's training gone, driven from his head; even the instinct that had brought him back to Theodoret's cathedral eradicated now. He held Sordio's gaze.

'We saw you,' Sordio said flatly. 'Over at the hall, in the rubble.'

The remembered texture of broken planking and bricks woke in his hands. Candia raised them and stared at ripped nails, bloody fingers.

Sordio's gaze went past him to the barred cathedral door. 'Do you think our mother never knew that he put you up to that place?'

'Bishop Theodoret is my friend.' The words left him unprompted. Candia opened his mouth in a gasp, tears filling his eyes, and giggled. 'Yes, he helped me to get into the university. Yes. The old bitch'd be proud of the return favour I've given him for that—'

He laughed helplessly. One dark man swung a splintered piece of two-by-four; he caught it on one up-raised arm, twisted it free of the man's grip, and whacked it back against the cathedral wall. The dull *crack!* echoed. The man stepped back. He stared at Sordio.

'Leave me alone!'

'You bastard, you brought them down on the Hall, you did that!'

Heat from the morning sun soaked into his bruised shoulders. He swallowed. His mouth tasted foul, but with the foulness of humanity: no copper-coin bitterness now.

'I'll say this.' He watched Sordio. A little older now, this last year gone by, a little stouter, with the muscles of a builder; wearing now the gold ribbon of the House of Salomon openly on his overalls. 'I went to the Lord Decan. I told him what was happening at the East-quarter hall. *You* told me.'

'Thirty-Six, you're my *brother*. I thought I could trust you!'

'You could. You can.'

A black beetle crawled in the dust on the cathedral's back step, abandoning the rubbish piled in the corner of the door. Masonry chilled his back where he leaned against the door-arch. Candia tensed. His body shuddered, shuddered uncontrollably; the thin beam of wood falling from his hands to the paving.

'I know exactly how many people died at that hall. I can tell you their names.' He shut his eyes, dizzy; opened them again to a blue-stained sunlight, and Sordio's sweating red face. 'It was better that some people should die now than most of the District die later. We had to take that decision. That was what we said. It's better—'

He swallowed with difficulty.

'Damn you, do it, then! Here I am. I'm telling you, the Lord Decan could wipe you out like *that*.' His boot crunched the black beetle into a chitinous smear. 'And what are we to them? They wouldn't waste time sorting out who's in the House of Salomon conspiracy and who's innocent. Remember Fifth District? A massacre!'

Somewhere, far away, a clock struck the quarter-hour.

A spar cracked across Candia's hip and stomach. He screamed. Two men moved in with fists. He staggered, tried a spin and kick; fell forward into Sordio's grip, gasping.

His brother's fist sank deep and hard into his stomach. Candia bent double, vomiting. Water blurred his vision, and he clamped his eyes shut.

Far above, a rustle of dry wings electrified the noon sky; and a line of blood incised itself across the inside of his eyelids. A distant mockery hissed in the sun.

—*Twice traitor!*—

'Clear the chamber,' Captain-General Desaguliers ordered. '*Move.*'

Sleek black Rat Cadets split up, crossing the great clover-leaf audience chamber. Desaguliers took up a stance under the vaulting of one intersection, watching ambassadors complain: Ger-zarru-huk protesting volubly, leaving at last with two Cadets gripping him firmly under the arms, his tail lashing; the Candovard Ambassador forcing his own contentious prince from the hall.

His scarred face creased, the smile sardonic.

'Messire, the generators? The human servants?'

Desaguliers picked his incisors with a neatly trimmed claw. Unlike the Magi, Lords and priests, he wore severe black sword-harness and studded leather collar.

'Leave 'em,' he directed the young Cadet. 'His Majesty'll spit blood if the precious lights don't stay on. When this is over, sling 'em in gaol for a week or two, until they forget they ever heard anything here today.'

The Cadet smartly touched her silver headband.

Desaguliers shoved through the press of bodies, checking for humans. The hot curtained morning brought a shiver to his spine. Premonitory, his scarred face creased into a frown. His black eyes, anxious for once, sought through the crowded ranks for a red-jacketed priest: one among many.

'Plessiez,' he muttered.

Hands resting on his plain sword-belt, he strode towards the dais and the King: narrow powerful shoulders thrusting a way between black and brown Rats. The four sets of double doors clanged shut. Cadets slid lock-bars into place, then moved to position themselves against the walls. Heat slicked Desaguliers' fur up into tufts. The noise and confusion of two hundred nobles, Magi and priests washed over him, and he wiped the fur above his eyes.

'Secure.' He made a low bow at the foot of the dais.

The Rat-King looked up from ordering pages to clear the silks and cushions, several pairs of eyes turning towards Desaguliers. The Captain-General's spine stiffened. Standing on the lowest step of the dais by one silver-furred Rats-King, Plessiez folded sleek hands and smiled.

'Messire Desaguliers.'

'Your reverence.'

The actinic lights brightened. Desaguliers heard a thong crack at the back of the hall, and a treadmill creak faster. Points of hard light shot back from diamond collars, from rings, from sword-hilts and from the black eyes of Rats. The smell of heat and fur made his snout tense rhythmically.

Lords Magi took their places in the first rank of the circle surrounding the bed-throne, and he moved a step aside as the seven Cardinals-General joined them. Across the room, he met Cardinal Ignatia's gaze, vainly searching for some hint of the future.

The Rat-King stood, one brown Rat offering a hand to the bony black Rat, the rest rising with some dignity. The knot of their tails stood out stark, scaled, deformed. With one movement the assembly bowed. Desaguliers, straightening, saw the Chancellor crack her ivory staff against the tiles.

'Hear his Majesty!'

All voices silenced, the only sound came from the hum and spark of the generators, the creak of the turning treadmills. The Rat-King stood in a circle, each Rat facing out across the assembly. Pages hurriedly finished draping the shoulders of each with cloth-of-gold cloaks.

The bony black Rats-King spoke.

'Captain-General.'

Desaguliers bowed, hands resting on his plain sword-belt. 'Your Majesty desires?'

'It seems Messire Plessiez survived the attack from the Fane.'

Tension and the fear of ridicule walked hot shivers up Desaguliers' spine. He glanced around, tail twitching. A few faces showed incomprehension. His eyes swept the Lords Magi and the Cardinals-General, seeing knowing smiles.

'Yes, your Majesty.'

Desaguliers made a low bow, going on one knee on the dais steps. His sword-harness clashed. That and his studded black collar were his only ornaments: a lean ragged black Rat in middle years. He lifted his head to meet the Rat-King's gaze.

'We should have been most interested to discover—'

'—what was said at that hall,' a brown Rats-King concluded. 'But you could not tell us, messire.'

'You could not tell us,' the bony black Rats-King smiled, 'that we knew of Messire Plessiez's mission. That he had our authority.'

Desaguliers studiously kept his face turned away from the little priest.

'I've done my best to investigate,' he judged it safe to say.

The black Rat glared down at Desaguliers, who began to sweat.

'Messire Plessiez made it clear just how long you were present at that meeting, before the Fane's acolytes attacked. You heard all of what was said there, and thought fit not to inform us of that fact.'

Desaguliers' whiskers quivered. His dark-fingered hand clenched by his side.

'We don't care to be deceived. We think that such an offence deserves summary dismissal—'

'—but that the little priest's evidence is not unbiased,' one of the silver-furred Rats concluded sardonically, leaning over from the far side of the circular bed. He fixed Desaguliers with eyes dark as garnets. 'We might advise you to prove your innocence, messire, and in fairly short order.'

The jabber and laughter of the Lords Magi and nobles washed

over him. He rose to his feet, and nodded once sharply: 'As your Majesty wishes.'

The bony black Rats-King turned his head, searching the ranks of nobles, Lords Magi and priests. Desaguliers breathed hard, sensing a respite but no escape.

'Cardinal-General Ignatia.'

The elderly female Rat stepped forward from the six other Cardinals-General of the Church, straightening her emerald-green robe.

'Your Majesty, I must protest at this sudden action of Messire Plessiez. He has been acting entirely without the authority of the Order of Guiry—'

'He has acted at all times with *our* authority and full knowledge.'

'I don't understand, your Majesty.'

Desaguliers smoothed his whiskers down, studying Ignatia's genuine bewilderment. A hot temper flared in his gut, and a fear. Whispered comments in the crowd located the fear: that something so obviously long-planned could occur without Desaguliers' police knowing of it.

The bony black Rats-King waved one hand, rings flashing in the artificial light.

'It seems to us,' he said mildly, 'that the pressures of the generalship of the Order of Guiry stand between you and your excellent scholarship, Cardinal Ignatia. We therefore promote a new Cardinal-General into your place, to enable you to spend even more of your valuable time in the Archives.'

Ignatia opened her mouth, closed it again, and fell to grooming the fur of one arm for a few seconds. Desaguliers caught her eye as she looked up, her gaze now lustreless.

'As your Majesty wishes. Who is my successor?'

Under his breath Desaguliers could not help muttering: 'You must be the only one in this room who doesn't guess!'

'Messire Plessiez,' the black Rats-King said sardonically, 'we invest you Cardinal-General of the Order of Guiry. Remembering always that poor service merits loss of such a position.'

Plessiez's head turned. He stared directly at Desaguliers.

The Captain-General's temper flared. 'I think his Majesty has no reason to complain of my service!'

In the crowd, several people sniggered. Desaguliers bit his lip, straightened and, having walked into the priest's trap, chose bluster to see him through it. He swept a curt bow to the black Rats-King.

'I *do* think you have no reason to complain of my service. If your

Majesty doubts me, my resignation is tendered now, this morning –
this moment. Let St Cyr have the Cadets.'

The silver-furred and the bony black Rats-King exchanged
glances. Desaguliers stood with his spine taut. One hand caressed
the hilt of his sword. His black eyes flicked to each one of the Rats-
King, bright with calculation.

'Yes . . .' The silver Rat smiled. The black Rat continued: 'Yes, we
agree. For a while, Messire Desaguliers, we accept your resignation.
Order Messire St Cyr to us after we have spoken to this assembly. It
will be politic to have him conduct this investigation. You will
resume your post when proved innocent of any deception of your
King.'

Desaguliers opened his mouth. His jaw hung slack for a second;
then snapped shut.

'Furthermore,' a black Rats-King said, 'St Cyr is to have the
overseeing of the artillery garden. Send your imported architect to
him as soon as is convenient.'

Desaguliers gave the briefest bow and turned away, not waiting
for a dismissal. Fury scoured him. He shouldered past five or six
Rat-Lords. Their laughter cauterised him.

At the far end of one clover-leaf, by the barred doors, he
abandoned caution and summoned one of the Cadets with a fierce
look.

'We must move earlier than I expected.'

'Messire?'

'St Cyr is to have the Cadets.' Desaguliers' scarred face twisted
into a smile. 'You might say I was fool enough to give his command
to him . . . Next time I'll make *sure* Plessiez is a corpse. Call the
others together. We'll meet at noon. All plans will have to be
advanced. Pass word on.'

The tall black Rat bowed, and slid away into the massed
assembly.

Desaguliers caught his breath with some difficulty, stared down
the dozen or so Rats nearest to him; and then cocked his ears as the
brass horns rang out again, silencing the assembly.

'We have called you here, also, to witness the promulgation of a
new law.'

The taller of the silver-furred Rats-King spoke, voice dropping
into the expectant silence. His incisors showed in a smile.

'It is not our intention to explain our policy, but to be obeyed in
what we say.

'For the immediate future, and for however long it may chance to
pass—'

'—and because we are a generous sovereign, wishing nothing more than to be loved by our people—'

'—we hereby revoke the penalties of treason and conspiracy outstanding against the human rebels now fugitive here in the heart of the world.'

A rumble of protest rose up into the vaulted roofs.

Desaguliers stared across the heads of the crowd, between translucent ears and nodding feather-plumes. The bright gold-cloaked figures of the Rat-King spangled light back, dazzling the assembled nobles.

'Therefore,' continued the other silver-furred Rats-King, his voice proceeding with the slightest-possible stutter, 'and as a gesture of goodwill, we promulgate the following law: that all men and women under the gold-cross banner of the Sun may be permitted to carry weapons in the streets and dwellings of the city.'

'*Never!*'

Against the crescendo of shouting, the Rats-King said something to the Chancellor, and that Rat slammed her ivory-and-garnet staff against the tiles and cried out: '*This audience is over!*'

Lights dimmed, Cadets wrenched curtains open, and sun and air poured in. Desaguliers pushed through the dazed assembly to be first out. He caught one glimpse of Plessiez as he went. The little priest stood on the dais steps, deep in conversation with the silver-furred Rats-King, smiling.

The carriage drew up outside one of the smaller and older of the Thirty-Six temples of the Fane. A clock down in North quarter struck quarter to the hour of eleven.

'Shit,' said the White Crow.

A granular sea-mist greyed the stone cornices and columns. The air below the mist made street-level humid, warm as bathwater. She hooked one bent frame of her spectacles in the V of her buttoned shirt, and pushed the brim of her hat up.

'I don't think this is one of your better ideas,' she remarked, dismounting from the carriage. Its springs creaked as the Lord-Architect got out after her.

'What's more—'

She turned her head to add another word of disquiet and stopped. The Lord-Architect Casaubon ponderously moved to position himself beside the rear nearside wheel. The White Crow's jaw slackened as he unbuttoned the flap of his blue silk breeches, reached down, stared absently back down the hill, and urinated fully and at some length over the wooden wheel-spokes.

'Oh, really!' The White Crow's exasperation gave way to laughter. 'There is a time and a place to exercise ancient privileges, and this isn't either one of them!'

Mist dissipated. Above the cityscape gliders flinked brilliance from their wings, circling about a central column of air.

'Nervous,' Casaubon explained, buttoning himself up.

'*You?*'

'Wait for us,' the Lord-Architect directed the carriage-driver.

The White Crow took a pace. Shadow fell cool across her back, where her linen shirt plastered sweaty skin. As if it were a talisman she raised her hand to her nostrils and inhaled human odours of heat.

A hooped arch broke the Fane's brown brick wall. Stepping under it, she saw other arches in other walls opening off to left and right. Across a small courtyard, and arch's bricks burned tawny in sunlight. Beyond, another lay in shade.

'Well, then.'

She stretched all fingers on both hands, palms taut, flexing sinews, in a gesture that she did not remember to be one church's Sign of the Branches. After that she tipped her speckled hat back slightly, and glanced up at the Lord-Architect.

'Suppose we leave this until another day?' she suggested.

'Suppose we don't.'

Brief shadow cooled her in the archway. In the small courtyard, heat bounced back from the worn brickwork. Silence drummed on her ears. Glancing back, the White Crow faced a blank wall: no sign of the arch by which they'd entered. She smiled ruefully.

'That one,' Casaubon said.

She walked towards the further archway. The Lord-Architect's blue satin frock-coat brushed her arm at every pace. Her left arm. Her right hand swung free, and she reached up to touch the hilt of her sword, and smiled to herself again.

'You never did miss a trick,' she observed.

The sky overhead curdled hot and yellow. Storm-lightning flickered above the windowless brick walls, almost invisible in the bright day. White Crow matched Casaubon stride for stride, through three enclosed courtyards: ears tensed for any noise, eyes searching for any movement.

Her saliva began to have the metallic taste of fear. Sweat made her skin tacky at elbow and knee joints, above her lip, and on each upper eyelid. She reached up and pulled her sword from its sheath.

'Valentine.'

'No. I need to,' she said. White sun flashed the length of the blade. Its grip fitted into her palm; and the weight of its pull on her shoulder felt comfortingly familiar. Anxiety tensed her back, prickled down her vertebrae.

She grinned.

'Last-minute rescues.' Her voice bounced back from the bricks of a fourth enclosed courtyard. 'Frantic escapes, reprieves on the gallows-steps, victory or defeat at the final instant, on the eleventh minute of the eleventh hour of the eleventh day . . .'

Casaubon's copper hair gleamed as he nodded. 'In short: the Decan of the Eleventh Hour.'

Urgency and excitement radiated back from the walls with the heat and light. With long-practised ease she reached up and slid the blade back into her shoulder-scabbard.

She turned her head to do it, and to look at Casaubon as she spoke, walking under yet another arch of the brick labyrinth. Turning back, she stopped in her tracks; Casaubon's cushioned arm bumped her forward a step; and she stumbled, wincing at her bare feet on gravelled earth.

The heart of the maze of the Thirty-Sixth temple opened before her.

The White Crow moved forward slowly into the large courtyard. High walls enclosed her, of small bricks once dark brown and now sun-bleached to ochre; the sky empty and sun-filled. Black dots floated across her vision. One of them landed on her arm, crawling among the fine red hairs.

'The old English black bee . . .' She raised her arm, blew softly, and the bee flew off.

'Made extinct in an epidemic.' Casaubon's hand rested on her shoulder. 'Master-Physician.'

All the ground lay marked in ochre and yellow and brown gravels, a labyrinth of patterns on the earth. She began to walk the knotted pattern. She did not raise her eyes yet, to see what lay in the centre of the courtyard.

Black roses thrust briars into crevices of the brickwork. The pattern brought her close to one wall, and she reached up to touch: black stem, black thorns, black petals; cold as living onyx or jet. The tiny bees swarmed about her. Their noise filled her head. She reached behind without looking, left-handed, and Casaubon's hand enclosed hers.

The soles of her bare feet burned with the hot earth. She stepped from that to brick paving, reaching the centre of the marked patterns. The Lord-Architect came to stand beside her. The yellow sun drenched the enclosed garden. A smell of hot earth and hot brick reached her nostrils.

A statue loomed in the centre of the courtyard, bees swarming over its crossed front paws. Brown unmortared bricks rose up into leonine shoulders, flanks, haunches, and a tail curved over one slightly stretched hind leg. Around the shoulders and head, drapework delineated in curved brickwork surrounded an almond-eyed face. The swell of breasts showed above the crossed front paws.

The White Crow shifted, eyes aching from staring up into the sun. The sphinx towered some sixteen or eighteen feet above her; shaped brickwork smoothly curving, sun-bleached, and crumbling here and there where bees nested in crevices. She sat down, cross-legged, ignoring Casaubon's expostulation; energy sucked by the heat.

Drowned dizzy, she wiped her red face and reached down to scratch her bare legs under the knee-breeches. The fingers of her left hand pricked with pain. She glanced down to see angry red pin-pricks where she had touched the bristles of the black roses.

Casaubon's voice, half-drowned in the silence of sun and bees, said: 'Time.'

She heard no clock. The hour sounded as invisibly as ripples under water, pulsing through her.

The sphinx's curved brickwork eyelids slid up.

Pupil-less ochre eyes gazed down, twelve feet above the earth. She saw herself and the Lord-Architect reflected there, in shining sand. Some frontier irrevocably crossed in her mind, the White Crow succumbed to a casual bravado that might pass for, or might become, courage. She removed her hat. She laughed.

Long lips curved up, and the great front paws moved, dust haunting the hot air.

'You are too early.'

The Lord-Architect knelt beside the White Crow. She stared at the back of his neck, the yellow-stained linen and heat-flushed skin.

'What do you mean, "too early"!' Casaubon protested indignantly. 'I might have been too late!'

The White Crow gripped the crown of her speckled black-and-white hat and fanned herself with the brim. Still sitting, she called up: 'Lady of the Eleventh Hour, who is Lord of the Ten Degrees of High Summer!'

The sphinx's eyes shifted to the red-haired woman.

'I'm the Master-Physician White Crow,' the White Crow said,

'and this is Baltazar Casaubon, Lord-Architect, Knight of the Golden Rose, Scholar-Soldier of the Invisible College . . .'

'*Yes.*' The ancient eyes filled with amusement. '*I know. I summoned him.*'

A stillness touched the White Crow; only her eyes shifting up to the man who knelt beside her. What she had forgotten of his wit and strength (not merely a very fat man, but a very large man also fat) came back to her with the rush of five years' forgetting.

Brick paving jolted as Casaubon sat down heavily. Peeling off the heavy satin frock-coat, and unbuttoning his embroidered waistcoat, he wiped his already-wet shirt-sleeves across his face, and gazed up at the Decan.

A heat-shimmer clung to the shaped bricks. The folds of the headdress fell across leonine shoulders, framing a face more than human. Articulated, impossible, the great body shifted to one elbow, hind leg stretching.

The White Crow ignored Casaubon's attempts to speak now that his immediate indignation had run dry. She gazed up at the god-daemon, not able to keep her mouth from stretching in a smile of pure joy. She put her hat back on the masses of tangled red hair, tilted it to shade her eyes. Her fingers flexed. They tingled for the act of an art so long unpractised.

The Decan's full-lipped mouth smiled. Her robed head bent, and her shining sand eyes fixed on the White Crow.

'*Child of earth.*'

'Lady.' The White Crow laughed. Sweat trickled down between her sharp shoulder-blades. The Decan's sun unknotted tensions in her body, smoothed them into a trance of heat.

'You sent for an architect and a physician of the Invisible College.' Casanbon, doggedly rolling up his shirt-sleeves, addressed his remarks to the sphinx-paw resting on the earth beside him. The paw lay large as a cart on the earth. Brick claws flexed.

'Divine One,' he added, as an afterthought.

Heady, as if she were ten years younger and still the woman who would speak her mind although god and daemon waited on it, she poked her finger into Casaubon's damp shoulder.

'Oh, now, you, hold it – *right* there. A *Decan* sent for the College's assistance? And you didn't tell me that?'

Sunned in the warmth of amusement radiant from the brick courtyard, the Lord-Architect said: 'Now, Valentine. You wouldn't be here if I had. I know you.'

'Yes.' The White Crow uncrossed her legs, rubbing at cramp in one calf. 'Yes . . .'

She rested her elbow along his shoulder. His shirt showed sopping patches under the arms and down the middle of his vast back. Sweat and metheglin reeked on the air.

'*This is not the appointed hour.*'

The White Crow made a grab for the Lord-Architect as he rose majestically to his feet.

'You're lucky I'm here at all!' he rumbled, ham-hands planted on hips. 'I bring you the best pox-rotted physician there is (who doesn't want to come), and the best living expert in architectonics (and *I* didn't want to come either, if your Divine Presence doesn't know that), and I get us both here, now, through *magia* run wild, and what thanks do I get for it!'

He stopped, swept up his satin coat, rescued the hip-flask from one pocket, and stomped to the edge of the brickwork to stare out over the knotted gravel patterns of the courtyard and coax a drop or two more of metheglin from the flask.

The hot brick paving quivered. The other paw of the sphinx fell lightly, so that, from where she sat between them now, the White Crow could have reached out a hand to touch both.

'*The best living – but I can raise the best of the dead. You passed a world of dangers – but we could unseam the world from pole to pole, in a heartbeat.*'

The White Crow laughed.

She was aware that Casaubon turned, that the freckles on his heated face stood out in a sudden pallor. All else vanished in the sandstorm and dust-devil gaze of the god-daemon, as the Decan lowered her head and focused her close gaze on the White Crow.

Nails digging into her palms, the White Crow said: 'Lady, and begging your Divine Presence's pardon, I know the Decans could unsoul the sky, untie the bonds that fasten the earth, untune the dance of the heavens; for all that is is held within the Degrees of the Thirty-Six.'

The brick lids blinked.

'And I also know,' the White Crow ended, 'how difficult it is to get thirty-six of anybody to agree to anything, and act as one.'

Furnace heat scoured the courtyard. Softer than the hum of black bees and the rustle of the roses, the White Crow heard the rare laughter of a Decan. She climbed to her feet. The muscles at the backs of her legs trembled.

'*She is a Master-Physician, to know the conflict and contention among the Stars so well. You have performed adequately, child of earth, in bringing her here. Welcome.*'

' "Bringing"?' the White Crow queried.

' "Adequately"?' the Lord-Architect bridled.

She could feel him clinging to his refuge of obtuse pride and alcohol, as she clung to wit or a studied carelessness: some scant refuge against the presence of the god-daemon informing mortal matter. Casaubon's plump knuckles brushed her chin, moved up to lift the tumbled mass of hair, silver-white at the temples. The power of ten degrees of the sky infused the courtyard: permitting no evasions, nothing less than truth.

'I made you keep me here. I made you listen to me. I made you come with me. Valentine.'

'Oh, I knew how you were doing it,' she said, 'but I let you, just the same . . . I did the hard bit when I hid here and researched the heart of the world for five years, alone.'

The White Crow pushed the brim of her hat up. She grinned, sun-dazed. 'And I'll do the rest that's hard when we leave here, and if we're alive at the end of it I will still thank you for finding me. But as for now—'

'—for now,' the Lord-Architect Casaubon picked up, turning to look into the Decan's slanting desert-eyes, 'I would be cautious, Divine One, with what I said before mortal kings. You, who read hearts and minds, know mine.'

The great paw moved slightly closer. The White Crow felt a radiance from it through her arm, ribs, thigh, and the left side of her body. She took a breath. Half air and half the soul of heat, it burned in her lungs.

'I wrote with woman's blood on the moon, because I saw the Great Circle four times broken.'

'*It will be broken again.*'

The god-daemon's breath touched her face, and the White Crow smelt bone-dust.

'*You are too early. For all things, there is a certain hour to act: that hour and no other.*'

The White Crow swayed. Black bees filled the air, mica-wings glittering. They flew exactly the sun-hot courtyard's patterns, holding the air above the gravel labyrinth. She reached out to knot the linen of Casaubon's shirt in one hand. Ghost-lines of darkness began to pattern the sky.

'*Shall pestilence in the heart of the world be healed? I have seen infinite generations board the Boat to be carried through the Night and back to birth. This is nothing in the eyes of the Thirty-Six Powers.*'

'Pestilence?' The White Crow frowned: calculating, bewildered.

The shining salt-pan gaze of the god-daemon fell on the White

Crow. A black geometry starred the sky. The White Crow rubbed her sweat-blurred eyes.

The Decan's robed head tilted to look down upon Casaubon, where the Lord-Architect stood between her paws.

'Shall we permit Salomon's House to be raised in the heart of the world, that it become the New Jerusalem? These things pass. The Temple has fallen once, and will fall again. This is nothing in the eyes of the Thirty-Six Powers.'

'Ah. I don't know about that . . . Divine One.' Casaubon wriggled his index finger in his ear, took it out, looked at the wax under the nail and, as he wiped it down his embroidered waistcoat, said: 'I ruled a city once. All of it built by line, by rule, by square; by order of hierarchy and just proportion of harmony. They tore it down. It's a republic now. The Lords-Architect are gone.'

The White Crow watched time-worn brick move as living flesh; the pocked and crumbling leonine body tense.

'We are who we are, and not to be vanquished by the reshaping of stone-masonry! That is nothing. But – The Spagyrus, the Lord of Noon and Midnight – shall He break the Dance?'

The White Crow slid her hand up to rest on Casaubon's forearm. Fine copper-haired flesh, sweet and sleepy: human. She reached up and removed her hat. The heat of the sky above the Thirty-Sixth temple struck at her neck and the crown of her head.

'It *was* broken.' Casaubon's arm slid around the White Crow's shoulders.

'A black miracle.' She rubbed her mouth with her hand and tasted salt. Her dry voice creaked. 'A Philosopher's Stone that gives eternal Death, death of the soul.'

'Such things unloose the sky and earth; untie the forces that hold world to sun, and flesh to bone.'

The White Crow's skin smelt to her now of sweat and sweet age, of middle years and high summer, of dreams enacted and powers taken up into unused hands. She brushed hair away from her eyes. The heat of it burned her fingers.

Casaubon's mouth at her ear, warm with alcohol, breathed: 'The face . . . Does she have the face of your mother?'

'How did you know that!'

'Because she has the face of my mother, too.'

'All things happen in a certain hour. An hour to act, an hour to fail or succeed.'

The courtyard hummed with the flight of bees, ceaselessly rising and falling. The scent of black roses hung in the heat-soaked air. The sphinx blocked all light, Her robed head raised against a yellow

sky pocked with the black geometries of constellations: the
hieroglyphs of reality.

'*Do what you will, children of earth. In one hour, there will be a magia
of pestilence. In one hour, the founding stone will be laid of the House of
Salomon. In this one same hour, do what you will.*'

The White Crow shivered, standing in the shadow of the god-
daemon. Lips curved, the baking-hot brick crumbling dust onto the
air. Lids slid widely open upon eyes as pitiless, amused and deadly
as earth's wastelands.

'*The hour of that day is not yet. You are come before your time.*

'*In that one hour, the Lord of Noon and Midnight will once more break
the great circle of the living and the dying: I prophesy. And in that one hour
the Wheel of Three Hundred and Sixty Degrees will fly apart into chaos: I
prophesy. Stone from stone, flesh from bone, earth from sun, star from star.
There shall not be one mote of matter left clinging to another, nor light
enough to kindle a spark, nor soul left living in the universe.*

'*In that one hour.*'

Movement caught her eye: the White Crow wrenched free of
Casaubon's arm, her hand going up to her sword. She froze, fingers
outstretched to grip. Above, in the yellow heat-soaked sky, black
lines etched animal-headed god-daemons with stars for eyes.

'*I give you both the day that holds that hour.*'

The sky shuddered.

A sense of turning sickened her. She slitted her lids to block out
the sky, and the sun that *moved:* shifting thirty Degrees across its arc
from the Sign of the Lord of Morning to the Sign of the Lady of High
Summer. Cramps twisted her womb, and she bent over, grinding a
fist into the pit of her belly, the pain of the moon waxing and
waning in a heartbeat.

'*At the precise moment that the Great Circle is once again broken – then
act!*'

The great paws of the god-daemon closed together.

The White Crow flung out both arms, pushing against the sun-
hot brick that writhed beneath her palms. She staggered, slipped to
one knee, sneezed violently as cold air forced its way into her lungs;
and scrambled to her feet.

A wall of tiny ochre bricks blocked her vision. Her dusty hands
rested flat against them. She pushed away, her eyes following the
brickwork up . . . to where it hooped above her head in an arch.

The first entrance-arch cast a dawn shadow into the street. No
coach waited outside. The White Crow stood alone, shivering in air
that felt cold only by contrast with the soul of heat. Her womb
ached with the loss of time passed.

'*Shit*-damn!'

Her voice echoed.

The White Crow swung around, taking in the dew drying on the cobbles, the dawn-mist turning the blue sky milky. 'Evelian! My rooms! Who's been feeding my animals while I've been gone?'

A citizen, out early, skittered past one corner of the Fane, and the White Crow yelled: 'The day, messire?'

Without turning or stopping, the man called: 'Day of the Feast of Misrule.'

'*That* long?'

She swung back, stabbing a dusty index-finger at the Lord-Architect, to realise that she stood alone and faced a blank gateless brick wall.

'—Casaubon?'

CHAPTER 5

Light spreads out across the heart of the world.

Down in Eighth District North quarter the barter-stalls open early, candy-striped awnings pearled with dawn's dew. Men and women argue the value of rice, portraits and chairs against pomanders, shoes and viola da gambas. The barter-markets will close in an hour: it is the Feast of Misrule.

In Thirty-First District morning is advanced. Children dig the heavy clay earth of allotments, unearthing shards of pottery with a peacock-bright glaze, where sun sparkles from the edges of broken telescopic lenses. Parents call the children in; it is the Feast of Misrule.

At the royal palace light slants into wide gravel-floored courtyards, glares back white from walls. Echoing: the clatter of guard-change, the rattle of hoofs. Even this early, heat soaks the thick-walled chambers where Rats await a special morning audience.

And down where Fourteenth District meets the harbour the sail-less masts of ships catch the first yellow fire of the sun. Tugs anchored; wherries moored; light stains the lapping water where ships lie idle, even the transients part of the preparations.

Ashen, the dawn touches the Fane. Light curdles, chitters; sifting to fall upon the ragged wings of daemons: acolytes rustle and roost. Storm-bright eyes flick open.

Light spreads out across the heart of the world, the dawn of the day of the Feast of Misrule.

Reverend Mistress Heurodis said: 'I cannot stay so long as I thought. It would hardly do for me to be seen with you.'

Archdeacon Regnault sat on the gutter step, sandal in one dark hand, fingering the ball of her aching right foot. She raised her head when Reverend Mistress Heurodis spoke, and laughed mirthlessly.

'I'm told by the novices that Reverend Master Candia took equally great care not to be seen with Bishop Theodoret of the Trees.' She pitched her voice to carry over the constant ringing of a charnel-house bell. 'They were together, I know that. I know nothing else. And that was thirty days ago!'

She stood, clutching one sandal in her hand.

'My time to search grows less. I'm needed back at the hospital now. We've never needed to heal so many sick with pestilence as this High Summer.'

Beckoning Heurodis with a nod of her head, she limped across the wide, tree-lined avenue towards the illegal cafés of the human Eighth District Southquarter, just opening or shutting with the dawn.

'If your Church didn't insist on healing those the god-daemons fate for death and rebirth' – Heurodis seized the trailing edge of her blue cotton dress, and picked a neat way between fallen leaves, cracked roadstones, and fresh dung – 'you wouldn't now stand between poverty and ignominy.'

Two- and three-storey sandstone buildings took a warm light from the sun, the cafés' shield-shaped signs glowing blue, crimson and gold. The smell of fresh water rose from newly washed pavements. Where the soapy liquid trickled into the gutters, it accentuated the dung-odours of the avenue.

The Archdeacon paused on the far pavement, waiting for the old woman to catch up. She squinted up at the milky sky, sighed, anticipating heat and the distances to be walked across the heart of the world when one's Church is too poor to afford carriages.

'A Sign's passed, but I won't give up. Tell me one thing,' she persisted doggedly, 'before you return to the university.'

The old woman in the neat cotton dress turned smoky-blue eyes on the Archdeacon.

'I have honest work teaching at the University of Crime,' Heurodis said, her thin voice firm. 'Why should I jeopardise it by becoming concerned in the dubious activities of the Church of the Trees?'

The Archdeacon stepped into the shadow of a eucalyptus tree, hearing its leaves rustle above her head. A rush of water from a shop-front wet her bare foot, and made Heurodis step aside with an irritated mutter. She made to take the old lady by the elbow and guide her.

'Ah! I didn't mean—' She shook her wrist, rubbed her elbow and stepped back from the Reverend Mistress. The white-haired woman smiled.

'What is it you have to ask me, girlie?'

The Archdeacon brushed the shoulder of her green cotton dress, and touched the scrolling bark of the eucalyptus for comfort. She

cinched her belt in another notch. The dappled shadow and light of
leaves fell across her black skin. She pointed down the avenue, to
one of the bars that, open all night in the heart of the world, now
began to close its doors.

'*Is* that Reverend Master Candia?' she asked.

Heurodis brushed tendrils of silver hair away from her face, and
shaded her eyes with a brown-spotted hand. The Archdeacon
followed her gaze into the open frontage of the café. Broken mirrors
lined the walls. Among tables and shattered bottles and the fumes
of hemp, a heavily built café-owner stood arguing with a man
slumped into a chair.

'Yes.' Heurodis rubbed her bare corded arms, as if with a sudden
chill.

The Archdeacon slipped her sandal back on her bare foot and
strode towards the café. The Reverend Mistress hurried after her.

'We'll take over here.'

The burly man turned a scarred face on the Archdeacon and the
Reverend Mistress. He nodded his head to Heurodis.

'If this bastard's a friend of yours, he's got a score to settle . . .'

Heurodis looked around, and slapped her hand down on Candia's
table. The burly man's voice died as she lifted her palm. Six or seven
silver coins gleamed on the scarred wood. Snake-swift, he brushed
the money over the table-edge into his hand, fisted it, and glared at
the old woman.

'You're mad! Using *coin*! The Rat-Lords will hang all four of us.'

'Then you'd better not tell them.'

The bar-owner met Heurodis's occluded gaze for a second,
turned, and stomped to the back of the café to oversee the
haphazard cleaning.

'Candia!'

The blond man sat slumped down so that his head was below the
back of the chair, his booted legs sprawled widely. His uncut beard
straggled to his collar. The buff-coloured doublet, open to show
filthy linen, had more slashes than sufficed to show the crimson
lining. He twitched at Heurodis's sharp tone.

'Reverend Master!'

The Archdeacon leaned forward. His warm foul breath hit her in
the face. She reached out, wound a dark hand in his hair and jerked
his head upright. Blond hair flopped across a face all pallor but for
sepia-bruised eyes.

The man muttered something inaudible.

Heurodis folded her hands neatly in front of her. 'It takes more
than days to get into this state.'

The Archdeacon straightened, looking around. Morning light showed unkind on upturned tables and the deserted bar. Dark wood scarred with knife-cuts and slogans reflected in shards of mirrors. She reached out and took a pail from one of the cleaners as he passed, and up-ended dirty water over the slumped man.

'Where's Theodoret? Where's my Bishop?'

The blond man reared up from the chair. Swearing, he threw out dripping arms for balance, opened his eyes and turned an uncomprehending gaze on the café and Heurodis and the Archdeacon. He stooped. One filthy hand went out to the nearest wall for support. An expression of amazement and embarrassment crossed his pale features.

Candia bent forward and vomited on the floor.

Broken mirrors at the back of the bar reflected the owner in conversation with two men. Both newcomers wore gold-and-white sashes; both wore clumsily adjusted rapiers and sword-belts.

Over the noise of retching, Heurodis said: 'Those are Salomon-men . . . We should move him from here, before they begin to question us.'

Gritting her teeth against the stink of vomit, alcohol and urine, the Archdeacon pulled one of the blond man's arms across her shoulder and guided (not being tall enough to support) him out into the avenue. A few yards on he fell against her, and she let him slide down to sit with his back against one of the eucalyptus trees.

Candia frowned, lifting a drooping head. He opened his mouth to speak and vomited into his lap, covering his doublet and breeches.

'It would be better, for his sake, not to take him back to the university.' Heurodis blinked in the sunlight.

The Archdeacon stepped back to join her. The blond man lay against the tree-trunk, head back, legs widely apart; moaning.

'Where did you go with the Bishop?'

She squatted down a yard from Candia.

'The novices saw you leave together. *Where did you take him?'*

A ragged band of crimson cloth had been tied about one of his wrists; days ago, judging by the dirt. A half-healed scar showed under the edge of it.

'He's been missing for nearly thirty days,' the Archdeacon persisted. *'Where did you leave him?'*

A light tap on her shoulder got her attention. She stood and faced Heurodis. Carts clattered past on the rough avenue. A few early passers-by turned to look at Candia.

'It's been nearly thirty days since the Reverend Master attended at the university,' Heurodis confirmed. 'I have not the least idea what he would be doing in the cathedral with low-life, but it seems a strong possibility that he *was*.'

The small old woman showed no disgust when she looked at the blond man sprawled on the pavement.

'He will need treatment, I'm afraid, before he can walk; and we can hardly carry him.' Heurodis's smoky gaze found its way to the Archdeacon's face. 'I have a basic grounding in medicine. And I, too, can remember drinking to drive away pain.'

'I can help him temporarily.'

Heurodis sniffed. Without a crack in her façade of disapproval, she nodded. 'Very well, then, but be quick. To be seen with one of you is bad enough, but to be present in public while you actually . . . Get on with it, girlie.'

The Archdeacon knelt down in front of Candia, one hand on his shoulder, one on the trunk of the eucalyptus.

Dawn mist cleared now, over roofs and alleys, and carts passed every few minutes, jolting over the broken paving-stones. All the drivers were human; no Rats visible. Heat began to soak up from the pavement, ripen the smells of the gutter.

Leaves rustled, rattled together.

A faint green colour rippled across the Archdeacon's black fingers. She brushed Candia's dirt ringed neck. He stirred, straightening; his eyes opened and blinked against the sunlight. A smell of green leaves and leaf-mould momentarily overpowered city odours.

Water brimmed in his eyes. A tear runnelled the dirt on his face. She saw him focus into himself; the loose-limbed sprawl tensing. She let a little more of the power of green growing things clear his sodden head and veins.

'Can you understand me?'

His thin dirty hand came up and touched hers. As if the faint green colour of spring leaves pained him, another rush of water brimmed over his eyes.

'He . . . did that, and it didn't save him . . .'

The Archdeacon glanced up at Heurodis. Healing momentarily forgotten, she tightened her grip on Candia's shoulder and shook him.

'Who did? I talked to builders, some of the builders on the Fane – they say they saw my Bishop there. Was that you? Were you with him? What happened to him?'

He groaned. Sweat broke out on his forehead, plastering blond hair down. His other hand came up and gripped her wrist.

'Ask – why did they let me go . . . and not Theo . . .'

'He's at the Fane? Is he alive and well?'

'Yes . . . no . . .'

His breath stank. The effort it took him to speak made the Archdeacon shake her head in self-disgust.

She reverently touched the eucalyptus-trunk, centring patterns of veins in leaf and flesh, letting energy rise. After a moment she let the colour fade from her hands, and pulled Candia's arm across her shoulder again, and lifted. He came up on to his feet with difficulty, weight heavy on her.

Heurodis's chin rose, looking up at him, flesh losing creases momentarily. 'Take him to my house.'

Trying not to breathe in his stink, the Archdeacon put her arm around Candia's body to support him. Under his shirt her fingers felt each rib prominent. His pelvic bone jabbed into her side. Heurodis, irritable at the increasing number of people on the avenue, moved to hook the Reverend Master's other arm in hers and push him into uncertain steps. He swayed as they walked, slow yard by yard.

'If I do anything, it's what the Thirty-Six want me to do . . . what they let me go loose for . . .' His voice slurred. 'People *talk* when they think you're drunk . . . I'm not drunk. I've heard things. Not as drunk as I'd have to be . . .'

His arms flopped loosely over the two women's supporting shoulders. His head dipped. His eyes shifted to the sky, watching under wary brows, afraid. The Archdeacon shifted her grip. His head turned, and he focused on the hawthorn pinned to her full bodice.

'Fuck your church! Fuck your arrogant beggarly church—'

He lurched free of the Archdeacon, ignoring Heurodis. His hair flew as he turned his face to the sky, to the Fane that blackened the south-aust horizon.

'Put *my* head on a spike like his, why don't you! Ask *me* why we betrayed the House of Salomon!'

A pulse of shock chilled her.

'Drunken hallucination,' Heurodis whispered.

'If one of the Salomon-men hears him . . .' The Archdeacon wiped vomit-stained hands down her dress. Bright, rising over roof-tops, morning sun dawned on the Day of the Feast of Misrule, warming the sandstone streets.

'Ask *me*. I know.' Candia sank to his knees on the paving. Tears slid down his filthy skin. He rubbed helplessly at his ripped doublet and breeches, and wiped his nose on the back of his bandaged wrist.

The Archdeacon steeled herself to walk forward and grip his arm.

Head down, he muttered at the broken paving. She only just understood what he said.

'Heurodis, Heurodis, I don't have the courage – no, I don't have the *talent* to do what we should do now.'

Dawn sunlight slid across the dial of Clock-mill as the loaded mules passed by its waterwheel. The balding man in the darned jerkin mopped his brow in the early heat and tugged the lead mule's rein.

Above, the blue-and-gold dial showed three hundred and sixty Degrees marked with the signs of the Thirty-Six Decans. The clockhands stood at five-and-twenty to six.

Mayor Tannakin Spatchet turned the corner out of Carver Street in an odour of mule dung. Two apprentices in silk and satin stopped and jeered. He stiffened his spine. A third girl, the gold-cross sash tied about her waist, shouted, and they ran off down the cobbles, bawling insults, late for their site. He drove the four mules around another corner as far as a narrow door, where he knocked.

One of the mules clattered its hoof against the cobbles, loud in the quiet street. The Mayor gazed up past the black wooden frieze of skulls and gold-chests and ivy to a window that stood an inch open.

'Lady! White Crow!'

He hammered his plump fist against the street-door. Distantly, above, he heard footsteps.

'Unh?'

A thin girl of fifteen or so opened the narrow door. Her yellow hair straggled up into a bun, and her blue satin overalls appeared to have a coating of orange fur and damp spots down the front.

'Unh?' she repeated.

Tannakin Spatchet, displeased at seeing the widow's daughter, drew in a breath that expanded his chest, showing off the verdigris-green Mayor's chain. 'Sharlevian, I wish to see the White Crow. Immediately. Fetch her.'

'Ain't here.'

'When will she—?'

'Ain't *living* here,' the girl snapped.

A voice from the darkness up the stairwell called: 'Sharlevian, who is it?'

'Aw, *Mo*ther . . . it isn't anybody. Only the Mayor.'

'Come back up here and finish feeding these blasted animals!'

Tannakin Spatchet heard Evelian's irritated voice grow louder coming down the stairs, and glimpsed her blue-and-yellow satin dress. The buxom woman thrust a half-grown fox-cub and a feeding-bottle into Sharlevian's hands, ignoring both their whines, and nodded briskly to him.

'Tannakin.'

He raised a finger, pointing at the upstairs window. 'Is she coming back?'

The buxom woman stepped down into the street, closing the door behind her. Her gaze took in the four mules and the roped tarpaulin loads that stood almost as high again as the animals' backs. One fair brow quirked up.

'I don't know that she *isn't*. What's all this lot? You've come for more talismans?'

'It's taken us thirty days to collect this to pay for the last ones, and now you say she's gone . . . Is there another philosopher in the quarter who can make protective talismans?'

'You're joking! Magus' Row is bare as a Tree priest's larder, and no wonder, after the last Sign.'

Evelian prodded the packing, and spoke without turning:

'Sharlevian's talking of nothing but this House of Salomon. All the apprentices are the same, and she – it's all these fool boys she hangs around with. A bitch on heat, if I say it who's her mother. I wish I didn't think that I'd be better off with friends among the Salomon-men, but I do.'

Tannakin let her vent the heat-bitterness of high summer.

'I've lost three lodgers in the last thirty days. I'm told the little Katayan's *alive*, but I've seen nothing of her. As for the White Crow . . . this is all hers?'

Tannakin Spatchet sighed. With his own bitter resentment, he said: 'It's little enough. Brass pans, some shelving, an old clock, some lenses, four cheeses—'

'I can smell the cheeses.'

'—a dozen tallow candles, and a ream of paper. The other loads are much the same. Mistress Evelian, in no way do I support the Salomon movement, in no way at all, but there are times when I would give my Mayor's chain not to have to barter, to be able to carry money and do with it what the Rat-Lords do.'

He saw her smile, but did not entirely understand why.

'We'll have to lug it all up these stairs and store it in her room. *Sharlevian!* If the White Crow doesn't come back,' the yellow-haired woman said, 'it can stand as my back rent.'

'Always the businesswoman—'

Tannakin Spatchet broke off, staring down the sunlit street into morning haze. Dark specks buzzed about the aust-west horizon: acolytes swarming about the angled Fane.

Evelian shaded her eyes. 'How often do you see that? Master Mayor, we're all going to need more than talismans to get through the next Calendar Sign.'

'*Hear me!*' The Hyena's voice crackled through the loudspeakers. The din of the crowd momentarily drowned out her words.

Zar-bettu-zekigal sat down on the step and unbuttoned her new greatcoat, cautiously letting the sun's early radiance warm her. She rested her chin on her fists.

The greatcoat, as matt black as her hacked-short hair, spread out on the marble step and the thrown-down yellow carpet. She curled her tail tightly to her body. The wash-faded black cloth of her dress began to grow hot in the morning sun, and she smiled and shrugged a stretch without moving from her sitting position. She kept one bare foot firmly on the stock of her musket that lay on the step below.

'We *will* build the Temple again, our temple, the House of Salomon: with just rule and line, for the Imperial dynasty to rule justly over our own people! We will build for ourselves, and never again for the Thirty-Six!'

Zar-bettu-zekigal yawned into her fists. Memory tracking automatically, she shifted an inch closer to the Hyena's plate-clad legs to watch every word. She gazed up, murmuring under her breath: 'Oh, you're beautiful! But see you, you're a child; just a baby!'

The Hyena stood on woven carpets, under gold silk canopies held by ragged silk-clad soldiers.

'We have been the servants of servants, the slaves of slaves, forbidden the least right, hidden in darkness, condemned to toil only for other! Now our buried birthright is uncovered, is come into the light; our day dawns, *this* day!'

She walked forward to the edge of the steps. Against the milk-blue sky, the armoured shoulders of the woman glittered silver; her scrubbed young face shone in the morning light. Zari watched the movement of her mobile mouth, the passion of her face; chopped-short brown hair flying, slanting red-brown eyes narrowed against the light.

'For them, now, nothing! We cut no more stone. We lay no more bricks. We dig no foundations. We draw no plans! Oh, they can force us to work – who denies it? But, if we're strong, who can force us to sleep or to eat?'

Behind the Hyena, gold-cross banners of the Sun shone: ranks of ragged soldiers crowding onto the steps of the Thirty-Second District square. The stink of gunpowder still hung in the air from a few enthusiastic musket-shots. Sword and sword-harness chinked.

'And when we die and are carried again on the Boat through the Night – who will they have then to build their power? Oh, who? None. For when we come again we will act as we do now: *we will not spend all our lives digging our graves and building our tombs!*'

The crowd's roar bounced back from the marble walls of the Trade Guild Meeting-halls, empty of their Rat-Lords now; together with the echoes of the Hyena's loudspeaker. Zari swivelled back on the step and faced forward, looking out across the heads of ten or fifteen thousand civilian men and women. In silk, in satin; their callused hands still carrying rule, trowel, wrench, or hod.

'But not only *I* tell you this.' The Hyena's voice dropped from passion to a passionate honesty. 'If it were only me, how could I ask you to act? I have hidden in darkness. I have hit and run, struck and fled again, damaging the Rat-Lords but never confronting them. I have not starved. I have not died, to refuse the Thirty-Six my labour. If it were only me, and these soldiers here, why would you listen?'

Zar-bettu-zekigal put in Memory the shouts in the crowd: half-audible, encouraging.

'So listen to one of your own,' the Hyena called out loudly. 'Listen to Master Builder Falke!'

Her foot kicked Zari as she stepped aside, and the woman looked down and grinned an apology. As the white-haired man moved out from under the shade of the silk canopy, the Hyena squatted down on her haunches beside Zar-bettu-zekigal.

'Hot.' Zari put the flat of her hand against the plate armour; the metal stung her palm. The woman pulled up her dark-red kerchief, shading her neck. A soldier two paces away held her laminated steel helm. The ragged Sun-banner drooped on a staff strapped to his back.

'Be hotter yet. This is early. It's going better than the last rally. Have you heard enough yet?'

'The Cardinal will want to know it all. He always does.'

A single line of Sun-banner soldiers kept the crowd back from the steps. The Hyena clanked down to sit beside Zari. The Katayan sat up and slid her hand along the hot steel to the woman's shoulders and, a little behind her now, began pressing her fingers down between armour and neck, finding points to release muscle tension.

'It had to work here.' The Hyena's voice rasped. 'After the last thirty days . . . Tell your Plessiez I gave the final order today. We're officially abandoning the areas under the city. Too much . . . *corruption* there.'

Zari dug her fingers in. 'See you, weren't there always haunt-ings?'

De
CŒMITERIIS.
five
ADYTIS ÆGYPTIORUM
Veterum

'*We cut no more stone. We lay no more bricks. We dig no foundations.*' Frontispiece to
Sphinx Mystogoga, Athanasius Kircher, Amsterdam, 1676

'Not like this!' The woman's plate gauntlet clacked against her breastplate. 'I wonder . . . I do wonder, now, what it was Plessiez had us do when we ran his underground errands. We don't get this sort of aid without our previous help being worth a lot. But after today it won't matter. We take charge today.'

White hair glinted in the sun as Falke stepped forward. His booted foot just missed Zar-bettu-zekigal. She glanced up over her shoulder.

Falke walked with gravitas, thumbs tucked under his new sword-belt. His white-silver hair, longer now, he wore scraped back into a pony-tail and confined by a heavy silver ring. The morning sun showed up the lines around his mouth.

Black silk strips criss-crossed his eyes. He moved uncomfortably, sweating in the sun's heat, with a sword hanging from his belt, and a mail shirt and surcoat over his padded grey leather arming doublet. Embroidered insignia caught the sun and blazed across the square, on his breast not a ragged Sun but the House of Salomon's golden Rule.

'My friends.'

His voice crackled out across the square, half-humorous, and self-mockingly indulgent.

'My friends, *I* have not gone into voluntary exile. *I* have not trained men and women to be warriors. *I* have not sabotaged the Rat-Lords, lived starving and tireless, fought without hope until I saw this day. No, I have not done these things. For that, you must go to the Lady Hyena and her people. And, conscious of that, I speak humbly after her.'

The flesh under Zari's fingers tensed. She began to rub her thumbs at the base of the Hyena's skull. The woman rumbled: 'And three weeks ago he was gibbering with terror in a sewer. Gods, but that man can make capital out of anything.'

'See you, you're absolutely right.'

Lost in the contact of flesh and flesh, Zar-bettu-zekigal grinned dreamily to herself. She cocked an eye at Falke, looking through his legs at the crowded square.

He raised the microphone to his mouth again.

'You've heard good oratory from many of us this morning. I'll disappoint you; I'm a plain speaker. I'm one head of one hall in the east quarter of Nineteenth District. That's one quarter out of a hundred and eighty-one; one District out of thirty-six. That's all. But I've learned things you have a right to know about.'

His head lowered for a calculated moment, then lifted to face sun, sky and the assembled thousands.

'From today, we do no work on any site. We have no choice. You have heard, and I have found out it's true, that his so-called Majesty the King will send in their troops to fire on you. And the priests of the Orders of Guiry, and Hildi, and Varagnac will come, and they will damn you with all ceremony. Let them! We can withstand it. We are stronger than that. We have no choice.'

Falke's voice rose.

'You will bear with me. None of you is a fool. We know the Rat-Lords exploit us and make us slaves, and we are old enough in the ways of the world not to expect better. But now we have – yes, I tell you today, now, this moment! – *now* we have the wisdom for which we searched. All of you know the Mysteries. You know the Interior Temple and the Exterior Temple are mirrors of each other, and of the greater Order.'

He rested one hand on his breast.

'If we had the knowledge, we said, we would build thus. Build in the shape of our souls, and compel the Divine to acknowledge us. We have been kept dumb and blind by the Rat-Lords, forbidden to build for ourselves, forbidden the knowledge of it; but no longer. Now, today, we have at last recovered the knowledge we lost – the knowledge they hid from us so long ago. Now, today, *we have the Word of Seshat*!'

A susurrus of words filled the air. Ripples of sound: lapping through the hot morning and the square, out to the pillared porticoes and marble frontages of the Trade Guild Meeting-halls.

'Look at them! There isn't a building site in the city that'll be working today.' The Hyena grinned. Her armoured heel hacked down on the marble. She turned a heat-reddened face to Zar-bettu-zekigal, impervious to the Katayan's skilled fingers.

'One minute everything's the same as it's always been, and then—' Her fist smacked into her palm. 'By the end of today we'll have a general strike. No building, no trains, no servants. Tell Plessiez that. And tell him Falke and I *must* know when his necromancy will take full effect.'

'I'll tell him.'

'Tell him I must know what happens at the Fane.' Her slanting red-brown eyes moved, some hidden fear stirring and suppressed in a blink. 'I must.'

'Shall I go to him now?'

The Hyena glanced up to where Falke still spoke, pale hands gesturing. The Sun-banner soldiers still stood, but much of the crowd sat on the paving-stones: clusters of people growing closer together with the steady increase in their numbers.

'Yes, and hurry back. Falke and I – we can start this, but we can't stop it once it's begun. It'll cross the city like fire: every slightest whisper will carry it! It's out of our hands.'

Zar-bettu-zekigal stood, picked up the musket and laid it back across one shoulder, and sketched a mock salute. 'Anything for you, Lady. Anything at all.'

'Leave that gun here!'

The woman put her fingers to her shoulder, only now sensing a tactile memory. The laminated steel plate blazed back sunlight. Zari blinked. The woman looked up at her.

'Take it, then, Kings' Memory. And take care.'

The airship and the warm bosom of the aircrew-woman long left behind, Casaubon's sparrow flies through skies where vultures rise on mesa-winds. Heat is a hard arrow under the bird's heart, piercing, piercing.

To either side rise up the cliffs, sand-banded mesas: ochre, scarlet, orange, white.

Reflected in the bird's obsidian eye is desert, blue sky, great horizons; the jagged battlements of a castle built into the mesa-side; the drowsy noon emptiness of a courtyard; the tower-window overlooking it.

The sparrow falls arrow-straight, kicks up a spurt of dust on the stone window-sill, hops on to the ring finger of the hand outstretched to receive her.

Hot morning sun and warm air poured in through the open windows of the palace corridor. Zar-bettu-zekigal, musket confiscated at the gates, swung her greatcoat off her shoulders and slung it across her arm as she walked. Her dappled tail curved up, poking through the slit at the back of her knee-length black dress.

'Messire!'

Plessiez raised a ringed hand in acknowledgment as he walked towards her. He gestured with finality to the four or five priests with him, giving orders, sending the last hurrying off as he came up with the Katayan.

'. . . and tell Messire Fenelon to attend me in the Abbey of Guiry in an hour. Honour to you, Zaribet.'

'I just came from the Abbey of Guiry, messire. Fleury told me you were here in attendance on the King.'

Outside the open windows, sun put a haze on the blue-tiled turrets and spires and belvederes of the royal palace roofs. The roofscape spread out, acre upon acre. Mist rose up from drying pools of water: the previous sundown's thunderstorm. Cardinal-General Plessiez drew in a breath, bead-black eyes bright, muzzle and whiskers quivering. He folded his arms and leaned up against the white stone corridor-wall.

'I have just had an audience with his Majesty, yes.'

A silver band looped above one of his translucent-skinned ears, below the other; a black ostrich-plume being clipped into it at a jaunty angle. A basket-hilted rapier hung at his side: leather harness black, buckles silver. Zar-bettu-zekigal grinned, seeing how he tied the cardinal's green sash rakishly from left shoulder to knot above right haunch; tail carried with a high swagger, silver *ankh* almost lost in his sleek neck-fur.

'I've much to do this morning. Now, the overseeing of the artillery garden . . . Zaribet, come with me; I shall need you as Memory then—'

'But not right this minute.' Zar-bettu-zekigal's eyes gleamed. 'Shouldn't Messire St Cyr be dealing with the artillery garden?'

Plessiez snapped his fingers as he turned, not looking to see if the young Katayan woman scurried down the corridor at his heels. Zar-bettu-zekigal tossed her greatcoat into the window embrasure and left it. She caught him up after a few skips, revelling in the sun-hot corridor-tiles under her feet.

'What did the King say, messire?'

Cardinal-General Plessiez slowed rapid steps. He clasped ringed fingers behind his back as he paced, and began evasively: 'Messire Desaguliers once removed, it would obviously be his second-in-command St Cyr, who gained control of the Cadets . . . St Cyr is not Desaguliers' man; he is mine. I put him in as lieutenant some years ago; hence he leaves to me what I desire to oversee; hence . . . I have said I will deal with the artillery garden.'

'And the King?'

Zar-bettu-zekigal smoothed back her matt black hair from its centre parting with both hands. She grinned up at the Cardinal-General: watching his severity and wry humour and affected military air with the delight of a connoisseur or an admirer.

Two approaching priests robbed her of what answer he might have given. Plessiez stopped to issue orders. Zar-bettu-zekigal leaned back against the double doors at the end of the corridor, palms flat against the black oak, her dappled tail coiling down to her bare ankles.

'Be Kings' Memory now,' Plessiez cut her off as he rejoined her. She pushed the doors open for him to pass through. Leisurely, she repeated the standard pronouncement: 'Messire, you have an auditor . . .'

Plessiez walked through the next hall to where, white in sunlight through leaded casements, the double-spiral stone staircase rose up through this wing of the palace. He paused under its entrance-arch for the young woman to catch up.

'You hold all our secrets.'

She glanced up from her footing on the warm stone steps, descending in front of him. 'No secrets, messire. What I'm asked, I tell to whoever asks me. When I've heard it as Memory.'

'And not otherwise?'

'Oh, see you, messire! I wouldn't take a question like that from anyone except you.'

Here in the stone shaft, air blew morning-cool. The Katayan rubbed her bare arms. Plessiez watched her with what, eventually, he had identified as a certain awe; as if she were some hawk come tamely willing to his hand without capture.

'That may be why we all use you as a confessional.' He caught the flash of her eyes, knowing and innocent; and his snout twitched with an unwilling smile. 'Or does the Lady Hyena, as yet, share more than the ear of the Kings' Memory?'

The Katayan woman fisted hands to thrust in greatcoat pockets no longer there. Instead she put them behind her back, tail coiling up to loop her wrists.

'I'm working on that . . . She wants to know when anything's going to happen at the Fane. And, see you, Master Falke is lying his head off.'

'Falke tells no lies that I don't know about.'

The jerk of her head, chopped-off hair flying, took in all the thirty-six Districts of the city invisible beyond palace walls. 'Her "Imperial dynasty" and the Salomon-men – they've started something they can't stop down there in the city.'

'I know,' Plessiez said. 'It will be soon. It has already begun.'

Leaving the stairwell two floors below, walking through a cluttered salon, he nodded a greeting to passing black Rats, to one of St Cyr's uniformed Cadets, and to an aide of one of the Lords Magi. The Katayan beside him skipped to keep up with his strides. Plessiez eased the green sash where it crossed the fur of his shoulder, onyx and silver rings clinking against the *ankh*.

In the next salon all the full-length windows had been flung open, and heat slid in on tentative breezes, bringing the noise of hammers and forges and Rats shouting. Outside the windows, a ruined marble terrace gave way to the artillery garden. Blue haze coiled up from stretches of mud not yet dried by the sun.

A brown Rat passed across the terrace, and the Katayan woman checked. 'I thought . . . it might have been Charnay.'

'No. Not yet.' Plessiez's finger tapped irritably against his flank. 'I believe the Lady Hyena's admission that she released her. That means Charnay is off on some fool plan of her own. And that's when one knows there'll be trouble.'

The ormolu clock at the far end of the salon struck seven times. As the tinny notes died, a Cadet pushed the doors open. He bowed deeply to Plessiez.

'Lord Cardinal, the military architect is here to see you.'

'Finally! Show him in.'

'He . . . ah . . .'

Plessiez glimpsed a shadow out on the terrace. The previous night's rain stood in pools, flashing back white sun through the rising haze of steam. The mud, rubble, broken joists, and the machines of the artillery garden were blotted out by the bulk of a man. The big man glanced in at the window, nodding to Plessiez. His copper hair shone. He hooked his thumbs under the lapels of his blue satin frock-coat.

'Messire priest, I am Baltazar Casaubon, Lord-Architect, Scholar-Soldier of the Invisible College, Surveyor of Extraordinary Gardens, Knight of the Rose Castle *and*,' the immensely fat man got in before Plessiez could interrupt him, 'Horologer, Solar and Lunar Dial-maker, Duke of the Golden Compasses, and Brother of the Forgotten Hunt. Where is Messire Desaguliers?'

Rubble and hard earth jarred the base of his spine. Candia's eyes jolted open. Sunlight spiked into his head. He moaned, lying back and leaning his face against rough-pointed brickwork.

'. . . it *is* a priest!'

'Not a real one.'

'We ain't got one, but we got her. Ei, priest, over here!'

Voices resounded in the warm air above his head. Yellow grass beside him grew up through shattered paving-stones. Silk- and satin-clad legs milled in front of his face: scarlet and azure and cloth-of-silver dazzled.

'—need any sort of a priest; we—'

'—see how things are here—'

'—necessary exorcism—'

'—a priest, *now*!'

Candia uncovered his face. A factory's sheer brick soared up into a blue sky. Above and beyond, he saw smokeless chimney-stacks. His head fell forward. Six inches from his nose, in the folds of a faded, tree-embroidered, green cotton dress, a black hand clenched into a fist.

A voice just above him said: 'I'll send you someone else from the Cathedral of the Trees.'

'No. We can't wait!'

'Not while they come all the way from Nineteenth District!'

Candia raised his head with an effort. He focused on a burly woman, arms folded, the gold Rule embroidered on her overalls catching the sun painfully bright.

'No,' she repeated. 'We want you, Archdeacon, before it's too late.'

Candia pushed his shaking fingers through his lank hair. As he moved, the cloth of his doublet and breeches cracked with dried liquid, and he smelt the stench of old urine and vomit. He pressed his shaking hands into his eye-sockets.

'Who? Where?' His weak voice cracked.

A familiar tart voice at his other side said: 'You're a fool, Candia. The university officially suspended you ten days ago. What did you do that was worth getting yourself into this state?'

He felt a slow heat spreading across his face. For a second his shame would not let him look up at Heurodis. Veins pulsed behind his shut eyelids, the colour of light through new leaves. The invading presence of that healing could no longer be denied.

'Heurodis . . .' He took his hands from his face, braced his shoulders against the wall, and pushed himself upright against the rough brick, ripping his buff doublet again. Morning sun dazzled. The young black woman beside him argued furiously with the burly carpenter. Workers crowded around in the alley, the movement confusing him.

'Stay here.' The black woman moved a step towards the factory, glancing at the locked gates at the end of the alley, and then at the elderly Heurodis and at Candia. 'I'll come back for you.'

'No . . .' Gesture and voice died; he leaned weakly against the wall, brushing fair hair from his eyes, ignoring filth.

'Yes.' Heurodis put her wrinkled hand protectively on Candia's arm, and kept it there until the black woman turned away. She raised one faded eyebrow at the Reverend Master then.

'Help me,' Candia said shakily. 'Now, while they're arguing. I've seen, and I've heard . . . Heurodis, I have to get back inside the Fane.'

'Of course,' Plessiez heard the Lord-Architect observe, 'I left numerous and very *detailed* plans . . .'

The Lord-Architect rested one ham-hand on a joist of the machine, some four feet above ground-level, and bent to peer under the platform. His left foot came free of the artillery garden's white mud with a concussive suck. He looked absently down at his dripping silk stocking and shoe.

'—which the factory could have accurately followed.'

'What caused your absence?' the Cardinal-General demanded.

'I assure you, messire, the last . . .' Casaubon paused invitingly.

'Thirty days.'

'The last thirty days have, for me, gone past in the blink of an eye. You may say, indeed, they passed in the space of a heartbeat.'

'I am well aware that you must be busy.' Plessiez, waspish, whipped his tail out of the mud, taking a firmer stance on the artillery garden's rubble. The immense shadow of the machine fell cool across his sun-warmed fur. His left hand slid down to grasp the scabbard of his rapier. He gestured for Zar-bettu-zekigal to approach. 'Are you suggesting that these particular engines have been built incorrectly? Is that where the difficulty of operation arises?'

'Oh, not *incorrectly*, not as such . . .'

The Lord-Architect rapped his fist against the lower joist near the massive rear wheel. The iron plates of the wheel casing quivered. His blue-coated bulk tipped lower as he moved a step forward, under the platform of the machine.

'. . . merely minor adjustments . . .'

As Plessiez watched, the fat man gripped a strut in one hand and pivoted, slowly graceful, easing his body down. One massive leg slid forward. He swung down to sit in three inches of semi-liquid mud and, on his back, pull himself further under the axle-casing with massive white-gloved hands.

'. . . a few days' work . . .'

Plessiez frowned. Picking his way across the rutted site, he stooped to look under the machine. The Lord-Architect Casaubon lay on his back in the mud, his blue satin frock-coat spreading out flat, soaking up rain-pools. As Plessiez started to speak, the fat man fumbled in the pocket of his embroidered waistcoat and brought out a miniature hammer. He reached up and tapped the iron axle. A sharp metallic click echoed back across the artillery garden from the royal palace wall.

'I don't have "a few days", Lord-Architect. These engines must be ready to move later today.'

Plessiez, irritated, straightened up and looked for the Kings' Memory. The young Katayan woman had her heels on the wheel-rim where it rested on the earth, eight inches above ground, her back to the axle, stretching her arms as far up the spokes to the metal casing as possible. The top of the wheel curved a yard and a half above her head.

Her chin tilted up, pale, as her eyes traversed the bulk of the engine above her on the wheeled platform.

'Zari!'

'I'm listening, messire.' The Katayan's chin lowered. She grinned.

Plessiez urbanely repressed the fur rising down his spine. The tip of his tail lashed an inch to either side in a tightly controlled movement. 'I repeat: I do not have days.'

The fat man grunted amiably. His large delicate fingers probed the gear-wheels above the axle. He took his hand away, staring at a glove now caked with black grease. He began to ease himself forward on hands and heels and buttocks, until he cleared the mud with a succession of squelches. The Lord-Architect stood up, cracked his head against the underside of the platform, and spread oil and mud in his copper-gold hair as he rubbed the crown of his head.

'Days,' Casaubon repeated firmly. He ducked out from under the platform. His silk knee-breeches dripped. Taking one hem of his frock-coat in a gloved hand, he cracked the cloth and spattered mud in a five-yard radius.

The Katayan wiped the tuft of her tail across her cheek.

Plessiez looked down at the glutinous white mud spattered across his fur and cardinal's sash. 'You may find this behavior acceptable. I do not. It is possible, Messire Casaubon, that these tactics are designed to obfuscate your inefficiency. I assure you that they fail.'

The Lord-Architect laughed. He swung a gloved grease-stained hand to clap Plessiez on the back. The Cardinal-General stepped away smartly, his heel coming down on a broken paving-stone filmed with mud.

'Wh—?'

Plessiez skidded, flailed limbs and tail to stay upright; a rock-solid hand closed around his arm and steadied his balance. Chins creased as the big man smiled, innocent.

'Careful, messire.'

'I am always careful. Thank you.' Plessiez met Zar-bettu-zekigal's gaze. The Kings' Memory leaned her fist hard against her mouth, eyes bright. Plessiez took a step back, gazing up at the metal-plated casings and turrets and ports and beaks of the siege engine.

Morning sun dazzled off the row of nineteen others ranked beyond it.

'Not my preferred line of work, really. Trained in it, of course. Could do you ornamental garden automata,' the Lord-Architect offered hopefully, 'or hydraulic water-organs . . .'

Plessiez narrowed his eyes to furred slits and studied the large man. Coming in moments to a conclusion that (had he known) it had taken the White Crow years to arrive at, he smiled, nodded an acknowledgment, and observed: 'Very well, we understand each other. I am somewhat in your hands, being at the mercy of your expertise, and you have a price which is not entirely orthodox. It may be granted, if it is not too impossible, messire.'

Casaubon beamed, blue eyes guileless. 'I could work faster if I knew what these engines are *specifically* needed to do.'

Morning light shone back from white earth, from distant windows and multi-tiered roofs, with a promise of later heat. Small figures dotted the perimeter of the site: engineers being kept back by St Cyr's Cadets. Their impatient voices came to Plessiez across the intervening distance.

'We *do* understand each other. Very well,' Plessiez conceded. His muzzle turned towards Zar-bettu-zekigal as she stepped down from her perch on the wheel. 'But, I regret, not in your presence, Zari. For the present this must be between his Majesty and myself – and now you, Messire Casaubon.'

'Must she go?' The big man's face creased in disappointment. 'Such a beautiful young woman. And a Memory, too? Lady, you should have told me.'

The Katayan leaned her elbow against the wheel-rim and her cheek on her hand. 'I did tell you. I yelled it in your ear. You had your head in the rotor-casing at the time, but I did tell you you had an auditor. Didn't I, messire?'

'Certainly.' Plessiez, sardonic, folded his arms, sword-harness chinking; looking from the King's Memory to the Lord-Architect, and absently picking pieces of drying mud from his left elbow-fur with his right hand. 'Is there anything else either of you would wish to know?'

'*I'd* like to know what these machines are for.' The Katayan inclined her head to the fat man, her tail cocked high. 'Zar-bettu-zekigal. Are *you* liable to need a Kings' Memory, messire architect?'

The Lord-Architect Casaubon took the young woman's hand between the tips of filthy gloved fingers and thumb, inspected it for a moment, and bowed to kiss it. 'Baltazar Casaubon, Lord-Architect, Scholar-Soldier of—'

Plessiez cut the man off in mid-flow: 'If you listen, Zaribet, you do it as a private person.'

The Katayan nodded vigorously, hair flopping over her black-hook eyebrows.

Plessiez let his weight rest on one haunch, thumb tucked into sword-belt, eyes narrowed against the sun; something of his poise returning.

'There are thirty-six of these engines. I've directed the production-line workers for the past week, getting sixteen engines on-station in the further Districts. These that remain must be functioning and able to move by noon, to be in position – at the entrances to the airfield, the docks, the underground rail and sewer termini, the main avenue to the royal palace, and at as many points overlooking the Fane as possible.'

He saw Zar-bettu-zekigal's head come up, her pale eyes raking armour-plating, gunports, stacked muskets on the platform, beaked battering-rams.

'You're going to attack the Hyena's people!' she accused.

'We face no serious threat from a few of the servant class who've latterly learned to hold a sword by the correct end.'

'No.'

Plessiez, startled, looked up from his footing on the rubble to meet the china-blue eyes of the Lord-Architect. The fat man absently wrung mud out of his coat-tails and shook his head again.

'As I understand it, these are spiritual machines.' Plessiez shrugged. 'Designed to protect my people against attack – by the servants of the Thirty-Six: the acolytes of the Fane.'

A shudder walked down Plessiez's spine. He momentarily shut his eyes upon a memory of Masons' Hall, butcher-red, a shambles. The early sun fell hot on his fur. He opened his eyes to the distant sparks of light from palace windows. The silence of work suspended hung above the artillery garden, as it had been poised above all the city since dawn.

Zar-bettu-zekigal's eyes narrowed against the brightness of the empty sky. She smoothed her dress over her narrow hips with both hands. Her dappled tail hung limp.

'Tripe!' boomed a bass voice: Casaubon shattering the quiet.

Plessiez, tight-mouthed, shifted his ringed hand to his belt-dagger. A momentary breeze unrolled like a gonfalon the hooded silk cloak of a Cardinal-General. 'Messire, if you would confine yourself to architecture and engineering—'

A large hand hit Plessiez squarely between the shoulders. The black Rat twisted his head, feather-plume blocking his view, to see a muddy glove-print on the back of his robe.

'*Complete* rubbish.' The Lord-Architect Casaubon beamed. 'That being the case, you'd only cover the Rat and Mixed districts. Wouldn't bother with a siege-engine for every district, including the Human.'

Plessiez opened his mouth to prevaricate, saw Zari hop from one bare foot to the other, grinning wildly, and Casaubon twinkle at her: 'I don't doubt he plans protection from the Fane. I'm no fool, Messire Cardinal. I can see thaumaturgy plain in a set of blueprints. As for these' – a jerk of the head at the towering siege-engines that set his multiple chins quivering – 'I'm an architect. I followed your exact design. Put these in strategic locations and you protect *everybody* – as far as that's possible, yes?'

Cardinal-General Plessiez shut his open mouth. He lifted his snout, raking the large man from copper hair to mud-dripping high-heeled shoes, and bringing his gaze to rest on the amiably smiling face. A brown smear of oil covered freckles, continued up into the cropped hair. The black Rat met the man's eyes.

'I assume that you need to know that,' Plessiez said, 'because I don't indulge idle curiosity, not with a matter that has taken years to conceive and execute, and which, besides, involves his Majesty the King. Even the curiosity of an excellent architect, messire.'

The Lord-Architect Casaubon inclined his head gravely, waiting.

'Yes,' Plessiez said. 'The intention is to protect as many people as we can, regardless of who and what they are. Rat or human. Or, if it comes to it, acolyte. You are liable to see apocalyptic matters today, messire, and if any of us survive it will be thanks to these machines which his Majesty has desired and I have designed.'

The Archdeacon's sandals scuffed on the concrete of the yard. Tawny grass sprouted up through the cracked surface. She raised her eyes to the tops of the surrounding factory walls. Grass rooted there, against a blue morning sky. A stink of oil and furnaces made her broad nostrils flare.

'A daylight possession? And not susceptible to talismans?'

'We've tried everything. It keeps growing.' The burly woman wiped sweat from her eyes. 'There have been small corruptions breaking through for ten days or more, but now the Rat priests and the Fane won't answer our messages.'

Inside the nearest factory-hangar door men and women leaned exhaustedly up against walls or lay on benches. The Archdeacon glanced back over her shoulder, seeing the alley; the Reverend Mistress and the blond Candia safely penned in by a locked gate and factory workers regarding them with suspicion.

'This way.' The burly woman in carpenter's silks led her past moulding and milling engines, standing silent and reeking of oil, towards the back of the building. In the unaccustomed silence, the bells of the nearby charnel-houses rang clearly.

'Your sick people here' – the Archdeacon pointed – 'is it the pestilence?'

The carpenter glanced back at her co-workers where they sprawled or staggered. The Archdeacon saw a whiteness of skin under the woman's eyes, a certain luminosity and sharpness about the broad features. Vagueness crossed her eyes from moment to moment.

'I'm Yolanda.' The woman stopped at the back wall. 'Foreman over in the next workshop. Well, priest—'

The Archdeacon pointed to a canvas-shrouded bundle in the corner, among broken glass and waste metal and sacking. The length and shape of the human body: on it, blotted red dried to blotched brown. 'Is that a victim of the possession here?'

A proud note came into Yolanda's deep voice. 'Garrard? He fainted and fell under the ore-carts out in the sidings. Hadn't eaten for five days, to my certain knowledge. We had a Sergeant of Arms down here, running back to the Rat-Lords, closing us down. We tried to get a real priest.'

She stopped, shrugged, eyes still on the shroud. 'Already on the Boat by now, and travelling through the Night. He always did like sailing . . . The possession is here, Archdeacon.'

The Archdeacon remained standing staring into the corner of the factory hangar. 'This man died because he tried to work without food or sleep?'

Yolanda folded her arms. 'He died because the Decans fated him to die today. More fool them. No foundries means no tools, no scaffolding, pretty soon no more building on the sites – no more Fane. They'll soon know how it goes. We're *willing* to work. Just not able.'

The Archdeacon cracked her dark knuckles, loosening the muscles in her hands. 'If the plague carries on, you won't need to starve or fatigue yourself, Fellowcraft Yolanda.'

'Here.' Yolanda pushed the small back door open.

Light from a clerestory window picked out the darker green threads woven into the Archdeacon's cotton dress: the pattern of roots, trunk, branches, leaves. She pulled her wide cloth belt taut. Her fingers touched the energy centres at her dark temples, at her breasts and groin and each opposite wrist.

'For all you despise my Church, I can't refuse to do my duty here. My name is Regnault.' The Archdeacon's voice sounded clear, cold. 'If I should be injured and can't do this, you must see to it: take Master Candia to the Cathedral of the Trees. Tell them Candia is to be questioned about Theodoret.'

'Candia is to be questioned about Theodoret—' Yolanda flinched back a sleep-dazed step as the door in the back wall began to drift open. She turned and walked rapidly towards the front of the factory, gesturing to other workers to stay back.

Regnault touched fingers to the peeling white paint of the door. She wrinkled her nose. A smell of rotten vegetation came through the open door: not honest decay, but touched with a corruption of flesh.

She entered, took one slow step into the long white-tiled room, and halted, the door swinging closed behind her, her eye caught by movement. A young black woman in a faded dress faced her from the far end of the room. Round-breasted, round-hipped; bushy hair throwing back a myriad points of gold light from the clerestory windows. Archdeacon Regnault gazed at her reflection in the spotted mirror, at the long row of porcelain urinals on the wall to her left, and the row of closed or open cubicle-doors to her right. Darkness prickled at the edge of her vision. Cold struck up through the tiling and her sandals to impale the soles of her feet.

'Root in Earth protect me.' Her whisper fell on dank air. She put her fingers to her breast, to the spray of hawthorn pinned there. She pressed the pad of her index finger against the thorn, piercing the skin. A bead of blood swelled.

'Above, beneath: branch and root—'

Breath-soft, she began the Litany of the Trees; letting her power push the pepper-scent of hawthorn out into the tiled room, expunging the smell of urine and faeces, tasting still a faint corruption in her mouth.

'Pillars of the world—'

Light brightened: sun through high windows. A watery *glop* sounded, close at hand. The Archdeacon padded forward, and suddenly stopped.

Her reflection in the fly-spotted mirror had not moved.

'—branch and leaf—'

The reflection raised a head subtly disfigured, and smiled with teeth too long and pointed.

'—leaf in bud: shelter and protection—'

The Archdeacon splayed the fingers of her left hand in the Sign of the Branches. Her right index finger throbbed. Blood fell to the floor-tiling in small perfect discs and ovals.

Something buzzed, close at her right hand.

Regnault halted between one step and the next, glancing sideways. The cubicle-door beside her stood half-open, opening inwards, disclosing muddy porcelain footstands in the floor-basin and the china throat of the open drain.

A furred body as large as her two fists hung above the toilet-hole, angrily buzzing. Yellow and black stripes, light glinting from whirring wings, multi-faceted eyes.

The Archdeacon turned from the mirror, stepping towards the cubicle. Water blinked in the open floor-drain: a dark eye in the stained white porcelain. The giant wasp shifted in the air, shifted again, faster than she could react. She stabbed her finger against the hawthorn again and sketched a sign in blood on the air.

'—the protection of the Branches that support the sky—'

The wasp lifted, buzzing, the vibration reverberated from the walls; rising level with the Archdeacon's head. Regnault flung both hands out at a level with her shoulders, spread her fingers and slowly closed them.

Dints appeared in the furred body-segments. Diaphanous wings glimmered emerald, the colour of spring leaves, and crumpled. The soft heavy body fell, still crumpling, to smack against the glazed china surface; slid down the shallow slope and blocked the open drain, feebly burring.

Sweat trickled down between Regnault's shoulder-blades. The step forward had brought her into the cubicle. Eyes still fixed on the dying wasp, she reached out a hand behind her to pull open the swung-to door.

Her outstretched fingers touched fur.

She twisted around, flattening her body against the pipework of the back wall. Her bare ankle brushed over the dead wasp. The door swung closed an inch, a foot, weighed by the heaviness of its burden.

Bulbous shapes – no, *a* shape – clung to the inside of the peeling cubicle door. Fragile insectile legs shifted for purchase. The throbbing soft segments of the torso glowed black and yellow, the glassy wings shattered a rainbow spectrum. The Archdeacon pressed herself back against the wall, heel kicking at the pipework.

The wasp's body, as tall and solid as she, clung quivering to the door, arching slightly at the division of its bulbous body, sting pulsing under the lower torso. Regnault's skin crawled. She looked up wildly to see if the cubicle walls could be climbed. Beyond the partition a deep buzzing note began, joined by another, then another. Sun through the clerestory windows glinted on rising wings.

The wasp that clung to the back of the door thrummed a raw increasing shriek.

'—heart of the Wood protect, the Lady of the Trees defend—'

A sharp click sounded outside the cubicle, at the end of the long room. She recognised the sound of a sandal stepping down on to a tiled floor from a small height: the height of, say, a wall-mirror.

She reached up, hands shaking, and carefully pressed each finger in turn to the hawthorn spray. With bloody hands she unpinned it from her dress, marking the cloth, tearing it into two handfuls of twig and leaf. Her skin cringed away from the insectile form clinging to the door, its translucent guts throbbing with half-digested food.

Poised, dizzy, she took a breath of oxygenless air.

Outside the cubicle, pacing footsteps traced a staccato inhuman rhythm. She glimpsed a brown ankle under the cubicle door, and a foot with claws.

Wetness touched her bare leg.

The fist-sized body of the dead wasp no longer blocked the drain. From its open throat a tendril of wet dark nuzzled. It touched her ankle, numbed the skin, left white puckered marks.

'Heart of the Wood!'

Both hands clenched on crushed hawthorn, she pivoted on one heel and struck the cubicle door solidly with her other foot, a handspan from the thrumming wings. The door banged shut, rebounded concussively inwards. She pitched into a forward roll through the door, hands tucked into her sides, bruising her shoulders.

The wasp ripped up into the air, its chainsaw buzz shattering the glass in the row of clerestory windows.

Regnault came up on to her feet, crouching on the tiles; threw her left hand's bunch of hawthorn full in the sharp-toothed liquid-fleshed mirror-face that fleered above her.

Bloody leaves, stained blossom: for a second outlined in green-and-gold brilliance. Light blinded. She dropped to one knee, edging back towards the urinals. Something black fell from the high ceiling. Shrieking above the saw-buzz of wasp wings, she flung her right hand's hawthorn, slipped, fell full-length on the floor.

The last whole windows imploded.

Black clotted liquid spattered her dress and skin, scalding hot. A rain of ordure pattered down for thirty seconds. She raised her head. Fragments of wing and black fur floated in the air: the wasps were no longer there.

Archdeacon Regnault put her wrist to her nose and wiped away blood. She smiled with the satisfaction of the craftsman. Silence pressed in on her eyes, deep and echoing. Slowly, painfully, she got to her feet; fingers throbbing and still bleeding, clots of faeces sliding to hit the tiles.

The wall-mirror hung shattered in the pattern of a hieroglyph. She read it; frowned suddenly.

' "Oldest of all, deepest of all, rooted in the soul of earth; who dies not but is disguised, who sleeps only—" '

The tiles under her feet rippled, ceramic shifting like water, and she fell to one knee.

A black stain oozed out from under the furthest cubicle door. Black liquid ran down from the urinals. A stink of blood and urine constricted her throat. She clenched her fists, forcing concentration out of pain, muscles tensing to push her towards the exit.

Her legs could not move.

The ceramic tiles under her foot and knee shattered, thin as cat-ice on a puddle. Tears ripped from her eyes as she fell into corrosive vapour. She clawed at the edge of the floor as she fell past it, caught a joist with one bleeding hand for the briefest second.

She stared down into vaulting flooded with liquid darkness, heard the voices calling her, saw in the glistening surface far below the reflection of her face: feral, sharp-toothed, grinning—

The joist grew wormy, holed and friable in the space of a breath. It crumbled under her clenching fingers.

She fell.

A sepia twilight, hot and brown, clings to discarded furnace-mouths, broken bains-marie and alembics. The Bishop of the Trees views them through the open door of his cell: unable to move, or turn away, crusted blood and sinew tightening below his impaled medulla oblongata.

'Why . . . will . . . you . . . not . . . let . . . me . . . die?'

He forces each word out with what breath he can gather into his withered cheeks.

Wings rustle in the heat. Basalt pinions settle to huge flanks as the Decan of Noon and Midnight who is also called The Spagyrus lays his tusked and tendrilled head upon vast paws.

—You're bait—

'Wh . . . ?'

The ebony lids slide up from basalt eyes.

—My servants questioned you for their pleasure. I am a god and a daemon, a Decan of the Thirty-Six: I know all that you could ever know. Still, I allow the acolytes their play—

Scales rustle as the immense head settles still further, yellow-crusted nostrils twitching.

Theodoret, Bishop of the Trees, turns his sandpaper-gaze to where the

Decan looks. Down in the wall of the Fane, above the deserted alchemical workshop, is set a glass bubble – no, a congeries of glass bubbles, each with their variant image of the heart of the world enclosed . . .

They cast a bluish-white light upon The Spagyrus, where the Decan sprawls under the Fane's crepuscular vaults. Perhaps it is that light – or the sun's not being in his Sign – or perhaps it is instinct: the most primitive instinct is smell, and Theodoret has that sense left to him still.

Each breath is rasping pain, each word formed through a torn throat and split lips; still, Bishop Theodoret forces words into the hot silence of the heart of the Fane.

'You . . . know . . . all . . . my . . . Lord – I . . . who . . . know . . . nothing . . . will ask you . . . a . . . riddle . . . What . . . can happen . . . to . . . make . . . a god . . . afraid?'

CHAPTER 6

ight advancing, mid-morning of the Day of the Feast of Misrule.

L Rafi of Adocentyn rolled over on the rug, kicking a foot against one of the Lord-Architect's locked abandoned chests.

'If I'd known we had theory-tests on Festival days, I'd never have joined the university! What is all this junk anyway?'

Lucas chose deliberately to misunderstand. From where he sprawled on his bed, surrounded by open books, he muttered: 'Geometry, one would hope.'

'Witty, Candover, witty.'

The languid king's son from Adocentyn hoisted himself up on an elbow on the rug, and plotted a course across a page with a dirty finger.

'Lucas, just *listen* to this question: *"The Five Points of the Compass lie upon a circle of 360 degrees, each one at a ninety-degree angle from the next . . . Draw a compass rose, and enter North, West, East, South and Aust at the appropriate positions."*'

Lucas shifted into a patch of morning sun, knowing he would be grateful later for shade. He gestured for Rafi to continue. The other dark-haired student propped the book up on its spine.

'*"Now draw the following quadrilateral triangle . . ."*'

Lucas leaned down, grabbed a sheet of paper and a lead pencil, and sketched for a few seconds. 'Like so.'

'You think so?' Rafi of Adocentyn sat up, scratching at the cleft of his buttocks. 'We're going to be sweating our arses off in Big Hall today.'

'The way things are here, lucky if that's the only problem we got.'

'Yeah, the Feast of Misrule won't be up to much.'

Lucas got up and stood at the open window, thumbs hooked in the back pockets of his knee-breeches. The warm air soothed his sun-scalded chest and shoulders. He looked down into the street. A mist so milky blue as to be almost purple clung to the roofs.

'At least you haven't been scrubbing latrines for three weeks.'

Rafi bellowed, thin mobile features convulsed. 'Shit, that Heur-odis bitch has got it in for you!'

'*And* the rest.'

'I think it's funny,' the other king's son said, 'but then, nothing that happens to me here is ever going to get back to Adocentyn if I can prevent it.'

The wooden frame creaked under Lucas's grip as he leaned out of the window, one knee up on the sill.

'What is it this time? Ei, *Luke!*'

He fell back into the room, struck the door-frame with his shoulder on the way through, ignored Rafi's shout, and hit every third stair going down to the street-door.

Heat struck down from a cloudless sky. Apprentices clattered past at the Clock-mill end of the side-alley. His rapid breathing slowed as he went barefoot over the cobbles to the other end of the alley and turned the corner.

Voices rang across the street: Evelian's snotty daughter, Evelian herself, and a woman just now halted with her back to Lucas.

Sun tumbled in cinnamon hair.

'I want my rent!' Evelian shouted. 'And where's your friend the Lord-Architect?'

'The gods know! No – they probably do. *I* don't.'

She stood, now, with one arm outstretched to the brick-and-plaster wall for support, her white shirt-sleeve half-unrolled. Sweat soaked the underarms; her uncovered skin glowed pink-red. Slung across her back, worn straps cinched tight, a sword-rapier caught the morning light.

'White Crow?'

His whisper cracked soprano, inaudible.

She brushed grit from the sole of her right foot with her free hand. Brick- or stone-dust powdered her smooth calves and the hems of her knee-breeches. A hat lay upturned at her feet, white felt speckled with black hieroglyphics; and she bent and turned and scooped it up, and her tawny eyes focused and met his.

'Lucas!'

She strode the few yards between them, flung her arms around his chest: breasts and belly and legs pressed the length of his stirring body. Her rib-cage moved rapidly as she panted, hyperventilating in the heat. He buried his face in her hot-odoured white-streaked hair. Careful of blade and harness, as careful of her fine-lined skin and solid flesh as of porcelain, Lucas closed his arms across her back.

'You're sunburned.' The White Crow swatted his chest with the brim of her hat, stepping out of his embrace. 'The mysteries of elapsed time . . . What the hell has happened to the trains and carriages? I've had to walk from the Thirty-Sixth District, and it's taken me hours.'

'You must be new here,' Evelian snarled sarcastically. 'Haven't you heard about the strikes?'

The White Crow smiled. 'I've been away, remember?'

Lucas watched her lips move in the sunlight. A fine line marked her lower lip: a thirst-split. More fine lines webbed the corners of her eyes and cheek-bones. Her cinnamon lashes blinked over pale eyes, in eye-sockets whitened by heat and sweat.

He bent his head, smelling the sweet odour of her skin, and kissed the gritted corner of first one and then her other eye.

'Grave-robber!' A possessive mutter from Sharlevian.

He straightened, ignoring the girl. The White Crow's mouth moved in some reaction too complex for easy interpretation. Shock still reverberating through him, Lucas yelled: '*What happened? What did the Fane do to you?*'

Sharlevian gasped; he saw her mouth gape comically. Evelian scowled. The White Crow pitched her voice above Mistress Evelian's renewed questions: 'I was gone, I'm back; I'll be gone again shortly, and after that I don't know!'

'But—'

Noise interrupted Lucas: a dozen apprentices clattering down the alley, cutting through the street to a Dockland site. A gangling dark boy snapped a punch at Lucas in passing; an older man jeered: 'Student!'

'What are the gold-and-white sashes?' the White Crow said at his shoulder. 'And was that *weapons* they're carrying? Openly?'

Lucas stared the gangling youth out until he turned, spitting, to follow the others. Of the dozen or so passing men and women, fully half had a striped sash and sword-belt around their shoulders or waists.

'The new Order of the— *Shit!*' A thrown pebble struck his knuckle. He jammed it into his mouth and sucked the cut. 'Of the Poor Knights of the House of Salomon. We've had street-fights with them at the university.'

'I did wonder. No one called me out on this.' The White Crow reached up, touching the hilt of her sword. Sunlight shone on the blue metal, the sweat-dark leather binding; and on the curve of her uplifted arm. 'It seems that the House of Salomon has changed greatly since the Mayor told me about them.'

'*Those* aren't Salomon men,' Lucas added. 'Just their followers.

White and gold are their colours. They're the sort who say you can wear the gold cross as protection against the plague.'

'There *is* a plague?'

Disquiet touched her face. Lucas regretted the dramatisation.

'Not really. Just the High Summer fevers are worse than usual. It's all rumour.'

'I need to know . . .' She shook her head, sun-silvered red hair falling about her shoulders. Lucas noted the falling cuff of her shirt: a stain of red wine not yet faded.

'. . . What *don't* I need to know!' she finished.

'Wait there, right there!'

'I'll be up in my rooms. Evelian—'

Lucas raced back around the corner of the building, up the street-stairs, into his own rooms, physical effort for the moment masking his wild excitement.

'The test's in an *hour*,' the king's son of Adocentyn grunted, arms full of texts, as Lucas shoved past him to rummage in a heap of revision-papers. 'They'll sling us out if we don't pass. Luke!'

'Yeah, yeah. *Got it.*'

He sprinted back, out into the morning air, seeing Evelian and her daughter still arguing in the street; leaping for the stairs and skidding up through the kitchen and into the White Crow's main room.

'Here. This'll tell you all you need to know about Salomon. It's put out by the woman who claims to lead the imperial dynasty.'

'The *what*?'

'You must know. Where have you been?' And then he froze, at the implications of that casual question.

The White Crow squatted, glancing into the fox-cubs' box. The chill of disuse and her absence cut through High Summer heat in the newly opened room. Junk stacked the corners, piled on chairs.

The mirror-table shone, glass side up, feeding-bottles scarring rings across its cracked surface.

'Fuck!' The White Crow bent to check the broken magus-mirror.

'Evelian wouldn't let me in here, or I'd have looked after it.'

The White Crow straightened. Her head came up as she turned a full circle, taking in neglected books and charts and lenses. The slightly fat-blurred line of her chin made his throat constrict. She prodded a heap of hand-scrawled messages resting on the table, tilting her head sideways to read one.

'I must follow up some of these names. And talk to Evelian about people she knows. Now . . .' She reached for the pamphlet he still held out, and her fingers touched his hand. He grinned foolishly.

'Damned black letter printing . . . Let me see. *Liber ad Milites Templi de Laude Novae Militae*. "In Praise of the New Knighthood"?'

'The Salomon men are behind the organised hunger-strikes up at the Fane. They've almost stopped all building going on.'

'Casaubon knows more about the Secret Orders than I do. Whenever he's been put now . . .' Her mouth quirked up. "One crucial hour" – and it turns out to be the Feast of Misrule. Lucas, don't let anyone tell you the gods have no sense of humour.'

Lucas scratched under his open shirt at sweaty hair. Bewildered, he said: 'There won't be much of a festival, with the sickness and the strikes. What do you mean, *when*ever?'

She absently folded the black-letter pamphlet, creasing it sharply, and put it in her pocket. 'I don't know for certain that the Decan did do the same to him. Pox-rotten damned idiot that he is, why didn't he tell me what he was up to! I wonder if it's too late to contact any more of the College?'

She rested both fists against her mouth, tapping them softly against her teeth, in the gesture of thought that brought Lucas's heart to his mouth. Then, still absently, she reached up to a shelf for a wooden box, opened it, and took out three small talismans on chains.

Cut into tear-translucent moonstone: a sickle moon. Into pearl: a nereid's trident. And into black onyx: the cold Pole Star. Some of the sweat-blotched red and white left her face as she put them around her neck. She stretched, and all but fell into a sitting position on the courtyard-window's sill.

'That's better. I'd forgotten what High Summer's like, here in the heart of the world . . .'

Lucas said softly: 'Are you well?'

She shoved her spread fingers through her hair, pushing it back from her face. The white at her temples gleamed. Resting with her back against the jamb, one bare foot up on the sill, she smiled exhaustedly up at Lucas.

'Yes, kind sir, I thank you for asking. But no,' she said, the smile vanishing, 'I'll have to be moving again. Damned transport would be out now, when I need to get across half the city. And I hate to break a strike.'

Lucas looked round at the star-charts curling on the walls, the cracked mage-mirror table, the stacked volumes of Paracelsus, Michael Meier, Basil Valentine. He walked to stand beside her, looking across the top of her head and out into the courtyard. Yellow grass sprouted up between the flagstones. A dark patch on the earth showed where Evelian irrigated the cherry trees; morning light dappling their long oval leaves.

'Lady, you don't need to be told how much I missed you, or how I feared you dead. I even ordered poor Andaluz to make enquiries at the Fane of the Thirty-Sixth Decan. My uncle is afraid of the Decans. He was not admitted, in any case. But you had been allowed in . . .'

She raised her face, and he lost track of his thoughts. He grinned: a rictus.

'I believe that I even missed your friend the Lord-Architect, gods alone know why; but I find myself hoping that he's well, as you are.'

The White Crow blinked as if thrusting away some disturbing image. 'I hope so, too.'

The heat and the white light that came in at the window dazzled Lucas. He rubbed his eyes.

'How could I forget what you said? *In this city, the soul can die, too.* I don't have to be a Kings' Memory to remember that. Lady, I've spent the days studying, learning, at the university; and all the time wondering: has it happened again? Has someone else been taken by The Spagyrus into the Fane and died – died, with no rebirth? And, if it had happened, had it happened to you?'

Lucas, having rehearsed the conversation for a dozen nights, lost the distinction between fact and fantasy, let the tips of his fingers touch her fine hair that the sun made hot.

'No, and no, is the answer. Believe me, you'd know! None of us would be here . . .' She slid off the window-sill to pace across the room, remove her leather backpack from its chest, and begin to throw into it gem-talismans, amulets, herbs, parchment and tiny bottles of strangely composed inks.

'And I suppose I'd better take Cornelius . . .' She slid a book into the satchel, paused, and added another. 'And the *Ghâya*.'

'What did the Decan tell you?' Lucas touched her shoulder as she passed him; the cloth of her shirt rough under his hand. 'You don't seem changed, and you've spoken with god.'

'You haven't been in the heart of the world long enough, Prince. You get used to living on god's doorstep, and you get used to some very practical divine intervention, when you live here. Hasn't anyone told you *this is Hell*?'

'I didn't know what they meant.'

'They might equally well have said *this is Heaven*. The gods are here, on earth. Live here, and you live cheek-by-jowl with what moves the living stars in their courses, and the sun, and the earth. When you die, Prince, you'll travel through the Night, and that's the same Night that exists within the Fane, *is* the Fane, grows with the Fane as it's built. Yes, I've spoken with god. Around here, that isn't too unusual.'

Lucas swallowed, wet his lips, touched by something that still clung to her, a scent as of sun-hot courtyards and the silence that stone breathes off under great heat.

'What will you do?'

The cinnamon-haired woman bent to pick up another piece of chalk and tuck it into the side-pocket of her leather backpack.

'I don't know what to do, except that it must be something a Scholar-Soldier *might* do – so I take this.' She touched her pack, her sword. 'And I don't know where, or when; but since it's The Spagyrus who caused this I suspect it's at the Fane, at noon or midnight. And, if I start now, I might just be able to walk to the Fane-in-the-Twelfth-District by noon.'

She tilted the mirror-table, catching sun from the skylight. Reflections danced on her neck and the underside of her chin. Her mouth twisted in a sideways smile.

'So much *magia* in the air! If I tried to use this, I'd be as deafened and blinded as when the acolytes attacked that hall. And it's the one time I would have risked *magia* to go from here to there without going between . . .'

Lucas frowned, thoughts racing. 'What did the Decan say you should do?'

'Heal. What else would a Master-Physician do? Of course, it would help if I knew who I was meant to be healing. And why the Decan wants them healed, instead of dying on their Fated day and passing through to rebirth.'

'You have a whole sick city to choose from.'

'Oh, Prince.' She straightened up from unfastening her sword-harness and slung the rapier and scabbard across the mirror-table, careless of further damage. 'That was gruesome enough to come from the Lord-Architect himself. You're learning.'

'Growing up,' Lucas said acidly.

'I have never doubted you were grown.' She twinkled. Shifting her attention before Lucas could say any of what crowded on his tongue, she added: 'I am to heal, and Casaubon, I think, is to handle the builders. The strike, I wonder, or the House of Salomon? She revealed nothing to him, nothing to me. Only assured us that we're in the right moment to act. And She should know, being a Decan.'

Lucas scowled. 'But if the Decans know what will happen in the future, then why—?'

The White Crow grinned. 'They make the future. They turn the Great Cycle of the Heavens: in the thirty-six divisions of Ten

Degrees. *But* . . . many of the Decans are in opposition to one another.'

'With us as game-pieces.'

'Oh, Prince, it's real life; it isn't a game.'

She was a little fey, he thought; and still with that air of the god-daemon about her, as if she could taste the power in her mouth, feel it crackle through her like static. He noticed how she favoured her left hand, the fingers pierced and slightly swollen, pin-pricked with black marks.

'White Crow, I can tell you something. You, or it might be more useful to the Lord-Architect.'

The savour of the knowledge had gone now, gone with the fantasy of her gratitude when she should receive it. He concentrated only on being as plain as possible.

'It started with my wanting to talk to Zari. Knowing she's alive. I haven't seen her yet, but I have seen that priest she went off with – the the one that was supposed to have been killed, and now he's a Cardinal?'

'And?' She bowed her head, adjusting the sword-harness so that she could buckle it about her waist, out of the way of the backpack.

'Plessiez and my uncle are old friends. I've met the Cardinal now. Between that and the Embassy files, I'm certain that he's got some very close connection with the House of Salomon, and with the woman that wrote the pamphlet, the one who claims to be leader of the imperial human dynasty.'

She nodded slowly. 'Yes. Lucas, I want you to do something for me. Find your friend, the Kings' Memory, Zar-bettu-zekigal. If your uncle knows her present employer, you should be able to manage it somehow. And if you can't bring her to me, try to find the Lord-Architect and take her to him. He'll need to know everything he can about the House of Salomon.'

'I'll do it,' the Prince of Candover said, 'after I've gone with you to the Fane. There are the acolytes. It's too dangerous for you to go on your own.'

She opened her mouth, and he cut off the sharp reply he saw in her eyes: 'Scholar, yes; soldier, yes; but have you been trained at the University of Crime?'

The White Crow's eyebrows went up. 'Well. You might have a point there, Prince.'

He watched her for a few more minutes, packing with the ease of practised preparation. The half-grown fox-cubs whined from their box.

'And if it happens again?' Lucas asked.

'It will. Once more. I have it on—' The White Crow paused.
'On very good authority. I can tell you the prophecy. *The Lord of
Noon and Midnight will once more break the circle of the living and the
dying: in that one hour the Wheel of Three Hundred and Sixty Degrees
will fly apart.* What I want to know is, if the Decan of Noon and
Midnight knows what that will do, which he must know, then
why do it?'

The White Crow broke off. Then: 'She cares nothing for plague.
That was apparent. So if She doesn't want me to heal the sick, who
am I to heal?'

'If The Spagyrus's alchemy—'

'I know what you're going to say. That that wouldn't be the
healing of a body from sickness, but of a soul from The Spagyrus's
black miracle: true death. I'm good,' Master-Physician White Crow
said, with a smile that never reached her eyes. 'I probably know
more about *magia* than anyone now in the heart of the world, the
Lord-Architect included. And I've done necromancy in my time.
But I wouldn't even know how to go about raising the truly dead.'

Lucas at last identified the energy that moved her: excitement,
and a wild fear.

'She said there would be a moment to act. She did not,' the White
Crow said, 'tell us what we should do. I wish Casaubon were
here . . . but I can't wait for him.'

'I'm coming with you.'

The woman made no objection, which at first pleased and then
badly frightened him. She hefted her pack onto her shoulders,
thumbing the straps into place, and walked past him towards the
window as she did up the buckles.

'There's more,' she said. 'Something new.'

The White Crow turned her head slightly, so that she looked
down into the courtyard and not at Lucas. Her fingers reached for
the warm wooden frieze interrupted by the window-frame: the
carved skulls and spades.

'Walking here this morning . . . I feel it every time my foot
touches the ground. There are focuses of ill and sickness, under the
city. Seven of them. Plague-*magia*, I think – corpse-relic necromancy. Either cast while I was gone, or grown stronger in the
meanwhile. And becoming more violent with every minute that
passes.'

'Necromancy.' Lucas swallowed, saliva suddenly thick in his
mouth. 'Lady, I think I can tell you something about necromancy
and Cardinal-General Plessiez.'

*

The heat of mid-morning stifled the small audience chamber. Lengths of fine linen, dyed blue, shaded the great windows; and brown Rat servants cranked the blades of a ceiling-fan. The Cardinal-General of Guiry waved other servants aside as he strode down the azure carpet.

'Your Majesty.' Plessiez knelt, with a flourish, on the dais step of the circular bed. 'I have news, best discussed confidentially.'

The Rat-King sprawled on silk covers. One dictated a letter to a secretary; another held out an arm for a young brown Rat page to groom it; two more played with tarot dice, spilling the bright enamelled cubes on the cushions they lay against. One plump black Rats-King sat himself grooming the knot of their eight tails.

'News?' The bony black Rats-King opened an eye. 'So we would hope. It grows—'

'—late, Messire Cardinal,' finished a fat brown Rats-King, this morning next to the black. He snapped his fingers, dismissing the servants to the five corners of the chamber. 'Well?'

Tension, like static in fur, crackled in the heat-heavy air.

'I have spoken with the architect, your Majesty, and corrected the fault in the drive mechanisms of the remaining siege-engines. They can be set to move whenever you command.'

The formal phrasing came easily. Plessiez kept his eyes fixed on a point just over the black Rats-King's shoulder. Before the King answered, he spoke again:

'Your Majesty, this was done by your will. I have always acted so; I trust that I always shall. You have had your necromancy performed, and by the end of this day there will be no one who does not perceive the result of it.'

One of the silver Rats-King put down the scroll he was reading. 'Then, all is well, messire.'

'Your engines are ready to be put in place, to ward off the acolytes if they attack.' Memory touched Plessiez's spine with a cold claw. 'But I beseech your Majesty, again, to approve the plan the Order of Guiry has suggested, and spare several such engines for the defence of Human districts.'

Heat soaked in through the linen curtains, and in the silence Plessiez heard the servants whispering in the corners of the audience chamber. The long-bladed fan turned slowly, as if through clear honey.

'St Cyr came to me today.' The bony black Rats-King spoke without acknowledging the Cardinal's last words. He smiled. 'The conspiracy of Messire Desaguliers – or perhaps *coup* is better, since he plans Our removal and replacement – is ripe now. St Cyr believes he and his disaffected friends will act in the next two days.'

'Remove the fool now, your Majesty.'

'I may yet have a use for Messire Desaguliers. But we did not—'

'—ask for your opinion in this, Messire Plessiez.' The fatter of the brown Rats-King spoke again. 'What else?'

Plessiez mentally shrugged, shifted one furred knee on the steps where it began to ache, and reported: 'It's five days, now, since anything at all was observed leaving or entering any part of the Fane. Your Majesty, I believe that means the *magia* begins to work upon them. We should protect ourselves.'

Three of the Rat-King spoke together.

'The humans—'

'—this High Summer fever is our pestilence in disguise. It begins—'

'—to thin down their numbers.'

'They will prove more tractable to our rule if there are fewer of them.' The bony middle-aged black Rats-King shifted, easing over on to his other haunch. 'Yes, Messire Plessiez, we are aware that you find that unpalatable. Government is a hard art, harder than your *magia*. Very well, order the engines to move out – between the hours of eleven and one, when the heat will empty the streets.'

Plessiez, rising to leave, adjusted the hang of his scabbard, and the cardinal's green sash; and at the last couldn't keep from his warning: 'Your Majesty, I know, may hope by this to weaken our masters' power, or even, it may be, to drive them to abandon their incarnation here amongst us. But consider that then we lose not only their oppression of us, but also their protection.'

'We *have* considered it,' the bony black Rats-King said. 'You may go and do as we order, messire.'

Plessiez bowed deeply, backing across the carpet to the doors. The brown Rat servants opened them soundlessly as he turned and passed through. The airless chamber slicked down his fur with heat. He paused for a moment in the palace corridor to groom.

'Lord Cardinal, a message for you.'

He took the folded paper from the brown Rat, expecting it to be Reverend Captains Fleury or Fenelon, or perhaps something from the military architect. He unfolded it and read:

I have urgent news but can't meet you now, messire. Be on the Mauressy Docks by noon. The laboriously printed signature spelled out *Lieutenant Charnay, King's Guard.*

'It's taken me an hour and a *half* to walk here.' Breathless, Zar-bettu-zekigal sat down heavily on the camp-bed. The trestles gave out a sharp creak.

'What does the Cardinal-General say?'

'Tell you in a . . . in a minute . . .'

The Hyena paced the length of the temporary pavilion. Sepia light through the canvas walls sallowed her face. Her scabbard clashed as she moved. Her plate armour hung discarded on a frame in the corner of the tent; the woman wore only her dark red shirt and breeches, sweat-marked in the close heat.

'Well?' She passed the document-covered desk, ignoring it for the moment, and finished standing beside the trestle bed, looking down at the young Katayan woman. 'What did he tell you?'

Muffled, clocks struck eleven. The harsh strokes barely penetrated the folds of the pavilion tent.

The young woman leaned back on her elbows on the bed, looking up. Her pale arms and legs glowed golden in the sunlight sifted through the canvas. Black lashes dipped once across dark eyes, before she shifted on to one elbow, reaching with her other hand for the shoulder of her black dress.

'I can't believe it: it's so *hot*.'

The Hyena folded her arms, with difficulty keeping a smile from her face. 'You're a Katayan.'

'I'm still hot!'

The younger woman, eyes holding the Hyena's, undid with accurate fingertips the hooks-and-eyes that ran down the shoulder and side of her black dress.

'You're as subtle as a brick.'

'Oh, but, see you, it *works*.'

Amused, exasperated, the Hyena shook her head. 'I don't have time for this, not now of all times. Tell me about Plessiez.'

The Katayan lifted her legs on to the trestle bed and rolled over onto her front, so that she lay on the discarded flattened dress, head pillowed on her pale arms. The matt-black hair of her head grew in a tiny hackle down her neck and the pale knobs of her spine, to transform into fur where her tail (wide as her wrist at the coccyx, but flattened) coiled down black and white.

'Don't you ever give up?'

'Never!'

The Hyena seated herself on the unsteady edge of the bed. She reached out and began to rub the younger woman's shoulders. Zar-bettu-zekigal lowered her head, lay with her nose in the crook of her arm. Something brushed the Hyena's shoulder; she started; realised it was the tuft-tipped tail.

'I'm ordering camp struck. Well enough for the Salomon men to fortify their halls, but the dynasty's used to hit-and-run.' She paused. 'We may need to be invisible before the end of today, to attack with no warning of our coming.'

Zari's head came up far enough for her to say: 'That why you shifted the tents down here? To Fourteenth District?'

The Hyena pushed her thumbs into flesh that barely cushioned sharp shoulder-blades, hot under her hands; bracing her fingers on the Katayan's skin. Shadows crossed the tent. No breeze moved the canvas walls. Outside, she heard the shouts of civilian infantry being drilled, spared a moment's thought for the sewer-taught soldiery and this district's militia.

'The Fane.' Her fingers dug into smooth skin.

'Messire the Cardinal says: *Memory, hear: To the leader of the imperial dynasty this message. His Majesty's own precautions will have taken place by noon. If you wish no retaliation, make no attack on them; they are not designed for use against your people . . .*'

The Hyena nodded impatiently. 'I know about the engines in the artillery garden. Zari—'

Still soothing the younger woman's muscles in rhythmic strokes, she found her hands moving as Zar-bettu-zekigal rolled over onto her back, until they rested on her small high breasts. The Katayan put her hands under the back of her head and grinned. A dappled tuft of hair marked her Venus-mound, and pale freckles dotted her belly. The Hyena moved her hands down over the sharply defined rib-cage.

'*Your own people's protection I leave to you. My best experts in magia foretell this noontide to be the moment of the Great Wheel's turning. Now, whether it be for the favour of my people or yours, I know not, but such a confusion is cast over all readings for our strange masters the Decans that I confidently anticipate—*'

Hardly holding in her impatience, she said: 'Yes? Yes?'

'—*anticipate that our bargain reaches its conclusion here. Lady, when the Fane falls—*'

The Katayan winced. The Hyena withdrew fingers that had spiked flesh, nodded.

'*When the Fane falls, which I believe will be noon today, then, it being everyone for themselves, I bid you farewell, Lady.*'

'Damn it, it is, it *is* today! Now – I'll give the alert.'

She sat back, moving to stand. Pale hands reached up. She stared absently down at the young woman, suddenly pulled her up to sit on the bed and threw her arms about her in a fierce embrace. Zar-bettu-zekigal yelped in her ear.

A voice outside the tent called: 'Lady Hyena!'

Ignoring Zar-bettu-zekigal's oath, she shouted back to the sentry: 'What is it, Clovis?'

'Vanringham's on his way through camp,' the muffled voice called. 'You said this time you'd see him, Lady.'

'Send him in.' She stood, strode to the desk, suddenly spun round in her tracks. 'Zari, out!'

'Ei, what?'

'You can't be allowed to talk to him. Out. Come on, out now!' The Hyena pulled her up by the wrists, and the Katayan came unwillingly to her feet.

Fists on bare hips, she glared. 'Oh, *what*!'

'The back way. Now!' She bundled up the crumpled black dress, thrust it into the younger woman's arms, head turned to catch the announcement of entrance. 'Vanringham's from one of the news-broadsheets. You can't talk to him.'

The dress dropped to the floor. The young Katayan woman's shoulders straightened. She glared up from under her fringe of black hair, taut with anger. 'I'm a Kings' Memory. I talk with whoever asks me—'

'Exactly, and you're not talking to the press. Now, *out* when I tell you!'

A horn blared outside the pavilion. The sound of mailed tread approached. The Hyena took a step forward. She watched as Zar-bettu-zekigal bent and scooped up the dress, clutched it to her bare stomach, and then hesitated.

The sentry outside called: 'Lady Hyena, the representative of the Nineteenth District broadsheet.'

The Katayan's head turned as the canvas wall of the tent quivered. Her chin came up. Hooking the dress on one finger, she slung it over her shoulder, sepia light sliding down her naked shoulders, breasts, hips and legs; and walked with something of a swagger to the curtained exit.

'Zari.'

Loud enough to be heard, the Katayan spat: 'If you didn't want a Kings' Memory, you had no business talking in front of one!'

Tail flicking, she strode out as the sentry and the new arrival came through the canvas passage; nodded a casual greeting at the gaping men, and walked out into the blazing sun.

The Hyena brushed the lank hair back from her face, sighing. The man escorted in, small and middle-aged, with white hair that stuck up like owl's feathers, turned his head back from following the Katayan's exit.

'*Do* you have a Kings' Memory in your employ, Lady?'

She ignored his question. Passing Clovis on her way to sit down, she said quietly: 'Call in the council of captains.'

Sepia light gleamed on the banners of the dynasty, draped white and gold at the rear of the tent. A flash of white light glinted from the armour-stand as Clovis lifted the curtain on his way out. The Hyena walked slowly round to sit behind the desk, facing the broadsheet publisher, the gold-cross banners at her back.

'Messire Vanringham, I want to show you something.'

She uncreased a folded broadsheet that lay on the table, on top of unfolded maps. Her own face looked up at her in shades of grey from the paper, slanting brows made heavy by shadow.

'I do not ever recall telling you, Messire Vanringham, that the army of the human dynasty is made up from "criminals escaped from oubliettes, the disaffected, the lunatic; and the young enticed by drugs or seduced by treason". Nor that "their leader, claiming imperial blood, is in fact the child of a shopkeeper and a Tree-priest . . .'''

The man scratched at his head, spiking the hair into further disarray, and then rubbed his nose vigorously and dug in the pockets of his stained doublet for his notebook. Unembarrassed, and possibly unafraid, he said: 'I print what I have to, Lady. Else I lose my printing press to the Rat-Lords.'

'Criminal.' She let sweat shine on his forehead before she added: 'But you need no longer suffer it.'

Light and heat momentarily glared as Clovis re-entered. Armour and swords clashed, the tent suddenly full of bright metal and gold-cross surcoats: eight or nine other captains entering with him. They knelt before the Hyena.

A little uncomfortable, Cornelius Vanringham looked at her across their lowered heads. The Hyena waited until she could see the professional hardness re-enter his gaze.

'We're ready to make the announcement today, messire. I want you to put out a special edition. Print it now, send it out to the five quarters here, and to as many other Districts as your delivery-men can reach—'

He made a protest patently not the one in his mind. 'But the strike?'

'The people will break it. This is for the human dynasty and the House of Salomon. And don't worry about your masters and your printing press.' She waited a heartbeat for the doubt to clear from his face. Seeing it would not, knowing the man's reservations, she grinned.

'Don't forget how far and how fast I've come. You'll believe me by the end of the day, Messire Vanringham. The story you'll print shall be this: that the imperial dynasty is at last ready to resume its place as the ruling power in the heart of the world.'

Heat-haze lay over the lagoon and the expanse of dockyards. Zar-bettu-zekigal hooked together the last hook-and-eye on the shoulder of her black dress, the cloth hot under her fingers.

'Bitch! Cow! Shitarse!'

She slammed her fists down on the balustrade of the bridge. A fragment of stone plopped into the canal below. She leaned over, staring down into the ripples. All the docks stood deserted. No barges sailed down from the arsenal; the booms and cranes of the Moressy dock-quay stood silent.

Faint but audible across the half-mile distance came the noise of the impromptu camp: imperial soldiers and the House of Salomon.

'Bitch . . .'

She leaned her elbows on the bridge, on clumps of grass that grew in the pointing. Eyes unfocused, she watched sun dance on the lagoon. Haze obscured sails on the horizon. Her gaze dropped, and her eyes abruptly focused.

'Oh, what!'

She put one foot on the rough brick, hoisting herself up; then slid down, ran barefoot down the further steps and ducked into the shadow of the canal bridge. 'Charnay!'

Cold metal slipped across her shoulder to lie against her neck.

'Don't be ridiculous!' she snapped. 'It's *me*.'

The rapier lifted. A deep laugh sounded in her ear. She turned. Burn-patches and scars marked the big brown Rat's fur, and her cloak and uniform were missing. She gave Zar-bettu-zekigal a confident smile. 'You've come from Messire Plessiez?'

Zar-bettu-zekigal shook her head.

'I sent a message,' Charnay complained, resheathing her rapier. 'He should have been here at noon.'

'That's an hour yet!' She saw the big Rat scowl. 'Charnay, where have you been? What's been happening?'

The brown Rat raised her head, listening for footsteps. 'Take me to Plessiez.'

'Can't. Kings' Memory business. Got to go back and find out if the bi— If she's got messages for him.' Zar-bettu-zekigal brought her tail up to scratch her upper arms, tingling from the sun. 'Isn't as easy as it sounds, but I have to. Charnay, where *were* you?'

'With the Night Council.'

'Who?'

The brown Rat opened her mouth as if to speak, then shut it. Transparently awkward, she cast about for something and finally pointed out into the lagoon. Heat lay white on the blue sea, on the sand-bars that lined the horizon. The sails of the small fleet of ships hung like faded washing, casting for every faint breeze.

'I've been watching that fleet come in. No pilot-ship?' Charnay said wonderingly. 'No tugs?'

Zar-bettu-zekigal narrowed her eyes and did her best imitation of Messire Plessiez. 'Charnay, someone once told you about changing the subject, but you never got the hang of it, did you? That's the strike. Now, what's this "Night Council"—?'

She grabbed Charnay's arm, and the big Rat winced as her fingers tightened.

'Charnay, wait! I *know* one of those ships. Those are the banners of South Katay!'

A smell of *magia* haunted the air like burning.

The White Crow tensed her fingers against the hot leather of reins, halting the brown mare. Hoofs broke the silence with hollow concussive noise. Something drifted past her field of vision, and she reached out with her free hand, snatching; and opening her hand on a black feather. She blinked back water, staring at the empty furnace-sky.

'In which it is seen,' she murmured, 'how a prince turns horse-thief. Very useful, your university training; we may yet make the Fane by noon.'

She pulled the brim of her black-and-white hat down firmly to cut the glare, squinting at the walls and shuttered windows of the Twenty-Third District's deserted street. Almost at the brow of the hill now. Despite talismans of cold, she wiped a face hot and sweaty.

'I hear something.' Lucas reined in the black gelding.

'I sense something.'

She lifted her leg over the saddle and slid to the street, slipping off her sandal and resting her foot on the flagstones. Stone burned her bare toughened sole.

'Seven focuses of plague-*magia*.' Two hours' riding left her throat sandpaper and her head pounding. 'And, yes, it's more than a summer pestilence. There are diseases of the flesh that have their resonances in soul and spirit.'

'How far away?'

'They're widely scattered. Even the nearest is a damn long way off.'

She forced concentration: cut out the weight of the leather backpack, the swinging scabbard at her hip, the mare's head lifting beside her shoulder and tugging on the reins.

'They're coming up to crisis-point now, I can tell that much. I could try to reach one – but if I even try to go for it, I'll miss The Spagyrus at noon. Damn. *Damn.*'

Lucas slid down from his stolen hack to join her. A red headband had been tied raggedly about his black hair, and a knife jutted through the belt of his knee-breeches. He hissed as his sandals touched the cobbles, and grabbed for the talisman at his neck.

'I meant that—'

A grinding roar drowned his words.

The White Crow straightened. The mare skittered back; reins jolted her arm and shoulder joint. Hoofs hit the cobbles inches from her feet. Automatically searching for *magia* words, she hesitated; her wet hands lost grip as the mare reared. Lucas swore, ducked back as the gelding kicked. Both horses clattered in circles in the street, the noise echoing from white porticoes; diminishing as they cantered back down the hill.

Lucas swore steadily and vilely under his breath.

'What-the-fuck-is-*that*?' he finished.

A machine rumbled towards them.

It towered level with the flat marble-balustraded roofs. The White Crow pushed back the brim of her hat, staring upwards at the bright metal housings that shot back highlights from the sun; at the two beaked rams like claws at the front, and the metal-sheathed ballista at the rear: a rising scorpion-tail. Brown and black Rats crouched on the carapace-platform carrying muskets.

'It's a siege-engine . . . It's a *Vitruvian* siege-engine . . .'

Noise thrummed through the flagstones of the street and the bones of her chest; she felt in her belly the juggernaut weight of it. Its massively spoked iron wheels turned with a ponderous inevitability.

Lucas's arm flattened her back against the wall. The noise roared into her head, spiking her ear-drums. She stepped back up onto a doorstep. As the engine drew level, the platform some eight feet above their heads, two of the blue-clad Rats lowered their muskets to point at the Prince of Candover and the Master-Physician.

'What—' Temper lost left her breathless. 'What about my fucking horse!'

Lucas's hand shook her arm. She turned to see him mouthing, inaudible, eyes bright; some convulsive emotion twisting his features. She shook her head, cupped her hand over her ear. He took both her shoulders in his hands, and turned her to face the front of the engine.

The throbbing machine backfired in a cloud of sweet-smelling oil and cut down to a tickover. She fingered her ear, wincing. In the comparative quiet, a voice above her said: 'Is it damned *passengers* now?'

The White Crow lifted her head. A metal trapdoor stood open in the upper casing. Filling every inch of the gap, an immensely fat man in rolled-up shirt and eye-goggles leaned massive elbows on the trapdoor rim. He reached up and shoved the goggles off his eyes, into his cropped orange-red hair.

A white mask of clean skin crossed the Lord-Architect's face at eye-level, clearly showing his freckles. The rest of his face, hands and arms showed black with oil and grease. He dabbed at his chins with a rag, small in his plump fingers, that appeared once to have been an embroidered silk waistcoat.

'Valentine!' He beamed. 'And my young Page of Sceptres, too. This city is remarkably short of transport at the moment, it would seem. Can I offer you a lift anywhere?'

Andaluz eased a finger under the tight ruff of his formal doublet, sweating in the docklands heat. Sun flickered up off the harbour water. The Candovard Ambassador stepped away from his private coach, signalling his clerk to attend him, and walked down the wide marble steps to Fourteenth District's north-quarter quay.

'But it's almost deserted. Dear girl, where are the other ambassadors?'

The clerk, a thin red-haired woman in black, shrugged. 'They were notified of the putative Katayan state visit, Excellency. Pardon me, Excellency, I don't even see a Rat-Lord here to greet them.'

Voices drifted on the wind. Andaluz risked a glance behind, across the sands of the airfield and the deflated airships, to where the marble buildings opened out from a great square. The size of the crowd, to be heard at this distance . . .

'They would have overturned us, simply for breaking the transport strike. I hardly blame the Rat-Lords for not being on the streets,' Andaluz said drily.

Across the lagoon, under the noon heat that leached all colour from the blue water and the bright flags, the unwieldy galleons spread all sail to catch the scant wind. Andaluz's pepper-and-salt brows met as he frowned, estimating. How long to come to safe anchorage at this deepest quay? He cocked his head, listening to a distant clock strike the half-hour.

'Noon,' he guessed. The clerk bowed.

'Excellency, if there are no lords here from the heart of the world, and no other ambassadors, I foresee that the King of South Katay will ask you many awkward questions.'

'Simply because I'm here? Dear girl, I can't ignore our duty because of that unfortunate fact.' Andaluz folded his hands together behind his back. Without a tremor of surprise, he added: 'But *this* young lady should be able to tell you considerably more about South Katay than I can. Claris, you'll have seen her with Cardinal-General Plessiez and myself.'

The clerk murmured: 'She's the one Prince Lucas wants to see? Shall I follow her when she leaves?'

'Of course,' Andaluz confirmed, mildly surprised; and raised his voice to call: 'Honour to you, Mistress Zar-bettu-zekigal.'

The Katayan woman trotted down the wide flight of steps to the quay, a brown Rat following her at a distance. She nodded absently to Andaluz, squatted down on the marble quay beside a silver mooring-bollard, and rested her arms on the metal and her chin on her arms.

'*Some*thing's wrong. See you, messire ambassador, when were you told this was happening?'

'Three days past, when the fleet passed the mouth of the estuary. You heard nothing from your august father?'

'Oh, if he's here three months after me, he must have left soon after I did. Takes close on a year to get here from South Katay.' The young woman straightened up and turned to sit on the bollard. As the large brown Rat joined them, she indicated the harbour with a sharp jerk of her head.

'See you, *some* of those are Katayan flags. That one isn't. Nor's that. And as for that last ship . . .'

Andaluz found the red-headed clerk at his elbow. She stooped slightly to speak in a low tone.

'Excellency, the last ship's banners are from New Atlantis. I recognise them – from my history studies at the University of the White Mountain.'

The Candovard Ambassador's head came up, chin and small beard jutting. He put a reassuring hand on the clerk's arm. Half his attention fixed on the King's daughter – she now leaned up against the big female Rat, pointing to the ships, chattering in an undertone – and half his attention on the ships.

'My dear,' he interrupted Zar-bettu-zekigal, 'will you do something for me? Will you count how many ships there are?'

'Oh, sure.' The Katayan's dappled tail came up, tuft flicking to

point at each one. 'The one with Katayan banners, the one with the
high poop-deck, the one with blue flags, one with bad hull-
barnacles, and one with what your friend calls New Atlantis
banners – six.'

Her tail drooped.

The big brown Rat guffawed, clapping her on the shoulder. 'Call
me stupid, girl? You've added up five and made six!'

Andaluz numbered them softly over in his head.

'One,' he counted. 'And one, and another one . . . another one,
and one more . . . and I see six of them still.'

The clerk nodded. 'So do I, Excellency.'

The brown Rat, still frowning, moved back towards the steps, as if
she had business urgently elsewhere. She carried her rapier
unsheathed now, and Andaluz had not seen her draw it. The
young Katayan ignored the Rat's muttered question. One pale fist
knotted in the cloth of her dress, black fabric bunched.

Her pale eyes met Andaluz's gaze. 'Those are oldstyle Union-of-
Katay banners. Not my father's.'

The Candovard Ambassador nodded. He planted his feet apart,
tugging his doublet straight, gave a glance to the sun's position, and
then stared out across the half-mile of water separating ships from
the dock.

'My dear, it seems to me that one of those ships must be the
Boat.'

Beetles and centipedes scuttled across the marble paving, fried by
the approaching-noon sun. Something rustled on her arm, and the
White Crow's fingertips brushed chitin: a locust skittering away.
She wiped her upper lip free of sweat. She could hardly look up at
the sky. The shadow of the siege-engine fell on her as welcome
shade.

'This really is the most amazing machine to drive.' The Lord-
Architect Casaubon beamed under oil-smears. His head lifted, chins
unfolding, as a clock chimed the half-hour somewhere down
towards the docks. The White Crow bit her lip to keep a grin off
her face.

'How long have you been now? Here?'

He gazed down from the engine-casing, rocked a podgy hand
back and forth. 'Since dawn, this day?'

'Yeah, that's about when I found myself.'

Catching the Rats' attention on her, she switched to a language of
more distant origin.

'I'm trying for the Fane-in-the-Twelfth-District, to enter at noon.

If not, it'll have to be at midnight. But I don't think we have that much time. And then there's . . .'

She flicked a brief gaze to the hot flagstones. Casaubon ponderously nodded.

'What lies below? Oh, yes. And almost ripe, by the feel of it.' His bulk shifted. 'Valentine . . . Pox rot the Decan; She robbed us of a month! We could have discovered the nature of this *magia*, and how to prevent it.'

'I can hazard a better guess than the great Lord-Architect Casaubon?' The White Crow wiped her wet forehead. 'Amazing. But talk to Lucas about the crypt under Aust-quarter. This is a plague-*magia*, responsible among other things for this High Summer pestilence. I believe I know who made it, but I don't know why. What advantage is it to the Rat-Lords to have humans sick now?'

She shifted one bare foot scalded by the hot paving, and raised it to slip on her shoe. 'And, if I go after it now, I'll miss entry to the Fane.'

The Lord-Architect rested bare arms on the engine-casing, wincing at the heat of sun on the metal, obviously feeling for a foothold in the bowels of the machine. Slowly he heaved his immense torso upwards. His shirt snagged on a rivet, tore free.

'Pox rot it, She gave me my own task to do; and I *must* do it. I must see the builders. If you haven't returned after noon, I'll come for you.'

He sat up and swung his massive legs over, slid down to the main part of the platform, and knelt to offer the White Crow a hand to climb up.

'If I can meet you, yes, we'll debate what we do next. If noon's the crucial time, then act as and how you can. I don't like the feel of the day.'

Metal rungs hot under her tender palms, she climbed the ladder; grasped his hand and swung to stand on the steel-plated platform. The Lord-Architect rose to stand beside her. Somewhere he had shed one stocking, and his shoes were caked with white mud.

'I wish,' the White Crow said, 'that She had been a *little* more forthcoming in what She wants us to do.'

From the height of the platform she could see how, ahead, the street opened up. She stared down the hill to the lagoon, the airfield and the rising slope of marble temples beyond, and – highest, farthest – the black aust-northerly horizon of the Fane-in-the-Twelfth-District.

'I do what I can, Master-Physician. I am only' – Casaubon put one massive hand on the stained shirt over his heart – 'a poor Arche-master and Master-Captain.'

'This is *serious*. Lucas . . . Lucas?'

Glancing down, she missed the Prince of Candover. His voice came from the rear of the engine-platform, as he scrambled up the metal ladder near the ballista and hailed a black Rat.

'Messire Cardinal!'

The Rats in Guard uniform fell back from the edge as the black Rat signalled. Sleek, a few inches taller than Lucas; he rested his ringed hand on the hilt of his rapier. The Rat stood lightly, tail cocked, black feather-plume at a jaunty angle, with a silver *ankh* at his collar, and only the rich green silk sash to mark him more than a priest.

'Where's Desaguliers?' The White Crow touched Casaubon's sweat-warm shirt-front. 'Those are Guiry colours. *That's* the Cardinal-General of Guiry? That's Plessiez?'

The Lord-Architect opened his mouth, shut it again, shook his head and made *later* gestures with his plump fingers.

The Prince of Candover walked down the platform, apparently unaffected by the sun-heated metal under his thin sandals. 'Messire Cardinal-General Plessiez. We've met, you may recall it. At the Embassy, with my Uncle Andaluz.'

The black Rat's snout wrinkled in a smile. 'And also, Prince, I think we met in the crypt below Nineteenth District's Aust quarter. But that I have not yet discussed with your uncle the Ambassador.'

'In a crypt!' the Lord-Architect snorted *sotto voce*.

Lucas's gaze moved across the White Crow's face, his own blank as any diplomat's; and she watched with a professional appreciation that momentarily, pleasantly, masked her urgent fears.

'The very question I wanted to raise, Messire Plessiez,' Lucas said. 'You'll recall I was with a Katayan girl then. Mistress Zar-bettu-zekigal – Zari. Her friends have been afraid she was dead. I'd very much like to speak with her again.'

The black Rat raised one furry brow.

About to speak, the White Crow hesitated as she felt Casaubon's voice rumble through his massive torso: 'I, also, think it would be rewarding to speak with the Kings' Memory. Valentine, you'll be unaware of it, but I met her this morning, in company with the Cardinal here. A most *delightful* young lady.'

She blandly ignored his last comment. The Lord-Architect's apparent smugness gave way to apparent pique. She smiled.

'You may be overstepping an archemaster's privileges, Messire

Casaubon.' The black Rat's expression flickered, the glint of anger in bead-black eyes.

'But,' Plessiez continued smoothly, 'in point of fact, I was about to suggest the same thing. I sent Mistress Zaribet to the great square in Fourteenth District with a message, and she may still be there. Perhaps, Prince Lucas, I could beg you to accompany us?'

Still in a distant language, the White Crow murmured: 'That one won't get as much out of the Prince as he hopes, though I see he'll try.'

'And your delightful foreign friend,' Cardinal-General Plessiez continued, 'who I take to be a practitioner of the noble Art? Madam, if you seek employment, I could find a use for a pro-gnosticator of fortunes.'

'As well as for a Lord-Architect?' the White Crow challenged. 'Who you seem to have riding in this monstrosity as well as building it—'

'Driving, not riding,' Casaubon corrected with mild hurt. 'Master Plessiez here has promised me an introduction to the leader of the House of Salomon, one Master Builder Falke, in the great square. Therefore I accompany him.'

'Falke?' The White Crow put her palms back against the hot metal casing of the upper engine, supporting herself. Between tension and delight, she grinned at Plessiez. 'So this Master Falke came out of the Eastquarter hall alive? I was told he died. But, then, I was told *you* died there, your Eminence. One can't trust rumour!'

Brown Rats in King's Guard uniform leaned at their stations on the engine's carapace, shading eyes against the brilliance, or check-ing the loading of muskets and calivers.

'You know Falke, madam?'

'I know of him. I know of you.'

The click of a rifle-bolt echoed back from the house-fronts. A sweet stink of oil choked the air, throbbing up as the siege-engine ticked over. Plessiez glanced over his shoulder at the Prince of Candover.

'I see . . .'

The Lord-Architect Casaubon interrupted: 'We can drive to our destination by way of the Twelfth District, Valentine. Certainly! You'd be late if we left you to walk.'

Plessiez opened his mouth to protest.

'Oh, certainly,' the White Crow deadpanned. 'I'll never get Lucas to steal me horse and tack again in the time left. Of course, if it weren't for this *thing*, we'd still have the mare and the gelding . . .'

Hot sun beat down. Marble roofs and frontages, gold and white against the blue, breathed back the silence that comes from hot stone. The tickover of the siege-engine came back from street and alley walls like the beating of surf, mingling with the offhand talk of the Guards as they patrolled the platform or squatted down against the shaded side.

The Cardinal-General frowned with an expression condemning bad taste.

'Madam, this is not a day upon which to make jokes.'

'I know, your Eminence. I know that better than you appreciate.'

The White Crow tilted her hat-brim down to shade her eyes. 'Let's speak of necromancy, shall we?'

Desaguliers walked past the turning treadmill, not pausing even to brush the sparks from his fur as they fell from the crackling chandeliers. One sweating human face turned towards him. He slapped the end of his tail against the bars. 'Get working.'

'Scum!'

Unbelieving, he swung back to throttle the whisper out of the naked straining worker. Before he could reach her, a Lord Magus in a golden robe appeared at his elbow.

'All's arranged.'

He felt a small hard object pressed into his palm.

'Watch me, then. Don't miss the signal.' Desaguliers, sweating in the heat of midday, the audience hall's closed curtains and artificial light, let a cynical smile appear on his lean features. 'I've known too many of these affairs be messy failures. This one has to succeed. If I go down, I'll take all of you with me.'

'We never doubted that, messire.'

Desaguliers left him, walking under the clover-leaf vaults of the great chamber, now bright with the flare of generated lights. He pushed between two Rats, one in blue satin, one in linen and leather; both feeding by hand and from the same dish their leashed human slaves.

A flurry in the thick crowd caught his attention. A tall Rat in the gold of the Lords Magi, awkwardly riding the shoulders of a female brown Rat-Guard, yelled a drunken toast to the four or five hundred packed into the hall: 'The King!'

Different voices chorused: 'The King and victory!'

'To our future without masters!' the Magus echoed, slipped, and slid to vanish from Desaguliers' sight into the crowd and a roar of laughter.

Pushing onwards, elbowing, the former Captain-General worked his way towards the circular dais-throne. The crowd grew thicker.

He thrust a way between four female Rats in guard uniform, a priest, a cluster of gallants quarrelling; stepped down hard on the long-toed foot of a dazed-drunk brown Rat and opened a gap in the front row.

The Rat-King sat among wine-stained cushions, under the incandescent glare of the lights. Receiving toasts, congratulations; waving away a messenger, talking to a priest in the robes of the Abbey of Guiry, bright-eyed with victory celebrations . . .

'Messire Desaguliers!' The younger of the silver-furred Rats-King raised a wine-goblet in ironic salutation. 'Have you come seeking your co-conspirators?'

Silence began to seep into their immediate circle.

'Conspiracy?' Desaguilers asked mildly.

'Janin, Reuss, Chalons,' the silver-furred Rat-king enumerated. 'And, of the Guard, Rostagny and Hervet—'

'—Volcyr, Perigord, de Barthes,' the bony black Rats-king picked up, turning away from the young female Guiry priest. 'If you have come enquiring for them, I recommend you seek them out in the palace oubliettes. But, then, you'll—'

'—be there in their company soon enough.' A brown Rats-King flopped down on his belly, tail cocked high, and wrinkled his nose dazedly. 'Drink, man! We'll settle your execution tomorrow. Things will be different tomorrow.'

'They certainly will.' Desaguliers spoke over the nearest of the crowd's ragged cheers. He made a low formal bow and, as he straightened up, added: 'You were well informed about the conspiracy, your Majesty. If not quite well enough.'

'Shilly.' The brown Rats-King closed his eyes suddenly.

'Are you still a danger, then?' the bony black Rats-King said. He sprang to his feet, dragging the knot of co-joined tails painfully towards him. Standing knee-deep in the silk cushions, he flung out a hand.

'Enough leniency. *More* than enough. Shoot him!'

The Rats nearest Desaguliers started, whiskers quivering; backed up hard against the packed crowd. The Guards around the dais raised their loaded muskets, struck tinder for the fuses. Someone at Desaguliers' elbow screamed. The Rat-King pointed again, shrieking: '*Shoot!*'

Elbows rammed into his ribs; feet clawed him, pushing away. Desaguliers, swordless, grinned a ferocious grin and kept his feet; watching the smouldering musket-fuses, praying that the Lord Magus' lent magic would – *once*, it only needs to be this once – work for him.

He flung up his hand and crushed the tiny glass sphere that he carried in his hand. '*Now!*'

The sputtering chandeliers died momentarily; then blazed up with a glare that lit the closed draperies like a gunpowder-flash. Hot splinters of glass rained down among screams. Desaguliers threw himself flat as a musket discharged, heard the shot whistle past his head and *thunk* into something with a noise like a butcher's cleaver hitting bone. Wet blood spattered his fur.

On his knees, jaw aching from some unrecognised blow, he heard what seemed at first to be a continuation of the bulbs breaking. The full-length windows shattered, draperies billowing inwards. Daylight blazed in, and dust.

Through clouds of dust and stone-fragments, Desaguliers saw the metal-tipped beak of a battering-ram. Panicked Rats all but crushed him as, now, they struggled as hard away from the windows as they had from the dais. Desaguliers sprang across the intervening distance and landed on the Rat-King's throne.

'*Nobody move!*'

The spur of the battering-ram, joined by a second, pushed collapsing wall and window-frames into the audience hall. Dust rained down on silks and satin and fur. Screams and cries echoed. A silver Rats-king sobbed. The vast bulk of a siege-engine rumbled through the destroyed wall and on to the inlaid-wood flooring, grinding up planks as it came. It blocked the shafts of sunlight spearing the dust . . .

'Here!' Desaguliers held up his hand, signalling to the Rats in Guard uniform crouching on the main platform, who now, swords in hand, leaped down and began shoving the crowd together in smaller, terrorised groups. One group remained on the engine-platform, firing a musket-volley into the King's Guards.

The leader, St Cyr, picked a way from the siege-engine between the wounded through to the throne, fastidiously wiping blood and dust from his black fur.

'Saw your signal,' he said. 'The rest are in position at the back of the building.'

Desaguliers looked down at the bony black Rats-king, crouching at his feet in the silken cushions.

'Your intelligence was good,' he advised, 'but not good enough. Think about how many more of these engines we may have stolen out of Messire Plessiez's control. And then you can be thinking about how the Rat-King, tomorrow, will still have a master. The senate of our new republic.'

*

The gangplank grated as it hit the quayside.

Six or eight very young children leaned over the Boat's rail, screeched, slid back; and the Candovard Ambassador heard their shrill voices calling, bare feet thumping on the deck, high above and invisible.

'Sir?'

Andaluz looked at the red-headed clerk at his elbow.

'My dear girl, you don't suppose that – No. He would be on the Boat when it docks under the White Mountain, not here. I mean my son.' A sea-breeze gusted in his face. He rubbed absently at his hair, feeling it stiff with salt. 'My late son. You'd recognise him easily, Claris. He bore a remarkable resemblance to my nephew.'

Noon shadows pooled on the white marble quay; from the brown Rat, the Katayan, and the two Candovards. Ropes strained from the bollard beside the four of them to the moored ship. Black tarred planks rose up above the Ambassador's head, plain and solid in the sun. He craned his neck and read the name of the Boat cut deeply into the hull. *Ludr.*

'An old word; it means "ship",' he said, 'and "cradle", and "grave" . . . The other ships are gone?'

The tall young clerk squinted into the light off the harbour. 'Yes, sir.'

Zar-bettu-zekigal pointed. 'It's still flying a Katayan flag!'

'Among many others.' Andaluz rested his hand on her shoulder, restraining her impatience.

'I don't understand.' The brown Rat, Charnay, padded back down the marble quay steps and halted beside Zar-bettu-Zekigal. 'When those five galleons were coming in, we couldn't see this one; and now we can see this one the others have vanished.'

'Oh, what! Haven't you ever seen the Boat before?' Zar-bettu-zekigal leaned back on her bare heels, tail coiling up to scratch at her shaggy-growing hair. 'See you, must be hundreds of 'em on board. Boat hasn't been in all this summer.'

Above, furled sails gleamed an ochre, sand-coloured white in the midday sun. From the decks came the clamour of children's voices.

'I can't stay here for this,' Charnay protested. 'I must find Messire Plessiez. The Night Council want him!'

Andaluz let their voices fade into the background. The sun beat down on his uncovered head; he blinked away heat-dazzles in his vision, sweating. Sounds came clearly: the shift of the horses, restless in the shafts of the coach up on the promenade, and, far off across the airfield and the square, the roar of voices . . .

The gangplank creaked.

Andaluz straightened, unconsciously assuming the position of formal greeting. Then his ramrod spine relaxed. He smiled wistfully.

A child some two or three years old staggered down the plank. Another followed it, dark as the first was fair; squatting to prod at the sun-softened tar on the plank. When she stepped onto the quay she took the other child's hand. Both walked away.

'They . . .'

Andaluz held up a hand to arrest Claris's words. He peered up at the light-silhouetted deck, seeing another child, two more; a group of a dozen Ratlings, burnished pelts bobbing in the sun. They clattered barefoot down the gangplank, swarmed for a moment about him, so that Andaluz looked down on the heads of small children, surrounded.

All silent now, all solemn; looking up at the Katayan woman, the Rat and the Candovards.

He knelt, reaching out, almost touching the arm of a small boy no more than two. The child looked with blue eyes, dark blue eyes so nakedly curious and real that Andaluz shuddered. He sat back, slipped, reached up to grip his clerk's arm. By the time he rose to his feet, the crowd of human and Rat children were beginning to back up on the gangplank. He stepped to one side.

'They forget. Travelling through the Night, they forget.'

One cried shrilly. Another laughed. All children, all under the age of three; they ran, suddenly, in the bright sun – running off along the quay, up to the airfield, down towards the promenade, scattering like a school of fish.

'No shadows.'

'What?' He looked where Claris pointed, at a small girl who plumped down trying to unpick threads from the mooring-rope: the hemp wider around than her small wrist. He saw only a tiny rim of black about her feet.

'They grow 'em in a few minutes.' Zar-bettu-zekigal stood on the tips of her filthy toes, peering up at the deck. The flood of children swept around her like a tide. Andaluz saw her reach out absently from time to time and touch a fair or dark head. He glanced around for Charnay. The brown Rat stood staring to and fro along the quay.

'He might have recognised me if he were here . . .'

A silence breathed off the tarred planks, muffing the creaking of the mooring-ropes. The voices of the children, not yet having speech, cried like distant gulls. Andaluz took out a kerchief and dusted his nose with some energy, wiped the corners of his eyes, and squinted up at the sun-drenched Boat.

A figure appeared at the top of the gangway, walking slowly

down to the quay. A tall man, thirty or so, with long black hair; his bony hand holding the paw of a brown Ratling. Andaluz, glancing down, saw neither had a shadow.

'Sir, I greet you.'

Their eyes met his, and Andaluz inclined his head, falling silent. A shadow of night still lay in their gaze. He stepped aside, bowed. The man and the Rat child walked past without a glance at Claris, Zar-bettu-zekigal or Charnay.

Another man appeared from the deck, then a sun-haired woman; two black Rats, fur dulled with the salt breeze; a young man with cropped black hair. Andaluz felt his pulse thud, once, before he recognised it as only a chance resemblance.

'I've waited a long while.' He looked at Claris. 'I can wait, it seems, a little longer.'

'If we're not needed, sir, may I suggest that we would be safer back in the Residence.'

The disembarking humans and Rats momentarily separated him from his clerk. Andaluz turned, brushed shoulders with Zar-bettu-zekigal, who stood gazing up at the pennants streaming from the mainmast.

'Lady, if you're going back into the city, may I offer you a ride in my coach?'

'Right!' She spun around, pivoting on one heel with dappled tail out for balance. Her grin shone in the sun. 'I need to get back to the square in Fourteenth's north quarter. So does Charnay. Can you drop us off there?'

Forming a tactful evasion, Andaluz began to speak, and cut himself off as he saw her gaze go over his shoulder and her sepia-brown eyes widen.

A voice shouted: 'Zar'!'

Andaluz saw the recognisable Katayan speech sink home into her as an arrow does. Caught with one heel resting on the stone quay, weight on the other bare foot, tail coiled down, she for a moment looked all child, bewildered as the embarkees from the Boat. He waited a second to see if he would have to catch her as she fainted.

Zar-bettu-zekigal whispered: '*Elish?*'

'Necromancy . . .'

The White Crow said: 'You heard me, Eminence.'

The Lord-Architect reached down one oil-black hand and touched her dark red hair, frowning. She saw Lucas's head turn, and his startled expression.

The black Rat, Plessiez, murmured urbanely: 'I fail to follow you.

What would a Cardinal of Guiry know about such heresies as necromancy? Come, come, you know as well as I do: there is a weak *magia* of the dead played with the discarded shells of souls, that is, bodies; but it has no power, and so is not worth speaking of.'

'And if souls died like bodies?'

The Cardinal-General appeared frankly angry. 'What nonsense. I won't listen to blasphemy. Under our masters the Decans, the dead travel through the Night and return on the Boat; there is no other death.'

The White Crow held his bead-black gaze.

'I'm a Scholar-Soldier, your Eminence, and while we travel you and I should talk.'

The black Rat suddenly laughed. His sleek jaw rose, light gleaming from his fur. The black feather on his headband swept the heated air.

'A Scholar-Soldier! Oh, come now. On this day of all days, to present me with some mythical human organisation—'

'This day?' The White Crow hooked her elbow over the steel rungs of the nearest ladder. She leaned back easily. 'Your Eminence, today's the Feast of Misrule. When servants beat their masters, Apprentices give orders to Fellowcrafts, Rat-Lords serve feasts to their human slaves, Cardinals tend humble priests – and the Thirty-Six Decans, it seems, leave the solving of cosmic riddles to poor, blind, stupid human scholars.'

She wiped her mouth, dry with the day's air; grinned at him with sweat-ringed eyes.

'And the Rat-Lords loose a plague amongst the human population of the heart of the world. Your Eminence, please. I do know about these things.'

Expecting no honest answer, she shivered when he inclined his head, his glittering black gaze still holding hers.

'Do you? Well, then, madam scholar. What can it alter, now, for it to be known? There is unrest. Order must be restored. With so many humans passing onto the Boat to begin their journey through the Night, they will be weakened beyond opposition to the King. Do you see?'

The White Crow absently lifted her free hand to her mouth, sucking dusty rose-scarred fingers. 'Truly, Eminence?'

The sleek Rat, black fur almost blue in the intense sun, shrugged lithe shoulders and gripped the hilt of his rapier. 'Madam scholar, what I have done I have done with my King's authority, and my own full knowledge. Now, if you will be so kind as to excuse me, I must finish the matter.'

'No, I won't excuse you.'

Her mouth curved up, a smile unwillingly rising; and she flipped her arm loose from the side-ladder, took the black Rat by the elbow and ushered him a dozen steps into one of the protruding sections of the upper platform that served as a shield against forward attack. She glanced back, seeing them out of earshot of the others.

He made no resistance, meeting her gaze with contained amusement.

'Well, madam scholar?'

'Master-Captain, as it happens.' She grinned. 'White Crow is my name.'

Above, the sky tilts towards midday. The weight of its heat lies heavy on her shoulders. The White Crow breathed a deep scent of oil, dust and harbour wind; shuddered with an instinct that presaged some manifestation of a *demonium meridianium*.

'Eminence, how can I convince you to talk to me? I've spoken to the Candovard Prince, and to others. I could probably give you the names of those who attended a meeting in Fourteenth Eastquarter's Masons' Hall, and tell you what was said there.'

She shifted, aware of the straps of her pack digging into her shoulder. The hilt of her sword-rapier scraped the metal carapace; the black Rat raised a furry brow.

She said: 'Someone had to be supplying the raw materials.'

All his lithe body stilled.

'Materials?'

'I've been asking myself questions while I was riding, your Eminence. Such as: What was a priest of Guiry doing with bones in an Austquarter crypt? I'm a Scholar-Soldier; I know that there have been four true deaths in the heart of the world. I may have known that before you did; I've been in the city a while.'

Some fragile accord, born of the hot sun and urgency and the knowledge of crisis, hung unspoken in the air between them. The black Rat nodded, approving.

'Master-Captain, you are a true practitioner of the Arts.'

She reached for the talismans at her throat, gripping them as if she could squeeze chill into her flesh.

'I guessed at where the bodies might be. In the city crypts. Where else do you put a corpse? And what other kind of corpse would give you the raw materials for necromancy? Hence this plague-*magia*. There's more to it, yes, but I believe what I'm saying is true.'

He smoothed down the Cardinal's green sash with a demure humour. 'Yes, Master-Captain. I think that I, also, believe that what you say is true.'

The White Crow touched his arm. Sun-hot fur burned her fingers.

'Eminence, tell me. *You need to.* I know. Don't ask me how I know. Not all the talents of a Scholar-Soldier are easy to analyse.'

The lean bulk of him blocked the sun, brought a certain coolness to her. The tender flesh of his nostrils flexed, vibrating wire-thin whiskers; and his voice, dropped to the threshold of audibility, contained a grating endurance.

'Can you take the weight of it, do you imagine?'

She shrugged.

'Messire, when one arrives at our age, it's with a baggage of emotional debts – and they're rarely repaid to those whom we owe. Others have taken the weight for me in the past. I'll do it for you now.'

He looked away, squinting at the bright sky. 'You are older than me, I think.'

'Am I?'

'Old enough to forget. What it is to *win* – you forget that. I can tell by the look of you.'

Wiry muscles shifted under the sleek pelt as he straightened, hind feet in the balanced stance of the sword-fighter. The blue sky glimmered beyond his sparkling gaze.

'I can have anything I want.' Plessiez laughed, musing. 'Luck put the Austquarter crypt in my way, and yet I have years enough of study to know what use to put it to. Luck put Guiry into my hands, and I had wit enough to take it. And if luck gives me a lever with which to move the Thirty-Six Themselves – well, why shouldn't the universe give me what I want?'

The black Rat exhaled. She smelt his breath, musky and metallic.

'So, I take a great part in this, and as great a responsibility. And, if I am honest, greater ambition – but I perceive you are aware of the goads of ambition yourself.' He looked back at her, nodded once. 'Oh, yes. It's apparent, if not relevant. And, to fall to the matter in hand, there have been other in as deep as I.'

The White Crow shut her mouth, which she had not been aware hung open.

'True. There were two other leads I'd have followed, if I'd had the time: a Reverend tutor of the University of Crime, and a priest from the Cathedral of the Trees.' She paused. 'Messire Cardinal, I don't know you, and I wish I did. I would like to know if *you* know what will happen, now, with your plague-*magia*.'

Softly he stressed: 'Not mine. Not mine alone.'

'No . . .'

They stood in silence for a moment. The black Rat snorted quietly, and gazed at the Guards manning the siege-engine with immense satisfaction.

'I have some conception of what approaches. But what is one to do? We have strange masters. And one may sometimes hope to outwit them.' Amusement, amazingly enough, in his voice. 'Madam, having come so far and so fast, and through such strange occurrences, I am ready to credit the existence of an Invisible College. Tell me, if you hazard a guess, what is to happen now?'

Fragile accord bound them for a moment in the sunlight.

'I've . . . been away. Eminence, this is how it seems to me.' Her acute gaze flicked towards him. 'I think noon will see another true death. Caused by that *magia* which you, and perhaps his Majesty? yes – which you have scattered under the heart of the world . . .'

He motioned with one hand, as if to say 'Go on.'

The White Crow took off her hat and fanned herself with the brim, and replaced it on her head. The sun burned hot on her hair. 'Only I don't know, messire, if you know all of what that *magia* is intended for.'

A sardonic stare met hers: as curious, and as cynical. The White Crow swallowed. Her shirt clung to her breasts, wet under the arms, her own sweat rank in her nostrils.

'I spoke with the Lady of the Eleventh Hour,' she said. 'We all speak with Decans, your Eminence. Me with mine, you with the Decan of Noon and Midnight, The Spagyrus.'

'The Order of Guiry's relations with The Spagyrus have always been most . . . cordial.' Cardinal-General Plessiez straightened. 'That really is enough, Master-Captain, unless you have practical advice for me.'

'You know what another death of the soul could do?'

'I conceive some idea.'

'Truly?' She stared. 'You knew what you were doing?'

A chill entered the Cardinal-General's voice. 'I believe I did.'

Their fragile accord parted as spider-thread parts in a summer breeze.

'I can't believe that *any*one—'

The siege-engine shook, motor roaring.

The White Crow gripped the jutting shield-wall. Plessiez's warm body brushed hers as he grabbed at the same support. She twisted to stare over her shoulder. The Lord-Architect had vanished: the engine-trapdoor stood open.

'*No* – I permit it!' Plessiez snapped an order; the Guards remained at their stations. The motor coughed a cloud of blue smoke and groaned as the wheels gripped the cobbles. Noise increased, plateaued. The beaked rams swivelled as the siege-engine ground to point north-aust.

The White Crow regained balance, the weight of pack and sword heavy on her. 'You'll allow this?'

The siege-engine thrummed, gathering speed. Streets flowed past. She rocked with the velocity. Ahead the sky turns ashen with the first finials of the Fane-in-the-Twelfth-District.

'It is no great detour. I have the time – and, possibly, I admit, the necessity – to indulge my expert engineer. I regret,' the Cardinal-General's voice rasped, pitched to carry over the metallic clash of gears, still with a mockery in it, 'I regret what you will find when we leave you, madam. It has been so for five days, for all of us; even for your kind – the Fane is closed to all entry now.'

Zar-bettu-zekigal pushed past Andaluz, dodging the Boat's speech-less passengers; and he shaded his eyes against the glare. A Katayan woman of medium height and in her middle twenties walked down the gangplank, peacock-blue satin coat and white breeches gleaming in the sun.

Her shadow lay on the plank, sharp-edged and blue.

'Elish? Oh, what! What are you *doing* here? How come you're on the Boat? You haven't been through the Night!'

'I did die, little one. I'm back now.'

Short black hair fell in curls over her pale forehead, a lace cravat foamed in ruffles under her chin; and she whisked a tail as black as her hair through the slit in the satin coat. 'Father told me the court seers predict ill fortune for you. I came to do what I could. How else could I get here and not spend a year travelling, except on the Boat?'

'Elish!'

Zar-bettu-zekigal flung her arms around the older Katayan woman, hugging her violently. The older woman patted her back. She raised her head, and Andaluz saw her smile as she met his eyes. He straightened his doublet and executed his best formal bow.

'Madam, I take you to be from the South Katayan court? May I, on behalf of the Candovard Embassy, welcome you here, and offer you any assistance that you may need?'

'Sir, I thank you. I—' The Katayan woman pried Zar-bettu-zekigal's head out of her lace ruffles. 'Zar'! Behave. What have you got yourself into *now*?'

Still with her arm about the woman's waist, the young Katayan faced Andaluz. 'This is my best full-sister, Elish-hakku-zekigal. Elish, this is Ambassador Andaluz; he's Lucas's uncle. Oh, dirt! You don't know Lucas. Or messire the Cardinal. We have to talk! I've been working as a Memory. Messire Andaluz, may my sister come in the coach with us?'

Andaluz smiled. 'Of course, child.'

'We'll have to take Charnay up to the square with us. *Charnay!* Get over here, you dumb Rat. And then there's the Hyena – Elish, you have *got* to meet her, she's wonderful!'

The black-haired Katayan smiled tolerantly.

'Another one of your true loves, Zar'? Messire Ambassador, I apologise for my sister. I would be extremely grateful for your hospitality; there are matters that I wish to discuss. I have some informal status as plenipotentiary envoy from South Katay.'

Andaluz lifted his head, scenting on the breeze something at once sweet and nauseous. It faded. He looked around at the sun and the sea and the white marble of the docks, deserted now but for the last travellers on the Boat, walking away into the city. The brown Rat had her snout lowered, listening to something that the clerk explained with short abrupt gestures. Andaluz saw both of them glance up the steps towards the airfield sands.

'You've walked in on a critical moment, Madam Elish-hakku-zekigal. I think the wisest thing that I can offer you and your sister is the protection of the Embassy Compound.'

'Oh, *what*!' Zar-bettu-zekigal stepped away from her sister, planting her fists on her narrow hips. 'I have to find the Hyena and Messire Plessiez. I've got work to do!'

'I really would advise—'

A screech ripped into his ear. Andaluz jerked around, one hand automatically clapped over his left ear, blinded by the sun off the lagoon-harbour. A blaze of red and yellow flapped in his face. He stumbled back.

A new voice called: 'Careful! You'll frighten him! Here, Ehecatl; here, boy.'

The brilliant-feathered bird scuttered in the air, circled, and fell to perch on the shoulder of a woman who stood halfway down the gangplank. Andaluz brushed furiously at his guano-spotted doublet and breeches.

'Madam, I really must protest!'

'Really? Then, please don't let me stop you.' The woman tapped her way down the gangplank, leaning on a bamboo cane.

Andaluz looked down at her as she approached. Skin shining a pale ochre, braided hair shining white, she stood barely as tall as his collar-bone. Lines wrinkled about her eyes as she smiled up at him, a woman some years short of sixty.

'Sir, I apologise. The journey's been hard, and I fear I've not arrived in time. Elish, help me with my baggage, please. I have two trunks on deck. Can you and your – sister, is it? – fetch them down here?'

The young Katayan gaped, then followed the elder with trepidation up the gangplank and leaned over to grab two cases, careful not to set a foot on the deck of the Boat. Andaluz rubbed his mouth thoughtfully, managing to conceal a chuckle.

'Sir, I don't know who you are.' The parakeet clung to her shoulder, guano spotting the crimson, purple and orange-patterned linen robes that swathed her. A small humming-bird hovered around her head, brilliant blue; and from a fold in the robes at her breast a dusty sparrow peered out.

'Candovard Ambassador, madam. My name is Andaluz. Welcome to—'

'An ambassador? How marvellous! *Just* the man I wanted to see.' She snapped her fingers. 'Elish, help your little sister, will you? Those cases must *not* be damaged, and they're heavy. Now, messire – Andaluz, is it? – kindly call me a carriage, and make sure that the horses are lively. I've much to do.'

The woman tapped past Andaluz, his clerk and the brown Rat. Andaluz caught a glimpse of gold sandals under the trailing robes. Sprays of scarlet-and-blue feathers had been braided into her long white plait. Now three bright humming-birds hovered in the air around her.

'Make haste!' She snapped her fingers again, and the two Katayan women fell in behind her, each with a small brass-bound trunk on her shoulder.

'Madam, I—' Andaluz moved forward, and found himself running up the quay steps to catch up with the woman. 'I don't think you understand. It's dangerous to be on the streets today. If you'll come with me to my Residence . . .'

Breath failed him at the top of the marble steps. The small woman paused, looking up at him with eyes bright and amber as the parakeet's. Laughter shifted in the lines of her round face. Shadows fell across her: high and distant, circling wings. Andaluz glanced up into an empty sky. When he looked down, the shadows remained.

Speaking with an inborn respect for *magia*, he asked: 'Lady, may I know your name?'

The older Katayan woman shouldered her trunk, sweating in the heat, and said: 'Messire Ambassador, this is the Lady of the Birds.'

'Luka to you, young man. Now . . .'

She smiled, disclosing crooked but white teeth, and rested her light hand on Andaluz's; a smile of such sweetness that he forgot his breathlessness and concern.

'First,' the Lady Luka said, 'I need to find my son. I believe he's here in the heart of the world. You may know of him. He's a Lord-Architect. His name is Baltazar Casaubon.'

The acolytes swarmed, their flight warping sky and light.

Warm dust skirled about the White Crow's ankles, blowing across the lichen-covered steps. Heat slammed back at her from the stone. Swinging the backpack from her shoulders and squatting, frog-like, she rummaged for a strip of paper written over with characters.

'C,mon, girl, come *on*; you haven't got all day—'

Echoes of her mutter clicked back double and triple from the Fane of the Decan of Noon and Midnight. Arches, pinnacles and buttresses reared above and around, blackening all the north-aust sky. She irritably rubbed the hair out of her eyes; pinned the thin strip of paper in a tight four-way loop about the hilt of her rapier.

A cracked elderly voice called: 'Here's another fool! Another one as mad as you are, young Candia!'

She risked a glance down the steps. The abandoned scaffolding shimmered in the heat. The path ran back between pyramids of bricks, gleaming like black tar under the sun, vanished among abandoned piles of half-dressed masonry. At the foot of the steps of the Fane a man stumbled as he walked, supported by the arm and shoulder of a white-haired woman.

The White Crow stood. 'Get *up* here. No, don't argue; get up here in the shelter of the arch. I don't know who the hell you are, but if you want to stay alive to regret this, *move!*'

She slung the pack up on her shoulders and gripped the hilt of her sword. The corded grip fitted her palm easily, smoothly; with the hard feel of something right and fitting. She raised her head.

High above, circling, swarming, no larger than birds or insects at this distance, acolytes flew restlessly up from pinnacles, gutters, high Gothic arches. One beast swept low, gargoyle-wings out-spread, bristle tail lashing the air. High-pitched humming chittered in the heat.

'Oh shit . . . *move!*'

A small old woman in a blue dress limped up the steps, one arm tightly hooked about a fair-haired man in his thirties. The White Crow grabbed the man's arm, thrust him under the overhanging carving of the great arched door; reached a hand to the old woman and dodged back with her, eyes still fixed on the sky. The acolyte hovered, wings beating, raising up dust.

'Saw you on the road behind me. What in gods' names possessed you to come here?'

'We might ask you the same thing, missy.'

The man's voice, amazed, said: 'She's a Scholar-Soldier.'

Heat reflected back from the dizzying heights of stone above, and from the great brass-hinged wooden doors. The White Crow coughed, smelling a sweetness of roses. She risked an eye-watering glance at the sun. Overhead: closing fast with noon.

'Not fast enough. Now, there's an irony.' Her pulse thundered away the minutes, beating in her head. She fingered the talismans with a sweat-slick hand, *magia* protecting against heat, not against fear. 'And if the damn place is closed anyway—'

'*Where were you?*'

Started at the man's intensity, she backed a step or two into the archway and glanced up at him. Fair hair flopped across his bruised-looking eyes. With one hand he made an attempt to pull a stained and stinking doublet into some kind of order, a gesture that degenerated into helplessness. His blue eyes glared.

'*Why* didn't you come to the university a month ago?'

Warm alcohol-stinking breath hit the White Crow in the face. Turning, eyes on the wheeling gargoyle-shape now riding an updraught, she snapped: 'Should I have?'

'We sent out messages for a Scholar-Soldier! We tried to contact the Invisible College for months!'

'Damn.' She stopped dead. 'Are you *Candia*? I've been asking Evelian about you—'

'Now wait just one moment.' The old woman's face creased into a frown, smoky-blue eyes darkening with anger. 'Do I understand you, Reverend Master? You've been in contact with these vagabond scholar-mercenaries? In direct contravention of university regulations? And just who are *we*?'

The man lurched forward. The White Crow grabbed his shoulder one-handed, found herself supporting half the man's weight. Now four shadows wheeled and skittered across the stone steps.

'Get back, rot you!'

Her left hand throbbed. She thrust him back, gripping the rapier, eyes never leaving the movements above, point mirroring flight by instinct and long practice.

His voice came from behind her. 'We prayed you'd come in with the new intake, a month ago. When I told Bishop Theodoret there was no one . . .'

Something that might have been a sob or a gasp of pain interrupted; his voice picked up after a second.

'I have to rescue him or kill him now, lady. *Where were you?*'

'Me? I've been here all along. The Invisible College never has been the best-organised—'

Cold air screeched across her skin; she whirled, thrust upward, darted back. The blade sank home, ripped free. A bristle-tail lashed the steps. White stone chips flew up, stinging her cheek. The lichen on the steps began to glow with a yellow luminescence. The beat of wings hissed in the air. Dark bodies dropped down from the soaring flock.

'We're going to miss noon by minutes.' Frustrated, she stared down at the heat-soaked abandoned building site; seeking cover, seeing only temporary salvation. Feeling through the soles of her feet the *magia* in the depths, necromancy boiling to crisis, that stirred the servants of the Fane to bloodlust. 'Minutes, unfortunately, will be enough. Damn, I think he was right: the Fane *is* closed.'

A spot of blood dripped from the rapier to her bare foot. She winced at the caustic impact. Waiting: waiting for the circles of Time to slide and interlock, mesh into the Noon that will open the Fane-of-the-Twelfth-Decan to mortals. Eyes running water, she stared up through circling wings at the sun still minutes short of midday.

'Girl!'

The White Crow swung round. The old woman stood at the great carved doors, one veined hand just leaving the bronze ring. At her touch the black wooden slab swung open a yard, and another. Sun-dusty beams of light slanted into the interior of the Fane.

'It's not time!'

Above, the chittering rose to shrieking-pitch. Dark wings tumbled across an air suddenly yellow and sere.

'Heurodis,' the woman said, folding a thin strip of metal and secreting it back in her cotton sleeve. 'Reverend Mistress, University of Crime. *I* have no intention of waiting out here to be attacked.'

The White Crow wiped her sweating face, pushing the silvered red hair back behind her ears. Aware that her mouth gaped open, she shut it firmly; caught the blond man's elbow in her free hand, and stepped smartly after the old woman, shoving the door to with her heel as she crossed the threshold into the Fane.

Silence shattered.

Raggedly at first, then in a roar, a hundred thousand men and women began to cheer.

'—*And now!*' Falke gripped the loudspeaker microphone tightly. '*The Feast of Misrule's truly started! With our strike-carnival!*'

The square rippled.

His silk eye-bandage blurred Fourteenth District's great square with black. Textures of cloth overwove the sunlight, snared the blue sky in threads. Falke blinked, strained vision.

The mass of people seethed.

He clenched his own hand at his side, seeing so many arms flung up, so many hands waving. Sweat ran down between his shoulder-blades; the heat of his mail-shirt robbing him of breath. Cheering racketed back from the distant façades of buildings.

'Listen to that!'

'I hear it.' The Hyena jostled his elbow, steel vambrace hard and hot in the sun. Through his shielding silk the visor of her helm flashed as she slid it up; red-brown eyes sharp. 'I see it. Now?'

'Now.' He wiped the sweat from his forehead, grinning. Abruptly he signalled.

Shadowless heat hammered him from the north-aust.

All this fifth side of the square lay demolished. Mansions torn down, ragged edges of brick and masonry and dug-up foundations cast aside in great heaps. Cranes and earth-movers rested, poised. He rubbed the silk tighter against his face, through blurred vision making out the sixty-acre clearance, the scaffolding at its entrance – and the great block of granite held in a cradle of rope and steel wire.

'Now, my baby . . .'

He shook his head and chuckled. A wind blew from the square behind him, carrying the smell of human sweat, of beer and sharp wine and the powder from muskets.

'Now's our time.'

The rope cradle creaked, inching round. He squinted at the cranes, unable to see the workers. Only the yellow-and-white Salomon colours. He paced four steps along, four steps back, booted heels kicking.

He cut the air with his hand: the lateral swing ceased.

Hieroglyphics shone on the great foundation-stone, newly in-cised; gleaming redly, as if the cut stone filled up with blood.

He turned his face up to the sky, letting the breeze cool his sweating face, turning back as the granite block stilled. Packed faces: painted, masked, laughing, calling; the rows of silent Rat-Lords at the nearer buildings' windows.

He touched the Hyena's steel shoulder. 'Wait for me here.'

He ran careless of obstacles down the rutted steps to the front of the site, the microphone clasped in his fist. Soldiers in imperial mail and citizen militia shoved the crowd back. Men and women reached between them, over their shoulders, hands outstretched;

and Falke waved good-naturedly, trotting along some yards until he swung and faced out into the crowd.

'*Long live tradition!*'

His voice echoed back from far walls, soft as surf in sewer-tunnels that riddle the docks. Paper streamers soared up into the air, and bottles; and he turned his face full up to the sun, careless of dazzlement.

'*Long live tradition, long live the Feast of Misrule!*' He paused, letting them quieten a little. '*Yes, the great and ancient Feast of Misrule . . . This annual day when all's turned upside-down – and we, yes, today, WE turn the world upside-down! Only this time, it STAYS this way! You see the stone. It is our stone, it is our foundation-stone: the founding-stone of the New Temple of Salomon!*'

Cheers broke out, doubled and redoubled.

He strode another few yards along the steps. A paper streamer glanced across his shoulder; he gripped it in the same hand as the microphone, waved it, grinned at the feather-masked boy, dimly seen, who'd thrown it. The boy pulled off his mask, eyes bright, mouth a round O.

'*The world turned upside-down – you've all heard that prophecy.*' The metal of the microphone, warmed and dampened by his breath, chilled his lips. '*Hear it and believe it! Oh, not the Rat-Lords; they don't matter now – although they may still think they do.*'

Falke paused, lifting a hand in ironic salute to the black Rats lining the overlooking windows. One looked down at a broken flower in his hand. Another, headband in hand, smoothed a feather. None spoke.

'*You will say they have been challenged before, these masters of ours. So they have. So they have. I was a part of that summer, fifteen years gone. Fifteen years ago, in Fifth District, when they cut us down in the streets – rode us down, for daring to refuse our labour!*'

Now he dropped his tone caressingly; walking down the scarred marble steps to the line of soldiers, touching hands with the people beyond as he walked along the front row, invisible to more than those few but letting the loudspeakers carry it.

'*I have never forgotten. You have never forgotten. Now we can erase it from our minds. Now, today, we labour only for ourselves.*'

He halted, lowering the microphone.

Faces, hands, swords, mail-shirts: the front row of the crowd a tapestry, sun-bright and raucous. His mouth dried. He swallowed with difficulty, blinking; the touch of silk strange against his lashes. He reached up and pulled the bandage free.

'*They have always betrayed us.*'

Tears streamed hot down his cheeks; a bubble of laughter in his chest for this final public hypocrisy. He snatched breath suddenly, tears of the bright sun becoming the wrenching tears of a man who assumed, until then, that he only cries for appearance's sake.

'*We can be true to ourselves.*'

Warm wind bathed his fingers as he held up his hand, poised; cut the air with one decisive stroke. He let his hand fall to his side.

Through his feet he felt the vibration of the Temple's foundation-stone settling into its place on the site behind him.

'*The foundation-stone is laid! Now feast and rejoice. Feast and rejoice – and build the New Temple of Salomon!*'

He laughed, recklessly reaching into the crowd again to grip hands; his tear-streaked naked face dappled with paint, daubed on by small children held up by their parents.

'*Now drink! Eat! Rejoice! BUILD THE TEMPLE!*'

Breathing hard, he stumbled back up the steps. A glare of silver: he seized the Hyena's plate-clad arm for support; leaned with his head down for a moment, breath sobbing, and then nodded.

'At last.' She signalled.

The imperial soldiers fell out the rank that held the crowd back. First one, then ten, then dozens of men and women ran forward and up the steps to the open site; meeting there the Fellowcrafts of the Masons' Halls. Falke gazed at the river of silks and satins, masks thrown down and trodden underfoot as the skilled workers swarmed over the foundations and scaffolding and cranes.

The Hyena held up her gauntleted hand, the soldiers linking arms again to thin the flow.

Falke covered his eyes, between sweating fingers watching the tide of masons, carpenters and builders spread out across the open ground behind him.

Exhilarated, the Hyena swept her arm in an arc. 'Look at it! We've done it.'

'I . . . hardly believe it.'

He retied his black silk bandage. The last of the first shift of workers walked across the steps to the site. The rest settled: men and women sitting down where they stood; bottles and food brought out, masks pushed up so that eating and drinking could begin. The noise of their singing, clapping and shouting beat back from the distant walls.

The Hyena yawped a laugh. 'No going back for us. Not now, whatever happens.'

The rising tide of sound drowned thought. He wiped his nose on the sleeve of his grey doublet, and rested both hands on his wide sword-belt. The ring-guards of the sword-rapier brushed his knuckles. Standing with feet apart, welcoming the weight of weapons, he peered through black silk at the crowded day. Faintly, through the shouting and music, a clock on the far side of the square chimed quarter to the hour.

'Ahead of schedule.' He smiled, finding his voice thick with the aftermath of weeping.

'*Ah.*'

'What is it?' He peered at the Hyena, straining to see which way she faced, what she stared at. 'Lady?'

'I think – right on schedule.' Amused surprise rounded her tone. 'This is effrontery of the first order. What does he think I'll do? Clovis!'

Clovis and a dozen other soldiers doubled up the steps to join her. Falke frowned. Shoved back, he elbowed his way to the Hyena's side, demanded:

'What is it? What's happening?'

The woman shaded her eyes against the sun, staring out across the great square. Frustrated, Falke followed the direction of her gaze. Waving arms, thrown hats and occasional muzzle-flashes from muskets: the rest a cloth-shrouded blur.

A groaning vibration came to him through the earth he stood on.

'All King's Guard by the uniform.' The Hyena's grin widened. 'Good firepower, but they're somewhat outnumbered. We'll accept their surrender. Clovis, take a squad down there and escort them here. Master Falke, can you see? There.'

A deep-throated mechanical roar drowned crowd-noise; and he wrinkled his nose at the stench of oil. Light glinted – from windows, stone surfaces. Swords? Gun-barrels?

Fine detail faded into sun-blaze.

Counting on a second's view before blindness, Falke snatched away the eye bandage. Tears ran down his face.

Shockingly close, rearing above the impromptu tents of the Hyena's camp and the crowd; beaked rams, hammered steel plates, curving ballista.

Midday sun gleamed from the blued-steel barrels of muskets, from unsheathed swords, and from the harness of Rat-Lords seemingly as small as children, crouched on the platform of a great armoured engine of war.

'There must be two hundred thousand people here!'

Lucas leaned tight into the steel wall-shield of the siege-engine, the metal platform hard under his knee. Curving hot metal sheltered his body ahead and to the side. From where he crouched, he could see the other King's Guard behind the shelters.

Tens, dozens, hundreds of faces turned upwards. Looking at the siege-engine. Faces caked with white lead and yellow ochre, the colours of the House of Salomon.

The engine's noise drowned all but the tolling of the charnel bells, coming raggedly from the quarters beyond Fourteenth District's square. His grip on the support-strut grew sweat-slippery. Blood pounded in his head, and his hand went automatically to the talisman at his neck.

'Casaubon! Lord-Architect!'

Lucas rapped on the hot metal of the engine-hatch. Heat throbbed from a bright sky.

'Slow down! If we hurt anyone, the rest'll tear us to pieces!'

'Pox rot it, I'm doing what I can!'

The thudding vibration of the machine diminished, the juggernaut wheels slowing. Heat shimmered across packed bodies.

The Lord-Architect Casaubon heaved himself up through the hatch, swore as his bare arms touched metal, and lifted his immense buttocks up to rest on the rivet-studded platform.

'And at that, we're almost too late.'

His stained linen shirt and corset obviously discarded somewhere in the engine compartment, sun pinked the slabs of fat cushioning his back and shoulder-blades. Black smears of oil covered his faint freckles, glistened on the copper hairs on his chest. He picked his nose and wiped the result on the metal hatch-casing.

'Let me get this thing on to its station and primed, and I'll shake the truth out of that sleek ruffian who calls himself a Cardinal! *Then* we'll see!'

The Lord-Architect reached up. Lucas stretched out a hand, gripped his; steadying the immense bulk as the man rose to his feet.

He let go, wiping his now-oily palm on the back of his breeches.

Casaubon drew himself up to his full six foot five, lifted his foot, brought it down, and with his stockinged toe hooked his discarded blue satin frock-coat across the platform towards him.

Sun hammered Lucas's scalp. He blinked rapidly.

'Nearly noon. The White Crow. She will be all right, won't she?' His voice thickened. 'Stupid question. She won't be all right unless she's very lucky. And that goes for all of us, doesn't it?'

The Lord-Architect reached into the voluminous pockets of his once white silk breeches and brought out a silver flask. Lucas reached across as the big man offered it, up-ended the flask down his throat, spluttered into a coughing fit, and at last managed to hiss: 'What *is* this?'

Casaubon scratched at his copper hair and examined his fingernails for oil and scurf. 'Turpentine?'

'What!'

'I beg your pardon,' the Lord-Architect said gravely, 'metheglin is what I meant to say. She's a Master-Captain, boy, and a Master-Physician. More than that, she's Valentine.'

'What . . . ? I don't . . .'

As Lucas watched, bewildered, the fat man slid down to seat himself with his broad back against the ram-casing. The Lord-Architect screwed up his eyes almost to the smallness of raisins against the glare off the page, and began to write painstakingly in his notebook, resting it against his bolster-thigh.

'There.' He tore the pages out with a delicate concentration, folded them, retrieved a gold pin from the lapel of his rescued jacket and pinned the paper shut.

Lucas hunkered down, resting his brown arms across his thighs. 'Well?'

'We arrive, but in time to do nothing.' Casaubon lifted his head, losing at least one chin. 'Get over to the University of Crime. Rouse the students. Give this to the Board of Governors – no, *don't* argue with me, boy. Tell them it's no use their thinking all this pox-blasted foolery is beneath them; they must act, and I'd be obliged if they'd do it now.'

'Explain to me just exactly how I . . .' Lucas stopped. 'You're serious, aren't you? I don't know why, messire, but the White Crow thinks you know what you're doing. Tell me how I get away from here and I'll give it a try.'

'Prince Lucas!'

The Lord-Architect lifted one copper brow at the new voice. 'Monstrous inconvenient.'

Cardinal-General Plessiez stepped out from the group of Guards on the platform and approached Lucas, pitching his voice over the crowd-noise. Sun shimmered from his black fur, from his *ankh* and green sash.

'An interesting woman, your magus, Prince Lucas. What can she hope to say to the Twelfth Decan?'

Buildings blocked the view behind them now; no sign of the marble terraces and the hill they had descended. Sun blurred Lucas's vision; he rubbed his eyes. Nothing to see from here. Not even that last glint of sun from her sword, herself a tiny blob of colour walking into heat-shimmer.

Sudden, clear, he feels the shade and cool interior of the house on Carver Street; a holistic flash of white walls, piled books, cracked mirror-table, and the woman's heat-roughened voice.

'According to you, there's no way into the Fane.' He attempted to eradicate hostility from his voice, achieved only sullenness. 'What's it to you, priest?'

'Still intransigent. I should have known when I met you. A King's son.'

Lucas frowned. On the north-aust horizon, around the Fane's black geometries, the summer air swarms thick with acolytes; gargoyle-wings beating as they hover, sink, aimlessly circle.

The smooth voice insinuated. 'And yet you're not with her now, messire. Did she just need a university student to steal her a horse when there are none to be had?'

The siege-engine creaked past the façades of ornate buildings lining the square. Pale plaster shot back sunlight and heat. Lucas stared grimly up at ornaments, strapwork, hanging flower-baskets. Rat-Lord spectators crowded balconies and windows. A brown Rat flourished a plumed hat; two drunken black Rats began tossing broken flowers down from pots on to the heads below.

'I can thieve,' he said. 'I don't have *magia*. She'd have been wasting her power protecting me. That's why I'm here and not with her.'

'But a magus—'

Something slithered across Lucas's bare ankle. A coiled paper streamer drifted across the platform, snagged, then pulled away.

Casaubon slammed his hand against the side of the machine. Iron echoed. 'What's happening, Plessiez? Where's your damned Master Builder? And young Zaribeth?'

A brown Rat called: 'Your Eminence!'

'You see we face some delay. The crowds,' Plessiez said silkily; and before he could be answered strode back to take a report from the Guard.

Lucas glanced back with a casual intensity, seeing the blue-liveried Guards positioned at each of the metal ladders. At the foot of the engine the crowd massed concealingly thick. The Lord-Architect beamed and prodded Lucas's chest with a fat finger, nearly overbalancing him.

'It'll work. You'll see.'

The black Rat, Plessiez, standing with the Guard, cast speculative glances up at the gleaming beaked rams and the high cup of the ballista. He murmured: 'We *must* stay on-station here at the south-aust side, at least until the stroke of midday.'

'Yes.' The Lord-Architect sounded grim. 'We must.'

Canopies of silk rose on this side of Fourteenth District's great square, great tents shining white and painted with the gold cross of the House of Salomon and the Sun of the Imperial Dynasty. Light glinted off laminated armour. Beyond the soldiers, scaffolding rose, great spider-structures of poles and platforms and cranes.

Lucas stood and shaded his eyes. 'Will you look at that!'

'It may have been wise to bring more men.' Plessiez walked to the front of the platform just as the Lord-Architect rose to his feet.

Heat shimmered over desolation.

A spiderwork of girders and scaffolding stretched away, covering sixty or more acres, the site rawly hacked out of the classical buildings surrounding it. Lucas stared at men and women swarming over heaps of brick and masonry. A great granite block towered in the foreground.

Lucas felt his skin shudder as a beast shivers. Realisation hit hard and sudden: a jolt of cold injected into the blazing heat.

'They've started building.'

He shot a glance over his shoulder, knowledge of foundation rites brimming on his tongue; silenced himself in the face of the Rat-Lords, and turned back to stare at worked stone, sunk in the earth, cut in proportion and inscribed.

'There is your revolution,' Plessiez remarked acidly at his side.

The Lord-Architect's head swivelled ponderously, surveying. His chins creased as he beamed, looking down at the Cardinal-General, nothing but innocence in his blue gaze.

'Wonderful! Obvious why they've started building now, of course. Someone's given them the Word of Seshat.'

Plessiez's fur, where it brushed Lucas's arm, prickled with a sudden tension.

Lucas looked up, met his black gaze. 'Yes, my uncle told me you have an interest in architecture, your Eminence. Human architecture. Speculative *and* operative.'

Plessiez stood four-square on the iron platform, balancing on bare clawed hind feet. A smile touched his mouth, the merest gleam of incisors. His head came up, the line of snout and jaw and sweeping feather-plume one clean curve in the midday heat. He turned his black eyes on Casaubon.

'Being a Lord-Architect, I suppose that would become immediately apparent to you. Yes. It's true that I put Messire Falke in the way of finding the lost knowledge he sought. I did not, until now, know the name of it. So the lost Word to build the Temple of Salomon is the Word of Seshat?'

'*Mistress of the House of Books, Lady of the Builder's Measure.*' From *Rituale Aegypticae Nova*, Vitruvius, ed. Johann Valentin Andreae, Antwerp, 1610 (now lost – supposed burned at Alexandria)

'Mistress of the House of books,' Casaubon said reverently, 'Lady of the Builder's Measure.'

The siege-engine inched forward, slowing now to a crowd-pressed halt. The Lord-Architect swung his arm around until it rested lightly across Plessiez's shoulders. He looked down over the swell of his belly at the black Rat.

'Why, Master Cardinal?'

A kind of relaxation or recklessness went through the black Rat. Lucas saw him look up at Casaubon, fur sleek and shining in the sun, one ringed hand touching his pectoral *ankh* while his scaly tail curved in a low arc about his feet.

'I thought it not amiss, in this time when all changes, if your people had a Temple of their own. You have built for our strange masters, and for his Majesty, and never for yourselves. I thought,' Plessiez said, a self-mocking irony apparent in his tone, 'that it might stave off at least *one* armed rebellion. We shall see if I am right.'

Obscurely angry, Lucas demanded: 'What did he pay you? This man Falke, you didn't give him what he wanted as a gift.'

Plessiez invested two words with a wealth of irony. 'He paid.'

'*You – halt!*'

The immense sweating crowd pulled back. Lucas stared down from ten or twelve feet high on to the square's paving stones. Across them clattered a woman.

The sun blazed back from her. He twisted his head aside, after-images swimming across his vision. Her mirror-polished armour blazed, sending highlights dancing across the metal carapace of the siege-engine and the Guards' uniforms.

Plessiez put up a narrow-fingered hand to shield his face. 'Lady Hyena.'

The woman looked up, a slanting-browed face framed in the open sallet helm. Her sheathed broadsword clanked against her armoured hip.

'Here in person, Eminence?' she grinned toothily. 'A mis-calculation, maybe.'

The black Rat beside Lucas shot one glance upwards, at the sun. 'I have no quarrel with you, Lady.'

'Nor with—?' She turned bodily, the sallet restricting her neck-movements, and pointed back to a man on the distant steps at the edge of the building site. 'Nor with the head of the House of Salomon? Don't make me laugh. Well, will you fire on the crowd or not? What say you? Do you take the chance?'

Lucas stared at the stranger. An excitement familiar from

exercises at arms in Candover tingled through his body. Readiness, anticipation – and no arms, no defences; and the black muzzles of armed Sun-banner men pointing full at the siege-engine. Lucas shuddered. The excitement still would not be killed. He knelt up, leaning one arm on the steel shield-wall, grinning fiercely at the human troops.

'Madam, have I offered you violence?' Plessiez said mildly.

The woman deliberately surveyed the towering engine, now coughing clouds of blue exhaust; the baroquely-cast beaked rams and the catapult. Sardonic, she observed: 'That's a fair offer of it!'

Now his thoughts slipped back into the taught mode, Lucas easily picked out snipers behind the tents, musketeers in the cover at the edge of the building site, armed men and women massing behind the first unarmed rows of the great crowd.

'I require nothing but to station this here as protection,' Plessiez said.

'What will you do now – sit quiet and watch Falke's builders?' She chuckled. 'Do that, then. I have a proclamation of my own to make, now that it's midday.'

At Lucas's elbow, the Lord-Architect Casaubon dug in his pocket and fumbled out a watch, flicked open the casing, and rumbled: 'Not yet. A few minutes.'

'White Crow said—' Lucas cut himself off. Imaging the woman, dark red hair tumbling, at the doors of the Fane: under the skreeing circles of daemons in flight. Noon. The Lord of Noon and Midnight. And which is it?

'Clovis, where's Cornelius Vanringham? Bring him. I want him to hear this.' The armoured woman, moving surprisingly lightly, strode to the front of the siege-engine. Lucas gazed down at her heat-scarlet face, dripping with sweat. She stared past him. 'Well, priest, you may as well hear it, too. You'd hear it before the end of today, be certain of that.'

Conciliatory, the black Rat bowed. 'As you wish, Lady. I shall be most interested to hear what you have to proclaim.'

'Only our independence.' Sardonic, her voice went harsh and honest. 'Only our freedom.'

Lucas shivered: a deep motion of the flesh that never reached his skin, that seemed to reverberate in his chest and gut. He looked to Casaubon.

'Go now,' the big man said quietly. His plump-fingered hand closed over Plessiez's shoulder, as the black Rat opened his mouth to call, tightening warningly.

Not pausing to consider trust, Lucas ducked back and slid on his buttocks past the Lord-Architect, hidden by the man's bulk. He stood, walked to the rear of the siege-engine; sat and slid and let himself fall from the edge of the platform in one movement. He staggered into the crowd with stinging ankles, thrusting between people with his elbows, tense for a shout, the crack of a musket behind him.

Bells chimed from the five corners of the square.

Noon.

Chill fell across him, cooling his chest, arms and back, welcome as cold water in the press of sweaty bodies. He felt muscles relax that had been tensed against the hammering heat of midday. Shadow swept across the square. And again, deep in his gut, his flesh shuddered.

A great intake of breath sounded around him, a simultaneous sound from the thousands gathered. Like wind across a cornfield, faces tipped up to the sky, ignoring the building site and the foundation-stone. Lucas raised his head, the corners of his vision filling with yellow dazzles.

Brilliant blackness stabbed his vision. Ringed with a corona of black flames, a black sun hung at the apex of the sky.

All the sky from arch to horizon glows yellow as ancient parchment. The twelfth chime of noon dies. Transmuted, transformed, in a fire of darkness: the Night Sun shines.

CHAPTER 7

'How the hell did you *do* that?' the White Crow demanded over her shoulder, padding down the steep flight of steps. 'You can't have done that; it isn't possible!'

The blond man touched one hand to the pale stone wall for support, leaning forward, frowning.

'It's . . . light . . . in here. I don't recognise any of this.'

He recollected himself and offered his hand to the old woman. Heurodis put one foot down, lowered her other foot to join it, then lowered herself cautiously down the next steep step. Her smoky eyes met the White Crow's.

'We don't do it often. We – that's the university, girlie – we can do it whenever we want to. That's something you indigent scholar-bullies will never master.'

'But you *can't—*'

The White Crow half-missed her footing. She turned her head, seeing white stone steps descending to an archway and a stone-flagged door just visible beyond. Above, the high ceiling of the passage glowed pale and deserted.

'It *is* light,' she said. 'And it wasn't for the first few minutes after we got in. I think I know what's happening outside . . . Reverend Mistress, you don't understand! It isn't a lock that keeps that threshold closed. It isn't *magia*, either; it's the power of god, the power that structures the universe. The interior of the Fane of Noon and Midnight doesn't *exist* outside those times; you can't just pick the lock and get in!'

'*We* can.' Heurodis grinned, showing all her long teeth.

Reverend Master Candia took Heurodis's hand and rested it on the White Crow's left shoulder. The age-spotted hand gripped with some strength. Candia loped down to the bottom of the flight of steps. His slashed jerkin shed fragments of lace, leaving a smell of stale alcohol on the air.

'And I thought seeing the impossible done couldn't surprise me any more!' The White Crow laughed aloud. Echoes hissed up the passage. 'I've always wondered why the university doesn't depend on Rat-Lords or human patrons. If you can do that, you don't have to. *How do you do it?*'

Heurodis stepped down off the last step and took her hand from the White Crow's shoulder.

'We're gods' thieves,' she said. '*And* we've stolen from the gods themselves, missy. Under divine sufferance, no doubt, but we have done.'

'Crime's a high Art.' Candia gripped the lintel of the arch, leaning to peer into the chamber beyond. One hand went to his belt, clenched into a fist. 'Heurodis is a great practitioner.'

'Here.'

Drawing her small knife from the back of her belt, the White Crow passed it to the blond man. His hand, which had seemed to search quite independently of his will, closed about the hilt; he stooped slightly as he looked down at her, nodding with a wide-eyed surprise.

'You trust me, Master-Captain?'

'I don't think this is a place for anyone to go unarmed.'

She hefted the rapier in her right hand, with her left reaching up to push a coil of red hair back under her hat. A wetness brushed her cheek. She rubbed her stinging fingers across her skin and looked down at a bloody hand.

'Lady, you're hurt.' He took her hand by the wrist, turning her palm upwards. A bead of blood oozed from the life-line.

'No. Or not just now anyway.' The White Crow winced, raising her left hand to her mouth, sucking at the pin-pricks made by black roses in the Garden of the Eleventh Hour. 'The stigmata of *magia*. Messire Candia, do you recognise any of this?'

'None of it, lady.'

Stone dust gritted under her sandals. The White Crow reached down and flipped them off, feeling the tension of stone under her bare feet. She padded forward into pale light.

Squat pillars spread out, forest-like, into the distance. From them great low vaults curved up, in arcs so shallow it seemed impossible the masonry of the ceiling should stay supported. The sourceless white light arced the ribs of the vaults with multiple shadows.

Her nostrils flared, catching a scent of roses.

'Why did you and . . . ?'

The blond man complied. 'Theo. Bishop Theodoret, of the Church of the Trees.'

'A Reverend tutor. And a Tree-priest. Of course.'

The White Crow knelt and strained her vision. A breath of warm air feathered her cheek. Distance blurred pillars, low vaults, more pillars. No windows: the light not the light of sun or moon.

'Why did you need Scholar-Soldiers?'

Heurodis, catching the question, snapped: 'Why indeed? What young Candia here thought he was doing asking help of the Invisible College, I'm sure I'll never know. Ignorant children, all of them. You, too, missy.'

Heurodis wiped a bony finger along the surface of the nearest pillar, sniffed at the dust, and wiped it down her blue cotton dress. In tones of waspish outrage she added: 'How the University of Crime could begin to trust an organisation that doesn't even work for *gain*—'

Reduced to complete speechlessness, the White Crow leaned her rapier against her leg, reached to pin her tumbling hair up out of the way under her wide-brimmed hat, and at last managed to say: 'You'll have to take that point up with one of the others. Come to think of it, I'd like you to talk to the Lord-Architect Casaubon. Rather, I'd like him to have the experience of talking to you . . .'

She walked forward as she talked, letting the words come almost absently, centring herself to the familiar heft of the sword in her hand, the weight of the backpack. Light slid about her like milk. The air grew warmer, out under the low-vaulted ceiling; and a glimmer of blue clung to the edges of ribs and pillars.

'If I had to guess, I'd say that noon brought us the Night Sun.' A quirk of humour showed as she glanced back at Heurodis. 'After today, I'm cautious about expressing an opinion.'

'Listen.'

She glanced up, seeing lines deepen in Candia's face; the blond man's air of permanent injured surprise giving way to an un-selfconcerned anxiety. He stumbled as he walked past her, away from the wall.

'What—? No, I hear it. Wait . . .' The White Crow moved forward and caught the buff-and-scarlet sleeve of his jerkin, halting him.

A deep wash of sound re-echoed from the pillars, hissing through the milky-blue air, losing direction against the white pillars and white vaults and white light. It died. The White Crow strained to hear. She walked forward, head cocked sideways, tracking it for some faint hint of direction.

'There . . .'

A faint green luminescence shone down one side of a low pillar, far off, where distance made the pillars small as a finger at arm's

length. Again the sound hissed, growing from inaudibility to a
harsh breath of pain. It sawed the warm air. Her chest tightened,
attempting to match that arrhythmic breathing. The White Crow
frowned, mouth open.

Candia grunted as if he had been punched. 'Theo.'

The White Crow looked to Heurodis. The old woman shook her
head, moving forward to take the blond man's elbow. His face held
some abstract expression of pain and memory that defied analysis.
The White Crow began to walk, hearing their slow footsteps behind
her.

Pillars shifted, perspective moving them in her peripheral vision.
Dry warm air rasped in her lungs. Deliberately barefoot, she walked
lightly on the balls of her feet, letting the sensations of the
flagstones guide her.

Between pillars, away in the milky light, she glimpsed a far wall.
She walked faster.

'Master-Captain!'

The hissed whisper broke her concentration. She gestured shortly
with her blood-wet left hand, ignoring Heurodis. More shifted in
the light than perspective could account for. Small hairs hackled
down the back of her neck. She slid from one squat round pillar to
the concealment of the next.

Greenness drifted into the granular milky light, coiling as if it
were steam or smoke and not luminescence; a light the colour of
sun through a canopy of new leaves. It touched the skin of her
arms, goose-pimpling them with cool. A stink of old blood caught in
her throat.

'Stay back.' The White Crow touched one bloody finger to her
backpack, stepping across the flagstoned space towards a door that
opened into a tiny stone cell. She looked inside.

Candia, behind her, whispered: '*Theo . . .*'

Shock hit: her sweaty skin going cold between her shoulder-
blades and down her arms. The White Crow bent forward and
retched. One hand to the door-frame, the other leaning for support
on her rapier, eyes blind with the tears of nausea, she vomited up
the bile of a day's fasting.

'Oh shit . . . Don't come in. Somebody keep watch outside.'

She spat, wiped her nose with the heel of her hand, took in a
breath, and stepped into the white stone cell. Its low step caught her
foot. She stumbled, staring ahead.

Stark against her sight, an iron spike curved up out of the
masonry wall. Blood and pale fluids had dried in streaks below it.
The White Crow stared at the head of a man impaled on the iron

spike. Undecayed, spots of blood still dripped from the neck-stump to the stained floor. White hair flowed down to where, red-dappled, it stuck to drying knots of vertebrae, slashed cords and tendons.

Only the head: the cell held no truncated body.

Dappled light shifted, green and gold. For a second the White Crow sensed the rush of branches, birds, steps through leaf-mould. A shriek of ripped wood echoed, the light shifting. She knelt, staring levelly at the creased labile face.

At his open conscious eyes.

Heurodis's sharp indrawn breath sounded above her head. The fair-haired man fell to his knees beside her. One dirty hand reached out as if he would touch the severed head. The White Crow caught his wrist.

'No, messire, I'm sorry. Not with the power here.'

Tears brimmed over the lower lids of Candia's eyes. Absently moving his knife, he picked with the tip of it under one thumbnail. Green light gleamed from the blade. 'My lord Bishop . . . Theo, tell me how. I'll do it.'

The White Crow got to her feet, eyes never leaving the severed head. Heurodis whispered, 'Take more than a knife, girl, when it's a god keeping that thing alive,' and the White Crow nodded, and risked a glance over her shoulder.

'Rot it! I thought as much.'

Outside the cell, the pillars of the crypt had vanished. The cell now opened onto a gallery, forty feet above the floor of a high-vaulted chamber large as the nave of a cathedral, white and gold stone gleaming in sourceless brilliance. The White Crow touched a knee briefly to the floor, kneeling to look up and out past the low arch of the cell's doorway.

Shafts of golden light curved over clustered pillars, soared down from perpendicular arches in dust-mote-filled curtains. And in all the hull-shaped nave no windows: light shafting from unappreciable sources. The White Crow tilted down the brim of her speckled hat, shading her eyes, squinting. High fan-vaulting and hollow arches hung bare, empty of roosting acolytes. Below, all the wide floor stretched out deserted.

'Leave . . . here . . .'

She shivered. Breath echoed back from the stone behind her, forced into painful speech: an old man's weary voice.

'Leave . . . here . . . Candia . . . I am . . . bait . . . for . . . you . . . Go . . . Go!'

The White Crow got to her feet. She turned. The man in buff and scarlet still knelt, facing the severed head. She winced, seeing how the features of Theodoret *moved*: wrinkled eyelids blinking, the wide mobile mouth shifting.

Heurodis's hands clenched in the folds of her cotton dress.

The White Crow sheathed her rapier and took off her pack, tossing the speckled hat down beside it on the flagstones. She unbuckled the straps, fumbling, hands shaking; breathed in to calm herself, and took out a cotton handkerchief and a metal water-flask.

'Well, I'm here to see The Spagyrus. I assume.' A ghost of sardonic humour touched her voice. 'This should bring him.'

She stepped past Candia and knelt, unscrewing the top of the flask, covering it with the kerchief and tipping it up. Water chilled the cloth and her fingers. She reached up and, with the damp cloth, moistened the cracked lips of the head.

She kept her eyes on that vulnerable mouth, shivered inside; finally lifted her gaze. Swimming with light, his grey eyes met hers, saw her plainly; and the old man's lips moved into an attempt at a smile.

'Pitiable . . . and . . . grotesque . . .'

'No, messire.'

The White Crow moistened the cloth again and applied it, words coming as randomly as her thoughts.

'Mistress Heurodis got me in here. She saved all our lives. Master Candia tells me you sent to the Invisible College. Tell me what you wish, messire.'

The Bishop of the Trees spoke slowly, painfully. 'Bless . . . you . . . child . . .'

All else put aside, the White Crow sat back on her heels, staring up into his creased face. The edges of her vision glowed with the light of forests.

'My name is Valentine. White Crow. I come from the Invisible College. I was fifteen years a Master-Captain; I'm a Master-Physician now. Tell me quickly. If anything at all is possible now, would you die, or would you have me try something other?'

Abrupt and arctic, silence dropped on the square, darkling under the black sun.

'Don't fear! We *know* what that means.'

The Hyena screeched. She flung her free hand up, pointing at the sky that now shone a deep and pitiless blue as the Night Sun took hold.

'The Night Sun! The sign! The hour has come. We are free of our strange masters, free of the god-daemons, free of the Decans, free of the Thirty-Six! You all hear it, you all see it, you all feel it!'

Her voice flattened against the still cold air.

She swung round, pushing between packed men and women, shoving her way from the siege-engine towards the steps. No lips moved. The crowd, silent, parted by unspoken consent to let her through.

'Feast and rejoice! Feast and rejoice and *build*. Hold our celebration while the Night Sun shines. And when it passes you'll see the day's light shine on a Fane standing open and empty, the Thirty-Six abandoning the heart of the world. And that heart of the world given over into our keeping, here: the imperial Sun dynasty!'

A middle-aged woman raised her head. Her silk carpenter's shirt hung in strips. Her face, caked thick with yellow and white paint, showed raw sores around her mouth and nostrils. She met the Hyena's gaze and showed her teeth.

'Clovis, damn you!' The Hyena strode up the steps, armour clattering; the only noise but for the siege-engine's throbbing motor.

Faces turned to follow. Silk and satin work-clothes hung in strips and tatters. A burly man stumbled from her path, face covered by a feather-mask. Many masks gleamed in the crowd: brilliant or dust-covered feathers clinging to faces, masking eyes, leaving mouths and sores uncovered. And still no sound: not a shout, not a whisper.

The blond man, Clovis, met her on the top step.

'Lady . . . what have we done?'

'*Plague Carnival!*'

The voice echoed down from the nearest building, where on balconies black and brown Rats gazed down with arrogant equanimity.

'Why not sing?' one called down. 'Why don't you dance now, peasants?'

Another pointed into the vast mass of people. 'A silent carnival! A plague carnival!'

'You don't amuse us!'

'Dancing's a sovereign cure for the plague, they tell me!'

'*Quiet!*' The sky shimmered from yellow to blue in the corners of the Hyena's vision. A smell of sickness breathed up from the flagstones. She rubbed her nose, eyes watering at the stench.

'Lay down fire across the building if they speak again. Over the heads of the crowd.'

A young boy stepped from the silent crowd and threw a handful of broken petals towards the balcony. He whisked a mask of owl's feathers from his face, sun gleaming on red hair and on his sores weeping white pus. Other masked revellers stood in silence, jammed shoulder to shoulder, crowding the dry basins of fountains. The Hyena followed the direction of every gaze.

In the pitiless blue sky, coronas of black fire licked out across the empyrean. Midnight at noon, night-fire: the black sun blazes.

'Clovis. Set up sound-broadcast. I'm going to tell them this is what we've been waiting for.' She spared one glance for the Rat-Lords on the siege-engine platform. Picking out an emerald sash, some humour curved her lips. 'We can all use . . . coincidences. Where's Falke?'

'Here.'

The man stepped silently to her side. He slid the black silk bandage from his eyes, raising his face to the sky. She saw momentarily in his unnaturally dilated pupils the twin reflections of darkness.

'We must hold the ceremony of the shadow. The building *must* continue.'

Her slanting red brows lifted. Directing troops to their places by hand-signals, she spoke now without looking at him, in a measured tone only a fraction from hysterical laughter.

'Whose shadow? Yours? *Have you seen what's in front of you?*'

The man gazed blindly across the building site.

'I've done without all else. I can do without my shadow to keep the Temple of Salomon standing.'

She pointed at their feet, then fumbled her hands back into plate gauntlets.

'Oh, damn your Craft mysteries . . .'

All their shadows fell bright, brilliant; fell through the dark air to shine on the broken stone.

'It's impossible. *Look.* You've to nail a shadow to the first-raised wall to keep the Temple standing. *All the shadows are lights!*'

Falke frowned, brushing a hand across his lips and the several tiny weeping sores at the corners of his mouth. The cagework-shadows of scaffolding fell bright across his surcoat, and the Hyena held out both gauntleted hands, glinting darkly.

'See! You have to depend on my troops now!'

She met his eyes, and his gaze blurred.

Falke stumbled against her, and she caught him with one steel-clad arm; spun to grip his shoulders and lower his dead weight to the broken paving. His eyes rolled up and showed only thin white lines below the lids.

'Damn pestilence, it's thinning us out faster than we can fight or build. Let's have some help here! Ho!'

The Hyena pushed greasy hair out of her face, pulled off her plate gauntlet to feel for his pulse. She glanced up for her lieutenants. Two of the people in her immediate sight – a dark-bearded man, a young boy – slid down on their knees and fell hard across the stones. She gaped.

Above on the scaffolding a scream sounded, and the thud of a heavy body falling.

'Falke?'

She grabbed his dark-streaked hair, pulling his head up, and stopped as he sprawled limply back against her; head falling back, mouth falling open. Tatters of black flesh ran across the skin of his face from mouth to temple, spread down his neck to vanish under his collar. Crisped, sere: as if plague-fever could burn up flesh in heartbeats.

She touched her bare fingers to his throat. No pulse.

Dark flames licked down into her vision. The Hyena stared across the open square. To left and to right, men and women sprawled across the paving; others leaped up or shouted for aid. A coldness chilled her bare hands.

With a child-like puzzlement, she looked down and touched the face of the man dead in her arms.

Brightness moved in his mouth.

The Hyena snatched her hand away. Antennae moved in the dead man's open mouth, quivering, wavering. Insect feet scraped for purchase on his lips. It crawled between his teeth, first a velvet body, and then the spreading black-and-white-mottled wings of a death's-head moth.

Frozen, not even able to push his body away, she watched the moth shake out its wings and sun itself on his tattered cheek.

A scrap of colour bobbed past her vision. A scarlet butterfly, wings dusted with gold, sharp against the blue sky . . . The Hyena looked at the boy collapsed on the next step down. From between his lips a pale blue butterfly crawled, took flight.

The death's-head moth flew up past her face, skull-markings plain on its dried wings. She covered her mouth with her hand, sick and afraid.

Under the generative chill of the Night Sun, all the air above the square glimmered, red and blue and black and gold, alive with whirling columns of butterflies and moths rising up from the mouths of the plague-dead.

*

'It's a bad joke!' Candia exclaimed. He rocked back on to his heels, standing up.

The White Crow grabbed at her arm as he caught it, pulling her up on to her feet. She twisted out of a grip that would leave bruises, glaring up at the blond man.

'*No*—'

Candia reached down to knot his fists in her shirt, leaning over her, breath stinking in her face.

'Break a Decan's power? Theo – you can't kill him, you can't heal him. How can you joke, and in front of him! I'll have no more of it. Hear me?'

'Messire—' The White Crow cut herself off. As gently as temper would let her, she closed her hands over the Reverend Master's fists, conscious of the pain in her left hand, of the dry warmth of the stone cell. 'Candia. I mean what I say.'

Flickers of green pushed at her vision, marbling the pale masonry walls. The blond man released his grip, reaching up to push hair out of his bruised-seeming eyes, gazing down bewildered. The White Crow tugged creased cloth straight.

'Lady, he . . . Death would be an act of mercy.'

'Trust me.'

'Trust a Scholar-Soldier?' Reverend Mistress Heurodis's acid voice sounded from the low arched door, where she peered out into the golden nave. 'Well, girlie, it doesn't matter; I think none of us will leave here, but you may try to end his pain.'

The White Crow turned and knelt. The stone, hard and warm under her bare knee, beat with an imperceptible tension. She looked up again at the severed head. The old man's eyelids slid half-shut over swimming grey eyes, and his mouth clenched.

'I . . . needed to . . . die . . . before . . . He . . . called . . . me . . . bait.'

Some choking pressure in her chest resolved itself into pity and anger, and she put out a hand and touched his soft skin, echoes of pain resounding on cellular levels. 'Take time to decide. We've got a little time.'

She sat back, grabbing the leather backpack and sorting through the books and papers inside.

Candia said thickly: 'Bait? For who?'

Heurodis's voice sounded above the White Crow's head. 'For all of us?'

The White Crow stood and moved to the door. She squatted, dabbed the gummed end of a paper strip at her tongue and pasted it

across the threshold. Her sallow fingers worked rapidly, fastening
the character-inked strips across the jamb and lintel. A certain
growing tension in the air held itself in abeyance.

She stood for a moment with her back to the three of them,
staring out into the golden shafts of light in the nave.

'My lord, I haven't heard you answer.'

'So . . . much . . . suffering . . .'

The White Crow turned and took two rapid paces across the cell,
catching up her sword as she knelt, resting her hands on the hilt
and her chin on her hands, words falling rapidly into the full
silence.

'I don't think I should help you die. I mean . . .' She gave a
helpless shrug. 'I don't know if I *can* give you anything better than
death. I'm a Scholar-Soldier; I can't work miracles. But, see,
someone is going to die soon – truly die, my lord, the soul, too –
and that's when the Circle is broken, and I can't . . . if it's you . . . if
that happens, we . . . I was told by the Decan of the Eleventh Hour
to act. But not how.'

Theodoret's creased features moved. Long seconds passed.

'My lord,' the White Crow said very softly, 'you're laughing at
me, I think.'

The severed head's bright eyes moved, meeting hers; and the
Bishop of the Trees, as if there were no one there but the two of
them, no old friend Candia, no Reverend Mistress, said: 'Do . . .
your . . . damnedest . . . woman . . . I would . . . live . . . like
this . . . if . . . I . . . thought . . . it would . . . hurt . . . The . . .
Spagyrus . . .'

Reverend Mistress Heurodis's bony finger tapped peremptorily on
her shoulder.

'You'll have to be quick, then, missy. Even one of the College
should be able to feel what's happening here.'

The White Crow reached one hand back through the air towards
the threshold. Blood tingled in her fingers, dropped to star the
stone. The divine, immanent in this cell, receded from her touch as
the long going-out of a tide; and for a second she leaned heavily on
the rapier for support.

'What . . . ?' Candia, his back resting against the wall, slid down
to a sitting position. The buff-and-scarlet jerkin rode up at the back,
pulling his dirty shirt and lace ruffles loose from his breeches; one
scuff-heeled boot lodged in the crack of a flagstone and arrested his
slide. He gazed up at Heurodis. 'You're both crazy.'

'Far from it, boy.' The white-haired woman paced across the cell
to peer out of the door, her voice coming back creakily. 'I believe I

saw this done once before, about fifty years ago now. Worked, too. Mind you, it killed one of the two other people involved.'

The White Crow rested her chin on the backs of her hands. The metal of the rapier echoed faintly with the tread of god-daemons. Without moving her head, she shifted her eyes to the Reverend Master.

'Candia, why did you come back here?'

'Back?' His head resting against the masonry, the man answered with closed eyes. 'We were seen entering, then? Yes. I was here before. We were here before. They let me go. After I saw what happened to Theo.'

Now his head fell forward, and he met her gaze.

'It took me time, lady, to find the courage to come back; and I found most of it in a bottle. Here I am. Useless. What did I think I could do? I don't know.'

The White Crow straightened, laying the rapier down on the flagstones. She held the blond man's gaze.

'Masons' Hall?' she said, too quiet for Heurodis's hearing. 'Could be, you came back out of guilt to be killed with Theodoret. I've known it happen among the College. Think that's true? Because, if it is, I can give you something to do that's almost guaranteed suicide.'

His bruised eyes blinked, startled. He unwillingly smiled. 'Lady, you're persuasive. What?'

A milky light began to seep through the joins of masonry, fogging the air in the cell. The White Crow put both hands to the flagstone floor. Strain tensed the stone. One of the paper talismans at the door snapped, a tiny *ppt!* in the silence.

'Paracelsus tells us . . .' A tiny smile appeared on the White Crow's face. With a certain droll formality, she straightened up and inclined her head to the Reverend Master. 'Hear a lecture, Messire Candia. Paracelsus teaches that in every body there is one bone, a seed-bone, from which the body is grown again on the Boat as it passes the Night. We being in the Fane, in that same Night through which the Boat passes, it may . . . it may just be possible, by use of *magia*, to heal that way. The seed-bone is here.'

The White Crow reached across, pushing her fingers through Candia's hair, touching his warm neck and the hard knob of bone at the base of his skull. Arm's length, the stink of his soiled clothes filled the air; but he raised his head with an insouciant carelessness, caught her wrist and growled: 'Shame me into it, would you? What would you have me do? I'd do it anyway.'

The weak voice protested: 'Candia . . . my friend . . .'

She saw his eyes shift, at last rest without flinching on Theodoret's severed head. 'I'll do it!'

'This *magia* needs a third person to draw strength from.' The White Crow took her hand back. 'Mistress Heurodis isn't strong enough in body.'

The white-haired woman grunted ungraciously. The White Crow shifted her gaze to the severed head of Theodoret, and met a bright humour there.

'We're strong. Of course, the chances are that it'll kill Messire Candia and me, too. I've never done *magia* inside the Night of the Fane. The gods alone know what might happen.'

'It . . . may . . . even . . . work.'

Reverend Mistress Heurodis walked across to Candia, cotton dress rustling, and rested one veined hand on the wall above him.

'Better get ready, missy. I'll tell him what he has to do.'

The White Crow nodded. Under her bare knees and shins, the flagstones began to pulse almost imperceptibly: their rhythm the rhythm of particles and electrons in their universal dance. Practised enough from five years in the city called the heart of the world, she recognised, far off, an approaching tread.

'I will . . . help . . . if . . . I . . . can . . .'

The White Crow's nostrils flared at a sudden scent of woodsmoke. Melancholy, sharp: tears sprang into the corners of her eyes. Momentarily the stone gritting under her blood-slick palms became the creased bark of oak.

Boots rasped. Solid at her shoulder, Candia folded his long legs and sat cross-legged beside the wall. A sharp odour of sweat came off him. The White Crow glimpsed, through milky light, Heurodis's hand just touching his bowed head. She breathed slowly and deeply.

'My lord.' The White Crow shivered, reaching up with her left hand. Her bloody fingers rested lightly on the crusting blood and mucus on the iron spike. The Bishop's creased eyelids lifted, lines of his face shifting in pain.

Milky light softened raw flesh and shining bone; glowed in his pale hair. The White Crow brought her other hand up to rest on the spike below the severed head. 'I may hurt you worse than He did.'

'You . . . cannot . . . child.'

She let go of the spike. Sword and pack spread around her, rose-pricked palm bleeding, the White Crow knelt before the impaled and severed head. Her right hand sketched a hieroglyph on air, skeining pale light into a net.

'Now . . .'

Her left hand went up to touch her uncovered hair. A bee crawled over the dark red coils to her knuckles, skimmed into flight; drowsing a summer warmth into the dry air. The netted air paled, glowing, thinning to the gold of sunlight.

The white-haired woman nudged him. Candia wet his lips and, ignoring how they shook, raised his hands. The White Crow took them in her own. With infinite care she placed them to cup the severed head of the old man, supporting his corded chin.

'. . . Grotesque . . . !'

Seeing that same laughter in the old man's light eyes, the White Crow, her hands outside the blond man's and holding them tight to cool kept-living flesh, grinned and said: 'Now!'

The lintel of the cell cracked. Gunshot-sharp echoes rattled away into the nave. A heavy tread shook stone.

'Now, damn you!'

Eyes squeezed almost shut, the blond man closed his hands tight about the severed head and lifted it off the metal spike. Her hands felt the dragging resistance of flesh through his. Iron grated on bone. A wet, hollow, sucking noise made her gag.

The stink of decay choked the air. A breathless scream cut off.

Her right hand slid to cup the ripped liquescing vertebrae as Candia cradled the severed head in his arms. The White Crow hesitated. A sweat-drop ran cold down the back of her own neck.

The *magia* light died. Imprinted on her vision, all three of them – old woman, young man and severed corrupting head – froze, caught in the stark whiteness of the cell.

'Now . . .'

This time only a breath, too soft for anyone but herself to hear it. The White Crow raised her left hand and slammed it palm-down on the point of the iron spike.

'Watch out! 'Way there! Coach coming through!'

A black-haired Katayan woman in a silk coat reined in the team of four horses, one boot planted up on the footboard. Beside her, gripping the corner of the roof, leaning down with tail outstretched for balance, Zar-bettu-zekigal brandished a torn white-and-gold banner and yelled enthusiastically.

'*That* way—' She stumbled and fell against the backboard, grabbing at the older Katayan's arm. 'Ei, *watch out*!'

Out of nowhere, men and women swarmed past the coach, running out through the dockyard entrance to Fourteenth's great square: fifty, a hundred, five hundred. One fell, lay kicked and beaten underfoot. Another pitched face down, and the lead brown gelding skittered in the shafts, half-rearing, refusing to trample the fallen boy.

'Whoa!' The older Katayan reined in again sharply. The coach jolted to a halt, wheezing back on its springs. Bodies thudded against the painted wooden doors. One of the geldings whickered, throwing its head up, eyes rolling. 'What the gods is this?'

Zar-bettu-zekigal jumped up. Balancing easily, dappled tail coiled back, she shaded her eyes against the black light and stared into the square. 'I see it! Keep us moving, Elish. Slowly!'

'Zar—'

'Trust me!'

She reached back, gripped the roof-rail, and swung down off the driver's seat; caught the wide open coach-window with one bare foot and let momentum push her over massing bodies of men and women streaming past. She plummeted into the coach's interior, landing sprawled across Charnay. The brown Rat hefted her off into the opposite seat, beside the Candovard Ambassador.

'We can't get through. No, wait!' She reached to grab the brown Rat's hand. 'One sword's not going to get us anywhere. There's a mob panic going on out there!'

She eased her rucked-up black dress down over her hips. Her eyes cleared, growing accustomed to the light shadow of the coach's interior. The Ambassador sat forward, peering through the opposite window, his grizzled face showing confusion. Charnay struggled with her half-drawn sword in the close confines. The silver-haired woman held up ringed hands upon which three sparrows perched.

'Ei! Clever,' Zar-bettu-zekigal appreciated. She leaned forward, hands locked, curving her tail up delicately to hold it invitingly before one bird. It cocked its head, stared at her with Night-dark eyes. 'Full-scale panic out there, Lady Luka. Shall we go back, try somewhere else – the palace maybe?'

'My dear girl!' The Ambassador, Andaluz, turned away from the window, his neat pepper-and-salt beard jutting. 'I would strongly suggest we . . . I would offer you the protection of the Embassy Compound, but as for what good that will be when *that* is happening I confess I don't know.'

Zar-bettu-zekigal looked at him in amazement. 'Oh, what! Haven't you ever seen a Night Sun before?'

She swivelled, resting her bare arms on the open window and her chin on her arms, eyes raised to the fiery blackness now at the sky's highest arc. Basking in the light shadows and cool beams, she said: 'Lady?'

Luka chuckled. 'Onwards, by all means, if we can. What is it you see?'

Zar-bettu-zekigal slid round in her seat, hooking one foot up under her. The small woman transferred the sparrows to her shoulders, where they nestled in the white-spotted robes. She met Zar-bettu-zekigal's gaze with eyes of a guileless blue.

'One of those siege-engines the fa— That your son,' she corrected herself, 'built for messire. It's here. Whoever's on it should know where both of them are.'

'Absolutely not. Most unlikely. We'll be overturned before we go much further.' Andaluz rested his stubby hand over the tanned hand of Luka. 'End this lunacy now, lady, I beg you.'

Zar-bettu-zekigal, about to sneer, ducked and slid back as the brown Rat finally hauled her sword from its sheath.

'Charnay!'

'They're only peasants.' Charnay smoothed her fur, translucent ears cocking; and grabbed the window-frame with one hand, pulling herself up to look out. 'They'll run when they're ordered—'

'They're running already and not from you!' Zari slipped back as the coach jolted. For a second all her view was sky through the window; deepest blue sky in which particles of darkness burned and danced.

Bright confetti colours dotted the sky.

'Stop the coach!' The Lady Luka trod heavily on Zar-bettu-zekigal's foot, leaning across the small coach to gaze out. Her feather-braided hair slapped Zari's mouth. Zar-bettu-zekigal scrambled up, glaring, opened her mouth, and the woman called:

'Elish-hakku-zekigal, stop the coach! Now!'

'Oh, what! See you, this isn't . . .'

The coach rocked on its springs, stopped dead. A horse whickered. Two bodies slammed against the door, running hard in the press of the crowd, then another: she glimpsed a white-and-yellow Harlequin face. Luka's hand slipped the catch and pushed the door open.

'Shit!' Zari scrambled across the seat, dropped a yard to the flagstones, and reached under the coach to release the steps. Grease smeared her hands.

Catching her foot, she stumbled.

Zar-bettu-zekigal looked down. A woman sprawled at her feet, eyes open and dead; the body of an older man fallen across her legs.

'It's a . . . battlefield.'

People still ran, away across the square. Where the coach halted men and women and children sprawled across the stained flagstones, the black tatters of plague racing across their flesh. Bright scraps of colour danced above their heads, crawled from between gaping lips. One veered towards her, and she jerked her head away, the garish red-and-blue of a peacock-butterfly filling all her vision.

'Souls . . .' Wonder in her tone, the Lady Luka took the Candovard Ambassador's hand absently as she descended the steps, Charnay hard on her heels. 'Souls. Such flight! But – no preparation, no burial, no summoning of the Boat? They'll be lost.'

A Rat's hand fell heavily on Zar-bettu-zekigal's shoulder. She started, looked up into the face of Charnay. The brown Rat carried her sword in her free hand, and now lifted it and sighted along the blade at a wheeling butterfly.

'I don't understand. How will they find their way to the Boat?'

Zari lifted her head to their flight: moths and butterflies fluttering like leaves, dotting the air . . . and rising. Slowly but with purpose, spiralling up towards the Night Sun.

'They won't. Oh, Elish.'

She heard the older Katayan woman's boots hit the flagstones, and her light tread as she stepped between the tumbled bodies. A warm hand took her arm. She pitched round, throwing her arms about her sister, burying her face in the sweet-scented lace ruffles of her shirt. 'Elish!'

'Little one.' Work-hardened hands held her back and head, crushing her dress, pressing sun-cooled hair against her scalp. 'Hush.'

'Hard times deserve hard measures.'

Luka's tone, sharp now, roused her. Zar-bettu-zekigal raised her head. The small woman stood with her arms outstretched, bamboo cane held up in one hand, head raised to the sky. Her feather-braided hair hung down over her breast, silver against the garish robes. The parakeet screeched, clinging to her shoulder.

Birds settled down.

Out of a clear sky, thrushes and starlings and hawks flew down, landing on the lady's outstretched arms. Sparrows, doves, pigeons, humming-birds – until her old arms bowed, and she flung them upwards, skywards. Zar-bettu-zekigal followed the gesture.

Dark under the Night Sun, birds circled. Great scarlet macaws, eagles, buzzards; peregrine falcons and merlins, mouse-owls and herring gulls, crows, ravens and vultures. Amazed, she hugged Elish tighter, deafened by the rush of great wings, wincing from the spatter of droppings that hit the flagstones; dizzied by the skirl of flight, hundreds upon thousands of birds flocking overhead.

'Follow! Follow-follow-follow!'

High as a jay's shriek, the old woman's voice pierced the air. She swept the bamboo cane high above her head.

A mottled black-and-white moth skittered across Zari's vision. A rush of cold wings sounded, whirring; and the scarlet parakeet seemed to halt in mid-air, beak snapping. The moth's body crunched. The bird flicked away on an updraught, beak pecking down the fragile wings.

'Elish . . .' Zari unknotted her fists from her sister's coat, knuckles white. A cold wind began to blow. 'Elish! What're they doing?'

Her heart thudded in her breast; Zar-bettu-zekigal felt it through her sister's flesh. The older Katayan said nothing, only stared upwards.

Swift, acute, cutting the sky: the great flock of birds circled and spread out, rising on dark wings, pursuing and catching and devouring the hundred thousand butterflies that spiralled up into the bright air.

Brick walls rose up about him. Lucas trotted to the end of another alley, pacing himself, holding in tight frustration. The alley opened into a crossroads.

Five identical ways led off: indistinguishable from all the other alleys. He cocked his head, listened. At least no footsteps now, no pursuers.

'Gods damn it!' He slammed his fist against the wall. Brickdust and plaster sifted down. 'I don't believe it!'

Lucas stared up at the narrow strip of sky visible between roofs. The black glare of the sun blinded him, dead overhead, no use for directions.

He picked an alley that might lead away from the square and began to run down it, loping, muscles aching. Within minutes he hit a division of the ways, paused. Lost.

Lost.

'I can't believe I did this.' His voice bounced thinly back from the walls and shutters. He banged on peeling shutters. No sound, no answer.

Claws scratched on cobblestones, loud in the silence. A hard hairy body pushed under his right hand. Lucas froze as it brushed his leg, looked down. A white dog.

'*Lazarus?*'

Not a dog, a timber wolf; turning its thin muzzle up to gaze at him with ice-blue eyes. Dust clogged the pads of the animal's feet. It let its jaw gape for a moment, panting; then gave a quick high-pitched growl and trotted off down one of the two alleys.

'Hey!' Lucas hesitated. 'Where is she? Were you with her? What the fuck – you're an animal. What do you know?'

The wolf stopped, gazing back with feral eyes.

Lucas stepped forward. Heat rebounded back from the walls of the buildings, built up a thin film of sweat on his skin that the sunlight cooled. He began to walk. The wolf, as if satisfied at seeing him follow, turned and trotted on, loping easily down the dry central gutter.

Dust thickened thirst on his tongue. Now the wolf began running, the rocking pace that eats up miles outside city streets; and Lucas, one hand pressed over his breeches pocket and the letter, sprinted after, panting.

'Hey!'

A corner, a narrow alley, a flight of steps; another long alley, cut right, cut left; a short alley—

He caught a gutter-pipe to pull him round the next corner. The street shone dusty, dark, empty before him. Disbelieving, he slowed, panting; walking slowly along past a high wall.

'As if I *believed*—' Incredulity sharpened his voice; he hit his fist against his thigh.

A murmur of voices came from a high window.

Lucas stopped. He narrowed his eyes against the light shadows cast by the wall, staring up at the building's clustered chimneys and high peaked roofs. Still staring up, he walked along the wall to the massive iron-railing gates that stood open.

Chimneys cast light shadows across the paving. Cool reflected back from the walls on three sides, light glinting blackly from the windows. Great stone stairways went up at cater-corners of the courtyard, the wooden doors at the top of the left-hand flight standing open.

The murmur of voices from Big Hall echoed down through open windows into the courtyard of the University of Crime.

From gable and ridge and roof, from finial and spire, from pinnacle and gutter they rise up.

Great ribbed wings scour the sky.

Their shadows fall across the heart of the world, falling not light as all other shadows do, but still black: black as pits on the streets and houses and parks below.

The Night Sun bubbles their skins like tar. They shriek, rising up into the air, soaring.

The heart of the world stretches far out to the horizon, its thirty-six Districts and one hundred and eighty-one quarters; each District cut on its austerly sides by the darkness of the Fane, tentacles of stone building piecemeal across the earth. Houses, palaces, inns, temples; courtyards and avenues, all empty now, no Rat-Lords, no humans, all lost or fleeing for refuge—

The acolytes of the Fane swarm, a hundred thousand.

Here they swoop low, bristle-tails beating the air, their thumb-hooked wings beating at the windowless Fane-in-the-Eighth-District. There they shriek, circling the buttresses of the Fane-in-the-Thirty-First-District.

They can no longer enter.

The Night Sun scorches their uncommon flesh, burning, burning.

Goaded they rise, blind with blood and fear. The Fane is closed to them. Over the city they swarm up, screaming.

Their Thirty-Six masters do not answer.

Clawed feet scrape the air: unflesh that can wither stone if it will. Wings beat: their breath can rip roofs from houses. Ears listen, hearing the beats of frightened hearts: the living who hide in their homes below and pray to the Fane's deafness.

Shrieking, they soar up into the burning black light. Gaining height to strike.

Plessiez clasped his onyx-ringed hands behind his back, gazing out over the building site of the House of Wisdom, Temple of the Two Pillars of Strength and Beauty, the Daughter of Salomon.

Abandoned barrows and diggers littered the earth, tarpaulins flapped loose over crates; drills, buckets, chisels and barrels lay on the ground and on the scaffolding platforms where they had been dropped. He stepped half a pace to one side as two black Rats, both in the lace and linen of minor gentry, carried the last of the dead men past by the hands and feet.

'The tents?' one queried. Plessiez inclined his head, glancing down at the body's heat-black and tattered skin.

'We need fear no infection . . . I believe.'

Dust still hung over the massive granite block by which he stood. From a blazing sky, dark light settled into the incised Word of Seshat, filling every carved channel. He rested his hand against the chill surface.

'As our great poet says, architecture is frozen music. A thaw would improve this greatly, I think. We'll have it demolished later.' He turned away from the site, now cleared of bodies, and walked down the broken steps. Without looking up, he added: 'How goes it?'

The Lord-Architect glanced up and winced. He wiped his face, smearing a white dropping across one dark copper eyebrow.

'Fewer butterflies,' he replied gravely. 'More birds.'

Plessiez nodded acknowledgment to a group of black Rats, merchants from one of the rich houses around the square; paused to exchange a word. To all sides now the square stretched away empty, but for the last of the impromptu squads carrying bodies to the abandoned Imperial tents. Careless, hard, cheerful: voices rang out. One ragged banner still flew, in the increasingly chill air.

'You have' – the Lord-Architect Casaubon drew on his voluminous blue satin frock-coat, and felt in his pockets – 'a monstrously tidy mind, Master Plessiez.'

Plessiez rubbed his hands together, restoring circulation. Giving a tug to his cardinal's green sash, he moved down from the last broken step to the paving, and into the bright shadow of the siege-engine. His scabbard jingled, harsh in the cold air.

'I see no reason these should not labour. Albeit minor gentry and merchants assume themselves too good for it.' A nod of his head to the velvet- and lace-clad Rats now milling in the square. 'I'll give orders later for some communal burial, some monument.'

'Later?'

Plessiez surveyed the crowds of his own kind, and smiled slightly. 'Oh, yes. After the present trouble.'

The Lord-Architect walked out a distance into the square and squatted down, studying the ground, blue silk breeches straining over his expanses of thigh and buttock. Rubbish still littered the paving about his feet: feathers, masks, coloured ribbons, abandoned food and drink.

'Then let me tell you . . .'

A glass with an inch of stewed beer still in it stood by the Lord-Architect's foot. He absently picked it up, drank the dregs, and rose to his feet again.

'. . . just by way of a warning, since you're too gods-damned ignorant to perceive it for yourself . . .'

Casaubon felt in his deep pockets. He brought out, first, a stale chunk of bread smeared with something brown, which he bit into and then returned; and then a small sextant. Holding this up to the Night Sun with greasy fingers, he spoke through a spray of bread pellets.

'. . . that there's plague, and the black sun, but your troubles aren't half-over yet . . .'

Plessiez crossed the space between them in three strides, seizing the fat man's arm. 'What do you know? Is this your Art?'

'. . . therefore,' the Lord-Architect concluded as if he had not been interrupted, 'kindly stand aside, master priest, and let me get on with my work!'

'What work?' He loosed the satin sleeve.

'*Plessiez!*'

'Wait here,' Plessiez ordered, turning to face the voice. The noise of hoofs echoed across the square, the rider driving hard between the clear-up squads; reining in to a reckless halt by the siege-engine. She swung down from the mare's saddle, a plump black Rat in the scarlet jacket and *ankh* of the Order of Guiry.

'Fleury?'

'Man, are *you* in trouble!' She caught his arm, drew him aside, her naked tail lashing nervously. 'I rode from the palace. Fenelon told me you'd gone this way. Let me tell you—'

'Wait.'

Plessiez signalled to the King's Guard, sending them to stations a little distance from the siege-engine; glanced at the Lord-Architect (the fat man's attention fixed on the Night Sun and his sextant); and drew the plump Rat into the shelter of the engine-platform.

'Now. And briefly.'

The black Rat priest blinked, her dark eyes wide. Specks of plaster clung to her fur; she smelt of horse-sweat and fear and cordite. Plessiez abruptly put his hands behind his back again, holding the one with the other, this time to prevent them shaking.

'Desaguliers holds the palace and the King.' She drew in a breath, began to relate in a machine-gun rattle.

Half-listening, half-absent, Plessiez narrowed his eyes against the cold wind skirling across the square. The shadows of birds, bright gold and fringed with light, fell thick across him, pelting like summer rain. Their cries diminished as they flocked higher, higher; drawn up after the swarm of brightly coloured insects seeking the sun.

'Your orders, messire?'

He reached out and ruffled Fleury's fur affectionately. 'My orders are to wait. We'll settle our discontented Captain-General, *and* St Cyr, when this is finished. Republic! What fools do they think we are?'

'Prodigious great ones?' The Lord-Architect Casaubon, padding back to the siege-engine, sat down by the heap of his belongings at the foot of the metal ladder. He beamed up at Plessiez, hooking on his heeled court-shoes, and pulling up one stocking that immediately slid back down around his ankle.

'I believe I can dispense with your services,' Plessiez murmured. 'The engine will do very well on-station here. Now, Fleury—'

'Gods rot your soul, I've half a mind to leave you to it!'

Bending, hitting his head on the under-carapace, the Lord-Architect moved under the siege-engine, twisting his head to peer up at the axle and gears. He reached up with delicate plump fingers, feeling among hard metal and grease. A sharp *clck!* sounded.

Plessiez stepped back. 'These men obey my orders, Messire Casaubon. I wouldn't want to have to arrest you.'

The fat man backed out from under the machine, straightening; cracked the back of his head on the undercarriage again, and stared ruefully up into the bird-shadowed sky. At the blue empyrean, the rising dark dots and confetti-colours; and the cold blaze of blackness at noon.

He sighed with something of a martyr's air: 'All in position?'

The bright shadow of the ballista fell across Plessiez, dazzling him momentarily. Courteous, while he raised a hand to call the Guard, he confirmed: 'Yes. One in each of the thirty-six Districts. Does aught else matter now? If you know of another danger, speak of it.'

The immensely fat man continued to stare upwards, while his ham-hands delved deeper into inner and outer pockets. 'Another danger!'

Casaubon, producing a lump of what appeared to be red wax from one pocket, and black chalk from another, took a last squint at the Night Sun and bent to inscribe curving lines on the paving-stones. Plessiez watched him backing away, rump in the air, periodically back-handing bottles or glasses out of his way. A laugh bubbled in his throat. He fought it down, fearing hysteria; drew his rapier and paced beside the pattern of hieroglyphs that curved around the Vitruvian siege-engine.

'What are you doing?'

At the simplicity of the question, the fat man tilted his head up for a second. 'Doesn't matter where the other thirty-five are, so long as they're in their Districts. Designed *this* one as the key. Activating it takes concentration, blast you!'

'But *why*? Is it what I feared?'

While Plessiez still fumed at the desperation he heard in his own voice, the Lord-Architect pointed with one filthy hand at the aust-westerly horizon.

'That's why.'

Whirling dark motes spun up from the spires and obelisks of the Fane. Plessiez automatically stepped back and raised his sword to guard position, staring as heads turned all across the square: Rats looking up from their talk and work to stare at the swarming sky.

The Lord-Architect Casaubon straightened up, and surveyed

Plessiez over the swell of his chest and belly with arrogant authority.

'Master priest, you and I have scores to pay off. In future time, if there *is* future time, I'll make it my business to discover if you were workman or architect of this plan. Certainly you're one of the pox-damned fools who thought necromancy was a safe *magia* to loose on the world. It may be, even, that you're the cause of Valentine's danger.'

Plessiez, his gaze fixed on the sky, heard a tone in the fat man's voice that made him glance down.

'I'll make time for you.' Casaubon grunted, hefting the chalk lost in his massive hand. 'For the rest – acolytes. The acolytes of the Fane. Had it occurred to you, master priest, that at this hour of the Night Sun they are masterless, too?'

Over the noises of birds and voices, over the humming and chattering in the air, and his own voice calling orders, Plessiez heard behind him the rapid urgent strokes of chalk on stone.

Throat raw with screaming, the White Crow sobbed in a breath and muttered a charm against pain. Stone grated hard under her knees and shins; against the side of her face. The stench of ordure faded in her nostrils, replaced by the sweetness of honey.

Kneeling, slumped against masonry, a hard tension pulled against the muscles of her arm.

'Did we . . . ?'

She opened her eyes to rose-pale light.

A deep hollow, man-sized, pitted the stone floor of the cell beside her. New, but smooth; as if time or the sea had worn it down for aeons. And cradled in that absence of stone she saw a foot, white and bony, a sharp shin, a knee . . . Her head jerked up.

A smell of honey, sweet and sleepy, sang in the air. The cell soared over their heads, white stone with a heart of rose burning softly in its masonry depths.

Candia knelt on the newly hollowed stone, bearded face gaunt now, his arm around the naked white shoulder of an old man.

'Gods! Oh, dear gods . . .'

The man's hands busy at his face touched flesh, white hair, nose, ears and lips; slid down to his Adam's apple and collar-bone and sharp-ribbed chest. Pale age-spotted skin all whole. Candia's buff-and-scarlet jacket swathed his hips; his thin legs and bare bony feet protruded from under it. His chest rose and fell smoothly. He broke into a sweet open smile.

All realisation in a split second: pain slammed her vision black and bloody. She doubled up. A scream ripped from her throat. Tears ran down her face. Still kneeling supported against the cell wall, she stared at her outstretched arm and hand.

Her left hand impaled, four inches down on the jutting iron spike.

Solid metal poked up from torn skin and flesh. Blood and white liquid ran down her arm, streaking red, drying. Her flesh trembled: the bones in her hand grated against the impaling metal spike.

'God-shit-*damn* it . . .'

A hand covered her eyes; she smelt a fragrance of lilac. Heurodis's voice said: 'Don't look. Wait. *There.*'

Something gripped her left hand, pulled it up, free of the spike.

Pain ripped through her. She rolled foetally on the stone floor of the cell, screaming, left hand held out and away from her body. Warm trickles of blood ran over her wrist.

'Lady.' A new voice, hesitant, well spoken; light with age.

She opened her mouth, screaming. A cold numbness took her skin, sank into muscle and bone.

The White Crow pushed herself up on to her knees, supporting herself on her right hand, sweating and dizzy. The old man knelt at her side, shrugging Candia off, labile face creased into a triumphant smile. She looked down. Both his hands clasped hers, the light of summer leaves shining out between the Bishop's fingers.

Pain ebbed.

The light of forests faded.

She covered their hands with her free one, squeezed his for a second longer. His grip loosened. The White Crow took her hand back, examining the wound. Red muscle gleamed at the edges, and a white bone glinted. A skein of dermis glinted over raw flesh. Pain. No blood.

'I could do more . . . if I were stronger.'

The White Crow met his grey brilliant eyes. 'I could learn from your Church, I think. Honour to you, my lord Bishop.'

'Master-Physician. You'd better see this.'

Heurodis's voice came from the cell door. The White Crow stood, staggered in the hollowed floor, bare feet kicking the discarded rapier and pack, and lurched over to lean up against the door-jamb.

All the twenty or so strips of paper curled up from the step and jamb and lintel and snapped, bleached into blankness.

'We'd better move, if we can.' The White Crow, straightening up, took a step across the threshold of the cell. It opened now into the body of a vast high-vaulted hall.

She looked back. Framed in the cell door, Heurodis held the arm of the Bishop of the Trees, supporting him as he rose to his feet;

Theodoret leaning part of his weight on the gaunt blond man's shoulder.

A voice, quieter than anything ever heard before but perfectly clear, spoke at her left hand.

'Child of flesh, he was bait – for a healer.'

Breath feathered her dark-red hair, pearled damp on her neck; a reek of carrion made her eyes sting and run over with tears. Her hand throbbed. Her legs weighed lead-heavy: she caught her breath, could not turn to where the voice came from.

Quiet as the rustling of electrons in the Dance, the voice spoke again.

'You could not have healed him if I had desired him truly to die.'

The woman has almost reached the sea again.

Andaluz hurries protectively after her, the coach abandoned. Her footprints, small and deep, wind across the sand of the airfield. His shadow pools in light around his feet. No matter how fast he walks, she is before him: her arms held up, the bamboo staff clasped in one hand, her bright-feathered silver braid penduluming across her back with her swift strides.

'Lady! Luka!'

Birds wheel above her head. Black-headed gulls, shrikes, cormorants: they swoop and skim the small woman's head or hands and rise, strong wings beating, in the wake of the flock that flies up to the Night Sun. Still they come, still they pursue.

'Wait! Dear lady . . .'

Sweating, popping buttons as he pulls the neck of his doublet open, Andaluz comes to the marble balustrade and steps overlooking the lagoon. He leans against the balustrade, panting.

'Luka.'

A sea-wind blows, sharp with the cold of ocean depths.

Black light shines down upon the marble terraces, the promenade, and the tossing waters of the lagoon. Onyx gleams flash from the waves. No one but Andaluz and the Lady of the Birds hears the rushing of that sea.

The docks stretch out, empty.

She stands on the marble steps that go down to the dock, staring to where the Boat moored. Nothing is there. The Boat is gone.

Andaluz, sharp pains in his chest, sees her raise her head and open her mouth: her cry is forlorn as a gull's, desolate.

Timber sleepers, jammed between the surrounding railings and wired down, blocked the entrance to the underground station.

'Break it open.' Plessiez smiled sardonically. 'The strike is over, I think.'

He stepped back as Fleury beckoned and a squad of Rats with dirty velvet robes tucked up into their belts began levering away wood and cutting wire.

The scrolled railings and steps leading down to the railway stood on the corner of the square and First Avenue, outside porticoed town-houses. A few yards from where he stood, a dozen Rats furiously piled up paving-stones and planks, barricading the doors.

'Soon have it done.' Fleury nervously tugged the scarlet jacket down over her plump haunches. 'Plessiez, what are you thinking?'

The pavement thrummed under his clawed feet. Plessiez glanced across the square. A hundred yards away the siege-engine glittered darkly under the Night Sun. Blue-liveried King's Guard swarmed over the platform, rolling out barrels of Greek fire for the ballista.

Of the Lord-Architect Casaubon, there was no sign.

'These houses aren't defensible. I'm opening a means of retreat. If the siege-engines fail us, we can take refuge in the underground tunnels and defend the entrances.' Seeing Fleury's eyes widen, he added: 'Go round. Pass the word on.'

Wood screamed, splintering. A sleeper tipped up, crashed down. Two Rats gripped another slab of wood and lifted it aside. Plaster and cracked tile fell down into the stairwell. Plessiez's nose twitched, scenting for anything strange, detecting only coal and stale smoke.

A voice spoke behind him.

'Messire, you're coming with me now. To the Night Council.'

'What?' Plessiez turned, the cold wind blowing dust in his eyes.

Under the blazing blue sky and Night Sun, a burly brown Rat strode towards him between piles of debris. Her coat showed charred and scraped patches, but from somewhere she had found a bright blue sash to tie over her shoulder and between her two rows of furry dugs.

'Charnay? Good gods, Charnay!' He kicked rubbish aside, stepping to grip her arms and gaze up at her face. 'You made it at last. Late, of course; but not too late, one hopes.'

Plessiez's gaze travelled past the brown Rat. He smiled. A pale black-haired young woman stood a few paces behind Charnay, hugging herself with bare and goosepimpled arms, head bowed. A dappled black-and-white tail hung limp to her ankles.

'Or did you find her for me, Mistress Zari?'

The young Katayan in the black dress shivered, not looking up. In

a low voice she said: 'You'll need a Kings' Memory. I'm here for
that, remember?'

A third member of the group straightened up from a crouch by a
pile of debris, brushing dust from a small hand-crossbow. A
Katayan woman perhaps twenty-five: black tail and cropped black
hair. She put her hand on Zar-bettu-zekigal's arm, the lace at the
wrist of her silk coat falling over her hand.

Plessiez frowned. Momentarily putting aside the bustle of preparation, the stranger, Rats running past on errands, and the
darkness seeping into the north-austerly horizon, he walked forward and put his hands on Zar-bettu-zekigal's shoulders.

'Why will I need a Memory now, little one?'

'The Night Council.'

'Don't be ridiculous. This is about to become a battlefield!'

He turned, opening his mouth to summon Fleury. Charnay
blocked his way. Irritably he put one ring-fingered hand on her
chest, pushing her aside.

Her strong hands gripped his sash and sword-harness, jerking him
to a halt. Startled, swearing, Plessiez felt his feet leave the pavement
as the brown Rat lifted him bodily, held him for a second six inches
above ground, and dropped him. Stone jarred him from head to
heels.

'*Listen to me, messire!*'

'You over-muscled oaf—!' He wrenched himself free. 'I have no
time for your customary *stupidity*.'

'Listen.'

Cold hackles began to walk down Plessiez's spine. He looked up,
meeting Charnay's eyes, seeing her blink slowly, slowly.

'They showed me how to get back to them. Down there.' She
pointed at the newly opened station entrance. 'That will do. They
want you, messire, and I'm bringing you to them. Either you can
walk, or I'll knock you down, or wound you and carry you down
there.'

Black sunlight beat down on her translucent tattered ears; on the
grimy fur of her flanks. In her face shone memories of brick tunnels,
of gibbets, of dangers passed and of whatever is unearthly in the city
that lies under the city. She drew her long rapier.

'I can't leave. I'm needed. I can't abandon these people!'

Zar-bettu-zekigal refused to meet his eyes. The other woman had
hunkered down again, sorting crossbow bolts from the debris on the
marble flagstones.

The brown Rat said: '*Now*, messire.'

*

They do not see where a greasy-haired woman crawls on hands and knees through the bodies outside the tents, shedding armour at every move as if some insect abandoned its carapace.

She half-rises, grunts, slides down to lope painfully along in the shadow of the wall, supporting herself with one or sometimes both hands.

The Rats watch the darkening horizon, not the edges of the square. Her dark red clothes disguise her somewhat in bloody shadows. Unwatched, she limps towards the entrance of the station; pauses once to lift her head and bark a hysterical laugh at the sky.

She slides into the stairwell and shadow. Following.

Zar-bettu-zekigal clung to the brickwork either side of the arch, squatting in the niche, her knees almost up about her ears. She peered through the narrow slit at the back of the niche where a brick had been missed out.

'Just more tunnels.'

Without turning, she kicked back with her feet and let go, arms and tail wheeling, landing four-square on the cinder track. Moisture dripped down from the roof of the tunnel. She turned, looted black ankle-boots crunching on the cinders. Elish-hakku-zekigal walked light-footed from sleeper to sleeper, the lantern swinging in her hand.

Ahead, in shifting circles of lamplight on brick, the two Rats walked. Zar-bettu-zekigal shrugged, plodding to catch up with the older Katayan.

'The birds will take them to the Boat.'

'What?' Zar-bettu-zekigal looked up warily. The hard toes of her unfamiliar boots caught on the railway sleepers.

'Souls. That's what she's doing.' Elish-hakku-zekigal held the lantern higher. Its barred light swung over the curved brick walls. 'The Lady Luka. She calls the birds to eat the *psyche*, the butterflies, before they're drawn up into the Night Sun. So that the birds can fly to the Boat and the *psyche* be reborn.'

Zar-bettu-zekigal's shoulders lifted. She took a deep breath, mouth moving slightly. 'Oh, what! I knew *that*!'

The woman smiled, her gaze on the diminishing parallel rails.

'Of course you did.'

Zari skipped down from sleeper to sleeper, hands thrust in her black dress pockets, head coming up as she gazed around at the tunnel, bouncing on her heels. 'Elish, why did Father let you come here?'

The older Katayan momentarily shifted her gaze from the rails to her sister. 'He doesn't know I'm here.'

'Oh, what! See you, you told Messire Andaluz that you're an envoy.'

'I could hardly tell him that I'm a runaway.' Amusement made the Katayan's tone rich.

Zar-bettu-zekigal slowed to walk beside her, looking up at the pale face nested among lace ruffles, the cropped black hair combed forward. She took one hand from her pocket and slipped it into Elish-hakku-zekigal's free hand. A black tail curved up to cuff her ear lightly.

'Elish, I love you.'

'I know you do, buzzard. And I intend to see we both come out of this crazy place in one piece.'

'Back there . . . up there . . . *will* those things from the Fane attack?'

The hand tightened on hers. Elish-hakku-zekigal began walking at a faster pace. Her face in the shifting lantern-light might have shown a smile or a grimace.

'Why ask me, little buzzard? I don't know everything.'

She jerked the older woman's arm sharply. 'You *do*!'

Elish-hakku-zekigal's laughter echoed down the tunnel. The black and the brown Rat paused to look back. She shook her head, sobering. 'Well, then. Yes. I think they will. That isn't our fight.'

The big Rat stooped slightly, the pole of her lantern in one hand and her drawn sword in the other. Yellow light shone on her brown fur, on her naked tail and clawed feet. She raised her snout to stare at the roof, incisors glinting.

'Are we right?' Zar-bettu-zekigal called.

'Certainly! I just have to work out—'

'—where we are?' the black Rat completed, *sotto voce*, after a moment.

'It's going to be fine, messire,' Zar-bettu-zekigal said as she came up with them.

Plessiez sighed. He carried a bull's-eye lantern in one hand, light glinting from the buckles of his harness, and his rings, and the slender drawn rapier in his other hand. The cardinal's sash glowed a brilliant green against his black fur.

'You had no right to drag me down here, away from . . .' He stared at Charnay still, adding in a lower tone: 'I would be happier with myself if I could regret the leaving more sincerely.'

'This way,' Charnay announced.

The big Rat padded away, following a curve of the line. Zar-bettu-zekigal squatted down on a sleeper, pulling at the hard metal of the rails where another joined it; looked ahead to realise the line split. She hastily knotted a bootlace and rose to her feet, following.

'Suppose a train came?'

'Suppose nothing of the kind!' Elish-hakku-zekigal reached out and ruffled her hair.

Zar-bettu-zekigal jumped from sleeper to sleeper, two-footed, grinning at the echoes coming back off the damp tunnel walls.

'How far down are we?'

'The lower levels,' Plessiez replied without turning.

Elish-hakku-zekigal lengthened her stride to catch up with the Cardinal-General. 'Two things you should perhaps be aware of, your Eminence. One is that we're being followed— No, Zar', be quiet!'

Zar-bettu-zekigal took her hands from her pockets and loped to walk between the black Rat and the Katayan woman.

'And the other is that your friend will have to take us off the track soon. You can't get there from here.'

The black Rat thrust the bull's-eye lantern at Zar-bettu-zekigal without acknowledgment, and she caught the handle just as he let go of it. Heat from the glass and metal warmed her hands. Holding it at arm's length, she saw a splinter of light: Plessiez now carried in his onyx-ringed left hand a triangular-bladed dagger.

Speaking across her head to Elish, the black Rat said: 'Who follows?'

'I can't tell who or what it is.'

'And the rest – you know about this 'Night Council,' I comprehend? And the ways to reach it? Oh, come – you've been in the heart of the world how long?'

Zar-bettu-zekigal muttered a protest, winced as the older Katayan woman's tail slapped her leg.

'She's a shaman,' she protested, ignoring Elish. 'Messire, you remember, when we came out from below last time, what we saw.'

Plessiez's upper lip wrinkled, showing white incisors. He quickened his pace.

A coil of mist brushed Zar-bettu-zekigal. She put her free hand up to her face, touching dampness. The metal surface of the lantern hissed gently, evaporating moisture.

'Look.' She held up the lantern.

The light cast Charnay's shadow ahead on to a bank of mist. Nitre-webbed brick walls vanished as mist thickened into fog. The brown Rat strode on, her lantern bobbing on its pole, becoming a globe of yellow light.

Plessiez's hand tightened on the hilt of his rapier. 'Well, we can't lose her now, I suppose.'

Zar-bettu-zekigal, conscious of her aching arm, held up the bull's-eye lantern, and took Elish's hand again. Her nostrils flared. Fog pearled on her dress, on the hairs on her arms; and she glanced up at the Katayan woman, seeing the sapphire at her throat dimmed by clinging moisture.

She stumbled, stared ahead. No tunnel walls. The clatter of her feet vanished into the fog, echoless. Three lanterns glowed, yellow in the mist.

'It smells strange.'

The black Rat briefly looked over his shoulder and murmured: 'Sewers.'

'No.'

'We're too far below ground-level for anything else, I assure you. Charnay, woman, slow down!'

Zar-bettu-zekigal shivered, chilled. She held the lamp and lifted her head to stare upwards, seeing nothing but fog, no tunnel roof. She pursed her lips to whistle for echoes; her mouth too dry. The lantern's muffled light could not even illuminate the cinders and sleepers underfoot.

'It smells . . . salt.'

Elish-hakku-zekigal's grip tightened.

Faint at first, on the edge of hearing, she felt the pulse and thunder of surf. A wind stirred the fog. She tasted seaweed and salt on her lips, pressing on faster to keep up with Charnay's lantern; brushing the black Rat's shoulder as she stumbled beside him.

'The sea!'

Wind roiled the fog, moving but not shifting it. The thunder of waves came from all quarters, the pounding of waves and the hiss of shingle sucked back. Zar-bettu-zekigal raised her head, neck prickling to the cold wind, searching for a lightness that would mark sky or sun. Wet air choked her. She loosed Elish's hand and stepped away.

'*No.*'

A black tail coiled around her wrist, pulled. She jerked to a halt.

'I want to see the sea!'

'No.'

Ahead, the bobbing lantern slowed. She caught a glimpse of Charnay, sword in hand, raising her snout to quest after a scent. Plessiez and the older Katayan woman hastened their steps.

'Oh, wait, will you!' Pebbles dragged at her feet and ankles, slid down her boots. Zar-bettu-zekigal stopped, bent, and put the lantern down on the beach; lifting her foot and reaching for the heel of her boot.

She froze. 'Elish! El!'

Brown pebbles crunched underfoot: friable, fragile. The lantern, standing tilted, shed illumination on the round shadow-pocked pebbles. All of a size: no larger than a walnut.

Tiny skulls.

Ragged eye-sockets caught shadow, lamp-light. Cranial sutures gleamed, black-thread thin; the articulate and precise joints of jaws shone. She stared, seeing some with lower jaws, some with only upper teeth; the ragged slits of noses. Thousand upon thousand, million upon million, stretching out under the fog in piled banks and valleys.

Underfoot, as far back as lamp-light shone, tiny crushed skulls marked their path. Zar-bettu-zekigal wavered, balanced on one leg, hand still gripping the back of her left boot.

'Elish!' She wailed. 'It doesn't matter where I put my feet, I'm going to break more of them . . .'

'I see it, little one. Keep walking.'

Zar-bettu-zekigal hooked off her boot, balancing one-legged, shook it and replaced it. She seized the lantern and lifted it. Fog swirled about her ankles, mellowing, concealing. The slope dragged at her feet as she ran after Elish-hakku-zekigal and the Rats.

'This place stinks,' she said bitterly. 'Ei, Charnay, aren't we there yet? How far now? Which way?'

She grabbed the brown Rat's sword-arm, fur slick and fog-dampened, shaking it. Charnay looked down at her.

'I forget,' she confessed.

'Oh, *what*—'

Plessiez, a yard or two ahead, interrupted. 'I think we've arrived.'

Lights shone through the fog. Zar-bettu-zekigal plodded on over the fragile beach, refusing to look down.

The fog thinned.

Ochre and red cliffs reared up before her and to either side; summits lost in distance. The sea echoed softly from wall to wall. A great amphitheatre of rock, in the flares of torches.

Warmth breathed from the stone, as if the sun had only just ceased to shine and it still gave back heat. Zar-bettu-zekigal stretched out her hands.

Hacked out of the bedrock brown granite, still part of the cliffs, great squared thrones formed a semicircle.

Zar-bettu-zekigal bent to place the bull's-eye lantern at her feet. Tiny skulls crunched under her boots. She reached back without looking, and Elish-hakku-zekigal gripped her hand. The older Katayan came to stand at her back, setting down her lantern, folding her arms about Zari's chest and resting her chin on the top of her head.

Charnay drove the pole of her lantern deep into the beach, brushing bone splinters from her fur. She straightened up.

Plessiez trod a few paces forward, past Zar-bettu-zekigal, until he stood at the focal point of those inward-facing thrones, lifting his head and resting his rapier back across the drying fur of his shoulder.

'Old . . .' Elish's chin jolted her skull as the woman whispered. Zar-bettu-zekigal gripped her sister's hand, pulling her arms tighter.

Silence breathed from the stone. Silence and a tension, the bedrock brown granite dense with aeons of geological compression.

The squared thrones jutted from living rock that continued above them into square pillars, soaring up. She tilted her head to follow; lost the sight in dim distance a quarter of a mile overhead. No sky. Nothing but foundation rock below the world.

Dizzy, she dropped her gaze to the empty thrones. Crude seats and arms and backs, smoothed not by artisans but by time.

'The carvings.' Elish's voice in her ear.

Lines marked the back of each brown granite throne, cut with no metal tools, cut with bone and wood and stone itself. She stared up at the human figures cut in stylised profile, the planes of muscle, the nakedness of bodies. She faced the central throne. Raising her eyes, Zar-bettu-zekigal followed the line of the giant figure's chest and shoulders. Scales marked the neck; the head not human but the head of a cobra.

She looked to the next throne, and the next. A man with the head of a viper, a woman whose black lidless eyes shone in the head of a python, a young man with the blunt head of a boa, a woman whose shoulders supported the blue-and-crimson head of a coral snake . . .

Movement caught her peripheral vision; Elish's arms tightened; she heard Plessiez swear an oath, and Charnay grunt with satisfaction. Colour and movement. Each figure changing as her eye left it, changing from bas-relief to solidity . . .

They sat each one high upon their thrones, the light of torches sliding on their bronze human flesh. Giant figures, twice the height of a man. The torches flared and glinted from scales, from lidless black eyes, from pulses beating in the white soft scales under serpentine jaws.

Elish's arms loosened. She breathed: 'The Serpent-headed . . .'

Now each of the Thirteen arose, standing before their thrones, scales shimmering, forked tongues licking between blunt lips; old with the age of granite, of bone, of earth.

Plessiez sheathed his rapier with a tiny click that echoed back from the towering walls. The black Rat raised his head, gazing at the giant figures.

'You are the Night Council?'

A scent of musk and sand-hot deserts breathed from the beach, from the miniature human skulls tumbled to the foot of the thrones. From the centre throne the figure arose, standing with brown hands resting on the granite.

Light shone on his human body, brown, smooth-skinned and naked; and Zar-bettu-zekigal let her gaze rise to where skin transmuted into scale and his spine curved inhumanly. Rearing up, haloed by hooded skin, the eyes of a cobra surveyed them with bright anger.

He spoke.

'Yeth.'

She turned from the cell doorway, staring out into the Fane.

'You could not have healed him, if I had desired him truly to die.'

White stone walls shone in sourceless light. The White Crow looked out across a floor littered with broken glass, alembics, bainsmarie and furnaces; eyes narrowing to witness the machinery of the alchemist. Flat glass bubbles, set in ranks into the wall, danced with moving pictures. She registered in peripheral vision outer views of the city. Past that . . .

This high vaulted hall opened into a nave, into a colonnade; into balconies, oratories, galleries . . .

So clear the air, no possible distance could make it blurred or diffuse. She saw into the heart of the Fane: all bright, all in focus. Colonnades of white arches hooped away, growing smaller in perspective; vaults shone and soared; galleries ran the walls, drawing zig-zag lines into the distance. All around: tower-stairs and loggias, porches and steps and halls starkly clear; white and intricate and shining as if carved from ivory and milk.

Glass rolled aside as she moved, ticking across the stone. She glanced down.

A rose-briar lay across the flagstones, jet-black, bristling with thorns. One withered leaf clung to the stem. Something had eaten away the petals of the remaining black rose. She raised her head, following it.

Insects crawled.

Cockroaches, locusts, scarab beetles, flies; a towering mass of bodies filled all the near end of the hall. Chittering, feelers waving, chitinous wings rasping; the insects crawled on a mountainous bulk that heaved although still.

The White Crow caught a glimpse of blackness under the mass, began to make out shapes. The circular rim of a great nostril, crusted with the bodies of locusts. Higher up the shapes of scales, cockroaches crawling under the rims. Tendrils of darkness sweeping back to where, through chitinous crawling bodies, an eye opens, disclosing a darkness greater than the Night Sun.

One-handed, she sheathed the rapier and beckoned the others to leave the cell.

He filled the whole space of the hall, so that she could hardly take in more than rising shoulders, basalt-feathered wings, tusked and toothed muzzle furred with insects. Cockroaches, locusts, black beetles; carrion-flies and scarabs; they clung, flew up a few inches, and fell to crawl again in worship over the body of The Spagyrus.

Dizzy with expense of power and sick with the receding tide of pain, the White Crow walked drunkenly across the flagstones until she stood before the Decan. A cockchafer burred past her face. Her head jerked back.

She held up her blood-stained and black-pitted left hand, and knelt to touch one knee to the stone floor.

'Divine One, Lord of the Elements, you healed him through me. I thank you for it.'

The shining basalt eyes closed.

The great body sprawled the length of the hall, flank up against curtain-tracery walls, head rising twenty-five feet into the air. Roses covered the massive paws and shoulders, clustered on the joint of a wing.

White light shone on living black basalt.

Clear now, unshadowed, she traced every lineament. Crusted nostrils, thick with hair and flies, in an upper muzzle that overhung the lower jaw by ten feet. Jutting tusks above the nostrils. Teeth spiking up from the lower jaw, digging into scaled cheeks; flowing tendrils around the head and tiny naked ears.

The White Crow got awkwardly to her feet. She heard someone kick glass as Candia, Heurodis and the Bishop came to stand beside her. The great eyes remained closed.

'Now . . .' She tapped her closed right fist against her mouth. 'What do we do now?'

'What we do now is . . .' Candia stepped forward, shaking out the stained lace of his cuffs, tugging his loose shirt into order. 'We play cards.'

'*What?*'

The blond man held out a filthy hand to Heurodis. The white-haired woman felt in the pocket of her blue cotton dress and brought out a thick pack of cards. Candia grinned, boyish, and she tutted.

'Tarot cards.' Elegant, faintly comic, he stripped off the binding ribbon and held the pack up one-handed, cards fanned into a circle. The White Crow gazed at images stained-glass brilliant against the white walls and the wreckage, against the million insects crawling, worshipping, on the living stone skin of The Spagyrus.

'You're out of your mind, Messire Candia,' the White Crow remarked quite cheerfully. 'You know that, don't you?'

He ignored her, scooping the cards into a pack again. Automatically his feet took him a few paces one way, a few paces the other; glancing up at the silent Decan as he spoke.

'Divine One, you'll remember me. My name is Candia. Reverend tutor, University of Crime. Now, my talent is the use of the tarot pack. Four suits: Swords, Grails, Sceptres, Stones. Thirty trumps. Watch.'

The White Crow craned her neck to look up at the god-daemon's face. Briars and black roses tangled in the scaled and tendrilled head, coiled to ring a forearm; rustling with the living garment of worshipping insects. The basalt eyes remained closed.

The blond man gave Heurodis his hand as the small woman seated herself limberly cross-legged on the flagstones. Theodoret stood behind her. Candia very carefully lowered himself to sit opposite. His long-fingered and dirty hands shuffled the pack.

Bemused, the White Crow moved to look over his shoulder.

'A reading of all eighty-six cards,' he announced. His fingers quickened, the pasteboard images flashing past. 'To determine the immediate and near future. My own method. Now.'

The man laid out three cards swiftly, slapping them face-down on the stone floor. Another three, then five grouped in a diamond with one in the centre. He paused. More sets of three, five and six.

'Hey!' She grabbed at his wrist, missing it.

The strong thin fingers dealt two more cards off the bottom of the pack as she watched. Candia glanced up through flopping hair, eyes bright. He indicated the backs of eighty-six cards with a careless gesture.

'Broadest reading, three cards in the Sign of the Archer. What have we got?'

Heurodis leaned forward, grunting, and turned over the three cards. The White Crow saw a castle struck by lightning, *The House of Destruction*, the knot of a shroud, *Plague*, and a skull with blue periwinkle flowers set into the eyes, *Death*.

'I think . . .' Candia's hand hovered over the cards. 'Probably not.'

He grinned at the White Crow, replacing the three cards face-down and then reaching out to them again. He paused, hand in mid-air, and gestured to her. 'You.'

She knelt cautiously and turned the three cards. The first, in bright colours, showed two children playing at noon in a garden, *The Sun*. The second, a man and a woman embracing, *The Lovers*. On the third, a hermaphrodite dancing among balanced alchemical symbols, *The World*.

'You can't do that!' Wide-eyed, she stared; aware of the dis-traction but not of when it had occurred.

Heurodis gave a long-toothed smile.

'I don't mean it won't work if you do. I mean that you can't do it!'

Candia fell to shuffling some of the lower cards, keeping *The Sun*, *The Lovers* and *The World* at the top of the reading. The White Crow stared intently, drew a deep breath and tried again.

'You can't sharp these cards. It isn't possible. They're constrained by the future. All the tarot's links are with what's going to happen; you can't cheat what's Fated!'

Fair hair fell across his eyes as he looked up. Practised, he shook back the lace cuffs from his wrists; a deliberate staginess in his gestures.

'Readings influence what will come, as well as being influenced *by* it.'

The White Crow stood, rubbing her calf muscle with her right hand. The humming of insects made her dizzy. An incredulous laugh bubbled up. She stifled it.

'You're telling me the University of Crime can sharp *tarot* cards?'

Heurodis said: 'Not often, girlie. But when we need to we can.'

Candia turned over a Ten of Grails, Three of Sceptres and *The House of Destruction* in the position of the Sign of the Wilderness. He lifted his gaze to meet the White Crow's, one brow raised; and when she glanced down it was to see the Ten of Grails, Ace of Sceptres and *Fidelity*.

'Damn you, you just might exercise some influence. Here. You just might. Are you a good cheat, Messire Candia?'

'The best.'

A breath reached her: saline, musky. Black basalt eyes opened, twenty-five feet above her head. The great lips moved apart, and she stared up at a cockroach picking its way across the living basalt of the Decan's skin.

'*Bait for a healer . . . which of my ten million souls here in the heart of the world, think you, is fated now truly to die? Can you tell, little magus? I tell you: they are already grievous sick.*'

Insects buzzed. The White Crow gazed up at empty vaulting over the Decan's head.

'I don't think to outwit omnipotency, Divine One. That would be stupid.'

'*My sister of the Ten Degrees of High Summer gave you a certain hour. You have not used it well.*'

She grinned up at the Decan: a rictus of pain, fear and defiance. She held up her left hand. The wound in its palm gaped, raw but not bleeding. Her fingers, red and swollen, bore pin-prick marks from the briars of black roses.

'All the same, aren't you? All Thirty-Six. The hour isn't over yet.'

'*WE ARE NOT ALL THE SAME . . . !*'

Echoes shuddered. Quietly, beside her, the Bishop of the Trees said: 'He's sick. His Sign is occluded.'

He reached down to his side, more firmly knotting the sleeves of the buff-and-scarlet doublet around his hips. He wore the makeshift covering with an old man's slow dignity. A faint green light began to gather about his fingers.

'No. I agree. But even so . . .' The White Crow shook her head warningly. 'This is the crucial hour. Plague outside, sickness in the Fane; and somewhere, somewhere . . .'

Great lips breathed carrion on the air.

'*They are far from here, and sick, and soon to die. Both the death of the body, and the death of a soul.*'

The White Crow cocked a jaundiced eye at the insect-ridden slopes of flank and shoulder rising, mountainous, before her.

'Yes? And will they die of the . . . same . . . sickness . . . ?'

She stopped. Her left hand burned, the pain connecting her to the substance of the Fane and the *magia* acted within it; and slowly, aloud, she followed the connection.

'You're the heart and centre of it,' the White Crow said. 'The truly dead, the plague, the death of souls, and the *magia* of necromancy. All of it begins here. Tell me, I know! I feel your power through the stone, I've spilled my blood here, I've healed a man with pain and your power channelled through me, and *I know*!'

She stopped to draw breath, grinning through tears that poured without volition down her face.

'One plague. Here and outside. *One* plague. Black alchemy . . .
Oh, they will die of the same sickness, won't they! It doesn't have to
be a human death, or the death of a Rat-Lord. Why didn't I think of
it! What death would really uncreate the world? *One of the Thirty-
Six!'*

Crowned with roses, worshipped by carrion-flies, his Sign
occluded by his power still immanent in the Fane about her, the
Decan of Noon and Midnight smiles.

'The most ancient question,' Theodoret murmured at her ear.
'*Can* the omnipotent gods unmake themselves?'

She ignored him. Theodoret stepped back to where Candia and
the white-haired woman bent over the spread of cards, their
intensity of concentration aware but not admitting influence of
even the Lord of Noon and Midnight.

'*I will let them play, little magus, until my Sign is past its occlusion. I
will even let your bait keep his life, for as long as is left to him.'*

Insect-clouds swarmed as the great body shifted, one hind claw
rasping at his basalt ribs. The great eyelids slid down, up; darkness
glimmering in the depths of the eyes. The voice dropped to
quietness.

'*We are not all of us alike: the Thirty-Six. We should not all hold equal
powers. I give you a secret, little magus. When the Great Circle flies in pieces,
then one of us will re-create it. And there will be not Thirty-Six but One
alone.'*

Carrion-breath stung her eyes. The rose-light smouldering in the
masonry flared: all the debris and pillars and stones white as skin
with blood beating a swift pulse under it.

'*I give you that secret, little Valentine. Tell whom you will. And what can
you do, now that you know?'*

The White Crow looked down at one whole and one injured
hand.

'If you're not afraid, Divine One, why stop me?'

'*Child of flesh, you speak of fear?'*

The White Crow laughed, water running from the corners of her
eyes. She reached up with her right hand as if she would touch the
Decan of Noon and Midnight.

'*Give* me my chance, then,' she challenged. 'What can it matter to
you, you who know all, see all, are all? Give me the strength to
search, and see if I find you out!'

Candia scratched at his overgrown blond beard and muttered:
'Shit!'

'Oh, I know.' The White Crow spoke to him without turning
away from the Decan. 'The most unwise thing, to challenge God—'

Pain stabbed her fingers.

She brought her hands up in front of her face, trying to clench them against the fire burning under the skin. Her white nails shone – shone and lengthened, splitting. Whiteness ran back over her hands and wrists and forearms.

'Wh-whaa—?'

Faint down feathered the backs of her hands. She raised them closer to her face, knocking them against some obstruction. Her head twisting, she seemed to knock her nose against her hands: a nose that lengthened, darkened, pulled up her teeth into its growth as her mouth shrank . . .

The Spagyrus' laughter shook dust from the high vaulting of the Fane.

Stepping back, stumbling, she fell. As she fell, her body collapsed into itself, folding impossibly. Her feet still flat on the stone, she seemed to be crouching only a few inches above the floor.

She threw out her arms for balance. The Fane wheeled.

'Whaaack!'

Briefly, far below, she caught sight of human faces turned up to hers in fear and awe. Air pushed up under her arms, sleeked down her body. Pain threaded her arteries with hot wires. Double images blurred her vision.

'Crrr-aaark!'

She swooped at the floor and a black shadow rose to meet her. Wide-winged, the tail fanning to catch the air; no mistaking that blunt beak and body. She skimmed the stone, wheeling to rise again on wide-fingered pinions.

Divine laughter beat against her, abrasive as sand and splinters of glass.

'*Search, if you will! If you can!*'

The albino carrion crow wheels and flees into the heart of the Fane.

Anger shining in his lidless black eyes, the head of the Night Council spoke.

'I fail to thee what *exthactly* is tho amuthing.'

Zar-bettu-zekigal buried her face in her sister's lace ruffle, little whimpering noises escaping her. An open palm hit her sharply across the ear.

'Behave! Zar'!'

She swung round, clasping her hands behind her back, kicking her heels in the bone beach. Her black ankle-boots crunched on fragile skulls no larger than walnuts. Fog touched her spine coldly. She gazed up at the thrones of the Serpent-headed, eyes bright.

'I didn't say anything!'

Dry heat radiated back from the endless cliffs, from the brown bedrock granite and the thrones of the foundation of the world. Twelve of the Serpent-headed seated themselves on their thrones; the last remained standing. Flaring torchlight gleamed on oiled human limbs, on naked hip and breast and muscular shoulders. On necks glittering with scales, serpent heads; blunt muzzles and the black lidless eyes of viper, coral snake, cobra.

'The, ah—' Plessiez coughed into his fist. Zar-bettu-zekigal tried to catch his gaze; he avoided her. 'The reason for this summons, messires?'

The head of the Council's sharp cobra jaw dipped, regarding the small group below. A black-bootlace tongue licked across his lipless mouth.

'We with to regithter a thtrong complaint. Grave thins have been committed againtht uth by the world above.'

'Excuth – *excuse* me.' Zar-bettu-zekigal rubbed her bare fog-dampened arms, digging in her short nails. By virtue of that she concentrated enough to call up across the intervening yards: 'Who are you, messires?'

The cobra head moved, lidless eyes fixing on her.

'Your thithster the thaman thould be able to tell you that. We are the Night Counthil. The motht ancient godth of the world.'

Zari turned rapidly away, hugging herself; bumped against Plessiez and looked up as the black Rat glanced down. Their eyes met.

'"Thithster".'

Zar-bettu-zekigal spluttered.

'"*Thaman*"?'

She caught one glimpse of Charnay's puzzled face and elbowed the Cardinal-General in the ribs. Plessiez looked, drew himself up, snout quivering, observed, 'Messires, I apolo— apologise for my companion,' stuttered a few more broken syllables and threw his arm across Zari's shoulders and guffawed, head down, weak, snorting with laughter.

'I thuppoth . . .' Unable to breathe, half-supporting his weight, she hugged his shaking body, nose pressed into the fur of the black Rat's chest. 'I thuppoth you think that'th funny!'

'Messire!' Charnay protested, outraged.

'Oh, he's gone.' Zar-bettu-zekigal struggled for breath, eyes brimming. She achieved poise long enough to add, '"Thithster"!'

the black Rat's body quaked with another fit, and she snuffled and burst into raucous laughter.

'Messire Plessiez!'

The black Rat straightened up, one arm still resting across her shoulders, the other clasped tight to his own ribs; looking at Elish-hakku-zekigal. He shook his head.

'Lady, I don't *care* any more. I've spent my life being diplomatic under the most trying circumstances and this, *this* is the end of it. Frankly, it's ridiculous.' He showed his incisors in a sharp grin, staring up at the cobra-headed Lord of the Night Council. 'Quite ridiculouth.'

'For gods' sake be careful!'

The black Rat ruffled Zar-bettu-zekigal's hair. 'Oh, I don't under-estimate the danger. You mistake me. This is too much. I no longer care.'

Torchlight flared on the mist behind Zar-bettu-zekigal. She gazed up at cold-eyed disapproving serpent heads. The heat of bedrock granite shone warm on her face. Unconsciously she held her hands out, warming them; the breathlessness of laughter tight in her chest.

'See you, I'm a Kings' Memory. You have an auditor.'

A burly male with the head of a python spoke from the fifth throne.

'We know what you are, mortal. We requethted your pre-thenth.'

Plessiez snorted. He stood with his weight on one clawed hind foot, tail coiled out for balance behind him, smiling cynically.

'Charnay, for *this* you took me away from a battle? Well.' He reached up to his neck, pulled the *ankh* from his collar and threw it on to the beach of skulls. 'By the time we make our way back to the world, it will be one which we control. I may have the best of it after all.'

Zar-bettu-zekigal swung one-handed on the pole of the lantern where it stood jammed into the beach, scooping up a handful of skulls, the brown bone light in her fingers. She crunched forward, ankle-deep, tossing the tiny bones up into the warm air.

'So what is all this? And what's it got to do with us?'

The first steps of the throne jutted out of the beach before her, each a yard high. She craned her neck, staring up the cliff walls. Distance or fog hid the summits.

'You are here to witneth our complaint and judgment.'

The cobra-headed figure placed his hands on the crudely cut arms of the throne, lowering himself into a sitting position. His human skin shone red as clay. The skin about his head flared, white underscales pulsing rapidly.

'You have polluted uth!'

Charnay guffawed, her eyes brightening with realisation. 'Oh! Plessiez, man, they all li—'

Plessiez trod down hard on the brown Rat's foot. She winced, puzzled, and fell silent.

'Mortalth, attend!'

'Whath'th the – I mean, what's the . . . ?' Plessiez shook his head and gave up.

'What'th the reathon for it? Thplit tongth, I thuppoth.' Zar-bettu-zekigal's eyes danced. 'That's what you get for being one of the Therpent-headed!'

Elish's hands closed over her shoulder, fingers jabbing hard into the hollow under her clavicle. '*Will* you be quiet!'

Zar-bettu-zekigal rubbed her hand across her mouth, looked away; saw in peripheral vision the Cardinal-General straighten, his expression gravely sober. She shoved the remainder of a handful of skulls into her dress pocket.

'El, they're *won*derful. You didn't tell me about this! What are they?'

'What they say they are.' Pale, calm, Elish-hakku-zekigal spoke to include Plessiez. 'Chthonic idols – not gods, except by virtue of human worship. Exiled beneath the heart of the world when the Thirty-Six took up their incarnations here on our human earth. The most ancient idols never died, only took refuge below.'

Plessiez raised an ironic brow. 'Their powers?'

'Intact.'

Zar-bettu-zekigal moved closer to Elish.

'Hear uth, and lithten well.'

Now the heat radiating from the stone became humid, steam sliding in snail-tracks down the granite. Wisps of vapour coiled up. The Lord of the Night Council stood again, pacing the steps before the thrones; turning to fling out one human hand, pointing at the skull beach.

'Thith ith not made by our hand!'

Zar-bettu-zekigal swayed, wiping sweat from her forehead, amazed to be too hot. A thick musky smell crept into the air, unstirred by the wind from the unseen ocean; and the noise of the surf faded, muffled.

'You pollute the world below. Your nightmareth come among uth. It ith *your* doing, Rat-Lord.'

The smell of green vegetation rasped in her throat, acrid and strong. She hiccuped, caught between the last paroxysm of a giggle and a sudden chill; reaching out for Elish-hakku-zekigal. Her sister's hand closed about hers.

Plessiez, not taking his eyes from the Night Council, muttered: 'Charnay! What have you told them?'

'Oh, everything.' The big brown Rat tugged her sword-belt straight and set the feather in her headband at a more jaunty angle. 'It was make a friend of them or find myself on one of your friend the Hyena's gibbets. Besides, they've been gods. What would you have me do, messire? I thought you probably wouldn't mind. You said don't tell anybody human and these people aren't human.'

The black Rat's face froze. He rested his long-fingered hand across his eyes, his shoulders momentarily heaving. 'You thought I probably wouldn't mind.' His eyes opened. 'Charnay, you are *unbelievably* stupid.'

Charnay shrugged massively muscled shoulders, brown fur rippling. 'Am I? *I* didn't plant necromancy under the heart of the world and then come back to admit it before the Night Council.'

'The Night Council doesn't care for the world above. What is there that I should admit to?'

Thirteen pairs of emotionless eyes looked down across the air. The cobra-headed god raised his hand.

'Very well, then. Behold.'

Tendrils of fog crept past Zar-bettu-zekigal and she rubbed her upper arms, feeling the skin damp and chill. A rustling filled the air.

The skull-pebbled slopes of beach *shifted* in the semicircle of space between the thrones; rolling back from granite curved and hollowed by time and scored with chthonic marks of bone, horn and wood. From the far-end thrones, two of the Night Council paced down to stand in the cleared space. One with the body of an old woman and the head of a krait, one with a young woman's body and the glittering crest of an iguana.

They met and grasped hands.

A wind began to blow.

Zar-bettu-zekigal trod back, bumping her shoulder against the older Katayan's breast. Hair tangled in her eyes. The wind blew colder, scoring her skin. Plessiez and Charnay lowered their snouts against the gusts, the brown Rat grabbing for the lantern as it fell.

A hurricane-wrench of air pulled the fog aside; light blazed in her eyes. She clawed hair from her face two-handed, shaded her eyes, opened her mouth to speak, and gaped.

The beach ran down to a black shore. Black water slopped thickly against the skull-pebbles. Debris tangled in the edges of the dark surf.

She put her fist to her mouth, staring. A corrosive vapour drifted, stinging her eyes.

All along the shore, as far as she could see, debris clogged the water-line. Broken wood and glass, the bodies of gigantic wasps; sodden entrails, a hand and arm rolling in the sea-drenched pebbles . . . The writhing bodies of ants, each as long as her forearm; a gouged-out eye; a basket-handled rapier rolling against the pebbles; a doll, and something dark-backed that broke the surface a little way offshore and vanished.

She stared offshore.

Ragged bedrock jutted up from the sea.

Giant tree-roots twisted up through the crags, splintering the ochre and vermilion stone. Glistening wet boles writhed across shattered blocks, stretching in island-ranges to the horizon. Zar-bettu-zekigal shuffled, turning, staring at the weed-covered stones, the masses of razor-edged shells clustering on ridges, the pods hanging down wetly from the giant tangles of roots.

Twenty feet away across the nearest strait, a man's body hung, head thrown back taut in agony. A thick root grew into his stomach under the navel, impaling him; his feet kicked against barnacle-covered rocks, razoring open his heels.

'Dear . . . *gods.*'

Zar-bettu-zekigal's hand moved to her mouth. She felt Elish tug at her shoulder; refused to turn away.

A figure hung over the screaming man, clawed feet gripping the wet bark, grinning with lengthened teeth. Its head turned as she watched. Subtly altered, strangely disfigured: the mirror-face of the impaled man stared at her. Pointed teeth smiled. The head continued to lift, to turn. It pivoted full-circle, neck cracking, until it stared down again at the pierced man: coughing quietly, laughing.

She looked just long enough to see how many human figures the root cages trapped, each accompanied by its distorted mirror-image tormentor; how far the islands stretched . . .

'I think I—' She faced about, spat bile on to the beach of tiny skulls.

'The pollution of nightmare. Dream-debris. Solid.' Elish-hakku-zekigal turned, embracing her, gazing back up at the semicircle of thrones. 'Solid. Real.'

The two of the Night Council paced back and climbed the steps to their thrones. Fog began to soften the horizon.

'You *infected* the world below.' The Lord of the Night Council
pointed a red-nailed finger at Plessiez. 'Necromanthy, *Magia* of the
dead, the truly dead . . . It ith your plague that kilth above, and in
the Fane, and allowth the Night Thun to thine. You brought it
below. Now you mutht dethtroy it.'

The black Rat's lip twitched, showing a gleam of incisor.

' "Kills above"?' Zar-bettu-zekigal asked.

Black serpent eyes turned upon her. Zar-bettu-zekigal shivered,
hacked one booted heel into the miniature skulls and looked away.
The voice echoed softly from the curving granite cliffs.

'We are not contherned with the above. Do what you will. We
do not need you. But we will not have you corrupt uth! Your
plague maketh their nightmareth real, here below.' The cobra-
head dipped, unblinking eyes watching. 'Memory, tell what you
have heard of pethtilenth.'

All laughter gone cold, she lifted her head and stared at
Plessiez. 'Oh, I'd rather tell what I've *seen* – up there. Now. But
you listen.'

She began speaking with the concentration of Memory.

' "*Plagues may exist in flesh, in base matter, and bring bodies to death.
And, we discover, there are other pestilences that may be achieved, plagues
of the spirit and soul. And there are plagues that can be brought into
existence only by acts of magia. They bring their own analogue of death to
such as our masters—*" '

'Not alone to such as those,' Elish interrupted. Zari saw the brown
Rat catch the remark and shrug carelessly.

' "*—such as our masters, the Thirty-Six Lords of Heaven and Hell, the
Decans.*" Is that what you want? See you, there's more. The Hyena.
"*Memory, witness. Certain articles of corpse-relic necromancy to be placed
at septagon points under the heart of the world, for the summoning of a
pestilence—*" ' She broke off, lifting her chin, staring at the Cardinal-
General. 'Did you know it would kill humans? Do this to them? *Did*
you?'

Charnay turned a surprised and blandly supercilious face. 'What
do you care? You're Katayan.'

'Messire!'

The Rat looked down over his shoulder. Fog dried on his black
fur, leaving it dull. He reached to place his hands on her shoulders,
long fingers warm through the fabric of her dress. She looked up at
brilliant black eyes; his whiskers unmoving, the light shining
through his ears.

She demanded: 'Did you?'

The black Rat removed his hands. He reached down to his

haunch, ringed fingers unknotting the green silk sash, brought it up two-handed and looped it over her head. For a moment he still held the two ends of it.

' "How now . . ." ' His incisors showed in a grin; his black eyes, feral, shone with a kind of fallen recklessness. Nothing to mark him as cardinal or priest now, all gone; he wore only silver headband and black plume, sword-belt and harness. ' "How now, two Rats! Dead, for a ducat, dead!" '

Charnay scowled. 'What!'

'I forget you're no follower of our great poets.' He reached to tug Zar-bettu-zekigal's short hair sharply, and swung round and strode back up the beach. Without lifting his head he called up to the Council: 'Messires, I'll do what I can. Charnay!'

'What?' The big brown Rat started, looked, and loped up the beach after him. 'Messire, I don't understand.'

Zar-bettu-zekigal started after them, touching the still-warm sash. She slid one trailing end across her shoulder to fall scarf-like down her back. 'Messire . . .'

Muffled screams echoed from the ocean, invisible in the thickening fog. Granular mist rolled across the beach, glimmering. It swept across the departing figures of the brown and black Rats.

'What will you do?' she shouted. 'Messire! What will you do?'

Mist blurred distance; she glimpsed his hand perhaps raised in salute.

'Your plathe ith not with them,' the viper-headed god said. His slender body seemed a young man's; his black eyes unblinking and ageless. 'We have your tathk, thaman-woman. You mutht be a guide back to the world above. Take what ith not ours, what we will not keep, and what you mutht.'

Zar-bettu-zekigal followed Elish's gaze.

A few yards from the beach of skulls, resting low in the shifting debris and black water, an unmoored ship floated. Twenty feet long, clinker-built of wood and coated in black tar. No oars. No mast. One curve from prow to stern.

No reflection of that hull in the mirror-black water.

'What . . . ?' Zar-bettu-zekigal took a few crunching steps down the beach. Fog made the inhabited islands invisible.

Behind her, Elish-hakku-zekigal chuckled.

Zari raised her head, seeing the boat still floating just offshore, growing larger as she stepped closer: thirty feet long at least.

A sibilant voice echoed from the amphitheatre of thrones: the cobra-headed Lord of the Night Council. 'We warn you. Your way will not be unoppothed.'

Zar-bettu-zekigal stared. 'It's the *Boat*. See you, I swear it; I swear it is!'

'Only when the Night Sun shines. Only when all laws cease for that certain hour . . .' Elish-hakku-zekigal's eyes showed a dazzled appalled wonder.

'Elish, don't!'

'Oh, you can *touch* it. Here, you can.' The Katayan woman strode past her, down the long skull-pebbled slope, splashing knee-deep into the black waves, ignoring her soaked breeches and the tails of her blue silk coat. Dark objects bobbed away on ripples, antennae feebly twitching. She gripped the edge of the Boat and expertly timed her leap so that it dipped, wallowed, but shipped hardly any water.

'Elish, I don't understand!'

The older Katayan woman stood up on the deck, gazing back over Zar-bettu-zekigal's head at the half-circle of thrones and the bed-rock foundations of the world. Each of the Serpent-headed now stood, left or right hand up-raised. A smile broke out on her pale features.

'Lords, I came here because of a prophecy. It was foretold to me: "Your sister will travel on the Boat." I didn't want her to die and so I came to give what help I could. But I see she *will* travel on the Boat, and living!'

'Act thwiftly; your time ith almotht patht.'

The Katayan woman's eyes glowed. She laughed; a gamine-grin very like her younger sister's. 'Don't fear. I can guide the Boat back to the world above. Zar'!'

Zar-bettu-zekigal padded down the slope to the edge of the sea. She slipped her boots off and slung them around her neck by the laces, wading out into black water icy about her ankles, her calves. She refused to look at what floated near her.

'The Boat?'

She reached out tentative fingers, laying them against the tarred wood of the hull. Elish braced a foot on the far side and reached down, grabbing her, pulling her up. She staggered and sat on the rocking deck, and felt her shoulders taken in a tight grip; Elish's blue eyes fixed on her face.

'You must jump ship the *instant* we get back. Once we're in the world above, none but the . . . dead . . . sail this Boat . . .'

'The dead.' Zar-bettu-zekigal gripped her sister's wrist. 'See you, what you told me: Lady Luka, people's *souls* – what's happening to what she's doing if the Boat isn't there!'

Elish-hakku-zekigal looked down, blue eyes suddenly vague.

'Who is Luka?'

Nightmares knocked softly against the hull. Zar-bettu-zekigal felt the tarred planks rock under her. The Boat drifted. Fog shut out the skull beach now, the vanished thrones of the Serpent-headed; fog hid the islands of splintered rock and flesh.

Droplets of mist dampened her face, clung to her lashes. She shook her head sharply. 'Elish!'

The black-haired Katayan woman swayed as she stood on the deck of the Boat. Water pearled on her blue silk coat, her lace ruffle. Her left hand, up-raised in a shaman's gesture of power, hovered forgotten. She stared at Zar-bettu-zekigal.

'Who are you?'

'I'd be obliged if you'd stop scaring the first-year students,' Reverend Master Pharamond said. 'We set the exam up to keep them out of harm's way while all this is going on.'

Lucas gulped air, injected authority into his voice. 'A message for the university. Urgent.'

A Proctor swung the heavy wooden door of the hall to, cutting off Lucas's view of the students at their desks; Rafi of Adocentyn half on his feet. The door muffled their rising voices.

'You'd better come with me, Prince,' Pharamond said.

Lucas let the small man steer him away from the hall door and down the sun-darkened corridor. The smell of wax polish and paper strong in his nostrils, he was abruptly aware of his clattering scabbard, torn breeches and shirtless state.

He reached up slowly, tugging the red kerchief from his head and undoing its knot. It smelt of sweat, of fear, of air made electric by the advent of the Night Sun.

'A message for the students and Board of Governors, from an Archemaster.'

Pharamond scratched his clipped beard with long strong fingers. A short sturdy man, he looked up at Lucas as he walked a half-pace ahead.

'Mmm. Thought as much. We're in emergency session; I can take you straight along with me. Assuming that there's some substance to this message, Prince?'

Lucas smiled crookedly. 'I'm the errand-boy, Reverend Master. But I can tell you what's going on out in the city *now*.'

'Oh, we know all about that. We've been subjecting it to some intensive research over the last month. I believe events are occurring much in the order that we predicted.'

Pharamond turned on his heel, boot squeaking on the polished boards, and threw open one of the carved wooden doors. He said over his shoulder, entering the large staff-room: 'But we can always use your help, boy. We need every hand here.'

An array of candles shivered in the door's draught. Dozens of them: jammed in pots and on bookshelves, on perpendicular-window ledges, wax-glued on the edges of tables and the backs of carved chairs. Fierce amber illumination banished the light shadows and the darkness of the sun. Two dozen faces glanced up as Pharamond entered.

'What's the news?' a freckled woman called from the table.

'All as predicted. We don't have much time.' Pharamond bustled across to where four long polished tables had been set together and whole geological strata of city maps unrolled across them. Gold-headed map-pins impaled the papers at intervals.

Lucas followed, automatically nodding respectful greetings, caught between being a first-year student and Lucas of Candover; all the while staring at the panelled walls, whose painted crests had diagrams pinned up over them; at scattered paints and quills, and bookshelves in complete disarray.

'Has Candia showed up?' a dark-skinned man asked, as Pharamond arrived at the table around which the group sat.

Pharamond stepped back, avoiding an elderly woman who pounced on the bookshelves and seized a scroll. 'I don't foresee that happening, Shamar.'

The scent of hot candlewax drenched the room. Two dozen men and women, their ages between thirty and sixty, crowded the map table. University gowns abandoned, flung down in disorder over the room's chairs and sofas, they worked mostly in shirt-sleeves and light cotton dresses.

Lucas stepped back as another woman left the table to grab a volume from the shelves and riffle through it rapidly. The dark man, Reverend Master Shamar, leaned across to stick a pin in a particular house or street.

'Nor Heurodis?' an old woman asked.

Lucas saw Pharamond smile, rubbing his long fingers together. 'I suspect she's out playing dice somewhere.'

'*Dice?*' His question came out involuntarily.

'Or cards.' Pharamond folded his hands behind his back, leaning over the map-table. 'Prince Lucas, I suggest you read the message to us here. We have a full session. It can be debated.'

Lucas felt in his breeches pocket for the folded paper. The gold pin pricked his thumb. Movement flickered beyond the distorting glass of the Gothic windows. In the dark sky whirled a multitude of specks. Birds? The Fane's acolytes? Both? He turned his back on the windows, unfolding the paper and holding it up to the light of a candle.

' *"Beneath Ninth Bank House, Moon Lane. Also beneath: The Clock & Candle at Brown Park. High Skidhill. North-aust side of Avenue Berenger. The Chapel of the Order of Fleurimond. Tannery Row. The Companile at Saffron Dock. These being respectively in the 9th, 18th, 1st, 31st, 5th, 12th and 27th Districts."* '

Lucas paused for breath, glanced up to see heads bent over the map-table, the men and women of the university muttering in suppressed excitement.

'Go on,' Pharamond said. 'Is there more?'

'Yes.' Lucas raised the paper again to the light, following the florid hasty script. 'He says: *"From Baltazar Casaubon, Archemaster, Scholar-Soldier of the Invisible College."* '

Pharamond grunted, black brows rising. 'A respectable Archemaster mixed up with those vagabonds?'

'My dear Pharamond, that was discredited years ago. A completely fictitious organisation. You'll recall Dollimore's excellent article in *Mage and Magia*. However . . .' The elderly woman who had asked about Heurodis rested her chins on her hand, staring down at the map-table. She pointed with a plump finger. 'This person *has* named all seven locations of the necromantic *magia*, and in two cases more accurately than we could. I believe we should listen to what else he has to tell us.'

'You know about the necromancy?' Lucas blurted.

Shamar glanced up, remarked, 'Discovered and monitored this past two weeks,' and went back to rustling the maps, dragging out a second set from under the first.

'It's come at *just* the wrong time. First term's always a bitch.' The freckled Reverend Mistress at the far end of the table looked up, her dark eyes meeting Lucas's. 'Your own attendance-record's pretty bad, Prince Candover.'

'Regis, this isn't the time for that!' Pharamond tugged at his black beard, made to lean down the length of the table, and had to move around to the side to stretch across and grab a chart. He reached back without looking, snapped his fingers, and took the golden pin that the elderly woman handed him.

' *Archeius-arcanum-elementum-hal-hadid-aurum-neboch!* '

His beard jutted as he raised his chin, gabbling through the incantation. Lucas saw him pass the pin through the nearest candle-flame and stab it into the map-paper.

A tall man on the far side of the table hitched himself up, looked, frowned, then nodded. 'That should hold it for now.'

'If we'd known the university was investigating . . .' Lucas scratched through the hair of his bare chest, gazing at the room from under dark meeting brows. His loosely buckled belt and stolen sword jingled as he shifted position, shoulders straightening. 'We might need what you know!'

'Candover couldn't *afford* us.' The dark man, Shamar, made a small gesture at the paper in Lucas's hand. 'Well? Read the rest of the *message*, lad.'

' "We . . ." ' The image in his head not Candover, the White Mountain, Gerima or any other, but red hair streaked with silver, and narrow shoulders in a white cotton shirt. He squinted at the Lord-Architect's scrawling hand:

' "*From B. Casaubon, Etc., to the Reverend tutors:*

' "*What I do now with the Archemaster's Art is against immediate danger. Time leaves me time for nothing else, until that's done. You are not above this battle, masters. Therefore this appeal to you.*" '

Pharamond snorted. The freckled Reverend Mistress held a map of Nineteenth District up to the darkness of the windows, impaling a point with a silver pin.

' "*You will realise, or I am mistaken in your Arts, how one single cause brings about epidemic in the city, powerlessness in the Fane, and the demonium meridanium, the Night Sun. Therefore this appeal . . .*" '

Lucas read with difficulty, hearing his own voice falling flat into the air.

' "*Masters, you are students of knowledge and wisdom. I put this to you plainly therefore.*

' "*It hath oft been writ, nothing can be done in magia without knowledge of that branch of Mathematics which is mystical and spiritual, that is, Mathesis.*" '

Lucas held the paper up, letting his gaze sneak past it. Heads around the table lifted, paying attention.

' "*To wit, Pico della Mirandola his eleventh conclusion: 'By numbers, a way is had, to the searching out, and understanding of everything able to be known.'*" '

'A mathematical analysis is the basis of a sound understanding, very true.' The dark Reverend Master Sharmar nodded thoughtfully, resting his chin on his hand, his gaze still on the piled maps. 'A man of learning, your Archemaster.'

'Not to say craft.' Lucas lowered his gaze and hastily read on:

' "*And to our immediate crisis this:*

' "*Doctor Johannes Dee his Book, writes how the gods, through their divine Numbering, produce orderly and distinct all things. For Their Numbering, then, was their Creating of all things. And Their continual numbering, of all things, is the conservation of them in being. And, where and when They shall lack a unit, there and then, that particular thing shall be Discreated." '*

'We're already facing a consensus reality breakdown.' Phara-mond stroked his beard. 'What would he have us do – pray to the gods to keep numbering the formulae of our existence?'

'Don't be ingenuous.' Regis snapped her fingers impatiently. 'What does your Archemaster say? What does he want us to do?'

Lucas cleared his throat and read into the attentive silence:

' *"You have amongst you natural philosophers, professors of Mathesis, physicists. You must set about numbering the formulae of the world: add your support to Those Who number All, in this hour when They begin to fail us.*

' *"Do this. Hold fast to the measurements and proportion of macrocosm and microcosm, as they become discreated – as it is the law that spatial, temporal, diurnal things be discreated when They cease to hold them in existence.*

' *"Break that law, masters.*

' *"Not merely the criminal law, but the laws of nature. Cheat physics, matter, energy, and form.* Break the laws of Mathesis. *No hope to counteract the equal and opposite reaction to the use of true necromancy now, no hope – but this." '*

All through the vast network under the heart of the world, lanterns and candles bob circles of light on brickwork. Rats and humans crowd the platforms and the train-tunnels where nitre spiders across curved walls.

Here and there, they fight.

Refugees: some sleep in an exhausted daze; some stare into noth-ing; some calm their children; some cry themselves into hysteria.

Even in the train-tunnels it is possible to hear the crashing collapse of buildings in the city above.

Refugees.

A female Rat in a torn scarlet jacket, the priest Fleury, crouches with her hand to the cinder-floor of a tunnel. Far, far below the heart of the world. Below (although she has lost all direction) Ninth Bank House, Moon Lane. Through long dark fingers resting on the earth, she senses something.

Silver gleams.

A substanceless petal brushes her snout, and she springs up, hand going to the *ankh* at her throat. Black petals drift down from the tunnel ceiling. Voices behind her shriek.

Now even an untrained priest can tell that necromantic *magia*

'It hath oft been writ, nothing can be done in magia without knowledge of that branch of Mathematics which is mystical and spiritual, that is, Mathesis.' Title page of *Monas Hieroglyphica*, John Dee, Antwerp, 1564

flowers beneath the city. Growing, still. Growing into its full power. Transmuted from its first design and purpose until, now, it is nothing its creator would recognise.

Black and silver, unbearably sweet: the haunting of roses throws out tendril and bramble and runner, choking the tunnel ahead, spreading rapidly towards her.

She has no desire to begin a panic stampede in the crowded tunnel.

Not until she sees the tide of nightmare flooding up in the wake of the haunting does Fleury break, scream and run.

Ribbed wings curdled the sky. Dust puffed out from between the masonry blocks of the wall. Desaguliers shouted a warning and leaped.

The wall of the palace's aust wing slid out, almost slowly, gathered momentum and collapsed into the courtyard with a roar and a whirlwind of dust. Flying glass and splintered beams battered the side of the commandeered siege-engine.

'Fire!' Desaguliers clawed his way back along the platform to the Cadets loading the ballista. One tripped the lever as he got there. The catapult shot up, slammed against the upper beam and halted, the machine quivering.

A scoop of Greek fire sprayed skyward, lashing the bodies of the swarming acolytes. The burning gelatine clung.

'It's not affecting them! They don't even feel it!'

Desaguliers slid into cover beside St Cyr at the back of the machine. Masonry dust drifted by, shadowing them with light. Screams echoed from Rats trapped in the collapsed building. St Cyr pointed.

'The Chapel! It's their next target.'

Black wings beat, falling from the sky. One acolyte gripped the roof with claws that sank into the blue tiles, bristle-tail whipping up to curve about a spire. Down, down: ten, fifteen, twenty of the Fane's acolytes covered the roof and walls, digging in with their fangs and clawed feet and the claws at their ribbed wing-joints.

Desaguliers touched his hand to his lean snout, brought it away bloody. His other hand ached. Dully surprised, he realised it gripped the stump of a sword. He prised his fingers open and let it fall, reaching across the slumped body of a brown Rat to take her rapier. He shoved a fallen pistol through his belt.

'Try to shift them from there?'

'We've taken thirty per cent losses, at least.' St Cyr flinched as the siege-engine shook, another bolt of fire catapulted skyward. 'We can't do anything else. Retreat, for gods' sakes.'

Desaguliers stared out across the great courtyard. The Night Sun glinted from shards of glass, from buckles and rings on fallen bodies. At least a dozen Cadets lay in plain view: most dead, one moving still, another screeching. The gutted palace cast shadows of light across split-open halls and chambers and kitchens.

Black shadows fell only from the daemons, shrinking as they soared, growing immense as they struck.

Over the crackling of fire and screams of the injured, he heard a roar. The roof of the chapel fell in, rafters jutting up like broken ribs. A scarlet-jacketed priest ran outside, his black fur burning. An acolyte swooped, beak dipping. Across the intervening yards Desaguliers clearly heard the snap of the priest's spine.

'Down into the lower tunnels?' Tired, he heard a question in his voice that a while ago would have been an order. 'St Cyr?'

'We can defend the train-tunnels. They'd be at a disadvantage if they followed.'

He looked at the other black Rat, smiling wearily.

'Give the orders, then. Retreat. Take whoever you can with you, civilian or military. Close the tunnels after you.'

Desaguliers knelt up, one hand on the hot metal of the engine-platform.

' "You" ?' St Cyr demanded.

Desaguliers rubbed his eyes, wincing at sandpaper vision. Burned patches charred his fur; a lean black Rat, febrile, running on nervous courage and little else. One shoulder lifted in a shrug, and he winced as his sword-harness chafed a patch of raw flesh.

'I'm taking a squad of the Cadets.' He jerked his head towards the last unfallen roofs of the palace, the shattered windows of the cloverleaf-vaulted audience hall. 'His Majesty. They can't be moved, not now. But defended – possibly.'

'No!'

'No, I know,' Desaguliers said softly, 'but loyalty's a hard habit to break. In the end.'

Before St Cyr could protest again he leaped from the metal ladder to the ground, running at full tilt across the wreckage-strewn courtyard, yelling hoarsely to the Cadets as he ran.

Warmth struck. Lucas glanced up to see heating-pipes running along the vaulted arches of the Long Gallery; stopped, his breathing suddenly shallow.

Machines towered to either side. A narrow space ran down the centre of the hall, diminishing into distance all of a quarter of a mile away. Bars of light-shadow fell from clerestory windows to a polished parquet floor. Lucas held up the five-branched candelabrum. The smell of hot wax dizzied him.

'Analytical engines!'

He strode forward, barefoot, the candles held high, sword and sword-belt clashing at his hip. His kerchief, knotted about his dirty neck, tangled with carved stone talismans hanging on chains.

Ranked to either side, cogs and shafts gleaming with darkness where the Night Sun's light shafted in, the great analytical engines rose twice his height and more. He walked staring at banks of dials, levers, ornamented iron handles; moved a step closer and held up the candles to peer at the interlocking network of large and small cogwheels, springs, iron shafts and notched gearwheels.

A small iron plate shone, dye-stamped with a factory's mark. *White Mountains: Candover.*

Hot wax spattered his hand.

He winced and set the candelabrum down, absently peeling the white discs of cooling wax from his skin. They left clean marks. He unknotted his red kerchief and wiped his hands and arms, conscious of dust, oil, bloody scratches; wiped his face. He smiled wryly, scratching through his hair, now grown long enough to catch in the chains of the talismans hung about his neck.

'Gerima would call me a base mechanic. And Uncle Andaluz—!'

He turned, decisive, and strode back across the floor to the Reverend tutors. Shamar waved his arms excitedly; Pharamond rubbed at his clipped beard, and gestured for quiet; Reverend Mistress Regis tucked her blonde-red hair back behind her ears and glared severely at Lucas.

'I suggest we send this young man back to the Archemaster with a message of some description. His class-record is not such that I think we'll find him useful in an emergency. You know how irresponsible these outland princes are.'

Heat touched his ears and cheeks. Lucas pressed on doggedly. 'The message said, cheat *mathesis*—'

Pharamond put his hands behind his back.

'There are certain numbers that control the Form of the world. The formulae of force, attraction, gravitation, celestial and terrestial mechanics. These the Decans number and keep in existence. As well as those formulae that create the shapes and souls of men and beasts; formulae written deep in our cells—'

'Oh, if we *could* cheat, yes!' Shamar interrupted the easy fluency of the lecture hall. His dark eyes glowed as he looked at the ranked analytical machines.

Lucas frowned. 'I don't understand—'

'Why should you think you could understand?' Regis snapped. 'You're a first-year student, and a mostly absent one at that.'

Shamar chuckled. A lightening of the tension went through the group. Lucas, for that reason, bit back a protest.

Regis added kindly: 'You wouldn't understand. And this is an emergency.'

Light caught in the corners of Lucas's eyes, blurring his vision with silver and blue. The levers and gearwheels of the analytical engines stood out black against the windows.

'I study to be wise, but I'm not ignorant to begin with!'

He drew himself up; all the bearing of Candover's princes coming back to him now: one hand resting on the hilt of his sword, his shoulders straight as he stared at the six or eight tutors of the University of Crime.

'Do you know who I am? The Emperor of the East and the Emperor of the West meet at my father's court! Do you think his wisest tutors failed to teach me how it is *mathesis* that holds the Great Wheel of the heavens in place? It's our serfs in Candover that build these mathematical engines! Now I'll tell *you* something.'

Regis's freckles stood out darkly. She opened her mouth.

'A magus told me,' Lucas said. 'A woman who isn't sitting here safe in the university! Do you know where she is, now, this minute? She's inside the Fane . . .'

He shook his head. 'Sorry. *None* of us is safe. But I'll tell you this. Yes, you can get these machines producing the Form-numbers of all things – stars, stones, roses, bricks, butterflies. You can run the formulae. What *good* will it do us? The White Crow told me what a Decan told her. All these formulae are going to be uncreated, finally, and for good. Now.'

Breath caught in his throat.

The scent of candlewax drenched the air. Muffled by glass, the shrieks of acolytes echoed across the university's courtyards. The silence in the hall pressed on his ears. Anger drained out of him; the last of court training reasserting itself.

'I apologise, masters. I *am* hindering you; I crave your pardon. Excuse me.'

He bowed shortly. 'What shall I tell Lord Casaubon when he asks why you don't act?'

Pharamond glanced away from the group of tutors: the elderly Reverend Mistress buttonholing Shamar, haranguing him; Regis stabbing a finger at both as she interrupted; four or five others clustered down the gallery by the ranked handles of the analytical engines.

The bearded man touched the handle nearest to him, cranking it thoughtfully. Cogs shifted; numbers rolled in the dial. 'Tell him we don't, imprimis, have the manpower—'

Lucas grinned. Air bubbled in his chest; he suddenly seized the smaller man by the shoulders.

'You do,' he said. 'You do! Just wait!'

'*Prince*—'

'Believe me, you do!'

He hit the door-jamb with his shoulder, racing out into the hall; feet hitting every third step down the great polished flight of stairs. Black light shone in from perpendicular windows; a scent of burning crept in through the creaking joins of the leaded glass. Lucas skidded across polished marble tiles and hit double-doors with both hands extended.

A burst of voices quietened; he gazed out at alarmed faces in Big Hall.

'Rafi!'

'What in hell is happening?' Rafi of Adocentyn demanded. He rapidly strode towards Lucas, who shut the door behind him and seized his arm.

'Get up to Long Gallery.'

'Oh, *what*? What are you on about, Candover?'

Lucas grabbed a chair from the nearest desk, climbed on it, yelled across the heads of the assembled students. The noise-level fell a little: fifty or sixty heads turning.

'*Listen!* Get yourselves up to the Long Gallery. Do it *now*. You're going to be running the analytical engines. If we do it right, we've got a chance of clearing up this mess!'

A flurry in one corner of Big Hall: the Proctor shoved into a corner and shouted down. Almost all faces turned towards Lucas. Students he recognised shouted questions, others yelled. As if by unspoken consent they began moving closer.

'I haven't got time to explain; it doesn't *matter* if you don't know what you're doing—'

'Nor you, Prince?' one voice yelled. Lucas laughed.

'Nor me, neither. *Listen*. There's a dozen Reverend tutors up in Long Gallery and they're wetting themselves because they can't run the machines on their own. Now, I'm going back up there. Come with me if you want. If you don't, then sod you!'

He kicked the chair aside as he leaped down; it skittered across the doorway. He ran out ahead of the crowd, Rafi of Adocentyn the only one close enough to catch up as he sprinted back up the stairs.

'Candover, what the fuck are you doing?'

Lucas's steps slowed. He heard feet pounding the stairs behind, and glanced back to see the Night Sun glint from fair and dark hair, students running, yelling, laughing with the relief of action. Caught up in action, only a few spared a glance for the world outside the windows.

'I don't know.' Lucas, dizzy with shouting, grinned at Rafi's narrow puzzled face. '*I* don't know. I'm trusting these idiots who teach us to know what they're doing. I'm trusting White Crow when she says Lord Casaubon knows what he's doing.'

The dark young man frowned. 'Those two that were at Carver Street? Gods, Lucas! You're crazy.'

Lucas grabbed the back of Rafi's neck, turning the young man to look across the top of the stairwell and out of a window that overlooked the heart of the world. '*Go outside and then tell me I'm crazy!*'

He swung the doors of the Long Gallery open, holding back the heavy oak. Rafi frowned, strode through. A girl followed, two more; a fair-haired Katayan; then a rabble of a dozen, then more. He stared at their excited shouting faces, searching for something, some conception of what had occurred outside the university in this hour of the Night Sun.

'I suppose,' Pharamond's voice came from behind Lucas, 'that they don't have to know what they're doing here to do it. *You, Hilaire, walk!* Shamar, get them sorted out, will you?'

Shamar raised his hand. The warm light gallery flooded with voices, with students who ran, shouting to each other; the Reverend tutor directing each to set a dial or crank a handle.

'Lucas, listen.' Pharamond sighed, resting his arm up against the door-jamb. 'Go and tell your Archemaster we'll do what we can, but probably it's not much. Yes, now we can run the numbers. But we can't cheat to prevent the discreation.'

Lucas froze. Half-suspecting, half-speculating, he looked across at the tutor. 'What would you have to do, for that?'

'Pattern compels,' Reverend Master Pharamond said. 'As above, so below. But the influence runs both ways. Our ciphering of the numbers of the cosmos is compelled by the divine numbering of the Decans, yes. But if we could cheat, and make Their numbering dependent on *our* results, here?'

Lucas stared.

'We don't do it often, boy, but when we need to we can – usually. We cheat with our results, and that cheats the world to comply with us.'

The dark Reverend Master, Shamar, approached the door and

paused as he came up with them. 'Pharamond, we've always said
we could do it, but could we? Really?'

'Not without the mechanical skills!' Pharamond nodded his head
sharply at the ranked lines of levers.

'Mechanical skills.' Lucas paused, breath tight in his throat.

'We'd have to gear the machines for the results we want, not the
results it'll give us now, considering what's going on out there in
the city. But . . .' Pharamond shrugged. 'The faculty's mechanics
aren't resident in the university.'

'Where will we find them?'

Regis's deep laughter echoed back from the Long Gallery. 'Find
them? *Find* them? In that chaos out there?'

'She's right,' the bearded man said. 'She's right.'

Lucas reached out and rested his dirty hand against the
stamped plate of Candover on the nearest engine. A quietness had
fallen in the Long Gallery, most of the young men and women
over the immediate excitement of their arrival. He heard their
voices, saw how they watched him speaking with the Reverend
tutors.

'I – it wouldn't be any use – well, it might—'

Regis snorted. Pharamond held up a hand, arresting what she
might have said; moved it to tap Shamar's shoulder for the dark
man's attention.

Heat coloured his face; Lucas shifted his feet, stared at the floor.

'I don't want my father ever to know this! That I've been mixing
with serfs, or with the trade of *thaumaturgike*, or— The truth of it is,
I know how these machines are put together. I think the Lord
Casaubon must know that: we've talked. I used to . . . to sneak
away and spend a lot of time in the workshops.'

The silence bit into him like acid. Somewhere down the hall, a
richly amused voice that sounded like the Prince of Adocentyn said:

' "Trade"!'

Raising his head, and with an odd dignity that belonged neither
to the past nor to Candover, Lucas said: 'Master Pharamond, I can
probably get these machines to do whatever you want them to. I
was in the workshops when the Mark Four was being designed. But
if you don't have any other mechanics here, and there's only me—'

Voices shattered the quiet hall: Regis protesting, Shamar protesting, and the bearded Reverend Master's voice drowning them both
out: 'Yes! We'll do it! We can argue afterwards if it was worthwhile,
if there is an afterwards. Masters, we stand in such a place that *any*
help we give is worthwhile. Regis, love, go and get the students
organised – Shamar, you, too. Good!'

He swung round, speaking over the clatter as they ran down the Gallery: 'Candover. Tools down there; if you need anything, ask for it. Take a look, then I'll tell you what you've got to do.'

'Yes . . .'

Lucas, Prince of Candover, unbuckled his sword and hung it by the belt on the back of the door. He walked across to squat, sit and finally slide himself down into the concrete sump under the first engine.

He picked up and adjusted a wrench, fingers black with oil; paused, looking up through the interlocking rods and gears.

'If this happens to help you, it's more than I have a right to ask.' Prayer not seeming relevant now, he contented himself with breathing her names: 'White Crow. Valentine.'

Loud footsteps clattered down the hall, each student going to set a dial or heave on a lever; shouting, voices edged half with fear and half with a wild excitement. Returning, Pharamond's voice vibrated with the same emotion: 'Do *exactly* what I tell you.'

Lucas, listening, reached up with the wrench to adjust the first gear.

Footsteps pounded past. Out among the debris and rubble of Fourteenth District's square, the last unwary Rats ran towards barricaded doors and tunnel-entrances. The undercarriage of the siege-engine shook deafeningly: liquid fire hissed up into the air.

'Ei, *you*!'

A torn edge of blue and yellow satin whisked past the Lord-Architect Casaubon's vision. A sharp and very solid finger poked him in the rump.

'Where's my bloody rent, you oversized fraud?'

Casaubon, straightening, clipped one ear-lobe painfully against the underside of the engine as his heel skidded in leaked oil. He grunted, backing out without turning until he could stand up.

'I *beg* your pardon?'

A woman of perhaps forty folded her arms under her ample bodice. Yellow coils of hair fell across her ripped satin dress. Oblivious of the now-deserted New Temple site, the other buildings' neo-classical doors barricaded with torn-up marble paving-slabs, ignoring the Guards up on the siege-engine platform, and the broken windows from which musket-muzzles jutted, Evelian stared up at the Lord-Architect with glassy determination.

'You heard me! You owe me a month's back rent! *Where is it?*'

'I – that is – unavoidably absent—'

Casaubon picked up his blue satin frock-coat, drawing it on over his filthy shirt. He drew himself up to his full six foot five, looked down over his swelling chest and belly, and shrugged magnificently. He spoke over the thunder of approaching wings.

'Mistress Evelian, I was, and *am*, busy. Now, if you don't mind—'

'That brat Lucas landed you on me, but the university's never heard of you; *they* won't pay me! If I can't get coin from them, I intend bartering those crates you left behind for whatever I can get for them!'

Casaubon absently retrieved a half-eaten lamb chop from an inner pocket, and paused in the act of biting into it.

'Are you mad? Absolutely *not*.'

'Calling yourself a Lord-Architect; I don't believe that for a minute.'

'Aw, *Mother*!'

A straggle-haired fifteen-year-old ran around from the other side of the siege-engine. She glanced up once at the brown Rats loading Greek fire into the ballista. A torn yellow-and-white sash had been tied over her plasterer's silk overalls.

'Get down!' She pushed the older blonde woman towards the side of the engine, her face upturned to the Night Sun.

'Don't *interrupt*, Sharlevian.'

The Lord-Architect Casaubon wiped grease off his chin with the back of his hand, smearing machine oil across his fair skin. He replaced the half-eaten chop in a deep outer pocket of his coat. 'Get under cover somewhere, rot you! I don't have time for this pox-damned nonsense!'

'Wanna go home,' the blonde girl said pugnaciously.

Evelian put her fists on her hips. 'I'm going nowhere until I get this account settled!'

'*Ah*.' A new, male voice cut in. 'Messire, do you have any authority here? Can you tell me who does? I wish to register the strongest-possible complaint—'

A *thunk!* and hiss from the ballista drowned his words. The Lord-Architect nestled his chin into three several layers of fat, looking down at a middle-aged, rotund and sweating man. A verdigrised chain hung about the man's neck.

'Tannakin Spatchet. Mayor of Nineteenth District east quarter.'

The Lord-Architect Casaubon rested his weight back on his right heel, planted his ham-fist on his hip, and raised his chin. He surveyed the woman, the girl and the middle-aged man; let his gaze travel past them to the battered façades of buildings surrounding the square, and the azure sky dark with acolytes and the Night Sun.

'A lesser man would be confused by this,' he rumbled plaintively.
'My *rent*—'

'We can't stand out here in the open—!'

'Severe damage to life and p-property—'

The Lord-Architect, ignoring the man's stutter, reached down
with plump delicate fingers. A dark glint shone among the links of
the Mayor's chain. He lifted a carved stone hanging on a separate
chain.

'You hired a Scholar-Soldier! Damn me if that isn't Valentine's
work.'

Tannakin Spatchet frowned, bemused.

'White Crow.' Seeing him nod, Casaubon let the talisman fall
back. Another glyptic pendant rested in the division of Evelian's
breasts; and a third, the chain lapping round several times, hung
from Sharlevian's left wrist.

A crackle of musket-fire echoed from the engine-platform above
their heads. Casaubon winced. Clouds of dust skirred up.

The Lord-Architect rubbed his stinging eyes, swore; grabbed
Evelian's elbow and pulled her into the shelter of his bolster-arm
as a daemon tail, a bristling thick cable, whiplashed down and
cracked across the marble paving.

Stone chippings spanged off the side of the siege-engine.

Evelian glared. 'My—'

'*Rent*, yes, I know,' the Lord-Architect muttered testily. 'Rot you,
get up on the machine. *All* of you. Safer. Move!'

He caught Sharlevian by the scruff of her overalls and pushed;
looked round for Spatchet and saw him already halfway up the
ladder to the platform. Following mother and daughter, the Lord-
Architect swung himself ponderously up the metal rungs.

'And stop that!' He batted one hand irritably towards the ballista.
A brown Rat in Guard uniform yelled for a temporary cease-fire.

Above, the wings of acolytes cracked the air. Bristle-tails lashed
down. The portico of a nearby house fragmented: stone splinters
shrapnelled. A balcony collapsed and spilled six Rats and two men
down into the rubble of the square.

The Lord-Architect Casaubon pushed through the Guards to the
back of the platform and knelt down. He folded back the deep cuffs
of his satin coat, and scratched thoughtfully in the hair over his ear,
peering down at the back axle.

Wheel-tracks and spilled oil marked their arrival, the tracks
diminishing back down the avenue by which they had entered the
square.

The Night Sun's black light gleamed on the marble frontages of temples, palaces, banks and offices on the surrounding hills; glinting from the horizons of the cityscape, from the very top of the Fane-in-the-Twelfth-District.

His china-blue eyes vague for a moment, he touched a filthy hand to his mouth, frowning. His lips moved, framed a word that might have been a woman's name. Inaudible in the roar of falling masonry, the shrieking and beat of wings.

'What are you *doing*?' Sharlevian demanded.

She collapsed into a sitting position beside him, silver-chain earrings dangling, narrow face pale. Remnants of yellow and white paint clung to her jaw and ears and hair-line. She clutched his arm, the bitten fingernails on her hand pulling threads from the satin.

'Hey!'

Casaubon's free hand went to one of his pockets. He dug in it, brought out a roast chicken-wing, absently offering it to Sharlevian. She sat back, disgust on her face. The Lord-Architect shoved the chicken-wing back; dug again, and his hand emerged clutching the small sextant. Still kneeling, he sighted up at the Night Sun.

He beamed.

'At *last*,' he said.

He prised his fat fingers under one of the iron plates on the platform, opening it up. The ends of two thickly plaited cables of bare copper wire shone in the Night Sun's light. Wrapping each of his hands in the tails of his frock-coat, he carefully twisted the cables together and slammed the hatch shut.

Sparks leaped.

He sat back, grabbing Sharlevian's shoulder. The girl fell against him. Heads turned at the searing actinic light.

For a split second it clung to the siege-engine: St Elmo's fire. Rat Guards cursed, swore, beating sparks from their uniforms. Mistress Evelian's gaze abruptly focused: she seized the Mayor's arm.

Searing blue-white light ran to the ground, to the spilled trail of oil staining the flagstones. Tiny blue flames licked up; then a thin rippling aurora-curtain of light. It sprang up from the spilled-oil trail, running powder-train swift back down the engine's tracks, down the avenue away from the square.

Wildfire-fast, spreading, running, the aurora-curtain of blue light sped up towards the distant hills, cornered, curved, divided and divided again: a brilliant track across the streets the siege-engine had followed.

The Lord-Architect Casaubon grasped one of the ballista struts. It creaked as he pulled himself up, foot scrabbling for a hold, until he saw the hills surrounding the docks and the airfield, the great city stretching away to every compass-point to the horizon.

Far in the distance other light-curtains began to spring up, thin as the spilled trail of oils from other siege-engines.

The electric-blue aurora tracery wavered, rising into the air, hovered at roof-level here, grew taller further off, shorter in other Districts. The Lord-Architect raised one great fist, punched the air; seams straining and at last popping under the arm of his frock-coat.

'Aw, I don't . . .' Sharlevian's puzzlement trailed off.

The light-threads of the labyrinth threaded the city streets, spreading far, far out of sight, following the oil-trails from specially constructed cisterns in each engine. Out through avenues and streets and alleys to all thirty-six Districts and all hundred and eighty-one quarters; netting the city that is called the heart of the world in a bright maze.

Sharlevian, at his elbow, wiped her nose on the back of her hand and sniffed. 'So you *are* an architect. They taught us the Chymicall Labyrinth in Masons' Hall. We build that pattern into our homes sometimes. But what *good* is it?'

One fat finger raised, the Lord-Architect Casaubon paused. His head cocked sideways as if he listened for faint music. The black shadows of the Fane's acolytes fell across him, across the square, thousand upon thousand.

Wheeling. Turning.

Thousands, tens of thousands wheeling and turning as one.

Unwilling, constrained, they wheeled in their flights: gliding on burning wings to fly the pattern of the labyrinth. And *only* the pattern of the labyrinth.

Casaubon lowered his hand. Breath touched his oil-stained cheek, a remembrance of the heat in the Garden of the Eleventh Hour: the roses, and the black extinct bees that fly the knot garden's subtle geometries.

'Don't they teach you apprentices anything in your pox-rotted Masons' Halls?' he rumbled. 'Patterns compel, structures compel. Will you *look* at that? Rot her, why can't Valentine be with me to see this?'

The acolytes of the Fane flocked, falling to fly the pattern of the burning labyrinth. Great ribbed wings spread under the Night Sun, blistering with its heat; bristle-tails flicked the air. Beaks and jaws opened to cry, cry agony.

Sparing no glance from blind black eyes for human or for Rat-Lord; tearing no stone from stone; uprooting no roofs now. Only gliding upon hot thermals, rising and falling; flurried wings lashing and falling again to a glide, compelled by the maze-pattern drawn in city streets that now they gaze on. Sightless gaze and are trapped, under the black scorching sun.

Across the city that is called the heart of the world, the labyrinth burns.

Pain hollowed each air-filled bone.

Cold air pressed every planing pinion as the white crow wheeled again, rising to glide down vaulted hills. A bird's side-set eyes reflected perpendicular arches, stone tracery, fan vaulting: a white desert of shaped stone.

'Crraaa-aak!'

Frosted air sleeked the feathers of her breast. She tilted aching wings, pain catching her in joints whose muscles still, at cell-level, remember being human. The scents of rotting hay, of weed left behind at equinoctial tides impinged sharply on her bird-senses.

'Craaa-akk-k!'

The white crow wheeled again and skimmed a long gallery. Age-polished stone flashed back her fragmented image, an albino hooded bird. She flew wearily from the gallery, wings beating deep strokes.

What use is it to search for the dying . . . ?

She lifted a wing-tip and soared. Pain flashed down nerve and sinew. She welcomed it. When her body no longer remembers that it was other and ceases to pain, she will have become what she is shaped to.

No one tell me that the Decan of Noon and Midnight has no sense of humour . . .

The internal voice seemed hers, forcing its way through avian synapses. Double images curved across the surface of her bright bird's eyes: the great pillars of the Fane seeming spears, soon to tumble into confusion as after a battle. The air resisted her wings so that they beat slowly, slowly; time itself slowing.

The great depths of the Fane opened around her. Masonry crumbling with age; floors worn down into hollows by aeons of divine tread. Lost ages built in stone: the Fanes that are one Fane, the inhabitation of god on earth. Built out as a tree grows, ring upon ring, hall and gallery and tower, nave and crypt and chapel. Growing, encrusting as a coral reef.

And as for what Rat-Lord and human empires rose and fell while this gallery was building, or what lovers and children died while these columns were cutting . . .

She stretched wide wings and lay herself on the air, letting it bear her; the voice in her head that is still Valentine and White Crow less frenetic now, slowing with the depths of millennia opening out.

They're not idols, magia or oracles. They're the Thirty-Six, the principles that structure the world. Why did we think we could go up against them? Why did we think that anything we did would not be what they ordained, even to the Uncreation?

'Craaaa-akk!'

She flew into the Fane of the Third Decan.

Into a hall in which cathedrals might have been lost, colours blotting her sight. Bright images burned in what should be perpendicular windows, but no light is needed to illuminate these shafts of colour. To either side they shine, fiery as the hearts of suns, scarlets and blues and golds: depicting dunes, lizards, beasts of the desert; ragged stars, comets and constellations long pushed apart by Time.

Depths swung sickeningly below her wings as she dived. Her instincts human, flight is precarious. She cawed, hard and harsh, the sound recognisable as a bird's copy of human speech.

'Xerefu! Akeru! Lord of Yesterday and Tomorrow!'

An ornate marble tomb towered in the centre of the nave, gleaming white and gold and onyx-black. Her wings held the air as she curved in flight around the pomegranate-ornamented pillars, the scarabs cut into the great base and pedestal.

A great scorpion shape crowned the tomb, thrice the height of a church spire.

White stone articulated the carapace of the scorpion: its high-curving tail and sting, great moon-arced claws. The segmented body gleamed hollow. Chill air drifted between the joints of the shell, caressing angular legs, clustered eyes. A scent of old dust haunts the air.

'Xerefu! Akeru!'

Time frosted the stone exoskeleton beneath her wings, shimmering as if ice runs over the fabric that, after aeons of divine incarnation, is no longer stone.

'We do not fear.'

Air whispers between the carapace-joints. The jointed tail quivers, a point of light sparkling at the tip of the hollow sting.

'We do not fear, as you do. We may choose now to incarnate Ourselves in the celestial world and not here on earth. Or We may raze this world and begin again. The game does not weary Us.'

The white crow wheeled across the cliff-face of the image, time stretching as she skimmed the distance between moon-curved claw and claw. Her heart pounded more rapidly than a watch, ticking away her slight bird's lifespan.

'Sick! Sick! You have! Plague here!'

Her travesty of human voice cawed, echoing from hollow shells. One serrated claw shifts. A shining globe-eye dulled as she flew past, and crumbling stone dust drifted down on the air.

'Xerefu! Akeru!'

The whispering air lies silent.

The hollow stone that incarnates the Decan of Beginnings and Endings, the Lord of the Night of Time, two-aspected and of two separate speeches, begins to crumble into fragments.

'Craa-akk-kk!'

Wing-tips beat down against unyielding air. The white crow folded wings to body and dived, feathers out-thrust to brake and sending her whirling into the passage and stairs to a crypt. Her wings clipped the corner of the wall. Falling stone misses her by a heartbeat.

Out of the crypt: now great rounded pillars rose up to either side of her. She flew on a level with their carved tops: human faces tall as ship's masts, with lilies growing from their mouths and eye-sockets. The corded stone columns sheered down into the depths of the Fane below. She flew too hard and too high to see what lies there.

The white crow flew under ribbed vaults, and into the Fane of the Twenty-Sixth Decan.

A ledge reared up.

One wing-tip flicked up in shock; she skidded to land, claws scrabbling, on an ancient surface. The white crow folded her wings. She raised her head, jerking her beak from side to side, rawly disgusted at ridiculousness no human eye can see.

Hard as mountains under aeons of permafrost, the ledge chilled her.

'Chnoumen! Destroyer of Hearts!'

The ledge ran around the inside of a domed round hall, the colour of old blood. Gold veined the red walls. Arched, huge; too vast even for echoes. Her bird's vision brought her sight of black line paintings on the dull red: thirty-six images colouring the walls around the three-hundred-and-sixty-degree circle. Too distant for their subjects to be deciphered.

'Chnachoumen! Opener of Hundreds and Thousands of Years!'

The floor of this round hall, blood red and blood dark, ripples: stone becoming liquid. She tilted her head, staring down. The stink of rotting weed dizzied her. Under the surface of the water, dark shapes moved.

'You have no business here.'

Translucent suddenly: glowing transparently scarlet as arterial blood, the interior sea ripples with white and gold light. Carved in planes of diamond, the coils of a great kraken fill up the pool. Tentacles curve, sinuous. The Decan of Judgments and Passing incarnate in adamant.

'Divine One!'

The white crow paces the ledge jerkily; cocking her head to one side to clearly see ahead. Scales shine on the beaked head of the kraken. But a dim film covers the golden eyes. She steels her voice to discipline.

'Divine One, if you created us you owe us something. You at least owe us the acknowledgment that we have universes inside *us*!'

The arterial scarlet of the inland sea lightened, becoming rose. The living diamond of the Decan's limbs coiled into rose-petal patterns. Liquid tones hissed from the domed ceiling and walls, amused.

'Why else should We take on flesh, but that for flesh has such universes within it?'

Her harsh crow's laughter lost itself in the spaces of immensity.

'To hurt? To be cold, to be hot? To bleed, kiss, fuck, shit? To eat? To love?'

'Child of flesh, We have loved Our creation, but nothing lasts, not even love.'

Her clawed feet slipped. A flake of red stone crumbled from the ledge.

She flicked into flight without thought, skimming down to follow it: this substance that should not be subject to time and decay. Her pinions spread, the wide-fingered wings of a crow. From the red water, rose light shone up through her feathers.

Heat scalded.

The stench of a butcher's shambles choked her. She flung herself up into suddenly blazing air, wings thrashing, blindly flying: one glimpse of water turned thickly bloody and the threshing of diamond limbs left imprinted double behind her eyes.

'Craa-akk!'

Gravity pulled her: not down, but onwards. The white crow spread her wings to their widest. The changing stone spun past below her feathered body. The names of Decans beat in the confines of her brain and blood: *Chnoumen, Chnachoumen, Knat, Biou, Erou, Erebiou, Rhamanoor, Rheianoor* . . .

A faint echo came down one high hall, a whisper caught out of time:

' "*I also know how difficult it is to get thirty-six of anybody to agree on anything and act as one.*" '

She cawed a crow's harsh bitter laughter.

A wall reared up before her. Her wing-tips brushed an arch of brick. Small smooth ochre bricks; the ghost of sun's warmth in their depth. The touch against her feathers froze her through to her hollowed bones.

Her feathered shadow skipped across a courtyard.

Black roses lay worm-eaten, tangled, dead in the Garden of the Eleventh Hour. The gravels of the knot garden lay smeared, patternless.

The crow's wings flapped slowly, curving into a descent.

A brown blight covered the brickwork eaten away by lichen. Grubs gnawed the leaves of black roses. Tiny curled dots showed on the earth, black bees lying dead.

The sky above shone brown, yellow, the colour of paper about to burst into flame.

'Divine One! Lady! Of the Eleventh Hour!'

The white crow wheeled, feathers cutting the air, gliding to land among ivy and lichen at the base of the great brick paw. The sand-bright sphinx bulked above her, mortar crumbling from between ochre bricks: the Decan of the Eleventh Hour, of Ten Degrees of High Summer, the Lady of Shining Force.

A crow is a large bird, some eighteen inches from beak to tail, and unwieldy: she landed heavily in a skirr of feathers. She raised her head, double vision shining with the ivy-bitten forepaws and breasts and head of the god-daemon.

'Divine One, you see all. Know all. Are all. The Decan of Noon and Midnight sends me. To tell you the Great Circle of the world breaks now.'

A sand-blast of heat breathes from Her curving lips.

'*It is so.*'

'To tell you. If it can be re-created from chaos. There won't be Thirty-Six, but One. I begin to see – why he wishes it. What other change – can omnipotence *desire*? What else could be impossible?'

The brick-curved linen draperies of Her head drift dust into the air. The lids of Her slanting eyes slide up. A gaze as pitiless as deserts impaled the crow.

'*I am omnipotent, child of flesh, and I do not desire non-being. If I tire of this world, I will make more. If I tire of the cosmos, I will make things other than universes. It has been long and long that I have guided the Great Wheel, long and long that I have created and changed it; it shall be longer still before I weary of all that is and all that can be.*'

Gravel chilled her bird-claws. Silence shimmered in the Garden. The white crow strutted on the earth, making a movement of wings and body oddly like a human shrug. She stabbed a hard carrion-tearer's beak at the air.

'He's weary. The Spagyrus.'

'*Flesh corrupts him. We do not weary unless we choose. It is not beyond us to forget, when we weary. Each springtime is the first of the world. Each winter the ending of an aeon. We need not weary of it.*'

'You can't let him!'

The Decan's head tilts, facing down to the earth; to the bird strutting among dead rose briars and the curled bodies of black bees. Aeons of deserts under noon fire and arctic cold burn in Her eyes, burn with the pain of fissure, dissolution, decay.

The white crow's wings open slightly, on the verge of panic flight.

'*Gods are not permitted, or hindered. If He can uncreate, then that is well. If He can uncreate us all, then that is well. All things done by the Divine are well.*'

'Naw!' The bird's croak sawed the air: comic, ludicrous before the Decan of the Eleventh Hour. 'No! You're wrong!'

'*The Divine are not wrong, child of flesh, for whatever we do is right, because it is We who act.*'

'You sent! Me! To heal!'

'*For then it would have been I who was right, and not the Lord of Noon and Midnight. Child of flesh, heal if you will. If you can. Until now, the hour had not yet quite come – but it has come, now.*'

'*Now.*'

'*It is time and the Hour is striking!*'

The white crow's feathers flurried as she strutted across the gravel, the earth that smelt faintly of mould, of rot, of corruption. Black bird-eyes glimmered, piercing. Her heavy beak stabbed the ground before great brick claws that, closing around her, could have cracked her like a flea.

Human speech cracked out of her as a thrush cracks a snail: shattering, raw.

'Who! Dies! Now! *Who?*'

The Decan weeps.

Lids slide down over Her eyes that hold deserts, rise to show the diamond-dust of tears. A shadow begins to cover Her breasts. Her head is raised as if she listens to the striking of some inaudible hour.

'*Cannot you tell, child of earth?*

'*It is he, the Decan of Noon and Midnight. How else may he hope to be One, who is one of Thirty-Six, unless he can uncreate and self-create himself? He must die, truly, to create himself again out of non-being, and if he cannot – why, then. Nothing. For Us all.'*

'How! Can! You! Allow!'

'We foresee it will be so. Create it will be so. Past his death we cannot see nor create.'

The corruption of plague shines in the desert eyes of the god-daemon.

Past speech, past debate, past miracle; the weight of aeons waits for the moment in which this may exist: true death.

'No! Hrrrakk-kk! No!'

Battered by a Divine suffering that no mortal flesh can behold, avian or human, the white crow flees, flying out into the Fane.

'You're a fool! Hrrrrakk! I won't! Let you! Do this!'

Wings beat, her frail heart pulsing urgency, sensing how in the air it trembles now; the striking of the noon of the Night Sun.

CHAPTER 8

Becalmed.

Black water slopped. Fog coiled across its cold surface. The one lantern's yellow light made no reflection in the water.

The forgetfulness of the Boat pulled at Zar-bettu-zekigal, at every cell in her body. Her eyes darkened with Memory.

'You always *call* me buzzard because I used to sound like one. When I was a baby. *Mee-oo*,' Zar-bettu-zekigal called. '*Mee-oo*.'

The harsh sound echoed back flatly from fog and darkness. She walked across the deck, the untied laces of her black ankle-boots ticking on the wood, arms wrapped about herself. 'See you, El, you remember that.'

The older Katayan woman sat cross-legged at the stern, by the lantern, one hand resting on the tiller of the Boat, lace ruffles falling over her wrist. A frown of intense concentration twisted her face.

'More.'

'Oh, what! See you, I'll tell you about the first time I ever met Messire . . . It was in an austquarter crypt. He said, *Students, Charnay, but of a particular talent. The young woman is a Kings' Memory.* And then: *You're young, all but trained, as I take it, and without a patron. My name is Plessiez. In the next few hours I – we – will badly need a trusted record of events. Trusted by both parties. If I put that proposition to you?*'

She squatted down in front of Elish-hakku-zekigal.

'Trust me, El?'

Sweat plastered the woman's black curls to her forehead; her pallid face seemed stained, under the eyes, with brown. Elish's lips moved silently, concentrating on the voice, following Memory's bright thread.

'I remember what you said to me when I left South Katay. *Learn hard, little buzzard, it opens all the world to you, and you're a wanderer. I'll be here to hear your tales*. I love you, Elish. I'll always come back and see you.'

Zar-bettu-zekigal knelt, hands on her knees, tail coiled up about her hips. She leaned forward to study the compass rose set into the deck before the shaman woman. The needle moved ceaselessly, swinging in five ninety-degree arcs around the circle, in turn to all five points of the compass. She sat back, willing Elish the power to steer through the amnesia of the Boat, stronger now with night and nightmares haunting its drifting.

'Listen, there's more—'

Outside her circle of Memory's voice, fleering mirror faces begin to gather.

The torch pitched forward, flaring soot across the floor.

His vision cleared.

Plessiez climbed to his feet, rubbing his haunch. Mist hung above him, choking the brick shaft they descended. He made to pick up the torch, and stopped.

The guttering torches on the stairwell shone down on a distorted curving brick floor that crested up, curved down in hollows, rippled out in frozen curves. The last of these steps had not been the last, once. It lay embedded in a tide of brick paving that had *flowed*, like water. His torch rocked in a deep hollow.

Brushwood rustled. Sound hissed back from the walls, with the drip of water. Nitre spidered white patterns. Plessiez stepped down into the hollow, bending to pick up his torch. Flames glimmered blackly along the pitch. The fingers of his other hand cramped on his rapier's hilt; the point circling, alert.

On the steps above a voice Charnay's and not Charnay's hissed: '*Go back little animal go back go die go away!*'

He spun, sword raised. 'What?'

Her blunt snout lowered, regarding him. She frowned. 'I said, this is strangely altered since the last time we ventured down here.'

'You – heard nothing?'

'Heard?' Charnay stared past him. A constricted passage some six feet high remained between roof and floor. This tunnel, lightless now, hissed unidentifiable echoes back.

'Bring another torch.'

The brown Rat trod heavily. Her scaly tail lashed debris on the steps: brick rubble, desiccated wood, the brown knobs of animal vertebrae. She tugged her stained blue sash across her chest, scratching at her furred dugs.

Brick gave way underfoot to earth and gravel.

He held up his torch, blinking. The yellow light and black smoke of burning pitch faded into a wider open space.

Twin gibbets now stood by the entrance to the catacombs.

Outlined in a pale silver glow, their nests of chains hung down, wound about bones, ragged flesh, cerements.

'*Those* weren't here before.'

Gravel crunched under the brown Rat's clawed feet. Charnay rested a hand against one of the white marble obelisks that flanked the opening, staring up at the inscription. She snorted.

' *"Halt! Here begins the Empire of the Dead . . ."* You always did have odd humours, messire.'

'*Magia* indicated this one of the septagon sites, not I.'

All perspective vanished in darkness. No torches burned inside the catacombs. Cold struck up from the gravelled earth beneath his clawed feet. A smell of nitre and dank mud sank into his fur.

'Charnay . . .'

Sound whispered back from the galleries.

'. . . you would do me a greater favour, I think, to go back up the shaft and guard the way against our over-enthusiastic follower.'

A hand clamped on his shoulder. The brown Rat stared him in the face, lowering her head to do it.

'I'm not in the business of doing you favours, Plessiez, man. I don't trust you. You see your own advantage in matters very clearly. I don't trust you not to work out some even more clever plot, and make things even worse.' She cut him off before he could interrupt. 'I don't *like* all of this. I want things back to normal. You're going in to put an end to this, and I'm going to be at your back every step of the way!'

She drew a deep breath. Plessiez, shaken, turned his gaze pointedly to where she gripped his shoulder. After a long minute her fingers loosened.

'You were compliant enough when it was a matter of a little sickness among the human servants, and the Decans our masters being persuaded to remove further off—'

'Ahh!' The Lieutenant spat. She held up the torch, shadows leaping violently in the gibbets' chains. 'You and his Majesty are a pair of fools, all of you. Now this dangerous nonsense with black suns and acolytes out of control – and you call *me* stupid, messire priest!'

A knob of bone rattled across the earth, rolling to rest at Plessiez's feet. 'I think . . . I think we should go back.'

Muted light dazzled his eyes as she lowered the torch, peering at him.

'Obviously we can do no good here; it was idiocy to suggest so.' Plessiez faced about, putting his back to the catacomb-entrance. One-handed and with some difficulty he sheathed his rapier. 'I

don't have the knowledge, I don't have the equipment for *magia*;
we should retreat and reconsider this. Perhaps return later, better
equipped. You as a soldier will recognise the sense in this.'

His tail twitched an inch one way, an inch back; he fell to
grooming the fur of his shoulder for a moment.

'*What?*' Charnay demanded.

'I've told you. We're leaving. We'll return here in due course.'

The brown Rat said: 'You're going in there.'

Plessiez leaned his hand up against the brown brick wall. Nitre
sweated under his long-fingered hands. He lowered his head for a
second, then lifted it, staring up at the rusting gibbet-chains, and
the white-painted inscription across the entrance.

'No,' he said, 'No.'

'Plessiez, man—'

'*I won't do it!*'

Echoes hissed off the low walls. Cold and damp struck deeper,
chilling blood and bone. A soft chuckle rustled through the chains
of the gibbets. The black Rat leaned dizzily against the brickwork.

'Now I envy you. Charnay, I would to gods I had your thick skull
and your ability not to foresee.'

The brown Rat lugged out her long sword, leaning the point on
the earth. She cocked her head to one side, a frown on her blunt
muzzle. 'Messire, *I* don't know what to do in there.'

'Neither do I!'

The black Rat rubbed his hand across his face, smoothing fur that
slicked up in tufts. His eyes glinted darkly, meeting Charnay's.

'Now, listen to me, Lieutenant Charnay. I suspect that when we
emerge on the surface it will be to find the servants, humans and
all, in confusion. H'm? Their temple destroyed, their ranks thinned
by pestilence.'

Plessiez picked at his incisors with one broken claw.

'His Majesty, gods preserve them, I fear to be dead, if what young
Fleury said is true. And the Lords of the Celestial Sphere, one might
prophesy, *returned* to that plane and only overlooking our earth
with their Divine providence. All which, if I am right, leaves clear
room for one determined in his aims. He – he and his friends,
Charnay – might do much, now, in the government of the heart of
the world.'

'*You're going in there.*'

The black Rat knelt, driving the shaft of the torch into the soft
earth and gravel. He got to his feet slowly. Black eyes bright, he
said: 'No. Not for my life. No.'

Silver glinted on the onyx rings on his fingers, on the headband that looped over one translucent pink ear and under the other; shimmered on the black feather plume that moved with his breathing. Nothing of the priest about him now: more gone than *ankh* and insignia. Charnay took in his febrile tension.

'I'm not a fool.' She shrugged. 'I know enough to be afraid. Leave *magia* alone and working for weeks, and the gods alone know what it's become now! But we don't have any choice. I told the Night Council that if you destroyed one of the seven points it would stop the necromancy working. Get in there and *do* it. You promised the little Kings' Memory.'

The black Rat turned his head, staring into the depths of the catacombs. He scratched at the back of his head, sliding a dark palm round to rub his snout as he lowered his arm.

'So I did.'

He shuddered: cold drifting out from the low arch of the catacombs. A visible pulse beat in the soft fur of his throat. His sword-harness clinked.

'What will you do now, my friend?'

The brown Rat, torch and long rapier in her hands, blocked the way back to the stairs. Her eyes narrowed. She thrust her torch at him so suddenly that he must grasp it or be singed; swung the sword up two-handed, and cut at the rusty chains.

Bones and cloth hit the earth; Plessiez skittered back. Charnay, backhanding, cut at the other gibbet. The rusty chains resisted; the rotten wood of the support cracked loud as musket-shot, teetered, and fell forward into darkness.

'Now you're equipped, messire. Now *move*.'

A hard knot of tension under his breastbone, Plessiez knelt, holding high the torch, swiftly and distastefully fumbling through the heaps of bones. What seemed most useful he wrapped in cerements; after a moment's hesitation tucking the bundle securely under his sword-belt.

'Well, then,' he said. 'Well.'

Damp cold prickled his spine, and he stepped forward with his tail carried fastidiously high. Smoke from the pitch made his eyes run with water. He raised the torch as he walked through the catacomb-entrance. Shadows of rib and pelvic bones danced on the cavern walls.

At his right hand rose the beginning of a wall of bones.

Forearm and thigh bones, laid crosswise like kindling and as brown, built up a retaining wall a head taller than himself. Into the space between the arm and leg bones and the cavern wall, ribs and vertebrae, carpals and metacarpals, pelvic bones and all else had been carelessly thrown. Along the top of the wall, jammed jowl to jowl, lay skulls. Rows of skulls jutting their eyeless long snouts into darkness, yellow incisors impossibly long.

The brown bone glowed, sprinkled with nitre as with frost.

Skulls, set into the walls of knobbed bone joints, made patterns of chevrons and *ankh*s; and long intact skeins of tail-vertebrae snaked around them, jammed in tight.

'We can be followed in here.' Charnay rescued the other torch, waving it to cast light down the curving passages and cross-passages of the royal catacombs. Another wall rose beside her; unencumbered with torch and rapier she could have stood in the centre of the passage and touched a hand to both.

'And outdistanced . . .'

Plessiez paced forward, torch high. Black shadows darted in the hollow rings of eye-sockets, in the channels of snouts, and over incisors still clinging to bony jaws. The brown Rat held her torch close to the white marble plaque, one of a number set into the wall at intervals.

' "*Behold these bones, the . . . the nest . . .*" '

Plessiez completed, rapidly and accurately enough to put down some of his terror, ' ". . . *the nest of each fledgling soul.*" Poor poetry, I fear, but his Majesty's taste was always less than highbrow—'

He broke off as the hilt of the brown Rat's sword nudged him. Without looking back, he walked into the catacombs and silence.

'And if it were only true, now, further in!'

The interior of the plague-tent shone, full of light-shadows.

Shock chilled her back to reality. Evelian stepped outside and let the canvas flap fall to behind her. She rubbed a work-roughened hand across her face.

'I've . . . found Falke for you.'

Her skin sweated, despite the Night Sun's chill. Slanting bars of light-shadow fell from the Imperial pavilions down into Fourteenth District's square. Gold-and-white banners hung limp, the canvas cloth now thickened with ice. Frost glimmered on shattered masonry, on abandoned muskets and greaves and shoes thrown together in a pile by the Rat-Lords' clear-up details.

'The master builder? Here?'

Through blazing black light, the Lord-Architect came towards her from the construction site, moving with a frighteningly rapid stride.

'He's . . . *Falke* . . . When he was a boy, we used to talk about all this. About House of Salomon and how we should build . . . I swore

I'd never get mixed up in it again after it failed the first time, but what would you? Poor bastard.'

She drew a noisy breath, huffed it out; dizzy with shock.

'*All* those poor bastards.'

The fat man's tread shook the paving-stones. She automatically stepped out of his way. She smelt machine oil and sweaty linen. The Lord-Architect Casaubon threw the tent-flap open, staring past her, to where the plague-dead lay stacked like winter wood.

'Rot him, I *needed* him!'

Casaubon pushed past her into the tent, the bulk of his body brushing aside her and the canvas with equal impatience. Evelian stared. Outrage flared in her, old temper reasserting itself.

'Damn you, man, what right do you have to say that? What right do you have not to care that he's dead?'

'Oh, I care!'

She turned her eyes away from the laid-out rows of men and women. Some wrapped in blankets or cloaks; some in summer clothing, still with the traces of lead-and-ochre paint on their faces. Afraid of how many she might recognise under the black disfigurement of plague.

'You *can't*—' Evelian stopped. The Lord-Architect Casaubon knelt down by Falke's body, one fat hand knotting surcoat and mail-shirt both at the shoulder, pulling him up into a half-sitting position, while his other hand searched the recesses of the man's clothes.

'Rot him, he knows things I need to know. Damn him for dying now of all times!'

White hair fell back from the plague-tattered flesh of the dead man; his mouth gaped slightly. A thin line of white showed under his eyelids. One hand flopped, too recently dead for rigidity. Casaubon handled the weight effortlessly, fat-sheathed muscles tensing. Evelian grunted.

'Not the joker you were in Carver Street now, are you, my *lord*?'

'Get out!'

Her heart pounded. She tasted blood, coppery and cold, on her breath; suddenly certain she had stayed too long away from her daughter. She stepped back.

Black air fogged vision, hiding the barricaded buildings around the square and the distant reaches of the construction site. Hiding the sky, beyond which distant wings moved; casting a veil of black across the streets, and the aurora-geometries of the labyrinth . . .

'Sharlevian!'

High above in darkness, the Fane's acolytes still screamed.

Fisting the blue-and-yellow satin dress, she tugged up the hem and stalked across the square. She strode through abandoned debris, guns and tankards, ribbons and trowels and flowers, kicking aside a broken marionette; running past where, head in hands, Tannakin Spatchet sat on the marble steps, to Sharlevian leaning back and kicking one heel against the foundation-stone carved with the Word of Seshat.

'*Mo*ther . . .' The yellow-haired girl didn't move out of Evelian's embrace; if anything, tightened her arms around her mother's waist. Evelian ruffled the girl's hair, then buried her face in it.

Footsteps clicked across the empty square, echoing back from distant buildings. A weighty tread.

'Archemaster, what will happen now?' Tannakin Spatchet's voice sounded flatly.

She rubbed her cheek against her daughter's warm hair and head, aware of the muscles tense in the child's back. Hiding her own fear, she put the girl back to arm's length and gave her a shake.

'There's my Sharl, eh.'

'Aw, leave off.'

The girl tugged her silk overall sleeves up to show her wrists, bracelets jangling. She shrugged Evelian's hands away.

'I heard something today.'

Caught by his tone, Evelian looked at the Mayor and found Tannakin staring at Casaubon.

'A prophecy, Lord Archemaster. This. *In one hour, the circle of the living and the dying shall be broken. In one hour, the Wheel of Three Hundred and Sixty Degrees will fly apart into chaos: stone from stone, flesh from bone, earth from sun, star from star. There shall not be one mote of matter left clinging to another, nor light enough to kindle a spark, nor soul left living in the universe.* Is this the hour?'

Evelian saw the fat man's blue eyes widen. 'Where did you hear that!'

'They say it has its origins in the Fane, messire.'

'Aw, yeah.' Sharlevian sniffed, resting her hands back against the Word of Seshat carved into the abandoned foundation-stone. 'That's been going round. Been lots of stuff like that.'

The luminescent shadow of the foundation-stone seemed to hold a little warmth. Her hands behind her back, wrapped in the folds of her skirt, Evelian drew courage enough to look up at blazing darkness.

'I never thought to see that come in my time. The Night Sun . . . Now will they leave us, the Thirty-Six? And wipe the world away and start a new one? Is the prophecy true?'

She looked down. A step or two below, his back to the square, the big man stood at eye-to-eye level with her. Anger tautened his massive shoulders.

'Are there other master builders here? Answer me, rot you! Who else would have the plans for the Temple? And workers, construction workers. I need them. I can't act without them!'

A cold wind blew. Tangled spars of light-shadow slanted from the scaffolding. Numbness bit at her feet and fingers. Evelian stared out at the glittering darkness of the Night Sun, eyes watering.

'You see where we are? You see what's happening to us?' She smiled, shook her head, one hand extending out to the deserted square. 'Those that aren't dead have run, messire. Now I've helped you search for Falke, I'm taking Sharlevian out of here. If it wasn't for *that*—'

She stabbed a finger at the distant siege-engine. Away from the stone of Seshat's warmth, black light clustered, hiding the aurora of the labyrinth, the trapped daemons.

'We shouldn't have listened to you anyway. We should have run when we had the chance!'

Tannakin Spatchet rose to his feet, pulling his greasy grey doublet straight. He gazed up at the fat man.

'Archemaster, I may say that I admire your skills in protecting us from the acolytes. We thank you for that. Now I feel it might be wise if we attempted to take cover, all of us. Ultimately it may make no difference, but then again . . .'

'Oh, Tan, for gods' sakes!' Exasperated, Evelian rubbed the corners of her eyes as she walked down the steps, as if the darkness might be in her vision and not in the air. Shock numbed her, left her whole seconds of calm normality before the chill reasserted itself.

'We used to hold a market . . .' She looked out towards the littered stone flags. Now faint metallic sparkles precipitated out of the air, falling to shine on porticoes and balconies. 'In Nineteenth's square, of course. Not here. Fourteenth is a Rat district . . . I don't suppose that matters at all now.'

She fisted her hand and touched it gently to Casaubon's arm, as she passed.

'That's what Falke wanted. But it's too late to think about that now, isn't it?'

The Lord-Architect sat, both hands palm-down on the frost-cracked steps, his head tipped back and leaning against the foundation-stone. Folds of satin coat blotted up moisture from the stone, that darkened his blue silk breeches. One of his court shoes lacked a heel now, and both stockings slid down his tremendous calves to his ankles.

'Falke could have given me the designs of the New Temple.'

He spoke so quietly that the silence almost drowned him.

'Mistress Evelian, deep structures have a power on the universe, witness what power the labyrinth has to compel the Fane's servants. The structure of building has that power, also; and I might have used it, if he had lived to tell me.'

The radiance of the Night Sun began to pulse: to tick, the time of some great heart or clock beating in it.

'I told the lady White Crow.' Tannakin Spatchet turned, hands fussing with his cuffs. The strands of hair combed across his balding head fell across his eyes now; and he jabbed an accusatory finger at the Lord-Architect. 'When she made us talismans, I told her that young Falke was a fool, and engaged in plague *magia* and bone *magia* and the Thirty-Six know what else! You had a month to act in. Why didn't you? Why wait until *now*? Until the Night Sun's here, and it's too late?'

'Ask the pox-rotted bitch who denied us a month to work in—!'

The air vibrated to a striking that might have been inside the ear-canal or over the distant horizon in another District. Casaubon's head came up. Copper hair fell over his forehead, straggling down to his eyes, and he gazed up through it. A liquidity swam in his eyes. The fine lines of his features, fat-blurred and buried, lost all good nature and humour.

' "When that hour strikes, then act—" '

His rounded delicate lips quivered with some emotion: anger or misery.

'Damn Her, the bitch! Treat an Archemaster like this!'

He reared to his feet, as if he would actually shake his fist towards the Fane-in-the-Twelfth-District. Some rigidity left his spine.

'Damned Divine mother of all bitches. Give me thirty days to prepare and I might have done something, but no! No! What's it to Her? Pick people up and put them down where it suits Her, no thought about what we can or can't do; Valentine to the Fane, me to this farce—'

Evelian, in a sharp voice that Sharlevian automatically winced at, snapped: '*Lord Casaubon!*'

To her surprise the large man's tantrum halted. He stared down at her, a faint pink colouring his cheeks.

'Damned Decans think they can play god-games.'

'Is that where Crow vanished to? The *Fane*? With you? You fool! That woman was a friend of mine, as well as a lodger; if you were

stupid enough to drag her into the *Fane*, of all places in earth and
heaven, then—'

'She's there now, woman! Willingly. Searching out ways to avert
your prophecy, Master Mayor.'

The Mayor reached to his throat, fingering a malachite talisman
carved with symbols.

Evelian reached behind and sat down on the steps without
looking, the muscles of her legs turned liquid. Stone jolted her.
She looked at her daughter, who shied pebbles idly across the
construction site and paused to hook up one coil of her hair with a
flashy pin.

'Sharlevian . . .'

The Lord-Architect stood as if he felt danger through the earth
beneath his feet. His gaze travelled through the abandoned chaos of
the construction site, staring towards the north-austerly horizon
and the black pyramids of the Fane-in-the-Twelfth-District.

Evelian looked up at him.

'What were you going to do? I think you had better try it, Messire
Lord-Architect.'

He shook his head ponderously. 'How? Given plans, given
workers . . . I could have at least built out the *ground-plan* of
Salomon's Temple. There were people enough here, before the
pestilence, for me to do it; but time ran out for us.'

Shuddering through bone and flesh and blood, Evelian felt the
striking of an hour. She reached up a hand as her daughter picked a
way back across the broken steps. The girl took it, staring at the fat
man.

'See you, Master Falke isn't the only builder. I'm an Entered
Apprentice.'

'Ah, love . . .'

Sharlevian pulled free of her hand, reaching up to twist her fair
hair into a worker's knot, pinning it securely, ear-rings jingling.
Plaster-dust stained the knees of her pink silk overalls. She smiled,
sly; excluding everything that lay outside her expression of pleasure
at her own intelligence.

'Why don't we build the Temple anyway?'

The Lord-Architect Casaubon looked at her in silenced disbelief.

'*No*,' the girl said. 'A *model*. There's enough stuff here. It's all
pattern, like you said. Oh gods, the lectures I've had in Masons' Hall
about *structures*.'

She sighed self-consciously. Evelian, gathering her blue-and-
yellow skirts and getting to her feet, said, 'Do you want a slap,
missy?' and then laughed at incongruous reflexes. 'Love, tell us.'

Abashed, the fair-haired girl mumbled: 'Doesn't matter what size it is, then, does it? Doesn't have to be full size. Still got structure, hasn't it?'

Casaubon's plump hands seized her by the shoulders. 'A model!'

Evelian walked past his padded torso, taking her daughter's arm. A long exasperation faded. She gripped both of Sharlevian's nail-bitten hands.

'Shall we do this? Or shall we try to take shelter?'

'Aw, Mother, *c'mon*. Might as well. Why not?'

'Right. Tan and I will help. Let's do it. Collect bricks – wood – nails – what nails – what you can. *Move!*'

She strode up the steps. Behind her Casaubon protested, 'There's no plans! No blueprints. I don't know what rituals he planned to use!'

'We'll build it how *we'd* want it to be. Who would it be for, after all?'

The fat man reached into an inside pocket and extracted a rule, a plumb-line and a notepad; the last of which he began to figure on rapidly.

Evelian climbed the steps to the site rapidly, and stopped with her hand on her stomach. Black sparkles fringed her vision. The smell of cold flared her nostrils; her breath fogged the air. She bent to seize the handles of an abandoned barrow.

Enthusiasm or desperation beat in her head with her pulse. Conscious of the Mayor at her side, unearthing bricks, tiles, bags of plaster, and stone fragments, she abruptly straightened up and began to laugh.

'Evelian.' Tannakin Spatchet stopped, hands deep in a toolbox, peering up at her over his much-darned doublet-shoulder.

It wheezed out of her, tears cold in the corners of her eyes. 'Tan, didn't you always want to be a hero? I did, when I was Sharl's age. This *isn't* what I had in mind.'

He straightened his back and threw a handful of chisels and knives into the barrow. A wind from somewhere began to tug at his doublet and patched breeches, and blow strands of thinning hair across his eyes.

'Evvie, I've never known you satisfied with anything.'

Her shoes lodged in the mud. She bent to free them, and to heave the barrow back towards the edge of the site.

'Look.'

Tannakin lurched through the soft earth and grabbed the barrow's other handle. As he pulled, he looked, and she saw him frown.

All else darkening, now, as if storms approached; some faint light yet remained. The abandoned foundation-stone of the New Temple glowed with a flickering warmth like firelight. It beat against her skin as they plodded back, the barrow jolting over the rubble. In its light, the immensely fat man sat with legs sprawled wide apart, reading from his notepad, directing Sharlevian and sketching with chalk on the paving-stones in front of the carved Word of Seshat.

'Let's have an open courtyard, too!' Sharlevian sprawled on her stomach, elbows outspread, careless of her silk overall. She reached over and planted two bricks, and a third, to form a plain arch.

'Main gates,' she announced. 'Build it in a rectangle or square, you can have a gate each side, people can walk in.'

The Lord-Architect reached across with the hand that enfolded his pencil and moved the bricks closer together, making the arch smaller. 'No coaches.'

'Oh, sure. Just so people can walk and the kids can play out of the way.'

Evelian heaved the barrow to a halt and left the Mayor to sort around in its contents. She gathered her skirts and knelt down on the broken marble.

'What are you doing?'

The Lord-Architect Casaubon measured a lath with his rule, snapped it expertly to length, and fitted it along the chalk lines of the model Temple.

'The proportions of great buildings should rightly be made the same as the proportions of the body, as Vitruvius writes.'

He knelt up, knees wide apart, silk straining to encase his huge thighs and calves. The top two buttons of his breeches had come undone, she saw, unequal to holding in his belly. His crumpled fleshy face wrinkled up with innocent concentration.

'Symmetry's the relations of the proportions of the part to the whole. As, the face – always the same distance from the bottom of the chin to the underside of the nose, as from nose to eyebrows, and eyebrows to hairline.'

He reached across, one fat finger tapping Sharlevian's chin, nose and forehead. The fifteen-year-old giggled, vaguely flattered; and Evelian's heart suddenly lurched for the normality of Masons' Halls and building instruction.

'Likewise, the length of the foot is one sixth the height of the whole body; the length of the forearm one fourth . . . And since man's a microcosm, and thus like the larger macrocosm, so the proportions and symmetry of the Temple, matching the body, can mirror the proportions and order of the cosmos.'

'*I'd build a garden. In the centre of the Temple. Laid out in pattern and proportion, but built of growing things* . . .' Heidelberg Castle and Gardens, engraved by Matthieu Merian from *Hortus Palatinus*, Salomon de Caus, pub. Johann Theodore De Bry, Frankfurt, 1620

'The cosmos isn't as ordered as all *that*.' Evelian smiled grimly. 'Allow for it being flamboyant and disordered from time to time, Archemaster.'

'Well . . . yes.'

'I'd build the place with room for people.' Sharlevian looked up, face smeared with chalk, totally unselfconscious. 'You go up to the avenues round the royal palace and *boom*! – it just hits you. You feel about *this* high. All those blocks, so massive – and you have to get up on the pavement or the coaches just knock you down. I'd build our Temple so people could sit around and just meet in the evenings, and there'd be places you could buy food, and the temple would look as though it wanted you to come in . . .'

'I . . . ah' – Tannakin Spatchet emerged from the depths of the barrow – 'I'd have the courtyard big enough to hold a regular market, and a place for the Market Court to meet, and somewhere to have a drink with colleagues when business is over . . .'

'And what a time you'd have with university students!' Evelian laughed. The sound startled her. 'Well, and why not? I'd like a place I could go to meet my old friends, a place that we'd helped build and was ours. No Lords! *And* I'd allow Temple coins, so that we could buy and sell in the Temple precinct, not barter. Even if that only happened there, it'd be a beginning. Say you – build your Temple and I'll run the bank for you!'

Her daughter giggled. Casaubon rubbed a cement-covered hand across his lapel, staining his coat.

'I'd build a garden. In the centre of the Temple. Laid out in pattern and proportion, but built of growing things: flowers, mosses, trees. A microcosm laid out in concentric circles, with the plants of each Celestial Sign growing in their proper places. I built gardens in my city . . .'

He raised his head, meeting Evelian's eyes.

'No Architect-Lords in that city now. Not any more. Oh, Parry's good enough to me. She's a senator in the Republic; she sees projects are put my way. But . . .'

'It should have a dome!' Sharlevian rolled over and grabbed the edge of the stone of Seshat to pull herself to her feet. She scrambled, careless of a rip in her overalls, to exhume an old leather bucket from a rubbish-pile.

'With the Celestial Signs,' she added, scratching with a nail on the interior surface. 'Or . . . Archemaster, will the Decans still be here on earth?'

Her tone had increased in respect since she saw the Chymicall Labyrinth function. She now eyed the Lord-Architect with expectation. Evelian smiled slightly, and caught the fat man's eye, and imperceptibly shook her head.

'Mistress Sharlevian, who knows?' He placed the makeshift dome on the central circular walls.

Tannakin Spatchet, peering down, said: 'Steps up to the main building – the flower- and fruit-sellers use them.'

'And fountains, to drink.'

'And let people draw on the pavements . . .'

Evelian shivered, ignored the coldness that bit at her fingers, and twisted wire in the proportions of golden mean and rule; watching it begin to take shape. Tiles propped up to form walls, bricks standing for outbuildings, the carefully measured wooden frame of the main building topped by its ridiculous bucket-dome – Casaubon and Sharlevian sprawling by it like children on a rug. Tannakin Spatchet unearthed a hose-nozzle, and ceremoniously set it in the tile-marked-out 'courtyard' as a fountain.

Evelian said: 'I thought you were a fraud when you arrived. I see I was wrong. I never did believe Crow's stories of her Invisible College – I see I was wrong in that, too.'

Casaubon's fingers, surprisingly delicate in their movements, wired lath to lath in parts of a growing framework. The skeleton hinted at outflung quirky grandeur: classical proportions extended into pleasing irregularity – towers, balconies, buttresses; comfortable small rooms, colonnades, courtyards.

'Not a fraud.' He placed another part of the framework on the chalked stone. It rocked. 'Just out of my depth, Mistress Evelian.'

Sharlevian, mixing mud in her hands, began to plaster the courtyard's outer walls smooth. Ignoring a broken fingernail, she sketched *trompe-l'œil* designs, so that her mother (closing an eye, squinting, forgetting scale) could see how the designs would lead one to perceive longer galleries and an apotheosis of images on the ceiling.

'I was hoping that at least *one* of the four of us knew what we're about.'

The Lord-Architect's gaze lifted first to her and then to the enclosing black light. His breath misted the air. He said nothing.

Four sets of hands built the model, in the warm shadow of the foundation-stone. The wooden-lath frame and hessian-and-plaster walls took on solidity. Rickety, makeshift, it none the less began to body out a shape.

The air shook again like a tolling bell.

Higher above the city that is called the heart of the world, birds soar.

The air is chill now, and thin. Below them the city curves with the curvature of the world. Eagles, wild hawks, cormorants and finches; bright parakeets and humming-birds: all frail feathers beat against the troposphere. Beaks snap. Butterfly-bodies crunch.

And still, higher and further, the bright blobs of moths and butterflies fly upwards. Drawn up by the black fires that sear the sky, hot and bitter as a plague-sore. Souls drawn up by the Night Sun that scars the sky as black tattered flesh scars the plague-dead.

Air thins in the frail bones of birds, but still they strive for height, striking at the bright insects, devouring.

A black-and-white death's-head moth bobs in the air, feeling on dusty fragile wings the cold of the Night Sun. The chill that will crisp the *psyche* into nothingness.

The death's-head moth flies up towards that oblivion, away from the beating wings of a dusty brown sparrow.

The black fire that does not give life but takes it: that can create only the death of a soul.

The white crow flew through the hollow body of the dying god.

A stone rib-cage soared above her. All hollow, hollow and white, that had been ebony: the Decan of Noon and Midnight.

The crow soared up, her wing-tips bending to the pressure of the air. Ice glinted on the pale stone ribs curving up to rise above her head.

'Hhrrraaa-kk!'

She flew through the void of it, vast as cathedrals: a gutted empty carcass. If stone can rot, this stone flesh rotted. It curved like a vast wall at her right side. Ribs, muscles, tendons clearly delineated.

On each lump of tendon and muscle, and lodged in the splintered crevices of bone, white wax candles burned. The yellow flames leaped in the draught of her wings. She felt their heat. Fire palely reflected in the stone flesh, warming no thaw in the frost.

Receding ranks of candles burned on each hillock and lump of petrified gut. The sweet smell of beeswax dizzied her. So far away that only avian sight detects it, the great ribs curved down again.

She beat frantic wings to soar up. The great spine of the Decan of Noon and Midnight jutted infinitely far above her head, vertebrae an avenue of spiked pillars hanging down into void. Light blazed back from the blade of a shoulder, vast as a salt-plain. Stone guts hung from stone ribs in profuse lace drapery.

Dust brushed her wing. She side-slipped in the cold air. A great slew of stone flesh avalanched down, raising dust and chill. Decaying, the rib-cage opened to the air beyond, a mist of gold and rose-colour that her bird's vision could not penetrate. From candle-starred heights another chunk of stone fell, alabaster-white, turning slowly in the air. She glided, caught in fascination; it roiled the air, falling past, tumbling her end over end; shattered in thunderous fragments below.

Weary, she skimmed the air, gliding down to flick her shadow (pale as ice) across the rounded joint of a limb, domed as great buildings are; rose again, straining, avian heartbeat ticking fast as a watch. The hollow between clavicle and jaw opened up ahead, flesh rotted away into stone-dust.

She beat her wings, straining to reach the gap. The great jaw-bones shed scales, marble slabs that might have stood for walls in the Temple of Salomon. An ache bit into what would have been her shoulders and the muscles of her breast. Cramp twinged. She wheeled and spun down – down – down; the floor of the body so great a distance below that she feared her strength would fail, and she fall despite her shape.

A colour: scarlet.

Far below, a man climbed slowly and painfully over the uneven surface between rib and stone rib, his bare feet slipping on the icy marble among the candles. One splash of colour: he wore, still, its arms knotted around his waist, Candia's buff-and-scarlet doublet.

Naked, his ribs showed bony as the Decan's.

'*Dies irae!*'

White silence shattered at her caw. She spread crow's wings, gliding down the pale air. Double images from her wide-set eyes merged as she focused on the man below.

'I take it to be that hour.' Theodoret raised his head. Grey eyes brimmed with mutable brilliance, following the curve of her flight. He shook the hair back from his eyes, smiling. 'Well, child? Young Candia believed help to be found in the Invisible College. You should have come before.'

'I did. The Decan. The Eleventh Decan. She moved me.'

'To this crucial hour . . .'

The white crow spread pinions to cup air, stalled, and gripped a splintered rib between her claws. She hopped from one jutting splinter of bone to the next. Warmth of candle-fire singed her breast-feathers, the stone under her claws icy.

'Oh, the world – is *always* saved. Always. In some form. Or another. What matters—' She forced breath from minute lungs in a toneless parody of speech. 'What matters – is what happens – to people. Individuals. They're not. Always saved.'

She tilted her head to look from one eye and gain a clear image.

Theodoret smiled, genuine amusement on his lined face. 'You're a very cynical crow, lady.'

She spluttered a caw that began in indignation and ended in something unrecognisable.

'But it *is* time.' Theodoret tugged the knotted sleeves tighter about his waist. He picked up a fallen bone spar or splinter from the floor, bracing his steps across the uneven flesh.

The white crow flapped into the air, landed scrabbling on the smooth side of a rib, and skidded down into the hollow between in a flurry of feathers. The Bishop of the Trees laughed. He trod onwards, bare feet unsteady on the icy stone.

'Craa-aak!'

She recovered herself, flapping up, curving in long glides back and forth across his path as he clambered over neck-bones, knee-deep in decaying stone-dust.

In the void ahead of her, a paler light shone down from empty eye-sockets vast as rose-windows, into the interior of the skull. The great head of The Spagyrus lay tilted, fangs wide as pillars crossing his half-open jaw. Wax stalactited the ledges of jaw and palate, and the curving roots of broken teeth: white candles burning with a pure flame. She flew wearily in the cold air, soaring up.

An old woman and a young man sat on the floor of the jaw.

Between them they scattered small cubes. The white crow skimmed the air above their heads, catching double visions of dice as she passed. Heurodis's smoky-blue gaze never wavered as she drew the dice towards herself and cast. The bearded blond man sprawled back on one hip, a finger tapping at his mouth; and as she passed he reached out and scooped up four of the six dice and tossed them down.

A feather falling – or is it rising? – against a blue sky: *Flight*. Meshing cogs and gearwheels: *Craft*. In a field of corn and poppies, two lovers embrace: *The Sun*. And – escaping its weighted cast towards the androgyne that dances masked, *The World* – the flower-eyed skull of *Death*.

An intensity of light burned about the bone-cubes, images bright with colour in that white desert. She felt through the tips of spread pinions how air and probability strained there; the edge of the field catching her, and she wheeled, gliding back towards the Bishop of the Trees.

'Not cards, now. Dice.'

She strained to fly a few yards further, stalled, and slid to nestle in a hollow part of the great jaw's hinge.

Theodoret paused, lifting his head.

'Can birds smell?' he asked softly. 'This is the way it would smell before snow, I remember when I was a child . . .'

'The world is not always saved.'

Tendoned, articulated, the machinery of the jaw rose complicated above her tiny niche. Stone chilled: she fluffed out breast-feathers. Her heart hammered. Candles dazzled. She cocked her head to one side, gazing out across the alabaster spaces. Candia and Heurodis at this distance two spots of colour, no more.

The vast curves of the god's skull rose, ledged with candles. Infinitely far above she glimpsed rose-light as another suture crumbled away into dust.

The whisper echoed again along the walls in fossilised flesh, vibrating in her hollow bones: *'Are you not gone from here?'*

Theodoret lifted his head. The crow, perched at eye-level, looked across at him. The candle-light shone on his silver-grey hair, finger-combed clean and curling to frame his lined face. His eyes shone, his lips parted slightly. The flesh of his shoulders and bony throat shone yellow against the Decan's alabaster ruin.

'No, nor likely to, my lord.'

He smoothed the doublet under his narrow buttocks and seated himself, with some effort, on the knotted marble.

'I have succeeded.'

The white crow opened her beak and cawed softly, the manipulation of the bird's larynx coming too easily.

'Divine One, think. Think. What you do. What you are. This sickness is – not necessary.'

'I know. It is my choice.'

Theodoret's gaze searched for some source of the disembodied whisper. Movement rustled. The crow shifted her stabbing beak, jerking her head around and her other eye to focus.

Whiteness moved.

A feeler vibrated on the air. Carapaces rustled. Carved as if from milk and ivory, moving blindly across the palate and teeth and jaw, white cockroaches crawled. Now that they moved, she saw them: marble scarabs clinging to splintered fangs, burrowing through deep and glittering alabaster dust. Intricately carved stone blowflies, and ants, swarming across the ridged floor of the vast skull-pan.

They approached the bare legs of Theodoret, where he sat calmly. She flicked into flight, curved down to skim the floor, and then reared up. Lack of her own human size had deceived her. Insects crawled, large as dogs or small ponies.

Stone feelers and legs rustled. Candle-flames glimmered on carapaces bright with frost. The rustling modulated, taking on a chorus-voice: '*I am the Thirty-Six. You cannot compel me. You cannot move me by pleading. Will you complain that I have done this, who am a god?*'

Her wings rose and fell, beating wearily. She fanned her tail feathers, gliding on a long curve to take her back to where Theodoret sat.

'Divine One, you forget—'

'*I do not forget. I know all that you know. I made the world and you.*'

The whiteness of stone blinded her. Aware to each side of her vision of pinions bending, forcing down cold air, beating hollow-boned, she cawed: 'I could tell you – hrraaa-ak! But I forget. I forget. I become. What I seem.'

Air roiled. From below and all around, the rustling of stone insects formed a voice: '*Will you require me to play by my rules? I am not so constrained. You desire your own shape, you bargain for it. But I perceive you, bone and blood and soul, down to the particles that dance below sense's awareness: I know what you know – and it is nothing.*'

The crow cried out.

Stone fractures, falling to splinters among the columns of limbs: far off, far off. Like thunder the echo resounds.

'*I am above your choices and desires.*'

She skimmed the old man's shoulder, curving in flight, dazzled by the light of candles on frosted marble.

'*For no reason, but my whim.*'

Pain slammed through her.

Every vein threaded with glowing wires, every bone weighed solid and fracturable; she whirled, flinching from the smooth marble that slammed into her body. Her head jerked up and back, neck cracking.

Gravity slammed her down. Her ribs burst wide, skin stretching, losing the goosepimple-lodging of quills. Claws uncurled, bones of feet stretching, stabbing. A sheer weight of body threw her down, wings spread out: spreading still although she couldn't move, knocked breathless, skin pushing out from beneath white feathers, skin and shaped bone—

Heaviness weighed her pelvis, her back. Fire coursed through her, cramp released from a cellular level; tears burst from her eyes, and she jerked her arms, moving them from the shoulders, to bury her face across her callused hands.

The woman lay face down on ridged marble.

'*I do not need reasons.*'

Loose feathers surrounded her hands.

She knelt back on her heels, staring at the white pinions and down that scattered the stone. Frost chilled her. She reached out hands palm-forward to the heat of candles on the ledge above her, and stared at short nails and skin. Not young: sallow skin with a minuscule incised diamond-pattern, healing from a cut here, marked (she turned the palms to her) with the calluses of pen and sword.

'Thank . . . you . . .' She spoke blindly, to the air. 'Thank you!'

A hot tear chilled down her cheek. She wiped it with the heel of her hand, wrapped her arms around her naked body and staggered to her feet. Her foot curled, clawing for purchase. She slipped, automatically throwing her arms out to the sides, not forward to break her fall; and other hands gripped her and pulled her to kneel by the stone on which he sat.

'Rest.'

'I don't have time—'

She raised her head and focused her single gaze on the old man. The Bishop of the Trees smiled. Her voice in her ears sounded like song. A smile moved her mouth.

'—but I don't suppose this matters now. Except to me.' She shivered, arms tight across her body. 'Except to me!'

Theodoret reached down, took one of her hands and unfolded it, and placed her fingertips against her temple.

Unfamiliar softness brushed her fingers. She leaned forward, staring into the smooth reflecting surface of the nearest marble, the skin about her eyes creasing as she squinted. Dark-red hair fell about her face and shoulders, curling finely, streaked with white.

In the hollow of each temple, just where the white hair began to grow out, a patch no larger than her thumbprint grew. White down, the feathers soft as fur.

'He doesn't need reasons.'

Before she could become fascinated, staring at her face in the shine of marble, she leaned her hands against the stone and pushed herself to her feet. Unsteady, she gazed down at Theodoret.

'I'm sorry, my lord. Scholar-Soldiers . . . I don't have *magia* now for this; all *magia* derives from the Thirty-Six powers of the universe, and they so weakened now—'

A grin stretched her face. Drunk on speech, she stretched up her arms: body stretching, shoulders, breasts, stomach, legs. Feeling the cold of ice upon her skin and the fretful warmth of candles, and she shook her hair back and laughed.

'—*Wonderful!*'

The Bishop of the Trees burst into laughter, rich and resonant. A wistfulness chilled the air. The rustling bodies of insects swarmed over the nearer stone.

With a crack that split air and sound together, the cathedral-skull split from tooth to eye. Intolerably bright, the rose-light glared in.

Stone poured down. Shards of marble rumbled down the slope of the inner mouth, bounding as boulders do in avalanches, resistless. The White Crow tilted her head and stared up at the falling rock, shafting through the air towards her. Breath made a hard knot in her gut.

'My lord Bishop, you are laughing at me, I think.'

She put both hands up to her head, fingers brushing the down at her temples. One knuckle nudged a gold bee-pin. All muscles tensed to take wing – pain threaded her human shape. She rose on the balls of her feet to run. Stone ripped down out of the air.

Unconsciously her hand tightened around the gold bee, loosened at a sensation of fur and whirring wings. She touched her fist to her mouth, breathing a name; threw out her hand. As the bee flew she stared up into hollow whiteness. Into mortal and divine substance fast decaying.

Taking his hand away from placing a piece of plaster, his fingers shook. Cold bit into his skin, blotching it white and blue. Casaubon stood awkwardly and tucked his fat hands up into his coat-armpits, squinting at the sky.

'Is it finished?'

Evelian grabbed his arm. Her hands didn't close about the width of his wrist. She jerked furiously at his satin sleeve.

'Is this finished? What's happening? What can we do?'

He took his arm away without noticing her grip. He felt in his left-hand pocket, then his right, one inside pocket and then the other; and finally from a pocket in the tail of the frock-coat unearthed a large brown handkerchief. He blew his nose.

'It . . .'

The white still-wet plaster model shone. Low buildings surrounded a courtyard, some entrances reached by cellar-steps, some by risers; all within a long wire-framed colonnade. Arches opened into the yard, too small to permit coaches, wide enough for walking. Steps and seats littered the yard at irregular geometric intervals.

Over it, the dome of the Temple rose, swelling up from the body of the complex: a dome to stand stunningly white and gold against summer skies, to be surrounded by doves, to be surrounded also by gardens – sketched in with chalk and a few uprooted weeds from the building site – growing with the brightness of roses. Open arches led from temple to gardens, from gardens to temple . . .

A model rocking on chalk-marked broken paving. Wired laths. Hessian. Plaster.

All precisely measured: to proportion, in symmetry, to scale.

'Given what it is, it's the best thing I've ever done.'

Casaubon reached up and scrubbed a hand through his copper-gold hair, leaving it in greasy spikes.

'Damn the whole lot of you. Your city, the Scholar-Soldiers, Decans, and me above all.'

His arm fell to his side. The black light glinted on oil and grease-stains on his satin frock-coat and breeches. His cravat hung unfolded over his open shirt. With no preparation, he sat down heavily on the top step; the marble vibrating under his bulk. He rested one cushioned elbow on his thigh, and the heel of that hand ground into his eye-socket.

'You all can rot, for all I care. I sent her into that place, promised her help I can't perform. I . . .'

He lumbered back up on to his feet.

'Of all the pox-rotten fools. She's good with *magia* and better with a sword, and I, *I* had to make her into a Master-Physician! Of all the stupid, *stupid*—'

Something brushed his cheek.

Startled, he raised a hand, lowered it.

A bee crept across his dirty knuckles, faceted eyes gleaming. Mica-bright wings quivered; its legs feather-touched his skin. Casaubon held his breath. The banded furry body pulsed, lifted into flight.

For one second he heard the hum of summer, of clear days, and the smell (too sweet, too rich) of rose gardens.

Metal clinked.

He knelt down ponderously, sweeping aside one of the skirts of his frock-coat, and felt on the paving until his fingers contacted metal. He straightened, opened his palm. Heavy, glinting with the black light, a golden bee lay in his hand.

'Lord Casaubon?'

The Mayor's voice.

Black light moved with the viscosity of honey. It thickened, rolled across the construction site, sliding down from the sky and the Night Sun. A hard metallic taste invaded his mouth. He spat, wiped his mouth on his satin sleeve.

'She needs me . . .'

The fading warmth from the stone of Seshat illuminated their faces. Shadowed eye-sockets, noses; glinting hair and bright eyes. The straggle-haired girl knelt by her mother, one hand gripping the woman's, intent on the model. Evelian leaned forward, yellow hair spilling across her breasts.

'I forget her for whole minutes at a time.' He smeared one plaster-wet hand down his shirt to clean it; weight resting back on one massive heel; brushing blindly at the grease-stains on the coat's embroidered lapels.

'So many years to find her, and then by *accident* . . .'

Water brimmed in his eyes and overran. Tears spilled down his cheeks, acid-hot and then cold in the cold air; running down cheeks and chins, runneling wet marks down his stained linen shirt.

'I never heard her speak of you.' Evelian's voice held wonder. 'I knew there had to be *somebody* the cause of it.'

He covered his face with his hand. As loud as a child, he snuffled, and wiped his leaking eyes and nose on his sleeve. He sucked in a breath and looked down at her with the total bewilderment of pain.

'What's happening to her? I thought' – his voice wavered, thinned, began to ululate – 'that I'd *help* her, gods rot her. Now. That I'd be able to . . . to *get* there, and . . .'

He rubbed his face with soaking hands. Tears and snot soaked the cuffs of his coat. He hiccuped, gasping in air; muffling a sob in the palm of one hand.

'I brought her into this!'

The chill on his wet hands burned in the Night Sun's enveloping cold. Arctic, a wind blew grit across the construction site. Sand tacked against his cheek.

His left hand tightened on the metal bee, and he opened it and looked down, watching beads of blood ooze out onto the plaster-stained lines of his palm. Cold numbed the pain. He folded his hand over the sharp wings and antennae, clenching hard.

'Valentine. *White Crow!*'

Cold blossomed.

As swiftly as if it were the light of some dawn, cold air fractured the world. Thick spikes of ice jolted down from the scaffolding. Marble paving crackled underfoot. He scrambled to his feet and stumbled, falling awkwardly, sprawling on his back with a heel caught in the skirts of his coat. The metal bee fell from his hand.

The Word of Seshat faded from the foundation-stone, remaining for a long moment imprinted on his vision.

In the dark he called out: 'White Crow.'

*

Broken marble littered the stone.

As far as her human eyes could see, ruined stone lay. From fragments small as a finger-bone to blocks the size of houses: all tumbled, splintered into a landscape of rubble. Occasional crags jutted up, white slopes yet covered with burning candles. A mist of light curled across the stone.

The White Crow stood with the Bishop of the Trees in a clear circle some thirty yards across.

A marble cricket, large as her hand and carved intricately, squatted on a ledge of the broken jaw. Its hind legs rasped together. The small voice sounded clear and perfect after the thunder of stone: '*Little animal, you are laughing at me, I think.*'

The stone under her bare feet crumbled, becoming friable and then dust. She sifted it between her toes. The White Crow smiled, not able to stop; sensuous in the new awareness of her self. She stood naked with no embarrassment.

Theodoret laughed.

'Why, what do you think I was doing, my lord Decan, while I lived in death here? I learned. There's much to be learned in the Fane, when only a miracle stands between you and death, and,' the old man said tartly, 'you wish that it didn't.'

'*You have learned to wish to die.*'

'No, my lord. *You* learned that of *us*. My young friend Candia always swore you pried too closely into mortal concerns and mortality.'

The White Crow squatted, running her hands through the dust of the Lord of Noon and Midnight. It sparkled on her fingers. Only the tiny voice remained now, guttering as a candle . . .

She sat back, bumping her bruised buttocks, grinning. The alabaster dust sparkled white and silver on her shins, in the red-gold curls of her public hair. She rubbed her hands against her nose, smelling sweat and frost and fire.

'The Eleventh Decan told me, Divine One. The Lady of the Ten Degrees of High Summer. You can forget, you can change your nature; it's only Rats and humans that have to live with limitation.' She stretched out a leg, examining bruises already yellow and purple. Fierce unreasonable joy fired her. 'Forget, change, become a miracle.'

'*I have made true death.*'

'Black miracles. Black miracles.'

'*And I will become One.*'

The White Crow gripped fistfuls of stone dust, sifting them out into the cold air. Abruptly she folded her legs under her buttocks, dug her feet in, pushed; and stood up without using her hands:

every muscle electric with energy. She turned, arms outstretched, letting the last of the dust fall.

Theodoret, his hands folded primly on his knees, said: 'I learned that I am a fool, for thinking to instruct one of the Thirty-Six. I learned that when the Decan of Noon and Midnight pretends ignorance of human conspiracy it may be because he is using that conspiracy; letting us place your true-death necromancy under the heart of the world; bringing the plague and the Night Sun and your sickness—'

All the joy of the Scholar-Soldier in her, the White Crow put in: 'Or else, being clouded by base Matter, only taking advantage of what conspiracies mortals had already put into action—'

'—and I learned, my lord Decan, that foolishness is not a province of humanity. But that,' Theodoret said, 'I always knew.'

The cricket's fretted hind legs ceased moving. White stone gleamed. No voice formed.

The White Crow gazed up at the old man. She touched his warm shoulder with a faintly proprietorial air and smiled. The air about them crackled, temperature falling towards sub-zero.

'I should despair.' She shook her head, grinning ruefully. 'It's this, I think. When you were healed, did you feel . . . ?'

'Master-Physician, yes.'

'As if it were impossible to be hurt, ever again?'

He put both hands on her bare shoulders, the touch of his fingers warm. Light gleamed in his grey eyes like water; silver and silky as his flowing hair. Briefly he kissed her, on the dark-red hair above her temples. The White Crow startled. His breath, warm and damp, smelt of cut grass.

'Now,' he said.

He turned, kneeling, burying his hands in the dust.

The last outcrops of rounded marble slumped into dust, white light blazing hard enough to bring tears to her eyes. She raised her head. Her heart beat in her ears and groin.

'I have learned,' Theodoret said.

A dank smell of leaf-mould penetrated her nostrils. The sole of her foot moved in some slick substance, and the White Crow looked down. Ankle-deep in stone dust, her skin sensed a moment's texture of river mud.

A faint light the colour of sun through beech leaves burns around the Bishop's hands – fades, fails and dies.

The Thirty-Six feel the great wheel of the world hesitate in its turning: pause, poise. Wait.

*

Some fractional movement above, where iron flood-doors hung suspended in grooves in the tunnel roof, warned Plessiez. He leaped forward as the chains and shutter crashed down.

'Plessiez!'

'Charnay, is all well?'

Her voice came, muffled, from behind the iron door. He picked himself up off his knees, realised that he stood in a brighter light than the fallen torch could account for.

The brown Rat's voice faded. His ears rang with the noise of the shutter's falling. After a moment she appeared at one of the close-barred window-openings where the tunnel doubled back on itself. 'I'll get round to you another way. Press on, messire. Courage!'

Under his breath, the black Rat murmured: 'And if what I find now is some way of slipping past you, regaining the surface?'

Sound scuttered at the edge of hearing. He snatched up the fallen rapier, the leather-wound hilt warm and worn under his palm. Here brown bones stacked the walls, racked up in barriers eight or nine feet tall; the close-packed knobs of bone broken only by jutting inset skulls. Plessiez moved cautiously down the wet slope. Ahead, the floor of the tunnel ran steeply down and the ceiling rose, until both widened out into the central cavern of the ossuary.

'A little short of omens and nightmares,' he whispered, sardonic, shaking.

The sound ran down ahead of him, hissing into echoes, not fading but growing; increasing in volume until it yawped up the scale into laughter.

'*Charnay?*'

Steep flights of steps angled down into the great cavern from other, higher entrances. Marble altars stood to each side, among the bones and obelisks. Light glowed on the smooth walls, rounded almost into bosses, brown strata hooping up with the curve of aeons. Black candles towered in ornate stands, each one lit. His shadow on the passage wall and the cave roof leaped, agile, frantic, despite his even pacing.

'Fool,' said the Hyena.

She swung lithely down from an entrance whose tunnel must cross above his. A basket-hilted rapier balanced in her right hand. Greasy hair fell down over her slanting brows, over the shoulders of her red shirt that hung torn to her waist. Her filthy red breeches were cut off at the knee; her bruised and cut feet moved without hesitation across the gravel as she ran towards him.

'Lady, you follow me fast enough to outdistance me.'

She yawped a laugh that made his pelt shiver.

Quickly he knelt and took the bundle of bones from his belt, tucking them under the nearest protruding wall. Skulls brushed his hand, friable and warm. He tightened his grip on his rapier. Without further speech he ran forward, seeking the flat cavern floor.

'*Gods*—'

Her blade leaped fire and light in the corner of his vision. He parried; scrabbling back to look wildly at what lay in the centre of the ossuary cavern.

On the far side, the catafalque of the Rat-Kings stood on a raised dais, on a dozen marble steps: a fragile lacy thing of white stone, engraved with the symbols of each of the Thirty-Six, with the insignia of the Churches – including Plessiez's own Guiry – of which the Rat-Kings would be titular head. Friezes of ancient nobles in procession circled the body of the catafalque, upon which, in equally execrable taste, a circle of seven robed Rats lay in a King. Under their bier, carved in precise mirror-detail, seven Rat corpses, their bony vertebrae intertwined, lay in various stages of stony decomposition: this one a skeleton, snout crumbling, incisors gone; the next a shrunken fleshly body, with tiny carved marble worms emerging from it; the next a petrified mummy . . .

Plessiez ignored the floridly baroque bad taste, staring past the dark-haired woman, past the blade that shot highlights from the candles.

'That—' Some bright sanity burned in the woman's eyes. For a moment she straightened from her sloping crouch, the animal gaze gone. 'Is *that* what they all were? What we took from you, what we placed under the heart of the world?'

They lay on the gravelled earth before the catafalque – the femur and tail-vertebrae and skull of a Rat, scarcely large enough to be adult. A scarlet ribbon tied them in curious knots. One long knobbed femur, a rib, a rib with vertebrae attached: the long decreasing series of tail-bones. They made a kind of irregular septagon shape, the skull and lower jaw-bone crowning it. Now Plessiez realised where the light came from. These, that had been new and scrubbed bones – boiled down for cleanliness – now glowed as white as roses in morning sunlight.

Fear shocked it out of him.

'Lady . . . four times the Divine upon this earth and by some black miracle caused a soul to die. We made our necromancy from their mortal remains.'

The Hyena's whisper hardly broke his trance: 'There's nothing there. *Nothing*.'

Red ribbon tied the bones in angled geometries. Red ribbon threaded the eye-sockets, attaching the skull to the bone framework upon which it rested. Ribbon, and the gravel on which it rested: all solid, all bodied into form and existence . . .

The whiteness of the bones, now, the whiteness of absolute negation.

'I saw them with butterflies all in their mouths,' she sang, 'seeking the Boat, and born again. But this . . .' The woman's tone dropped to growling speech. 'This isn't death, but *nothing*.'

Plessiez raised his eyes. The woman, unarmoured, stood as if she still wore the Sun's ragged banners; brows come down over her slanting dark eyes. Yellow shadows moved at her feet, mottled and smelling of heat and dust. She met his gaze. Her eyes dulled: flat, cunning, bestial.

White light shone from behind her. The arctic negation of that light chilled him: so small, so bright.

'They are the bones of the truly dead.' He stared around. At the whiteness sifting down upon the catafalque, upon the stacked bones of the royal dead: each with the seed-bone removed, each long since boarded the Boat and travelled the Night and returned again.

The chill of the earth faded under his clawed feet. Numbness replaced it, radiating out from the tiny pile of bones in the centre of the cavern.

'You may not blame me, lady! Blame the Decan of Noon and Midnight, who thought fit that Guiry should share his alchemical work—'

Bare feet scuffed gravel. Her sword swung up. He knocked it aside, metal clashing harshly, echoing up into the cavern's dry heights.

'It didn't shock you.' Her breath sawed. She flung her free hand out, pointing at him. 'I saw. Falke died. I saw your face. They all started to die. It didn't – even – *surprise* you. You *knew* the plague would hit us—'

On the walls of the ossuary cavern the shadows of the woman and the black Rat danced: sword-blades engaging, darting, each movement exaggerated, each swirl of the Rat's plume, each stoop-shouldered dash of the woman. Laughter yammered, drowning the hiss of bare feet on the earth.

'—ours and the Decan's, the same pestilence—'

'*Wait!*'

His long wrist pivoted. He beat her blade back, wrenching his shoulder. Gravel bit his heels. His panting breath echoed back off the walls with the clang of metal. Habit took him to guard position; found him the snap in her concentration and lunged – parried, beat her blade down and jumped back.

'—*you* the same cause—'

The woman crabbed sideways three steps and scooped up a brown thigh-bone from the ossuary heap nearest, weighing it in her left hand. The bone-wall groaned, teetered.

'You're by far a better demagogue than fighter.' Plessiez trod forward, his eyes meeting her dulled flat gaze. Anger burned him breathless. And fear. 'You're a fool, get out.'

'Yes, a fool. Yes, a fool to listen, ever, to you. I am the last now: the last of Sun and Roses. If I *am* a hyena, I can make you carrion!'

Highlights glinted in the woman's eyes, the eyes of a woman no more than adequate, he would guess, with a blade; but now flat and hard and cunning, echoing the yellow shadows that moved with her, mimicked her movements, padded in shadows, laughed in-human laughter.

White light burned.

Now multiple shadows danced on the cavern walls. Brightness scarred his vision. He risked a lunge, continued it on into a run: dashing for the flight of stone steps leading up to another exit. In one loping jump the woman made the lower step: rapier darting up at his breast, he parried, skidded to one knee, staggered up, breath hot in his mouth.

He grabbed at his belt, finding the main-gauche lost somewhere; lunged again, one foot on the bottom step, drove her up three steps;, brought a heel down half off the edge of the sheer flight; leaped backwards and landed on the earth, left hand and tail out for balance. She half-loped and half-fell down the steps towards him.

The point took his gaze away. He only sensed her hand move.

Reflex brought his left hand up. The thrown femur jarred his wrist, clattered away on the floor. She lunged, leaping from the steps; and he bound her blade and kicked, crouched, whipped his scaled tail hard across her ankles. She fell.

She pitched past him, into the ossuary wall that she had loosened the bone from: in a rush and shatter of femurs and skulls and ribs and pelvises the mass of dry brown bones avalanched down on her. She sprawled face-down, greasy hair flying, one bare foot scrabbling for purchase. In the same second he fell forward into the furthest extent of his lunge and felt the penetration of flesh clear up the blade.

Through his grip on the hilt he felt his own pulse or the last fibrillation of her heart.

A Rat skull bounced across the floor. Vertebrae scattered like dice. The bone-pile slid to an unsteady halt, balanced up like kindling. The woman sprawled, partly covered in splintered brown bone, the half-inch-wide blade jammed up through her stomach and under the lowest rib. Blood rivuleted, staining her shirt; a dark stain marked her breeches as bowel and bladder relaxed. Her bubbling, blood-filled breath echoed into silence.

The rapier blade scraped a rib as he withdrew it, bracing his clawed foot against her shoulder.

Light tore. In the whiteness of the bones of the truly dead, a rip appeared.

Tumblers click, numbers roll.

In the university building Lucas scrambles from under the meshing gears of an analytical engine. There is no noise, no smoking oil, no ripping metal. Only an intolerable strain that holds the fabric of the air taut, taut.

Away across the heart of the world, a makeshift lath-and-plaster model of a building glows, moon-bright. A fifteen-year-old girl on her knees beside it, ear-rings jangling, breaks into tears at something she cannot explain: perhaps simply the extravagant order and complexity of its proportions.

Enamel-imaged dice, scattered and chipped, lie among the discarded Thirty Trionfi cards, in a hollow of whiteness where a man and an old woman fall, fall endlessly.

Breaking strain. As if in the weak forces that glue the universe together, some sudden slippage could be felt. Strings pulling apart, order losing its probability.

Plessiez staggered back, sitting down on the bottom step of the nearest flight of stairs.

Blood pooled from the rapier's point to the earth. He sat staring at it, how it glistened in the white light. His chest heaved. He brushed his wrist across his mouth, touched matted fur; touched it again and took his hand away.

One cut ripped his lip, just over the left incisor. He tasted blood, not knowing until he felt the slick matted fur on his right haunch that she had wounded him twice. Numbness began to fill the cavern, hiding the pain. Feeling the weakness of her deep wound, he with shaking fingers unbuckled his sword-belt and rebelted it tightly around his haunch as a tourniquet.

'Well, now . . .'

His voice, even at a whisper, sounded loud as gunfire in a

cathedral. He wiped the rapier, fumbling it; leaned the point on the gravelled earth and pushed himself upright.

With a sharp snap, the blade broke.

The black Rat staggered. His naked bristling tail whipped out for balance. He stood, eyes half-shut, peering at the clouded air before his face. The white light leached colour from the fallen bones, from the great catafalque and the ossuary cavern itself. He gazed up at the dark tunnel-entrance to which the stairs led.

Plessiez looked back.

The great Wheel falters, loosens and forgets the unheard cadences of the Dance of all things; particles of earth and stone and bone dissolve upon air.

He let the broken sword fall.

One hand clenched hard enough to drive rings into his flesh.

Not a light, but a leaching-away of substance.

The earth beneath his numb feet not lost in brilliance, but dissolving into air, and air itself dissolving into nothingness . . .

Plessiez squatted down awkwardly, one arm resting across his unwounded knee, staring at the bones.

Moments ticked past, marked by the slow spreading of blood from the murdered woman. A tension thrummed deep in the stone. On the edge of audibility, Plessiez sensed the loosing of bonds in the heart of the earth. The bones and their red ribbon imprisoned his gaze, nested in the warm whiteness of oblivion.

He spoke softly.

'Now we are the same, you and I . . . Myself stripped gradually and willingly of all I've earned: cardinal's rank, priesthood, power, and friends and skills. And you stripping the heart of the world until nothing remains. True death. Your portent in the sky: the Night Sun – there by a god's conjuring, and mine. Well, we are the same.'

He lifted his snout, looking up at one of the stairs and exits.

'No matter how fast, I would be very close, still, when it happens. So where is the point of running?'

One translucent ear twitched. He heard no sound of Charnay, lost in the ossuary labyrinth; and the rattle in the dead woman's throat would not be repeated.

'Believe that I did not know you would be like this – but, then, one is seldom sure of outcomes, dealing in matters pertaining to the Divine. Does The Spagyrus regret you, I wonder?'

Above his head, the stone roof of the cavern creaked.

'And I am like you in this: I admit of no possibility of victory. Even though I think I perceive – I *think* – a method towards it. But you could not expect it of me.'

Talking to the bones as if they were his mirror image, the black Rat slid down to sit on the gravel: the nearer stones leached of colour and substance.

'Well, and if it were fire I might manage that, and if it were flesh and blood there's *her*—' One slender dark finger pointed to the corpse of the Hyena. 'But hardly of use, I fear, with the life departed from it. Death's no cure for entropy.'

A large chunk of stone dislodged itself from the roof and fell, cracking the corner from the catafalque of the Rat-Kings. Part of a carved rose rattled down the steps. The smell of blood and ordure began to lessen, and even the chill in the air became mild.

'*But*—' The black Rat argued obsessively, leaning forward. 'You could not expect it of me. Even if I willed it, even if I saw nothing else to be done, even if – and it is possible, oh, I grant you it is possible – I *desired* it, well, still the flesh would not let me. That has its own desire for survival.'

He lay down now, on his side, tail coiled up to his flank, and one arm cradling his head. His black eyes glowed. With his free hand he reached out, testing the limits of absolute numbness near the bones: the milk-white bones glowing in brilliance.

Expecting a pulse of tension, it brought tear hot into his throat to feel, through fingertips, the sensation of fracturing thin ice, of falling suddenly from the step that is not there—

The knowledge of how short a time before the world split and rolled up like cloth burned in him. His eyes half-closed. White light split into rainbows.

'Well,' he said.

Plessiez, *ankh* and priesthood discarded both, all conspiracies broken and bloody, lying on one elbow now, as if to read, or by the side of some lover, reached out and with a gentle touch took hold of the infinite whiteness of bone.

The ceiling of the cavern cracked and fell.

High above darkness, high above where the labyrinth in city streets gutters and dies; high above the straining wings of eagles, and soaring into the face of darkness, flies a moth with death's-head markings on its wings.

Airbreathed wings of dark fire reach out.

The Night Sun's blackness burns, a beacon. In the thin air, thinning with height of atmosphere, and with the loosening charges of electrons, the moth beats black-dusted wings furiously, rising, reaching up—

A sparrow stalls in the air, snaps, crunches the moth's soft body. Its gullet jerks twice, swallowing.

The wind thins.

Caught in dissolution, in air dissolving; the strangeness of matter that is its body fading, the bird begins to fall.

And suddenly the sky is gold.

'Messire!'

Through rock that tumbled down, immense and slow, great boulders bounding and crushing heaps of bones, Lieutenant Charnay dodged and lumbered down the longest flight of steps, sword-rapier in hand.

She ran across the floor of the ossuary cavern, moving fast, sparing one glance for the dead woman; heading for the slumped black figure before the catafalque. Shouting, voice lost in the roar of splintering rock.

She flung herself to her knees beside Plessiez and turned him over.

And stared into a face so changed she might never have recognised it if she had not, once, met his grandfather.

His black fur was now faded grey; white about the jaw. His shrunken body moaned as she held it, light as sacking. Under his loose pelt, his ribs and collar-bone jutted in stark angles; slim fingers reduced to thin bony sticks.

His head fell back. The flesh of his ears had turned translucently grey; and, as he blinked slowly, she took one look at his eyes – milky with cataracts – and turned her head aside to vomit.

One of Plessiez's age-withered hands grasped a skull's lower jaw: brown and old and fragile. A coil of red ribbon ringed his wrist. All the nails of his hand were cracked, yellow, waxen.

His other hand moved feebly. She dropped her sword and clasped it.

'Plessiez, man.'

The black Rat, whiskers quivering, raised a hand that trembled. His head bobbed on his thin corded neck. He peered at her.

'And I had always wagered' – his thin voice shook – 'that I would not live to die old.'

A roar from above warned her. She had one second to look up at the falling rock, to see how many layers of the catacombs now fell in towards their foundations. Plessiez groaned. The brown Rat tightened her grip on his hand. She threw her body protectively across his, at the last reaching out for her sword.

*

Stone soughs into dust.

A weakness as of internal bleeding hamstrings her. The White Crow presses both fists into her stomach under the arch of her ribs. Body shaking with sudden cold, teeth grinding, she sits down hard in the alabaster whiteness.

Maggots boil up like milk.

Their soft bodies slide against her skin. Revolted, too weak to stand, she reaches out a hand to sketch a hieroglyph on the air. Her hand drops to her side, the powerless shape left unfinished.

'He's dying—'

Waves of maggots belly up, silky and cool about her shins and ankles. The solidity of what stone remains under her begins to soften.

Quietly, the White Crow laughs.

'Theo, my lord, you did say "corrupted". The divine and demonic souls of the universe don't decay into *maggots* when they die! Oh, he learned this of us.'

The absence that weakens her grows now, as if her heartblood leaks away through weakened aorta and ventricle at every pulse. At some deep level of cells, still resounding from the miracle of shape-changing, the White Crow shivers into dissolution.

She shouts: 'You didn't have to do this! You're a god; even these rules don't bind you.'

'He chooses that they do.'

Theodoret stands, Candia's doublet still kilting his waist. Age-spotted skin gleams sallow in the growing intensity of light breaking down. His red lips part, he frowns; his head high, grey hair flowing.

'Young woman, the Thirty-Six were fool enough to choose to exile the Church of the Trees and degrade their worshippers. I've suffered from that all my life. Don't tell me about Divine capriciousness and stupidity!'

She twists around on her knees, smearing the crawling maggots to a paste. Effort burns her lungs. As if the cells behind her eyes dissolve also, her vision whitens.

'Ahhh—'

Not her vision, it is the world that whitens. She perceives with preternatural clarity this last moment; her voice hissing in her ears like static: 'He's dead!'

Weakness grows, pressing against her skin from inside. A void too large to contain. Her numb fingers no longer feel each other, nor her arms pressed to her sides; thighs drawn up tight to her belly and breasts.

Her fingers, touching her flesh, feel the decaying voices of the

Thirty-Six. Scholar-Soldier, student of *magia*, Master-Physician: she
has the skill to hear their last cry, fading in the wake of dissolution—
    And something else.
    'Listen! *Feel!* Something's happening.'
    The old man looks sharply down at her. 'What is it?'
    Far across the city that is called the heart of the world, echoes of
destroyed *magia* vibrate. She, in the wasteland of ruined marble and
maggots, points up at his hands. A faint luminescence clings to
them, the colour of green shadows and sunlight.

Above the city, the sky is suddenly gold.
    Dusty wings beating, the sparrow falls. In the bird's bead-black
eyes, reflected clearly, the Night Sun is over-spotted with a leprous
golden light.
    Flat as an illustrated manuscript, the sky over the heart of the
world sears yellow as fever.

Voices thundered in her head. Visions blurred her eyes. The smell of
corruption choked her, sickly sweet. The White Crow retched, dry
heaves that twisted her gut.
    'Don't hesitate!' The White Crow lifted her head and shouted.
'*Now*, my lord Bishop, now!'
    Wood-sunlight limned his bony fingers. The old man's eyes
narrowed, wincing. 'He hurt me, hurt me unbelievably. I can't find
in me the charity to forgive him.'
    Acerbic fear tugged her smile crooked. 'You don't forgive gods,
Theo, my lord, the day for *that* isn't in the calendar. And what can
you expect from a Decan who's had entirely too much contact with
humans?'
    ' "Too much"?'
    His beaked nose jutted as the corners of his mouth came up,
deepening the folds of his skin. His brows contracted, and the skin
around his eyes wrinkled. Sudden laughter spluttered in his voice.
    'What can I *expect*—?'
    She fell forward on both hands.
    The sweet smell changed.
    Her hands slid in the cool flesh of maggots, and it changed. On
hands and knees she stared down. White rose-petals covered her
hands, buried them to the wrists; she knelt on them. The thick
heavy sweetness of roses breathed up from crushed flowers.
    She knelt up, head lowered, staring at the wave-front of white-
ness travelling away from her among crumbled marble: the heaving

bodies of grubs transmuting to flowers. She bent and pushed her hands forward into the mass.

Thorns snagged her skin.

Her skin, tanned, gold by contrast with these white petals and green spiked stems; her skin that smelt of sweat and dirt, now stitched across each arm with the dotted scars of rose-thorns. A bead of blood swelled. She lifted her arm to her mouth and licked.

'Oh, but *what*—?'

She began to laugh.

'Above, beneath: branch and root . . .'

His voice from behind her resonated with a calm casual expectancy. She, magus, Master-Physician, echoed him joyously; feeding the power of the words into the world: 'Above, beneath: branch and root—'

'Pillar of the world . . .'

A bramble coiled her ankle, the spikes too young and soft to do more than tickle. Roses fingered their way across her thighs where she sat; coiled up an arm; spread into the masses of her dark-red hair. She shook her head, white petals fluttering down, the corners of her eyes wet with laughter.

'Oh, hey—'

Ten yards away, he stood with his back to her. The old man, the Bishop; his hands folded calmly behind him, his chin a little raised. The wave-front of generation pulsed out from where he stood. 'Leaf in bud: shelter and protection.'

'Light of the forest . . .'

She stood up, naked, the white roses hanging heavy in her hair. A scent of them breathed on the suddenly blowing breeze. Heat fell down across her shoulders, unknotting the muscles there, relaxing her spine; so that she stood with her weight back on one heel and reached up with both arms, stretching up to light that glowed gold and green.

Spikes pushed up through the drifts of white roses.

She took one step forward and then another, unsteady on her feet; and twigs poked up, growing, sprouting into the air, knitting the air together about them – great clumps of blackthorn and may, elder and wild roses: sparkling with green shoots, pale in the light.

'Protection of the branches that support the sky . . .' Saplings jutted from the earth around his feet. Brown twigs, one looped leaf spiking up from each.

'Heart of the wood . . .'

'Oldest of all, deepest of all—'

Blackthorn grew, tough wood spearing higher than her head now. She felt how it knitted earth together within its roots, beneath the roses; how it knitted together, too, at microcosmic levels, binding energy, possibility, structure.

'Rooted in the soul of earth—'

'Who dies not, but is disguised; who sleeps only.'

'Heart of the wood!'

On the nearest branch a tiny leaf uncoiled, bright green beside the thorn-spikes and white flower. So close that she crossed her eyes to focus on it, giggled and stepped back. Leaf and flower together, spidered now with flowering creeper, the horns of morning glory, columbine, old man's beard, and ivy: green and white and dappling the light with new shade.

The White Crow spread her arms wide.

She traced through her fingertips the divine and demonic in the structure.

'Theodoret! Theo!'

Heady: oxygen and excitement filled her lungs. The light of her inner vision blazed green and gold, filling her veins. Beech saplings sprouted from the earth all around her.

She walked barefoot, wincing as a sharpness dug into the sole of her foot; stopping to balance and pull out a thorn, and on impulse kiss her finger and press it to the infinitesimal wound and smile, smile as if her face would never lose that expression.

Warmth shone down.

Warmth bloomed up from the earth beneath Theodoret's feet. Runners of ivy criss-crossed the ground, the leaves of other plants poking up between. And between one step and another the coiled heads of a myriad shoots unfurled, unwinding into flowers, and she walked knee-deep in bluebells with the old man.

A dappled light shone on him, silvering and greying his hair by turns: a light of trees only yet potential.

'You're doing it!' Joy filled her; she shouted to the growing trees.

'I can reach him, child – *just*.'

Wind creaked through the branches of trees grown tall, skittered over a ground clear of undergrowth in this newly mature wood.

As far as she could see, the perspectives of the wood stretched. New leaves shimmered on trees, bluebells misted the distance. Far off, far away, in the heart of the wood . . .

The White Crow let her arms fall to her sides. Aching, she stared; keeping the long sight down into the centre as a part of her; hidden, dangerous, glorious.

She turned.

This way the trees were not so thick, and she glimpsed past them a light of rose and gold: swirling, granular, hot.

'You . . .'

'Me,' Theodoret rasped.

He pressed back against the smooth bole of a grown beech tree behind him. Sunlight and shadow spotted his bony chest, dappled his legs and thighs. He pressed his hands and spine against the bark.

The waves of generation sank back.

Unsteady, the White Crow staggered towards him.

A tendril of ivy crept around the bole of the tree, looping the old man's wrist. His skin darkened, silvered. Before she could draw breath his skin cracked and fissured, merging so swiftly into the lumps and curves of the beech-trunk that she had no time to turn away her gaze.

The tree grew.

He grew with it, embedded into the wood. His long mobile features darkened to green, to silver-brown; his hair flowed out across the bark, rooting down into it.

He opened his mouth and called a word of healing.

She fell down, the leaves and fragments of bark imprinting her flesh.

The call echoed into the heart of the wood.

His jaw strained open, strained further open, and she thought it must surely crack; his head tipped back and growing into the heart-wood of the beech.

Two sprouting pale-green leaves poked from the corners of his mouth.

Swift, swift as thought they grew; jutting out like tusks and coiling back, growing into the trunk of the beech.

'Theo! My lord Bishop!'

She pulled herself to her feet, craning her neck to see the tree. Already the trunk was too vast for her to perceive all of it, and its leaves and branches shadowed the world. The coolness of forests shivered across her skin.

'*I have found him.*'

A cool heartbreaking wind blew around her, out of the heart of the wood. Awe dried her throat. Sweat slicked the skin of her elbows, behind her ears, her thighs: blood and cells burning, warm with a knowledge of solidity. She shook her hair back and craned her neck to look up through shedding petals.

The sense of an old story rose in her, unbelieved, unconquerable; and she gazed up into the heights of branches and green leaves.

'*Now . . .*'

Her spine shuddered, prickled the hairs at the back of her neck. She touched her fingers to her mouth. Vibrating at cell- and DNA-level, voices sang in her flesh: thirty-five of them. Voices of the Decans of Hell and Heaven.

Something tickled her hand. She lifted it. Blood-heat, imperceptible, red liquid trickled from her palm and dripped to the earth. Blood smeared the sweating flesh of her knee, her ankle. The black bee-stings of the Decan's maze throbbed, her left hand raw and swollen.

'*Act—*'

'*Act now—*'

'*Channel us—*'

'*We will inform you—*'

'*Breathe in you—*'

'*Speak in you—*'

'*Open our Selves to you—*'

A sand-bright voice, clearer than all others, thrummed in her human flesh: '*We made you in Our image and with Our power. You are all star-daemons. My child, my lover, my bride of the sun and widow of the moon, call down the universe now. Heal!*'

Sprawling naked, without sword or book, her suntanned flesh scratched with the thorns of impossible roses, the White Crow reached out. With her left hand she drew hieroglyphs, skeining down the bright air to twist in *magia* patterns. Watching how the light shifted, as leaves shift in a high wind; feeling for the moment and sensing it—

At some level above or below perception, binding took place.

A sapling birch brushed her arm, white bark peeling like paper. Transparent green leaves sprinkled the branches. Heat burned into her back.

The dappled light of beech shade fell cool across her skin.

She reached up, holding her hand in the sign of protection. The feedback of power between microcosm and macrocosm, Scholar-Soldier and the elementals, filled her with an electric energy; drawing power down the chains of the world from the Thirty-Six houses of the heavens.

She sprang up, barefooted, stamped a foot down into new grass. Beeches surrounded her, growing up to the invisible sky. Their great boles towered like pillars, soaring up a hundred feet to where they arched together, new green leaves rustling, and a bird sang.

Divine and demonic: demonic and divine.

Tall slender branches rose as pillars to the sky, meeting overhead in arches of new foliage. Birds sang in the branches, caterpillars and woodlice crawled among the roots.

A mass of broken marble lay embedded in the earth. Walking closer, she gazed up at it. Solid, some fifteen or twenty feet high; cracked and fissured and gold, still, with the light of extinguished candles. The last of the ruined mortal matter that had hosted a goddaemon. The White Crow walked close enough to touch, to feel the cold radiating from it.

She drew rapidly, smearing blood from her hand in complex astrological and cabbalistic signs on the broken surface of the marble. A frown indented the dark-red eyebrows, and she rested her free hand against the stone as support, leaning her forehead on that arm. The scrawled signs covered a half, two-thirds of the rock. The symbols grew cramped, smaller as the surface became more crowded; and the White Crow frowned in concentration, muttering the remembered first prayers of training.

'O thou who are the four elements of our nature, and the hundred elements of nature itself; Powers; star-daemons; rulers of the Thirty-Six Houses of the sky and Earth . . .'

'Draw down power. As above, so below. You are Our creation and We created you kin to Us. Draw power down the linkages of the world and heal!'

The stone split under her fingers.

Cracking like a shell: sliding, splitting; stone fragments falling to splinter on the floor of the wood. She stumbled back. Her hand dropped, lifted again to draw with bloodstains on the air. Rubble fell away, echoing like gunshots, from the massive shape disclosed.

In a shaft of sunlight, great wings unfurled.

Ribbed wings opened, glowing first pearl and then pale rose and then gold. The wind from their beating knocked her from her feet. Earth hit her. She grunted, breath jolted from her body. Grass and twigs imprinted her bare stomach. She raised herself up and rested on her forearms.

A great muzzle dipped, vast dark-gold eyes opening. Scales glinted on monstrous cheek-bones. Tiny naked ears flicked alertly. Tendrils floated upon the air, anchored across the head and around the eyes. Tusks jutted up alongside the pit-nostrils, crusted with deposits of adamant crystal. The overhanging upper lip wrinkled.

She hardly breathed. 'Lord of Noon and Midnight.'

The leonine body unfolded, rising from marble fragments to stand forty feet high: spotted yellow as a leopard, brown-gold as a hyena. Great wings sheathed. Lids slid up to narrow the eyes watching her. The full closed lips curved.

'I had forgotten how it is, to become so young . . . I had forgotten how it is to forget . . .'

Miracle beat in her blood, staggered her feet, so that she stumbled to her feet, head fizzing as with wine. She held out one hand empty of sword, the other empty of scroll; grinning up into the newborn face so hard that it hurt her jaws.

The overhanging muzzle dipped. She flinched. Closed lips touched her. She smelt fire, comet-dust, the green breath of trees.

'Where's Theo? Divine One . . .'

The massive head lifted. Ivy coiled, ringing the tusks with white and green. Insects crept in the folds of the upper lip; woodlice and wild bees and lizards. She stared up into eyes liquid with golden blackness; smelt from the delicate-lipped mouth a scent of cut grass. A shiver walked up her spine, exploded between her shoulder-blades.

'Forget, change, become a miracle.'

The voice sounded like the rustle of leaves, like the echo of sound in great spaces of stone.

'I had forgotten what it is to change! Each spring is the world's first; each winter the ending of an aeon; each summer the high and changeless meridian of pleasure. Now is the millennium. Now I see!'

The great long-muzzled head lifted. Wide nostrils and mouth encompassed a speckled darkness, the yellow darkness of sun in shadowed cavities of wood. The god-daemon shifted, haunches sinking, wings curving up to frame the high shoulders. It sat immovably in the cathedral of trees.

She shook.

The tension of green hung in the air; paused, poised, hesitated; hung in balance.

The Decan, The Spagyrus, Lord of Noon and Midnight, reached out one clawed limb and touched the bark of the great beech tree. White flesh and bone tumbled into shape: the old man sprawled in the grass. The White Crow held out her right hand, and the Bishop of the Trees seized it and pulled himself to his feet.

'We . . . did it.' He laughed, dazed, face creasing.

The White Crow gazed up through shifting beech leaves, the brightness of the green tingling in her blood and vision.

'Yeah. We did it and here's the end of it . . .'

The voice of the Twelfth Decan rang through the aisles of the trees, deep and new. His sandstone-and-gold pelt rippled.

'End? No. I perceive . . . We perceive . . . that We have erred. No, this is not the end. You have scarcely been admitted across the threshold of miracle. It is the beginning, now.'

The ancient voice burned with energy and new fire. In the Scholar-Soldier's head it echoed with the voices of the Thirty-Six who make up the circle of the sky.

'*Now We see that We should not for so many aeons have concealed Ourselves in stone. Now We throw down the Fane. And now . . . We will walk amongst you.*'

The White Crow craned her neck, staring upwards.

All the flat gold of the sky softened, turning to great towering masses of brilliance that paled: here to rose, there to pink and gold . . .

The sky shredded; stretching and pulling apart. The depths beyond glowed blue.

Clouds parted, the sun's beams turning them gold and pink. Parted, pulled aside, no trace of the flat gold sky now; only a heat and a brightness that dazzled her.

A white-yellow disc brought water to her eyes.

She stared up into the infinity of a blue summer sky.

'Captain-General, something's happening!'

Desaguliers straightened, leaning his musket and rest back against his haunch. He stared up at the top of the barricade where the Cadet crouched. 'Did no one ever train you to make an exact report? *What* is "happening"?'

The young Cadet – a slim black Rat, hardly more than a Ratling – clung with tail and one gloved hand to the shattered joists of the palace wall. Powder-burns scarred his livery and smooth-furred snout.

'I don't know!'

Desaguliers, hearing battle-fatigue in the young Rat's voice, leaned his musket against the barricade's bricks, joists and jewel-studded furniture; drew his pistol, and loped along to scramble up the slope.

A stray shot spanged off a corner of the demolished wall. Desaguliers ducked, glancing back. Nothing new – the main palace hall broken open to the sky, slashed with the light-shadows of the Night Sun, and barricaded from the courtyard where human refugees hid behind rubble and risked shots with captured weapons.

Darkness clung to masonry, illuminated only by powder-flashes. The blue light that mazed the streets sank into dimness. Desaguliers rubbed his sore eyes. The wings of acolytes overlapped the sky, flying down to cling to broken walls, precariously leaning roofs.

'They're . . . not attacking.'

Desaguliers, hand poised to give the signal to fire, hesitated. 'Not yet, I think.'

Ribbed wings folded, obsidian claws clutching coign and balcony and gutter, bristle-tails coiling: by tens and dozens the acolytes settled on the besieged palace.

He turned his lean snout, staring down from the barricade into the body of the hall. Shattered glass and treadmills, torn drapes, the inlaid floor splintered with soldiers' running feet; here and there the black smears of extinguished fires. Blue-jacketed Cadets lined the barricades, steadying muskets on rests or cleaning swords black with daemon blood.

Clustered in the centre, under the last remaining arch of that clover-leaf roof, away from attack and falling walls, eight Rats clung together. One brown Rat nursed a bloody arm, resting back in the arms of two black Rats. A silver Rat trod down a scarlet robe under one hind claw, clutching at a bony black Rat. They clung. The fattest black Rat lay on broken marquetry flooring, curled around the clump of intergrown tails that he clutched to his furred stomach.

'They're *not* attacking, messire.'

Desaguliers narrowed his eyes, stroking his scarred cheek. 'They're going to come right over us next time they try, that's obvious. Messire Jannac, is your blade dull yet?'

'Er, no, messire.'

'We're going to move down into the nearest train-tunnels while this lull lasts.'

'But his Majesty?'

'We're going to cut his Majesty free; it's the only way we'll move them.'

'Messire!'

He turned his head, swearing at the Rat daring to protest; stopped dead, staring at the Cadet. A pale light glinted on his black fur, shone from the young Rat's broken nails and sword-hilt. Desaguliers raised his head.

The light-shadows blurred and vanished. Above, the world lightened to yellow, to gold, to brilliance.

He raised his eyes, staring up to where the Night Sun had blotted the sky, and looked directly into the white-hot disc of the noon sun.

Desaguliers scrambled up on to the highest point of the barricade, careless of fire; eyes running tears in the brilliance of daylight, the summer sun's heat like fire on his pelt.

He grabbed a metal rod projecting from the rubble, blotted his eyes with the fur of his arm, and stared out across the city. Across the courtyard, where men and women walked out wondering into sunlight; across the city roofs black with clustering acolytes, to the great darkness in the north-aust.

Walls and buttresses tumbled, falling slow into clear air.

Desaguliers beckoned wildly, aware of Jannac climbing to his side. 'Do you see, messire? Do you *see* that?'

'The Fane!'

Black walls splintered, shifting, falling. Arched roofs crashed down into naves. Desaguliers felt through clawed feet the rumble of the impact; sound twitched at his ragged ears. Dust billowed up from the Fane-in-the-Seventh-District, spires crumpling, falling like rows of dominoes. The breath of a smell came to him in the summer air: dank stone, opened crypts, and something that choked his throat with unshed tears.

'The Fane!'

He sheathed his sword, loping up to cling to the edge of the broken wall and lean outwards. Shadow skirred across him. He jerked his snout up. The daemon-acolytes beat their wings, spiked tails clutching the palace masonry, beaked jaws open and screeching.

Dust and haze thundered up in the north-aust sky.

Captain-General Desaguliers shaded his eyes with a callused shaking hand. Gripping brick with his other hand, he leaned out and squinted to the aust-west. Far distant, down in Eleventh District, the midnight silhouettes of black masonry collapsed . . .

'It is . . . it *is* destroyed.'

About to call down in triumph to the Cadets, Desaguliers choked on wonder.

He had swivelled round to climb down, and now faced the Fane again. Colour danced: scarlet, green, blue, white and purple.

From out of the Fane's black rubble and ruin, from tilted pillars and crumbling buttresses, from ogive windows and broken spires, plants began to flower. Roses, hawthorn, forget-me-nots, apple blossom; orchids and cowslips, blackberries and alyssum; out of season and out of time, growing, spilling out of the ruins like a lava-tide . . .

Below him, the Cadets rested muskets and sheathed swords, climbing the barricades to walk among bewildered men and women in temporary truce. The Rat-King milled in confusion. Desaguliers stepped, slipped, slid a yard down a tilted limestone slab, grazing his haunch; grabbed the torn stone edge and stared, wordless, at the Fane.

Among the ruins of millennially old stone, miraculous flowers opened petals to the summer sky, spilling down into the city streets.

The wings of acolytes rustled agitatedly on the roof above. Desaguliers looked up to see each beaked muzzle pointing at the Fane's ruins in dumb expectancy.

Grey heat burned her bare shoulders.

She threw her head back, muscles unknotting from tension; feeling her rose-tangled hair hot under the sun. A granular grey summer's heat burned in her, fogging her vision; pricking her skin with ultraviolet, loosing all strains.

She stared up into a blue sky.

Open, blue: the sun an unbearable white hole into heat and light. One glance upwards blinded her, tears pouring down her cheeks; she saw, smeared, to each horizon: north, south, aust, west and east, the city that is called the heart of the world.

At every horizon, the Fane is tumbled into ruin: obelisks jutting like broken teeth, buttresses fracturing into stone lace, roofs falling, walls split, open to the summer air.

'*We have chosen Our new way. We have hidden Ourselves for too long. Now We choose to walk amongst you.*'

All Fanes are one Fane.

Her feet are conscious of hardness, that she walks now on brick paving, and she stares up – in a courtyard where pottery brick walls collapse – at the stone-warm image of a sphinx.

Black bees swarmed frantically, the air full of buzzing black dots. The White Crow walked forward, hands gently brushing bees aside, their furred feet tickling as they crawled across her bare shoulders. She lifts her head.

'*The Wheel turns. The Dance begins again.*'

'You'll . . . build again?'

Terracotta full lips smile, anciently and with warmth. The Decan of High Summer, the Lady of the Eleventh Hour: a sphinx-shape that towers high above the woman; heat radiating back from sun-warmed brick flanks and head-dress and heavy-lidded eyes.

'*We have confined Ourselves to the Fane too long,*' the Decan's voice repeats, attendant with echoes, until it seems that all the Thirty-Six are speaking in a confusion of voices. '*My Master-Physician, all that the Divine does is right, because it is We who do it. Come.*'

The White Crow's feet stung with the reverberation of a brick paw falling to the ground. She swayed, staring up. Moss-crusted flanks stretch, great shoulders arch; the vast body of the god-daemon rises from the earth. Impossible, articulated, the incarnate stone flesh moves; shining in the noon sun with the brilliance of deserts.

The footfall's reverberation shook her flesh. The White Crow stumbled, half-walking and half-running. The shadow of ancient stone fell across her, and she, legs turned rubbery, staggered to walk beside the god-daemon as the Decan slowly paced forward.

'Come. We will walk out into the world.'

Parquet flooring, hot with impossible sun, burned his palms.

Lucas slid out from the pit under the last analytical engine in the Long Gallery and stood up. Other students crowded the doors, the high windows, clamouring. Black grease smeared his hands and arms. He reached to grab his discarded doublet with filthy fingers.

'It's the sun!' Rafi slapped his bare shoulder, running past. 'It's daylight out there! *We did it!'*

Bodies jostled. Lucas floated in their movement, hardly conscious of it; aching with weariness from wrench and gear and rod, eyes stinging with tiredness. He let himself be carried down the grand stairway into the university's entrance-hall.

'Outside!' A blonde girl hammered the door-beam out of its socket with the heel of her hand.

Above his head, the carved applewood beams shimmered. He raised his head. Summer heat and light flooded in through the opening door. A sharp sweet smell drifted in.

One pale green spot appeared on the wood. It swelled, bubbled up, unscrolled into the air – a leaf. A veined green leaf. Lucas pushed his headband further up his brow, shifting the hair from his eyes, gaping.

All the beams supporting the roof burst into leaf. A tide of green swept through the hall, leaves unfolding, rustling; springing from the wood of beams and panelling and doors, darkening the sunlit hall to a green shadow.

Lucas pushed into the throng of students and Reverend tutors, finding himself carried towards the door. Pink blossom burst out on the now-knotted beams.

'The sun—!'

A silence fell. Lucas stepped out into the courtyard, the other students slowing as they pushed out into that wide paved space. Briars wreathed the great sandstone staircases rising up at cater-corners of the yard. Glass windows shimmered, river-bright. Acolytes clung to the towering chimneys, bristle-tails writhing down among flowering wooden window-frames.

Pharamond caught his gaze across the heads of other students: the bearded man with his hair dishevelled, his face dazed. 'We did it. We cheated the laws of nature!'

Lucas brushed his arms, the faint dew and wind raising the small hairs down his forearms. Black machine-oil glistened. Over the courtyard and the open gates, an early-summer sky clung to roofs and streets and spires. A sky hot and soft and pale with heat.

A Katayan student clapped his hands rhythmically, broke off, caught a dark-haired woman's hands and pulled her into a dance-step. Lucas, to his own astonishment, picked up the clapping rhythm. Two girls snatched up soft-thorned briars, weaving them into garlands. Processional, ragged, yelling, the students burst open the university's iron gates.

Lucas stifled fear under fatigue, triumph and sheer blinded brilliance. With each step the sun shone more brightly, until he had to turn his face away from the blaze and look down at his black shadow on the paving. He passed under the main gate, and a shower of green leaves flew about him, brushing his shoulders; white and pink apple blossom whirling into the air, petals clinging damply to his skin.

The heat reflected from alley walls and bright windows, smelling of dust and dirt, of manure, of bird's feathers and fruit-stalls and drying washing. Fragments of song burst up into the air, one student beginning a catch, someone else drowning it. A shatter of glass made him stumble. He turned to see Regis, the sun bright on her freckled face, standing ankle-deep in an arcade window and passing out bottles of wine.

The yellow-haired Katayan male knocked against Lucas as he stumbled past, chanting an unrecognisable song:

'Now we shall walk—

'Now we shall walk—

'Now we shall walk amongst you—'

A flash of white caught Lucas's eye.

He staggered into a run, breaking for an alley-entrance, panting, legs spiked with pain as he turned and ran up the hill. The bleached sky burned above.

Its shadow dark on the cobbles, the silver timber-wolf trotted quickly around corner and corner.

Heart hammering, lungs burning, Lucas caught up. He ran from the last houses, out on to the abandoned building site surrounding the Fane-in-the-Nineteenth-District. A confused impression of abandoned scaffolding and stone, of black marble and jungles of flowers blurred his vision.

Like lava it ran down the hill into the city, a resistless tide. Daisies sprouted from guttering, ivy from door-posts; wild roses threshed up into great banks of scent and colour. Sparkling mosses thrust up from roof-tiles. The wind filled his mouth with the scent of cherry and roses and stocks, slowing his steps until he paced, resting his oil-grimed fingers on the ruff at the wolf's neck.

Exposed under the pitiless noon sky, he momentarily shut his eyes. His palms sweated. Anticipation pulsed under his ribs, in his guts. His hand closed hard over the wolf's rough pelt. Lazarus whined.

'Lazarus! Hey, boy!'

Lucas's eyes flew open.

She trod the chalky ground of the site, dust whitening her bare feet and ankles, her face tilted up to the summer sky. A warm wind tugged the masses of dark red hair that fell about her shoulders, hair whitened at the temples, and wound with white roses that shed petals as she walked. Brown smears of dried blood marked her left hand.

She walked naked in the summer's heat.

He mouthed her name. He heard the skitter of gravel as she kicked it, walking across the site; saw her head come down, eyes sky- and sun-dazzled, and a wide smile spread across her face. Now, closer, the young man saw how dirt creased in the folds of skin at her elbows and jaw; how sweat shone on her forehead and breasts. Dust paled her dark aureoles, glimmered in the dark-red curls of her pubic hair.

'Lucas.'

He reached out with both hands, cupping her bare shoulders. Oil smudged her skin. She smiled, the skin crinkling around her tawny eyes; tilted her head a little to the side. Flowers spiralled across the chalky earth, coiling up about her ankles. He smelt her warm sweat, tasted salt as he kissed her mouth and licked her cheek. Energy sang in her skin, pulsed in her blood; the backwash of some tide not yet gone from her consciousness.

'Lucas . . .'

Her arms came up under his, tightening around his ribs and across his back. Her breasts pressed against his skin. He grabbed her to him, probing her mouth with his tongue, suddenly and appallingly inexpert. Some tremor shook the body he held: laughter or disgust? He gripped her more tightly.

He felt her hands slide down and unhook his belt, smoothing his breeches down his hips, guiding him to sheath his aching and too-ready flesh in her transformed body.

The sparrow soars down from the heights.

This is the same midday heat that would drive it to shelter under eaves, or seek out a dust-bath to flutter feathers cool. Now, dropping to earth, the bird's unblinking eyes take in the heart of the world.

*White stone wings extend, hissing in the clear air. The sparrow stalls, flicks
to perch on a vast extended finger. It cocks its head, taking in the naked and
narrow-hipped body that lounges upon the wind. An eagle-head dips,
golden eyes blinking. A dream of feathers blows about the god-daemon's
stone skin.*

*The Decan of Daybreak, Lord of Air and Gathering, lifts his finger and
touches – so delicately – his colossal carved beak to the bird's head.*

'See . . .'

All the austerly horizons burst into flame with flowers.

Air shimmered over the model, over the single bricks that formed a
makeshift wall around its five-metre-square plan. Walled and gated
by bricks, interior gardens sketched with chalk, domes and halls
slapped together from hessian and wet plaster on a wired lath
frame. A model rocking on chalk-marked broken paving.

'Ah.' The Lord-Architect Casaubon looked up as a shadow fell
across the scaffolding and bricks and masonry of Fourteenth District's
square where he sat. 'I thought you'd be along, sooner or later.'

A vast sphinx-shadow covered the broken paving and the granite
block engraved with the Word of Seshat; darkening the shabby
makeshift model of the New Temple.

The Decan of the Eleventh Hour stands against the sun, the warm
and glowing substance of Her incarnation wreathed with trailing
wild roses. Black bees swarm about Her face, nest in the crevices of
brickwork drapery. The summer breeze blows from behind Her,
scented with desert dawn and arctic night.

'Well done, little lord.'

The Lord-Architect climbed ponderously to his feet, rump
momentarily skyward; tugged his blue silk breeches up and brushed
with one ham-hand at the dirt on his shirt and frock-coat.

'I know what you've come to do.' His china-blue eyes blinked
against the new sunlight. He rubbed his stomach and gently
belched. 'Hadn't you – I beg your pardon, Divine One – hadn't you
better get *on* with it?'

'Hurry is for mortals.'

One copper eyebrow lifted. The fat man opened his mouth,
hesitated, and shook his head. He began to feel through each of his
deep coat-pockets in turn. At last he unearthed a tiny notebook and
pencil.

The Lord-Architect stripped off his voluminous blue coat, spread
it over an expanse of step, and eased himself down to sit on it. He
balanced the notebook on his immense thigh, and licked the pencil
thoughtfully.

'There is something yet to do, little lord.'

The Lord-Architect Casaubon lifted his head from his writing. He pushed up his shirt-sleeves with the pencil still folded in his plump fingers. A line of tiny neat letters marked the notebook's page.

'I said, there is—'

A grin creased its way across the fat man's oil- and plaster-stained face. He spread one open palm. 'Divine One. *Do* it. I always had a taste for a good miracle myself.'

Radiant and stinging as the sunlight, divine amusement beat against his skin. He rested his chins on his hand, and his elbow on one vast up-raised knee, and held the tiny notebook up.

'I see . . .'

Heavy-lidded eyes close, open, with leonine slowness. Sun gleams on high cheek-bones and nose, shines back from tiny ochre bricks and the white dots of roses. The salt-pan whiteness of Her gaze fixes upon him.

'Knowing all, then, you will not need Me to tell you that she lives.'

A shudder passed through his flesh, shaking his chins and belly. He wiped a sweat-drenched forehead, smearing plaster-dust in clumps into his hair, and breathed in sharply. For a moment he sagged in relief. Then he tapped the notebook against his delicate lips, hiding a broad smile.

'No – but I thank you for the thought.'

'If you are not damned, little architect, it will not be the fault of the Thirty-Six. Very well, then. Your expected miracle. See now what I conceive it necessary to do!'

Light blazed.

In that second he saw no lath-and-plaster domes, no brick colonnades or chalk-drawn gardens, only the deep structure of order and proportion and extravagant flamboyance that lies in particles, cells, souls.

Breath knocked out of him, the Lord-Architect sprawled on his back. He grunted, getting himself up on to his elbows.

'Madam, I congratulate . . . you . . .'

The stone of Seshat lay embedded now in a wall, mortared in with a cement that seemed to bear the weathering of many seasons. Beside it, before the Lord-Architect's startled gaze, mellow red brick soared up into a foliate gate. He stared through the opening, too small to admit a carriage, across lawns flanked by comfortable low colonnades. A fountain shot thin jets into the sunlight.

'Oh, I do,' he said. 'I do.'

Beyond the fountain, wide steps suitable for traders' booths or just for resting rose to a rotunda and tiled dome; its arches open and without doors to close them.

Somewhere beyond the main body of the temple, a campanile put delicate brick tracery into the summer sky. He stared at the ledges, balconies and open belvedere. His gaze fell to gardens, and clear through the gateway came the sound of river-water.

'*Look* at it . . .' A woman's husky voice sounded above him. Casaubon pushed himself up to a sitting position beside Mistress Evelian.

'It was bound to happen.' Pride crept into the fat man's voice. 'Such acute construction ought never to be wasted—'

'Sharlevian!'

With eyes for nothing else, not even the presence of a goddaemon, the yellow-haired woman ran through the gate, catching up the hem of her dirty blue satin dress. She flung her arms around a figure in pink overalls, swinging her daughter's feet off the ground.

Tannakin Spatchet, hovering on the edge of their joy in embarrassment, caught the Lord-Architect's eye. The Mayor drank from a pottery jar, lifting it in salute.

Behind him, spreading out through the grounds that now seemed to fill all the site-space lying behind the square, black and brown Rats, and humans still in the remnants of carnival dress, wandered wide-eyed up from the underground tunnels. Talk sounded gradually louder on the air.

Casaubon stood and walked under the arch of the gateway. He rested one brick-grazed hand against the wall. Flesh curved, creasing his face into a ridiculous and ineradicable smile; he swept his gaze across the Temple grounds – cool passageways, wide steps, seats, fountains; the glimmer of mosaics in the ceiling of the great dome; distant tree-tops, and the explosion of blossom, and the growing crowds – and finally swung back, arms wide.

'Didn't I say, the best thing I'd ever done! Oh, not as magnificent as many, not as *grand* – but for the *form* of it! That structure all but compels them to rest, to walk slowly, to talk peaceably—'

'*Compelled? Invited, rather. And was it your conception, little lord? I think it was also the woman's and the child's, and the other man's there.*'

'Well . . . Yes. I admit it. Baltazar Casaubon doesn't need to fear sharing credit, Divine One.'

Her head rises against the blue summer sky, incarnate, ancient and young. Black bees hum around her shoulders and flanks. The Decan of the Eleventh Hour raises Her head and gazes into the heart of the sun itself. The full curved lips move.

'*So . . . but yes. Yes. Haste is for mortals – but there is still one thing to be done.*'

The deck slewed.

The Boat, gripped in a midnight current, raced into noise and darkness. Clawed hands tore at the hull, wood shrieking as it ripped. Zar-bettu-zekigal staggered back and forth across the deck, boot-laces flapping, hacking her heel down on nine-clawed hands, spitting at catfish-mouthed human faces. She swallowed, saliva wetting her sore throat.

'I can keep this up all night if it helps. Isn't *anything* I don't remember.'

Far up, in the vaults of darkness, a line of white glimmered. Zari narrowed her eyes. In her moment's inattention, the humming chant behind her faded into vagueness.

'Elish!'

'I hear you, Zar'. What happened then?'

'Oh, she told me to get out of the tent. I had it *just* where I planned and she – all *she* cared about was that I shouldn't talk to the press!'

Zar-bettu-zekigal let the stream of words come. She balanced on the moving deck, knees aching at the shifts of balance. Water curved up – *up* – in a great hill: obsidian-black, sharp with rills and knot-hole eddies. Above and ahead, at the crest of the rising water, whiteness foamed. Zari's hand shot out and grabbed a thwart.

'And why *shouldn't* I talk to Vanringham? I'm a Kings' Memory! I can talk to anyone I like!'

A chuckle. 'But can you stop?'

A whisk-ended tail whipped about Zari's ankle. She glanced back. Elish-hakku-zekigal sat cross-legged at the tiller, one elbow hooked about the black wood; her free hand tapping a shaman drum-rhythm on the deck. Her cornflower-blue eyes gleamed in the guttering light of the one lamp.

'Need you, little one. Who else could keep my memory stirred?'

She began to hum, deep in her throat: a shaman chant. The hairs rose down Zar-bettu-zekigal's spine, and the familiarity of it stirred a reckless joy in her. She jerked her head, hair flying.

'And that? Up ahead?'

'I think, for good or ill, the end of us. Hold on!'

The roar of the impossibly-rising hill of water deafened her. Zar-bettu-zekigal whiplashed moisture from her tail and tottered back across the deck.

'Steer us away from it – across the current!'

'Trying, little one. Come help.'

Zari set her narrow hip against the wooden tiller. It shook against her hands. The lantern on the stern-pole swung wildly, sending faint light across the water. Filament-mouthed faces shone in the blackness. Crustacean claws lifted. Something with fleer-eyed malice swam frog-like at the bows. She braced herself hard against the tiller, turning to stare ahead.

'Hey!'

Fish-eyes gleamed in nebula-clusters, burning green and gold in sudden brilliance. A ripple of gold ran through the hill of water, spider-threading infinite depths.

'El, what is it!'

'Baby, I'm here; it's all right—'

A wave rushed down the hill-slope, battering the prow of the Boat. Spray soaked Zar-bettu-zekigal. She shook wet hair from her eyes, swearing. The Boat dipped, wallowed; she dug heels into the deck and heaved the tiller hard over, looked up into darkness, and her heel skidded. She clung to the wooden spar.

The darkness curdled, cracked. She rubbed salt water from her streaming eyes, staring up. Overhead the blackness flaked, crumbled . . .

The god-daemon lay calm among waters.

Light shone between granite horns.

He lay between rows of cracked grey pillars, sea-washed, carved over with hieroglyphs; and incised in the flagstones around the plinth she saw, sea-worn, the signs of the Thirty-Six. Black water threshed and foamed against living stone.

Zar-bettu-zekigal looked up from vast webbed black hands gripping the plinth, to caprine forearms, to shaggy throat and shoulders. The great horned goat's head towered above into darkness: cracked grey granite, informed with the presence of the Decan.

'Divine One.' Elish-hakku-zekigal bowed her head, not losing her grip on the tiller.

Tor-weathered, the shaggy granite flanks shed sea-foam and beating water. The mountain-range of shoulder and spine and haunch stretched away into darkness to where, far off, his scale-crusted tail lashed black waters to storm.

A rich smell dizzied Zar-bettu-zekigal. Rich enough to drown out the oil, fish, ooze and excrement that composed it; rich with the energies of generation and corruption and growth. She sneezed and wiped the back of her wrist across her face, leaning out over the hull of the Boat to stare up at the god-daemon.

'Oh, hey . . .' Utter contentment in her voice. 'Elish, I've *seen* one!'

The older Katayan spluttered into brief laughter.

'Say you, you have. And if it's not the last thing we ever see, then doubtless I'll never hear the end of it!'

Between the coiled sky-reaching horns a white disc burned, burning with the blotched stains of lunar seas. Light fell across the deck of the Boat, shining on her, and on the older Katayan's face, turning it stark black and silver.

Stone flaked: the eyes of the god-daemon among the waters opened.

Zari kicked a heel against the deck of the Boat, tilting her head to judge their speed as they rushed up to where the hill of water crested: to where, head lowered, the Decan of the Waters Below the Earth watched seas pour away into infinity. The roar of the waters falling all but drowned her shout: 'If he doesn't do something, El, we're finished!'

Great slanting eyes opened, liquid darkness staring down from under stone lids. The moon's light sent hard shadows across the horns and ears and muzzle, across the vast lips curving in an ancient slow smile. Far, far above her head, the coiled horns shone red with strings of roses: minute as blood-drops against the disc of the moon.

The dark of the Decan's eyes glimmered on foam and sea-fret. She felt her mouth go dry. As if it swung into dock between pilot and tugs, the Boat curved across the rising hills of water and slowed, slowed and stopped before the web-fingered hands of the god-daemon.

Her neck hurt, craning to look up. Raw throat, drenched and dripping coat, chilled to the bone: all became, for that instant, unimportant. Zar-bettu-zekigal gazed up at the long caprine face, the stone goat's muzzle whose beard jutted forked bone and forked wood; sea-serpents and crustaceans infesting the crevices.

Crumbled to bone at elbow and shoulder, none the less, green leaves sprouted to cover the great mountain-range spine. Moss spidered across the stone, fresh green. Seaweed sprouted bright yellows and ochres between the vast webs of fingers.

Nightmares swarmed about the distant flanks, small as pismires, that were large enough to swallow the Boat complete.

'Lord Decan!'

With a peculiar pride in courtesy, she looked into the stone-lidded eyes and bowed her head. She couldn't keep from grinning widely, excited.

'Zar'.' The older woman stood and stepped away from the tiller, her black-furred tail whipping around Zar-bettu-zekigal's wrist and tugging her aside.

'Oh, what!' She pulled herself free.

A cluster of red roses sprouted on the Boat's black-tarred thwart. A green runner coiled the length of the tiller. Barbed green thorns shot out of it, serrated leaves unfolded; a whole hedge-tangle of pink dog-roses weighed the tiller into stillness.

Serrated fins scraped the hull. Water slopped. She wiped her wet hair off her forehead and licked her lips; tasted the faint sweetness of ordure and gagged.

Moon-crested, lying between the Pillars of the Waters Under the Earth, the Decan bent its horned goat-head. The great-fingered hands shifted.

The waters boiled.

A heavy weight dipped down one side of the Boat. Zari stepped back, bumping her shoulder against Elish-hakku-zekigal where the shaman woman stood quietly at the prow. The Boat rocked again.

'Oh, hey . . .'

Only a breath, almost silence. She squatted on her haunches, leaning to stare at the wet footprints tracking the empty deck. She smiled in wonder. Shifting and shifting again, the Boat rocked and settled deeper into the waters. She stared up at the stone upon which the Decan lay, seeking for footprints wet among the carved flagstones of the plinth, but it towered above her head.

Crowding, overlapping: sourceless shadows of men and Rats stained the deck.

'Elish.' She touched one finger to a swift-drying mark (the print of a small Rat, by the size), feeling no substance by it. She stood. The air across the deck curdled, somehow full. She tugged Elish's satin sleeve and grinned. 'Passengers!'

'I thought it would never . . . Something's changed.' Elish-hakku-zekigal raised her eyes to the god-daemon. 'Again, the Boat carries the dead.'

Stone lips curved in an ancient uncanny smile; pursed very slightly and blew. The Boat rocked. The curve of the falls shot back gold light from black water. The lantern, guttering, tipped to the deck and smashed. She grabbed at the side of the Boat, Elish's hand catching her shoulder.

'We're going to go over!'

The shaman Elish-hakku-zekigal lifted her head and began to hum in the back of her throat. The chant for finding homecomings sounded, soft and quiet under the roar of waves. The current grabbed the Boat suddenly enough that it jolted Zari off her feet. She scrambled up with skinned knees.

Elish sang.

Zar-bettu-zekigal kicked off her black ankle-boots. She ran forward and leaped up, one foot either side of the sharp prow; knelt for a second and then stood, tail coiled out on the air for balance, wind lashing short wet hair back from her face.

'Hey!'

She pushed down on the balls of her feet as the prow dipped, rode the push upwards; yelling in unmusical concert the shaman chant, kicking out at a webbed hand grabbing her foot. A filamented mouth gaped, teeth gleaming. The crest of the hill of black water rushed closer.

'*Go, little ones.*'

A breath on the waters, warm as spring; a glimmer of fire, sea-green; and the voice of the Decan: '*Go back to the world.*'

She turned her head, sketched a bow, coat-tails flying. The prow fell away from under her feet; she slipped, banged her knee, and knelt to stare ahead at the beating crest of waters now all white fire and lace about the Boat—

'Look!' Elish broke her chant for a second, rushing forward beside her and pointing down. 'Look, the stars!'

Monstrous forms clung to thwarts and prow, fish-mouths wide, gaping for water; screeching. A clawed finger raked wood into splinters beside Zari's foot. She bent and grabbed a boat-hook from its ledge under the rail, scrambled up the prow, stabbed down among masses of green flesh and scale thick enough now to slow the Boat.

The rising wave crested.

Below, above, all around: she stared up dazzled at the stars in their Houses, burning in the Three Hundred and Sixty Degrees. Elish's warm hands gripped her shoulders. Dark and day spun across her sight, wheeling, turning . . .

Sunlight dazzled.

Zari heaved herself up to stand on the prow, one arm flung up against the sudden light. So all the later, famous pictures show her: a young black-haired Katayan, coat flying, arm raised as she beats down the swarming nightmare-monsters under the Boat's prow. She balances there, beneath her the tumbling bodies of nightmares, all framed by the great onyx-and-marble Arch of Days where the canal flows from the grounds of Salomon's Temple.

The older Katayan woman stands by a rose-shrouded tiller; her head back, her mouth open, chanting to the sun that shines full on her face.

Sun dazzles.

Canal-water boiled in motion, light shafting up and blinding her: the clawed and tendril-mouthed horrors diving for the depths. Zar-bettu-zekigal straightened, shaking out her wet greatcoat.

'*Ei!*'

'Now, Zar'!'

A tail coiled around her wrist and jerked. She staggered to the deck, avoiding the mast – the mast? – and glared at Elish-hakku-zekigal. A crowd of people jostled them.

Women, children, Rats, men, Ratlings. The deck shone, shadowless.

'*Off*, now. Move!'

Strong hands gripped the shoulders of her coat, pushing her across deck towards the gangplank – the gangplank? – and her heels skidded as she dug them in and staggered, clutching at a splinter.

'Say you, yes – but we both—'

'I came this way; I can go this way: I have to guide the Boat: now will you *leave*?'

Zar-bettu-zekigal staggered onto the gangplank. She let her shoulders slump in acquiescence. The heavily laden vessel wallowed. She folded her hand back and grabbed the solid vertebrae of the older Katayan's tail, and let her full weight swing them both to fall across plank and canal-water and tow-path.

The canal walkway whacked her between the shoulders. Dimly she heard shouting, cheering; sensed the movement of the great vessel on the waters. Pounding footsteps approached; dozens, hundreds.

She hitched herself up on to her wet elbows, raising one knee, her own tail twitching. The older woman sprawled, rubbing the base of her wrenched tail.

'Don't want you dead. Want you here. With me.'

'You shave-tailed little idiot!'

Twin masts shone black against a blue summer sky, the rigging bare. The Boat drifted in the canal, between gardens, people running up from far away, joining the growing crowd. Elish-hakku-zekigal stared.

She began to hum absently in her throat.

The vessel straightened, swinging to point away from the Arch of Days. It began to glide, weighted down by passengers who cast no shadows; to glide away in the sun . . .

Elish shot her one broad grin and staggered to her feet, shaking out her coat-tails and lace ruffle. She walked unsteadily down the canal path, lifting her head, singing the guiding chant, her eyes all on the Boat and not on the front runners of the crowd who fell back, cheering, to give her passage.

Sun blazed.

Zar-bettu-zekigal felt a hand at her shoulder, at her elbow; and grabbed wildly as they swung her up on to her feet. A man shook her hand, another wrung her other hand; a woman threw her arms around her and kissed her.

Over the heads of the crowd the shaman chant sounded, high and clear.

She laughed, shook hands, kissed back; began to walk shoulder-by-shoulder with men and women in rags, recognising no faces; walking with small red-faced children, and brown Rats in the rags of King's Guard livery.

'Oh, hey, I know *you*.'

She elbowed herself a space as a small man fought through the crowd to her side, falling back a few yards from the people that flocked around Elish as she sang.

The small man, his white hair standing up like owl's feathers, grabbed her hand and wrung it. With his other hand he felt in the pockets of his greasy cotton coat and unearthed a broadsheet which he thrust at her. She dropped it.

'Nineteenth District broadsheet—'

Cornelius Vanringham dabbed at his sweating forehead. Two men at his heels raised cameras, flashbulbs popping. From another pocket he rummaged out a notepad and a pen, waving them at her in an explanatory manner.

'We were interrupted before. I wonder if I could talk to you now. Please.'

She shoved her hands deep in her greatcoat-pockets, swirling the hems, which steamed a little now in the drying sun. A great swath of the crowd slowed, staying with her rather than with Elish. Her head came up, and she walked with a kick-heeled strut, feeling the dust of the canal walk hot under her bare feet. She smelt sweat and wine and roses. Heat blazed out of a hazed blue-grey sky.

'Oh, see you . . .'

Voices at her shoulder fell silent, others further back hissed for quiet. Attentive silence spread out like ripples in water. The crowd jostled her, human and Rat, as she sauntered in the wake of her sister.

A grin quirked up the corners of her mouth. Hands in pockets, she shrugged, superbly casual.

'. . . Just *ask* me. I can tell you! I'm a Kings' Memory. What do you want to know?'

Candia, sprawling down on a stone horse-block, scratched at thick blond stubble and spread out stained pasteboard cards. A dazed child's wonder blanked his expression.

Brilliant image succeeds brilliant image, no tarot card what it has been before, all new and strange and altering again even as he turns them: lions coupling in a desert, a river flowing uphill, a steel-and-granite bird circling a star, a throned empress giving her child suck . . .

Acolytes clung to every projection of stone above him, gripping gutters, façades, strapwork and chimneys; staring down into the overgrown university quadrangle.

The black gelding grazing loose by the block raised its head and whinnied, sweat creaming its haunches, eyes white and wild. Candia glanced up. He sprang to his feet, the cards scattered.

'My lord! Theo!'

He put his arms carefully around Theodoret's shoulders, embracing him. The Bishop returned the grip, careless of the younger man's sweat-stained and filthy shirt.

'My friend, I haven't thanked you—'

'Don't. It took me long enough to come back, and I had to be pig-drunk to do it—'

A shadow halted him in mid-word. Behind the white-haired man, bright in the sun, a sandstone-and-gold shape paced between tall university buildings that only shadowed His flanks.

'Lord Spagyrus.' He swallowed, mouth dry. 'You live, still?'

'*Yes, little Candia, I live. I live again!*'

The great head lowered, tusks gold against the sky, tiny scaled ears pricked forward. The scales of the Decan's muzzle glinted. The Bishop of the Trees reached up and laid a veined hand on the tip of one down-jutting fang, just below the vast nostril. Breath stirred Candia's hair. An almost-mischievous smile creased Theodoret's face.

'*I am the elixir, I am the prima materia, I am the stone that touches all, the marriage of heaven and hell. I had forgotten,*' the Decan's soft voice boomed, echoing in sandstone courtyards where the slim leaves of bamboo sprout from shattered windows, '*and I perceive that I have erred, the while that matter clouded me.*'

Candia shoved his straggling hair back under its sweat-band, put his fists on his hips, and glared up at the Decan of Noon and Midnight.

' "Erred".' He eyed the Decan with an exasperation long since past the point of caution. 'Erred! Would you like me to tell you about it!'

'*The error is not one that concerns you.*'

Candia rubbed the back of his wrist across his mouth. The horse whinnied again. His breath came back to him, rich with the scent of the dusty yard: sweet, salt, rose- and dung-odoured. Clamour continued to sound outside. Through the archway, across the District to the harbour's marble piers and aqueducts, to the far south-aust horizon where tides of flowers flowed.

'Who, then?'

'*These.*'

To each roof-ridge, chimney, gable and gutter, the dispossessed Fane's acolytes clung. They roosted restlessly, membraned wings furling and unfurling in the new sun, obsidian claws gripping stone and metal. Candia tilted his head back, staring up into slit-eyed beaked faces.

Malice and pain stared back.

'*They suffer.*'

Candia grunted. 'Good. They made us suffer for centuries.'

Daemon-wings flared open, beating the bright day into dust-storms. One beast clung head down on lead guttering, picking with its beak at new vegetation, spitting dumb hatred down at him.

'*They are Our just instruments. They have no minds to recall, else they would remember how you sought to betray fellow-humans to them.*'

The Decan's scented breath skirred dust about Candia's feet. He sank to one knee in the courtyard, head high; his mouth opening and closing several times.

'*I have always been able to rely on mortals for treachery.*'

Stubbornly suppliant, Candia remained kneeling, a ragged blond man squinting against the light. A resonance of his swagger and competence of a Sign ago haunted him, now, much as he haunted this deserted university. The Decan's shadow fell across his flopping hair, his filthy shirt and breeches.

'*These are only animals. Death is death to them; their generations do not return. Except in the darkness behind the eye and in the Fane, they have no voice. We must make some end of these servants of Ours, now that We walk out into the world. What would you have Me do? Tell Me what you would do, little Candia.*'

The Fane's acolytes raised restless muzzles to all five points of the compass, sniffing the blossom-scented wind, searching for the Fane.

His face heating, Candia muttered: 'Why ask me? I'll answer for

Masons' Hall. It was my choice. As for these butchers, they were
your instruments!'

'*Tree-priest, you suffered most. What would you?*'

'Lord Decan, it's you I can't forgive.' Theodoret's veined hands
spread in a Sign of the Branches, faint sparks of green and gold
flowing under the skin. 'I'm an old man, therefore familiar with
discomfort. You and they gave me pain that should have killed—'

'*Forget.*'

'You haven't yet paid for that!'

'*God does not pay. We do not incur debts. Whatever We do is well and
right, because it is We who do it. Who can deny that?*'

Candia muttered: 'Bollocks!'

A raw tone echoed back from the courtyard's walls. Candia only
knew it much later for a Decan's laughter.

'*It is true that much is different now, but that does not change. But give
an answer. What shall be done with these?*'

Candia stared up at the misshapen bodies. 'Freeze them into
stone for all I care, and let them stick there until the city's
demolished!'

Prescience gave an image of how it would be, clear as a tarot card:
each massive building lined with rows of stone guardians, bodies
frozen in a rictus, rain streaming from their open beaks . . .

The Decan's full lips parted. One gold fang dulled with his
summer breath, birthing the beginning of a word.

'No!' The day's heat dappled on Theodoret; he seemed to move in
shade and the shifting of leaves. 'Lord Spagyrus, no.'

'*Why not so?*'

'Animals are innocent murderers, Divine One.' The Bishop's
ascetic mouth wrinkled, distaste mingling with resignation and a
certain sly justice. 'You should pay something, Lord Spagyrus. What
penalty one asks of the Divine, I don't know. Perhaps you should
pay by taking responsibility. They are yours, these daemons.'

'*We have no use for these servants now. What they did, We will do
Ourselves.*'

Spitting temper, Candia pushed the hair back that flopped into
his eyes. 'Call *that* taking responsibility!'

'*I perceive that I have erred. See how I will pay.*' Grave humour
echoes; like the Bishop's young beyond its years, and fully
cognisant of dubious moral standpoints. '*Let them have speech and
souls. I create them so. I create them free of Us!*'

'Speech and souls—'

Candia grabbed the Bishop's arm, pulling himself to his feet. The
old man's lips opened, anticipating, awed.

'Praise the Lord Decan!' a gargoyle-figure shrilled, hanging head-down from a high gutter.

'Praise be buggered!' A raucous cry. Bristle-tail lashing, a daemon uncurled black wings and flew up to hover over the roof. His eyes gleamed amber. 'He's thrown us to our enemies, that's all He's done! They'll take revenge for what He made us do!'

Beaked muzzles rose, opening, and harsh voices cawed in competition with one another.

'We're different now; Rats and men won't hate us—'

'*Won't* they!'

'I have a right to be here; it's our city, too!'

'No home, here; no place for us—'

'All ours! Sky and roofscape, all ours.'

'But I want more than that—'

'The Lord Decan will tell us what to do!'

'Not me, he won't tell!'

Wings rattled in the heat, circling; shadows falling to dazzle Candia as he gazed upwards. Apprehensive of the copper taste of blood, he waited for that ancient warning of their presence. Nothing came. Black ribbed wings, moth-eaten brown furred bodies, spiked long tails – mortal gargoyle-daemons swarmed above the university quadrangle.

Theodoret's elbow dug his ribs. Through the archway, black specks began to rise in confusion across the whole district. Dumbfounded, Candia scratched at his blond stubble.

'The Rat-Lords aren't going to like this. His Majesty *really* isn't going to like this.'

'Choice. Knowledge and choice. I think I *am* revenged. Let these have all our problems! Let them deal with us, and his Majesty – *and* the Thirty-Six in the world, and—' The Bishop suddenly guffawed. 'My friend, no one's going to like it!'

An elderly gargoyle-daemon on a gutter linked clawed thumbs across her flaking breast. Her ribbed wings, drawn down, furled about her shoulders, gleaming tar-black and smelling of old buried stone. One finger moved to scratch under a drooping dug. She stared down at Candia and Theodoret with a light in her eye.

'Who *asked* you to like it?'

Andaluz rolled down one black woollen stocking, folded it neatly on the canal steps beside its twin, and lowered his lean feet into the water.

Early-afternoon sun shimmered, light webbing his pale skin. He flexed his toes in the cold water.

'I assure you, Lady Luka, this canal is real enough. Although to my knowledge it's never been here before—'

He broke off, spreading his hands to acknowledge the city of wonders; shook his head, smiling.

'One says that of so much. What's one canal!'

The plump silver-braided woman walked in a swirl of bright robes to where he sat. She shaded her eyes with her hands. 'In a city of wonders . . . !'

Andaluz slid his heavy doublet off his arms and shoulders, letting it fall carelessly on the steps. He unfastened a button-toggle of his shirt. Sweat dampened the cloth between his narrow shoulder-blades; heat drove sixty years' chill from his bones. He lifted one foot from the canal and hooked his arm around his knee.

'Luka?'

She gazed at the sky: at the heat-hazed, soft grey-blue, empty of all birds. Past her profile, the new wide waterway here opened out into the harbour. Heat and summer's brightest light glared back from the marble palaces that lined the great canal. Andaluz left wet splashes on the marble as he drew his feet from the water and stood up.

'Lady, what is it?'

Marble-and-gold steps and walkways paralleled the canal, running down to where the light flashed from the sea-harbour. Hot on the air came the smell of the sea. Miles of city fronting the harbour shone now in the sun, bright with apple and cherry and blackthorn flower.

She turned to face inland. 'Listen!'

The buzz of the approaching crowd grew louder. The Candovard Ambassador stood barefoot, in shirt and breeches, scratching at his grizzled hair. He reached down towards his discarded doublet. The movement arrested itself midway: he straightened, resting his hand on the woman's arm.

'Luka, dear lady, tell me—'

'There!'

A sudden black spar reared over the heads of the crowd. Appearing between the frontages of palaces, where the canal curved back into the city, the prow of a black ship glided into sight.

The smell of tar came to him in the hot sun, sparkling on the planks. Great black masts towered, white sails belling from them. A sweet rich scent set Andaluz to rubbing his eyes; he frowned, focusing.

Sails hung in tangles against the sky, great curtains and draperies of roses depending from the rigging. The flower-sailed ship glided deep and steady in the water, no hand at the wheel. Figures lined the rails. Ripples lapped the marble steps at Andaluz's feet.

'It's the Boat! Dear lady—' He turned to her, eyes bright with a sudden comprehension.

One of her slender fingers pointed. 'And it's young Elish!'

Crowds of people walked the canal paths. Noisy, hand-in-hand or arms about each other's shoulders, sweating in the heat and calling to their neighbors on the far canal bank, the people of the city crowded out into the sun.

Between a stocky brown Rat and an elderly Fellowcraft, the Katayan walked. Her pale face raised, she moved her mouth; he could hear nothing of what she chanted. The power and joy of it beat against his skin, as hot as the sun's light.

'Madame Elish!'

He pushed his way forward between people and embraced the thin woman. She shifted her gaze from the Boat, the wall of the hull towering beside them as it glided slowly towards the sea.

'Ambassador!' She caught his hand and swung him to walk on with her to where Luka stood waiting. 'You must know, messire, I lied to you. I'm no envoy.'

'My dear girl, I don't care whether you are or not; you're infinitely welcome.'

The great vessel began to slow. The Katayan woman, licking her lips and drawing in breath, chanted a few soft syllables. She ran forward to grip Luka's hands, laughing down at the middle-aged woman. Andaluz caught his bare foot on a stone, staggered against someone in the crowd. A tall bearded man smiled and handed him a wine-flask.

Andaluz began to shake his head, stopped, took the wine and drank. 'My thanks to you, messire.'

'Welcome. Welcome!'

'Oh, see you—' A hand gripped his bare elbow. 'Messire Ambassador! Isn't it *won*derful?'

Andaluz ran his finger down the younger Katayan's palely freckled jaw-line. He smiled. 'Mistress Zari. My nephew, if he yet lives, wishes you found. Do you know this?'

'Nephew – oh, *Lucas*.' Zar-bettu-zekigal chuckled. 'Oh, *he'll* be all right. He's a good kid. Ask him from me what's he going to be when he grows up.'

Andaluz roared with laughter, pushed a way for them between men and Rats to Luka's side. The older Katayan knelt, bending to drink from the canal's clean cold water. The Lady Luka stared out across the great canal at the heavily laden vessel.

She held up a hand, gripping her bamboo cane. She nodded, once, the motion folding the soft skin at her throat. Andaluz stepped to her side. Her head moved on bird-delicate shoulders; she looked up at him.

'They're here.' She spoke barely above a whisper.

Andaluz strained to hear over the crowd's babble: voices and sudden laughter, a dropped bottle, a Ratling's squeak. He frowned, hearing only a gull's cry and the creak of rose-laden masts.

'I don't—'

The gull cried again: sharp, desolate, joyful. Andaluz stared at Luka. He lifted one hand, touching the feathers wound into her single braid.

Shadows of bird's wings fell across her, across her silver hair and orange-and-purple robes; across his blunt-fingered hand.

'Oh, lady.' Sudden tears constricted his throat.

The woman lifted both arms. Rings glittered in the sunlight. Her orange scarves swirled. Tiny bells on her leather belt jingled, soft as hawks' jesses. Bright-eyed, she laughed; raised her voice and called out an answering gull's shriek.

Dots flocked in the high haze.

Silence spread out into the crowd, Luka's voice soaring over theirs. Andaluz stood quite still, arms hanging at his sides, mouth slightly open; openly relaxed into his own amazement.

They fell down from the sky – soaring in great squadrons, clouds, flocks: hawks and eagles, gulls, thrushes, humming-birds; owls and cormorants and wild geese; chaffinches and peregrine falcons and sparrows . . . All the air full of wings, whirring, full of dusty feathers and bird-calls and droppings; thousands of birds circling in a great wheel that had, in its eye, the silver-braided bird-woman.

Andaluz softly said: 'Oh, my dear lady . . .'

Luka's raised hands shot forward. The cane reached up towards the black vessel riding the canal. A great herring-gull caught the hot still air under its wings, curved in flight to skim across the water and land on the rail of the Boat.

A thrush flicked to land on a coil of rope.

Luka reached her hands out across the water. Hard concentration furrowed her face. Bird after bird flew down, soaring towards the high invisible deck.

Andaluz stared at figures crowding the rails, figures with no shadows. He felt his own heart beat in his throat.

'So many dead . . .'

The Boat settled into the water. Flocks of gulls and starlings

circled the flower-draped sails. They dipped, curving flights to cross
the deck.

He moved as close to her as he dared, eyes still fixed on the Boat.
Ripples ran across the canal from its hull, dazzling in the summer
heat. He took a great breath of humid air. 'Is that what I think?'

The small woman gazed up, plump face beaming. She fumbled
her cane; pulled the orange-and-purple robes looser at her neck,
and rubbed sweat from her forehead with the heel of her hand. She
rocked back and forth on her sandalled heels.

'Yes, my birds carry them back to the Boat, and, yes, the Boat will
carry them through the Day and back to birth again . . .'

Andaluz stared up. A hawk clung to the Boat's nearer rail. It
raised half-open wings, head down, hacking a harsh call. It
choked.

The bright body and wings of a butterfly unfolded from the bird's
beak, hacked into the air by its strangulated call. Andaluz laughed.
Drunkenly, the bright *psyche* flew up to cling to the bottom of a
rose-woven sail.

Elish-hakku-zekigal chanted, her voice croaking quiet as a
whisper. The Boat moved out, no faster than walking pace, flanked
by crowds on either side of the canal now; gliding on towards the
lagoon.

A vast crowd of bright moths and butterflies clung to the Boat,
almost hiding the black wood with gold, scarlet, green, purple,
azure. Bird after bird swooped down to the deck, then soared up to
fly off across the city . . .

Figures at the rail glided past Andaluz. A black woman in a faded
green gown, who stretched her fists up to the sun and laughed,
silently, as if she couldn't have too much of the light. A man
pushing between two brown Rats to lean on the rail, milk-white
hair blowing in the summer wind; gazing down at the crowd with
wide pit-black pupils. A slender black Rat in a scarlet priest's jacket,
who touched a white rose to her furred cheek and held her other
hand close by the rail, admiring how no shadow marked the
wood . . .

More, more: too many to see and note.

'I—' Andaluz abruptly turned to Luka. The woman rubbed at her
wet eyes with plump fingers, smiling up at him. His own eyes ran
water. He folded his arm in hers, patting her hand, and lifted it to
his lips and kissed it.

She smiled with a brilliance that outshone the sky.

Elish-hakku-zekigal touched his arm and pointed. Her chant
croaked on, breathless, unfaltering. Freckles stood out on Zar-

bettu-zekigal's pale skin. The Candovard Ambassador stared upwards, following her gaze.

Six yards above, at the black rail, a shadowless woman leaned her chin on her arms and frowned as if memory troubled her. Slanting black brows dipped over reddish-brown eyes webbed around with faint lines. Broken butterfly-wings tangled in her short greasy hair.

'Lady!' Zar-bettu-zekigal's hand jerked up, stopped, fell to her side. 'Lady Hyena!'

Warm wind brushed the woman's face, smoothing away the frown. A ragged Sun-banner sashed her red shirt; and she fisted the cloth in one hand and rubbed it against her cheek, her glance sliding away from the Katayan girl.

Andaluz rested his arm across her shoulders. 'She'll come back, Mistress Zari. If not to you, then to others.'

Zar-bettu-zekigal broke from his embrace. 'Oh, what! I know *that*—'

Her greatcoat swirled about her pale calves. Loping strides took her ahead, paralleling the woman at the rail. Her hands fisted at her sides, black against dazzling light and water, as she came to the carved steps where the canal opened out into the lagoon.

A frown dented the woman's slanting brows.

Suddenly the woman grabbed at her hip, as if she expected to find a sword there. She thrust her way down the rail, limping, pushing her way between men and Rats; walking level with Zar-bettu-zekigal.

No shadow marked the deck.

A sweet smile broke over her face, relaxed and content. She stopped, standing still; and – as no other on the Boat – lifted her hand in farewell. Andaluz glanced down. Zar-bettu-zekigal's eyes glowed.

'Did you see that! She said goodbye. To *me*!'

The Boat moved out into the lagoon, prow turning towards the open sea. A humid wind shifted the masses of roses, and the rose-leaves sprouting from rail and bow and spar. Limpid water rushed against the curving tarred planks of the hull.

Andaluz shaded his eyes with his hand. Sweat slicked the grizzled hairs on his skin. The Lady Luka gripped Elish's arm for support and lowered herself to sit on a step, easing her sweat-pink feet into the cool water. He stepped down beside her, resting one hand on her rumpled robes.

'Andaluz, look!'

The harbour water flows, a net of diamonds; and in lucid depths adamant limbs now stir: Chnoumen, Chachnoumen, Opener of

Hundreds and Thousands of Years, implicit in the lines of sun on water.

'Things can't be the same after this . . .'

A tread behind warns him, that and the sudden silence of the crowd.

Towering over the marble-and-gold palaces, Her ancient terracotta smile secret and triumphant, the Decan of the Eleventh Hour walks amongst Rats and humans that scurry like ants about Her feet. Bees hum among the roses that chain her, sweet and white in the afternoon sun.

Andaluz tastes salt and sand in his mouth.

'I wish I knew my son were here and safe.' Luka raised her head, surveying all; bird-bright glance softening with dreamy reminiscence. 'He was always so delicate as a child, my Baltazar. His chest, you know. He never did take *care* of himself.'

Andaluz bit the inside of his cheek firmly. 'Ah . . . yes. Mistress Zari's described Lord Casaubon to me so well that I feel I already know him.'

The younger Katayan woman gurgled. She caught a light-standard and pulled herself up on to its marble base, gazing over the heads of the crowd, searching.

Luka patted her silver braid, twisting a feather more tightly in it. 'I know he's never been too proud to ask his mother for help; that's why I came at once. I'd never *say* that to Baltazar, of course. He'd be dreadfully embarrassed. Did he look well when you last saw him?'

' "Well"?' Zar-bettu-zekigal grinned and pointed. 'See for yourself, Lady. Ei! *Lord-Architect!*'

'Baltazar!'

Luka elbowed her way between people. Andaluz at her heels. Andaluz glimpsed copper hair as a head turned.

An immensely tall and fat man walked beside the Decan of the Eleventh Hour, stately and beaming. His shirt hung out of his breeches, unbuttoned, stained black with machine-oil. The two top buttons of his breeches had gone missing, and both stockings were unrolled to his ankles. He moved massively, the crowd parting in front of him.

Luka hallooed: 'My little baby *boy*!'

The Lord-Architect Casaubon stopped, sat heavily and abruptly down on the top step of the quay, put his padded elbows on his vast knees, and sank his face into his hands.

'. . . Mother.'

Slowly the Boat moves into distance, hazed in the afternoon heat; gliding down the path of sun-dazzles on the water.

Still from the sky they pour down to follow it, the birds that fly from thin-aired heights; and, high above, white stone wings curve on air: Erou, the Ninth Decan, Lord of the Triumph of Time, soaring in the changing brilliance of the sky.

'We will never be the same again.'

Into the silence of gathered tens of thousands, a clear voice sounds: the Decan of the Eleventh Hour, Lady of the Ten Degrees of High Summer, whose gaze now scatters miracles over the god-haunted heart of the world.

'Death is not final—'

From the Fifth Point of the Compass they come, walking out from the ruins of the Fane into the world. In the great Districts that stretch across a continent, bells ring in abbey towers, ships' masts burst into flower, women and children and Rats and men clasp hands and dance, in chains and pairs, through streets, and through the midnight-marble ruins.

Stone-bodied, immense, beast-headed: god-daemons stalk streets and parks and avenues, squares and palaces.

'—only change is final; and now it changes again!'

After millennia of construction, thrown down now and laid waste, the Thirty-Six Decans walk out of the Fane's ruins and into the world.

CHAPTER 9

White heat-haze lies over the full-leafed summer trees, shadowing their green canopies blue.

Where she lies, in tall cow-parsley between field and formal gardens, damp grass and shadow imprint her body. Borrowed shirt and breeches shade her from sunburn.

Up on the hill-slope, past garden fountain-jets ten metres tall and impromptu open-air feasting, the rotunda of the New Temple curves across the sky. Warm brick, pennants and flags, tiny dots of faces where people walk in wonder along its outer balconies . . .

Time enough to go back to crowds and questions in a few minutes. The woman lies in the grass, hearing birds sing; now gazing down past where the Arch of Days lies invisible under the foot of the hill, past the new canal, to distant hills hollowed with blue shadow.

A large figure approaches, down in the valley, walking along the canal path. Frock-coated: copper hair glinting a clear quarter-mile.

The White Crow rolled over on her back, staring up through the dust of meadowsweet, reaching up with scarred hands to play with the swarming black-dot haze of bees. And abruptly shifted, sprang to her feet, and began to run back up the hill towards the Temple.

A distant clock chimes.

Blazing white light reflected from pale gravel and a pale sky. Zar-bettu-zekigal sprawled on the fountain's marble rim, knees and black dress spread apart, nostrils flaring to smell the day's heat.

'I know the answers to every question now.'

'Every question?' Lucas pulled at the neck of his shirt. He lifted a wine-bottle to his mouth and drank. The young Katayan woman sat sideways on the fountain's rim, one foot up on the marble, her black dress falling down between her knees and over her tail.

'I'm a Kings' Memory: I know.' She snorted. 'Which is more than *they* do.'

Sheaves of paper lay scattered on the gravel about her feet. Black-letter, with illustrative grey-and-black photographic images, and narrow columns of print. The fountain's odourous spray speckled them with water.

'Vanringham got *this* out fast enough! Listen.' She hauled a sheet of paper out from under her other heel. *The Moderate Intelligencer*'s still-damp ink marked her fingers.

' "Visiting student Prince Lucas of our far-flung colony of Candover played a curious part in events. It is creditably reported that he authorised the students of the University of Crime to go on a spree of looting, they only being discouraged at the last by the disclosure of his background in the mechanic trade—" '

'What!' Lucas, choking on a swallow of wine, sat up and grabbed the paper. 'I'll sue!'

She shuffled paper-clippings, dropping a small pair of silver scissors on the gravel. 'Here's another one. "Rumor speaks of the late Master of the Hall in Nineteenth Eastquarter, Falke, being instrumental in preventing the late outbreak of plague from worsening." Ei! *Won't* I talk to Vanringham! I told him everything true, and he's just distorted it all!'

Lucas turned the page of Thirtieth District's *Starry Messenger* over, reading aloud.

' "Accusations against Reverend tutor Candia of the University of Crime have been dropped. It was reported that Master Candia had dealt with persons unbecoming to the reputation of the University of Crime, and was to be dismissed from his place on the Faculty, but after representations from the Church of the Trees—" ' Astonishment edged Lucas's tone. ' "—from the Church of the Trees all charges have been dropped." '

'Oh, say you, that's because of this.'

Zar-bettu-zekigal proffered Eighth District's *Mercurius Politicus*.

' "Bishop Theodoret instrumental in dismissing Black Sun; makes overtures to the Thirty-Six; intervention of this *gaia*-church successful; The Spagyrus ratifies new status for the Church of the Trees; see pictures page six." '

'Pictures?' Lucas took the clipping, peering at silver-and-grey images of the Cathedral of the Trees and that square's gallows, a tiny figure in the foreground recognisable as Theodoret. The cameraman had, quite sensibly, made no attempt to include the Decan, but a vast shadow lay across the foreground of the square.

At Theodoret's side, small and bright, stood the White Crow.

Breath stopped in Lucas's throat, left a lump past which he could not swallow. Zari's voice faded from his consciousness for a minute. Lucas gazed across the gardens to the canal. Small boats bobbed on the water, where music and laughter sounded. He smiled, almost hugging himself.

His fingers remember the touch of skin.

'If we'd known how it would end . . .' He scanned her narrow face, searching for differences from the young Katayan in the university's courtyard, and in Austquarter's crypt and the palace throne-room. Memory nagged. With sudden discovery, he said: 'Plessiez? I heard that . . . I haven't seen him. Is he . . . ?'

Zar-bettu-zekigal looked up, her lively features still.

'Elish – my sister Elish-hakku-zekigal, she's a shaman – she did a vision. She told me. She sees true. She saw Messire Plessiez at the end, underground, somewhere where there were bones . . .'

Her fingers slid to the sash about her waist, a length of green silk casually knotted around her black dress.

'You can say what you like about the university. And about your old White Crow. It was Messire who went in to break the *magia*. Elish saw – and then her vision couldn't see through the dust: the whole cavern-roof caved in and came down on him. Him and Charnay, too.'

Her eyes, sepia with Memory, shifted.

'I wish I could have seen him on the Boat.'

Lucas took the *Tractatus Democritus* broadsheet between finger and thumb, staring at the print without reading it. He grunted cynically.

'Cardinal Plessiez? He had no more conscience than a fish has feathers! If you ask me, it's a good thing he didn't make it.'

The paper tore, snatched out of his hands.

'Mistress Zari? I didn't mean . . .'

The Katayan hunched her shoulders, bent over the heap of broadsheets, and began with frightening care to scissor out clippings from the remaining papers.

Passing humans and Rats brushed by him; Lucas stood and stepped back with automatic courteous apology. He backed further away from the fountain. Bright silks shone on the far side of falling screens of water.

Up on the terrace, in front of the open pillared rotunda where many danced, a crowd blocked the path. Men and Rats pressed in on the White Crow, shouting questions. She laughed; her hand resting on the green-and-gold sleeve of the Bishop of the Trees.

'Damn. Why does he have to be there? Or any of them? Well . . . Well.'

He shrugged and began to walk up towards the terrace.

*

Abandoning press cuttings, Zar-bettu-zekigal dipped the tuft of her black-and-white furred tail into the fountain, lifted it above her head, and shook a fine spray over herself. Cool water spotted the shoulders of her black dress. She crossed her ankles and leaned back, supported precariously by her arms on the marble fountain's wide rim. Her face up-turned, eyes ecstatically shut, she dipped her tail again – stopped, sniffed, opened her eyes, and turned a disgusted glance on the green fountain-basin.

'Ei! What a stink.'

'Low-quality lead piping,' a voice rumbled, its owner invisible through the falling fountain-spray. 'My dear child, ought you really to do that?'

The Lord-Architect Casaubon strode magisterially around the fountain-basin, mud-stained satin coat over one bolster-arm, his shirt unlaced and his sleeves rolled up. Black oil and grease smeared his blue silk breeches and braces. The rag with which he wiped his face looked as if it might have been an embroidered silk waistcoat.

'Very inferior work, all of this.'

'You just can't trust miracles any more, messire architect!'

Zar-bettu-zekigal flicked her tail in greeting. Water-drops cartwheeled in the sun.

He beamed. 'Trust miracles? From now on you can!'

The distant clock sounded again. On its last stroke, the sound of trumpets clashed out. Jets shot up fifteen or twenty feet from twelve surrounding fountains. Zar-bettu-zekigal put both hands up to push suddenly wet hair out of her eyes, nose wrinkling at the stronger low-tide-mud stink. A burst of complicated music blasted from sound horns in the statuary.

'Ei!' Zari cocked one black eyebrow.

The Lord-Architect looked down his nose, chins and the considerable expanse of his belly at the fountain. A pained expression crossed his features at the sight of carved nereids spurting water from their breasts, and ragged sea-monsters jetting water from nostrils and every other orifice.

'Florid.'

He slung the blue satin frock-coat on the marble rim, careless of one sleeve trailing in the water, searched the pockets, and brought out a metal hip-flask.

She rolled over on to her stomach on the marble. 'I want to talk to the Bishop of the Trees and Master Candia. About inside the Fane. And Lady Luka, how she got here. Have the whole story.'

Startled, the Lord-Architect met Zari's eye.

'I'm . . . ah . . . not certain where Mother is.'

'I told her *you* were up in the rotunda.' The Katayan stretched, water-spotted dress already drying in the heat, and grinned at his evident relief.

The music ceased abruptly, with a mechanical squeak. The jets died. Shadows, precise-edged, blackened the steps and the flagstones and lawn around the fountains. Her own elbow-and-knee-joint shadow, tail up, coiled into a florid curve worthy of the fountain's statues.

'*Hei!* Master Casaubon!'

A blonde girl in pink satin overalls swaggered up, silver chains jingling about her neck and wrists. She threw herself down on the marble rim between Zari and Casaubon, sparing no glance for anyone but the Lord-Architect.

'Mistress Sharlevian.' He kissed her bitten-nailed fingers and waved a casual hand. 'You two aren't acquainted, I believe. Entered Apprentice; Kings' Memory . . . Mistress Zari, I was about to ask – have you seen young Lucas of late?'

Zar-bettu-zekigal shifted from her elbows to lie on her side, opening her mouth to answer. A sharp voice cut in: 'Oh, Lucas. *I've* seen him. He went off looking for that red-headed cow who's one of my mother's lodgers.' The girl pushed tangled yellow hair back out of her eyes. Her silver-chain ear-rings glinted. 'Always mooning after her, dozy old bag. Well, she's welcome to what she gets, that's all I can say!'

The Lord-Architect raised both copper eyebrows.

'Kids!' The girl sniffed, wiping the back of her wrist across her nose. She leaned her arms back on the marble, weight on hip and heel. Under the remnants of paint, her complexion had a child's clearness. 'I don't know why I go around with kids. I mean, that boy – poke-poke-bang and it's all over, y'know? I wanna go with men who are worth the time.'

Zar-bettu-zekigal smothered an exhalation of breath, for once without useful comment. The Lord-Architect opened his mouth to speak, rubbed his chins bewilderedly and shook his head. Sharlevian leaned to one side, her breast pressed against his shoulder, her breath warm and moist against his ear.

'What I say is, why go out with a kid when you can go out with someone . . . mature?'

Zar-bettu-zekigal coiled her dapple-furred tail sensuously across the girl's thigh and, when she had her attention, grinned. 'Maybe Lucas feels the same way.'

'Of all the—!'

Sharlevian stared from Zar-bettu-zekigal to the Lord-Architect and, as it became apparent that he would make no response, reddened, stood, and stalked off.

'It's true, he's looking for White Crow.' Zar-bettu-zekigal stared up at the rotunda's terrace, seeing the Prince of Candover and a dozen House of Salomon officers, and no Bishop Theodoret. No White Crow.

'Anyone would think,' the Lord-Architect rumbled, 'that that woman is avoiding me.'

Zar-bettu-zekigal crossed her ankles, rested her chin on the backs of her hands, and directed her gaze to Casaubon. 'No! Go on!'

Horn and harpsichord ring out, lazing down the late afternoon. Human and Rats take refuge under trees' shade. Water-automata play. Hot scents of wine, dust and roses fill the air, spreading out across the miles of the New Temple's gardens.

Lazy under that same heat, the air and the cells of flesh vibrate with the voices of Decans: more speech between the Thirty-Six in this one day than in the past century.

The black Rat St Cyr stood with the Bishop of the Trees, watching a play.

A few planks rocked on top of barrels, with the canal and the nearest wall of the Temple for a backdrop. On the impromptu stage, a ragged grey-furred Rat brandished a banner:

> *'Not sun of pitch, nor brightest burning shadow*
> *Daunted our noble King – they lay*
> *A-quiver, pissing in their satin bed,*
> *Whether the threat came from a friend or foe.*
> *Twice-turned, a traitor saved them. (Saved myself*
> *A life of luxury in the world to come!)*
> *Witness, you renegades, what is gained by such*
> *Devotion as I showed my lord the king!'*

Both humans and Rats in the crowd cheered.

'I perceive,' the Bishop of the Trees observed, 'that that is intended for Messire Desaguliers.'

'You're right.' St Cyr chuckled. He paced elegantly forward through the mixed crowd. 'Well acted, messires!'

A woman appeared at the old man's elbow. The paleness of the Fane marked her. Sun brightened her dark-red silver-streaked hair, caught up at the sides and shining with roses that tumbled down on to her shoulders. Minuscule down-feathers grew at her temples. St Cyr, a little awed, bowed.

She grinned at Theodoret. 'Let's get out of here before they get on to the Fane again. Mind you, I think they do *you* very well . . .'

Theodoret's beak-nose jutted. He swept the green robe up from his bare feet, snorting back laughter. 'Say you so?'

Behind them, from the stage, the harsh *caw!* of a crow rang out.

'Much better than they do me. I don't know what that Vanringham's been telling people, but I regret his source of news caught me when I was in shock enough to be honest!'

'Zar-bettu-zekigal is an engaging child.'

'She's a plain nuisance. I remember thinking *that* when she arrived at Carver Street.'

St Cyr followed the direction of her gaze, seeing the woman spot the young Prince of Candover and frown. About to comment, he found his arm seized; she walked between himself and the Bishop of the Trees, away down towards the gardens.

'Hey!' The White Crow gave a loud hail as they came under the shadow of beeches. 'Reverend Mistress! Heurodis!'

Sun and shadow dappled the old lady and her companions. St Cyr made his bow to the representatives of the University of Crime.

'Feasting and rejoicing is all very well.' Reverend Mistress Heurodis's face wrinkled into a smile that showed her long white teeth. 'However, we ought not to miss our opportunities.'

She leaned on her cane, regarding with satisfaction the procession of students, largely first-year Kings' Thieves and Kings' Assassins, passing with jewel-boxes, candlesticks, portraits, gemmed books, rings and *ankhs* from the earthquake-tumbled ruins of the Abbey of Guiry.

St Cyr raised furry brows; thought better of it.

'Zu-Harruk!' The old woman snapped a yellow flower sprouting from the head of her cane and tucked the blossom behind her ear. Her smoky-blue gaze rested unimpressed on miracle. 'Come here!'

A tall yellow-haired Katayan student staggering under a box of altar regalia stopped, grunting, while she clucked and, with a jeweller's eye, abstracted a number of the smaller and more perfect diamonds.

'Don't dawdle!' she advised. 'When you've transferred this to the university, I trust I've trained you well enough to go on to the other Abbeys and the royal palace?'

'Yes, ma'am!'

The old lady ignored St Cyr, and rapped her cane against the White Crow's elbow. 'We have a reputation to keep up.'

THEATRVM
VITÆ HVMANÆ

'*Well acted, messires!*' From *Rituale Aegypticae Nova*, Vitruvius, ed. Johann Valentin Andreae, Antwerp. 1610 (now lost – supposed burned at Alexandria)

'Er. Mmm. Doubtless. Yes.'

'Now that's *his* trouble.'

She pointed between sun-soaked trees to where Reverend Master Candia sprawled, asleep.

'No sense of duty. With all due respect to you and Theodoret and the Rat here, the man hangs out with Tree-priests and Scholar-Soldiers; he just isn't *respectable* enough for the University of Crime.'

St Cyr sees the White Crow laugh; glance anxiously back over her shoulder.

Heat beats back from the courtyard's brick paving.

In shadowed colonnades, they shelter; eating and drinking, weeping, searching for known faces. Rat-Lords in their lace and velvet elbow women in factory overalls. Quarrels break out in corners.

A silence.

Shrouded in dark wings, stooped, casting a shadow purple as plum-bloom, a gargoyle-daemon paces across the New Temple's courtyard and stoops to pet a child.

Inside the rotunda of the New Temple, the Mayor of the eastern quarter of Nineteenth District, a little dizzy from the afternoon heat, accepts another drink from a man in Master Builder's overalls.

The man fingered the chained talismans about Tannakin Spatchet's neck.

'Our consortium is naturally interested in the – shall we say? – the mass production of these talismans that warn of daemons' presences.'

Tannakin Spatchet glanced past the man. Under the great arch, between two of the great sandstone pillars that opened to the courtyards, old blankets and cushions had been thrown in a heap. Eight or nine draggled Rats clustered there, talking, preening, snarling for pages to groom them. No courtiers flocked to them.

Their co-joined tails were lost in the cushions. He saw the eyes of a silver-furred Rats-King fix on him.

Beyond, in the courtyard, a gargoyle-daemon leaves a human child, and fixes its amber gaze on the Rats.

'Sir.' He bowed stiffly to the man, nothing the House of Salomon's ribbons on his overalls. 'You may find such talismans don't function now. All things change.'

The man protested. 'But you know her! The Master-Physician, White Crow. You *know* her.'

'I flatter myself that I have some influence in that quarter, it's

true. Yes. Excuse me.' The Mayor put the Master Builder aside
gently, weaving through the crowds towards the Rat-King. 'In case
things don't *all* change, I have to discuss the repeal of a few local by-
laws.'

Lucas walked by the food-booths in the Temple grounds, letting his
feet carry him without direction except that necessary to walk
through the crowds. He knocked the elbow of a brown Rat, who
turned with a curse and then shrugged her shoulders.

The White Crow walked with strangers and friends. He dogged
her, at a distance. On one terrace he stopped, between great lead
figures of sea-monsters spouting a fine spray of jets.

'Young Lucas.' A voice rumbled at his elbow.

'Piss off.' He looked sourly up at Casaubon.

'Is that any way for my page to speak to me?'

The fat man seated himself with his legs apart on a stone bench,
mopping at his brow with a lace handkerchief. Sun glinted on his
copper hair. One garter had come unravelled, and his silk stocking
sagged down his immense calf.

'If I *were* your page . . .' The Prince of Candover sighed, crossing
to the bench and kneeling down. He tugged the fat man's stocking
up and tied the garter in a flamboyant bow below the knee. 'I'd
quit. You're impossible!'

Casaubon rested his elbows on his knees, and his chins on his
hands; face peering out from among the froth of white lace cuffs. 'Is
that any way to speak to your prospective cousin-in-law?'

'What?'

Without lifting his head, the fat man nodded. Lucas stared down
past the nereid fountains to the lawns.

A small man in Candovard formal doublet, his hair grizzled
black and white, stood holding both a woman's hands in his. The
woman, plump and swathed in orange robes, was recognisable
from Vanringham's broadsheet photographs: the bird magus, Lady
Luka. She said something, her face shining; and the Candovard
Ambassador flung his arms around her, burying his face in her
neck.

Lucas breathed: 'Andaluz . . . ?'

'He may not have any *magia*; but, then, my lady mother has all
the political sense of a sparrow. They suit extremely. So. Your
uncle, my mother; I'm her son, that makes us cousins *de facto*—'

'Oh no!' Lucas groaned.

In tones of great hurt, the Lord-Architect remarked: '*I* think they
make a very nice couple.'

'I . . . you . . .' He turned back to the terrace. The White Crow moved among velvet-clad Rat-Lords, and masons in silk overalls. 'It's just . . . it's just too much!'

The Lord-Architect patted Lucas carefully on the shoulder. For once he said nothing at all.

White sea-mist cools the flanks of the Thirty-Sixth Decan, wading in the heat-haze between city and garden.

Sun blasts Her ochre bricks pale, dazzles from roses that trail in Her wake; is dimmed only by the brilliance of Her eyes. Her cowled head lifts.

In the heat-soaked summer sky, Erou, Ninth Decan, Lord of Time and Gathering, shadows Her with white marble wings. His muscled body slides the air, angel-wings feathering horizon to horizon, and He smiles, meeting Her gaze.

Particles, electrons, strings, weak forces: Their pulse beats with the Dance.

In the middle air, a small and sharp *crack!* sounds.

Pale in the sun, a premature celebratory firework scatters green sparks across the sky.

Lucas craned his neck, watching through the garden's trees the thin trail of smoke over the rotunda. No further explosions sounded.

A tall man in dockside gear called: 'You the Prince?'

He left Rafi of Adocentyn and the other students to impressing young Entered Apprentices, and loped across the grass.

'I'm Lucas.'

'Met a woman. She lookin' for you.'

A hard pulse hit him under the ribs. Lucas nodded.

'She say her ship just come into Fourteenth District harbour,' the man observed. 'Calls herself Princess Gerima of the White Mountains, Gerima of Candover?'

Outside the rotunda, the White Crow paces a colonnade between tiny mirror screens, set in vast ornate metal frameworks. Like the congeries of bubbles in the demolished Fane-in-the-Twelfth-District, the screens glowed pale blue.

She pauses to stare into them, seeing scenes of revelry in other Districts. Down by the factories, and in the docks. Across the estuary, up in the high hills, and far across the continent to all points of the compass . . .

The White Crow looks into an oval screen. Swirling iron petals cup it. The image shows humans and Rats together at a banquet on Seventeenth District's beach, so far to the east that the sun's light has faded, and they revel by torches and pastel light-spheres and the rising glow of the moon.

She fists her hands, stretching her arms up in the afternoon heat; bones and muscles creaking. The sun dazzles in her red-brown eyes.

Her mouth moves in a quiet smile, feeling a gaze resting on her back.

The black-browed woman caught up her formal gown, lifting the hem as she raced up the terrace steps to Lucas and hugged him.

'I didn't know what was happening when we arrived; three days out from land the portents started, and such sudden miracles seen at sea! But you're safe. You're safe.' Gerima drew breath, pale face flushed under dark curls. 'Tell me. Which is she?'

'Over there. In white.'

'Her? I thought she'd be . . . younger.'

Lucas moved out of his sister's embrace, rubbing the back of his sweating neck. He looked from Gerima to the Scholar-Soldier further down the terrace. 'I don't care if you don't like her!'

Gerima smiled at the red-haired woman.

'Like her? But I met her while I was looking for you; she's the magus who was in the Fane! But that's wonderful! When you (gods forbid) inherit the throne from father, what better to have as a queen than a woman with *magia*?'

She put her short curls back from her face, features sharpening with concentration.

'If you're serious, we can have the wedding later this year. Father will take you out of the university. You ought to give him at least one grandchild before you leave White Mountains again. Don't you think? And she could teach at the University of the White Mountain while we train her in statecraft . . . What's the matter, Lu?'

The Prince of Candover pulled down his knotted handkerchief and wiped his forehead, his head turning uneasily between his sister and the White Crow. He opened and shut his mouth several times.

'Maybe,' he said at last, 'we should think about this.'

The Princess Gerima of Candover, passing by the Master-Physician White Crow, concluded their earlier and longer conversation with a short wink.

*

Mid-afternoon drowses; long, lingering, with somewhere the scent of fresh-cut grass.

'It's a climate of miracles now . . .' Theodoret touched a blunt finger to the White Crow's temple, and the chick-soft down growing there. 'All these people are thinking that tonight is for rejoicing and tomorrow for putting the world back together. But it'll be a different world when they do.'

'They know it.'

The White Crow reached down and scratched in the ruff of a silver timber wolf. The wolf scrabbled in the soft earth at the edge of the flower-bed, nosing a bone to the surface, and trotted off with it in its jaws.

'Scholar-Soldier, are you waiting for the moon?' Bishop Theodoret asked. 'To see what might be written on it?'

She opened her mouth to reply and stayed silent.

The Decan of Noon and Midnight, afternoon sunlight soft on sandstone and gold flanks, paced between flower-beds and fountains. The tusked and fanged muzzle lowered, moving in the ancient smile. Where He passed, people stopped their talk and knelt on the cool grass. The White Crow smelt stone-dust, and the distant burning of candles.

Theodoret's face creased into a smile. 'The man will catch up with you sooner or later. Heart of the Woods! Talk to him, lady, and then I can stop avoiding him in your company. I have somewhat of a desire to speak with your architect-magus.'

A gargoyle-daemon whirled leathery wings, roosting on a balustrade; cawing something softly to a man who stood beside her and did not kneel to the Decan of Noon and Midnight. One Rat in red satin folded his arms insouciantly and stared at the sky. A little distance away, young Entered Apprentices continued their dancing.

The Spagyrus touched His lips to the fountain, raised His head, passing on. The White Crow scooped her hand in and tasted, lips numbed with heavy red wine.

'Who knows *what* may happen?' She grinned. 'My lord Bishop, I think we should have another drink, before they dispose of the lot.'

'Not much chance of that, I would have thought.'

The White Crow gazed down into the gardens, at men and women and Rats. 'Don't bet on it. Some of this lot could out-drink a miracle, no problem.'

In a further garden, Captain-General Desaguliers swept his plush cloak back with ringed fingers. Medal-ribbons fluttered. The white ostrich plumes in his silver headband curved up in a fan, one dipping to brush his lean jaw, almost blinding him. The jewelled harness of his sword clanked as he walked.

'Well, now . . .'

He gestured expansively. Four Cadets walked with him, each similarly overdressed; the tallest – a sleek black Rat – stumbling over the hem of her cloak from time to time. Desaguliers belched. He leaned heavily on the shoulder of the gargoyle-daemon.

'I think we should serioushly talk . . .'

'I agree.' The harsh caw, muted now, didn't carry further than this corner of the garden. The elderly acolyte-daemon waddled on clawed feet across the grass, her shabby wings pulled cloak-like around her shoulders. Her claw-tipped fingers clasped each other across her flaking breast as if she prayed. 'Messire Captain-General, I offer no apologies for what we were before—'

'No, no. 'Course not. Victims of circumstances. Superior orders,' he said owlishly, bead-black eyes widening.

'Had we been otherwise then . . .'

Desaguliers pushed himself upright, halting the gargoyle-daemon with a pressure of his furred arm. He laid his snout across her shoulder, crumpling his ear against her beaked head, and pointed with his free hand.

'See them? Tha's his Majesty the *King*. Just needs a little looking after, is all. Going to call a meeting, me and the Lords Magi 'n' others, form a Senate.' He stopped, puzzled. 'That isn't what I was going to tell you. What was I going to tell you?'

The gargoyle-daemon's body shifted under his arm as he felt her draw in a long breath.

'What *was* it, messire?'

In a rather less slurred tone than he had been affecting for the past few minutes, the Captain-General put his mouth so close to her that his incisors rubbed her small round ear, and said: 'Lot to worry us now. These rabble peasants will want things their own way. 'N' your people, too. Got to make sure we can come to arrangements. Sensible arrangements.'

'Exempli gratia?'

The black Rat's whiskers quivered. He blinked. 'Oh. Yes. For example, we – the new Senate – we keep his Majesty in order. And you, you tell us about *your* masters.'

'Who are no longer our masters.' The gargoyle head turned to follow the passing of a Decan's shadow in the sunlit air. Desaguliers prodded the air with one dark finger.

' 'Zactly! We got the King sewn up. *You* keep us posted on the Divine Ones. Well, then! Elbow-room for everybody. Then we'll set about the peasants.'

He snatched a goblet of wine from the tall black Rat. The gargoyle-daemon's clawed wing unfurled, and her fingers reached out and gripped the metal, indenting it. Desaguliers stood, arms hanging at his sides, amazement on his lean scarred face. The daemon, wine spilling, none the less got most of the goblet's contents into her beaked mouth.

'Urp!' She scratched at her flaking brown-furred dugs. 'Outwit the Divine Ones? While they dwell amongst us, out in the world? Well . . . *urp* . . . Who knows? We might do it at that . . .'

The cover of the sewer stood open.

Zar-bettu-zekigal picked the petals from an ox-eye daisy and let them fall, one at a time, into the darkness.

She listens: hears no yawping laughter, that hyena-hysteria quieted now. Hears no rush of waves upon hot and mist-drenched shores. No immensurate wings.

Now she is still, only the dappled-furred tail twitching; straining to hear in the foundations of the world the Serpent-headed Night Council. Below her bare feet is silence and a hot pregnant blackness.

For lack of a grave to put it on, she throws the ravaged flower down into the dark.

Lights hovered in the air, globes of pale fire, unsupported. They dotted the gardens, transparent against the long evening light. Now that the sun sat on the aust-westerly horizon, their pastel colours began to glow.

The lights clung to the pillars and dome of the open rotunda, shining down on a chequerboard floor of ash and ebony. Couples moved in wild measures, coats and robes rustling; music chimed.

Surrounded by questioners, the White Crow stood at the edge of the open-air dance-floor. With one hand she gestured, answering a tall brown Rat's question; the other held a spray of cherries that she bit into, nodding and listening.

Zar-bettu-zekigal elbowed through the crowd until she got to the Lord-Architect.

'Ei, you!'

The Lord-Architect turned on one two-inch heel, the satin skirts of his frock-coat swirling. Dirty silk breeches strained over his thighs and belly, failing to button; and leaving some inches' gap between themselves and a shirt black with machine-oil.

'There you are!' A delighted smile spread over his face. He took her hand in gloved fingers and bowed over it. His copper-red hair had been scraped together at the back, and a tiny tuft tied with a black velvet string. 'Honour to you, Kings' Memory.'

'Care to dance?' she said.

'My honour, lady.'

Zar-bettu-zekigal touched the fingers of her left hand to the Lord-Architect's arm, resting them on the twelve-inch turned-back cuff's silver braid; rested her other hand in his; hooked her tufted tail over her elbow, and stepped out into a waltz. Someone called her name, and she grinned, hearing a scatter of applause.

'I heard about the Chemicall Labyrinth. So that's what those machines were for! Damn, I wish I'd seen it!'

The Lord-Architect lumbered gracefully into a turn, narrowly missing a Rat in mauve silk. 'I adapted the little priest's design.'

'If not for him and his Majesty, there wouldn't have been a plague. But then, if not for him, it wouldn't have stopped. I *wish* he could have been here.'

They swung close to a pillar. Looming by it, some eight feet high and with night wings furled about his shoulders, an acolyte-daemon gazed with yellow eyes at the dancing. She smelt his cold breath.

'H'm. A little uncouth, perhaps,' the Lord-Architect admitted. 'But, then, they'll have had little experience of this sort of thing . . .'

Zar-bettu-zekigal nodded to Elish-hakku-zekigal in the crowd as she danced by; and lifted her head again to the Lord-Architect.

'I've been talking to your lady. She's not bad, y'know? I should have got to know her while she was in Carver Street. Don't suppose I'll get the chance now.'

China-blue eyes looked down at her.

'You suspect her on her way to Candover?'

'Oh, what! Don't you?'

The gentle pressure of his fingers steered her towards the edge of the dance-floor. Sunset put the long shadows of the pillars across the dancers.

'I'm going to take steps,' he announced.

Somewhere between affection and cynicism, Zar-bettu-zekigal demanded: '*What* steps?'

The fat man looked puzzled for a few seconds. 'Perhaps . . . Yes! Perhaps I should finish my poem?'

'What p—?'

Zar-bettu-zekigal stared after him as he walked away.

'*Poem?*'

A hand tapped her shoulder. She glanced back. Resplendent in sky-blue and iris-yellow satin, Mistress Evelian of Carver Street smiled down at her.

'You left owing me rent— *Oof!*'

'I'm so glad to see you!' Zar-bettu-zekigal hugged the woman harder.

Evelian settled her puffed ribbon-decorated sleeves, tugging her bodice down over her full breasts.

'And I you. Zaribeth, don't be heartsore for too long.' She flicked the Katayan girl's cheek with her finger. 'I want to see you happy.'

Away from the dancing-floor, the Lord-Architect Casaubon felt absently through the outside left-hand pocket of his stained blue satin frock-coat, then the right-hand pocket; and finally abandoned them both and investigated an inside breast-pocket. From this, he brought out a large speckled goose-egg.

'For a member of the Invisible College,' he remarked, 'you seem to be remarkably visible.'

The White Crow, sitting at the end of the abandoned banqueting-table, shrugged. 'I wasn't planning on staying here anyway.'

He tapped the goose-egg against the marble buttock of a *putto* on the nearest balustrade, a delicate and economical movement that knocked off the top of the shell. Egg-white ran down his plump fingers.

'*I'll* cheer you up . . .'

He lifted the shell to his mouth, tipping it as he threw his head back. She watched in awed fascination as his throat moved, swallowing.

'I have a present for you!'

He belched, wiping his mouth with the back of his fat hand, and dropped the now-empty egg-shell. He looked down over his swelling chest and belly at the rose-haired woman.

The White Crow folded her arms and glared up at him in exasperation.

'A present. OK, I'll buy it. What present?'

The Lord-Architect, satisfied, leaned back against the marble balustrade. She heard a quiet but distinct pop. The Lord-Architect heaved himself off the stone, and put his hand into the satin coat's tail-pocket.

He brought out a handful of crushed shell, his fingers dripping egg-white and egg-yolk.

'*Knew* I had another one somewhere,' he observed, picking off the shell and licking his fingers. 'Now . . .'

The White Crow put her head in her hands and groaned.

With his moderately clean hand, the Lord-Architect Casaubon reached into his buttoned-back cuff and pulled out a folded sheet of paper.

'It's a poem. For you. I wrote it.'

He swept the skirts of his coat back in a magnificent formal bow, beamed vaguely, and wandered away down the terrace. The White Crow rested the folded sweat-stained paper against her lips. Dark red brows dipped.

'You don't fool *me* . . .'

She stared at his departing back.

'. . . not for a minute.'

The carved limestone balustrade pressed hard against her hipbones. Zar-bettu-zekigal leaned over, shading her eyes against the level sun. Day's heat beat up from the stone. She shrugged the black greatcoat more firmly about her thin shoulders, wrapping it across her chest.

She watched the red-headed woman walk away down the lower terraces towards the fountains and flower-beds, a paper clutched in her left hand.

A voice spoke acidly behind Zar-bettu-zekigal: 'Yes: the eminent Master-Physician. I perceive, as our poet says, that there is an upstart crow amongst us – "a player's heart, wrapped in a tiger's hide" . . .'

'Tiger's heart wrapped in a woman's hide!' Zari corrected automatically.

And spun on her heel fast enough to stumble.

A very large brown Rat wheeled a chair to a halt on the gravelled terrace. In the wheelchair sat a stooped and frail black Rat, his fur grizzled to grey, and white about his muzzle. A healed scar marked his upper lip above the incisor.

His body reclined half-drowned in the emerald silk and white lace of the Cardinal-General of Guiry's robes. He lifted yellow-cataracted alert eyes to her face.

'Messire . . . ?' Her voice cracked. 'Charnay! Messire Plessiez, you . . . Oh, messire, it is you!'

She flung herself down beside the chair, throwing her arms around him, burying her face in the warm silk and fur. Gravel scarred her knees. His shaking hand stroked the back of her head. Long fingers unsteady, chill. She sat back on her heels, feeling his fragility; her eyes wide.

'Messire, how . . . ? *Is* it you?'

'Charnay, you may go and gladden your heart by getting drunk.'

'Yes, messire!'

'While I talk with Mistress Zari. Apparently I have things to tell her.'

Charnay grinned and slapped Zar-bettu-zekigal's shoulder as she passed. Long-shadowed, she loped down the steps to the lower terrace, scarlet cloak flying; swaggering towards a group of Cadets, lithe young male Rats. Within a few seconds she sprawled at one of their benches, bottle in one hand, and with the other pulling the most drunken of the male Rats onto her knee, her tail waving cheerfully in the air.

'Zari.'

The black Rat gripped the chair's arms and, with effort, stood. His gown rustled against her cheek. She stared up. Age left him sharp, fragile, acute. Abruptly she scrambled to her feet and offered her arm.

He rested weight on it as he walked along the terrace, favouring his right leg. She breathed, dizzy, the warmth of his body, the odour of his fur; all the fragile lilac scents of age. She glanced back. Beside hers, his shadow ran stoop-shouldered and long on the gravel path.

'You will be told all, Kings' Memory, never fear. Somehow one never seems to keep anything from you.'

Awed, she looked up into his gaunt face. Of the sleek duellist, the sharp priest, only echoes remain in that flesh. She wound her dapple-furred tail anxiously about her ankle as she walked.

'You *died*, messire. Elish saw you.'

'Such an accusatory tone!' His sardonic marvelling broke in a shallow cough. The Cardinal-General lowered his lean muzzle. She followed his gaze. To the green sash that, under the open greatcoat, she wore as a scarf.

'But how?'

'You ask me that, in this world of Divinity run riot?'

As if some wing brushes between him and the sunset, Plessiez is dazed with a momentary awe.

'The past later. Other matters first, I think; concerning the future, whatever shape that may or now may not hold—'

He broke off.

'I am asking you this very badly.'

'So far, messire, you're not asking me anything at all.'

A wheezy chuckle escaped him. He looked back to the interior of the New Temple, where a table composed of Lords Magi, the

District's master builders, and two former acolyte daemons settled down to banquet. Zar-bettu-zekigal paused as he did.

He spoke without looking at her.

'I ask you to leave your university training. Oh, continue it if it pleases you, but you scarcely need it; Memories like you come once in a generation. Leave. Leave and be my Memory now, for what years of work are left to me.'

Her thin lips quivered. A little hoarsely, she said: 'I like the plea for sympathy, messire.'

Plessiez's delicate fingers closed over her arm. She opened her mouth hurriedly, falling over syllables, and he halted her with a smile.

'Walk with me. Don't answer yet. I'll answer your questions, and tell you what use I put my lost years to – and whether I had sooner died than lost them.'

Zar-bettu-zekigal frowned.

Plessiez continued his slow pacing; a thin and fragile black Rat in silk robes and lace, an emerald-studded *ankh* nestling at his collar. His clouded dark eyes blinked.

'I could lie to you. No other lives who knows the truth except myself. And the Decans, one supposes, who know all. I would sooner tell you now than have you discover it later. I must tell you how the Lady Hyena came to die – came to be murdered. And then make your answer to my request, if you will.'

The young Katayan woman loosed his arm and moved a pace ahead.

Hot and level sun blazed in her eyes. In the arch of the sky, the first stars showed. Scents of roses and cooking-oil drifted up from the gardens and courtyard.

His voice finished:

'. . . and that is what happened. I can tell you no more.'

He waited. She turned.

'Messire!'

All condemnation, all solemnity burned out of her by a fierce joy; grinning widely, fists on her hips, greatcoat swinging open as she moved. The sunset light blazes her shadow long across the terrace, as in future years their influence will cast a bright shadow on the city.

Gracefully and with dignity, she dipped one knee to the gravel terrace, taking the black Rat's hand and kissing the ring of the Cardinal-General of Guiry.

Plessiez snatched her to her feet, holding both her hands tight in his; long jaw tight with repressed emotion.

'Oh, see you, messire; and I thought age was supposed to make people reform!'

The black Rat recovered himself enough to smile sardonically. The Katayan woman linked her arm in his, walking slowly, giving him all of her strength that he needed for support.

Black bees throng, swarming in the flowers that weigh down the city's gutters, blossom from ships' masts in the harbour. Their noise is all heat, all summer, all dusty sunset days.

The Decan of Noon and Midnight, Lord of the Spagyric Art, turns His face to the setting sun. The ancient smile widens. At His feet, children play in the Temple's spouting fountains, shrill cries undaunted, not yet called in to bed.

Sunset glared from ivory-and-gold statues, from the rippling water of the ornamental lake, and from the bright flowers of the formal gardens.

'Damn.' The White Crow leaned forward and bit into the hot vegetable-roll she carried. She spilled grease on to the gravel and her borrowed shirt and breeches. 'Ah, I'm still not used to this. Arms and legs and things . . .'

'That's what you get,' the Bishop of the Trees observed, 'for being given the bird.'

She shied a lump of pastry past Theodoret. It ricocheted off the back of his marble bench, fragmenting. Ducks from the ornamental lake squarked and pecked it up.

'But, you see . . .'

Candia, insouciant in buff leather and scarlet silk, arranged empty wine-bottles along the edge of the lake. His blond hair flopped forward. As he set the first of a handful of long-stemmed rockets in the bottles, he completed: '. . . I know why that happened to her.'

The red-headed woman's eyes narrowed.

'Go on.'

'Obviously, because it's always quicker as the crow flies.'

'*Can*dia!'

Unrepentant, the Reverend Master grinned at the Bishop. Theodoret, on the bench, linked his hands across his stomach. 'Therefore, as you might say, she decided to wing it . . .'

'One of you is a man of the cloth,' the woman observed, 'and the other doubtless recovering from the shock of recent events, *otherwise—*'

'At least,' Theodoret added, 'she got me off the hook.'

The White Crow bit into her vegetable-roll again, glared at the Bishop, and observed through a mouthful of pastry: 'That's what you get for being stuck up!'

Candia squatted, removing a tinder-box from his breeches-pocket. 'Who says you can't play dice with the universe?'

'Aaw!'

Candia chuckled. 'Something the matter with her?'

The White Crow licked grease from her fingers. She stood up. Inside the breast of her shirt, a folded paper rustled, scratching the skin as memory scratches at peace of mind.

'You two deserve each other,' she said. 'I might come back when you're being sensible.'

Candia struck flint. Theodoret inclined his head graciously at the White Crow's departing back, and then jumped as the rocket hissed skyward.

Softly explosive, pale against the still-bright sky, the first of Reverend Master Candia's fireworks exploded in a shower of red sparks.

Gas-lamps gleamed. The sky above glowed almost a pale mauve, the sun sitting on the horizon, heat still soaking from the stones. Stars shone in the top of the sky.

The White Crow walked by the canal, and the Arch of Days, holding the stained paper up to the level sunset light.

Her lips moved as she read, silently testing the words:

> 'You are a banquet for a starving man,
> All sweet savouries in your flesh presented.
> Of this food I offer you the plan
> Anatomised and elemented:
> Freckle-sugar-dusted thighs
> Cool and cream-smooth: enterprise
> The drinking of these syllabub sighs;
> This table laid out in the candle's flicker
> Garnished with sweat's tang and the body's liquor.
>
> 'Lady, your dish delights the tongue:
> Hot crevices and subtle flavours.
> I taste your breasts, your skin: undone,
> Abandoned, gluttonous, to your savours.
> Such intricate conceits demand
> A Paradox. You understand:
> I sit to feast, and yet I stand.

Save that, for me, for this one time at least,
I would not come unbidden to the feast.

'Such banquets, self-consumed in mutual pleasure,
Display a goddess' skill in their erection:
Giving, receiving; both in equal measure
Of which I'm expert to detect perfection.
But this feast her own guest invites,
None may enjoy without those rights,
So I go hungry from delights.
Lady, I love you: I leave love behind me:
Or, if you love me, follow me, and find me.'

Elish-hakku-zekigal, finding her silk coat knotted in the red-headed woman's fist, pointed away from the New Temple in bewilderment.

'The Lord-Architect that Zar' keeps talking about? He left. No, I don't know where. If you look, Scholar-Soldier, you'll see the moon is marked in blood. A signal.'

The woman let go of her coat, scowling.

'Damn, the Invisible College can be *any*where!'

'I remember once he spoke to Zar' of a city he built as Lord-Architect. Would he return there?'

The White Crow abruptly grinned.

'No . . . Thank you; but I've just worked it out. It doesn't matter where he's planning to go from here – I know where he'll be *before* he leaves.'

Clock-mill strikes the hour in Carver Street. Wheezing metal machinery clangs.

She does not even pause to see how sun, moon and star-constellations on the dial are different now.

She kicked the door without knocking and entered his room.

The Lord-Architect Casaubon sat in the iron claw-footed bath. She saw very little water: his bare knees, elbows and stomach jammed together to take up almost all the room. He looked up as she came in, eased himself a little, and brought the soap up from a lap invisible beneath bubbles.

'Yes?' Innocent blue eyes, under a draggled mop of copper-gold hair.

'I want to talk to you.'

The White Crow pushed the door shut behind her without looking, and slid the lock-bar across.

'I'm hardly at my best,' the Lord-Architect complained.

Amusement tugged up the corners of her mouth. 'It's how I remember you.'

She padded across the floorboards. Patches of sun falling in at the window made the wood painfully hot under the bare soles of her feet. A scent of herbs came from the stacked crates, and the less identifiable scents of wax and perfume and badly cured parchments.

The Lord-Architect gripped both sides of the bath, hoisted himself up an inch, and slipped back. Water slopped up, splattered on the floorboards. The White Crow stepped back, laughing. Casaubon folded his massive arms across his pink stomach, with an air of injured dignity. The soap slid down his chest and plopped into the water between his legs.

'Talk to me about *what*?' he demanded, irritable.

'Poetry!'

She covered her mouth with one fisted hand, looking at him for a minute over her knuckles.

'Too easy,' she said. 'You're the same and I'm the same – we're *not*, but somehow we've grown in the same way. It's as if I'd never left.'

The Lord-Architect Casaubon looked up at her loftily. He flicked water from cushioned fingers and held out a demanding hand. The White Crow grabbed his hand, heaving to help him from the bath.

Her heels skidded on the floorboards, his hand wrapped around her wrist and pulled. The White Crow swore, startled, sprawled face down across his chest, and slid to sit in his lap and six inches of soapy water. The Lord-Architect let go of her hand, and bent a painful inch forward to kiss her, bird-delicate, on the lips.

'Shit-damned-cretinous-moronic—!'

She slumped back against his thighs and knees: padded as pillows. One of her heels skidded for purchase on the boards, but obtained no balance. She sat back in the hot soapy water.

'You might as well,' Casaubon said, 'have a bath while you're here?'

'*Cas*aubon . . . !'

The White Crow pushed flattened fingers through the tiny copper curls on his chest. She shook her head. Reaching his cheek, she patted twice, hard enough to sting. He sat very still, arms hanging out of the sides of the bath.

'I can't be here any longer' – he made a sideways movement of the head that took in the city called the heart of the world – 'and not touch you.'

His large hands came up, moving delicately as watchmaker's fingers to unbutton her wet shirt.

The White Crow drew his head forward to her breasts.

Left To His Own Devices

CHAPTER 1
Masters of Defence

Eighty feet above the London pavement, rapier strikes against dagger.

That sound echoed across the flat roofs with a sliding crash. Cymbals. A salt taste leaked down to Valentine Branwen's lips. She squinted against the sun, accentuating the lines at the corners of her eyes. Flexed her hand, still feeling the tingling impact through her dagger's blade to its hilt.

'Not close enough.' Valentine grinned.

A young woman in a loose tank top and shorts faced her. The young woman switches on. Valentine watches it: the slight shift of spinal muscles, the replacement of foot position, the vaguely blank look in the eyes. Valentine felt her opponent's tension in her own muscles; let it wash through without touching her. They began to cautiously circle.

The young opponent – and she *is* young, no more than eighteen – holds a swept-hilt rapier in her right hand, and a thirteen-inch dagger in her left hand. The 80 degree sun flashes from the windows of Centre Point. Another young woman sprawls against the door to the stairwell, paging through *Cosmopolitan*. Voices come up from the street below, with the smell of warm lager.

Take it all in. See without seeing. Everything equally important. The bleached blue sky leaches colour from the brick stacks on the roof. Paint peels on the waist-high iron railing at the edge of the building.

Her opponent's rapier lunges.

It has happened before Valentine considers it: the cut-away parry that she does with her dagger, stepping in close to the younger woman's body, and how she places the blade of the dagger (the sole weapon she is using at the moment) quickly against the young woman's belly.

'You're still *thinking* about it, Frankie.'

Frankie Hollister's rounded shoulder muscles shifted. She smelled pleasantly of sweat. Her thick, gold-brown eyebrows scowled. 'You're a lousy tutor!'

Valentine moved away, the concrete gritty under her bare feet. Sun burned her shoulders under her loose white tank-top vest. She let herself become aware of the Gothic plainsong hissing out of her other student's Walkman, and squatted down beside the teenager, her wing of dark red hair falling across her shoulder.

'Start a work-out routine.'

One headphone temporarily lifted. 'It's too *hot*.'

'Rue . . .'

'Well, I didn't want to be here *anyway*. I only put in for it because *she* did.'

'Please yourself, sweetheart.'

A rapier *whicked* through the humid air. Nothing extraneous left her mind. No spurt of adrenaline. Valentine still thought: *eleven o'clock Friday morning and already too hot to practise, there's iced tea in the flat below, drama students are a pain, Rue Ingram is ignoring me out of nothing more personal than idleness.* Only her hand, cued by the sound and Frankie Hollister's ink-blue shadow in her peripheral vision, moved the dagger strongly up to catch the rapier blade between guard and ricasso, before it struck her back.

'You *do not*—!'

She drove sideways and down from her crouch, hitting the concrete with her left shoulder and rolling, and put her right hand into the hilt of her own rapier, and came up gripping it.

Grit clung to her biceps and back, and her knee under her cut-off brown denims. The sun lasered off windows, off car sunroofs far below; pooled shadow at her feet. She took one stride, another: positioned her back as much to the sun as could be.

Hearing only the sound of blades, she missed a metallic groan. The iron fire-escape creaked.

She feels the disparate weights of a blade a yard and a half long, three quarters of an inch wide, in one hand, a blade fifteen inches long in the other. Her dagger foot is advanced, her dagger hand forward; her rear hand and rapier raised, point steadily aimed at her opponent's eye—

'—*do* not *mess about with swords!*'

Frankie Hollister's blade thrusts, low. Valentine hacks it down viciously with her dagger. The younger woman is holding her sword far too loosely, expecting a dojo's usual mannered duelling. Expecting theatre combat.

Valentine's blow bounces Frankie's sword's point off the concrete. The girl yells, her right hand slipping off the hilt and tangling in the steel loops of the curved guard. Valentine steps forward, body-charging. She collects Frankie's sword with her dagger and hammers it left, trapping it across Frankie's body. Her impetus slams the young woman back against a brick stack, trapped by Valentine's weight.

The air jolts out of the young woman's lungs. Her face is pale and shiny. *I may have broken her wrist*, Valentine thinks.

Rue Ingram dropped her magazine and stood up, black mass of hair falling over her pale face and pale shoulders. A girl in a red flower-print dress, with a satin elastic hair-band worn around her wrist, and Walkphones jerked out of her pierced ears. She is looking beautiful, in the way that they do. 'Leave her alone, you cow!'

Valentine pushed her face into Frankie Hollister's, sheathing her dagger without looking, still holding her sword with the blade pointing down. 'I am teaching you to fight for the stage. I can teach you the real thing if you prefer. With live blades.'

A drop of blood bulged on the young woman's arm. Pressure behind it broke the meniscus: it dropped down to her elbow in a sudden run of red.

Valentine flicked her nail contemptuously along Hollister's practice blade. The rebated or blunt edge was flat. A burr of bright steel, knocked up where the blades had made contact, pricked like a metal thorn.

'File that down. Then we'll try again.'

'Cow!' Frankie said. She licked the blood from her arm.

A new voice spoke from the top of the rusting iron fire escape.

'She's right. "Cow". And, I may add, "bully".'

A fat man stepped delicately from the iron platform to the roof. His age indeterminate, he appeared somewhere between thirty and forty. He stood over six foot four inches tall. His white cotton shirt sleeves, rolled up, bulged over bolster-layers of flesh. Great patches of sweat soaked his underarms. His hair shone copper red, bright as fuse wire.

Valentine stared for whole seconds. Caught, she decided dazedly, by seeing him out of context. Hell, he shouldn't be back in this *country*. For something like a minute she took in the vast bulk of him without ever formulating his name.

'I must apologise,' he said gravely to the two younger women. 'She has a fierce temper. God knows I have cause to know that – but do I complain?'

The fat man carefully placed the ivory jacket of his suit on a brick stack, lowered himself on to it, and struck an attitude.

'I do not,' he concluded. 'Although I have been a martyr to this temper of Valentine's—'

'Class dismissed,' Valentine said absently. And when there was no movement in the corner of her eye, she projected her voice without raising it. '*Now*.'

A whiff of sweat drifted across the hot roof. The sun shone on his copper-red hair, curling in a hacked-off crop. Too-blue eyes surveyed Valentine from a fat, freckled face. The man mopped his chins with the tail end of his tie, ignoring the sweat mark that resulted.

'You aren't even going to introduce me,' he said mournfully. 'And such pretty ladies, too.'

'Yeah, introduce us!' Frankie Hollister looked up from massaging her wrist. Valentine noted absently that it was functional, that the girl looked grim, that Rue Ingram was supporting her friend with an arm around those bare shoulders.

'Frankie Hollister, Rue Ingram, two of my students from the London College drama course.'

'I apologise for remaining seated. Most impolite. The effort of the climb.' He gestured with one fat-padded hand at the fire-escape steps. For all that, his immense chest and belly did not rise or fall rapidly, and despite his size he was not panting. He favoured the eighteen-year-olds with a beam. 'I, of course, am your instructor's husband.'

'You're *married*?' Frankie grunted at Valentine.

Rue only watched, dark eyed.

Valentine was not yet used to the road silence. No noise of engines, of gear-changes and horns. Only faint voices came up from the street, and out of a window somewhere there was music. It would be the silence weighing on her that made her reluctant to break it, and put an absorbency of sweat across her forehead.

'This,' she said, 'is Baltazar Casaubon. Now *go away*.'

'But I've only just got here,' he protested in hurt tones.

'I don't mean you!'

'Oh, good. You want me to stay, then.'

Valentine Branwen took a deep breath, then another. Hyperventilation and the sun made her dizzy. She sheathed the rapier she still held by touch, left thumb at the mouth of her scabbard, right hand guiding the blunt blade home. 'Rue, Frankie; same time next week.'

Baltazar Casaubon lumbered to his feet and began gallantly

helping Rue Ingram pack her gear into her sports bag. Valentine folded her arms and watched all the small delays of departure. The sun was heavy on her head. A thirst rasped in her mouth.

When their footsteps had died away down the interior stairs of the building, and Baltazar Casaubon turned away from the roof door, she stared at him for a long minute. He yanked his tie loose. A shirt collar button pinged.

'Shouldn't you be home in the States,' Valentine Branwen said acidly, 'with your *wife*?'

The pedestrianised cobbles of Neal Street run south towards Covent Garden. Baltazar Casaubon indicated a café a few yards further on, as he breasted the waves of shoppers.

'You don't want me in your flat,' he said mournfully. 'I understand. That's your home ground. I don't feel hurt. I can understand that you want to talk on neutral territory. Public, even.'

He seated himself under a meagre London tree at one of the pavement café tables, cramming his bulk with difficulty into one of the uneven-legged plastic chairs. He leaned his elbows expansively on chairs to either side of him, ignoring the glares of overcrowded tourists.

'A mineral water, I think.'

The woman dumped a ski-bag of swords beside him. Although concealed, they rattled metallically. His own meagre luggage – an augmented portable PC in an ABS plastic case – he kept clamped firmly between his swollen ankles.

'How did you find me?' She gestured at the computer. 'That?'

With pudgy fingers he searched in his shirt pocket. He proffered a business card now soggily wet with sweat, curved where it had rested against his chest. The lettering was still legible. *White Crowe Enterprises. Swords and software.*

'I expected something a bit more high-tech than chasing down my business card!'

'Your changing IDs are hard to follow.' He beamed. 'But I can always find you. Even when you abandon the software industry to become a fight instructor, God save us.'

He let her bring the drinks out, and when she did, he said nothing, only burying his face in his glass and lifting it. His eyes slitted closed against the sun. Clear water spilled down his neck. His chins jerked. He lowered an empty glass.

'Ah . . .' One fat finger scraped around the inside of the glass, collecting the slice of lemon. He put it in his mouth and chewed.

A lingering odour of petrochemicals and dog-turd pervaded

midday. The woman sitting opposite him leaned back into the dappled shade of the sapling. Her white tank-top hung loosely about her shoulders. Her knees under her cut-off brown denim shorts were scabbed. She smelled of exercise-sweat. Sun gleamed from chained bicycles beside her, a man's earring beyond, and her own shadowed eyes.

When he saw her last, her hair was dark red and her eyes tawny. Now her hair has silver at the temples. Her eyes are silver, too. She is wearing mirrorshade contact lenses. He sees himself, white and copper and incredibly small, reflected therein.

'You are my wife,' Baltazar Casaubon observed mildly. 'I distinctly remember the wedding. I wore white. You didn't.'

'*Casaubon!*'

Loud enough for two small Japanese girls to startle as they walk past the table. Baltazar Casaubon graciously inclined his head and murmured, '*Hontō ni sumi-masen.*'

One giggled. '*Dō itashimashite!*'

Baltazar Casaubon's empty glass was almost lost in his huge hand. He jiggled it hopefully, turning to Valentine.

The red-headed woman leaned back in the white plastic chair. Her tone, vehement, nonetheless pitched itself under the ambient street noise.

'I just don't believe this! Remember me? I'm the one whose lover and father of her children turned out to have a wife he was still married to – except you didn't tell me this at the time, and you certainly didn't tell me when we were getting married. Or indeed, afterwards.'

'Oh, *that* wife,' he acknowledged cheerfully.

'You lied to me! You never told me. You never *told* me!'

Casaubon broke eye-contact. Valentine closed her eyes. A time passed in silence.

Giving up on her theoretical generosity, he hailed a waiter, and ordered several bottles: some water, some wine. 'I still don't understand why you're angry.'

'What do you *want*?'

He opened his mouth, but before he could speak, she cut across him.

'No, no, don't bother. I know what you want. You want me to do something for you. I don't know what it is, but you want me to do something for you. You always bloody do. Well, you can just bugger off!'

He attempted an injured look. Not sure of its success, and deciding that the extreme heat must be putting him off, he unscrewed the cap from one of the bottles of water and upended it over his head.

'Oh, Jesus.' Valentine Branwen brushed fruitlessly at her sprayed bare arm and tank-top. He distinctly noticed her shift around in her seat and face away from him, staring at the shop windows opposite. Her body language said volubly that she did not know him, had never met him, was nothing to do with him.

He scrubbed a hand through his soaked hair. 'Valentine—'

'Excuse me, miss, is this man bothering you?'

Both Baltazar Casaubon and the red-headed woman looked up at the café's waiter.

'You'll never know . . .' Her voice was uneven. 'Thank you. No. It's fine.'

They sat for a while. Lulled by the rhythm of people walking past, up and down Neal Street, into shops and out, and lulled also by what proved to be a quite reasonable wine, Baltazar Casaubon lurched with a jolt out of a half-doze. His water-soaked shirt front and trousers were almost dry. Valentine had leaned her elbows on the unevenly balanced plastic table and was watching him.

She said, 'You went back to her.'

'You asked me to leave,' Baltazar Casaubon riposted, with great dignity. Then he frowned, lips pursed. 'I might almost say, you threw me out.'

'What gives you the right to even *speak* to me?'

The whole street smelled of summer heat. In between the people wearing cotton skirts and jackets, the bare arms and sandalled feet, Casaubon picked out a man looking into the window of the bookshop opposite. The man wore casual jacket and trousers. He also knew which window commanded a reflection of the outdoor café tables.

Quite neutrally, Valentine said, 'I know you're still doing US Defence work.'

'You do keep track of me!' He smiled, smug.

'Not especially. I stayed in contact with a few of our – *my* colleagues, after I left. Sometimes your name gets mentioned. That's all.'

He scratched at his great belly, under his shirt. Another shirt button came away in his hand. He regarded it thoughtfully. 'I don't have any accommodation in London at the present.'

'Now *there's* a surprise.'

'I knew I should have taken you to bed first. That way you'd have been far more amenable.' He frowned. 'What are you laughing at?'

The woman had always had a bark of a laugh. It turned heads at the nearer tables.

'No.' Her mouth was an odd shape. 'No, you don't charm me into whatever it is. I know how you work. After all these years, I know.'

He threw his arms wide, exposing his great belly. Several café patrons ducked. Another shirt button pinged. 'Do it, then! Leave me to sleep on the streets! Why don't you hack into the Home Office and have me deported? Why not—'

Her finger placed on his lips silenced him. He took the hand, pressing each of her knuckles in turn to his lips.

'You're not going to walk away,' Casaubon said reasonably. 'You might as well sit down and let me tell you all about it.'

Valentine Branwen shoved her chair back with strong wrists as she stood. She leaned her knuckles on the table, and her body-weight on her arms.

'Sweetheart, it isn't enough to be funny, and charming. You know, I used to think there would be some way I could tell when you were lying to me? But there isn't. It's just how you are.'

A flash of light reflects from her mirrorshade lenses.

'I don't think you understand why what you did hurt me. That frightens me, because I can't *make* you understand. It frightens me, because I'd take you back tomorrow. Just stay away.'

Baltazar Casaubon leaned back. The plastic chair creaked. Absently, one of his fat hands slid down round his belly to scratch at his crotch. He frowned, sniffed at his fingers, and looked up at her again.

'I would stay away. But I need your help.'

The man watching window reflections dawdles back towards the café. He is wearing a different jacket, and sunglasses, and a small child holds his left hand. It is his own child, but then, his particular government department commonly employs such methods.

He sees the unknown woman's palm hit the plastic café table, bottles jolted and rolling. Her voice is loud enough that it turns heads within a radius of thirty metres.

'*No.* I started White Crowe Enterprises to get away from all that. Jesus Christ! I don't see you for eighteen months, and you come back, and it's *this*?'

CHAPTER 2
Programmed Sunlight

Four days later, on the Monday that they officially closed London, Rue Ingram stood in the narrow court behind Shaftesbury Avenue and Neal Street and burned her wedding dress.

Moisture steamed up, drying in the early dawn heat. Piles of satin fabric lay on the rain-wet cobbles. The wedding dress's cream-and-peach sheen crisped in the flames, consumed, turning black. A stink of paraffin stung her nostrils. She wiped the back of her wrist under her nose.

'Are you sure you know what you're doing, miss?'

The voice interrupted her thoughts. Her head lifted sharply. Old brick buildings surrounded her, four and five storeys high; the iron fire-escape clinging to the wall at the end of the court.

Under its pierced metal steps, a man leaned against the far wall.

A man in his thirties, perhaps; blond, hairy, shambling, scruffy, *big*. Boots laced up to the ankles. Slightly bloused combat trousers and a sand-coloured sweatshirt. A cluttered web-belt locked around his waist gave some further iconographic suggestion of the techno-military.

'What are you doing?'

'What business is it of yours?' Rue Ingram rubbed the heel of her hand into her eye socket, tears slick against her skin. A waft of smoke caught in her throat and she coughed, thickly.

'I'm a cameraman.'

She raised black eyebrows at that.

'For the rolling-news satellite channels.' He tapped his web-belt equipment.

'Yeah? Which one?'

'All of them. Some. A fair proportion. I'm a freelance.'

'Oh, *sure*. I know what *that* means. And before you ask, no, I don't do "modelling".'

Her hair plastered the back of her neck, above the scooped neckline of her black cotton dress. The fire's heat added to the already-hot summer morning. Pain tensioned the cords of her throat.

As if bewildered to find herself there, she said, 'That's it, now. That's it. Finished. The deadline's passed. Oh, hey, I wanted London closed as much as anyone! But he *could* have got residence. He *could* have applied. Bastard.'

The man shifted his back from the brick wall, straightening. Maybe younger than thirties, the beard makes it difficult to tell.

'I'm Miles Godric. Why don't you come for a drink after I'm done here?' He glanced up at the strip of sky visible between buildings, that now glowed a yellow-white, pregnant with heatwave. 'You look as though you need one.'

Rue Ingram stared at the smouldering cloth at her feet. Bodice and veil burnt to ashes, but the vast panelled skirt barely half consumed. She kicked at it with a sandalled foot. 'Rolling news. You want eye witness stuff. Reactions of the public to Fortress London. You can just go—' She sniffled.

'But you could use someone to talk to.'

'A more foolish man than I—'

The voice cut across Miles Godric's. Rue glanced upwards. Up where the fire escape passed a fourth-storey room, a fat man leaned large arms comfortably on the windowsill. She said, 'Who? – Oh. We met a couple of days back?'

'A man more foolish than I,' Baltazar Casaubon revised, no more grammatically, 'would ask you what you were doing.'

The slightest lift of tone made it into a question.

'I'm burning my wedding dress,' Rue Ingram said dourly, 'what does it look like?'

'It looks like a mess,' he observed, 'and in my backyard, too.'

A conviction of tragedy turning by some sleight of hand to farce took hold of her. The red-haired man leaned out of the window, vastly fat shoulders and torso filling almost all the frame. He pursed delicately-chiselled lips, staring down at the burnt cloth.

'I suppose you and your invisible friend wouldn't like to come up here and talk about this?'

Rue Ingram, bewildered, was about to speak when the shambling man ducked out from under the stairs and stood in the court, where he became visible to the fourth-floor window.

'Would you be Casaubon? Mr Baltazar Casaubon?'

The older man leaned several chins upon his hand, and his elbow on the windowsill, and gazed down at the court as if he gave the matter serious consideration.

'I might be,' he conceded. 'Who are you?'

'Miles Godric; you faxed me to meet you in this . . . yard.'

'Godric . . . ? Godric! Ah. I *know* I faxed you. You were the only name in her address file that looked like a media person. Hate media people,' Baltazar Casaubon concluded diffidently. 'Hungry little rats out for their own aggrandisement.'

Miles Godric shrugged large shoulders, as if he only took in the surface of what the fat man was saying. 'Is that fair?'

'You came, didn't you? I suppose you'd both better come up. Top flat. Go around to the front – the stairs back here are less than safe, I warn you.'

The fat man vanished back inside. Rue Ingram gaped up at the empty window. 'Wh—?'

Miles Godric took her elbow, staring up in the same direction. His grip felt strong. 'I think you should come in. You need to sit down.'

She ran a finger round under the neck of her dress, the black cotton already wet with perspiration. A soft smell of skin made her breathe in sharply, in pain. It seemed that her lover's own smell, incised upon her body-chemistry, remained with her in his absence.

'What's your name?'

She snarled, 'What's it to you?'

The last licking tongues of flame died. The wedding dress, a heap of black-and-cream cloth, lay marked with smoke and dust. She stirred it with her foot, then bent down to rip a section from the hem free and stuff it in her pocket. 'Oh . . . Who *is* he, anyway?'

'You don't know Baltazar Casaubon?' Miles Godric pushed damp blond hair out of his face. His eyes, meeting Rue's, were pale, throwing the pupil into sharp relief. Lion-eyes.

'I met him for two minutes last week. If I knew who he is, I wouldn't ask.'

'Last week? I didn't realise he'd been in the country that long. He's— I'd rather explain afterwards.' Godric smiled, broad shoulders unconsciously hunched as if he were attempting not to loom over her. 'It gives me an excuse to ask you out to dinner.'

'Oh, get *real*.' She swung on her heel, the brick walls towering above her; walked out into the street, steeling herself against the blows of the sun's heat. Her eyes automatically slitted. She felt the front vee of her dress for the UV shades hooked there, hurriedly putting them on.

Miles Godric caught up with her as she lost impetus at the junction with Neal Street.

He edged her a few steps down, past shops and cafés, to an entry-phone and entrance, the door already clicking open.

Miles Godric found the tiny fourth-floor kitchen smelled of toast and cat urine.

His gaze slid across the closed door that must lead to the rest of the apartment, took in window, fire-escape, and a man built large enough that manoeuvring between table and sink required his total concentration. Baltazar Casaubon. A man whom he has never met. He knows his reputation. And Miles Godric once had the man described to him closely enough that all is familiar.

Miles hooked his thumbs over his web-belt. 'You don't mind if I record this.'

The small recorder locked to his belt was already online; the larger shoulder-slung one he now set down among the piled dishes on the kitchen table.

Baltazar Casaubon sighed sweatily. Standing, he looked down from what Miles Godric guessed to be six foot four or five; over chins, towering chest, and immense belly only just constrained by his trouser-belt. With a sudden effort he tugged his shirt-tail free of voluminous white trousers and pulled the shirt off over his head.

Momentarily muffled by shirt, the fat man observed, 'Burning your *wedding* dress?'

The dark-haired girl snatched her anti-UV shades off and glared at him as he emerged, ruffled. '*So?*'

Baltazar Casaubon wadded his shirt, regarded it for a moment, then scrubbed his neck and under his armpits with it, and tossed it into a corner of the kitchen. Fine red hairs protruded through the string vest that he wore.

'Well, really,' he said mildly, 'if you must—' And then held out his arms.

Miles watched the girl allow herself to be enveloped in an ursine embrace. Fists clenched at her mouth, she sobbed and bubbled. Miles's eyes stung in sympathy with her gut-wrenching sobs.

He checked his light-levels.

'She a friend of yours, Mr Casaubon?'

'It would seem so.' Looking down, the fat man added, 'Have some hummus.'

The girl stepped back out of his arms and regarded with suspicion the dish of elderly chickpeas that he held out.

'There are—' She coughed, losing throatiness. 'There are whole micro-ecologies evolving in there.'

'Do you know, you remind me of a dear friend of mine. What do you want, boy?'

Miles Godric, at least a decade too old for that 'boy', rested his hip back against the kitchen windowsill. A faint air, already warm, slid into the room; smelling of dust, vinegar, and dog-shit. A less perceptible, more metaphysical scent impinged itself on his instincts. The smell of something happening, times upon which events pivot.

'I got your fax. Yes, I want to record a public announcement by the greatest link-architect of the decade. The greatest renegade link-architect, I should say.'

'Hhrrrmmm . . .' The fat man scratched in his copper-red hair, studied his nails for scurf, and flicked it on to the floor. Straggling sweaty hair fell over copper brows. A search through his trouser pockets elicited a rubber band. He smoothed his hair back in one ham-hand, fastening the band around the tiny pony-tail at the back of his neck. He met Miles's gaze with guileless blue eyes.

'Even with the advantage of youth on your side,' Casaubon rumbled, 'you may still meet someone whose nerve is of a better quality brass than yours.'

Miles schooled his face to cool interest, moving across the kitchen. Window light cast the fire-escape's angular shadows across Baltazar Casaubon, the leaf-shadows of an iron forest. Good introductory shot.

The nameless girl, sucking a finger loaded with hummus, mumbled something inaudible; removed her finger; concluded, '. . . *really* don't know why I'm in here . . .'

'You're in here because I invited you in.' The link-architect sighed. 'Both of you. For my sins. Do you drink lemon tea?'

Miles nodded agreeably. 'Sure. Tell me—'

'Because if you *do*, there's tea in the cupboard, and a lemon around here . . .' Plump-fingered hands waved at the tiny cluttered room. '. . . somewhere.'

Miles hooked the big recorder around to face the closed door, crossed the room, tried the handle, and pushed it open.

'Good grief,' he said mildly.

He walked through into the long, wide room beyond. Its street window opened to the roofscape across Neal Street. Sun slanted in, hot and white, bleaching the floorboards.

And, hard and harsh, and at right-angles to it, *other* sunlight slanted in from a 'window' filling all of the partition-wall between the room and the next building.

Miles padded forward, the boards creaking under his booted feet, staring at a second sun. At blue sky and a warm sandstone cityscape below; domes, pillars, colonnades, piazzas . . .

And touched the finger-thin flat screen monitor fixed to the partition wall. Even close, perfect definition fooled the eye; his stomach churning with the apparent drop outside the apparent window.

He smiled. 'That's what I *call* a monitor.'

The girl passed him, walking to get to what breeze flowed in through the streetside window. Her heeled sandals clicked on the boards, picking a way between a jumble of High Street-available hardware: Apple Macs, Amstrads, old Spectrums, keyboards lashed together in a tangle of wiring; telephone cables running in bundles; monochrome PC monitors stacked three high and a dozen wide.

Miles Godric looked past the gash High Street stuff to the ex-GLC Crays, guessed at the remaining room being similarly occupied, surmised in a moment of sheer amazement the high bandwidth of information going into and out of this flat.

The girl eyed the hardware with momentary interest. 'Hey, I bet you can do stuff with this! But what a kludge.'

'The gear may be a kludge, but the programming must be elegant.'

'I have to go . . .' Her suddenly tear-heavy voice bounced dissonances against a background track he at last identified: Tull playing *Said She Was a Dancer*. Her hair, loose and with braids in the tangles, hung down black about her rounded, tanned shoulders; her skin smooth and odourous with summer. Her young, pale face shone with sweat.

True and false windows cast double shadows on the floor. On the big monitor, small green figures over Brunelleschi's dome read 07.45 a.m. Miles focused through the garage-clutter at disc-strewn desks in front of the main window.

'I rarely contact the media,' the large man began, consideringly, from the kitchen doorway.

He was interrupted by the sound of footsteps hammering up the stairs. Miles turned his belt-recorder to the room's further door, letting its arc take in hardware, monitor, and the stained double mattress in the corner.

The door banged opened, hip-shoved by a woman with her arms apparently full of cloth bundles.

Miles Godric felt heat climb up his fair-skinned face with one heartbeat, drain away in the next.

'*Valentine?*' Casaubon startled.

'Hi, Ms Branwen,' the girl snuffled, apparently unsurprised at the woman's presence in the flat.

The newcomer dropped what she carried on the pale floor-boards, in a patch of programmed sunlight. The light blazed back from her clothes: a muddy doublet and black breeches. A fisted hand rubbed the small of her back. Her black hair, obviously a wig, flashed with the blue gleam of a crow's wing. It was styled just short enough to rub the edge of her white linen collar.

'Baltazar . . . ? What the *fuck* are you doing in here? Jesus Christ, I told you to get lost! I meant it. You're *not* staying here.' Her eyes slitted. 'Did you break in over the weekend?'

'Of course,' the fat man said equably. 'What on earth are you doing dressed up like that?'

Godric thought, This isn't *his* flat. And then he thought nothing, only stared. He registered her voice. The way she stands. Saw her gaze move around the room as immediate anger faded and she realised she was not alone.

'Rue, this isn't a Friday, what are you doing here?'

And then, finally, her gaze intercepted Miles. Her mouth shut up like a trap.

'How very useful,' Casaubon said, 'that you should have a freelance cameraman as a friend.'

' "Friend" isn't quite the word for Miles and me,' the woman said grimly. 'How are you, Miles?'

You didn't return my calls, how would you know how I am? Miles hooked his thumbs under his web-belt and watched her. 'I didn't know you'd moved to Seven Dials, Val. Do I take it I was contacted at random?'

Tiny crow's-feet crinkled at the corners of her eyes as she stared at Baltazar Casaubon. 'By someone poking around in my secure files.'

The woman tugged at her black woollen sixteenth-century knee-breeches, unbuckled a belt from her waist, and let belt, scabbard, and a long sword clatter to the floor. Her fingers fumbled at her scalp. She pulled the black wig off, shaking free a mass of dark red curling hair. It fell across the shoulder rolls of her quilted Renaissance doublet.

'I do a lot of this,' she said coolly. She might have been addressing Casaubon or himself. 'Not that it isn't more trouble than it's worth, with London closed. You should have seen me coming back. I got stopped at every customs post and passport check on the Northern Line.'

A thin *skree* of steel: she squatted and drew her blade and sighted along it, her arm at full extension. 'And if I have to explain one more time that this isn't "a medieval sword", it's a Renaissance military rapier with a swept-hilt, then I swear I'll make a kebab of the person that asks me!'

The girl, Rue, stepped forward. The movement catching Val's eye, she lowered the blade's point to safety. A curious smile tugged at her mouth as she stood.

'To what do we owe the pleasure of *your* company, Rue?'

Baltazar Casaubon said, 'She was out in the court. She was burn—'

'I don't want to talk about that!'

In the silence left by the girl's tearful outburst, Val sheathed her sword.

'Let no one say I don't take my games research seriously.' She scratched her sweaty hair, and smiled sweetly at Baltazar Casaubon. 'Elizabethan historical re-enactment. Wars of Religion. There weren't enough Papists to take the field this time, so I had to leave the heretic Protestants and join them – can't disappoint the public. At least we won. They won. Well, you know what I mean. Somebody won.'

The fat man waved his arms. The floorboards flexed under his advancing weight. *'Damn it, Valentine, you quit because you said you wouldn't do any more simulation war games!'*

'Different games.'

She stirred the cloth bundles with her foot. A cloak, a black leather doublet, a wig, a purse . . . effectively a disguise: the more so because it appears to be not disguise but costume.

Miles Godric met her eyes. Silver brilliancies. Deliberately professional, he said smoothly, 'How long have you been back in contact with Baltazar Casaubon?'

She inclined her head, as if to an opponent's touch in fencing. 'It only feels like centuries. Exactly which channel are you with these days, Miles? I've lost track.'

Baltazar Casaubon remarked, 'Primarily with *Hypershift!*, I believe, but not on a contract. One can't choose one's wife's lovers, of course, but one would have thought a better-quality channel . . . Damn it, I suspect we're about to star in some gutter-press extravaganza.'

He paused.

'At least, I hope so. I demand to *star*, at the very least.'

' "Demand" to star?' Miles queried.

'In exchange for your presence here. At, if I may say so, one of the great historical events of the decade.' Another pause. Baltazar

Casaubon absently dug a finger in one nostril, removed it, and wiped the result on his trouser-leg.

'Event of the century,' he corrected himself. 'If not of several.'

'I want to talk to you,' Val said. Miles winced at the tone that meant trouble. The fat man remained impervious.

The woman walked across the room and squatted by a kettle that stood on the floor, plugging it into the only singly-used power point in the room. A thin steam began to rise. She busied herself with mugs and some black granules from an unmarked paper bag.

'I am *not* going along with this. You're on your own. Both of you,' she added sourly. 'Rue, you want a cup?'

'Uh, no.'

Miles's fingers checked sound-and-vision levels, swiftly and automatically. Excitement over and above the professional flared, without cause or evidence; his breathing shallow with anticipation. He kept his gaze on her bright face. 'Never mind the bloody tea, Val. I never could get a straight answer out of you—'

'Know exactly what you mean,' the fat man rumbled.

'*What* are you not going along with?'

Squatting, she rested her forearms across her knees; tea-spoon in one hand, chipped mug in the other. The soft hairs at her temples were dark red, with strands of purest white. She tapped the bowl of the tea-spoon softly against her full lower lip, only her eyes shifting up to meet his.

'Whatever it is, I'll bet he can't do this without me.'

'Don't be ridiculous,' the fat man said loftily. 'I merely wished to give you an opportunity to participate.'

Spoon clattering into mug, Val threw both down, straightened, crossed the room in swift strides, and was seized up out of her path into an embrace by massive arms; Baltazar Casaubon's face buried in her neck, her arms about him, his hands grabbing her so that the linen shirt rode up out of the back of her breeches.

She removed herself with two practised blows from her elbows.

'Oh bloody hell – Miles, we're out of sugar. Suppose you go out and get some. We'll talk when you get back. Talk *alone*.'

'But it was Mr Casaubon I was to film!'

'*Miles, don't argue.*'

Miles Godric collects cameras, recording equipment, and his shaken thoughts.

'Sure,' he says. 'Twenty minutes.'

CHAPTER 3
Simulations

Rue Ingram was barely aware, through swallowed weeping, of the door banging behind Miles Godric.

The fight instructor flopped on to the mattress, on the floor. She rolled up her sleeves, dabbing a clear liquid from a bottle on to the bruises on her arms. Then she took off her woollen breeches and silk hose, streching her barefoot legs. Her linen shirt covered her to mid-thigh. One large yellow and purple bruise marked her shin, lesser ones spreading in a chain from thigh to knee.

Hurts, Rue thought.

'That was *my* interview! How dare you interrupt?'

'That was my ex-lover! Who gave you the right to poke around in my encrypted files?'

'*I* shall make tea,' the fat man said pointedly, removing himself and the kettle to the kitchen.

Rue picked up and unsheathed Valentine's military rapier and swung it experimentally. Fake sunlight from the big monitor flashed. Knuckleguards scraped her fingers. The weight of it pulled at her wrist.

'You really *fight* with this thing? Not stage fighting? Not to a script?'

The older woman said, 'Yes, I fight.'

The blunt edge chilled Rue Ingram's thumb. She let the sword fall on the stained mattress. Tears pushed over her lower lids. She pulled back from emotion.

'What's that smell?'

'Witch hazel,' the woman said. 'It helps bruises heal faster.'

Not the usual Friday tutor. No professional *hauteur*, only a pragmatic intention to treat her minor injuries, regardless of dignity. The woman's eyes were edged with faint lines, and the bones of her cheeks stood out under taut skin. Her body under the loose skirt moved with a compact energy.

Rue wandered aimlessly across the cluttered room, the bevelled screens of old monitors reflecting her a dozen times. The rattle of crockery and muffled curses sounded in the kitchen.

'See this?' Rue reached into her dress pocket. Her hand cupped the thin weight of a cut-throat razor. She flicked it out and open. Metal snicked. Valentine Branwen came instantly alert, with a tremor of complete responsiveness to the position of the knife.

Slightly shaken by the difference in her, Rue said, 'See that? When I fight, I don't mess around with blunt blades. I'm not *playing.*'

'You'd be better off if you were.' Inevitable laughter, sardonic and slow, faded from Valentine's voice. 'You've never used it.'

'I will! If I need to, I will. I might need to. It's protection.'

Rue wrist-flicked the razor shut and dropped it back into the pocket of her dress. The weight gave the black cotton one more unnoticeable crease. She paced restlessly. From the kitchen came an increasingly pointed rattle of crockery.

'Jesus, Ms Branwen, don't you ever walk down the street? Half of Former Europe is living rough on your doorstep! It's *why* they've closed London. To keep the refugees out. You ought to be on our side, you have to live here too!'

Valentine Branwen pulled the linen shirt off over her head. She shook her hair loose, emerging from her sole remaining garment. She stood, naked, muscle-weary, arms raised; the room's double sunlight blazing back from her white skin. A few dark red hairs feathered the aureoles of her breasts, and her triangle of lush hair further down glittered reddish-black. Rue's breath caught under her sternum.

Valentine said crisply, 'Do you want to know the only thing I learned from playing soldiers? It's how *often* you die . . . and don't get up again when it's game-over.'

Grief wiped out momentarily by anger, Rue had no vision of how all the subdued language of her body shifted, transmuted to a hard power and determination; a metamorphosis from grub to skull-winged black butterfly. 'This city is my home! These people should go back where they came from!'

Dark oblate bruises marked Valentine's upper arms, and the outside of her thighs. The older woman fingered each reflectively, ticking them off, and glanced up. 'There comes a distressing tendency to total up lumps and bruises as if they were real battle scars.'

She felt under the mattress on the floor and pulled out a sleeveless white t-shirt and a crumpled pair of white Levi 501s. Standing to dress, she added, 'Not that there haven't *been* scars. It's when you catch yourself becoming proud of that, that you know you've lost it.'

From the open kitchen door, the fat man's voice rumbled, 'Damn it, Rose of the World, you have a macabre taste in relaxation.'

'*I told you to get out!*'

'*And* you know better.'

Turning abruptly, the woman's bright face shone against the monitor-skies over Florence. Rue almost looked for the breeze that swayed the cypresses to move the woman's hair. The multiple humming of hard discs sounded thick, like honey.

'Rue, sweetheart, someday I'll show you some of the stuff I'm working on.' The woman's thumb slides along a shelf of labelled discs. *Shatterworld. Lace and Leather. Tactica.* 'For now, you're going to have to love me and leave me. I need to talk to—'

'You can't—' Dizzy, breathless, balance gone from that centre that lies at the base of the skull, Rue Ingram forced herself to begin again. 'You can't have all this and just write *games* software with it! It's obscene. Nobody over twenty-five ought to be allowed to handle technology. You don't understand what it's *for*.'

'It's for commercial interactive multi-user Virtual Reality games at the moment,' Valentine said grimly, 'and it's for paying my bills. There are worse games.'

Rue suddenly snivelled.

Baltazar Casaubon, with a tray, in what he obviously supposed to be an undertone, rumbled, 'She's *upset*. I found her outside, burning a wedding dress.'

'A *wedding* dress? Why the hell would she – oh, never mind. Not now.' Valentine sighed. 'Here. Have this tea. Sugar's good for shock.'

Casaubon, whose tea it was, looked momentarily affronted. Then, with a grand gesture, he shoved a teetering stack of machine code printouts from a chair. 'Sit down, Rue. I shall not ask questions. I am not an inquisitive man.'

Alone, in someone else's flat, not wanting to think, not wanting now to be alone, Rue doggedly continued.

'You just spread *crap*. I've played VR games. All this bullshit about multi-national corporations with artificial intelligences, street runners with surgically implanted data ports. It isn't going to *be* like that.'

'No. It isn't going to be like that. It already isn't like that.'

Valentine seated herself cross-legged on the sun-warmed floor-boards by Rue's feet, moving with a fight instructor's grace. 'Do you know what I used to do for a living?'

'What?' Rue stared.

'I flew virtual F16s. Or, I should say, I *wrote* virtual F16s. And virtual M1 Abrams tanks, Apache helicopter gunships, aircraft carriers, satellite submarine detectors, cruise missiles. Half of the UCS military's SIMNET is mine. And I wrote the landscapes for wars. The reason the landings in Iberia worked at all is because the infantry knew the Virtual country backwards, forwards and side-ways before they ever got there in the flesh . . .'

Valentine smiled.

'I used to talk to brat-hackers in the States. They'd harangue me about Drexler and the nanotechnology revolution, and how we're going to send Von Neumann machines to the stars, and meantime down here there's going to be nothing but corrupt and outdated nation states powerless before the subversive hacker anarchy . . . It makes good copy for commercial games. And I like it.'

'You're sad,' Rue sneered.

'I know the alternative. You start off with smart shells – and you end up with bolt-action rifles, making your own ammunition. Former Europe. Urban civil war, where the water and the power and the medical supplies break down; and you won't be program-ming anything because the telephone network doesn't function, and the dark fibre cablenet has been blasted sky high, and even the high-tech sensors on military equipment have degraded . . .'

'My – this guy I know – he's in the Forces . . .' Rue rubbed the heel of her hand across her eyes, and then under her nose. '*You* don't like the information revolution because it's wiping out your world; how they did things in your day!'

'I wasn't aware my day was over,' Valentine said, not waspishly. 'Sweetheart, I think your cyberpunk dystopias are . . . infinitely fragile and valuable. Looking at technology on its own is naive. The old power structures can swallow hacker anarchy and never burp.'

Baltazar Casaubon, returning with his own tea mug, stated, 'The last thing that child stands in need of at the moment is a lecture.'

Caught up in the argument – anything but think or feel – Rue yelled, 'But they don't understand it! They don't understand how the world *is* now.'

Valentine Branwen buttoned her white jeans taut across her flat stomach.

'Sweetheart, they don't have to understand it. You don't have to understand something to exploit it. And now, if you'll excuse me, I have an intruder to throw out of *my* flat.'

Gridlocked, abandoned cars blocked Monmouth Street and snarled into a metal kaleidoscope around the pillar of Seven Dials. Closed London's sparser crowds dotted the street. Miles Godric identified the nervous, card-clutching men and women in bright clothes as foreign tourists, and those mixed in with the locals as refugees.

His boots jolted on the hot, cracked paving stones.

Warm air moved against his face. He touched the microphone attachment on his web-belt shoulder strap.

'Val Branwen, ex-star of the US Department of Defense, is back in contact with her husband Baltazar Casaubon, notorious hacker, data-thief, and possibly the 90s' most versatile and intelligent constructor of hypermedia architecture. It seems neither deliberate nor willing. But does it imply she's doing more than write commercial games software? What announcement does Baltazar Casaubon want to make to the public . . . ? Is this connected with rumours of an explosion of discoveries coming out of the MultiNet as more of it comes online? Val hasn't changed. I've heard far too much about Baltazar Casaubon from her. Am I only seeing him through her eyes?'

'Spare some change, please? Spare some change, please?'

A woman in filthy man's overalls leaned out of the gaping door of a BMW. Her red-rimmed eyes fastened on Miles. Her hair shone pepper-and-salt through the shattered windscreen, bright with sunlight and grease.

The inside of the car was draped with old cloth, rucked up into rat's-nests on the back seat. No sign of who might have owned it, once; it took on the contours of the homeless now.

Miles Godric met her flat gaze; saw a tinge of anger in the woman's face. Curious refugees: leaving a six-bedroomed house and two Mercedes cars abandoned in the wreckage of Paris or Florence; inarticulate, dispossessed of the middle class.

'Spare-some-change-sir-please.'

On the opposite side of Earlham Street two men in late middle age shared the contents of a bottle in a brown paper bag. Their blotched red scalps almost met, bent over it. One's gaze flicked up, met Miles's and skidded across him as if he left no retinal image.

'I don't carry money,' he explained, his voice gentling, 'I'm not a tourist. Sorry, love. Look, try down Shaftesbury Avenue.'

Her hand closed over his forearm, broken nails digging into his skin. Fast and without fuss, he dug his own nails into the joint of her wrist, forcing her fingers to release.

The usual unhappy thought went through his mind: Someday *I* shall end up like this.

The Seven Dials pillar gleamed, its faces blue and gold in the rising sunlight. Counting exits, Miles Godric crossed two streets, entered a Chinese supermarket, and emerged a few minutes later with sugar, rice, noodles. Those who lived in the abandoned cars looked dully at him as he passed. He thumbed the smallest belt-camera online, relying on picture compensation to edit out his movements, and scanned the long line of cars.

Background material, he tells himself.

Finally frustrated, he checks his watch, sits on the bonnet of a broken down Jaguar, and takes his sub-notebook PC out of his backpack. Practised hacker access to the MultiNet via a mobile phone link gives him, within a quarter of an hour, tax and health records on Val Branwen (uninformative), the telephone bill for modem use to the Neal Street flat (phenomenal, but still less than it should be), bank statements that feature regular small payments to odd sources (unspecified), and no information on Baltazar Casaubon whatsoever. Querying a civilian and a military subNet in California adds nothing.

No record of her marriage. No record of any association with Casaubon. Some mention of himself, twelve months ago. Otherwise squeaky clean.

'Someone's interested in you, Val . . .'

He has seen this kind of thing before when hackers tamper with their own records, but this goes beyond that. The marks of absence are over everything. It appears to be very similar to what happens when security forces encrypt information because they themselves are interested in it.

For a minute it bothers him more that his name and the address in Docklands are on file than it does that the PanEuropean Security Services are obviously monitoring Val Branwen, and have been for some time.

Since before Baltazar Casaubon went 'missing' in the USA, in fact.

Miles Godric walked back up out of Earlham Street. A sudden stench hit his nostrils. He looked down and swore, and scraped his ankle-boot against the kerb, scraping off the worst of the wet horse manure.

Up ahead, where Neal Street and Monmouth Street come to an intersection with Shaftesbury Avenue, a rider slumped along on a hack mare with the motion of a sack of potatoes. Ban the internal combustion engine and they'll use anything.

A dozen or so tourists, bright in crimson and azure shirts, raise their cameras to photograph the horse and rider.

He leaned his shoulder against the entry buzzer.

No answer.

Checked his watch: thirty minutes.

No answer. At all.

The outer door closed behind Rue Ingram as, finally, she left.

Silence in the flat. Early morning sun.

'Why don't you,' Valentine asked, pronouncing each word with individual precision, 'just fuck off and die?'

Baltazar Casaubon grabbed at his throat with both hands, fingers sinking into multiple chins. He gurgled. His body stiffened from head to heel. He tipped backwards, and fell.

Pivoting on his heels, he pitched backwards and hit the floor, rigid as a board. Three desks, a monitor, and two filing cabinets jolted six inches into the air and crashed down. Dust shot up from between the floorboards. A stack of discs ricocheted down the metal shelving.

Valentine, simultaneously thinking *I am* not *going to laugh* and *Is he hurt?* snorted uncontrollably. She wiped snot and spit on to her bare wrist. Her eyes watered.

Baltazar Casaubon remained suspiciously still.

'I hope you *have* cracked your skull,' Valentine snarled.

Casaubon lay still. Without moving, he murmured, 'They'll never get me down those stairs on a stretcher. I shall starve to death on your floor.'

Amusement vanished in irritation. 'Casaubon!'

'After all the effort I go to, to entertain you . . .'

'I don't want to be entertained, I want you out of my life.' She sighed and sat down on the mattress. 'That's not true, of course. What I want is you back in my life, but without all those annoying little faults. Bigamy. Burglary. That kind of thing . . . How's that for irrational? You are what you are. And if you attempt to seduce me while I'm in this mood—'

Casaubon's hand scuttled back to his side.

'—I shall rip your testicles off, varnish them, and wear them as ear-rings. Who knows, maybe I'll start a mass trend.'

'How many testicles do you think I've *got*?'

His mock alarm brought her close to laughter.

'Perhaps you could re-grow them for each occasion,' she said whimsically. 'A new fashion line. Baltazar's Balls. Look, this is all very nice, but now you're leaving.'

He lifted his head, regarded the room, and flopped back to the horizontal.

'I could try, this thing is more important than both of us?' he said hopefully. 'I guess the troubles of two little people don't amount to a—'

'Don't you dare!'

Valentine rested her arms on her knees, sitting foetally; after a while she pulled her discarded linen re-enactment shirt into her arms and sat with her nose buried in it, smelling the ingrained scent of wind and turf.

'Are you going to tell me what this is all about?' she demanded.

'Of course not,' Casaubon said reasonably. 'Somewhere out on those roof-tops is a vibration-sensitive laser microphone trained on our windows – do you want me to tell the whole *world*?'

Valentine sighed.

'I suppose we can always go for brutal isolation.'

CHAPTER 4
The Language of Angels

'Civilians talking about war,' observed the PanEuropean Minister of Defence, 'is like virgins talking about sex, I have always thought.'

Flight Lieutenant Wynne Ashton hesitated. The middle-aged woman sitting in the co-pilot and gunner's seat of the Mark 7 Lynx helicopter turned her head and smiled at him. A helmet hid her blonde hair. Her voice sounded through his headphones again.

'I wonder what civilian *experience* of war counts as? Heavy petting, perhaps?'

'Uh, yes, ma'am. I mean, I don't know, ma'am.'

Ashton unnecessarily repeated the last three items on his flight check list, thumbed the cut-out to advise the tower that he was ready, and glanced back once over his shoulder. The cramped interior of the Lynx, made even more cramped by the very basic eight-man seating riveted in, was full of men in suits with shades and, he suspected, Heckler and Koch P7s and MP5s. The roar of the turning rotors a foot or so above the cabin roof meant non-radio-mediated speech was impossible.

Acknowledgement came through from the tower. The sun sparkled across the canopy; the leather seats were hot to the touch. Ashton, without fuss, lifted off from the French airbase and up and forward into the July sky.

'Good machine,' her voice said.

'The Mark 7's OK.' He eased the cyclic forward.

'You've flown combat missions.'

Nose down, to obviate at least some of its forward visibility problems, the Lynx drove ahead. He took the helicopter up to two thousand feet, gaining a few degrees of welcome coolness, and the machine dropped a step in the air as they came over the edge of the hills outside Rouen.

'Yes, ma'am.'

'Tours of duty in Central Europe, in Iberia, and West Africa.'

Ashton thought at first that, being a politician, the woman had taken a quick flick through his file to make him feel noticed. However, the likelihood – or *un*likelihood – of the PanEuropean Defence Minister bothering about the good opinion of a Rapid Reaction Force chopper pilot who is purely taking her from Rouen to London with appropriate cargo of security people . . .

'You didn't take out residence in London in time, Lieutenant.'

'No, ma'am.' Awkward, he wanted to vocalise a set of confused feelings that had been clear at the time. That it had seemed unjust to use his military qualifications to get him residence when that would be the only reason for his acceptance. That he would feel exposed and isolated in London.

'Although,' the woman's voice changed slightly, 'you were engaged to be married, Lieutenant Ashton?'

The Lynx drifted sideways a little, and he corrected, corrected again, and found himself with the first pilot-induced oscillation since training school. Behind the mirrored visor of helmet and HUD he could feel his skin grow hot.

'You obviously know a lot about me, ma'am.'

She ignored that effortlessly. 'Engaged to a girl called Rue Ingram. I don't want to know why you decided not to marry her, Lieutenant. I do want to know about Rue Ingram. What she does. Who she is. I thought you might be able to tell me.'

The air thrummed, and the grey disc of the rotor blades held steady in their apparent position towards the top of the windscreen. The Lynx chuntered north across the void at a hundred and eighty miles per hour, sky clear, no wind, rising thermals.

'I don't know what you want to know,' Ashton said. 'She's a drama student. She works part-time in a London shop. A theatrical costume shop, round the back of Shaffesbury Avenue. She lives in Seven Dials as a resident. She's going to be nineteen this year. She doesn't drive. She's not very mature, ma'am – I mean, she doesn't understand why I couldn't be in the UK all the time, or see her all the time. I don't think she wants to do anything much except talk to her girlfriends.'

Curiosity overcame military formality.

'Ma'am, why do you want to know about Rue?'

Johanna Branwen, the Minister of Defence for an area from the Carpathians to Carthage, said, 'I like to know what company my daughter is keeping.'

*

Water hissed, creasing back from the slow prow of the *Carola*. A smell of rank Thames water permeated the deck of the tourist riverboat. The smell of the estuary, not of the sea.

Casaubon, in view of the public nature of the place, had let himself be persuaded into wearing a shirt. Now he was not entirely certain whether the oversized, short-sleeved silk garment with the red hibiscus-flower pattern was a mistake.

'They'll know you're in England.' The woman watched a big Saab paralleling their course on the Embankment. She wore her hair differently, and two years longer. 'I've got used to having my phone tapped and my electronic mail monitored.'

'They will know I'm in England. I'm counting on it.'

'What?'

A computer with no modem, no incoming fibre or data discs, cannot be hacked into or corrupted: it is in brutal isolation. Casaubon pitched his voice under the racket of a hundred and fifty *bona fide* tourists, driven out of central London's canyon-streets by the reflecting hammer blows of heat. Difficult to pick individual voices out of the ambient noise background. When faced with the subtlest surveillance techniques available, old-fashioned physical isolation often works.

'No one will touch *you*.' Valentine sounded cynical. 'You're the leader in your field. They'll cut you a lot of slack before they pull the plug. They think there isn't anyone else who can do what you can do.'

'The same was said of you.'

Sweat stuck his shirt to his back between his shoulder blades, and clung warm and damp where it was belted under his trouser waistband. Sweat left Valentine's face shiny, where she turned it up to the sun. The red flush of a burn already marked her cheekbones and the tops of her shoulders.

'I'm taking a chance, little one,' he said. 'I think that when you did what you did—'

'Which was what, exactly?' she bristled.

'You ran away from California and stuck your head in the sand, and decided to let Mummy protect you while you piddled away your life on PC games . . .'

'I don't have to hear this!'

'You can hide here under your mother's security blanket for as long as you like, but you're not living! Damn it, woman, you have responsibilities!'

Buildings seemed to jut up directly from the flat water. Sun-coloured brick warehouses, office buildings with the interior walls scraped out, and goldenrod and birch saplings growing from the crevices. The river here smelled of dust. The noise of the riverboat engine echoed back from the walls of Docklands.

'As I say,' Casaubon continued, 'when you ran away, I don't think it was because of the little differences we were having.'

'About whether you'd actually married me or some bimbo, you mean?'

'She isn't a bimbo, she's a perfectly respectable doctor of medicine. You shouldn't let your natural jealousy warp your judgement. But I digress . . . I think, little one, that the reason you left California wasn't the "project failure" you told the Department of Defense had occurred. I think you *solved* the particular problem you were working on. I think you solved the algorithm. And then you ran.'

Nothing, then, for three quarters of an hour; nothing but trying to soak in every whisper of coolness from the river water. They chugged further downstream, in a wider river, in sight of the Thames barrier. He saw her shading her eyes against light off the water too bright to look at.

She said at last, 'Why travel so many thousand miles . . . ?'

'Because the same thing has happened to me. I made a breakthrough in the area *I* was working in. And, like you, I destroyed all records except my personal ones, evaded security, left the US, and . . . vanished.'

The tourist commentary crackled unheard over speakers. The boat reversed its course. Women in cotton dresses smelling of sour perspiration changed their children's nappies. The White Tower floated by on the bank, lost in leafy tops of plane trees.

Baltazar Casaubon gave a smile of surpassing sweetness.

'Besides, little one, I assumed that you would still have all your contacts at the Yates Hospital research department.'

They came back almost as far as the pleasure boat dock before she nodded an ambiguous *yes*.

Miles Godric woke, still huddled waiting into the doorway of the Neal Street flats. There were a few pennies in his lap, and one of his lighter camcorders was missing. He swallowed the foul taste in his mouth and scrumpled his sun-hot hair. The skin on his nose was crisp.

'You took your time.' He focused on his watch. 'Jesus, it's three o'clock in the afternoon!'

Their two shadows cooled and covered him. Miles saw that the fat man now wore a scarlet shirt, and a pair of scarlet cotton shorts, with which his copper hair seemed expressly designed to clash.

Val Branwen unlocked the street door. 'You'd better come up.'

Baltazar Casaubon cupped a huge and protective hand around the woman's shoulders. While not appearing to be appreciated, he was not immediately rebuffed.

Miles Godric stood and followed. His belt camera panned angles, searching the sunlit stairs as he climbed up after them to the fourth-floor flat. Liquid soaked the centre back of his T-shirt. The air seemed liquid also, like breathing mud or fur. He leaned against a landing window, breathing hard, sweating harder. For a moment he remained, head down, resting his forearms on the sill, until the pain of the sun-hot wood made him move. He lifted his head.

No smell of exhaust. No noise of vehicles.

From a mile south the sweet sourness of Thames water drifts to him; that and the dung-and-cooking-oil smell of the streets. The heat hollowed his lungs. Visions of the dirty green river and the cooler air over it haunted his flesh with tangible desire.

One summer when we all lived on Neal Street . . .

Possible opening words for the video commentary spooling through his head. Variant styles. Sweat stung his eyes as he blinked at the pale sky, the world held in a translucent bubble of heat: 90°F and rising.

Hard rock music pounded through the third-floor flat's door. It cut off abruptly when the door to Val's flat closed behind him. The woman balanced on the balls of her feet; a lithe stance ready to take off in any direction. Heat slicked the red hair damply to her temples and neck. Sweat darkened the white T-shirt between her breasts.

'Smile for the cameras.' A demure sarcasm sounded in her voice. 'Miles, I've set up a demonstration.'

'But you haven't been back here.'

'I borrowed the Yates Institute's terminals. They're used to seeing me there for story research.'

'Sorry. Not awake. I – that's a private medial research facility?' Belatedly, he gave her the statutory hypermedia warning. 'You're online and on record.'

'Good,' Casaubon approved.

Miles straightened, hands at his belt, touching to check, automatically, the standard levels of light and colour. The online code burred under his fingers, home base responding. Metal and plastic slicked his wet fingers. He walked through into the apartment's double sunlight.

'I'll talk you through some of it,' the woman said.

'Mmmmrgh!' Casaubon protested, wandering back in from the kitchen. He slumped into the swivel chair in front of the wall monitor, a bowl cushioned in the crook of one arm, from which he ate with a tablespoon. He waved the spoon mutely.

Valentine Branwen licked a spatter from her bare arm. 'Oh, you're welcome to it if you prefer to—'

She made a face and interrupted herself, looking over the link-architect's shoulder and inspecting the contents of his bowl, which appeared to be lumpy and consist of various shades of pink. 'What *is* that?'

Baltazar Casaubon removed an emptied spoon from his mouth. 'Loganberry icecream and tuna-fish.'

'Oh.' The woman paused. 'Fine.' She added thoughtfully, 'I see.'

The fat man put another loaded spoonful into his mouth and said indistinctly something that might have been, 'With Tabasco sauce.'

Val glared at him. 'It's *your* damn demo. *You* do this.'

'Oh, very well . . . I, ah, am a link-architect. I do the architecture of information space; that is, a database cross-indexed to within an inch of its life.'

'We can assume some background knowledge among *Hypershift!*'s viewers,' Miles said more acidly than he intended. 'Tell me what's new.'

The link-architect, Casaubon, put his bowl down on the floor and padded amiably over to stand beside Miles Godric, resting his bolster-arm across Miles's shoulders. 'You understand, it's the freedom from linear text. When it's possible to access texts at any point instantaneously, we have what is sometimes called information-flight. *All* information co-exists, simultaneously . . . the creation of indexes, cross-indexes, and maps to where one is in the information-space become crucial, hence,' he inclined his head, 'myself. Minds become disorientated when information comes in no linear progression. That's why one needs link-architecture – the creation of ordered multiple links between pieces of information.'

The fat man paused.

'Is that good, do you think? I can do it again, if you like. Do you think,' he peered at Miles's belt, 'that you caught my good profile?'

'The channel will do their own voice-over in any case.' Miles took a deep breath. 'That way it won't sound stilted.'

He needed both hands, then. Val Branwen threw him a headset and gloves, and he stood, dangling the goggles in his hands for a minute and looking at her quizzically. A red tendril of hair was plastered to her forehead by sweat. In her sallow face, her eyes gleamed reddish-gold.

'Put them *on*,' Val said, overly patient. He couldn't help but grin. He cabled the set into the most powerful of his camcorders. As he pulled the goggles over his eyes, he saw her have the grace to give him her own most self-mocking smile.

VR space.

A pale light glows in the depths, grey and glittery, with a hint of wings. The airless room tightened about his throat. He swallowed. The gloves are hot on his hands.

'How does it operate?'

'No different from any other. Hold on, let me just . . . oh fuck it – wait a minute . . .'

A faint tremor of his flesh argued a movement cancelled before it began: the hooking of his thumbs under his belt. The solid web-belt, with its comforting heaviness, from which direct-line cameras and sound detectors hang like weapons. His boots are hot on his bare feet, but their heels sustain him. His uniform a carapace to bear up and shape what lies within.

A breath of hot wind touched his cheek. From the window? He tensed.

Around him the pale light opens. A gothic roof arched up into vaults of darkness. He squinted at the stained-glass windows, eyesight adjusting, moved forward and cracked his knee against clear air.

'Sweetheart, you're too old to walk around when you're in VR . . .'

Valentine Branwen's voice comes from frighteningly close at hand. The other side of a high definition image in which the walls are fifty feet away and the wide tombstone-studded floor between Miles and them empty.

He grinned approvingly, moving his hands. Jerkily, the nave of Westminster Abbey shifts around him. The pixel images are blocky, geometric, cartoon colours. The marble busts that clustered in niches along the walls began to speak. He pointed a gloved finger.

'. . . *hypertext and the problems of information flood* . . .'

'. . . *late nineteenth-century Romantic poetry* . . .'

'. . . *steam engine, and the homogenisation of Time* . . .'

'. . . *food additives addressed* . . .'

'. . . *battle of Plassey and consequent colonial expansion* . . .'

Miles turned his head, knowing the field and focus of his hardware independent of his movements. The busts of appropriate statesmen, poets and soldiers, scientists and academics mouthed their particular subjects, white marble lips moving simultaneously in animation.

Light slanted down from the gothic windows, casting rainbow shadows on the flagstones. Each tombstone set flat into the floor had a named subject. Miles pointed his gloved finger at the one nearest to him.

The cathedral shifted, jolting as if a hand-held camera swung round and pointed downwards. The tombstone rose up, with a gritty squeak, and the high-definition viewpoint jolted down the steps into a crypt beneath, where each coffin was labelled with subsections of that subject. He grabbed at air, his balance gone, and bashed his knuckles against something in the invisible apartment.

A rumbling voice murmured, 'Let me follow up a few flightpaths for you.'

Inner ear fooled by the eye, he feels his muscles tense and relax. The crypt floor drops away. The world folded up and poured itself into one of the labelled coffins, that unfolded out into structured shelves, ladders, webs . . .

He flew.

Fast as snowflakes in a blizzard, word- and image-menus flashed up before his eyes. A storm of pictures, sorted so rapidly that he could not comprehend. Information flight through video tracks, sound recordings, statistical charts, novels, and dense texts.

'As far as I can see,' Miles spoke blindly, 'this is standard Art-of-Memory indexing: you find your way around Virtual Reality by associating icons.'

'It's a little more sophisticated than the standard version, but the principle's the same.'

'This isn't the breakthrough you indicated.'

Val's voice said, 'This? Oh, this was just Baltazar proving to me that what he's got, works. The breakthrough isn't anything to do with Art-of-Memory indexing. Look, I'll run my demo.'

He slips off one glove for a minute and checks his belt equipment. It is downloading this quite happily. Glove on.

'Running *School of Night*,' Val's voice says, and the audio hiss runs over her voice, and becomes a tacky lutes-and-sackbut introductory track. Val never did think much of music, he remembers that.

The glittering greyness becomes a room with white walls and a low, beamed ceiling. The boards are bare. Men in stockinged feet move about the floor. They are men in ruffs, doublets and knee breeches, practising swordplay. Three, five, ten figures at least, in a dazzling display of multiple virtuals.

Miles recognised Val's preoccupations. He thinks he knows, has seen in one of her books, the woodcut she has chosen to animate here. It gives him an odd stab of familiarity, and then a moment of insecurity: he is, after all, blind with goggles and deaf with audio playback, in a room with his ex-lover and her husband whom he cannot see.

The pixel quality has little of the geometric blockiness of most commercial VR. Only a faceted quality remains: the walls, the swords, the faces of the duellists glitter as if covered with fish scales. Miles pushes his hand forward. The specifically engineered tolerances of the pressure glove give him a feel, albeit muffled, for the hilt of the sword on the bench beside him.

Red letters run across the top of his vision, exactly where (he notes wryly) a military HUD would run. ALL THE WORLDS A STAGE™. *A ShakespeareWorld Franchise Production*. It blips out before company and copyright details appear: obviously not pasted in yet.

'You must never,' a main character says, walking into his field of vision from the left, 'grip your man's weapon unless you have upon your left hand the *guanta da presa*, which is to say, a gauntlet with fine mail rings sewn upon the palm of it. Then you may catch at his sword-hand wrist when you will, and pull it across your body to twist and break the small bones of the elbow.'

'That,' says another main character, who seats himself on the bench at Miles' right, 'is Master George Silver, who is our chiefest exponent of the Art of Defence. And yet, sir, there are other arts, for those who would investigate them.'

The sound quality is good, although to his ear it is perfectly obviously Val's voice run through a synthesiser.

'You may parry to strike down his sword arm,' says the grey-haired, stocky man in Elizabethan dress, swinging a sword with a simple cruciform hilt as if it weighs nothing, demonstrating upon the empty air. 'And when you have struck his arm down, strike your hilt up full into his face, and send the bones of his nostrils up into the brain and so slay him. Or kick up his heels with your left foot, and throw him a great fall. Good day to you, Master Marlowe.'

Miles turns his head and the viewpoint world adjusts itself with no lag at all. Now this one *is* an animate portrait: the painting of a red-haired twenty-four-year-old in a flashy doublet, arms folded, eyebrows black, cheeks red as a young boy's. The poet and playwright Christopher Marlowe.

Experimentally, he quotes, ' "All who love not boys and tobacco are fools".'

'Sir, I could have heard you quote other of my words with more satisfaction, but few with more pleasure.' The 'portrait' Marlowe is different full-length, stockinged feet stretched lazily out, a long-stemmed pipe in one hand, the implicit smile become a grin. 'Now, sir, to business. Are you initiate in the Art you see here, or would you become initiate in others? The play of swords is sweet, the play of minds sweeter; sweetest of all, sweet magick, tis thou has ravished me.'

It is commercially obvious which the cue words are. Miles Godric suggests, 'An initiate in magic?'

'A true science magick is, master; full of lines, characters,' a blip here, which Miles guesses to be an ill-remembered quotation, and the audio track picks up again, synchronised with the red lips, 'and many do practise it here in Gloriana's kingdom. Abjuring the illusions of the common day, we enrol ourselves a School of Night, wherein we may seek all knowledge, forbidden or no.'

Voice track cuts out. The airless grey abruptly returns. In mid-air a crack opened into emptiness. Into unbearable brightness – the sunlight of Neal Street. In peripheral vision he saw more. Her hands lifted the goggles. The dark glowing air was patched with unreality.

Miles Godric stripped off the gloves, his skin sticky with the summer heat. He blinked at Val with the feeling, familiar from commercial VR games, of having been gone a long time somewhere indefinable.

'*Some* of your enthusiasms wore off on me,' Val Branwen commented. 'I'm calling my expert system "Marlowe" . . . It's a follow-up to the big game I did last year; I had an expert system, "Virgil", games-mastering INFERNOWORLD™.'

Baltazar Casaubon muttered, 'Oh *dear*.'

'Rumour on the MultiNet has it that—' The feeling of having been gone a long time, flying through information space, stayed with him. '—that what you're talking about is DNI. True?' he persisted.

The woman's gaze immediately went to Baltazar Casaubon. The big man sat monitoring the Virtual Reality programme on the wall monitor.

'We OK?'

'Of course.'

An almost imperceptible excitement tensed the line of her shoulders. Miles caught it on camera. The hairs on the back of his neck hackled. Framing a question, he opened his mouth to speak and was interrupted.

'How long do you think it took me to key in and cross index that particular association-tree?' Valentine Branwen asked. 'The physical programming of the data, and putting it on to a database?'

The sun blazed in that quiet room in Neal Street. No traffic noise or fumes, no music; only the quiet.

Miles, statistics at his tongue-tip, guessed. 'Images, sounds, animation . . . I'd say something on the order of six to eight months.'

'I'll tell you,' Valentine Branwen said. 'Four hours. But, true, that doesn't include time spent setting up the CAT-scan and magnetic resonance equipment.'

A chill touched him, and the trigger of adrenaline-rush, and hope. He did not say *that isn't possible*. With some deliberation he touched the stud at his belt that would give him direct voice-comment over the video. He panned in on Val.

'Let me just make that clear. You're saying that you constructed that VR sequence within a space of *hours*? Today?'

'Yes . . . Let me quote something to you. The president of the Royal Information Society, on June fifth of last year.' She opened a video file on the wall monitor. A dark man behind a rostrum.

'The task we face in translating the collected knowledge of humankind on to computer databases is as great a task as the construction of paved roads, where once there were only footpaths. When we have done this, the speed at which we can use information moves from walking-pace to high-speed racing-car mode. But the sheer time taken in constructing programs, and the architecture of indexes that will link them, and most of all the sheer physical effort of scanning in the data, means that decades will pass before we have any true realisation of what information-flood means, and what it will do to our society. It is unfortunate, but there is no way around the physical facts.'

Miles nodded. 'Yes. The President said that at Rouen. I was there. And you're saying that there *is* a shortcut? That you can load data in hours that, even with teams on full time, it would take months to get online?'

With the sting of adrenaline-rush comes a kind of switching on. He caught without effort the best camera angle: the small, red-haired woman with the window's light blazing back from her white jeans; and at her back the immense form of Baltazar Casaubon hunched over gimcrack monitors.

'Oh, the hardware isn't that difficult. Medical laser scans, magnetic resonance – the technology has existed for years. But not the ability to process the result. Not the link-architecture to deal with the sheer volume and complexity of direct-brain data.' He saw her look, a little bemused and wondering, at the fat man.

'A prototype, working, safe method of direct neural input of information from a human mind into a computer.' He stated it flatly. 'Direct neural input. DNI. Would you confirm that, Mr Casaubon?'

'Hhrmm. Yes. Obviously.'

'You're saying this at the moment without any proof. Tell me,' Miles said. 'What do you need the hypermedia news for?'

'I would have thought that was obvious. We need to get this out into the public domain. We want commercial offers.'

'Out?'

'It is, at the moment,' Baltazar Casaubon said gently, 'technically – legally – the property of the US military.'

Miles Godric stared.

'But you won't, immediately, mention that.' Valentine Branwen shook the hair back from her face and stretched, arching her back. One fisted hand reached up towards the ceiling. Joints and tendons popped. She gave a long, rested sigh. 'We need a massive campaign for multinationals to come in and buy the system.'

Rather blankly, his mind racing, Miles asked. 'And then?'

'Then?' Her voice changed. He saw her stroke the grained wood of the windowsill, touch being the ultimate test of reality; and put her fingers to her mouth, still with the tactile memory of wood. 'And then, one supposes, everything is different.'

'You think people will just come and—' He shook his head. 'You think I'll *tell* people they should come to this project and get their brains minced?'

Baltazar Casaubon leaned back from the bank of monitors. He scratched through his greasy copper hair, beaming. He ignored the provocation, and waved an expansive hand.

'Of course they will. *You* will. Especially after all the hypermedia news coverage, when you volunteer to be the first man read by DNI in a public demonstration for all the scientific, medical, and IT establishments.'

'When I *what?*'

The fat man abruptly stood up from the monitors, rising to his full height. 'Good *God*, what's this country coming to? The government in power when I left would never have tolerated this! I bring this back to PanEurope and some piddling little cameraman whines that it isn't *safe?* Where's your guts, man? True, the National Security Association and Federal Bureau of Investigation have us under surveillance – but I assure you, they won't be able to interfere if the media acts quickly enough.'

Miles raised his eyebrows, recognising a wrong intonation in the genuine anger. There is more to be uncovered here. This is only the surface.

Casaubon rumbled, 'Your place – your *business* – is to help us get this story out. We're not obliged to give explanations of every little qualm we may have.'

The woman sat down in Casaubon's vacated chair, one bare foot up on the desk. She smoothed the white denim over her knee and glanced up from beneath copper-red lashes, smiling slightly. 'Miles, it's a prototype. These are adult games we're playing. Weigh it up – is this something you want?'

The fat man muttered: '. . . plenty of *other* . . .'

Miles looked at his hands. The fingers just perceptibly shook. He is twenty-nine this year. In one holistic flash he sees it: all the city, all doors opening, the respect and resentment that success forces.

Notoriety. Status.

Reward.

CHAPTER 5
Johanna

The PanEuropean Minister of Defence stared at the walls of the unisex toilets in the Federal PanEuropean Defence building. *Johanna Branwen eats babies!* someone had scrawled. Under it, neatly, someone else had printed *yes but at least she peels them first.* Johanna Branwen smiled appreciatively. When the plumbing in one's office breaks down, one discovers such treats.

She left the cubicle and paused in front of the full-length executive mirror. The habit of fifty years is not advisedly broken: she checked her image for how it could be read.

The yellow interior illumination shone kindly on her face. It softened the lines of her plump chin. Businesslike, she flicked steel-and-silver curls out from under her tracksuit collar; repaired her scarlet lipstick; dabbed on a little more of her distinctive musky perfume. A wide, thin mouth, with only a hint of fullness in the lower lip. Her eyes are long and tilted, her lashes fading.

'Mmm . . . ?'

She pushes her fists back and plants them on her hips, the black fur-collared jacket swinging open. Under it she wears a scarlet track suit, Nike trainers, large amounts of subtle gold jewelry. It does no harm to be seen to be losing the battle against plump flesh, not at fifty-three. It relaxes people. A soft body indicates a soft mind.

She checks her wrist. Rolex watch-and-wrist-VDU. She clip-locks the jacket, remains staring down at her fingers. They show her age: brown-spotted, with raised veins and the blue tinge of poor circulation. She wears warm, clumsy, brown wool fingerless gloves – but not when observed. Now she strips them off, takes one last mirror-check.

'You'll do, girl. You'll do.'

The security guard fell in by her side as she left the washroom. She climbed the flight of stairs back up to her office. The plate glass bullet-proof windows glittered. Siesta weather in London. Not ten in the morning and the sun made the low-rise cityscape outside shimmer. Finials of white Baroque stone pierced a deep blue sky above the complex's major courtyard. Polarised ogee windows burned back light. She noted the guard sweat, despite the air-conditioning. She rubbed her own hands together to warm them.

'Files,' she said, passing through the outer office. Her Principal Private Secretary Morgan Froissart hastened to stand, smartly, abandoning a clutch of microdiscs. 'See that I'm not disturbed.'

'Minister.' The second secretary began diverting calls.

'Put that stuff back on screen, Morgan.'

Morgan Froissart followed her into her inner office. 'Certainly, Minister.'

She sprawled into her padded leather chair and sank her chin down into the fur of her jacket collar. Customarily, the air-conditioning is turned off in her office. She began to feel warmed. She watched the man sweat across his face and under his arms, and smiled. Life is full of small satisfactions, if one knows where to look.

'And these are?'

'The initial reports from the diplomatic bag from Washington, dated two years ago. I've isolated mentions of Professor Branwen, Minister.'

She gave a lizard-smile. 'Play it, Morgan. Play it.'

She leaned forward, resting her lips against her thumbs. Her fingers still blue-white with circulatory disease.

'These premises are secure.' Morgan Froissart gave the obligatory reminder. He voice-keyed the first report.

Johanna Branwen fingered the fur at her collar. Small body-language movements that are less a giveaway than a deliberate broadcasting of uneasiness; a warning, as it were, that someone might suffer the side-blast of this one.

The wall-VDU bloomed into colour. An image of a small, white-walled interrogation room. She would have recognised the style even without the recorded head-up display figures. The Confederate American States.

'The security complex at Dallas, ma'am.'

'Yes.'

' "*I know nothing about a fire supposed to have destroyed data. I know nothing about any fire supposed to have destroyed records. You have all my computer time logged. You know how much time I've spent in the department, you know exactly what I've been doing. What else is there to say?*" '

A thirty-something woman, voice ingenuous to the knowing ear. Sitting on a plain chair with one knee hooked up and her hands clasped around it, the red hair pinned back from her sharp-eared face. This is two years ago: she wears her hair differently now. Valentine Branwen does not physically take after her mother, to any great degree. But there are similarities.

' "*I'm quitting because I have ethical problems now working for the military. I don't expect you to understand that. You can debrief me as much as you like – I'm clean.*" '

'So that was her story, at that time. She was never proved to have undertaken, ah, extra-curricular activities. I imagine, however that she did.'

'Probably, ma'am.'

'She must have known at that point that she would be removed from Confederate government custody. Extradited back here.' Johanna rested her chin on her thumbs. 'Morgan, take a note. The custodial sentences on the escorts who failed to bring her back to Rouen should be increased. Say, four years. No: five. It seems this is more serious than was at first thought.'

'Yes, ma'am.'

'Run *Casaubon*. The interrogation in March of this year.'

The fat man, sweating, in a room in San Jose.

' "*Why try to persuade me to implicate the people at the Department? Ridiculous. I may have misused materials and worktime, but nothing has come of it that need concern you.*" '

'Are they talking about the same thing, Minister?' Morgan ventured.

'One has to assume so, but . . .' Johanna shook her head. 'What do we have from April to June?'

'Various sections of the Defense Department being shut down due to "compromised security", and their staff being pretty roughly investigated.'

Her secretary voice-cued sound and vision. After a moment he decreased the sound of the beatings. Johanna Branwen recovered it to full stereo.

'Their security people are right, of course. Something like this can rarely be put down to the invention of any one person, even if he is,' Johanna Branwen said distastefully, 'a "computer wizard". Morgan, make sure that we keep unofficial access to Confederate records. There will be no overt cooperation with us, I think.'

'No, ma'am.'

The PanEuropean Minister of Defence stood and moved to her window. The undulating London cityscape rolled away from her, low-rise windows flashing back the sun. She shivered and pulled the furred jacket closer around her neck.

'Why are they stupid enough to seek *public* exposure? My damn daughter,' she said. Her Principal Private Secretary, hearing that, heard for the first time the speech-patterns of Valentine Branwen from her mother's mouth.

'We know where her husband is now, but legally, Minister, we can't do anything about it. Nothing criminal has yet been proved against him here or in America.'

'What I want you to do,' Johanna Branwen stated clearly, 'is to lay false information in her records. Criminal acts, mental instability, whatever seems appropriate. Both of them; the man too.'

'Minister. Ah . . . That kind of disinformation can be very difficult to eradicate afterwards, Minister. And the security services themselves are much better placed to excuse such an action, if it ever became known it had taken place.'

Johanna Branwen tucked her cold hands up into her armpits. She did not bother to look at Morgan, knowing how the light from the unpolarised windows made her a black silhouette against the sun's glare.

'I want it done under my control, and I want it done *now*. I see only one hope for this situation. My daughter and her colleague must be completely discredited, to the point where no one – least of all the commercial corporations and the scientific community – will believe a word they say.'

CHAPTER 6
Criminal Proceedings

A horn blared ceaselessly, jammed on. Barking dogs answered it. Rue Ingram skirted the gates of the British Museum – washing flapped on lines strung between the NeoClassical pillars, and a gang of eight-year-olds played football with tin cans in the court-yard – and ducked into the tiny noon shade of a plane tree.

'So that's your tame video journalist boyfriend,' Frankie Hollister said.

Rue stretched, heat-sticky. The bark of the tree rubbed dust against her bare shoulder. 'He's not my boyfriend!'

'He shows you advance videos of the news.'

'He came round to the refectory because he heard her say what college I was at. He's a journalist. He just wants me as a source.'

'Yeah!'

Seeing Hollister's grin, Rue abandoned what she had been going to say. The car horn rasped. They walked on under the summer trees.

'So all this was when?'

'Monday.' Rue added, 'That *was* her on *Hypershift!* news this morning.'

'Give you that one,' Frankie Hollister drawled. She jerked her head, flipping the short gold-brown hair out of her face. Her hands, fisted, dug deep in baggy cotton dungarees pockets. 'She *undressed* in front of you?'

Rue Ingram nodded.

'Gross.' Frankie shuddered theatrically. The black cotton strap of her overalls slipped down her bare, dark shoulder. 'She's *got* to be over thirty. Wrinkles and bags. Urrgh.'

The smell of sun-washed flesh stayed in Rue's memory, her own or the woman's, she was not sure which; together with the slow beat of *Said She Was A Dancer* and the glitter of light from the whole-wall monitor.

'Yeah, it was pretty gross. I wasn't thinking about that. What it is, she was all over bruises. From real swordfighting.'

'C'mon, don't kid me. He beats her, right. They do that.'

'Nah. And I don't think she thought anything about undressing.' Rue stopped. Her long, slender black brows came down into a scowl. 'I think she was just . . . unselfconscious.'

Frankie Hollister snorted. She swaggered ahead down Great Russell Street, fists still in her pockets, not waiting for Rue's half-run that brought her up level. They walked across to Tottenham Court Road.

'Maybe *we* could go on one of these battles,' Frankie said.

'Oh, *swords*. You and swords. *Again*. The swords aren't the *point*. The bruises . . .'

Heat blasted back from the walls of buildings and the windows of shops, stung up from the metal carapaces of abandoned cars that paved the road four lanes wide.

'Does she know you're one of us?'

The sun beat down on Rue Ingram, on the back of her neck; and she swallowed nausea. She slitted her eyes against the sun's light reflecting from walls and pavements. 'She knows. I told her.'

Frankie, small and bouncy, strode ahead as if heatwaves couldn't touch her. 'Guess I ought to ask her some questions, then. Make sure we got nothing to worry about.'

Summer's brilliance forces the gaze down. Down from the deserted windows of Centre Point, diamond-bright against the sky; down from the roofscape against the cloudless blue. Down to the street, the people, the parasols and icecreams.

'Christ, they've even got up this far!' Outraged, Frankie Hollister jerked her head at a refugee Basque woman with three ill-dressed children, sheltering from the heat in a gutted dormobile. A scatter of possessions marked it as an inhabited vehicle. 'We're gonna have to do something about this. And *soon*.'

Four hours later, across London, Miles Godric stands talking to a newscaster colleague, Eugene Turlough, in the garish corridors of an independent research hospital.

'The process is based on a multiple magnetic resonance scan of the brain, modelling a holographic representation of synapse activity. That's experimental, but it isn't new – what's new is the architecture of the master program that interprets the raw data as memory.'

'Yeah . . .' Eugene Turlough wiped his hand across his red face. Sweat soaked his T-shirt, blotting the *Hypershift!* logo. Miles' senior editor (talking across the crowded room to the senior editor of *Newsbytes*) flanked his other side. The hospital gown left Miles paradoxically chilled and too hot under the lights of the cameras.

'So the medical side's a souped-up brainscan.' Turlough, morose, cradled a glass in the palm of his sweaty hand; a half-inch of yellow media party wine slopping. 'So it's . . . Miles, if you volunteered for this, you're mad. See *why* you're doing it. You're going to be able to ask your own price for freelance work after this. But that's assuming you don't get your brains fucked here.'

'At least I'll make main headline spot – either way.' Godric spoke with a new confidence that he saw raise hackles up Eugene Turlough's spine.

A nurse in pale blue that could have been an informal, if severe, day dress touched Miles's arm. He nodded, smiling, and walked across to the trolley and lay down. The noise of voice-over commentaries sparked like wildfire through the room. He heard Val Branwen's urbane irony, being interviewed. The clipped webbing about his waist was comforting: sound and vision linked to base, his words to be recorded in realtime.

In the cold whiteness of the theatre anteroom, he lay absolutely still. Medical staff moved smoothly from machine to machine. The competence of professional practice seemed unostentatiously but clearly written in their movements. A memory came into his mind of Val sighting down the length of some damn antique sword: the movement of her wrist framing that same competence.

'Miles.'

Her voice spoke so appositely that it was a moment before he turned his head. 'Come to see if I've changed my mind?'

'Have you?'

'With the entire London hypermedia corps out there?' Miles Godric looked at her from under long fair lashes. 'You know me better than that. I guess you know me better. Baltazar Casaubon didn't assume I'd do this without talking to you first.'

'You think? Well, maybe you're right.' Offhand, as if what she says is routine; her thoughts quite different.

'I hear there have been representations from the American embassy this morning. Will your mother make any comment on this?'

The woman mirrored his own professional expression. 'Keep trying. My answer to that is still *no comment*. I just wanted a word with you before the scan.'

Irritated at his momentary heartfelt gladness in having her to talk to, Miles Godric said, 'Which particular word would that be?'

She choked on laughter. 'I knew hanging around Baltazar Casaubon wasn't doing you any good! Ah well. The word, I suppose, is flexibility. Don't be surprised. When the neurons start firing, you'll get side-effects that aren't easily attributable to memory-readout. You may feel some sense of interaction with the structuring program – the linking-architecture – but Baltazar assures me it's because this is a prototype, there's still some odd feedback. I've felt it myself. It's a bug we'll iron out.'

She leaned up as one of the nurses moved across and swabbed his arm, injecting a syringe with almost-painless smoothness.

'Remember, if you've done any meditation or relaxation, practise it as you go.' Val touched his arm. 'The beta-blockers ought to do it. Memory's a fragile thing, and what controls learning and reading is chiefly levels of tension. We won't get much out of you if you're in a chemical state of anxiety. But Casaubon told me you test out low-aptitude for fear.'

'You mean—' His voice slurred. He felt for the beltcorder, adjusting sound levels by touch. 'You mean this is a highly public occasion, so don't fuck up my chances by being terrified?'

She chuckled. 'That's what I mean. What did you choose for a subject-reading?'

'*Tamburlaine*.' He saw her dark red brows indent. 'Baltazar knows. Well, you put Marlowe into my mind. I don't know if I ever told you, back when I did my media degree, it had the videos of Olivier's *Tamburlaine* and *Doctor Faustus* on it. Not a thing one admits to in journalism.'

He played for a smile: got it. She touched his cheek with the pad of her index finger.

'So we'll get lit. crit. out of you, will we? Now that I do have to see! OK, I don't think there's anything else. Go for it, guys.'

His attention shifted, charming the medical staff; a word and a smile distributed here and there, until the hard base of the scanner was under his spine, his shaven skull under a cap, and firm in the padded clamps. A faint *whirrr* was the only sound of the scanner sliding into position.

He opened his mouth to start a commentary and gave a small, dry cough, the ridges of his mouth desert-dry with tension. He began again. 'The process of the scan has been fully explained to me, as has the theory of memory data reading. Baltazar Casaubon is as yet not ready to disclose full details to the public, although specialists in his field are studying his evidence – are subjecting his evidence to intensive study—'

He stopped. *Live* transmission, not a tape for editing. Well, too late now. And to have some (not unprofessional) evidence of tension here . . . ? May be no bad idea.

'My first question, naturally, is: does DNI work? And my second? That's another question entirely . . . If direct neural input is possible, I want to know – is what it reads the objective truth, or a subjective lie?'

A silence spiked behind his eyes.

He began quite consciously to let go of fear.

'Let's see what we can get.' Valentine Branwen cued the Sony wall monitor to montage, and it split between the theatre where Godric's body lay motionless, the skull encased in a vast wheel of machine; the medical staff calibrating read-outs; and Baltazar Casaubon, sweating between keyboard and icons. The audio track piped through his continual mutterings.

Fortunately they were, Valentine reflected, too mumbled to be decoded, even if English had been the first language of most of those present in the Yates Institute teaching room.

Keiko Musashi sipped coffee. 'Thank you for a most interesting demonstration.' The Japanese representative for Sony-Nissan kept her eyes fixed on the monitor. After a moment she added, 'There is no representation of the downloaded data?'

Valentine split the screen again to display rapid lines of machine code. 'Regrettably, this will be of little value until structured in analogue form.'

'Ah.'

'*Hontō ni sumi-masen.*' Valentine bowed her head briefly.

The screen divided again to give a blurred and jerky image. She heard a mutter behind her. The image was perfectly recognisable as a shot of the main reception area of the Yates Institute, but a *cinéma vérité* shot: point of view Miles Godric.

'Such an image might be reconstructed from the security cameras,' Pyotr Andreyev said, speaking for the Pacific Rim consortiums.

'We have some pre-arranged data to download, to avoid any possibility of fraud.'

The man from Kazakhstan sank back into his chair. Curiously, in this room lit only by neon tubes, the walls surrounded by channelled white marble slabs, and smelling of disinfectant, he did not seem out of place. Valentine had downloaded his data and found no medical training.

'There are many implications to this new technology,' Keiko Musashi said, 'if it can be brought past the prototype stage. For entertainment, for teaching skills, for financial dealings, for legal affairs. It is quite breath-taking.'

Valentine Branwen seated herself on the edge of the table and poured herself coffee.

'I may,' she said, 'have had more to do with the entertainment division of all your corporations during the past two years. Prior to that, as we all know, I was one of those unworldly researchers desiring only knowledge, working for the Confederate government.'

A small, ironic laugh acknowledged what she said. She nodded at Pyotr Andreyev.

'Being unwordly, you comprehend, I may not understand commercial matters. However, I do have some understanding of patent law, company law, and the necessity of dealing adequately with it, which is why all Mr Casaubon's agreements will be finalised through Fisher, Pitman and Trott, here in the City. And you will appreciate, also, that other multinationals apart from the Pacific Rim will be approached.'

'Of course,' Keiko said.

'Baltazar Casaubon will sell on what seems the best promise of development,' Valentine said, 'and on no account will he sell this process to a company which is buying it to suppress it. That's his only condition. Let's begin the discussion.'

'*Kso!*' On screen, the fat man swore aloud, and began to re-program the secondary sequence from the beginning.

The late evening sun shone in through the hospital's high Victorian windows, slanting light and lessening heat on to the hypermedia crews, ubiquitous in black jeans, tracksuits, sweat-shirts; no face much over thirty. Valentine Branwen let her gaze slide past them to the editors in summer suits and dresses. Older. She shrugged her shoulders back, a movement that loosened muscles and tension without being obtrusive.

'You,' Baltazar Casaubon said, 'would rather be in the field.'

With his words came a sensory memory so strong as to be almost hallucination: the smell of grass, sun on dried dung, mud and wool and linen; black-powder gunshot. Her eyes automatically narrowed. She shrugged, this time for effect.

'Why do you think I do re-enactment battles? They have solvable problems. Easily solvable.'

'But the implications of them are no less . . .' The link-architect paused for a word. '. . . questionable.'

She put her fingers on the creased arm of his white suit, thoughtful, aware of an implicit distance between them that only might be to do with the occasion; a distance forgotten in the last few days' frantic work, but now remembered.

A camcorder whirred online. Eugene Turlough's over-heavy stomach drooped over the waistband of his black tracksuit bottoms. He spoke with alcohol-fuelled clarity. 'Mr Casaubon, can you tell us why this is such a significant invention?'

The fat man beamed. 'Significant? *Earth*-shattering! I have, here, successfully married together medical technology with a hardware system capable of recording, accurately, the hard-memory levels of the human brain. And, crucially, with a software system of link-architecture *capable* of dealing with that amount and complexity of information.'

'So you can turn electronic slush into eidetic memory record.' Turlough's eyes had a slight glaze, counting footage-seconds. 'Why is that "earth-shattering"?'

Valentine Branwen raised her head. The window light dazzled her vision and struck a brilliant red from her hair, an entirely selfconscious gift for the camcorders – saint in a shaft of heavenly light, Joan at the stake, Prometheus in the self-bought fire.

'What we do,' she said, 'is keep inventing the wheel. There was a time – I think it was somewhere around the year 1250, some of you may remember it—'

A chuckle went round the crowded room. Her eyes crinkled as she acknowledged that.

'A time when you could learn everything there was to know about one given subject. And perhaps know a little about most others. That time was over by the end of the Renaissance. The Scientific and the Industrial Revolutions brought us more knowledge in any one field of study than any one person could assimilate. And more fields of knowledge than the Middle Ages could imagine existing. In our own century . . . any specialist field has divided and sub-divided, there's no way I can know my field, and know about – say – link-architecture in detail as well.'

The room was quiet but for the subliminal whirr of camcorders. Urbane irony touched her tone.

'I can't explain this in soundbites. When you put it out on hypermedia, you'll flag references for what I've first said, so that anyone who's interested can follow up what I'm saying now. What I will say. And what the Yates Institute has said; what the PanEuropean Ministry of Defence claims; what the beginnings of hypermedia invention were . . . And that's the way the human mind works. It follows expanding webs of knowledge. And in the cracks between the webs – if you'll pardon a mixed metaphor – is the wheel we keep reinventing, and the wheels we haven't invented yet.'

She rubbed the back of her wrist across her face. Her long-sleeved white cotton shirt hid bruises, trapped heat.

'Somewhere in what the human race *already* knows are the Big Science answers to cancer, crop failure, a technology that will take us out of the solar system, and the answers . . . The answers to questions that we don't yet know enough to ask, because the concepts themselves are still hidden down those cracks. We don't find them, except on rare occasions, because the human mind is too small. Self-programming DNI computers will *not* be too small.'

A man raised his hand. Baltazar Casaubon indicated him with a wave of one broad-palmed hand.

The questioner spoke with a northern accent. 'None of this is new, Mr Casaubon. We've been promised information flood for years now. What's different about this?'

'Time,' Casaubon rumbled. 'Simply time. The limitation was always the speed at which knowledge could be physically got into computers. And then the time that it takes to put in all the cross-links, the roadmap-architecture necessary to read it. Crudely, sir, this system reads the human memory as fast as the human memory works – holistically, almost instantaneously. That means information flood within a few years, rather than fifty or a hundred.'

'Accurate information? Doesn't memory blur facts, forget them?' *Newsbyte's* prime news reporter: Pramila Aziz.

Casaubon's ponderous head inclined. 'A reasonable objection. Knowledge input through the human brain might be more sketchy than that scanned in from print and video, and more prone to error. However, the advantage of this hardware is that it reads at the *eidetic* level of the brain, where everything is photographically recorded.'

Aziz said, 'So this process could read the mind for, say, evidence in a criminal trail?'

'Only under certain very limited circumstances, Ms Aziz. The mind must be relaxed, trusting, unanxious. Or else the result is neurochemically ruined garbage.' Baltazar Casaubon clasped his hands over the head of his ivory walking-stick. 'Of course it can't read minds for interrogation. What a supposition. As if I'd write link-architecture for a program that could. I'm not a fool, you know.' He beamed encouragingly at Valentine Branwen and the assembled journalists. 'Intelligence is not making the same mistake twice. Genius is not making the same mistake *once*.'

A voice from behind the bank of camcorders and lights said, 'Is it true that the US Defence Department is claiming joint ownership of DNI, Mr Casaubon?'

Casaubon smiled. 'This is mine, to do with as I choose – and I choose to sell it to the highest bidder.'

A man stood. Valentine recognised Eugene Turlough again, his eyes fixing on hers.

He said, 'Professor Branwen, is it true that in America you first worked for, and then disclaimed all connection with, the Department of Defense? That two years ago you fled the US? Now you're with a man rumoured to have stolen data on three continents. Ms Branwen, is it true that you have been clinically treated for regular psychotic episodes?'

An irresistible smile spread across her face. Valentine Branwen laughed. She saw the clear, relaxed sound diffuse a little of the room's tension. 'You *have* been listening to my commercial competitors, haven't you?'

Eugene Turlough looked past her. 'Mr Casaubon, may I ask you a question?'

The large man leaned his immense weight on one hip and the walking-stick, and gestured expansively with his other hand. The camcorders duly took in white suit, sweat-stained shirt, his greasy red hair still fastened in a tiny ponytail with a rubber band.

'Is it true,' Eugene Turlough asked, 'that there are six paedophilia charges still outstanding against you in PanEurope for offences against the Revised Child Protection Act?'

CHAPTER 7
'The Wondrous Architecture of the World'

'Don't you dare walk out on me now!'

'You have not,' the large man said, miffed, 'gone out of your way to make me feel welcome. Now you tell me *not* to go—'

'*Casaubon!*' Valentine Branwen glared. The strong urine smell of the Gentlemen's toilets made her blink. Her voice, forced low for secrecy, bounced off the tiled walls.

Baltazar Casaubon reached down and under and unzipped his trousers, facing the urinal. 'You said to me, I distinctly remember, when we came here at the beginning of the week, that you would help me up to a point, and then I was on my own. I'm just on my own a little earlier than I anticipated. It is not,' he said, 'a problem.'

The sound of his running urine echoed. Valentine absently hit the button of the wall hand-drier, in case of microphones, and spoke under its roar.

'You do *know* what kind of a tightrope you're walking here? You're trusting to the fact that the NSA and European Security won't cooperate. For how long? You're trusting Johanna to protect me, and protect you by default. For how long? You're assuming that six multinational corporations won't care that they're buying something you don't actually own—'

'They don't care. If I'm not mistaken, they're in the process of attempting to steal it even as we speak.'

Casaubon shook out the last drops, zipped up his trousers, and moved to the washbasin. Halfway there he stopped, glared downwards, and eventually shook one ponderous leg.

Valentine turned the tap on for him. 'I thought we had ten days maximum. We made it to six. Time out, game over. I'm not going back out there on my own!'

'They won't hurt you, little one.'

'Hurt me! *Hurt* me? They're spreading all the dirt they can think of over me, and I've got a business to run! How long do you think White Crowe Enterprises is going to last once some of the mud starts sticking?'

'I'm sure your other contacts in interactive media will be only too pleased to make you a *cause célèbre*. You can always,' he said pointedly, 'ask your lover Miles.'

'He's not my lover! He's a lousy fuck! There: are you happy?'

Like most taps in hospitals, these had long spatulate handles enabling them to be pushed with an elbow. Baltazar Casaubon pushed off the tap, moved to the hand-drier, and dried his plump fingers through two cycles of warm air.

Footsteps sounded outside in the corridor. A hand tried the locked door, despite the OUT OF ORDER notice she had tacked up. The footsteps moved away. Common garden-variety stupidity.

'Is he a lousy fuck?'

'No, he's quite good, actually. Out of bed, though, he's piss-boring.'

Baltazar Casaubon, somewhat smugly, remarked, 'I'm never boring.'

'*He* was never a bigamist!'

'You do harp on things, little one. I've noticed that. It could be a mistake, all this obsessing. You might become—'

'—boring,' Valentine said in unison with the fat man. 'Yes. Very witty. I've heard it before. *I thought this was important.*'

'You're a businesswoman. I've given you my power of attorney. Johanna will protect you up to a point. I'm sure I can leave the financial and contract side in your capable charge.' Baltazar Casaubon unlocked the door, surveyed the corridor, and looked back at her. 'Or not, as the case may be.'

'Baltazar, don't you dare!'

The door clicked shut behind him.

Silence. Two minutes. Three. Five.

She swung around, paced two steps forward, two steps back, constrained by the small space and slippery tiles. '*Shit!*'

A startled *Newsbyte* editor and a Sony-Nissan aide collided coming in together. The OUT OF ORDER notice was not now in evidence on the front of the door.

Embarrassed, Valentine Branwen walked quickly out of the Gentlemen's toilets.

Through the hospital windows, the last light drained from the sky.

The outer wearing of clothes has its effect on inner confidence. Back in combat pants, T-shirt, and camera belt, Miles Godric regarded the crowded room with only slightly disturbed ease, and broke away from the other journalists, practised at the ending of interviews. His newly shaved scalp itched and he rubbed it, making a wry mouth of wounded vanity. But it is a visible and honourable campaign scar. He moved swiftly across to Eugene Turlough while replaying the previous two hours' hypermedia record. Towards the end of the disc:

'—*regular psychotic episodes?*'

'Oh shit!'

'—*paedophilia . . . offences against the Revised Child Protection Act?*'

'Eugene, you asshole, so what! They're *Hypershift!*'s story!'

The man's jowls were red and wet. 'If it's a scam, we have to have been seen to ask the awkward questions first. Yeah? So don't tell me my job, shitbrain.'

Miles grunted, shaking his head, and turned his back on Turlough. His camcorder focused in on Val's face, now slack with concentration, almost ugly in its absence from exterior stimuli. Slowly brilliance returned.

'I'll take you guys through some of the text version first,' Val Branwen announced, 'that's probably easier. And we seem to have some pretty clear bits. Miles, are you coming over to see what you produced?'

He walked across to where she stood.

'I'm into the Yates mainframe. Take a look at this. I've run the raw data through the particular form of link-architecture invented by my friend here—' The red-headed woman looked up. Miles Godric automatically glanced up as she did. There was no sign of the fat man.

'Where's Casaubon?'

'In the washroom, I suppose. Avoiding any more awkward questions.' Valentine Branwen straightened up from her terminal, hand in the small of her back. She seemed oblivious to the hypermedia journalists crowding the bank of monitors, jacking in their own systems. A kind of careless confidence emanated from her, arousing a – memory?

Something speared his head from eye to cortex. Not a pain, but a memory, a memory of—

He shook his head, and scratched his shaven scalp.

Eugene Turlough pounced. 'Disorientated?'

'To tell you the truth, hangover. Christ, I knew I shouldn't have gone out drinking last night!' He fixed a convivial smile in place, faking it from the eyes and not the mouth, and leaned one arm on the monitor, so that he could see past Val's elbow.

'Up and running,' she announced.

A muted sound went through the journalists, part excitement, part scepticism. Miles's automatic smile widened. The muscles of his face felt stiff.

'Take you through the prepared version of the text . . .' The woman clicked icons. He leaned down to study the section of page presented:

> in sharp contrast to *Doctor Faustus*,[23] whose internal dialectic is concerned not with the acquisition of knowledge,[24] but with the damnation of free will and NeoPlatonic magic,[25] *Tamburlaine*, its eponymous hero, the peasant conqueror of Asia, is a thought-experiment in will, ambition, and achievement (shorn free of Christianity, Renaissance ethics, and all plot save the protagonist's headlong, bloody rush into victory) set free to play in the Elizabethan theatres, and to remain (for reasons about which it may not be valid to conjecture) a money-spinner and byword, quotable to the point of parody for a generation, and surpassed by only one other play.[26] The shepherd-general of Asia

---

[23] *The Plays of Christopher Marlowe*, ed. Roma Gill, Oxford University Press, 1971

[24] *Radical Tragedy*, Jonathan Dollimore, Harvester Press, 1984

[25] *The Occult Philosophy in the Elizabethan Age*, Frances Yates, Routledge & Kegan Paul, 1979

[26] Marlowe, *The Spy at Londinium*, 1610, ed. Jeremy de Cossé Brissac, Cyprian Press, 1910

'I'll get the database to check that against the original.' The woman shifted small, muscled shoulders under her white shirt. He saw how, without appearing to, she kept her attention on the room; taking in the reactions of the editors and journalists. 'OK, there's the text-page, from a standard university database. And here's what we got from you.'

His text scrolled through:

> in sharp contrast to *Doctor Faustus*,[23] whose internal dialectic is concerned not with the acquisition of knowledge,[24] but with the damnation of free will and NeoPlatonic magic,[25] *Tamburlaine*, its eponymous hero, the peasant conqueror of Asia, is a thought—

'Yeah!' Miles hit his fist against the console.

'It could be a set-up,' *Newsbyte*'s Pramila Aziz said ungraciously.

'It could be. But it isn't. At the moment,' Valentine Branwen said, 'DNI recording needs all the help it can get. If you're expecting perfection – not yet. OK, let's take a look at Miles's independent visuals . . .'

Miles Godric stared at the wall VDU.

At first the image seems a substandard graphic. Then it shifts into near-photographic focus. A man in golden Renaissance armour, on a stage backed by sky-cloth; other actors around him in armours of stark white, red, and black, Val keyed in sound:

'Nature . . .'

The actor's voice boomed with theatre-projection, false in any video recording but here reverberate with power:

> *'. . . that fram'd us of four elements*
> *Warring within our breasts for regiment,*
> *Doth teach us all to have aspiring minds.'*

Eugene Turlough, at Miles's shoulder, protested, 'That's not the video. But there aren't any live recordings of . . . it could be virtual. It could be a fix-up, virtual cut-and-paste.'

'That would have been about the time I was at Oxford. He was an old man, but – Jesus Christ. Is my memory *that* good?' Miles said wonderingly. 'It was a pretty naff evening, there was this girl; I wasn't really paying attention . . .'

Val Branwen smiled, nothing faked in it, the flesh around her eyes creasing warmly. 'But this has everything Miles Godric knows about Kit Marlowe. Play texts. Textbooks. Performances. Especially performances.'

'Let me through.' A blonde woman with sharp blue eyes elbowed her way in beside Miles.

The face, vaguely familiar, he identified after a second. 'Louise de Keroac?'

'The year above you,' she said crisply. 'I went to that performance. There aren't any live recordings. But there's something I remember – something he did. Is there more of this? Keep it running.'

On the wall VDU, the actor abruptly swung around and put his back to the audience; his voice nonetheless sounding out clear and yearning:

> *'Our souls, whose faculties can comprehend*
> *The wondrous Architecture of the world,*
> *And measure every wand'ring planet's course,*
> *Still climbing after knowledge infinite,*

And always moving as the restless spheres,
Wills us to wear ourselves and never rest
Until we reach the ripest fruit of all . . .'

The figure raised armoured hands to the great sun at the back of the stage, drowned suddenly in a flood of yellow light:

Why, this is Hell, nor am I out of it!

'Yes.' Louise de Keroac shook her head. Her blue eyes swam with tears; her hand on Miles's shoulder was warm with sweat. 'That's what he did, that last night. That's not from *Tamburlaine*, it's from *Doctor Faustus*. That's how it *was*.'

'Damn it, it works!' Eugene Turlough rested a hand on Miles's other shoulder. 'Miles, first, for *Hypershift!* readers – you went through a whole battery of medical tests before and after, and we'll get the results through soon, but subjectively: have you had any ill-effects from your experience?'

He saw Val spread hands (bruised olive and brown across the knuckles) in a gesture of assurance.

'Nothing to speak of,' he lied.

He hooked his thumbs under his web-belt, weight on both hips. Decisions, always taken in some split second between the webs of chronology. Decisions, and what are their motivations?

'Professor Branwen, I realise this is a prototype.' Miles smiled publicly. 'I've been Mr Casaubon's guinea-pig. You owe me first rights to a hypermedia feature – let me have first access to the complete version of that recording.'

Val nodded. 'Sure, Miles.'

The editor of *Newsbyte* was the first to take him aside.

'As I understand it, Mr Godric, you're not on exclusive contract to *Hypershift!*. Our channel network would be very interested. I'm thinking of a figure in the area of three hundred and fifty thousand pounds initially. Then royalties.'

'I'm thinking of a seven-figure sum,' Miles Godric said.

Darkness.

The landing outside the Neal Street apartment creaked under a cautious, massive weight. A shade slid across shadow: the door closing.

Baltazar Casaubon clasped a briefcase to him as he bent to lock the door. A scrabble of claws, and a rat – pale in the light from Neal Street's one remaining streetlamp – peeked out between the folds of his white suit jacket.

'Sssh,' the link-architect advised.

He padded heavily down to the entrance.

Outside, across the road in Monmouth Street, a bonfire burned in the wreck of a van. Dark figures swarmed around it. The link-architect moved, for his bulk, surprisingly softly; skirting the fire's light. He tucked the case under one arm, carrying his ivory stick lefthanded.

Newly planted surveillance cameras suffered inexplicable break-downs in their programming, blanking out realtime and replaying shots of an empty street.

Towards the end of Earlham Street a noise startled him. He gripped the swordstick's handle and pulled. A slender blade shone in the city darkness. The sounds stopped and did not resume.

The link-architect Baltazar Casaubon padded away down narrow alleys. Above, visible in newly carbon-dioxide-free skies, a full moon burned.

She knew as soon as she put her key in the lock that the flat was empty.

Empty places have a sound to them. Unmistakable. She went in and shut the door behind her, and stood in the room for a time, in the orange radiance of the streetlamp outside the window. Little licks of orange reflected back from dull monitor screens. Red and green LEDs blinked on timers.

I guess that's it, then.

She checked, just the same. No portable. No clothes. Even the rat's cage gone – although not the pungent, pleasant smell of it. Not yet. Give it a day or two.

Sometimes (the right biorhythms, her own excitement, some-thing) his skin has a dry, fuzzy, electric quality to it. Then, she can spend hours roaming his body; not that there isn't enough of it; lying in the sun, their uncurtained window not overlooked, time to grow sweaty and then dry.

She logged on to an old Powerbook, one of the five machines connected into a net within the flat, and ran a check on her own security systems. Tampered with. This one is probably US Military Intelligence. That one is MI6. The MI6 one is almost an old friend: she knows the operator's tricks of thought. These are probably commercial taps. This one here is very good, but it can't crack her public key encryption.

Besides, there is nothing here to find. Her multiple redundant back-ups are thirty jumps away, through telephone exchanges, hidden under false names on university databases. She always has liked universities.

Knowing she won't sleep, she downloads the latest trawl of files from the MultiNet, answers her e-mail, plays with bulletin boards. Tries for her own amusement to crack her way back in to the database at San Jose. At least manages to hide her identity from the tripped security expert systems. Tinkers with some of the ramifications of ALL THE WORLDS A STAGE™. Kit Marlowe, playwright and spy and games master, bringing the player character to the rooms of Elizabeth I's chief minister, Walsingham. Her voice synthesised to that of a dry old man:

' "It is white angel-magic, surely, that which you do seek. Our great magister, Doctor John Dee, sought it for many years in his Enochian congress with the spirits of God. It is the language of the angels of God, in which tongue men may speak to one another only the truth".'

She leans back from the keyboard mike.

And thinks, *I wonder if I did the right thing?*

CHAPTER 8
No Sword No Intention

Two weeks later, in the Pan European Ministry of Defence:
    'Minister, you have parliamentary debates on Tuesday and
Friday. Two meetings of select committees, one this morning
and one this afternoon; reports are in the appropriate multimedia
files for presentation.'

Her Principal Private Secretary continued to read the diary file
aloud.

'You have an official dinner on Wednesday, and you have been
asked to speak; the speech department are delivering that for your
final approval this evening. Your club holds its AGM on Thursday.
You have meetings with delegations on Wednesday and Friday
mornings. There are some other appointments I'm holding off on
confirming until I have your approval.'

Johanna Branwen swivelled her chair round to face the office's
full-length, bullet-and-bomb-proof window. The dawn sunlight
gilded her face. She sat with her right arm hanging down,
monotonously opening and closing a Hawkeye II lock-knife. Practising without looking the single-handed finger-coordination of the
movement to open, and the manipulation of the lock-release to
shut. The blade's edge shone rainbows.

'In the days when I was my own secretary I kept this sharp for
opening letters. There were jokes about its other uses.' She let her
lips curve. 'Useless for e-mail, of course.'

She snicked the blade shut and laid it down flat on the desk,
ignoring Morgan in favour of the other man present. 'What advice
does the department have for me?'

Her latest military adviser, a young man with shaven hair,
observed, 'We can leave the conflict in Germany to the news
media, ma'am. Nothing decisive is anticipated in the next week.
I've advised your speech-writing department to make some

pronouncement on the casualty rate – it's well below the expected ten per cent, which you should capitalise on immediately. It will rise to fourteen per cent as soon as we have to fight for Bonn.'

She watched him. A broad-shouldered boy in his early twenties; boots polished, brown fatigues tailored and pressed. He answers not quite by the numbers, but that possibility is always there.

'I could certainly put that into the speech for the Japanese trade delegation at the Guildhall. Our better morale, superior training. Then revise it to underdogs fighting against the superior firepower of tyranny, if it comes to Bonn.'

'It must come to that, ma'am.'

Pleasantly mild, Johanna Branwen said, 'But I think it may be expedient for there to be peace. A temporary cease fire.'

He frowned. 'Ma'am, with respect, if you don't carry the military victory through, the campaign will have been pointless.'

'Ah, the single-mindedness of the soldier's view . . . I must thank you for your help.' She sat back, in an attitude of dismissal. 'Your commanding officer will be receiving a full report from me. Join-ville, isn't it? It's unfortunate that you're not of the right calibre to become a permanent military adviser to a minister, but I'm *sure* this won't prevent the forces using your no doubt excellent capabilities in some other respect . . .'

She had the minor pleasure of seeing him colour a splotchy red and white. The boy saluted and left. She chuckled to herself, making a note on the e-pad.

'They will send me these idiots,' she said cheerfully. 'Morgan, call up the files, will you.'

By the time Morgan Froissart had done that, the cheerfulness faded. Dawn's slanting light showed up the lines of her face, and there was nothing soft or humorous in that hardness.

'I have the latest update, ma'am.' He slid a microdisc into the console. She swivelled to watch the wall-VDU. Very little of the displayed schematic graphic is now green. Some sections are amber. By far the most of them are red.

'These are our breached security systems,' Morgan said. No drama in his voice. 'As you are aware, Minister, in the past two weeks we've experienced increasingly massive leaks. Multiple users who shouldn't be there.'

'We *must* order a new system.'

'With respect, ma'am, we can't order a new system. This one has been makeshifted and adapted over the years. By now it's unique. We wiped and went to back-up tapes, but they are corrupted too. It's been suggested to me that the operating system is corrupt, and not the software.' Morgan appeared unusually frustrated. 'None of the experts can explain to me, ma'am, why all kinds of security have been breached. All they tell me is that, even if we close down, we don't know what else has been planted to be activated later.'

Her hand went to the desk and wrapped around the warm metal of the lock-knife. Absently she slid the blade open, clicked it shut. 'We can work on isolated systems – but hermit computers have their limitations. Certainly the Ministry can't be run that way.'

'This has progressed appallingly quickly in two weeks, ma'am.'

She clicked her fingers and the wall-VDU darkened. No light in the big office now but the dawn, orange in the east. She shivered and keyed the daylight-fluorescent panels, blinking in the welcome additional blue-white light.

'I have some little appreciation of the field,' she said. 'The sheer degree of complexity required to breach all the different kinds of security we have . . . And yet we can't *not* put data into the system.'

She turned away from the window, looking philosophically at the big man, who stood with his broad shoulders straight and his back erect; and Morgan Froissart looked back at her. Practised enough to school his expression away from panic.

'No single attack should work against all systems,' he said, 'because of the multitude of different operating systems. And yet it is.'

'The stages of technology,' she said ruminatively. 'You see, we're past the stage of new technology being used to do the old technology's job but faster. We're well past that. New technology does things now that can only be done with new technology. And we depend on it. We *have* to use the databases. We *have* to use the nets. We can't close it all down. Nor can we risk continued data corruption. Everything would grind to a halt. Chaos.'

'Apparently our virus-killer software programs are useless.'

A silence followed. He added tentatively:

'It's beginning to show up in other ministries' databases. The news will break—'

'I *know*!' Johanna Branwen put the lock-knife into her jacket pocket. She shrugged the jacket collar up, and brushed silver-grey curls out from under its edge with both hands. 'Is it a virus? That is the mark of the man my daughter married. I believe he must have generated this program-corrupting virus. And . . . I don't doubt but that she is assisting him.'

'We can pick up your daughter whenever you give the word. US Military Intelligence has gone back on standby.' Morgan shrugged.

'Admittedly it would happen in the full glare of publicity, during this direct neural input affair, but it could easily be done.'

' "The full glare of publicity"? Really, Morgan. You've been watching too much satellite news. The question is, how much of that kind of "publicity" can we bear? And – actually, I think we can stand a great deal, Morgan, provided no one permits this to be made into a *cause célèbre*. It's probably useless to further discredit Valentine. It's certainly becoming essential that we have her husband.'

'Do we assume she knows where he is, ma'am?'

She can, with a little effort, think of Valentine as someone else. Someone else's daughter. Whether she can do this when she sees the woman, she doesn't know. But certainly she can act without compunction where Baltazar Casaubon is concerned.

Johanna Branwen says, 'Find them.'

The wall of the Docklands apartment came into focus. A hazy sun shone in, warming the painted brickwork. Two weeks mostly without sleep, interrupted by cat-naps and unconsciousness. Miles automatically groped towards the keyboard for morning TV. He rubbed his eyes. Sleep-gritty vision gave him the time on the wall screen's inset chronometer: 05.03 a.m.

'Shit! I'm wasting time.'

He rolled over, under dirty sheets, aware of the early satellite news, paying minimal attention to the local headlines.

'The Prime Minister today stated that there will be further financial incentives offered by the government to those residents of London willing to sell their houses in the dormitory towns. Next: another customs post has been set up on the Victoria Line, owing to the high influx of tourists this July. Our special report—'

'Ah, *shit*!' This time he means *Hypershift!*'s early morning magazine slot.

Frustrated, he hit his forehead with the heel of his hand; rolled over, and punched the pillow. The white cotton indented; slowly relaxed. He sat up, struggling into crumpled combat pants and staggering from the bed to the balcony, the wooden planking already warm from the dawn sun.

I'm losing it. I'm losing the money. I should have had this taped and ready to go. Christ, two weeks!

A breeze raises the hairs down his back.

Two dogs snarl at each other in the alley between the warehouses. He leaned over, looking to left and right, seeing the rusting cars that blocked each of the crossroads; some smoke going up from a cooking fire in the gutter near a Fiat Uno. A dark hand reached out of the car body and turned a skinned rat upon a spit.

Too early for the streets to be safe. Too late to try to go back to sleep.

He turned, staggering back into the sparse apartment, picking up the diary-corder off the top of a stack of printouts. His voice sounded odd even to himself. Worn down to the bone.

'Further notes on my direct neural input recording . . . I can't make this make sense! Everyone knows that Christopher Marlowe never wrote a play in 1610 called *The Spy at Londinium*. It isn't even recorded as a lost text. Hell, Christopher Marlowe *died* in 1593, May 30 . . . But here it is, in the databases. And I can't find even *one* academic record that doesn't take it for granted that the play exists, and that it had its first night in the year 1610.

'Could it be a lost play? But they quote from it. All of them: Boas, Ellis-Fermor, Bradbrook . . . And there's no way the play can have been discovered after I left Oxford. Some of the references go back to 1905. I don't *understand*.

'All of them say it's a genuine Marlowe play. But that isn't the important thing. The only thing is. Is. *Fuck*.

'Only schizophrenics get personal messages from the TV set. Is that what's happening here? Was Eugene right when he said it would fuck my mind? Do schizophrenics think sixteenth-century plays were written to give them personal messages? Is that what I am?

'Do I, honestly, think that this is some sort of a *communication* with me? Because that's what it felt like, I swear to God: like something *talking* to me.'

The satellite news soundtrack blipped, breaking his concentration and he glanced up to see a still graphic of a man. Caught leaning on an ivory walking-stick, free hand scratching at the seat of a pair of white cotton trousers that strained to encase his bulk; the light from the research hospital's windows striking copper fire from his hair.

'UK headline news. There is still no news on the missing American scientist Baltazar Casaubon, last seen at the June launch of the controversial direct neural input method of computerised mind-reading. Michael.'

'Thank you, Eugene. Direct neural input, or direct-brain reading of data, has aroused protest world-wide from civil liberties groups. A ministry spokesman said today that it is not government policy to interfere with commercial developments of multinational cor-porations not based in the UK. Sony-Nissan and Pacific Rim representatives were unavailable for comment, and representatives of the US Department of Defense issued no statement after seeing the Prime Minister yesterday. No arrest has yet been made of the controversial computer scientist Baltazar Casaubon, rumoured to have been charged with child sex offences. Eugene—'

Two weeks.

Am I going crazy?

Miles Godric stood still for a moment. Outside, a quarrel of sparrows skittered across the opposite warehouse roof. Their noise ceased and he threw down the diary-corder, picked up the webbing and clipped his camera-belt about his waist as he ran for the stairs, grabbing up a sheaf of printouts as he went.

'Block,' the older woman advised.

Rue Ingram gripped the hilt of the bastard sword in sweaty gloved hands. The canted blade hung in her vision, unfocused. Trying not to look at the woman, the woman's eyes, the woman's smile; but to take in passively the whole field of vision: backyard court, flagstones, brick wall, building, fire-escape, woman, sword.

Movement flashed to her left. She dropped her guard position, and caught Valentine Branwen's sword. Halted: slammed into the angle between cross-guard and blade. Blocked.

'Hey!' She grinned, wide enough to hurt the muscles of her cheeks. 'Hey . . .'

'Aw, Jesus, it was about time. We been here three days running and that's the first time she's let you use the thing properly.'

Frankie Hollister sat across the bottom rung of the fire-escape, in the diminishing shade, bare feet up on ironwork, ankles crossed. One sweaty fist pushed the hair out of her eyes.

'You're just jealous because you can't afford private tuition now,' Rue needled.

'I will not,' Valentine Branwen said, 'teach this to you, Frankie, so that you can take some irresponsible gang of children out on the street with it. Term's over. It's not my business any more.'

'You're teaching *her*.'

'So I am. But she has more sense than you do.' The woman smiled lopsidedly. 'In another day and age I would have taught sword. Now all I know is how to create two-edged swords of another kind entirely . . . OK, OK. Practise with the quarterstaff, Frankie. The drill's the same.'

Rue rubbed moisture out of the hollows of her eyes.

Brilliant light sleeted down into the court, shadows shrinking towards noon. Thirst dried her lips. She frowned, squinting the blaze out of her vision; bounced on the balls of her feet, and swung the hand-and-a-half sword in a cautious, pulled blow.

Silver darted. Valentine's blade flashed in a half circle, parrying her own sword through. The shock of metal scraping metal tingled in her hands. Her grin remained, wide and wider.

The woman said, 'So are you thinking of re-enactment, Rue?'

Concentration never missed a beat. Rue Ingram moved smoothly back, evading a strike, came in again; was suckered to the right for a block, and the woman's sword tapped her lightly on the meaty part of her thigh.

' "Think of it as a three-foot iron bar",' Frankie Hollister quoted, bored. She rested a wooden *bokkan* over her tanned shoulder, ignoring drill. 'That's what it looks like the way you guys are using it.'

'Because at the moment she has to think about it. Engrave reflexes on her unconscious mind. Input instinctive programs.' Valentine moved springily, her body at ease with the motion of the sword. Each pulled blow landed with no apparent effort, no strain on her wrist. 'Get the unconscious programs running, trigger them with an attack – which I won't do at the moment, Rue; that comes much later – then the whole thing moves faster.'

Safe within the circle of teacher and pupil, Rue Ingram thought block, parry, blow. Not wanting to think but to feel, react.

'I couldn't get out to – ow. Shit, you had me there. I couldn't get out to do re-enactment now. Not now they've closed the borders.' Rue hitched up the strap of her dress. 'My father's talking about taking the government grant for selling our house, and moving up to Manchester or Bristol or Newcastle. But London's still the information capital. He won't move out knowing we can't move back in again later.'

'I been in and out since they closed the borders.' Frankie's voice came from behind. 'S easy. You just got to look like a tourist, is all.'

'What, you, an incomer?' The older woman's voice was lightly teasing.

She put in an attack and Rue swooped to parry it through, metal on metal, a clear ringing sound that Rue had thought she would love and in combat mentally filed under *extraneous noises*.

'If you moved out would you meet your fiancé again?'

Rue blocked, wildly, catching a knuckle against the cross-guard of the woman's blade, and stepped back to strip off her leather glove and suck the finger. Pain or something like it started tears that she blinked back.

She rested the rebated sword back against her shoulder. 'If he couldn't stay here for me, why would I want to leave and go out to him?'

A *thukk!* sounded at her right side, and Rue looked, and her own arm was up, and the sound had been metal against wood. She froze, staring at Frankie's *bokkan*, that had whistled in at head-height and was now stopped, held by her own raised blade.

'I don't . . . I didn't . . .'

'First there is *no sword*.' Silver eyes glinted. The older woman even ignored Frankie. 'When the blade becomes an extension of your arm. You don't strike "with the sword", you just strike your opponent's body. And then there is *no intention*. You're not even conscious of seeing the weakness, the blow; you just find you've moved. No sword, no intention. Rue, I think you're starting to learn. Hollister—'

'Val! Val Branwen!'

Rue Ingram automatically lifted her head. The voice came from the entrance to the court. The glint of video lenses caught her gaze. She put the hair back from her hot face. 'Miles?'

Almost not recognisable: the shaven scalp grown out into a yellow-silver crewcut that has the paradoxical effect of making him seem more broad-shouldered. His pale skin reddens with sunburn.

'What is it?' The red-headed woman knelt to lay her military rapier flat. She stood up, stripping off sweat-softened leather gloves and shading her eyes with one arm. 'What's the matter?'

Learning how to see, Rue studied the line of Valentine Branwen's shoulders, silhouetted against inner-court windows, seeing how the muscles relaxed into honesty. *She isn't really that surprised to see him*.

Brown shadows lined his cheeks, hollows thick with stubble a shade darker than his hair. Rue thought *he's older*, and then *no, he's ill*. A belt pulled his combat trousers in to gaunt hip-bones. He cradled a bundle of printouts in his arms.

He ignored Rue, ignored Frankie; spoke to Valentine Branwen as if no one else was there. 'Where's Baltazar?'

'I wish I knew. To tell you the truth, I'm surprised *I'm* still here.'

Rue Ingram sat down on the flagstones, resting the medieval bastard sword across her lap. A bar of light from the flat blade flashed across the man's face. Nothing registered.

'I need to see him!'

'You and every other hypermedia. Not to mention the Ministry of Defence.' Valentine Branwen frowned. Her tone changed. 'Real problems?'

'Oh, sure. Yeah, that's for sure.' He rubbed his face with the heel of his hand and, as if startled, felt the rough stubble with his fingers.

His brows lifted. He moved his mouth as if he tasted something stale. Rue saw his pale eyes were red-rimmed.

'I need to speak to him about the link-architecture on direct neural input data,' Miles Godric said.

The woman stared back at him. 'Really?' Blankly unconvinced.

He changed tack. 'I can tell you *most* of what you've been doing.'

Rue, listening for glibness, heard honesty.

'The Yates Institute – half its funding comes from the Confederate Department of Defense. I checked up before your press launch. Now the Defense R & D boys have got your DNI systems back to play with, so they're happy. *Except* – so have the European Ministry of Defence. And so have the commercial companies. In Europe, the States, the Far East – No one can sit on it now!'

Rue slid her fingers down the blunt sword blade. Sun made the metal hot and harmless.

The man said, 'I've got contacts. You were right; no one was going to go public on this at all. You forced the military's hands. Successfully. Now they *want* Baltazar Casaubon.'

The woman raised a red eyebrow. 'If all this were so – and with cameras online, I'm not going to say anything about it – *if* that were true, then it's just the mechanics of the arrangement. You knew what we were doing. It succeeded: end of story.'

'*You look at this!*'

Miles's voice rang off the narrow court's walls. Rue winced, startled.

'*You look, Val.* This is a printout. From the data you recorded off me at the press launch. Listen—' He flourished the paper. It rustled in the noon heat. 'I don't remember any of this. I wouldn't. It's crap. Marlowe never wrote a play in 1610 called *The Spy at Londinium*. He was *dead* by 1610, dead fifteen years! OK, I thought, so it's a program glitch, Casaubon fucked up, DNI doesn't live up to its claims. And then I started reading this.'

Rue Ingram rested her cheek against the blade of the sword. Its blunt edge indented her skin. She sighed for the training, impatient now for the interruption to be over.

'You too, Ingram. Listen.'

Startled, she sat up. The man's eyes, rimmed with sepia shadow, fixed on her. He held up the printout and read aloud:

' "The Spy at Londinium, by Ch. Marlowe, Gent. Act One, enter Lady Regret." '

His voice echoed flatly in the narrow court. Frankie Hollister rested her nose down on her crossed forearms, back curving, shadows marking every indent of her spine. The red-haired woman began to pace, slowly. Rue swallowed with a mouth suddenly dry.

Miles Godric said, 'This is Lady Regret's speech:

> ' *"Under fair nature's eye, within this yard,*
> *Now Phoebus' chariot mounts the morning sky,*
> *I'll make a pyre of every gift he sent.*
> *This gorgeous robe of tissue, like the moon*
> *Glazed over with the silver of the stars,*
> *Its bodice trimmed with fine embroidery—"* '

'What?' Rue said. And then, 'Burning a dress. It's talking about burning a dress.'

Miles startled, then nodded. 'That's right; drama student. Checked you out a couple of weeks back. Listen.

> *"Its bodice trimmed with fine embroidery,*
> *And every panel of it figured o'er*
> *With pictures of the happiness I lack—*
> *I mean, the scene of my defeated love;*
> *My marriage to this faithful-faithless man.*
> *Here let it lie. And I will set my tinder*
> *To cloth as fragile as my delicate flesh:*
> *So let it burn—"* '

His halting delivery faded on a dry mouth. He added, 'Then there's a stage direction, "She fires the cloth. Enter a spy." Then the spy says:
"A strange sight, e'en for these degenerate days!
What do you, maiden?" . . .'

Rue dropped the broadsword. Metal clashed, echoed back from the high buildings. She snatched the printout from his hands, tearing it, and looked down at the paper.

SPY: A strange sight, e'en for these degenerate days!
What doe you, maiden, wailing in this place
Like Hecuba?

REGRET: Say whats your business here?
I feele no urge to speak of this defeat.
I'lle warrant you your business is far off
From questioning mee, who know not what you are.

'Original spelling.' Rue became aware of Frankie craning to read over her shoulder.

> SPY: Madam a scribe is what I am. Or if
> You like it better saye I am a spy.
> News is my business, sought amongst the court
> And retailed at a price that is aboue
> The jewelled stars that hang at heauen's ear.
> (I would haue heauen's ear too, an I could,
> To hear thatte newes which I myself create.
> I must discharge my poison where I can.)
> Now speak:what strangenesse is this?

> REGRET: O regret!
> I rue me that I answer what you ask.
> As you may see, I burne my wedding dress.
> Our cittie is besieged (you know that well)
> Like to a landlock'd island, girt about
> With greedy hands that seek to rauish us.
> My once-sworn loue now dwells without these walls.
> I cannot be cojoin'd with him in loue
> Because he left me ere the gates were shutt
> To follow warres in lands I do not know;
> An *Icarus* vpon the fields of blood,
> High o'er the land of our most ancient foe.
> Go tell it to the court, tis news enough:
> Him I cannot follow. This my grief.
> Of my life's joys I call him now the thief.

> SPY: You burn all colour. Blacks youre funeral pall,
> And yet the colour may become one faire,
> As it is said, jett lacks not opulence
> Because he has night's hue, so grief adorns.
> Drink with mee lady it may ease your minde
> To tell your grief—

> *Enter the fatte clowne*

> CLOWN: A man more fool than I
> Would seek, fair child, to know your cause of grief.

'That's us.' She stared at Godric. 'The first time I met you. *That was us*. Here. What the *fuck* do you think you're doing? I didn't ask to be put into any play! That's private!'

Valentine Branwen's hand on her neck, flesh against warm flesh, steadied something of the dizziness in her head. Rue looked a question at the older woman.

Who said, 'If this is a joke, Miles—'

'You look at the bibliography I've printed out. If it's a joke, I'm getting academic references for it that go back nearly a century!'

Breath failed the blond man. His pale eyes screwed up, as if pain clamped around his temples. He hit the printout, ripping the top sheet of paper. Rue read *THE SPYE AT LONDinium by Ch. Marlowe Gent. Printed by Master Rich. Alleyn at St Pawles Churchyarde 1610*. The man thumbed through, sticky-handed, and slapped another page into Valentine's hand.

'Read that! It's a fucking eight-page bibliography. *Where does that come from?'*

Valentine's hand slid away from Rue's shoulder. The woman tapped her bottom lip with her thumbnail. 'You checked this out against university databases, obviously. Did you look at any early print sources?'

'Print? Where would I get time to do the legwork? I called it up through databases—' Godric stopped dead. Rue saw him nod, once, and a shadow leave his eyes, to be replaced by anger. 'Primary sources. Original print books. They won't say anything about a new Marlowe play – because it's a fucking electronic *forgery*.'

Rue reached out and tugged the printout from his grip.

Valentine spoke slowly. 'Miles . . . it couldn't . . . but I can't see any other explanation – I think the program must be somehow recasting your DNI recording in the form of a four-hundred-year-old play. Christ alone knows *why*. Maybe something corrupted the data.'

'Val, it *isn't* all my recording. There's stuff here I couldn't know! She never told me about this guy she was supposed to marry!' He turned away from the older woman. 'Rue. Is there anything in this that's about him? That *you* didn't tell me?'

She searched the paper. Letters blurred in her vision, loss of concentration unfocusing her eyes. At last she said, ' "To follow—" *wars*, is it? "—in lands I do not know." Icarus. I never told you he was a helicopter pilot. I never told you he was posted to France.'

The printout concertinaed out of his hands, spilling across the dusty flagstones. Rue fell to her knees between them, knocking against the older woman's muscled leg; scrabbled among the papers as Miles Godric squatted beside her, and Valentine at last went down on one knee to rummage through the coffee-marked, half-torn pages of text.

Frankie Hollister, still sitting on the fire-escape, grunted and watched.

'How long have you been snooping on me?' Rue demanded.

Miles Godric sat back on his bare heels. An edge of one camcorder on his belt grazed her arm. 'How much did you talk with Baltazar Casaubon about your boyfriend?'

'I didn't. Are you saying this is *his* idea of a joke?'

The older woman gazed at Miles Godric. She let what paper she held fall to the flagstones. Her eyes squinted against the sunlight. 'The play's incomplete.'

'It's all fragments. It doesn't,' he said, 'it doesn't actually read like Marlowe. It reads like every Renaissance dramatist I ever had to study for my degree, in collaboration.'

'It could be just that. Your memories of reading them. A freak arrangement of data.'

'How did the program learn to do that? And where does the other data come from? And, Val, that isn't what it feels like. It feels . . . like there's something there. When I play it back. Something . . . there.'

The silver lenses blink. A tremor of genuine disquiet? Or something else? Dazzled, Rue dropped her gaze, seeing the mess of papers through green and purple after-images.

Godric said, 'I need to find Baltazar! There's more about the "clown" in here, listen:

> *"Go bid the spy devise most cunningly*
> *A plot by which we may o'erhear the man:*
> *This clown's a very oracle for news.*
> *And all who wish their Delphic questions answered—"*

Then a lot of mythological references, then:

> *"He hath a room, more fell than Faustus's,*
> *In which he practises a rare conceit:*
> *Devices like to Bacon's brazen head*
> *That spoke and said,* Time is, was, and will be,
> *Speak unto him, and tell him far-off news.*
> *This clown, master of witty devices,*
> *Perils his fat soul: spy, go seek him out . . ."* '

Rue sat, legs sprawling under the thin, hot cotton of her skirt. Valentine shook her head.

'*Where is he?*' Miles demanded.

'I don't know.'

'Bullshit!' a female voice interrupted. Rue, startled, stared over her shoulder at Frankie Hollister. The short girl sprang up, letting the *bokkan* fall, and shoved her fists in her dungarees pockets as she swaggered over to Valentine.

'I seen you two together that time. Don't tell me *you* can't find him. Not if you want to. Don't give me that crap!'

With some satisfaction the blonde girl squatted and rested her arm across Rue's shoulders.

The weight of flesh made Rue sweat in the noon heat. She shrugged free and knuckled Frankie's arm. 'Get off!'

'I want two things understood, Miles,' Valentine Branwen said softly. 'The first is that you turn your video equipment offline now, and you put it back online when I tell you to, and that's the way it is.'

The man reached to his belt controls. She watched him.

'The second thing is, Rue, you and your little friend will have to come too. Just for the moment, I don't want anyone sneaking off to the news media.'

She touched the spilled printout.

'Maybe . . . I can find him if I can think like him.'

CHAPTER 9
Earlier that Same Morning

A liquid plop sounded.

Baltazar Casaubon wiped his massive hand across his face without bothering to open his eyes. A sticky substance smeared his fingers. He wiped it down his shirt, and sat up. His eyes opened.

Pigeons wheeled over Trafalgar Square.

The sun, not high enough to have burned off the dew, struck against the sides of buildings all down gridlocked Whitehall, and flashed in gold from the spires of the House of Commons. He wrenched his neck one way, then the other, creaking; and grunted.

The ABS plastic computer case jabbed into his massive flank. He got slowly to his feet, and stretched. One shirt-button pinged, losing itself among the pigeons grazing on early tourist grain.

'*Mon pauvre ami!*' A coin clinked on the guano-spotted pavement.

The link-architect Casaubon yawned jaw-crackingly wide, stretched his bolster-thick arms, and swooped to pick the pound coin up. He looked, but the tourists had wandered off towards Nelson's Column.

'*Merci bien,*' the large man rumbled. '*Mille fois.*'

No traffic sounded in the Square. All the air shone clear, sun delineating the NeoClassical columns of the National Gallery with a pristine grace. He grinned widely, and wiped the remains of the pigeon droppings off his faintly-freckled face. He belched. Rummaging under the lip of the fountain found him the shoes and jacket he had used as a pillow.

'As to that . . .' His voice rumbled, deep in the morning air. He hooked one shoe on, a finger under the trodden-down heel; then the other; and shrugged himself gratefully into the creased and stained jacket. '. . . *now* we shall see what we shall see.'

He made a faint gesture by way of brushing himself down, and strode off across the square, and then down an alley, past St Martin-in-the-Fields church into Adelaide Street.

'Hey, mate, got any change?'

He took his absent-minded gaze off the Victorian gothic roof of Charing Cross Station, the sun sliding down its spires as morning advanced. Two men in dirty sleeping-bags lay half-sitting in a doorway; a girl with cropped yellow hair squatted beside one, a cigarette hanging from her fingers.

'I do believe I . . .' The pound coin came easily to his searching fingers. He proceeded to turn out each pocket, slinging his case by its strap over his shoulder.

'What you got there then, mate?'

'That's his change of clothes,' the girl said. 'Off for an interview, he is. "You've got the job, what's your address, then?" "Er, third cardboard box on the right, Trafalgar Square." "Well fuck off then we ain't got no job for you!" That's about the size of it, innit?'

'You.' The link-architect pointed a massive, fat finger in her direction, and beckoned magisterially. 'Come with me.'

'Oh yeah. Want me to do that, do you?'

The girl glanced at the younger of the two men, who shrugged to his feet. His sleeping bag had split at the end. He wore it as a robe. They followed as the fat man, head high, walked down past the entrance to the Underground station.

'It's obvious when you think about it.' Baltazar Casaubon waved his free hand. 'How ridiculous the damned thing is. You know what's being taken away from you? *Time*. Time for the important things like making love, and good food, and arguing about what kind of Art is truly moral. Don't you agree?'

The man scrubbed at his stubbled cheeks with a hand upon which the nails were blue and blackened. 'I think you're a fucking nutter, mate.'

A dozen men and women were gathered around the standpipe at the corner with the Strand. Baltazar Casaubon queued to take his turn, and cup plump hands to hold the freezing water, and rinse his face and neck.

He looked up, copper-red hair sleeked wetly to his forehead. 'I'll show you,' he said.

Another two or three people joined him on his majestical promenade along the pavement of the Strand, appearing out of abandoned cars and shop doorways. By the time he reached the bank fifteen or so men and women crowded his heels, hacking coughs into the morning air.

'So now what?' the blonde girl demanded.

The link-architect thoughtfully picked his nose, and wiped his fingers down his once-white shirt. He looked about him helplessly. Then he beamed, and bent over (knocking an older man three steps back with the collision) and picked up an abandoned pencil from the pavement.

He walked along the bank's frontage to the cash dispenser, and, on the white marble above it, carefully inscribed two numbers. He entered them into the cash point, fat and dirty fingers poising delicately to tap each numeral. And then he stood back.

The machine whirred.

A grinding sounded, down in the depths; vibrating through the paving stones. A harsh ratcheting sound started, stopped, and picked up again. The cash point cover slid up.

Twenty-pound notes slid down the rollers, jammed, and slid out, pushed by the force of notes behind them. Ten, a dozen, a hundred, two hundred . . .

A flick of wind caught them, and the ten- and fifty-pound notes that followed, a whole stream, darting up into the air above the Strand like birds; and the street-sleepers at first stared, then grabbed, then chuckled, and bellowed, waking others, frightening the first businessmen coming in from the station; and all the while the link-architect Casaubon leaned back on his ivory sword-stick and watched the notes pay out: the financial artery cut and spouting into the street.

The blonde girl saw him go, but – both hands, all pockets, and the front of her T-shirt crammed with notes – didn't bother to follow. With a biro she carefully wrote on her arm, in blue ink, the numbers inscribed above the cash point.

By midday the knowledge of the numbers had spread as far as Southwark, and by two o'clock the banks suspended business.

CHAPTER 10
Owls and Other Birds of Prey

The noise of a drill echoed down from dusty heights, drowning out a clock striking three. Valentine Branwen glanced up at the scaffolding and plastic-shrouded building at the end of Monmouth Street, and then back at the outside of *The Greene Lyon*. A cardboard notice in the pub window neatly lettered NO WORK BOOTS OR OVERALLS.

'OK, OK, I'm *going*.' Frankie Hollister pushed her way rapidly back out through the swing doors.

'Can't find a working phonebox hardly anywhere these days.' The short girl glared. 'I got through, though. The woman says you can come over. Sounds a right old bag to me.'

Valentine Branwen raised an eyebrow.

From inside *The Greene Lyon* a voice shouted something undecipherable but hostile. Swaggering a little, Frankie caught up with Valentine's rapid walk. She said, 'I can't go in half the pubs round here.'

'Why not?'

'Because I'm a Hollister.' A pause, as if it should be self-explanatory. 'Hollister Construction, yeah? See the sign back there? My father's sacked half the labourers on this site. So there's pubs I can't drink in because there's too much hassle. Not trouble, I don't *mind* trouble; just hassle. And then there's other places I can drink because I *am* a Hollister – there's a lot of us. Me mum was the only girl among nine boys, so there's all them, and my sisters' husbands. See?'

Valentine nodded with something that might have been nostalgia. She remained aware of Rue Ingram hovering at the girl's elbow, and of Miles Godric walking as if the solid pavement were rubber under his feet. A horse-drawn dray loaded with cladding rumbled up St Martin's Lane towards the building site, in a slow weave between burnt-out vehicles cleared to the sides of the road. All conversation ceased until the noise passed them.

'We're not that rough,' Frankie Hollister said. 'There's some of our lot I wouldn't mess with. There was one got sent down for GBH and armed robbery – he didn't *do* the armed robbery, but the law came round and did his place over and said he assaulted them. They didn't have any evidence and they were deliberately winding him up. But he wasn't a Hollister, he was one of me brother-in-laws' cousins, I think. They think I'm dead thick, going to college.'

The short girl shrugged her dungarees up over her shoulders, the cloth showing gaps where safety-pins held the straps together. Grime ringed her neck, London's black dust. Valentine looked from Frankie to Rue.

Oh, Frankie. The original, of which the other is but a pale copy. But my time's run out, I think.

They turned into Long Acre, the street shining in the afternoon heat, tourists scanning those shop windows not boarded up. Mark Knopfler on lead guitar sounded from a ghetto blaster. Below the Victorian brick skyline, glass and steel frontages glittered. She tasted air growing cleaner by the day.

'Miles . . .'

Camcorder lenses glittered, mechanically alert. The man walked hunched in the heat, fingers whitely gripping the pile of printout. She withstood an impulse to put her arm around his muscular torso.

She shook her head, feeling her sun-hot hair brush her shoulders, shuddering with a kind of physical realisation of the city itself: brick, stone and mortar, river and gulls and burnt-out cars; still thronged with people, still the heartland of her soul. 'You've got first rights on the inside story of DNI: you can ask your own price for your next career step. You're *OK*.'

'Not if I hand in a story that sounds like a schizoid hallucination!'

He gripped the mass of paper he cradled. The pallor of his skin glowed in the high afternoon light.

'Direct neural input had powerful enemies. They've gone quiet,' Miles Godric said, surprising her with his coherence. 'Or have they?'

She looked at his hair, roots growing out very fair, and the thin beard that lined his cheeks; and met his pale eyes, with a vision of how he would be in twenty years time, older, confused, compromised; but undefeated.

He said, 'You didn't use e-mail because hackers read e-mail. You used a public phone, not the one in the flat. You really are trying to get out from under.'

'For a couple of hours, maybe.'

'Jesus Christ, woman, did Baltazar even *think* about what he was doing? Direct neural input – it's a secret policeman's wet dream! We're close enough to a fascist police state as it is. Yes, OK, fear screws up the reading, and it's fragmentary, but it'll be improved, there'll be drugs—'

Seeing that he would speak piecemeal, she did nothing but make a small prompting noise.

He said, 'That's if anything genuine is coming out of it. *If* it is.'

She came to a halt as they crossed the top of Neal Street, the two younger women some yards ahead, and he stopped with her; and lifted his head to stare at the clarity of the summer sky.

'But when it turns out garbage like this—!' Miles hugged the printout tighter to his chest. Valentine watched him: heat-stricken, eyes rimmed with sweat. His hands pressing flat against the paper, as if that meant he would never have to read the words again.

'I almost hope it is garbage. Even if I never see any money out of it if it is.'

'But is it garbage?' she said. 'Where does a "play" come from, how can it exist? Does it invalidate DNI?'

Valentine Branwen fisted her hands and stretched, shoulders relaxing in the pressure of summer's heat. Still ozone summer; and the horizon a hazy white-blue. She licked her lips, this time tasting grit. The entrance to Covent Garden tube loomed.

'It's one of two answers,' she said. 'It does. Or it doesn't. And, believe me, I want to know which one it is just as badly as you do!'

After an hour and three-quarters of changing lines on the Underground, Rue Ingram stood in an outside yard watching a big copper-haired woman bite into a peach. Juice ran down the woman's muscular forearm, blotting the faint gold fuzz of hair. The woman wiped her mouth with the back of her hand, and put the peach-pit between her back teeth and cracked it.

'Baltazar who?' she enquired. 'Never heard of him.'

Rue looked tentatively at Valentine Branwen.

Who shoved her shirtsleeves up, and pulled the tail of her shirt out of her jeans, flapping the cloth to circulate air over hot flesh. 'How are the kids behaving?'

The big copper-haired woman spat out the fractured peach stone. She appeared to relax. 'The boy's fine. I left him reading the *Financial Times*. The girl's an unholy terror.'

'*Tell* me about it . . .'

They seemed to overflow the small yard behind the wooden fence: Rue with Frankie, the cameraman with Valentine Branwen, and the big woman in dungarees. Rue craned her neck. The afternoon sun gleamed on the woman's hair (the colour of fuse-wire), on pale and freckled flesh. A face that is young except for crêpe-skin around the eyes: forty or so.

'And White Crowe's still collecting cute little girls.' The large woman winked at Rue Ingram. Frankie gave her a blistering glare. 'And reporters?'

Rue glanced at Miles Godric. The camcorder lenses glinted at his web-belt, his knuckles were white around the sheaf of paper.

The teacher of sword, the sun bright on her bush of dark red hair and on her white shirt, prodded the large woman's denim-covered belly.

'Are you going to let us in, or are we going to stand out here and fry?' Valentine asked acerbically.

'Baltazar hasn't been here, you know. She thinks you know where he is.'

A voice from inside the block of flats called, 'Dorothea!'

The big woman pushed the front door open and led the way in.

Out of the sun, indoors, Rue blinked retinal after-images out of her vision. A council flat front room full of furniture and perches. Something stank.

'My mother keeps owls,' the large woman explained, just as Rue realised that the copper eyes staring at her from every corner blinked. A pointed wing lifted, stretched. 'And other birds of prey. It means the place stinks of droppings, we keep very odd hours, and the fridge is full of dead mice. Have some icecream?'

Her surprisingly delicate hand appeared out of the dimness. Rue Ingram stared at the dish of chocolate-chip icecream.

'You don't want any?' The big orange-haired woman walked past Rue. She hitched one large haunch on to the edge of a desk, snagging her torn denims on the old wood. She rested the dish against her large cotton-shirted breasts. Through a mouthful of icecream she said, 'Waste not, want not!'

Rue watched how the tiny room, hot despite all open windows, made the woman's fair skin flush pink; freckles deepening across her wide forehead and cheeks. Her massy orange hair was escaping from its braid, sneaking tendrils across her heavily muscled arms.

'Really, Dorothea, where are your manners?'

'Sorry, Mum.'

'Pour the tea.' A white-haired woman, tiny in this family of large, self-indulgent redheads, spoke from an armchair. She frowned critically at Dorothea. It was unclear, at a second glance, whether this glare was intended for her daughter or for the Scops Owl, fully grown and barely five inches tall, that gripped her own outstretched finger. She turned to Rue Ingram. 'My name is Luka, my dear. Please sit down. Your friend too.'

Frankie remained recalcitrantly standing, fists buried in her dungarees-pockets. Rue held back something that might become hysterical laughter and took the teacup Dorothea passed to her. She tasted the appallingly weak tea. 'Um, thanks. Yeah. Thanks.'

The old woman began feeding something yellow and red and furry to the Scops Owl from between her withered lips. She could be no taller than four foot six. Her silver hair hung down her back in a braid as thick as her daughter's arm. A few bright hawk feathers had been woven into the strands.

She abandoned the Scops Owl reluctantly. 'Valentine, my dear, with all respect to the way you and Izumi choose to bring them up – I simply cannot cope with both your children! Not even with Dorothea's assistance. And she can hardly be absent from work for ever.'

Rue balanced the fancy tea-cup and saucer. She looked to Valentine Branwen for a cue.

'Izumi will have them back in California soon. I've booked a flight. I need to show Baltazar something before he goes back to her.' Valentine hesitated. 'Miles, if I can take the printout—'

'No!' The man blinked in the indoor summer dimness. He locked gazes with Valentine, ignoring everyone else in the room. 'I want to see Baltazar Casaubon *now*.'

Valentine halted for a half-second, her gaze sweeping the room. She did not take notice of Rue. She grinned, winked at Miles Godric, said, 'Don't go away!' and vanished back out into the corridor.

'She doesn't believe he's not here. I'll keep an eye on her.' Dorothea rose up and slouched out of the room, still carrying her bowl of icecream.

'Well, now.' The old woman, Luka, turned back. 'I don't believe I know your name, young man.'

'He's Miles Godric,' Rue said, when she saw he wasn't going to. She put the cup and saucer down on a spindly table. 'Are you Baltazar Casaubon's mother?'

'Yes, my dear.' The old woman beamed. It was time-faded, and aided with dentures, but Rue recognised it: the link-architect's benevolent, unselfconscious beam.

'Do you know, I grew up on an estate like this?' Miles Godric suddenly gave an absent, cut-off chuckle. 'Flat-blocks, no gardens, and always knowing out there it was *London* . . .'

He took an automatic foursquare stance, catching all the room within the range of camcorders, adjusting contrast levels.

'I knew the way out when I was eight – university, networking, technological specialisation. I made it.'

'Oh fer Chrissakes!' Frankie moved with a swing to her elbows that threatened every ornament, dresser, coffee table, and hooded hawk in the tiny crowded room. Belled jesses jangled. The low mutter of bird sound rose to shrieks. She strode across to the back window. Rue saw a square of common grass beyond the glass. 'Let's stop pissing about. We don't have to stay here. C'mon, Rue.'

'And you must be the young lady I spoke with on the telephone. "Frankie".' Luka lifted the Scops Owl. It blinked amazingly large furry eyelids at Rue, opened its beak, and hissed. A thin strip of leather held one of its legs, wound between the old woman's fingers. It threw itself forward ferociously, straining the leather, hissing. A dropping splashed white-and-black on the hem of Rue's dress.

'I love it.' Rue grinned. 'A little pitbull owl.'

The heat did not lessen. It altered in quality from stunning to stifling. Lulled, the hawks stood motionless on their perches. Miles Godric, with one careful fingertip, stroked the back of the Scops Owl's head. 'Val brought us a long way round to get here, but I could find the place again. I'll just keep coming until I find out what's going on. Until I find Baltazar Casaubon.'

'I haven't seen my son. The police have asked me the same questions.' Luka stood up, placing the owl on a perch and her empty cup on the one table that seemed out of place in the room. A stout desk, covered in paperwork, with a battered large monitor and keyboard. The monitor displayed a 3D exploded graphic of architectural plans.

Rue sauntered over, eyeing the incomplete drawings. An inset in one corner of the screen showed what was presumably the finished plan: a spired and multi-floored anachronism large enough to be an office block or major museum. Luka's voice at her elbow said:

'Dorothea has no sense of the Classical virtues. No order, harmony, restraint. She will persist with these Baroque monstrosities. They're so . . .' The old woman sought a suitable classification. 'So flamboyant.'

'I like 'em.' Rue picked up the 1996 desk calender. Still on June.

'He's *not* here?' Miles sounded dazed.

Rue walked across and shook Miles's shoulders. His muscles hardly tensed against her. 'Of course he's not here! Haven't you been listening? Aw, for fuck's sake!'

'Language,' Luka said critically. 'You young girls are much too excitable, I've always said so.'

Rue fisted her hand and punched Miles in the ribs. He grunted, pained, rubbing his side; and suddenly focused. 'You're not too old for a good shaking—'

'We need you to be with it!' she snarled. The heat of the afternoon made her sweaty, breathless, short-tempered. 'I don't understand what's going on. I'm in this too! That play . . . Valentine acts like she doesn't know, but it's just an act. I don't believe her! I want to know what's happening!'

'Yeah!' Frankie hefted her slipping dungarees straps up over her shoulders.

'Ah.' The small white-haired woman tsked. A flurry of wings in the sun-dark room came from a tethered peregrine hawk. Rue, turning, flinched from movement, and felt claws prick her own scalp. She reached up with over-controlled patience and coaxed the Scops Owl on to her forefinger.

' "Ah"?' Rue said. 'What does *that* mean?'

'People often react to my daughter-in-law that way. If I were Baltazar I doubt I would permit – but there: old women become interfering old biddies. I won't interfere.' Her thin face creased. Rue watched all the parlour's light shine in her eyes.

'I don't get it.'

The old woman moved her gaze quite deliberately to Frankie. Frankie Hollister wiped at the back of her sweating, dirty neck; and suddenly looked confused.

'Really,' Luka said.

Stillness came, suddenly catching up: the long, hot walk over; the flat dim and shining. Rue replaced the owl and put her hands up, and smoothed her straggling black hair back from her face. Her palms felt hot. She ignored Miles Godric's stare, concentrating now on the old woman's face.

'I think you'd better tell me what you mean.'

'I'll put it as plainly as I can,' Luka said. 'My dear, if you're sleeping with my daughter-in-law, she won't leave Baltazar for you.'

Valentine stood in the kitchen, regarding the street through the window, her face blank.

'The police have been here several times,' Dorothea said. 'I think my brother has been very careful not to come here.'

'But a message? He has to have left a message somewhere!'

A rhythmic noise intruded itself over her attention threshold.

Dorothea moved back down the entrance hall, looked, and then came to lean her immense bulk against the door-jamb, finishing her icecream. 'Something's up.'

'Not the kids?'

'No. They're safe.' Dorothea straightened broad shoulders. 'But I think you'd better come out now and deal with it.'

CHAPTER 11
Brutal Isolation

A twinge of hunger surprised Valentine as she paced down the corridor behind Dorothea. She glanced at her watch and found it after six. The summer afternoon light streamed in through the open front door. She squinted against the rising dust.

An olive drab Lynx, rotors heavily turning, stood on the piece of common grass between the flat blocks. Soldiers in woodland camouflage ringed the perimeter. She could just make out, through the helicopter's windscreen, a man in a suit.

She showed teeth in what might have been a grin, raising her voice over the idling engine. 'OK, Dor. I know who it is. You want to take the kids out to Covent Garden for an icecream?'

The big woman nodded. 'Jay already told me to. He's smart, your boy. Weird, but smart.'

A brown-haired boy of perhaps eleven stood waiting quietly on the path, ignoring the helicopter, his black trousers neatly pressed and his white shirt buttoned up to the neck. A three-year-old girl crouched by the fence, sun bright on her orange curls. Her summer dress was rucked up around her chest, and she squatted, chuckling. She was peeing ornamental patterns in the dust.

'I haven't really seen them long enough this time. It'll take them a while to get used to me again.' Valentine looked wistfully at the little girl. 'Phone before you bring them back here.'

'Trust me.'

Luka entered the hall, closing the door to the front room behind her with a cold deliberation. Her blue eyes were milky as the sky. '*That person* has come here. Tell me when she leaves.'

The old woman stalked towards her kitchen.

Somewhere in the next flat a sound-system plays *Your Latest Trick*, and Valentine paused for a second, slowing her pulse to the beat. Then she turned and went into the front room.

Rue and Frankie stood together by the open window; Rue whispering uncomfortably in the smaller girl's ear; Frankie leaning back against the sill with her ankles crossed. Miles Godric sat bolt upright on the sofa.

Johanna Branwen sat at Dorothea's desk. Her gloved fingers flicked across the keyboard. The monitor glowed faint rainbows under sunlight. 'Interesting . . .' Johanna leaned back and stretched her arms out wide. The white fur collar of her jacket framed her plump, lined face and steel-silver hair.

Valentine looked her up and down. The woman wore a startlingly white tracksuit and Nike trainers. Gold bracelets clinked on her wrists; gold flashed at her ears and fingers.

'I was just discussing with Luka the inadvisability of having illegal anti-surveillance equipment in your house,' the woman's familiar voice said. 'She chose to leave. You're sending my grandchildren away. Permit me to send these other children with them.'

'You took your time getting here.'

No surprise at that comment showed on the middle-aged woman's face. Caught in the automatic power-plays of conversation with Johanna Branwen, Valentine suddenly sighed. 'I *didn't* expect you in person. Let's talk. Really talk.'

'I don't believe I'm familiar with that experience where you're concerned.'

There was a smothered laugh. Johanna Branwen glanced over her shoulder at the two girls.

'You find that funny? Mmm. Interesting. Frances Amy Hollister, aged eighteen, student, four juvenile convictions for – let me see – driving without a licence, arson, being in possession of proscribed substances, carrying an offensive weapon. To wit, one sharpened steel comb.'

'Aw, *what*? Fuck you, man.'

'And Rue Ingram. No criminal record, as such; but there was that abortion you had last year. Did you ever tell your lover that you had become pregnant, before he was posted overseas? No, I beg your pardon, this was your previous lover. The married man.'

'That's a lie!'

'It *is* a lie,' Frankie Hollister wailed. 'I'm her mate. I should know.'

'Perhaps you should. But obviously you don't.'

'That's enough.' Valentine Branwen walked across the small, hot room. Birds of prey stretched, hooded beaked heads questing. She put one hand on Rue's shoulder, one on Frankie's. Feeling the hearts beat through sweat-sticky flesh. Holding the two of them. 'So she has access to Home Office records. That's not exactly surprising.'

' "She." You don't call me "Mother",' the older woman stated. 'You don't call me anything, I notice. Not even "Johanna".'

Valentine squeezed Rue's shoulder, then Frankie's. 'Go.'

'Yeah.' Frankie Hollister swaggered across the sunlit room, reached down and took a handful of biscuits from Luka's plate as she passed, stuffed them in her mouth and went out spitting crumbs. Miles Godric got unsteadily to his feet.

At the door Rue turned her head. Valentine met her gaze. A tall, leggy girl; black hair falling on to sun-golden shoulders; her creased black dress marked with the droppings of owls. One of the merlin hawks cried. Valentine looked away from the intensity of Rue's stare, and moments later heard the door close.

'Shit, why do you always do that? Why try to destroy people?'

'They'll have forgotten it by tomorrow. Turn round and let me look at you.'

'Don't say "it's been too long". You know what I look like. You'll have seen enough security tapes of me over the last couple of years.'

Slowly, she turns. Aware of grime on her white jeans and shirt; aware of sweat-patches under her arms, and the summer smell of hot flesh. She tucked strands of dark red hair away behind her ears.

'You look older,' Johanna Branwen said.

'How much heavy support did you bring with you?'

'They don't let me go anywhere without security, I'm afraid. One of the penalties of being a cabinet minister. Morgan is in the helicopter. The rest, I assume, are where they usually are. I think it's more than time that I spoke to your – to Baltazar Casaubon.'

Valentine looked down at her own callused hands. 'Sometimes, when I wonder how I got to be such a bastard, I think about you. Then I know. I learned it from an expert.'

'That's pathetic.' Johanna Branwen got up from the desk. An inch or so smaller than her daughter, but somehow giving the impression that her sight-line is an inch or two taller. She walked across and closed the louvre window. The sun-dim room grew hotter and more stifling. The hooded birds became quiescent.

She said, 'The truth is, that what we find out, as we get older, is that we are not nice people. It may be the last illusion one loses. Only pride restrains us from cruel and immoral acts. Pride in not being that sort of person.'

She undid the belt of her jacket, and drew off her pale leather gloves.

'And some of us, as well, when we learn enough about ourselves to stop pretending we care about injustice, go further and learn that we love gratuitous cruelty for its own sake. And the thing is—'

Valentine felt her arms gripped. She looked levelly into the older woman's eyes.

'—the thing is, *it doesn't matter.*'

Hands grip her, hands that are older than hers but the same shape. Blue-white at the fingertips. Raynaud's Disease. The smell of these hands is familiar from memories too deep to despise: memories of when chairs were tall, and the ground close and interesting, and hands were there to wash you clean. The hands of someone tall, who settles the frightening world into intelligibility. The hands of a smart, strong, beautiful mother; to whom (as it should) the world comes to listen.

Valentine reached up and detached the older woman's fingers. She held the cool hands for a moment. 'Casaubon's not here. Hasn't been here. And there's no message.'

'Really?'

A tremor in those cold hands. The fragility of older flesh goes through Valentine like a knife of pity. She loosens her grip. 'I used to – worship you. I wanted to be just like you, in control of everything, making everything do what you wanted. It would have frightened me, then, to think there could be something you don't know about. Or that if you do know – which wouldn't surprise me – you don't know what it means.'

Valentine held out her hand to Miles Godric, who had remained standing. She took the scrolled-up printout, reversed and scrolled it the other way, flattening the paper out.

'I expect,' she said, 'that you will have seen this.'

Rue looked at the soldiers who lay with their rifles around the perimeter of the common ground. She walked down the path, skirting the yellow grass beaten down by the military helicopter.

The blonde girl said, 'Is it true?'

'Frankie, you're *Catholic*. What was I going to say to you?'

There were several men, not in uniform, wearing jackets despite the heat. Two of them began to walk around the path. The noise of the idling rotors made it difficult to speak. Rue went with them when they reached her.

'Just a few questions,' one shouted. 'Purely routine.'

The other showed an ID that seemed official.

She believed them, being realistic about it. *They'll have checked us out, down to dental records. If she's a cabinet minister's daughter, then I guess they know all of what Frankie and me have been doing at the dojo. This is just procedure.*

It was not until she was climbing awkwardly up the step into the body of the helicopter, smelling hot oil and metal, deafened by the rotors, that she properly saw the pilot. His mirror visor was pushed up.

Her automatic glance at the plain-clothes officers made her think, by their faces, that this was not a surprise to them.

'Wynne?'

Flight Lieutenant Wynne Ashton said something to his helmet mike. Sweat pearled his skin, what she could see of it under the equipment and flight suit. That skin that smells of spices.

'Well, Jesus,' Rue Ingram said, her voice breaking at every word, but her head up, 'isn't *that* just wonderful?'

'Not now,' Ashton muttered, obviously painfully embarrased.

' "Not now." ' Rue from ignorance or pain could ignore the idling rotors, the turboshaft engine, the weight of the aircraft and the accidents that might happen if the pilot's attention wandered. '*You* can tell *me* "not now"?'

'Rue . . .'

'Oh, you can remember my name. *That's* nice.'

The visor curves down, blanking her vision of his eyes, and sunlight slides across it as his head moves away.

'Go fuck yourself,' Rue said. And then, 'How could you just *go*? You didn't even speak to me!'

His head did not turn.

'Shit . . .'

She was unsure whether he heard her. She moved, stooped, to sit on one of the bolted-in metal benches. One of the plain-clothes officers fastened a lap-strap across her body, and leaned back wiping owl-shit off his cuff.

Frankie Hollister reached over and held her hand tightly.

The heat of the airless room dizzied Valentine. She leaned over Johanna Branwen's shoulders, watching the older woman's face as the woman began to read.

'A play.' Her eyes slid down the cast list. She looked at Miles Godric. 'With a "Ladie Johannah". And a "Valentinia". This was a poor joke.'

Miles Godric wiped his face, hand rasping over his scruffy beard. Valentine waited for him to say something.

'Ah.' She grinned at Johanna. 'I forget. You terrify me because you're my mother. I was never afraid of you as a cabinet minister. Other people are. Miles, she's seen this already. I'd put money on it.'

'Wait outside.' Johanna Branwen watched Miles Godric to the

door. As it closed behind the big man, she began to read aloud, quickly at first, and then more slowly. 'Let me see: "the Ladie Johannah" has a speech here . . .

> *"My damnèd daughter fled the Western Land*
> *As sly thieves flee, my agents circumventing—*
> *And mark me, servant, those must be abused*
> *In keeping with my curious wit's desire:*
> *Condemn them to a lower prison cell*
> *For five long years; and for my daughter's fate*
> *Let her be calumniated with all vile*
> *Rumour, and her feckless husband too.*
> *The world must well believe that they are mad,*
> *That done – and other lies which I'll suggest—*
> *They'll speak in Sphinx's riddles to the world,*
> *And not a world of words will be believed." '*

Johanna gave a chuckle. 'Interesting. I would have sworn the security systems around my office were impregnable. But then, of course, there's no such thing as an unsurveillable target. But why this doggerel? And why try to pass it off as direct neural input?'

Valentine said, 'You're not shocked that I now know you were behind the smears.'

'I'm hardly ever shocked, you should know that.'

'Yes.'

'And if this is an attempt to do it—'

The older woman broke off. Valentine looked up from the coffee-and-guano stained papers. Johanna held two sheets of printout in her hands. She sat down, without looking behind her, on the sofa. A Tawny Owl blinked at her with flat, back-lit gold eyes.

'And that,' she said, 'is one of the penalties of an extremely rapid reading-speed. One takes things in too quickly. Takes in the poison with the apple, as it were . . .'

Valentine sat beside her. The soft sofa threw them together, hip to hip in close proximity. The cool of the woman, in that summer afternoon heat, brought back other, older memories. Valentine traced down the page with her fingertip. 'Let's see? Um . . . a "Secretarie" says:

> *"Ambassadors from foreign potentates*
> *Would speak with you; and you yourself will speak*
> *And dine with those who curry favours from you . . ."*

Then "Johannah":

> *"See you this blade? It hath an edge so sharp*
> *Nought in this world may match it, save my wit,*
> *Which so excels the common run of men*
> *That you may rightly say, I rightly rule." '*

Valentine raised an eyebrow. 'Oh. Your knife. Did you say that?'

Johanna Branwen leaned forward, her hands clasped together in her lap. 'After a fashion, I may have . . . implied that. But one would have to know me better than most to guess at it.' She began to pull on soft leather gloves.

Valentine read on. 'Stage directions. "Lady Johannah as in a dream. Enter to her her child Valentinia, attended by demons, at several doors." Demons?'

The older woman said, 'We all have demons.'

Valentine read aloud. ' "First demon":

> *"We come as heralds of the coming day*
> *When Dies Irae is loosed upon the world.*
> *All that men know, all men now shall share   " '*

She stopped, and began again:

> *' "All that men know, all men now shall share,*
> *As once Pandora loosed upon the world*
> *All ills and sores that tetter on your skins.*
> *O Man! Beware. At her hand, hope was left.*
> *What hope for you?"*

Then "Mephistophilis" . . .

> *"All in the balance lies.*
> *Whether this be the work of my Dread Lord,*
> *Or whether it shall be that after this*
> *Man shall partake of angel qualities*
> *Having the angels' knowledge of the earth,*
> *Remains unknown until this fruit is tried." '*

The sun's warmth filled the room, filtering in golden. The smell of droppings and dead meat stuffed the nostrils. Luka was in the kitchen, banging pans. Starting with the old peregrine on the corner perch, the hawks screeled. Wasps buzzed. Valentine breathed out a long breath. '*Did* you dream?'

'Good God! In the middle of a heavy day with parliament sitting? No, I did not dream.'

'I . . . You had me worried there for a minute.'

Johanna snorted. 'This is pure fiction.'

'Is it?' Valentine said. 'Is it? Impure fiction, at least. Oh, I *see*.

"VALENTINIA": "We make the world anew. Not shame nor pity
Stays our hand. What though disaster come?
Power's not bred without pain, nor love from mirth.
We choose to loose the dogs upon the world:
Heralds or hell-hounds, let Time choose their courses."

"MEPHISTOPHILIS": "How is this different? How is this the same?"

"JOHANNAH": "The governing of man, for good or ill,
Is mine. Such a Medusa's art it is,
It hardens we who wrestle it to stone.
Pity I have not, love I never knew.
Thus you'd excuse me, daughter of my womb,
For actions taken when my course is plain.
How then, for actions similar, excuse you?
Necessity we both claim for our god."

"MEPHISTOPHILIS": "Bred in one cradle, sister more than mother;
Fighting the world behind the self-same blade.
How could you fail but recognise the other,
Mirrored in action, thought, desire and deed?
But like likes not its image painted well:
Avoids it as it were the mouth of Hell." '

Valentine paused again. And then, as if it were not the first thing in her mind, said, 'So this never actually happened. So what? There are personal database records. Psychological profiles. *That's* what's going on here. Some process is synthesising data.'

'Synthesising?'

'Extrapolating. Creating. That's my guess. It's like the "Spy" and "Lady Regret" scene between Miles and Rue – it isn't what did happen, it's what *should* have happened. It would have helped Rue to talk, then. And this—'

Johanna Branwen interrupted. 'You realise, this kind of inter-polated fictional conversation makes the more genuine sections useless for blackmail.'

'If I'd ever wanted to use them for that, yes. Is that what you thought?'

The older woman said sharply. 'Don't be ingenuous. It was always one of your worst faults.'

Valentine let out a long, relaxing sigh. 'I admit it.' And, after some seconds' thought, let the remark stand on its own.

Johanna Branwen said, 'Who created this recording? Whose idea was it to use surveillance techniques to produce, for want of a better word, a psychodrama?'

'This is what Baltazar Casaubon's system architecture produced out of what the medical scans read from Miles's brain activity. Nothing more. Nothing less.'

'Perhaps something more.' Johanna gripped Valentine's arm. 'What is being that creative? Is there anything else you want to bring to my attention before I find your Baltazar Casaubon?'

Guard down, pretence abandoned: the immediate feel of total honesty is heady. Drunk with it, Valentine said, 'Only that I think he dislikes you with as much reason as you dislike him. You're jealous. And he has to deal with the parts of me that are you. Because, oddly enough, I won't abandon them. They are part of me.'

After a moment, Johanna Branwen said, 'Personal matters aside, one of the matters I urgently want to take up with your husband is the current plague of database security corruption. I take it he's responsible? No, you needn't answer. No matter. This is more . . . more than I had anticipated.'

The woman brushed the fur of her collar back from her scarlet lips, murmuring into the Rolex comlink. Steel-and-silver curls plastered her forehead in the enclosed heat. Nonetheless, as the middle-aged woman stood up, Valentine saw her shiver.

Valentine started to speak: thought better of it.

Johanna Branwen regarded her daughter. 'You worked on artificial intelligence projects for the American military.'

'Yes, everybody did, at one time or another, but we didn't get anything. Just complex expert systems. You think *this*—' Valentine stared. Her mirrorshade lenses obscured as she blinked, rapidly. '*Be real*. Things like artificial intelligence don't happen by accident!'

'No.' The older woman stood. 'They don't, do they?'

CHAPTER 12
In the English Renaissance Memory Garden

Early heat echoes from the enclosing brick walls of the Garden of Scents.

Miles Godric typed, with one unsteady finger, *Ten mins. flying time north London. No border checks. Security safe house? Ministry of Defence? Ministerial w/end retreat? No contact media!* and encrypted the file on his subnotepad.

Another blazing morning's sun is hot on the cloth of his combat pants, already burns his fair-skinned muscular arms under his short-sleeved T-shirt. He feels bare and unbalanced without his video equipment.

'Of course I'm scared,' he admitted. 'I'm not stupid. You're a very influential woman in this government. I've already stretched things about as far as I can go. Technically I'm an accessory to industrial espionage, if the US ever decide to prosecute Baltazar Casaubon.'

'Military espionage,' Johanna Branwen corrected mildly. 'I think you'll find it carries a higher penalty.'

Miles rubbed the socket of his right eye, hard, and blinked through retinal sun-blotches. His palm rasped against his beard. 'It hasn't been declared an illegal act, yet, Minister. And I've got a contract. Despite your forcing me to sign the Official Secrets Act.'

'Purely a formality,' the minister says, with a note of humour in her voice that Miles reinterprets at least twice. 'Curiously enough, I'm still not averse to you making a substantial and satisfactory amount of money out of this, Mr Godric. It's merely that the national interest will have to be satisfied before you do. Otherwise, regretfully, I will authorise your extradition to the Confederate States.'

Carrot and stick.

Madam a scribe is what I am. Or if
You like it better saye I am a spy.

He remembers how Val's expert system 'Kit Marlowe' grinned at him, a morphed portrait of the past in a VR future world. Doctor Faustus. More than anything, Miles thinks, I need to understand what has happened to me. No access to databases, MultiNet, his own neural recordings. He feels bereft.

'You'll have to let me go in first,' Val Branwen said, not to him. 'First. Alone.'

She knelt on hot flagstones, face bent close to the sparse camomile that covered an area around a sundial, inhaling the plant's scent. She wears a pair of expensive spectacles with thin gold rims, mirrorshade contact lenses abandoned in their compulsory trip north. Even Val's stuck without cleanser. Miles Godric grinned, leaning his large body further back on his bench, under the mild shade of a palmate-leafed creeper.

Two ornamental stone fish fountains spouted water, splashing in the silence.

' "Go in"? Impossible. Even if he were located.' The minister, Johanna Branwen, stood unprotected under the blazing sun. A middle-aged woman with expensive perfume and high quality sports clothes. Familiar from morning studio briefings, but never known. He may have processed a feature on her about three years back, it isn't clear in his mind. Until yesterday he has never spoken to any politician outside of his technician's role.

This is too much, too high, too dangerous.

Try as he might, he can see no physical resemblance between the two of them. Val might take after some hypothetical father, he speculates, assuming anyone had ever dared engage Johanna Branwen in anything so carnal as coitus; and his rambling mind snapped back into focus after twelve hours of lights, caffeine, interrogation, stimulant drugs, and a small cream-walled office with heavy-duty recording equipment that hadn't seemed to belong in the house here.

The Elizabethan candy-stick brick chimneys are all that can be seen of the palace, over the green tops of the pleached lime walk. Miles breathed in lavender, camomile, roses, and a hundred other plants of whose names he would never bother to become aware. Plants cared for by people who exist to function, not to be noticed by those with power or privilege.

He *wants* that privilege. Has he wanted it so badly he has permitted something terrible to be done to him?

'If Baltazar has any sense he'll be out of the country by now,' Miles said.

Both the women turned their heads to look at him with identical expressions.

'Ah. Now I know what it feels like to be *completely* superfluous.' He eased back, brows raised, and dropped his hand down to the bone china cup of coffee in which (despite it not being past nine in the morning) he had required a lacing of brandy.

Val sat back on her heels. 'Shut up, Miles. OK, Baltazar might have run. I don't think so. I think he's still in London. He will run, if you send MI6 and the Met and the army down on him like a ton of bricks. Let me handle it.'

'Ridiculous. Even the supposition that you might do that is ridiculous.'

'You'll frighten him off, you'll never find him. I know what he's like! If he's *really* interested in not being found, it'll take you months. Years, maybe.'

Miles hears an unspoken conclusion to that sentence: *You haven't got that long.*

The early sun coloured the brick walls peach. Heat beat down on the garden, in whose thickets of leaves and fleshy stems some dew remained still moist. Birds called. The bright colours of nameless flowers shimmered. A bee drifted past, body hanging at an angle in the air. Lack of sleep and close interrogation left him with a mind able to slip its ratchet. The coffee and brandy bit at his duodenum.

The younger woman rose without swaying, balance utterly sure. He flexed blunt fingers. The feel of her shoulders and curved back, taut under the white shirt, is not so distant from his memory. He finds himself thinking, without any real sense of connection, of her thin waist, and the Ingram girl's thin arms, and the huge solidity of Dorothea Casaubon. Flesh to be romped over, kneaded, dived into.

'Withholding information on a matter of national security would be an indictable offence in peacetime. As matters stand, I'm afraid it's rather more serious than that.'

'I don't know where he is!'

'Yet you assume that you can find him.'

'It helps that I know what I'm looking for. I was married to the man, remember? That beats a security services psychological profile any day!'

Miles abandons the empty cup and the bench, lurching to his feet, scuffed combat boots trudging the brilliance of the garden walks among flower beds. White Classical statues haunt the undergrowth. He notices that the sundial is wrong by an hour: Pan European Standard Time. Its verdigrised copper glows.

This place is full of *but*. The military helicopter landed on the gravel car park in front of the hall unchallenged, but. No perimeter security is visible, but. His interrogators did not state what department authorised them, but.

No one has said he is under arrest. But.

He can't hear a rifle cock, but every time he comes within a certain distance of Johanna Branwen a small red dot appears on his chest. A red-dot laser sight. The same dot appears, too, on Val's white shirt if she approaches the limits of secure distance.

'It's *my* Marlowe play!' he calls. 'Recorded from in *here*.' Hitting the side of his head with the heel of his hand. Wincing. 'Jesus H. Christ, do you *know* how much I'm going to lose in income if I can't use this?'

'Please be quiet, Mr Godric.'

Something flicks past him with a whirr of feathers. A bird, he realises, and straightens up from a low flinch with embarrassment.

'I'm sick to death of *shut up, Miles*.' He walked to Val, looking down at her sun-caught face. She blinked. 'I want to know what you've done. Whatever the status of direct neural input software, that isn't all that's going on here, is it?'

The woman shrugged.

Miles closed his big hands on her shoulders. 'No. No, you don't do that to me. I know that most of the medical tests I've been put through in the last twelve hours are to do with neurological damage.'

'Oh – no, that isn't it. There's nothing.' The red-headed woman shrugged again, a little helplessly, backing off; and snatched off her spectacles, clutching them in her palm. Her gaze went briefly to her mother.

Johanna Branwen seated herself on the wooden garden bench. She inhaled scent from the lavender beds.

'As far as my people can find out,' she said, 'the public auction, if I may call it that, of direct neural reading of the human brain, preceded by only a few hours the sabotage of security in government, City of London financial, police, military, medical, university and social services databases.'

'Sabotage of security?'

'Beginning with my own ministerial database.' The older woman looked at Val.

'Police? Military? . . .' Miles said.

'Across the board,' Johanna said, distastefully, in verbal quotes, as if the cliché were painful to her, and added with no more stress, 'I hardly think it to be coincidental. Since my government has as yet had no ransom demands, and no political leverage from . . . elsewhere, it seems to me that Baltazar Casaubon, having surfaced here, is a likely candidate for such irresponsible sabotage.'

'Sabotage,' Miles repeated for the second time, and caught himself with an impatient shake of the head. 'Security compromised. Government files, defence projects, bank accounts, industrial patents, credit records—'

> *We come as heralds of the coming day*
> *When Dies Irae is loosed upon the world.*
> *All that men know, all men now shall share.*

'Anyone else would have made capital from it before now?' he speculated.

'I cannot imagine otherwise.'

'This is going to break!'

'Of course. It already is. People talk,' the minister said dismissively. 'We are containing the problem, but cannot continue indefinitely, which is why I am not willing to allow Baltazar Casaubon any chance of leaving the country.'

The sun makes the stone of the sundial hot under his forearms where he leans on it. The hot metal bites at his skin. Miles Godric breathes deeply of the scents of the garden. His eyes follow the flick of bees across the marble whiteness of nymphs, fauns, satyrs.

'That many different databases? Could even Baltazar come up with something that would crack the security of so many different operating systems?' He frowned. 'There's a theoretical easy back door into Unix, but that doesn't apply to . . . and there are so many ways to encrypt data!' He held up his subnotebook in Johanna's direction. 'Ok, you can run an algorithm that will crack the password on my public key encryption files, but it won't give you a result within the lifetime of this galaxy! The possible numbers are too huge. You're talking encryption depending on two *eight-figure* prime numbers.'

He sat down, spine to the stone sundial, careless of the camomile crushed under his boots. The scent drowned him. 'Unbreakable security codes. It's the classic mathematical thing – the travelling salesman formal Non-P problem. You have a map of PanEurope and you want to work out the quickest route by which the salesman can visit every city once only, without backtracking or crossing his route. Two cities gives you two possible routes. Three cities gives

you six routes. Four cities gives you nine . . . no, twenty-five . . .
no: I forget. When it gets to sixty cities, forget it. The factors
involved are so complex that the processing required to work this
out would take several lifetimes of the universe, and even then you
wouldn't know if it were the best route, or just 98 per cent best . . .'

A voice chuckled. It was Val, but Val watching Johanna
Branwen.

'Now I feel like little Rue,' the red-headed woman said, 'telling
you *But you don't understand the information age!*'

'I have people to do that for me,' the cabinet minister said
tranquilly. 'Besides, I do know the mathematics of Non-P problems.
Why does one's child always assume one to be living in the past? I
know that without unimaginable amounts of processing power,
which no one has, data security cannot be breached. And yet it
is.'

The shadow on the sundial imperceptibly moves.

'What you do,' Valentine Branwen said, 'is, you spend four years
working on security projects for the US military. You don't work
out a way to solve Non-P problems. Eventually you develop an
algorithm that *converts* a Non-P problem into a P problem – makes it
solvable in a feasible amount of time, with a best-case answer.
Which is the same thing, really.'

Her hand touches Miles Godric's muscular shoulder. He stares.

Johanna Branwen glances at empty air. It is the first and only
sign Miles has had to confirm that they are being recorded.

Val says, 'I put the algorithm in a piggyback program with the
direct neural input software. I knew that was going to get spread
round a *lot* of databases. I wanted everyone to have access to it. I'm
good at viruses that virus-killers can't detect. I put the code-breaker
algorithm into a self-replicating worm virus – with an expert system
to activate it at random intervals.'

Silence in the garden.

Miles Godric, weakly, said, 'Oh, Jesus.'

'Not unless he's an expert programmer.' Johanna Branwen's
voice is deeper, richer, dropping into notes of irony and unbelief
that Miles has never yet heard. 'Baltazar Casaubon could be this
stupid, this irresponsible. But that *you* could. Valentine, Valentine.
You knew what the implications were. Are. *Why?*'

'Because I can,' Val Branwen said. 'Somebody told me – we're
not nice people.'

'A software program that opens encrypted files, disseminates
information,' the minister said. 'I begin to see the shape of this . . .
artificial intelligence program.'

'Mother, there is Baltazar's architecture, and there's my algorithm; there is no artificial intelligence project!'

The heat swells a bubble of scents: shrub, border plant, climbing vine, flower. Miles Godric sneezes once, minutely, like a kitten. Wiping his nose, surprised, he said, 'There could be.'

He saw that both of them were staring at him.

'Something,' he said, 'produced *The Spy at Londinium*.'

Johanna Branwen walked through the palace rooms as if they were her home.

Valentine carried her shoes in her right hand, bare feet padding over the parquet flooring. This seemed to be one of those Elizabethan country mansions, just short of a royal palace, that had ceased to be fiddled about with in the eighteenth century. If she cared about it she could have identified it. Portraits looked down from pale green and white walls on to white-and-gold furniture.

In the high-ceilinged, sunny drawing-room that they entered, men in suits quietly vanished into corners, except for one burly man with a Parisian accent who matched his steps to Johanna as she moved to close the French windows. He spoke rapidly to her. Valentine looked out at blue sky, tree-tops. No traffic, no twentieth-century buildings. The occasional military vehicle.

Heavy desks occupied one side of the room. She wandered over to a workstation, dropped her shoes, and attempted to log on to whatever political, military or security mainframe might be available.

'There is,' Johanna's voice said beside her, 'the matter of your children. My grandchildren. I think they should stay in England.'

'With you.'

Valentine ran an immediate self-check on the system. It gave her, almost incidentally, their geographical location.

'Neither your bigamous ex-husband nor his first wife, admirable though her genetic research programmes may be, seem capable of raising motivated children.'

Valentine sat back. Her gold-rimmed glasses slid down the sweat on the bridge of her nose. ' "Motivated".'

'I should hardly like them to grow to adulthood resembling their father. Or, indeed, their mother.'

Valentine swore and attempted to hack into the Land Use Registry by a different route. That failing, she abandoned it for import and export registries. Data flicked by on the active colour screen.

'Whatever makes you think I'd let you take Jared and Jadis?'

'I can't imagine. Unless it's the way you let their father have custody, and leave their upbringing to his family or to Izumi Teishi's family.'

'I wouldn't give a dog into your care, never mind my children.'

'Oh, *Val*entine.'

Specialist medical equipment orders gave her the first clue. She hacked into the London hospital administrative databases. Some of the dates on the orders seemed reasonable. Metropolitan Police records? Abandoning the connection with Land Registry, still unavailable, she resorted to transport firms. Guessing, she ran several quick data searches. She sat back in frustration.

'Izumi's maternal. They like her. California's – well. California, I suppose.' Valentine glanced up. 'I won't have Jared and Jadis anywhere near the PanEuropean war.'

'Not even vicariously, when Jared hacks into SIMNET? He is quite bright for an eleven-year-old.'

Restricted information, pride and oneupmanship become, Valentine thinks, sickly in private matters, no matter how effective in the public sphere. Bloody old woman.

The hum of hard discs behind her, and the conversations of Johanna's staff, made no more than a surface impression on her mind. For the sake of it she took a broad scan through Social Welfare mainframes, and blinked at the ease and quantity of files available. An alarm went off somewhere behind her. Johanna quieted the voices with a gesture.

'Is that really relevant?' A waspish note in the older woman's voice. 'Or are you merely curious as to the damage you've done?'

'Merely curious. As to my children . . . I would rather let Izumi have them. They love her. It's safer.'

'Than me?'

'Than *me*.' Valentine hacked into her own small network back at the flat and ran a retrospective on modem use by anyone other than herself.

'Now that's odd,' she mused. 'OK. I know where he is. Even if I don't know why he's there.'

There was a silence from the rest of the room, and a second's startled glance from Johanna. Actually startled. Valentine smiled.

'Oh, come on. I know the man. I know what I'm looking for.'

'Are you certain?'

'Of course not. But it's my best-guess result. You can see for yourself . . .'

Johanna leaned over, one soft cold hand gripping Valentine's shoulder. Her perfume drowned the smell of sunlight and cigarettes. She was shorter than Valentine remembered.

She said, 'He's in a theatre?'

Rue Ingram and Frankie Hollister walked down the steps together from the anonymous modern office building. They did not look at each other. When, as if by mutual decision, they halted on the pavement, neither spoke to the other.

Gridlocked cars stretched away down Whitehall from the Ministry of Defence building. Summer nights are cold enough to wake pavement sleepers at four a.m. Snotty-nosed children, up for hours, watch Rue, watch Frankie. A man in blue slacks moves away from the side road as if he has been waiting for them. A clear-complexioned young man with short hair and a skinny, muscular body.

'Rue?'

She recognises what the flight lieutenant wears when he's off-duty.

'Rue, are you all right?'

Frankie Hollister begins to plod away east. Back towards home. Rue follows. She ignores the building beside her, only her shoulder on that side is tense, as if she is hunched slightly away from the concrete and glass.

'I knew you'd be released.'

She makes no answer.

'Rue.' A hand on her arm, stopping her walking. She looks down at it.

'I brought you this,' Wynne Ashton says. What he holds is an old, very creased piece of paper. She unfolds it. Poster-painted. Childishly painted.

He says, 'My mum – my adopted mum – she keeps some drawings I did in primary school. That's her, my dad, and me.'

All three the same: blobs with yellow hair, pink skin.

'They know one of them has to be me because it's the smallest.' He watched her closely. 'Twenty-five years ago, if you wanted to adopt a baby, you could only get babies of colour. That's why I won't take Closed London citizenship. It's a fraud. The only reason *I* qualify is because I'm serving in the armed forces. Do you understand, now, why—'

Rue Ingram tore the painting across once and dropped it, and walked away.

His resonant voice behind her said, 'Bitch!'

*

An hour in the Garden of Scents sunburned his forearms painfully, and reddened the tender skin at the nape of his neck. Miles Godric sprawled on gravel, his back against the walled garden's brick wall, smoking a French cigarette he had bummed off one of the security guards at the wrought-iron gate.

'He's in a *theatre*?' Miles stared up.

Val's face against the sun was invisible, her hair a red corona.

'What the hell is he doing there?'

'A disused theatre,' Val corrected herself. She squinted behind her UV spectacles. The faint throb of a helicopter echoed from all points of the horizon. 'I suppose because it's the least likely place.'

Miles stood and ground out the cigarette under his boot. Its scent mingled with the scents of the garden. A soft, large white rose brushed his face. He saw Johanna Branwen standing on the steps leading down into the garden, conferring with a secretary. Shadows pooled at their feet. He longed for the shade of the lime walk behind them.

Now Phoebus' chariot mounts the morning sky . . .

'Let me guess. The minister *now* says she plans to keep you and me in protective custody until the security teams snatch him?'

'Something like that.' Her hand, browned from long training in the sun, stroked the petals of the rose. She sniffed at her fingers. She swung round, facing Johanna.

'If something goes wrong, if he's hurt, shot, how are you going to explain that?'

'Don't be ridiculous, Valentine. I'm fully aware of his value as a resource, if nothing else.'

'By the time you can mount a security operation, he won't be there. For Christ's sake, Mother, your data security is fucked! Every time you use a phone, a modem, shortwave radio . . . He can watch what you're doing, while you're doing it!'

> *Devices like to Bacon's brazen head*
> *That spoke and said,* Time is, was, and will be,
> *Speak unto him, and tell him far-off news.*
> *This clown, master of witty devices,*
> *Perils his fat soul: spy, go seek him out . . .*

'There is,' Miles Godric said, 'something I have to tell you.'

Neither of them paid attention. Val Branwen, face taut, fists clenched, body-language of a fourteen-year-old, yelled, 'He'll see who's coming in, and the only person he'll stay still for is me! You have to let me go in alone and talk to him. Jesus Christ, I want to know what's happened as much as you do!'

'And have both of you vanish?' The minister spoke softly. 'I'm sure I can convince your ex-husband that your future happiness depends on his cooperation.'

> *. . . Whether it shall be that after this*
> *Men shall partake of angel qualities*
> *Having the angels' knowledge of the earth . . .*

Whatever it is, it talked to me.

Still missing the weight of cameras at his belt, Miles walked forward until the red dot sight appeared on his sand-coloured T-shirt. He scratched through his dusty hair, and tried not to loom over the older woman.

'If government security is falling down around your head, that has to be a primary concern. Maybe as a newschannel man that's what I should be most interested in, but . . . Minister, it's *my* neural input that was used here. If there *is* an artificial intelligence, or the slightest beginning of something that could lead to one, then that's what I've been interacting with.'

Johanna Branwen watches him in the Renaissance garden.

'I've gotten tired,' Miles says, 'of being told things are not my concern. I'm doing my job, Minister. Wire me up. I'll go in with Val. I'll tell Baltazar it's a live link out to the rolling news media. Online and on record. Tell Baltazar Casaubon that's how you'll guarantee his safety – nothing can happen on camera. I'm sure you can make it *appear* that the broadcast is going out.'

A half smile appears at the corners of her mouth. Familiar from satellite news broadcasts, from hard copy paper news.

He said, 'Baltazar Casaubon created the software for direct neural input, and Val solved the code-cracker algorithm, and do you know what, Minister? If this is a true artificial intelligence that's come out of their project, you need to be first with it. You need to go cautiously. You *cannot* afford to lose either of the people who created it.'

CHAPTER 13
The Armour of Light

Baltazar Casaubon was not in the riverside office-block basement that did duty as the Rose Theatre Museum.

Valentine Branwen gave the museum's PR equipment a cursory glance, left Miles puzzling, and walked towards the fire exit.

'Val—!'

Valentine walked outside. The stink of river mud hit her. Midday sun blazed down. She welcomed the heat, the smells; all equally enjoyable to her sensual appetites.

'Down here!' a muffled voice called, as the fire door clanged behind her.

She walked across to a wall and leaned her arms on the brickwork. A breeze blew off the river Thames and into her face. Barely cool. And smelling of fish, of weed, and of diesel-engined tourist boats. She lifted a hand and waved to a passing passenger cruiser. Distant hands waved back.

She leaned further over and looked down.

Sitting with his buttocks overflowing a sunken oil-drum, and his white trousers rolled up to his vast knees, Baltazar Casaubon sat spread-legged with his bare feet in the river. Scum ridged his ankles. He wiped a muddy hand through his copper-gold hair and beamed up at her.

'Hello, my little one. Thought you'd turn up before long.'

The mud smells of mortality. Here the wooden wharves crack with the heat, and green-shrouded rocks jut up from the shoreline. A few yards away in tidal mud, a half-sunken bicycle trailed weed from its rusted spokes. A gull swooped low, calling.

He seemed, physically at least, to be unharmed.

She warned, 'I've got Miles Godric with me.'

Baltazar Casaubon stood. His feet sucked deep into the mud. His head down, ponderously watching where he stepped, he began to make his way ashore. She reached down one arm, impulsively, and when he had gotten ashore he reached up and took it, smearing her wrist with cool mud.

'If I were you, I'd hurry,' Valentine said.

'Oh, I think Johanna – it is Johanna? – will contain her impatience, don't you?' He picked his nose magisterially. 'This is a most wonderfully insoluble conundrum!'

Valentine glared at him with tawny-orange eyes. 'I'm glad somebody thinks so!'

Miles Godric thought, Don't I remember this from a school trip, once?

The surviving parts of the Elizabethan Rose Theatre – post-holes, pit floor, and audiences' hazel nut refuse, mostly – seemed crushed under the low concrete ceiling of the office-block basement. A clerestory window let some sun trickle into the stuffy room. Around the walls, hologram projectors and Virtual Reality stations cluttered the bare boards. Tacky strip-plastic labels advertised (erroneously, he noted) *Shakespeare's Rose*, together with live actions of *Doctor Faustus: The First Night*. His mouth quirked, reading that.

'The hologram equipment?' the red-headed woman suggested. As if she had guessed the right answer to a problem without knowing why it was the right answer.

'The hologram equipment.' Baltazar Casaubon stripped rapidly to his string vest and underpants, and seated himself at a table with his immense back to the museum exhibit. He hunched over a keyboard and flat-screen monitor; a half-empty bottle of Lambrusco rosé at his elbow.

Miles rubbed at his face. Sweat filmed his skin. He panned automatically, sweeping the piles of equipment it was obvious did not belong to the museum: old monitors, chip circuit diagrams, camcorders, other stuff. The implant mike behind his ear approved: *'Lots of anti-surveillance gear in there, Miles.'*

Morgan Froissart's voice.

'I'm keeping you on realtime recording.'

He thumbed the acknowledgement key.

'Baltazar. You're online and on record.'

'Oh yes. I know.'

Miles walked across the room and dumped a printout into the fat man's lap. He ignored Baltazar's startled yelp. The stack of paper slid, concertinaed, and began to cascade to the floor.

'I know about the algorithm. I want to know what else is going on!' Miles hooked his thumbs in the back of his camera belt, watching Casaubon's flushed, startled face.

'Algorithm?' the man squeaked.

Val squatted down on her haunches. She swept the printout into a pile, picked it up, and dumped it back on Baltazar Casaubon's table.

A small smile, instantly extinguished, crossed his fat features. 'You did it. You actually did do it.'

Baltazar Casaubon glanced back up over his shoulder. The woman nodded once, only a slight movement of the chin; her expression preoccupied. Something between the two of them cut Miles out: a communication as wordless as it was exclusive.

'I thought it must be you,' he said smugly.

Miles snapped, 'Have you read this?'

'In part.' Obediently, the fat man thumbed up the first page. His delicately-shaped lips moved silently as he read.

The small, airless room made Miles ache for rain; for cool drinks in a bar; for forgetfulness. The long silence was broken only by the flick of pages as Baltazar Casaubon skim-read the remaining verse.

Miles snarled, 'Never mind the bloody play! I want to know why it exists. What it means!'

Baltazar Casaubon lifted his nose out of the stage directions and gave him a pained look.

'I think it's a damned nerve! "Fatte clowne", indeed!'

'Never mind your vanity.' Valentine wiped a blotch of bird-shit off one sheet of the printout. 'Re-access the original neural record. I want to look.'

'And I don't even get more than fifty speaking lines in the whole—'

'*Casaubon!*'

'—play. Psychodrama. Whatever term you prefer. I have *finally* got the system up and running again,' he added, with more hurt dignity than seemed possible for one man to accrue. 'I was merely pondering my next action when you arrived.'

'The "play" is a fake.' Miles spoke quietly. 'And it could be said, couldn't it, that that discredits direct neural recording?'

Baltazar Casaubon regarded him with a glacial calm. 'No one said information technology was going to be one hundred per cent reliable. There will always be lies, and misinformation, and primary sources are few and far between, and even the provenance of *those* is not proven. To think otherwise is to be technophile and simplistic.'

'I—' Miles spluttered.

'And besides, this is not direct neural architecture as I structured it. What it has produced is an electronic data forgery – of a kind. The question is,' Baltazar Casaubon finished magisterially, 'what nature of forgery? Done how, and for what purpose?'

A crackle broke the silence. Miles looked to see Val Branwen, one hip resting up on the rail that surrounded the sixteenth-century architectural remains, tinkering with the tuning of her wrist VDU. It was quiet enough in the museum that he heard the broadcast clearly.

'—and the stock market panic brought on yesterday by the major High Street banks closing their public services shows no sign of abating. Tokyo and New York are expected again to follow suit when the markets re-open.

'A government spokesman strenuously denied that the integrity of confidential data in MI6 and the Department of Social Welfare has been compromised.

'Rolling news channels this morning carried excerpts from the confidential medical records of Members of Parliament, Chief Constables across PanEurope, and the Royal Family. A High Court injunction failed to—'

'Sabotaging the banking system was a mistake,' she observed.

'I don't make mistakes,' the fat man said loftily. 'Although I admit sometimes my timing may leave something to be desired.'

Val snorted. 'You're telling me! You're sitting here, and I know what you're thinking about. US security snatch squads. European SWAT teams. The Ministry of Defence and the Metropolitan Police. You're scared shitless.'

'Far from it,' the link-architect said loftily. He sat before monitor, phone, fax, and modem; glancing shrewdly up. 'Far from i— That wasn't a siren, by any chance, was it?'

Miles saw the woman momentarily let her hand rest against the greasy curls of hair at the back of the fat man's neck, as if his flesh warm against her knuckles comforted her.

'All this is probably just an expert system run wild.' She sounded unconvinced. 'That's all.'

The link-architect rested his immense elbows on the desk, and his chin on his interlaced fingers. 'The trouble with you two,' he mused, 'is that you worry too much.'

Valentine cuffed him smartly across the side of the head.

The midday sun slanted down into the room, scattering across the improvised control desk. Smartcard modules lay in heaps. Casaubon made a long arm across the desk and picked up a sandwich, spilling jam across a keyboard as he bit into the bread.

'Whatever it is . . . it seemes to be an integral . . .' The fat man spouted crumbs. '*Integral* part of direct neural architecture.'

Miles reached down a finger and touched the spilt jam, and lifted his finger to his lips. Strawberry. A movement flickered in the corner of his eye. A fat white rat, its fur spiky with jam and butter, sat up beside the corner of one keyboard and cleaned its spring-wire whiskers. Baltazar Casaubon snapped his fingers. The rat ran, jumped, clung to his shirt, and scuttled up to sit on his broad shoulder, scaly tail dangling. Casaubon put his finger up for it to chew on.

'The question is, of course, why a sixteenth-century play?'

Miles stared him down. 'No – the question is, where did the additional input-data come from?'

Casaubon reached up across his expansive chest to scratch the pet rat behind its ears. Val Branwen leaned across him to access the system.

'The question is, why isn't it a plain recording of data? Let's find out,' she said.

Movement glinted in the corner of Miles Godric's eye. He fell silent.

The museum stage equipment began to show active tell-tales. A pale hologram light bloomed in the centre of the cramped room. Grey and glittery, with a hint of what might have been wings . . . The airless heat tightened about his throat. He swallowed. The holograms focused.

The Rose Theatre, reconstructed from a few fragments of wood and stone: octagonal white-plastered walls surrounding them, blue sky over their heads and over the peaked, thatched roofs of the galleries. Polished, painted wood gleamed.

Sunlight blazed out of invisible sources, glaring so that his eyes ran. He wiped the back of his wrist across his eyes. The hologram projection machinery vanished, hidden by three-dimensional images of raised stage, pillars, galleries crowded with Elizabethan play-goers (mouthing conversation in silence). The bare stage's back wall was painted so that it appeared, *trompe-l'œil*, as carved and columned; rioting with cherubs, Greek deities, angels, clouds, myth-ical beasts, and golden suns. The interior of a painted temple . . .

He shook his head and looked away. At the hologram's edges his vision skewed; then museum door and desk were plain and clear. The fat man had his head bent over the keyboard, muttering.

Val Branwen, dazzled, stared past him at the hologram scene with rising excitement. He turned back.

On the stage wall, among painted Renaissance cherubim, a

dispatch bike rider in leathers leans his way through the celestial traffic. Below, a train-rail gleams in the hills of Arcadia.

'Tampered with,' Casaubon announced, with satisfaction. 'Now we shall see . . .'

Miles stepped forward. A blot of dark light appeared an apparent few feet in front of him.

He focused his eyes on a tiny image that hung in mid-air, wings beating furiously. Minuscule blue eyes gleamed in a face surrounded by brown curls. The pink, naked *putto* sketched a bow, mid-air.

'Very funny,' Miles Godric said acidly.

The voice that issued from the speakers sounded several feet to the right of the *putto's* not-quite-synchronised lips.

'Baroque cherubs aren't to your taste? I can alter that. Remember, you contain *anima* and *animus* both within you.'

The voice itself . . .

'You heard a recording once. Very old. Of the last *castrato* singer.'

. . . a truly strange voice, one for which he has no referent; too low for a woman, but with nothing at all of a man about it.

The hologram blinked. An androgynous image grinned at him, hair auburn, eyebrows black, cheeks red. It quoted, 'A great reckoning in a little room . . .'

The VR 'Kit Marlowe' – and yet, not quite. Miles Godric screwed up his face, striving for concentration. The image of a young woman, or a young man, sat on the edge of the raised wooden stage. Across its black T-shirt was printed THIS IS NOT A RE-HEARSAL . . . As it twisted around to look into the wings, he read the back of the shirt . . . THIS IS REAL LIFE.

A demon peeped out from the uncurtained wings of the stage, and darted back.

'This is – you – you're Baltazar's link-architecture. I . . . *remember*.' His throat felt sore, constricted as with influenza. He swallowed several times without releasing that feeling. 'It is an artificial intelligence system.'

'Not precisely.' Now its hair is lion-yellow.

Sweat ran down his back. Seen close up, the resemblance is undeniable. His own face: reversed, as in a photographic image rather than a mirror, the image the way the world sees it. Leaner, younger, but none the less his own. A feather of hair shone, plastered to its forehead by apparent perspiration.

'You can call me system-name *Mephistophilis*.' A light-slip, disorientating as a landslip. His androgyne-self slid down to stand in front of him, dressed now in a sixteenth-century scholar's long buttoned black gown, still with the same appallingly familiar face.

'This shape becomes me best . . .' It surveyed him with guileless pale eyes. 'Shall I tell you what I am? And then we'll move on to the interesting stuff. Lines, circles, signs, letters and characters: Ay, these are those that Faustus most admires. Can you record me?'

Too deep a voice, too many harmonics and familiarities in it for ease of mind. Miles put his hands on his belt. 'I can record holo-images.'

He turned his back on the creations of light. 'Who wrote this program?'

Baltazar Casaubon leaned back in his chair, which creaked alarmingly. The white rat still squatted on his fat shoulder. 'Miles, my boy, this is your neural recording. It appears to have altered again.'

Val muttered, 'Miles, speak to it. Try to trigger another sequence.'

Miles turned back. The illusion of depth stretched the museum room out to the back of a bare stage. On the edge of hearing, Baroque music played. The androgyne sat again on the edge of the stage, legs jutting out from under the scholar's gown, heels kicking against the boards.

Miles rubbed his hand across the back of his neck, feeling sweat, and muscles tensed as hard as rock. 'Explain, then. You're what – a a computer-analogue written into the system, to make it accessible? Part of the link-architecture. A talking index. An expert system.'

The androgyne hooked its arms about one raised knee, resting its chin on its arms. Behind it, decoration crept up the pillars that supported the stage canopy: strapwork, cartouches, cherubs. The underside of the stage canopy glistened gold and blue, painted with sun, moon, and astrological constellations. The soundtrack mocked. 'Listen to the man who talks to architecture!'

Miles hesitated. Val's arm brushed him as she came to stand next to him.

'Anthropomorphism. It isn't the first time I've treated a reactive system as intelligent.' He grinned. 'What always got to me about the Turing test isn't how many programs pass it, but how many human beings fail it.'

Val chuckled, her tone for a moment almost as low as the hologram-image's. 'It sounds so self-directed. I swear it, Miles, it could be. It just could be. A real artificial intelligence . . .'

Morgan Froissart's voice prompted in his ear. '*Mr Godric, ask about the database corruption that's going on – ask if this is responsible. Ask if it's a side-effect of this program.*'

Miles opened his mouth to speak.

The hologram said, 'No, it isn't, not in the way you mean. And it isn't corruption, Miles Godric. Corruption is the last thing it is.'

Baltazar stared. Val Branwen took a sudden step forward. Sun leached into the museum hall. Distortion whorled in the image's hands. Used now to that photographic but altered resemblance, Miles began to feel some control coming back to him.

'It's accessing transmissions. It *is* using the code-cracker.' He demanded, 'Self-test. Explain what you are.'

The androgyne figure gathered its legs under it and stood, hands spreading out, taking in all the stage.

'I gave you the printout,' it said, in that low rich voice that was his, but somehow neither a man's nor a woman's. 'Did you ever see a play? And then did you ever go and see the same play put on by some other company? The words are the same, but the play is *different*. The experience is different. If you like, the text of the play is the stage upon which the experience takes place. The text remains the same, the play – the result – is different. Does that answer your question?'

Miles, a little blankly, said, 'No.'

The programmed hologram continued to speak. 'What you had recorded was eidetic memory, Miles. Memory from, if you like, the left hand side of the brain. Hard memory, like hard text. And what you get back from me is the play . . .'

It smiled. 'I'm not an Artificial Intelligence. I'm an Artificial Unconscious.'

CHAPTER 14
Games Software

Johanna Branwen sits in warm sunlight, blinded by goggles. The minutely faceted VR image she regards is that of Francis Walsingham, spymaster to Queen Elizabeth I. She recognises his features from one of the portraits in the gallery here.

'Neural networks?' She spoke over the VR game's soundtrack.

Morgan Froissart's voice concealed less of his exhaustion than his unseen face. 'It's one of our department's theories, Minister. You asked them to expedite possible models. If the architecture for the code-breaking algorithm were to have spread, corrupted a neural network experiment somewhere, that might account for what Mr Godric is currently interacting with.'

'It sounds unlikely to me.'

The virtual room she sits in is low-ceilinged with lead-paned windows, and a show-off pixel sunset going on outside over Elizabethan London. A tavern in Deptford. She has not, in two attempts at the game, managed to avoid historical necessity: the games-master expert system 'Kit Marlowe' lies once again dying through a stab into the eye. The player is on her own.

Walsingham says sadly, *'Master Marley could not be allowed to live and speak of this white magick. These Cabalistic wonder-working words are not for the common people. It is a secret of state, which we cannot allow freely to be known, for if all men knew and spoke the arcane tongue of angels, and thus spoke nothing but truth, how then might government be accomplished?'*

'My daughter fancies herself a satirist,' Johanna remarked.

'Another theory, Minister, is that direct input of brain activity into data storage, once it reaches a certain level of complexity, achieves consciousness spontaneously in the same manner as the human brain.'

'"Philosophy is odious and obscure,"' Johanna quotes, within the game and outside it.

Walsingham's trunk-hosed agents, feminine in ruffs, but with nothing effeminate about their thick-bladed chopping swords, move to guard the door of the tavern's upper room. One says, '*She knows the language of the angels. Shall I silence her mouth for ever, master?*'

Morgan Froissart, edgy and unseen, says, 'Quite, Minister. Another theory is that your daughter used the same expert system to structure the virus that dispersed the code-cracking algorithm as she did for SHAKESPEAREWORLD^{TM}. That would have incorporated her expert system into the architecture structuring direct neural data. But not, however, the historical period bias.'

Johanna moves the VR glove, triggering a games token she acquired early in the sequence. Her virtual hand removes the velvet mask from her face. Cleverly, a mirror on the tavern wall behind Walsingham shows her her own virtual features. Chalk-white maquillage. Tight, dyed auburn hair. Tudor nose. Her own yellow-tawny eyes.

Walsingham's jaw relaxes behind his thick beard. Amazed, he blurts, '*Your Majesty*—'

Morgan Froissart said, 'However, Minister, Miles Godric is known to have played the prototype version at your daughter's flat, before his neural output was recorded. Therefore, an interaction between his DNI and the original expert program . . .'

'Well done, thou good and faithful servant,' Johanna says lightly, and the virtual Walsingham bows his head in smiling relief. Removing the VR headset, she surprises an identical expression on Morgan Froissart's face.

'Minister?'

'It's of no consequence.' Johanna Branwen stops laughing. 'This theory accounts for the downloading of Godric's neural data in verse form, is that it? What are they doing?'

Morgan crosses the drawing-room towards the cluster of suddenly agitated technicians. A sky even more flamboyant than that over virtual Deptford lights the room orange. Johanna clicks her own monitor to the surveillance channel, studies the raw unprocessed camcorder image.

The screen abruptly blanks.

'I'm no tool of a police state. You can no more interrogate me than you could interrogate anybody's creative subconscious.'

The hologram display of the Artificial Unconscious grinned, mimicking conversations in voices a shade deeper than its own resonant tones.

' "Where were you on the night of the tenth?" "Fish!" It won't *work*, Miles.'

Its hologram lips continued to move just out of synch with the sound.

Bewildered, Miles Godric threw his hands up, gesturing helplessly. He turned to do a camscan that took in the dusty reality of half the museum hall: the fat man bending to let the rat scuttle down off his shoulder and into the pocket of his jacket hanging on the chair, and Val Branwen with her hands fisted and resting under her chin, an expression on her face that defied deciphering.

'What use is an Artificial *Un*conscious?' Miles demanded. 'What fucking use is a *subjective* database?'

Mephistophilis's image laughed. 'As well ask what's the use of any kind of creativity.'

Val Branwen leaned her small, muscular shoulders back against the room door. 'Do you know, you haven't triggered the same sequence again even once?'

Miles repeated, 'What use is an Artificial *Un*conscious?'

The contralto-tenor voice said, 'Miles Godric, do you want to hear what more I have to say? Shall I make spirits fetch you what you please? Resolve you of all ambiguities?'

He looked into the hologram of his own face, the image younger and more ambivalent. Taken from personnel records a decade ago. Acknowledging a limitless curiosity, he nodded in consent.

The speakers say, 'But this play will run without an audience.'

A dead channel hissed in his ear.

All outgoing transmissions of his camera equipment appeared to be functioning. But no response to the query key. And no voice of Morgan Froissart in his ear-mike. Nothing but dead air.

Instantly, he envisions the panicked transmissions among the soldiers and security officials, from however great a distance they are surveying the Rose Theatre; pictures the howling sirens, alerted marksmen, cordons thrown around the South Bank.

'Oh, shit,' Miles Godric says, fruitlessly attempting to punch a signal through. '*Shit*. This is where the roof falls in.'

Morgan Froissart held out the secure video-phone. 'It's the PM for you, Minister.'

Johanna Branwen nods, absently.

He said, 'With the Home Secretary, on a conference line.'

Johanna takes the phone. 'David. Richard. Yes . . . I concur. No. Regrettably, no. You are aware that there are no transmissions at the present moment that can be considered secure?'

The phone quacked.

'Oh, absolutely,' Johanna Branwen agreed. 'Only in person.'

The link-architect Casaubon lowered his head ponderously and sniffed first under his right armpit, and then under his left armpit. He beamed with amiable surprise.

'Oh, good . . .'

He got to his feet and padded across the room, and bent down to rummage in his discarded white jacket's pocket. His hand came out wrapped around a container tiny among the massive folds of his flesh. Cheerfully he upended it into his other hand, and began to pat and smooth handfuls of talcum powder under his arms, across the deep creases of fat at his chest and stomach, and between his tree-trunk thighs and behind his knees.

The air turned momentarily white.

'The heat,' he explained to Miles Godric.

The slick, sweat-abraded flesh at his elbows, chins, balls, and buttocks eased with application of the cool powder. He sneezed, inhaling by mistake, and put the tin of talcum back in his jacket pocket. He continued to prod through his heap of discarded clothing.

Godric waved his stocky arms. 'How can you be so calm! There are armed SWAT teams, police cordons around Southwark—'

'In which case I see no reason not to look my best, and be comfortable.'

Baltazar Casaubon, head bent, concentrated on pulling on the pair of white cotton trousers that, although marked with Thames mud and pavement dirt, were the cleanest garments in the pile.

'You used me! You let them think they could keep you under observation through me!'

'I used you,' Casaubon agreed.

Knowing that agreement can short-circuit anger. Or give a few useful moments of shock to manipulate. Memories of days arguing on committee, back-stage politicking, smoke-filled rooms and deviousness are clear in his mind.

'And I have no objection to being under observation. I merely prefer it to be a little more personal.' Baltazar Casaubon straightened and turned. He looked at the sharp, hungry face of the man. The sunlight slanted in through the closed shutters. Through the clerestory windows, the river gleamed in the heat that just began to lessen. The edges of the hologram projection twisted vision. Casaubon looked at the frozen image, then back at Miles Godric.

'Are you angry?' he marvelled, voice rumbling deep in his chest.

'This is a story some men would give their life to see, *boy*, and you're complaining that I chose you?'

He slitted his eyes comfortably in rolls of flesh, watching the younger man. Miles Godric moved with explosive sharp gestures.

'It's all out of control! Isn't it? What happens now, Baltazar? Do you know? No. Does she? No!'

'No,' Casaubon confessed. He sat down at the desk. The white rat poked twitching whiskers out from under a collection of micro-monitors. He winked at it. The rat turned tail and vanished.

'They're going to blame me,' Godric said. 'I'll never get a free-lance commission again.'

'My heart bleeds!' Casaubon got to his feet, towering a good six or eight inches over the younger man. He pointed with one pudgy finger at the frozen hologram, the androgyne figure in the archaic scholar's gown. 'Never mistake the nature of Mephistophilis. Do you hear me, boy? No matter how good a deal it seems – the nature of Mephistophilis never changes. I offered you a story. More than *a* story: *the* story. How direct neural input will happen and why the world won't be the same any more. And you have it, and you tried to command money and power by having it. But then you made a deal with Johanna. Now,' Baltazar Casaubon rumbled, 'she's col-lecting. Godric, I want you here, I want your recording equipment working, I want no argument about it.'

'I can't get a channel out!'

'You can still record.'

'Record *what*?'

Valentine's muffled voice, from the museum door, looking down Park Street, said, 'Here they come!'

Casaubon surveyed the room rapidly. He hooked his sandals out from under the desk and slipped them on, treading down the heels; and moved to position himself in the slatted sunlight from the clerestory windows. He listened for the faint whine of Godric's camcorders focusing.

The door banged open, one black-hooded man breaking to the left, the second to the right, and the third barrelling straight across the room to end up with his back slammed into the far wall, machine pistol trained on Casaubon. Casaubon made no extrane-ous movements. The door swung on its broken hinges. An order cracked out, outside. There are also the ones you don't see.

Valentine Branwen walked in, escorted, beside a plump, middle-aged woman.

The SAS team continued to cover entrances and exits.

Baltazar Casaubon returned his attention to the armed man

nearest himself. 'I regret,' he said, 'that I can't offer you any refreshments. But I suppose you can't drink on duty anyway?'

Something that sounded suspiciously like, 'No, sir,' came from under the black wool balaclava. The remainder of the team twitched.

'Johanna!' Casaubon drew himself up to his full height and directed a smile of wonderful sweetness at the woman following Valentine in. 'A pleasant surprise.'

'I think, neither.'

'Well, true,' Casaubon admitted. 'Even you had to realise – the more that secrecy becomes impossible, the more the powerful must do things in person. I thought you might be along.'

The woman rucked her jacket collar up around her ears, shivering, and regarded Miles Godric. 'What is the point of that, Mr Godric? None of your transmissions are being broadcast, as I have cause to know.'

'He can record,' Baltazar Casaubon said mildly. 'It's historic.'

'It's irrelevant,' Johanna Branwen said. 'There is, regrettably, no way to put this genie back in its bottle; however, there are successful measures that I am empowered to take.'

The plump woman glanced briskly from Casaubon to her daughter. 'City finance, medical records: these are minor inconveniences. The fact remains that, temporarily, you have caused a breakdown in the systems of government. The Prime Minister is of the opinion that the only option remaining is to put the country under martial law until things can be controlled.'

Valentine blurted, '*Martial law?*'

Johanna Branwen walked across the museum floor and stared up at the hologram theatre, and the still image.

'Regrettably, I have had to inform the Prime Minister that I cannot exercise that option. My advice to him is to sit on things, cover up, and hope no one realises how destabilised things are until we have them back under control. Given the war in Europe, we can't afford any more upset.' She spoke crisply. 'Administrative chaos is one thing, the market crashing is another; civil unrest, on the other hand, is absolutely not allowable. Fortress Europe only retains the UK and small areas of France and Spain; we *cannot* afford unrest here.'

Casaubon leaned on the back of the chair at his desk. It groaned but took the weight. He moved to seat himself comfortably in it, belly slumped down on his thighs, the rolls of flesh on his back bulging over the back of the chair. He hitched up the knees of his white cotton trousers. A cooling breeze blew in through the clerestory windows.

'Martial law.' He beamed at the armed team surrounding them.

'I have said that is not an option. Much as I regret it. The Prime Minister concurs.'

Valentine, voice unconsciously high, said, 'You can't avoid social unrest!'

Johanna smiled. 'I can avoid being out of office at the end of it. A combination of "open government" ideology broadcast by us, combined with apologies for the system breakdown, ought to do it. Now.' The woman swung around. 'You will release flawed copies of the codebreaking algorithm into the system to muddy the waters. Hopefully that will devalue the original to some degree. You will then work on encryption until either you achieve new security measures, or it becomes apparent that you are unable to do this; in any case, we have a safe and secure location in which you can pursue your research.'

Valentine shook her head. There was a noise Casaubon thought might have been a snuffled laugh. When the red-haired woman raised her face, it was very drawn. Johanna Branwen turned towards him.

Casaubon lifted a copper-coloured eyebrow.

She said, 'This is not a central European regime. Therefore, unless you do resist arrest, you are unlikely to meet with an accident resisting arrest. I think that is something of a shame. You will, however, cooperate with the authorities in analysing the nature of this artificial intelligence, produced however accidentally, and in continuing your research into direct neural input.'

Swivelling his chair, Casaubon spotted the half-eaten sandwich on the desk, seized and bit into it, and through a mouthful of bread and jam observed, 'Not all my software is contaminated with the little one's expert system. What the multinationals have bought will work very well recording eidetic data. Information flood will happen. Openly. From now, we live in glass houses, Johanna. Glass houses.'

She ignored him.

'*You*, however—'

He saw the shambling big man flinch, Godric's hands seeking reassurance at the controls of his cameras and not receiving any. Pale eyes blinked.

'—I don't need.'

'I'll sign whatever you like. You can have my files. This film.' Miles Godric's voice shook. 'Look, I'll sign the Official Secrets Act, I don't want anything to do with any of this, I just want to go back home and do my job. You can trust me to be responsible. There's no way I'm going to disclose anything. It wouldn't be in my interests, would it? I'm not going to be that stupid, am I?'

Casaubon wiped his fat hand across his face.

'Well,' Johanna Branwen said. 'Mr Godric, you can be the public face of the government here, if you want to.'

Ah. Yes.

It compromises him, and it gets him reward. He consents to be their public apologist and broadcast on behalf of the government, to keep things under control. He becomes part of it, Baltazar Casaubon reflects. And thus safe? Who can tell.

Godric shook his head and scratched at his beard. His eyes were small, bright. 'Thank you, Minister. I'll try to justify your trust in me.'

Casaubon heard Valentine snort. The big man coloured.

'Baltazar, it didn't even occur to you not to do this, did it?' At *this*, Godric's jerked thumb took in hologram, troops, the entire concept by implication.

Casaubon slitted his eyes against hologram sunlight. He wiped his forehead ponderously, and then wiped his hand down his trousers. He gave a great, honest laugh. Genuinely puzzled, he asked, 'Why would I not do any of this?'

' "Never mistake the nature of Mephistophilis"!' the man quoted. 'Fucking hell, Baltazar!'

The armed guard with Johanna, at her nod, escorted Miles Godric out of the museum. Casaubon watched the departing recording equipment with a sigh.

He swallowed the last of his sandwich and rose to his feet. Noon blazed from the hologram stage, from Elizabethan Southwark, and he reached down with sticky fingers to poke at the keyboard. The arrested image of the androgyne jerked into movement, stopped again. The remaining armed men in the museum room became alert to it, without it being possible to say how this was apparent. He swore under his breath.

'Damnable thing . . . ! I spend three quarters of my time trying to get it to give me anything at *all*.'

The armed Special Forces soldier beside him, with an appearance of instantly regretted curiosity, asked, 'What does it do when it's not dumping data, sir?'

'It writes reasonably good modern song lyrics.'

Silence in the sun-dim museum. Valentine: her narrow shoulders hunched, thumbs hooked over the back pockets of her white 501s, all her posture that of a sullen brat. He could not stop the smile that creased his face. And the steel-and-silver woman: Nike-shod feet braced apart, arms wrapping her jacket over her thick crimson tracksuit; gold earrings catching a heavy spark of sun.

'No one,' he said gently, wonderingly, 'has ever seen anything like this before.'

He sequenced numbers, symbols, and operant codes in rapid order; entering where necessary the identity of the person to be addressed. 'System-name *Mephistophilis.*'

The woman wrapped her jacket more tightly around her body. 'The program intercepts audio-visual transmissions. And taps data sources. Then it synthesises an end-product, with which one may, to a limited extent, interact.'

Hurt, he protested, 'You're simplifying something of stupendous complexity. Why, I don't fully understand it myself, yet. You may be interested to know, Johanna, that it defines itself.'

He watched her flinch, very slightly.

'What we have here,' he said, 'may be the prototype of something definable as artificial intelligence, but it calls itself – calls *itself*, mark you – an Artificial Unconscious.'

It halted her momentum. He saw that. She lowered her head, jaw down, looking up from under her brows, and it went through him like a blade: Valentine's gesture.

'Artificial *Unconscious*? I . . . see. Do I? No. No, I don't believe I do.'

'I'll show you,' Casaubon offered.

'No! No. Send me a report. I don't need to see.'

And then the hologram image moved.

CHAPTER 15
Street Fighter

Ten o'clock and the light beginning to die.

Footsteps picked a sharp rhythm down the Tottenham Court Road tube station corridor, hesitated, slowed further; and then picked up speed again, heading back in the opposite direction.

Rue Ingram glanced up from where she knelt, lacing on her combat boots, and glimpsed a vanishing back. No one else came up the steps towards this exit. She grinned, feral. Holding down a hard tension.

At her side, a voice said, 'Aw, shit. Anybody got any tape?'

Instantly and without looking, she handed the boy a roll of black insulation tape; which he began to wind around his boot to keep the loose sole on.

Some nine or ten youths rummaged in innocent rucksacks. The last sun slanted down the steps from Tottenham Court Road Underground entrance, picking out the filth and graffiti on this first landing, shining on the Soldier-Saints as they geared up. Rue spared a glance for the electronic newsboards above her head, glimpsed . . . *DATABASE CORRUPTION CONTAINED, PAN-EUROPEAN MINISTRY OF DEFENCE CONFIRMS . . . GERMAN SKIRMISH REPORTS TO FOLLOW . . .* and turned back to fastening her combat boots.

'OK!' Rue stood. She tugged the black assault vest down, tightening the fastenings; checking the handle of the commando knife in its sheath. The buzz of illegality ran through her. Tonight is different. Because of what has gone before: different.

Beside her, Frankie grinned with more than usual manic enthusiasm. 'Another tour of duty! Here we go!'

A tall, fair boy shrugged into an expensive but too-small blue flak jacket that barely came down to the bottom of his ribs; oblivious to their mockery. 'So are the south river guys here?'

'Maybe.' Rue fastened the web-belt and pouches around her waist. She shook out the folds of the long black skirt she wore over ripped tights. In a warning undertone, she said, 'Frankie's mad tonight.'

'Fuck, that girl ain't ever been nothing *else* but mad.'

Two brothers marked each other's faces with camouflage paint, green and black on brown. The rest – putting on shirts tightly buttoned to the neck, solid boots; webbing, headbands, ragged strips of cloth tied about their biceps – yelled at each other, voices rising.

'Move out.' Frankie touched Rue on the arm. 'Let's *do* it, guys.'

The roof of Rue's mouth tasted fizzily dry. She picked up her heavy sports bag. She swallowed and ran, boots clattering, up into the last evening light and Oxford Street. The pounding of her boots seemed to contain and shape her anger, making a fierce rhythm out of humiliation.

A tourist turned a whitened face as they flooded out into the open, his mouth a square of shock. Junction of Oxford Street and Tottenham Court Road. Gridlocked taxis, long-abandoned, shone with chitinous black carapaces. Further down she saw vans, trailers, a burnt-out bus. Rue kicked a waste-bin on its steel pole, laughing to hear the noise echo.

'Hey *fucker*!'

'Yo, Frankie!'

Rue shucked into the sleeveless leather jacket, newly painted on the back with the sword-that-is-a-crucifix insignia of the Soldier-Saints. Feeling suddenly outclassed, for all its expense, by the gang of crop-haired young men and women in overalls, boots, and black headbands that surrounded her and Frankie.

She shook the hair out of her eyes, tying her own ragged headband on. It is peach and ivory silk, scorched at the edges. 'Let's go!'

The short girl swaggered past, her eyes squeezed into slits against the western light. A bottle of brandy cradled in her arms, the red of her cheeks could have been alcohol or remembered anger.

'We going to do a sweep.' Frankie's free arm swung out. 'Mark this fucking street. Clean the shit out of it for good, while they're drugged out of their fucking brains!'

The sky was a darkening clarity over high roofs. Somewhere an audio news broadcast sounded: '—*unsuccessful attack on the city of Bonn at 2 a.m. this morning*—' She recognised the anchorman Eugene Turlough's voice.

Control slid away, willingly abandoned. Rue Ingram linked arms with Frankie and the tall black youth with her; beginning the rhythmic chant, the stamping; the slow, dangerous progress that kicked over bins and the last rug-displays of the street traders; kicked in one unbarred shop window in a glorious scythe of plate glass; marching up the wide street.

Furtive figures slipped from abandoned cars ahead; vanishing into the half-light.

'Flush 'em out! Extended line!'

The street-wide linkage of arms dissolved into a scatter of kneeling figures.

Rue dropped down and scrabbled the gun out of her sports bag. Blued metal. Heavy. Hopper magazine. She worked the lock-and-load, lifted it, sighted along the crude metal sights and pulled the trigger.

The gelatine-and-paint missile scarred orange down the side of an abandoned Mercedes.

'*Mark* them!' Frankie yelled. She lifted her own paint-gun and fired rapidly, repeatedly; dying a shop window in an arc of blue spatters; and hit a man in a decaying parka.

Two other men moved off, swearing. Rue aimed, felt the thunk of recoil, and one yelled and slammed his hand into the side of his head, and took it away orange. Indelible orange.

'We *know* what you are!' Her voice ripped her throat. 'Everybody can *see* what you are!'

She shot again, branding another for public recognition, public abuse. The magazine rattled, emptying, empty.

'Hey—' She caught Frankie's arm. The short girl jerked loose.

'What's *that*?'

Voices from up ahead: screaming and shouting. Rue poised for flight. 'Is that the police?'

A laugh from the short girl stung, acidic, and Rue coloured.

'Shit, no! Sent the south river guys along to Oxford Circus, they're coming up towards us now. Hey, Dinnie!'

A sandy-haired boy stopped, knelt down, and carefully took from his pockets two plastic bags, kept upright. He unwrapped half a dozen bottles filled with clear liquid, and with wet cotton strips trailing from their necks.

'Shit, Frankie!' Aghast. 'Shit. That isn't what we do.'

'It's what *I* do.'

Light bloomed in the young woman's hand. Rue noticed, by contrast, how the sky above was velvet blue. A yellow circle of light. Twilight.

And will they still be in that flat on the estate?

The tingle of Rue's blood slowed, chilled, and she met Frankie's eyes soberly.

'You're going to hurt somebody.'

'That's right. I am.'

And then the bottle sprouted a tongue of fire as Frankie hurled it in a half-arc, and shattered ahead in a spreading semicircle of flame. Hot air blasted back in Rue's face, singing her eyebrows. She swore.

'Aw, fuck it, I can't throw the damn things far enough!' Frankie Hollister sat down on the pavement, legs apart, gasping through laughter for breath. 'I can't – throw them away – from me!'

'Christ, you're a mess when you're pissed.'

'Yeah, an' you too, sober.'

'We've done enough. They've called the police by now. Let's go.' She raised her voice. 'Bug out! ERV! *Bug out!*'

'Oh, I don't think I want to, just yet.' Her precise imitation of Rue's accent was cruel.

'I don't care what you want, Hollister. You're coming with me.'

'I want to do some more of these. Yo. One more guy won't beg off of tourists. Or steal my tax money for Benefits. Yo . . .'

'For Christ's sake, who cares about money—'

'Not *you*. *You* don't have to. You got your sugar mommy, that fucking middle-class dyke. And *why* didn't you tell me about that married guy?'

The tiny flame bloomed again, kissed the rim of a bottle. Rue saw Frankie's eyes bright in the light, fascinated, staring affectionately as the cotton rag burned down. Holding the burning bottle in her hand.

'Oh for – just throw – *throw* it!'

Panic spilled bile in her throat. She reached down and grabbed and threw in one smooth motion, made efficient by terror of fire and explosion. The petrol bomb wobbled in its flight, thunking through the window of an abandoned van. The shatter of glass and the *woof!* of flame loosened fear in her. She fell down on to her knees and stared at the burning vehicle.

A hand waved silently, trapped behind the glass.

CHAPTER 16
Mephistophilis

There are armed men cordoning off the Rose Theatre museum, helicopters over the streets, Special Forces troops in the auditorium. Johanna Branwen flinches, nonetheless, when the hologram image moves.

The stage speakers broadcast, in broad Confederate, '*Yo, marine!*'

Johanna endures the inside-out shift of vision that a change of holograms causes. The Elizabethan theatre becomes gunmetal grey: the scene the interior of a Chinook troop-carrier helicopter. Taken from newsreel clips, translated into three dimensions. Tropical sunlight blazes from nowhere into its open belly.

She wiped the heel of one hand slowly across her eyes. English heat is different. 'That's . . . ?'

'I said *Yo!* You deaf, soldier?'

The strident voice's Confederate accent is not native. Johanna focuses on the hologram figure's face, briefly reminded of young Rue Ingram and then revising her impression. This face is much younger than its original is now.

The military kit is out of date. Green combat fatigues. Ammunition pouches. Cloth-covered helmet. Grenades hanging from outdated webbing. Jungle boots.

This is what they copy, the children, from films and T/Video. War games fought with the paraphernalia of the war-before-last. As always.

She hesitates.

'Hey, Jo, they *your* files, man.' Not androgyne now, the figure sprawls against a metal airframe, one foot up on the bench, an M16 assault rifle resting across her plump hips. She wears combat fatigues open to the waist; under that a green T-shirt stained with sweat. Dog-tags. Soft black curls plaster her forehead. She grins, wide-eyed. She is young. Nineteen. No lines of fat around the chin; but her hands are white and pinched.

'This is a joke.' Johanna pauses in fastening her jacket against the evening chill. Watches, fascinated.

The *castrato* voice rasped, 'No joke. It's Mephistophilis, man. None other. All things that move between the quiet poles shall be at my command . . . But her dominion that exceeds in *this* stretcheth as far as doth the mind of man.'

There are microphones in the interactive museum technology: it must be accessing them. ' "This"?'

'Knowledge. Power. *War*.'

The voice spoke just out of synch with the lips. Johanna moved to one side, then to the other, her eyes fixed on the three-dimensionally solid hologram on the Rose Theatre's non-existent stage. 'You're stealing – co-opting – system-space. That's coming through a satellite-delay.'

'Via the Confederate West Coast. It's a simple principle.' The sweating fat man beamed. 'How pleasant to have an intelligent audience. I confess I don't entirely understand this military ambience.'

'I served abroad,' Johanna Branwen cut him off. 'When young.'

The hologram figure stands up, slinging her M16 from one shoulder by its strap. Her shoulder patch is that of the European Volunteer Force. The curly black hair that will one day be steel-silver is tied back with a headband, ripped from one of the combat jacket's torn sleeves. Her eyes are bright. 'And I will be thy slave and wait on thee, and give thee more than thou hast wit to ask. How much wit you got, grunt?'

Johanna, testing, repeated back, 'And I will be thy slave . . .'

'And I will be thy slave and wait on thee, and give thee more than thou hast wit to ask. How much wit you got, grunt?'

The same words, the same intonation. Johanna relaxed slightly into a self-referential checking of her image, a deliberately softened tone of voice.

'This is not from a direct neural recording. The Defense Department personnel records, I assume? It's an interesting simulation, Baltazar, I grant you, but—' The self-deprecating, I'm-ordinary-folks chuckle. '—we don't have time for it.'

The hologram-figure threw up her hand, appealing to the skies. 'You princely legions of infernal rule, how am I vexed by this villain's charms! From California has he brought me now, only for pleasure of this damned slave.'

'I am hardly a slave,' Johanna said drily, and then, *'California?'*

Mephistophilis chuckled. 'Constantinople, in the original, but what's a quote between friends?'

Testing again, Johanna Branwen repeated with her original inflection, '*California?*'

'You some piss-poor excuse for a politician, you know? Never knew no politician that wasn't. We'd've won if you politicians had let us.'

That *you politicians*, from that young, unforgiving, known face . . .

'Hey, I got to make the best I can with what I find in here. California mainframe battle simulations, future war tech stuff. You know all about that, Jo. No use for it – yet.' The figure hunkered down, tapping a global map that now glowed under her feet, superimposed on to the steel stage flooring. 'Local wars. That's all there is these days. Local wars. Skirmishes and insurrections. Too bad, huh?'

Consenting to interact, Johanna said, 'A war economy would boost prosperity. However, one can never *regret* the lack of war.'

Mephistophilis raised her head. Beads of sweat slid down her face; darkened the torn combats. One hand came up to brush the hair from her forehead. 'Don't *give* me that shit. Is it not passing brave to be a king, and ride in triumph through Persepolis? You love it! We

> *never rest*
> *Until we reach the ripest fruit of all,*
> *That perfect bliss and sole felicity,*
> *The sweet fruition of an earthly crown.'*

So. Not Faustus, for me. Tamburlaine.

'Clear the room,' Johanna said, projecting her voice without raising it. With articulated and smooth precision, the armed men vacated the room for the twilight of Park Street. 'This . . . particular interaction could all be electronic fakery. My daughter writes games software, after all.'

'Nothing to do with me.' Her daughter shrugged. 'Your files have been cracked, I guess.'

The hologram light-slipped, returning for a brief moment to its Godric/Marlowe figure in a scholar's gown.

'All electronically stored knowledge, free to all.' The amused, multi-sexual voice soared as the figure threw up his arms. ' "Why, this is the Invisible College, nor am I out of it!" '

The fat man raised an eyebrow, and peered thoughtfully at the voice recognition codes on the monitor. 'Of course, there was nothing to say it wouldn't have a sense of humour, too.'

Johanna shook her head, and raised the Rolex communicator to her mouth. 'Morgan, I'm about done here.'

Light flared as the hologram interior of the Chinook helicopter reappeared on stage. The hologram figure swung to her feet, one slender hand resting protectively on the shoulder-slung M16. Green eyes gleamed. Dirt and sweat marked her face. 'It's happenin'. You could'a used this – got right to the top – but you blew it. Man, you are *history*. Old woman, get your dumbfuck ass outta here!'

Old woman. Watching that scorn, that so long forgotten young face, she really has only one thought. *Why couldn't my daughter be like this?*

The fat man remarked mildly, 'I must say that one gets entirely fitting responses from Unconscious software. You're not impressed?'

'By the technological achievement? Infinitely. By the result? An oracle is useless if it tells one only what one already knows. I don't need to be told that I enjoy my work. Or that I'm ambitious.' Johanna met her daughter's gaze cheerfully. '*Quelle surprise*. Pious warnings, I regret, won't alter me now. Is this what you wanted Mr Godric to record, to make some attempt to coerce me? Do you think I'm worried about the disclosure of some . . . some pop-psychodrama? I'm sorry to disappoint you. The satellite channels will no doubt make their usual meal of all this, and good luck to them, if it takes their small minds off more important concerns.'

'More important?'

'Let us merely say, I would sooner hear my private life broadcast than, for example, the firing codes for our nuclear deterrent.'

She pressed the communicator again.

'You will both, I may add, be kept in custody separately.'

'Oh, don't be ludicrous!' the fat man snapped, testily. 'The little one and I will have to work together on this.'

Valentine looked at him. A cool breeze blew in through the shutters. Johanna inhaled the evening odours of the river, and the distant café kitchen smells of cooking. The fat man's stomach audibly growled.

'Preferably before dinner,' he added.

She rubbed her numbed hands one against the other. 'You don't question this "oracle", I notice?' she said to her daughter; and watched the old expression come to the child's face.

'But what have you ever done,' she continued gently, 'except run away?' She looked at the hologram. '*Deserter*. Do you know, I thought you might eventually make something of your life? I got

you dual citizenship; I thought when you followed me into the
Forces . . . but there. I never expected any child of mine to make
such a sprawling *mess* of her life.'

Her daughter shrugged.

Her child Valentine has crow's-feet at the corners of her eyes,
behind the gold-rimmed spectacles; a few white hairs. Her child
is over thirty. Over thirty-five. What does that make me? she wonders. Old? I am not yet ready to give it up, any of it.

'Of course,' the fat man ruminated, 'there was no guarantee that
the collective unconscious would be a pacifist.'

'Collective unconscious?'

The fat man grimaced. She assumed it to be a smile: on his flesh-
drowned features it is difficult to determine.

'Don't you think? What else would you call an artificial intelligence that works randomly, on dream-logic, and can access and
download any data? No conscience and all creativity. The collective
unconscious of the information age. I am uncertain,' he confessed
tolerantly, 'whether this is the original program we're accessing, or
one of the copies. Mephistophilis appears to have proliferated.'

'Baltazar, I could just have you disappeared,' she snapped. 'There
are probably any number of people who can duplicate your
research.'

'Our research,' her daughter corrected her. 'However accidentally. I solved the algorithm. I wrote the virus. I estimate five months
to infiltrate ninety-five per cent of global databases. Whatever
this is, there's going to be a lot of it about – and there isn't one
damn thing you can do about it.' Her voice took on a thoughtful
note with which Johanna was long familiar. 'I suppose you could
call this data corruption. Corrupted with change. But the world
always is.'

The fat man belched, and gently massaged his vast stomach.

'These devices would have been invented anyway, in the course
of things, but gradually, and subject to prohibitions, and you people
would have found ways to preserve government security,' Casaubon said. 'I'm putting all of this into the open at one go. Victory
here belongs to whoever gets in first, before counter-measures can
be devised. You knew you were too late, Johanna, when you were
able to find me this easily.'

'I don't know if you're clinically certifiable.' Johanna shook her
head. 'Megalomania? Delusions of grandeur?'

'Hardly delusions,' he said. 'Johanna, Johanna. Sometimes the
important thing is not the message of the oracle, but merely the fact
that it is *here*.'

Johanna Branwen stared at the stage. At the hologram figure: the girl's unlined face, active body. Her potential for what, forty, fifty, sixty more years?

Abruptly, she flailed at the theatre equipment control board, hitting it with her gloved fists. The projection equipment squealed. The hologram sun vanished. Johanna blinked at the dimness in the endlessly long falling of the summer's night.

'And what do I do with you now?' she mused.

'Nothing.' Baltazar Casaubon's fat features became perfectly serious. 'What you cannot do, as the Artificial Unconscious says, is coerce creativity.'

She looked at him.

'Without undue modesty, I must confess that there are probably two or three men who could do what I've done here. Who could fully understand it. Who may be able to replicate, constrain, control it – eventually. Is *probably* good enough, Johanna?'

'Possibly,' she said.

'I got the algorithm out successfully,' her daughter Valentine said. 'Now you're desperate for new security measures, and I'm damned if I'm going to help you. This is the window. This is where everything happens, in the space between now and when you do get secure encryption again. You can have my files, if you don't already. Work on counter-measures. See how long it takes.' Her eyes are red, golden, bright; with a brilliance that is more than a reflection of the hologram. 'That's just inevitable technology: invention and counter-invention. But there *is* going to be open government, information flood, chaos. People are going to know what they're not supposed to.' She added quickly, 'What he had developed was dangerous. What I had developed was dangerous. And someone else would have developed direct neural recording or a decryption algorithm in time. Putting them out *together* – that's the only way I could see of doing it safely.'

'Safely!'

'And you cannot,' Valentine said, 'coerce me. Simply, you can't make me work for you, because I'm not afraid of you.'

'I never wanted that,' Johanna protested.

'You couldn't even make a secure facility to hold me, now. Not if you want me to work. That must cut you down to the core.'

They stared at each other.

'Well.' Johanna picked thoughtfully at the fur of her coat collar. 'There is physical violence.'

'I'm walking out of here. With Baltazar. With Miles, if he wants to come. You can stop me if you're willing to hurt me.'

Johanna rapped her gloved knuckles against the hologram projection machinery. Without the illusions of light, the museum was dingy. Only the cold stone floor of the Elizabethan theatre remained. Outside, she could hear radio transmissions squawking.

'Yes, I thought it might come to this,' she said. 'It isn't over yet.'

CHAPTER 17
War Games

The last light leaves the sky over gridlocked Oxford Street. Rue Ingram shudders.

'Oh fuck. Oh fuck.'

Burned, crisping black, the flesh melting . . .

'*Jesus.*'

Careless of whether there might be petrol left in the abandoned vehicle's tank, careless of the fire's heat beating against her face, Rue knelt on the pavement and stared ahead. The broken-down van held fire: a glass and steel bubble. The stench and smoke of burning upholstery threaded the night. Footsteps sounded, Soldier-Saints running towards her.

'I . . .'

Flesh melting, trailing slime down the inside of the windscreen. No scream, no sound. She coughed, surprised into vomit that stained the front of her dress.

'. . . no!'

The tall youth, holding himself with laughter, pointed at her.

'What . . . ?'

Rue Ingram stood, brushing embedded grit from her knees.

The van burned smokily. Still it was possible to see, through the van's windscreen, the tangled straight arms and legs of Oxford Street shop window dummies.

Melting wax, burning wax.

'I'm going home.'

'Oh, what!' Frankie Hollister rested an arm up across her shoulder, leaning, breathing alcohol into the night. 'We haven't finished yet. I want to find a car with some of those bastards still living in it. I want to do that to them.'

Rue put her hands against her own hot cheeks. 'That's going too far!' Her eyes caught movement. 'What's . . . *police*!'

Far down Oxford Street hooves clattered, mounted police coming up at a canter. The light from burning cars shone on their visors and clubs, slid down the horses' gleaming flanks.

'You and me, we can't – if they get us again— Scatter!' Rue yelled.

Frankie, hot-faced, shouted over the noise, 'Regroup at Covent Garden!'

Six or seven teenagers loped across Oxford Street and away into side roads that Rue knew would take them up Tottenham Court Road, round the back of the British Museum and then south. A dozen of the Soldier-Saints ran with her and Frankie. Rue ran, boots pounding the pavement, leading the rest down into the alleys back of Soho Square.

Breathless, harsh whispers:

'Oh, shit I . . .'

'Frankie!'

'Little motherfucker's crazy . . .'

'Gear down.' One of the brothers spoke. 'They're gonna be here soon, let's go.'

'Did you see what she—!'

'Christ Jesus!'

Nervous laughter echoed off the walls of buildings. Behind them the stink of burning tyres choked the road. The churning black smoke covered the last of their retreat.

Rue Ingram slid the zip of the sleeveless leather jacket up to cover her assault vest and the hilt of the commando knife. The webbing she unclipped, looped over one shoulder. The weariness of relaxing tension unstrung her muscles, so that her legs were glue and rubber.

'Oh God . . .'

Frankie leaned back against a brick wall, face upturned, sweat running channels of dirt down her skin. Without directly looking at Rue, she said, 'You're shit at this. You know that?'

In the night-neon of Soho, among gridlocked cars and blaring strip-joints, Rue hears something. The road smells of horse dung. She kneels, going into cover behind an abandoned car. *He* taught her this. Passed on snippets of bootcamp training, amused at her interest. Wynne Ashton, amused and derisory.

'I'm not shit! Wynne taught me!'

'Guess that's about *all* Wynne taught you.' Frankie Hollister does not move to get into cover, but she lowers her head and looks bright-eyed at Rue. 'Last Easter I told him you'd never leave London.'

'You told him—'

'I told him you were sleeping with another guy. He didn't even ask for a *name*, Rue.'

'Oh, Jesus, Frankie.'

Rue stares up, neck hurting, from beside the car.

'Waste of time.' The blonde girl stripped off her jacket, dropping it on the pavement, over the crumpled bin-bag in which she had concealed her paint-gun. She moved slowly. No more rapidly, she walked off south-west into Soho.

'What do you mean, a waste of *time*—?'

Vanished: gone into streetlamps and neon and the darkness between tall buildings.

Crouched at her elbow, a tall fair girl said, 'You wanna go on somewhere else, Rue? Mark some more of them?'

'Wait!' Rue held up a hand for silence. She glanced over her shoulder. None of the Soldier-Saints visible, and that's how it should be: all in cover. She strained her hearing.

Frankie.

No.

No . . .

'There!' She pointed. 'Fuck, they've got police horses round the back of us. Let's get out of here!'

Rue Ingram runs. Hard behind her, and faster, a horse canters across closed city streets.

CHAPTER 18
A Grave and Gallant City

The light shines blue, with a cold clarity only seen at dawn. Miles Godric gazes up at the cloudless sky over Adelaide Street. The haze will come later, after dawn: for now it is 3.30 a.m. and sparkling.

Street refugees, mostly middle-aged men and women, sit around a brazier. The coals glow, almost invisible in the new sunlight. Far overhead, pigeons wheel whitely over St Martin's church, vanish down below the skyline to settle in Trafalgar Square.

'Val – where are you going? What are you doing?'

The red-haired woman grins at him. Her eyes are puffy with lack of sleep, and she walks with a slack-boned step, but she is, nonetheless, grinning. 'You'll find out. You can broadcast it for Johanna.'

'*Val.*'

'Oh, I don't mind. Why would I mind the open society? I invented it, after all.'

'Not so much of the *I*,' Baltazar Casaubon rumbled.

The big man – and he stood a good two inches taller even than Miles, as Miles was once again reminded, standing beside him – coughed, and pulled his creased white jacket around his massive shoulders. He absently poked a finger down towards his pocket.

A pink nose and vibrating whiskers emerged from the top of the pocket, nipped Baltazar Casaubon's questing forefinger severely, and vanished back into the voluminous folds of silk.

'I don't think Spike likes cold mornings . . .' The fat man sucked his bleeding finger.

'For God's *sake*!' the red-headed woman said. 'Keep that animal out of sight!'

Casaubon anxiously regarded Miles Godric, the refugees, and the paying customers across the street entering an all-night vegetarian café. 'You think there'll be a panic?'

'I think we'll have everyone crawling over you going *eeuuw! ain't
it cute!'* Valentine said grimly.

Baltazar Casaubon instantly assumed the demeanour of a man
who was not carrying his pet white rat upon his person.

Miles, exasperated, demanded, 'But where are you *going*?'

The fat man's eyes lowered, gazing south down Adelaide Street to
Charing Cross Station. Miles wonders if he is envisaging the Surrey
countryside invisible beyond: Surrey and Sussex and the Channel,
whose tunnel opens in countries where other languages are
spoken.

Where other wars are fought.

They have been back to the Neal Street flat. Miles does not know
what they have packed; except, of course, for the bundle of swords.
By this, knowing Val, he assumes she is not returning.

He nodded a greeting to the men and women clustering round
the brazier, and scrubbed at his cropped yellow hair with dirt-
rimmed nails. The early sun warms his skin. Easy enough for the
government to turn him into a babbling nobody, the kind of crazy
in a dirty parka who stops you on street corners with stories of
cover-ups, conspiracies. It's only a matter of perspective. Down here
among disbelief, drugs, violence; how long before it would be true?

His belt cameras record.

Miles Godric turned to face Val Branwen. She stood at the door of
the vegetarian café Cranks, looked back over her shoulder, and
beckoned as she went in.

'You know that I'm recording this officially.' He spoke to the fat
man beside him. 'You don't even care, do you?'

'Food, boy,' Baltazar Casaubon growled, clamping a huge hand
on to Miles's shoulder. 'There's always time for food.'

'But—' But *Johanna*. Does she really just want me to record these
two? Not stop them? And then do what?

Through the plate glass of the café he can see Val, sports bag from
the Neal Street flat slung over her shoulder, vanishing into the
restroom.

'Perhaps it's time I took up my responsibilities again. I am not,'
Baltazar Casaubon confessed, 'a young man any more. Make
no mistake, I'm not *old*. By no means. But it is past time I settled
down, chose something to do, and did it with some effort, because
otherwise,' the big man said, 'I shall have done nothing but
wander.'

'Nothing! Direct neural input architecture is nothing, I suppose.
And the Artificial Unconscious?' Miles shook his head, muttering.
' "Nothing"!'

'That? Mere playing with gadgetry. Nothing of much importance. You wait,' Baltazar Casaubon promised, 'now that I have *real* access to research, and let me loose on art and architecture in this country; on mathematics and military engineering, music and the stage: *then* you'll see something. Assuming I am ever heard of again. Johanna is not a woman of her word.'

'What will *she* do?'

No need, between them, to specify who is meant by that *she*. Baltazar Casaubon's head swivelled to the door through which Val Branwen had entered Cranks.

'I don't know. I have never known.'

Miles Godric understands in those words a history between the two of them longer than he can understand, no matter how many hours of interview he may have with Casaubon, or how close he has been to Val.

Through the plate glass window he sees her emerge into the café again.

She wears a white shirt that moulds itself to her narrow shoulders, and brown wool breeches, and she carries a brown, gold-studded leather doublet slung over one shoulder. Rapier and dagger dangle from her sword-belt, nothing awkward in her management of the hardware. Dark red hair pinned up. He sees that she has woven white-feather earrings into the hair at her temples, gleaming in the morning sun.

'Excuse me,' the large man said. 'I believe that it's time that I went and changed.'

The fat man edged himself around Val Branwen where she stood in the doorway, shading her eyes against the light. She beckoned. Miles walked as far as the street corner. Arm's reach away. 'Are you going with him? Or are you just seeing him across the London border? Are you going together?'

She smiles. There are lines in that smile. She is old enough that a night without sleep lets him see how her face will look when she is fifty. Sallow, warm skin. Some of the lines around her mouth are new since he and she were lovers.

'All these questions. For *Hypershift!*? For the ministry? That's the same thing for you, now.'

'Yes. I suppose so.' He reached down and touched the controls on his belt pad. Main camera offline. Main transmission offline. Backup visual record offline. Store transmission offline. 'I can stand being a highly paid government spokesman. It sounds safe. I was never what you might call an investigating reporter, Val. But – I don't have to start the job until working hours.'

She reaches up to touch him, touch his face; and he catches her hand. It is small, held in his stubby fingers and large palm.

'As my mother said, it isn't over yet.'

Her hand is cold. Colder than one would expect, and he considers that Raynaud's Disease is inherited.

'I'm going home,' he said. 'I can't record if I'm not here. And I can't say where you're going if I don't know. I'm sorry to miss the end of this.'

She grips his hand once for goodbye. Flesh to flesh. 'But you will know everything. Ultimately. We're all behind glass walls now. I'll tell you the stuff I never told you,' she said whimsically, 'before you go to the bother yourself. My father died when I was four. Johanna has always been Johanna. I ran off at thirteen, got myself a false-age computer ID, worked, worked as a hooker, put myself through university, went into military training, went with mercenaries to Central Europe, went to the US – every time she caught up with me, I ran. Until one night I realised the solution to the Non-P algorithm was staring back up at me off the screen. And then I ran back home.'

'And now?'

'Oh, now. That's the question . . .'

'Don't tell me,' Miles said. 'There are already things I wish I didn't know.'

'Then I guess you'll have to learn not to ask. If you can.'

Miles turns and walks away into the streets around Charing Cross. Looking for unmarked helicopters, for plain-clothes security operatives, for anything that will tell him what is happening.

Warm air drifted out through the open café fire-doors. Rue Ingram slipped inside Cranks, bone-weary, two of the boys and the young-est girl at her heels.

'That's it. We're safe. Sit.' She pointed to one of the stripped-pine tables. They collapsed into the seats. She made her way towards the counter.

'Two decafs. Two orange juices.' She felt around in her skirt pockets for change. Used to paying for the others; to be the only one able to pay for the others. But the difference now is that it is by her choice. A kind of weariness that is not of the body possesses her: a pleasant melancholy.

She took the two decaffeinated coffees to the table and returned to the counter for the juices.

Four a.m., and those half-dozen men in the corner are the first of the market traders, coming up in allotment carts that smell of veg and dirt. Four a.m., and the groups down in the main part of the café are the last of the has-been brat-hacker drinkers, hanging out into the early hours; black leather and mirrorshades and faces too old for their clothes. She nodded to a couple of her father's friends there.

'Yo, Rue . . .'

The black youth's soft murmur reached her. She followed his glance to the door. A dozen or so men and women came into Cranks by twos and threes, greeting each other as they passed the door; coming up from the Underground or across from Covent Garden.

Plumed hats bobbed. She noted their long jerkins, breeches, bandoleers, belts cluttered with draw-string purses, and lace-collared shirts; and hardly had to look for the muskets and swords they carried rolled in blankets.

'Oh, *what*,' the black youth, Pete, muttered.

Rue Ingram eased down into the curve-backed chair beside him. She rested her elbows on the table. The belt and webbing were uncomfortable zipped under her sleeveless leather jacket. Slowly she pulled down the zip and shrugged the jacket off, careless of who might be watching. Rolled it and shoved it in the sports bag with the paint gun.

'Looks like the Protectorate Civil War Society. Or the Carolingian Sealed Knot, maybe. I always forget which is which. They'll be going out of London. I forgot: she told me there was going to be a muster somewhere down south this week.'

'She? Aw, your "Valentine Branwen", I suppose.'

''S right.'

After a few minutes' pause another group began to drift in from outside. A clatter drowned conversation: plate armour set down beside tables. The men wore fifteenth-century doublet-and-hose, those without gowns shivering in the dawn's chill; and the women walked bundled up in kirtles and shawls. Queen Carola's army ignored them. Rue Ingram leaned into the aisle, looking at the scabbarded swords in their blanket-bundles.

'You won't like them,' a voice said behind her, 'they're a War of the Roses society that go under the name of *Sir Nigel's Company*, and they don't permit women to fight.'

'Oh, what!' Rue swivelled round in her chair. Two tables away, no longer screened by the market traders, Valentine Branwen raised a decaffeinated-coffee mug.

'Valentine?' She stood; took a brief look at the other three Soldier-Saints – Alice, Mike, and Pete half-asleep – and walked back to join the red-haired woman. The woman's shirt was creased linen, the collar and cuffs a foam of dirty lace. Doublet and breeches were brown. Rue saw that she wore her sword-belt, the blade tied into its scabbard with peace-strings. She looked weary.

Rue said, 'You told me there was going to be a muster. You might have told me when. When will you be back?'

Valentine said, 'Rue, you're very beautiful, do you know that?'

Rue blushed. 'Aw, *c'mon*. Get real.'

The woman had her elbows on the pale pine table. She rested her chin on her interlocked fingers. Light showed the crêpe skin at her throat, the lines fanning out from the corners of her warm eyes.

'Sweetheart, you're not doing anything with your life here, are you? Have you ever thought about California? Or mainland Europe – I used to hold a commission in the PanEuropean Forces before I went to the UCS, you'd be perfectly safe with me. Or there's Nihon.'

'You *got* to be joking!'

Valentine stared.

'And what,' she said acidly, 'is so laughable?'

'Jesus, you're thirty-*six*.'

'You bothered to find out.' One red-brown eyebrow went up. 'Hellfire. Sweetheart, you think anyone over nineteen is an old fart, don't you?'

Rue stood hesitant, confused.

'I take it,' the older woman said gently, 'that you're not interested in going on a trip with me?'

'No!'

The woman's mouth moved. Sun through the café window shone in her dark red hair, in the feather-decorations at her temple, and from the hilts of her weapons. Rue looked away, wiping at the paint-ball stains on her skirt.

'Why do that?' the woman said suddenly.

'Why? Oh – it's an excuse. All of this. Mark the refugees for deportation, and they'll open Closed London again. An excuse. They'll never do it. But . . .'

Rue lifted her head, pushed her fingers through her now-lank hair.

'But, it's so difficult to stop. Because what no one told me is that – despite *everything* – I'd enjoy it so much.'

'You should keep up with the swordfighting.' The woman reached down. 'Here's something. To remind you of the virtues of blunt blades. Here. Take it. I'd move soon, if I were you. I understand the police check out the all-night cafés after street fights.'

A toilet flushed loudly in the Gents, and Baltazar Casaubon

walked out. In costume, Rue saw, bemused. The fat man wore white silk knee-breeches that didn't do up over his capacious belly. The cloth was stained with slops from the bottle of red wine he carried. His calves and feet were stockinged, but otherwise bare. He carried a pair of heeled court shoes tied by the laces and slung around his neck, resting in the folds of a silk shirt and badly tied cravat. Something sky-blue and silk and voluminous over his arm might have been a coat or a cloak.

He rumbled, 'Damned health food. Turns my guts.'

'That,' the woman said, 'is because you never let yourself become used to it. If you're good, I'll buy you a burger at the station before you go.'

'Really?' He perked up. 'And chips?'

Rue looked at her gift. She weighed on her outstretched palms the heft of Valentine's drop-hilted parrying dagger. The diamond-sectioned blade glittered in the dawn light. She slid it into her left hand and the pommel nestled against the heel of her hand, fitting perfectly.

'I guess I better go find Frankie. I didn't tell her yet, she's got a rep job to see her through the summer to next term,'

'Good luck,' says the fat man.

When she lifts her face she is, through wetness, smiling with a brilliance to equal the early light. 'But when will you be back?'

The morning chill froze Johanna Branwen's fingers. She halted in the entrance of Cranks, standing in the down-draught of warmth from the door heater and lazily surveying the café.

'Ah . . .'

She made her way steadily between the tables. Her thick-furred jacket snagged against wrapped sword hilts and the sleeves of badly made doublets. The men and women who glanced up found themselves muttering involuntary apologies. She drew up a chair and sat down at an empty corner table.

Just faintly through the soles of her feet she felt the passing of the first Underground trains.

'Valentine.'

Her daughter looked across heads from the counter queue and met her eyes. Johanna beckoned. Valentine Branwen muttered something to her fat ex-husband and walked across to stand with her fists on her hips. 'What the fuck are you doing here?'

'I have something to say to you and your husband.'

The early summer morning glitters through the plate glass windows. 4.30 a.m., pavements still dark with dew; the sides of buildings white with roosting pigeons. The smell of the river drifted in: mud, and dead weed, and diesel. Johanna slitted her eyes momentarily against the brilliance, anticipating the longer, hotter days of the continent as soon as unfinished business could be concluded here.

'You don't . . .' Her daughter's face creased into a frown. 'Look, you're not here to – apologise, or anything? I don't want this to get embarrassing.'

A small smile curved Johanna's lips. She shook her head, filled with a contrary liking for the woman her girl has become. She reached over and tapped the pommel of her child's sword. 'You look ridiculous wearing that in public.'

'Only because it's not a live blade, Mother.' A smile. 'How do you *expect* me to carry it? It was designed to be worn.'

'Bring your ex-husband over here.'

Her daughter's heeled period shoes clicked on the wooden floor. Johanna watched her back as she moved. Narrow shoulders in a white shirt; brown knee-breeches and hose; the dark red hair braided over her head in barley-rows, and white feathers wound into the hair at her temples. Vivaldi played on the café's sound-system. She felt a chill, precise melancholy; and at the same time a sprightly joy. She rested her plump chin down on her gloved hands. Her daughter, returning, put a mug of apple-tea in front of her. Steam coiled upwards.

'Sit down,' Johanna said crisply.

The fat man, following, beamed. He inspected the nearest chair, mug in one hand and a plate balanced in the crook of his elbow. Finding the chairs all too fragile, he put his back against the wall and slid down into a sitting position between her and Valentine, near a small pile of bags and cases. He dug one finger into the plate of lemon cheesecake, sucked it, and made a purse-mouthed face.

'Heavy on the lemon,' he remarked. 'Johanna! There was absolutely no necessity for you to come and see me off. None at all. I assure you, my time-keeping may not be superb, but I shall have no difficulty in ensuring that I catch the cross-Channel train.'

'Two things,' she said.

The fat man scratched at his head, leaving traces of cheesecake in his orange-gold hair. She watched him steadily for several seconds, turning then to look at Valentine. She put out of her mind's eye the superimposed memories of a younger girl, in the holidays from boarding school, with that same sober, ironic wariness in her eyes.

'And this is the first.'

The café doors opened behind her. A large woman entered,

seeming taller by virtue of the orange hair coiled up into braids on top of her head, and wearing a smart ivory silk suit. She carried a notebook PC clamped between one fat elbow and flank.

'Now. About this Alexandria Project,' she said.

Dorothea Casaubon seated herself at their table.

CHAPTER 19
Omnia Mutantur

'There are more violent forms of intimidation and coercion,' Johanna said thoughtfully. 'I thought, however, that what I would do is bribe you. You specifically, Baltazar.'

She watched her daughter. The younger woman's face froze. The large man choked on a mouthful of cheesecake, spraying brown fragments on her scarlet tracksuit. She brushed them off.

'*Bribe?*'

'Like so many people,' she said as she watched him, 'you are under the illusion that there is nothing you want that badly. Dorothea, please?'

Dorothea Casaubon's large hands flipped up the cover of her notebook PC. Working the tiny keys with difficulty, she accessed and displayed a sequence of screens. A large Baroque public building. Optical disc storage units. Dark-fibre communications networks.

'A storage and access facility for information. I think,' Johanna said lightly, 'that they used to be called libraries. I forget how many terabytes of storage capacity are planned for installation. Certainly it will be globally unique. This is only the first building, the whole complex will be the size of a small city. Accommodation, entertainment complexes, fully equipped research laboratories – you'd be surprised what you can do with a defence budget when you try.'

Dorothea Casaubon pushed up the ivory silk sleeves of her suit jacket and leaned back in her creaking chair. 'You *are* paying me. Good. I was beginning to wonder.'

Baltazar Casaubon looked up at his sister. He jerked a cheese-cake-covered thumb. 'You design for her?'

'I do now.'

'Ah.'

The copper-haired woman wiped sweat from her face, smearing

her lipstick. She blithely crowded Johanna with her elbow as she removed a mirror compact from one pocket. Lining her mouth, she muttered indistinctly, 'Why "Alexandria", though?'

Baltazar interrupted Johanna before she could reply.

'Good grief! Does no one have a classical education these days? The Library at Alexandria! One of the seven wonders of the world. It contained all the books in the world,' he said softly, 'and it was burned.'

Johanna smiled.

'I've come from arranging shared funding with Confederate America, the Japanese trade-sphere, and Australia. I have also arranged a Middle Eastern site for the storage facility. Quite near the historical Alexandria – a genuine publicity coup. Building can start in three weeks.'

She rubbed her fingers together and felt the painful pricking of returning circulation.

'I shall use it as a flagship. We must ride the wave of information flood.' She tried the phrase out on her tongue and smiled. 'I must have Morgan contact the speech-writing department. Open government. A due concern to ease the transition to new forms of society. And what could make me appear more liberal than funding the re-established Library at Alexandria? "Information for all." There's a slogan. I'm sorry to say,' she concluded, 'that there will not be a place on the staff for you, Valentine.'

Her daughter's shoulders moved in the slightest shrug.

'However, Baltazar, I should like you to consider taking the position of Director.'

The fat man's freckled face reddened. For once he said nothing at all.

Johanna continued, 'The salary is one hundred and twenty thousand pounds per annum. Duties won't interfere with your own research. A full staff at the Library at Alexandria will handle heavy publicity, concentrated work-schedules, and – let no one say I'm changing sides to be with the winners. No, indeed.' She put her fingers into her hair at her temples, smoothing the slick curls back over her ears. The café lurched with the momentary dizziness of sleeplessness.

'A few years ago I could work through the night and never think about it.' She gave a blurry smile. 'Well. What do you say?'

'Keiko Musashi offered me a position with Sony-Nissan.' He avoided her daughter's gaze when he said it. 'Continuing neural architecture research.'

'*And?*' Valentine demanded.

'I told Keiko-sama I should not, as it transpired, be joining her.'

The red-headed woman frowned. 'What did she say?'

Baltazar Casaubon dug his finger deep into his ear and examined what he had extracted. ' "*Bakame!*" '

' "Bloody fool".' Valentine chuckled.

'Ah . . .' Johanna began to pull on a pair of soft leather gloves. 'But that isn't the point, is it, the research? The point about the Alexandria Project is that it will have a staff of three thousand, and an associated staff of twice that number. In effect, a small city – and you can run it. If you want to. Say the word.'

The fat man said quietly, 'It's redundant.'

'What?'

'Before it's built. Johanna, who needs a physical library? What's the point of storing information, of concentrating it?' He shrugged. 'When you can have it all, now, anywhere, independent of geography.'

Dorothea Casaubon nodded vigorously.

'It's the mistake of thinking knowledge can be restricted to one head.' Dorothea eyed her brother's cheesecake enviously. 'You're all running around in pointless circles. I was getting the code-breaker algorithm off *public* bulletin boards as shareware ten days ago.'

'*What*?' Johanna stared, appalled.

'Hackers are like that.' Dorothea shrugged, her immense breasts moving under her ivory silk jacket. 'It won't be that long before there are bootleg copies of direct neural input architecture. Johanna, you never did understand the hacker mentality. We don't care about all this authoritarian garbage.'

'Neural architecture is worth hundreds of thousands of pounds!'

Dorothea said, 'We just want to see how he *did* it. Play with it ourselves. Money doesn't matter.'

'If hackers are so bloody subversive,' Valentine demanded, 'how come they're all employed for vast salaries by multinational corporations, and they can't organise a union worth a damn? If young hackers are going to change the world, why do they spend all their time playing multi-user dungeons and worrying about how high-level their wizard is?'

The fat man murmured, ' "Shoot the liberals".'

'I say shoot the techno-liberals – what did you say?'

'Nothing,' Baltazar Casaubon said. 'Nothing at all. I wouldn't dare.'

'I'm *right*,' her daughter Valentine said.

'I'm hungry again,' Casaubon said. 'Do you think there's any remote chance of concluding this and getting some more food?' He turned bright eyes up to Johanna, beamed, and in an undertone said, '*I* knew we could trust the hacker network to distribute the software. It seemed a reasonable fall-back plan.'

'Thank you, Dorothea. You can leave the files.'

The big woman rose, awkwardly. Her gaze skated over Johanna's daughter. She looked down at her brother. 'It's time you did something you can be recognised for, Bal. Make the family proud. Don't you think?'

The fat man grumbled under his breath.

The café door swung closed behind Dorothea Casaubon.

Johanna Branwen removed her gloves and cabled the notebook PC into her mobile phone with hands upon which the fingers were pinched white and purple. 'Whether it's redundant or not, Baltazar, you want it.'

'No.'

'No? Shall we see,' she said, 'what the idiot-savant of the psychological world has to say about it?'

At the touch of her finger, software began to upload on to the notebook PC.

'Although I must say,' Johanna added waspishly, 'that if there is one thing the government probably *doesn't* need, it's an online counsellor. Are we ready?' She keyed in the query.

The screen clears, then scrolls text.

⟨*I have returned in signs and characters – this shape delights you best?*⟩

Versatile program. She approves.

'Let us see,' Johanna says, 'what you really would do, left to your own devices, Baltazar. Consult the oracle. Ask it.'

She sat back, staring him down, smiling. If he asks it, he is obeying her. If he refuses any part of this, he looks a coward in front of her daughter. These little double-binds are simple to set up, wonderfully effective in play.

'No?' she says, after a minute. 'Then let me. I wish it had been an artificial *intelligence*. It could be controlled far more effectively. One can't get a straightforward answer out of it – more like a novel than a slot machine.' She smiles, devil's advocate. 'One gets out of it what one is capable of understanding, rather than objective knowledge. Almost an artist's perspective. Which makes it harder to misuse.'

'Of course it can be "misused",' Valentine snapped. 'It's a purely liberal superstition to think that anyone who can comprehend what Art is telling them must be moral. Art isn't a democracy. I don't think an Artificial Unconscious is any more moral than a rabid dog. It just does what it does.'

The fat man knelt up to the table, entered codes on the keyboard, crashed, swore, re-booted, re-booted again; and sat back on his stockinged heels. Text scrolled rapidly across the nine-inch screen.

Her daughter smiled wryly. 'Oh – *I* get it. In the form of a screenplay this time.'

‹INTERIOR, SAN FRANCISCO APARTMENT, DAY

A young VALENTINE BRANWEN turns away from the 26th floor window. Behind her we can see San Francisco and the Bay.

VAL: Casaubon, I'm going to need the main monitor.

CAS: Hrrrrhmm . . .

VAL: *Now* will do!

The young BALTAZAR CASAUBON slouches on a swivel chair that creaks under his bulk, the VDU remote-control vanishing in the flesh of one hand. We see CASAUBON put his free hand on his shoulder and cover VALENTINE's fingers lightly resting there, without looking away from the wall-screen.

CAS: Inna minute . . .

VAL: Are you test-running – oh, what the hell! *Ca*saubon!

We see CASAUBON chuckle, the motion rumbling through his flesh. VALENTINE's fingers tense. CASAUBON clicks the remote control, absently, morse-fast, his eyes flicking across the divided screen. We can see on the split screen a page of novel-text surrounded by technical diagrams (the heroine's starship), time-lines (following a single character through the story; it gives spreadsheets on two minor villains at the moment), a video of the landscape over which a star-battle is taking place, with soundtrack; and selected chunks of the author's biography.

VAL: You're not still viewing that tripe!

CAS: We-ell . . .›

Johanna looked up. The fat man's pudgy finger rested on the *Hold* key. His eyes were bright.

'Pleasant memories?'

Her daughter raised her head from reading upsidedown, and said softly, 'An amalgamation, I think?'

'Yes . . .'

‹*CASAUBON reads effortlessly and holistically: skipping from battle-scene to the love-scene preceding, forward to one of the heroine's tragic deaths; running a rock video of the soundtrack, pausing to take in a scan of all other titles dealing with similar matters, fiction and non-fiction; and inserting top right a TV interview with an academic critic.*

CAS: Just a little relaxation, my Rose of the World.

VAL: I need the monitor. And you need to be using this properly! Any time this *year*, Casaubon.

VALENTINE reaches over his shoulder and removes the remote control.

VAL: I know that one. It's the pirate version of *Sun Magic*. It isn't relaxation, it's tripe, pure and simple!

CASAUBON lifts his head lazily and pulls VALENTINE down to kiss her. He rubs his cheek against her shoulder.

CAS: This from the woman I found making a novel out of the hyper-indexed version of Machiavelli's *Prince*?

VAL: That's different!

CAS: Splicing in it, as I recall, with segments from *The Three Musketeers* and the Olivier *Richard III* . . .

VAL: Yes. Well.

If someone resting over a man's shoulder can be said to shuffle, VALENTINE shuffles. She bites at his ear. CASAUBON winces.

CAS: Now.

CASAUBON stands up. The chair's metal screeches as he uses it for support. He stretches his arms, then tugs off his vest.

CAS: I suppose one had better change for company.⟩

It is better than she supposes, when she looks up. Tears are running down the man's motionless features, dripping from his chins.

⟨*CASAUBON unbuttons his trousers and kicks his feet free of the crumpled material. He removes a pair of crimson underpants, patterned with butterflies, and faces her, naked.*

CAS: At least I waited to undress. I thought you'd given up collecting little girls.

VALENTINE grins at him, and sighs between amusement and admiration.

VAL: You know damn well I think you're magnificent.

CASAUBON strikes a pose, hipshot, nude: hands clasped at the back of his head.

CAS: *And* magnificently endowed!

VAL: How would you know? I've seen it a hell of a lot more recently than you have!

CASAUBON flirts his eyebrows at VALENTINE, reducing her to giggles, and picks up a pastel pink cotton shirt. Surveying it, he sniffs, shrugs, and wrestles his arms into its sleeves.

'It could have happened like that.' He does not touch Johanna's daughter but he looks at her. 'In Neal Street. Little one . . .'

VALENTINE hooks the cloth free of CASAUBON's elbow and buttons the shirt across his swelling belly.

FX: DOOR BUZZER.

VALENTINE picks up the entry-phone and listens. We see her frown. She puts the receiver slowly down.

VAL: It's a woman. I think she says her name is 'Izumi Teishi'. She says she needs to speak to you?

Quietly, without annoyance, her daughter reaches over and shuts down the notebook PC. 'I think that's enough.'

'Do you?' Baltazar Casaubon wiped his streaming face. 'Little one, I could read it all day, if I didn't hurt so much.'

'I think that's kind of the point.'

Her daughter Valentine has red-brown eyes, but there is no seeing them behind mirrorshade lenses that glint, and reflect the pale surfaces of stripped-pine tables, and the blue sky curving outside the window.

Johanna leaned forward. 'And now you're going to listen to me while I tell you the second thing that you need to know. Or do you need to know? I think, in any case, I need to tell you.'

She lifted the apple-tea and sipped. The hot ceramic brought a welcome warmth to her hands. She held the mug cradled while she spoke.

'Valentine. I have your fingerprints, and your DNA coding. I have your retinal prints. I have several years' worth of statistical analysis of your computer-use styles, which makes them perfectly identifiable. And I have access to police and MI6 files, Home Office and credit-card databases, Social Welfare and hypertext journalism.'

Johanna drank again, and the apple-tea scalded her throat. Tears started in her eyes. She stared at them: the small red-haired woman and the large man. The early sun cast their shadows across the polished wooden table.

'Valentine, I may not be able to stop you hacking into the occasional bank for food money, but I'll get you thrown out of any accommodation. I'll make sure you never have credit or a cheque-book. I'll make it certain that you never get a job again. That you never hold any kind of professional status. Never get any State benefit. Never get through Customs.' She switched her gaze to the window, briefly. 'I'm making sure that the only place you have left to go is the pavement, with the other refugees.'

Johanna looked back. She made a small, snorting chuckle; very quietly.

'I'm not a complete monster. I won't interfere with the children going to Izumi Teishi. You may even see them occasionally – provided that you visit me at the same time. I don't think that's too much for a grandmother to ask, do you?' She allowed a calculated pause, and added, 'Your ex-husband can be employed at the Alexandria Library. He at least *can* work, whereas you never will. I regret the inevitable friction this will cause between the two of you.'

She sees them look at each other.

Is it triumph she feels? Or is it merely relief at the shifting of such a long-term, dead-weight, Gordian knot? Johanna Branwen drains the mug of apple-tea. She inhales the last incense-heavy scent of it, and puts the cooling ceramic mug down. Her gloved fingers shake very slightly.

'And that's all.' Johanna pushed her chair back. The legs screeled across the floor. She stood, staring down, and caught the gaze of the fat man. Baltazar Casaubon had his head cocked to one side.

She met his eyes, expecting customary benevolence.

She blinked with sudden shock.

Miles Godric paused for human interest footage on his way home through Charing Cross station, listening to the conversations under the noise of a harpsichord playing something cold and tinkly on the PA system. A few men in medieval costume seemed to be having an argument, in broad south London accents, over where their pass-ports were, and how would they get across the GLC border *now*?

His gaze, flicking across the crowd, caught sight of a woman at the coffee stall. Orange hair. Broad shoulders. A head taller, even, than most of the male commuters around her.

Dorothea Casaubon, on her own.

He glanced up at the Departures board. A Channel train leaving in nine minutes . . .

Dorothea Casaubon. A big woman wearing a suit: ivory silk jacket and skirt. With earrings composed of hawk feathers and tiny polished bones. Her wrist-deep massy hair down about her shoulders.

Knowing all objections: the woman one of *that* family, ten years older than himself at the least, and not particularly a friend of his. Bad beginnings, and no more than the stirrings of attraction to put against that. And what is she capable of, being *his* sister?

Knowing all this, Miles scrubs a hand through his beard, blinks pale eyes, and – the first decision, but not necessarily the hardest – walks across to speak to her.

'That is *not* all.' Baltazar Casaubon rose, magisterially, to his feet; still cradling the plate of lemon cheesecake.

' "Johanna is not a woman of her word",' Johanna quoted, standing facing him. ' "It's past time I settled down, because otherwise I shall have done nothing but wander." Baltazar, you *want* this. The sweet fruition of an earthly crown. You want the Library.'

The big man gazed down at her. The first sun shone in through the café window on his stained cravat's creases, and knee-breeches, and the shoes slung around his fat-rolled neck.

Baltazar Casaubon rumbled, 'It's a bad error to think a person stupid beyond contempt, simply because they are the scum who have taken your daughter from you. You never took the time to discover adequately how I think. Yes, I want this position. No, I won't take it.'

He has the look of a man hearing bolts and bars collapse, a door swinging open. And then, with a sudden uncertainty, he finishes, 'But trying to make your daughter a non-person . . . I confess I did not expect that.'

At last she looks at her daughter.

Expecting shock. Expecting that blind, beaten expression that is Valentine's fury from small child to teenager. Whether that is a current expression of her daughter's Johanna doesn't know, not having been with her in so many years. Certainly it is not the way she looks now.

'Is that a challenge to me – beat the system?' Dancing, her daughter's eyes; and suddenly Valentine swivels around in her seat and puts her heeled shoes up on the table, and stretches her arms as if they will crack. 'I *won*der . . . And in any case, it can't be done. You can't do it. Jesus Christ, Mother. How many times have they lost *your* medical records? How many times has someone stolen your bank code? The higher the technology level, the more there is to fuck up, be honest. You can't make me a non-person, you don't have the control over the information.'

Valentine smiles.

'Especially not *now* . . .'

'Haven't you been listening to anything I've said!' Johanna quiets her voice and breathing.

'Of course.' The fat man sounded hurt by the imputation. 'Of course she has. You said something about sleeping on pavements . . .'

'Valentine, you have nowhere to go! You *have* to come to me.'

'Do you really think there won't be a subculture of the information have-nots?' Valentine says. 'I've slept on pavements before.'

'And a lot more people will be sleeping there because of you!' Temper gone now, leaning clenched fists down on the table, Johanna spits out the words. 'Prices, inflation, crashes . . . Have you any idea of what life is going to be like with *this*? I think you've finally succeeded in shocking me. The economy's gone, and how long before it's the telephone network off, and water, and power? How long before London is part of Former Europe, without even the benefit of a *war* to cause it!'

'You don't know that it will be a total collapse.'

'You don't know that it won't!'

Johanna's bones ache with the early morning. She has had the victory and it aches somewhere down deeper in her bones. The mental readjustment to ambiguity takes hardly a blink; she has had to do more and harder in her time. Still, there is time for one more effort. To make her daughter *see* the position she's in. And then: '*Why*, baby? Why? What you've chosen to do is . . . unforgivable.'

'It's nothing of the sort,' Valentine said. 'Or maybe it is, but it wasn't a choice. It wasn't a choice between good and bad, order and anarchy. It never is. It's a choice between the good of the powerful and the welfare of the powerless. Look at what you *can* do – even legitimately, you control the legislation, the army, the police, the money. Who else has that kind of power? Not me. Not anyone else I know. We never will.'

Johanna manages a sceptical smile.

Valentine leaned forward. 'The choice is between things getting worse for just the powerless, or things getting worse for everybody.

It's rock bottom pragmatism. I choose the option where everybody suffers, so I can include those in power. Because otherwise only the powerless suffer.'

'You arrogant little girl,' Johanna said.

'Of course it's arrogance. I know how to create knowledge. I made the Non-P algorithm possible. If I can do that, I have some responsibility to decide what happens when I've done it! If I can. If I have the chance. I had the chance, this is it, make what you like of it. I thought, this way there's a chance something better might come out of it. As opposed to no chance at all.'

'It's too late to stop the chaos of a world with no privacy.' Johanna blinked. 'Which may be worse than the fascism of a world with invasive mind technology.'

'Risk isn't better than security but it's the only possible choice. History's on the side of the random hacker. You might call what I've done fighting fire with small tactical nukes!' Her daughter's gaze is, at last, hers. 'But it's better the powerful and the powerless should both be in the shit, when the only other choice is just the powerless in the shit.'

Johanna's clenched first does not dent the notebook PC, merely rattles it across the café table. Her daughter places sallow fingers on it Vivaldi on the café sound system is replaced by Pachelbel.

'As for me . . . ask yourself what the Artificial Unconscious can do,' Valentine said. 'It can answer questions we haven't asked yet. It can give amoral, pragmatic solutions to political problems – but it won't give them secretly. It can't keep a secret.'

She paused and leaned her chin on her fingertips.

'It'll make one hell of a military computer. What happens to battle simulations when you can process infinitely more data and come out with a real-time answer? Does it become possible to process a genuine war while you fight, and win because there are, now, no unforeseen actions? What happens when you do it, fully aware of enemy movements, and they fully aware of yours?'

'What will you do, now?' Johanna asked. 'Will you come home with me?'

'I thought it was so easy. Life the way it was. I'd built up a reputation in the entertainment industry . . . Baltazar had just built up a reputation!' She grinned, and then grew reflective, studying the fat man's features. 'And I knew where you were if I should ever want to see you. Which I didn't.'

'Answer the question!'

'I'm going back to the Confederate military,' Valentine said, 'because they need me now. I'm going back to do something about the specifically military applications of direct neural input and the Artificial Unconscious – God knows, someone has to. It has to be someone who's not afraid of dirty hands. And I know how the military mind works.' She, for the last time, curved her mouth in that grin that is always Valentine's. 'I do have responsibilities, you know.'

'I begin to see how this works. I can always find you,' Johanna says, 'glass walls work both ways.'

Neither of them appeared to have heard her speak.

The fat man tugged at his costume breeches, casting a speculative eye at the morning outside, and began to pull on what was (now he unfolded it) a deep-cuffed, many-buttoned frock-coat.

With a dignity that even Johanna had, as spectator, to admit, he said, 'Haven't I proved that you can trust me?'

The red-haired woman looked up, crossed heels still resting up on the table. 'I told you you didn't understand, sweetheart. You frighten me even more, now. What sort of people are we? What are we capable of?'

'I love you, little one.'

'You love a lot of people.'

'I do. Not the way I love you.'

Johanna, acidly, put in, 'This is very touching – from a married man.'

Her daughter Valentine acknowledged that with a quirk of her mouth. 'I guess . . .' She scratched under her arms, through the linen shirt. 'It isn't that simple, I guess. But, give it a year or two and we may sort ourselves out. I have hopes.'

' "A year or two".' The large man thoughtfully folded his napkin about his remaining cheesecake slice, and tucked it squashily into one voluminous pocket. 'I'm coming with you to California. Now.'

'No. Not yet.' One hand steadies the scabbard of her rapier, the other reaches up to touch his arm. 'Soon. When things have changed.'

Baltazar Casaubon beamed. 'Ah, but I never did do what you told me to, did I?'

Johanna steps out into the air that is bitter, not with the bitter cool of sunrise in stone streets, but bitter as wormwood. Faustus is dragged down by devils in the end, no matter whether they be theological or interior demons. Undefeated on the field of battle, even Tamburlaine at last just – dies.

Pigeons wheel up towards the blue and pink sky.

She looks down at the paper that her hand, fiddling in her pocket, turns between curious fingers and brings out into the bright sunshine. Part of Godric's printout. It is the Epilogue speaking at the end of *The Spy at Londinium* when all (in a most unJacobean and unMarlovian device – an Artificial Unconscious can be most creative) are, from spy to clown to lady, narrowly escaped from death.

Johanna Branwen halts by the back railings of St Martin-in-the-Fields. A young man looks up from filthy blankets crusted with summer dust and says, routinely, 'Spare some change, please?'

Johanna reads aloud to him.

> '*Epilogue:* Kit Marlowe *speaks:*
> "*Pleasures and pastimes in the city prove*
> *Grave danger and great joy excite the mind.*
> *Some narrowly escape the reaper's blade—*
> *One in a tavern, brawling with a spy,*
> *Escapes to vaunt the pleasures of old age.*
> *The blade drew blood but failed to take my life.*" '

She takes a breath. The line of sunlight creeps down St Martin's spire.

> ' "*Thus come I, visioning a greater city.*
> *Closed London's river, bright as Hellespont,*
> *Makes a wide strait between the past and present.*
> *This London's people flow its mighty streets.*
> *Themselves a river, in a city chang'd—*
> *Though hungry earth would huddle me in death,*
> *I preach no city of the afterlife*
> *(Though after, life is chang'd beyond recall),*
> *I prophecy no virtue, nor repentance!*
> *My future's drawn in colour, with blood's scarlet,*
> *The black of death; withal, the gold of power,*
> *For after Kingship beggars will still strive.*" '

And now she smiles.

> ' "*Of all, delight in hazard most endures;*
> *Power's pleasures do not live with certainty,*
> *They rise from danger as the Phoenix's fire:*
> *As we, her children, burning, mount still higher.*
> *—Omnia mutantur noset mutamur in illis—*" '

The young man stares at her. 'What the fuck use is this, lady?'

'Its price is above rubies,' she says cheerfully, handing him the screwed-up paper, 'but, unfortunately, mine is not.'

Is her Swiss bank account already dry? Has the PM seen her encrypted files? Does she still have security clearance to the Ministry of Defence building? Ah, two can play at those games. And doubtless will.

'What's the foreign stuff?' the young man calls after her.

' "All things change",' Johanna Branwen translates, ' "and we change with them".'

Finding her own kind of freedom in the presence of risk, Johanna Branwen walks cold into the dawn down Adelaide Street, through to Trafalgar Square, where among fountains, with rotors turning, the military helicopter waits.

The Architecture of Desire

We had fed the heart on fantasies,
The heart's grown brutal from the fare
—W. B. Yeats
Meditations in Time of Civil War, VI

CHAPTER 1

'**B**ut I don't understand *why* the servants have to form a collective,' the Lord-Architect said plaintively.

His huge bulk shifted as he leaned back, swivel-chair creaking, and prodded a fat finger into the air.

'*And* I don't see why they have to eat at the same table that we do!'

Winter light shone through the tall windows, slotting down from the glass cupola onto his tilted drawing-table. A smell of heat and sea-coal filled the immense room. A draught chilled his stockinged calves. Morning whiteness illuminated high ceilings; plaster-mouldings; walls covered in plans, drawings, charts of tensile strength; and the T-square and tracing-board hung up over the Adam fireplace.

'In addition to which,' he added, with dignity, 'I have more important matters to consider.'

'Oh, listen to him!'

A plan scrolled up, rattling, as he took his bolster-heavy elbow off it. He scowled. 'Rot it!'

The White Crow grinned. She added: 'I can think of at least one good reason why they should. Hazelrigg and the rest have been indentured here for the past forty years; the last time *I* saw the place I was hardly older than Jared; and I know as much about farming and estate-management as you do about – about, for example, music!'

The Lord-Architect appeared hurt. 'I can sing.'

'Mmm. One could say you have a way with music. One *could* say King Herod had a way with children.'

The White Crow sprawled back in the deep armchair. In her right hand, awkwardly, she held a blackletter pamphlet. Six or seven other pamphlets rested across her lap. Her studded brown leather doublet and lace-linen shirt unbuttoned, she cradled a baby in the crook of her left arm while it suckled at her bare breast. She divided her time between reading and beaming aimlessly into the middle-distance.

'It's bloody Elias Ashmole again!' One-handed, she brandished a sheaf of papers. 'Here's Lilly in *The Starry Messenger*, and Ashmole in *The White King at Liberty*, and damned if they haven't dragged that fool Aubrey in. The next thing, we'll have John Evelyn and the whole Astrologers' Observatory putting out this rubbish! This war's gone on for years, thank you very much, and it isn't going to stop for the prophecies of a couple of fifth-rate astrologers. I'm going to have to get up to London and collect the next lot of pamphlets.'

'I've got it!' Oblivious of her, the Lord-Architect Casaubon dipped his index finger into the inkwell and began to smudge in shadows on the full-frontage drawing. The furred hem of his wide sleeve trailed through the standish.

'What did I tell you!' His fat finger stabbed the columns of figures on papers that slid rustling to the carpet. 'A *direct* correlation – the fewer floors on any tenement, the fewer snatch-purses working the building. The fewer corners for nips and foists to hide and spy out victims. If the number of walkways is cut, then *down* goes the number of Abraham-men and silver-priggers. Design it with no more than one entrance to a courtyard, there's but one way out past the Watch – and your thief goes a-looking for some other ken.'

He rubbed his wide forehead absently with his finger, smearing ink across copper-red brows.

'Let me rebuild the St Sophia Rookeries and I'll have their thievery and thuggery down by nine-tenths in a year. It's perfect!'

'*Now* all you have to do is persuade the Protector to let you do it.' She paused, her sardonic gaze vague.

'It would drastically lower the crime rate . . . little one?'

'Every faction has to have its astrologers,' the White Crow finished morosely, 'and they're going to catch up with me sooner or later.'

'Sooner,' the Lord-Architect hazarded.

'*Thank* you, Casaubon.'

She absently dropped a kiss on her child's hair. Bright enough red to be orange, the hair curled in tiny, damp sweat-rings. The smell of milk and baby clung to her fingers along with the printer's ink.

'Regarding the collective – I say what I said at thirteen.' The White Crow shifted the baby in her arm. Her index finger stroked the child's lip and her own breast. 'If I *wanted* to run a hotel-sized kitchen, or enough staff to keep a city parish in order, or be landlord to four farms, then I'd have *asked* to do so.'

The light barred her face, calling out fire from her dark red brows, and citrine light from her irises.

'To which I add now: why shouldn't the whole lot belong to the people who work it? I don't. God He knows my family never did.'

The Lord-Architect raised a brow at her, appalled. 'Mad. Completely mad.'

He witnessed her expression of disquiet, as if panelled walls and high, bright ceiling and the blazing fire rebuked her. She rallied:

'*And*, if we don't eat at the same table, you won't get to hear gossip about Hazelrigg's mistress. Or how the work's going, down at the excavations. Or what Rowland's sister wrote to him about news in town. Nor will you be able to collapse young Denzil with what I, for one, regard as fairly feeble wit. True?'

In tones of injured dignity, Casaubon protested, 'That is hardly the point!'

She let the pamphlets slide to the floor, sitting up to put the child in the bassinet. The open hearth-fire roared hollowly at her back. The White Crow hitched up her belt and leather breeches and walked across to the windows. Her boots, soundless on rugs, scraped the scrubbed pine boards. She leaned both hands against the window. Her breath fogged the cold glass.

'It isn't as bitter as yesterday. *Told* you it was going to snow.'

A yellow light emanated from the cloud-cover, the sky lighter than the cast wing's roofs and the forest beyond the grounds. Black specks showed against it. Below, white clots of snow feathered down the air to skein the earth.

Baltazar Casaubon, Lord-Architect, tugged his fingerless gloves on more securely. He scratched at his short, copper-red hair, flicking scurf from under his nails. He picked up his goblet of mulled wine and cupped it with both large hands for warmth.

'When I ruled my own city, servants knew their place!'

'Firstly, it wasn't your city; secondly, it's a republic these days, and no great wonder; thirdly—'

The Lord-Architect interrupted: 'Why aren't you wearing your sword?'

The woman swore.

Her voice echoed the length of the long room, sharp in the cold air. She turned from the window and marched to his table.

Casaubon sat back, startled. Standing at the back of the tilted drawing-table, she was tall enough to rest her arms on it, and her chin on her arms, and gaze at him. Faint lines contracted round her narrowed eyes. Studs glinted in her brown leather doublet; lace fell crisp from collar and cuffs.

'I apologise,' she said sweetly, 'for mention of the word *Republic*.'

The Lord-Architect slammed down his goblet of mulled wine.

Rivulets spilled down onto the sleeves of his velvet robe; trickled down the scrolled paper, the table, and onto the furred hem of his gown.

He wiped his mouth. 'What sort of a Scholar-Soldier can you call yourself, and not wear a sword?'

He tugged the voluminous green velvet gown more tightly over the shirt and breeches that strained to encompass his stomach, and climbed massively down from the chair. Rolls of flesh shifted. From his full height of six feet, five inches, he looked down at her over the swell of chins, chest, and belly, reaching a sticky finger to her cheek.

'Little one . . .'

Cold made her skin pale, lucid under dark red hair drawn up in the Scholar-Soldiers' six braids. He touched softness. At each of her temples, and no larger than his thumbprint, a patch of white down-feathers grew: sleek, soft, merging into the white streaks of her hair.

She caught his fingers, pressing the padded, dirty flesh to her cheek. 'You weren't born to understanding servants. True enough. Yes. I should remember. No, really, you're doing *very* well.'

The Lord-Architect stamped one stockinged foot. 'Death and furies! I will not be condescended to in my own house.'

'*Whose* own house?'

Deadpan, and with quick calculation, he reprised. 'I will not be condescended to in your own house!'

He almost had her: her mouth twitched.

One of the room's double doors clicked open. A stocky fair-haired boy, perhaps eight years old, entered and reached up to the ornate handle, pushing the door closed behind him. He pulled at the turned-back cuffs of his diminutive frock-coat.

'Mama, Hazelrigg says you had better come to the yard-gate.'

'In this weather?' Casaubon remarked. Through the glass, on the terrace, snow whitened the flagstones to invisibility.

The White Crow began absently to button up her shirt and doublet. 'Why does he want me, Jared?'

'Mama, he says there's a troop of mercenary soldiers just riding onto the estate.'

The White Crow clattered down steps into a stone-floored kitchen, ducking her head to avoid hanging hams and pheasants. Fumbling, fingers paralysed with cold, she slid sideways between the grain-bins and barrels and through into the outhouse.

Hazelrigg reported, 'Abiathar and Kyril are round the back, ma'am. Young Denzil can ride to the next farm?'

'He'll never make fifteen miles in this.'

Hazelrigg, a stocky, dark man, bundled in a frieze coat, pushed the brim of his hat up and spat into the settling snow. 'Destructive bastards, soldiers.'

She slung the cloak over her right shoulder, leaving left hand and sword-side unencumbered. 'The Lord-Architect has the children safe.'

She stomped across the yard, boot-heels skidding on the film of white. Warm only by contrast with yesterday's bitter cold, the raw air bit into her. Snow stuck to her eyelashes as she glanced up, looking to see Achitophel's bell-mouthed musket projecting from under the eaves. Cold air seared her bare jaw and ears.

Hooves clattered, muffled on the driveway.

Men on horses loomed through the now-driving snow, huddled in cloaks and hats; the sharp lines of musket barrels jutting up from their silhouettes.

The White Crow narrowed her eyes. Grey bulks emerged against the pale clouds. A horse and rider; another; two more. One. Two. And three more horses, each with two riders tandem on the back.

'Yeah.' Cynicism in her tone, that Hazelrigg clearly heard, and a prepared knowledge. 'So where's the rest of them . . .'

She brushed her wrist across her eyes, clearing wet flakes. Automatically, despite the absence of belt and blade, she tucked her sword-hand up into the opposite armpit, flexing fingers for warmth and readiness.

'Madam!'

The leading rider attempted to rein in a big dapple mare. The beast dropped her head between her shoulders as soon as the grip on the rein slackened.

Horse-breath huffed, clouding the raw air. The White Crow stepped forward and touched a hand to the horse's foam-rimmed nostrils.

'Are you their captain? You're killing this animal!'

A boot passed within inches of her face as the man swung down from the horse. Snow chalked his felt coat and tricorne hat.

'Madam, I apologise. We gambled with the weather and lost. The beasts suffer as we do.'

He took off his hat. Oddly brilliant eyes gazed down from a lined face. Snow settled into the glossy brown curls of his full-bottomed periwig. A man perhaps forty: riding some eighteen stone, and well over six feet tall.

'I have the honour to command this free company of gentlemen-mercenaries.' Hat in one hand, the mare's reins in the other, he contrived to sweep a passable low bow.

Her gaze went over his bent back. The other riders sat slumped in the driving cold particles of ice. One gelding whickered.

'Are you the lady of the house, madam?'

Under the coat, faded lace showed at his throat. A scabbarded sword clinked. Snow crusted on scuffed boots. His strong, large-featured face contrasted sharply with the curled wig and lace.

The White Crow stood bareheaded, ignoring the snow soaking through her hair and cold on her scalp. 'I'll show you the road to the next estate.'

'Madam, earlier this morning I had the honour to give your residence – distantly visible as it was before this confounded snow – as a rendezvous for the remainder of my company. They will arrive here soon.'

'How many is the remainder?'

The big man turned his head, calculating horses and riders present. 'Enough, madam.'

'We'll send them on after you.'

One deep-cuffed hand moved to rest on his hip. He squinted up at the house eaves through the snow. 'I'll wager not. You can hardly muster more than ten men, I think; and not so many expert with arms. Madam, it pains me to be impolite. I swear it does. You have food and shelter, my company stand in need, and I have business here.'

She met his brightly dangerous eyes, hearing equally compounded bluster and humour.

The White Crow lifted her head, looking round at the circle of riders: hard and weary faces visible under the brims of plumed hats. She shook the cloak back from her shoulders. Cold cut through her body.

'It isn't as if I haven't stood in your shoes, Captain. But no.'

Without shivering, without faltering, she raised her warmed hand and sketched a complex sign on the air.

A rose-and-gold luminescence tinged her fingers, brilliant against the falling snow. Where her hand passed, air coalesced and tingled: shone the colour of the absent sun. Ground thrummed underfoot.

Snow like a handful of thrown gravel stung her jaw. The temperature plummeted. Air contracted: blasting icily across the riders, ripping at hats and cloaks, numbing hands. A musket clattered to the cobbles. Men swore.

A watery light emanated from no clear point, unless it was the hands of the White Crow. The little dappled shadows of the snow flocked to her feet. Blue shadows on white snow.

The whiteness rose and flowed about her ankles, warm as fur.

She cast the colour of bone and ivory, dipping her hands to skim and touch the wind-devils of snowflakes. Wind-devils that whirled out, hardened, began to become solid . . .

The shapes of great snow leopards prowled across the yard. Blue patterns their pelts, shimmers over muscle and ligament, shadows their great jaws, and sits in their eyes of flowers. The colour of bone is cold in their mouths.

One brown gelding screamed. Its head jerked up and pulled the reins from a dismounted mercenary's hand, and its forefeet rose, hung pawing; and the bugling scream ripped out as it backed, jostled, and half-reared again. The other horses began to back and fret.

The White Crow paused with one hand halfway to her dagger. She drew no confirming blood.

'Madam!'

Still holding the mercenary captain's gaze, his face blue-white in the sudden freeze, she all but completed the air-drawn hieroglyph, then dropped her hand to the dapple mare's neck.

Potential predators faded into greyness. The exhausted horse whickered and raised her head.

Snow ran into water around the White Crow's boots. Yard-cobbbles gleamed. Sudden warmth breathed into their faces.

'*Magia!*' The captain swore.

A horse clattered back. One sword among the group snicked back into its scabbard. She heard startled whispers.

'My name is White Crow. Master-Physician Valentine White Crow, of the Invisible College. Now. If we don't have muskets, I suspect you don't have *magia*. Probably we could discuss this in a civilised manner.'

The man's gaze went past her. The White Crow took two steps back before she glanced over her shoulder.

'Excuse me.' Three skidding steps took her across the wet stone. She grabbed the Lord-Architect's fat arm as he walked into the yard. 'Casaubon! What in damnation do you think you're—'

'*CALMADY!*'

The White Crow fingered her cold ear, a pained expression on her face. ' "Calmady"?'

The Lord-Architect, beaming, lumbered between horses and riders to enfold the mercenary captain in an ursine embrace. 'Rot it! Pollexfen Calmady!'

Captain Pollexfen Calmady studied the hole in the heel of his stocking. He eased down in the wing-armed kitchen chair, one boot still on, sinking his chin into the yards of lace swathing his throat. 'That's luck. Death and damnation, but it is!'

The heat of the oven fireplace beat against him.

'Post sentries, Captain?'

'Post lookouts for Bevil, death take him.' Calmady shut his eyes. The gentleman-mercenary's footsteps departed.

'Messire Captain.'

Without moving anything else, he opened his eyes. Half a dozen mercenaries, in various states of disarray, lounged in the great fireplace. A pale snowlight shone on the kitchen's whitewashed vaults. He smelled salt bacon, herbs, and sawdust.

A redheaded woman of perhaps thirty sat with one hip up on the scrubbed table. She watched him with tawny-red eyes.

'Messire Captain, I want some answers.'

'Apply to your husband for them, madam. I confess myself so exhausted, I couldn't plead my case were I before the Lord Chief Justice herself.'

'Try.'

Slowly, he finished unbuttoning his frieze coat, letting it fall open. Melting snow crusted his scarlet silk breeches and the embroidered hem of his scarlet waistcoat. He sighed.

'Calmady of Calmady,' he rumbled. 'That is my lord Gadsbury; *that* is Lord Rule; over there you'll find Lady Arbella Lacey, Sir John Hay, Margrave Linebaugh, the Countess of . . . but they have manners enough to introduce themselves.'

He saw the woman's mouth tighten.

Lord Rule, black periwig somewhat wetly draggled, swept the plumed hat from his head and made an exquisite bow. 'Servant, ma'am.'

'Likewise, madam, likewise.' Bess, Lady Winslow, flashed paste rings, whirling a lace kerchief in a flourish. She stretched one silk-breeched leg to the fire, hand casually resting over the larger of its patches.

'I don't like gentlemen-mercenaries.' The woman's mouth remained tight. 'I don't like your particular brand of noble brutality.'

'As Physician-magus, madam, you're at liberty to dislike what you please.' Pollexfen Calmady watched snow-light glint off the last remaining gold rings on his large fingers. 'Were you both scholar and soldier, as some of your College are, we should find a less cold welcome.'

'I am – I have been a Scholar-Soldier. As for the present, your welcome depends solely on your conduct in my house.'

She slipped from the table to stand on the stone flags, hands cupping elbows, looking at him with her head cocked to one side. He let her hostility slide by him. He leaned forward, smothered in the riding-coat, to pull off his other boot; failed, and snapped fingers for Gadsbury. The stocky man knelt and dug his fingers into leather, mud, and slush.

'Any sign of him, Gadsbury?'

'Not yet, Captain.' The boot jerked free.

'Boy's a damn *fool*.'

Gadsbury grunted agreement, rising. 'Anyone who doesn't make it through this soon isn't going to make it at all.'

Cold blasted through the cracks of the kitchen door. A few particles of snow dusted the floor. Calmady rested his foot down, wincing as the stocking-hole let bare skin touch the flagstones. Beyond the snow-pasted glass, a blizzard whirled. The wind's buffets echoed through the kitchens.

'Light the lanterns.' The redhaired woman signalled to a clutch of country-dressed men and women whom Calmady assumed to be the servants, and turned back to him. 'Messire Captain, you—'

Thunderous bangs rattled the kitchen door.

Lord Rule, having applied his eye to the crack, wiped sleet from his face and wig and unbarred the door. It clanged open. A cluster of figures stumbled in, shedding cloaks, shouting. Calmady sat straighter in the chair. As they saw him, they quietened.

'Captain—'

'Report first—'

'—Captain!'

A familiar gangling figure pushed his way forward to the fireplace, swept off his triple-plumed hat, and bowed to Calmady, scattering snow over flagstones and Bess, Lady Winslow, impartially. The woman-mercenary swore. The boy pushed his long yellow curls out of his face.

'Father – *Captain*, I mean – we did it!'

Lieutenant Bevil beamed with a sixteen-year-old's enthusiasm. The tip of his sharp nose shone red in his cold-mottled face, and a drop of moisture hung from it. He fumbled, stripping off lacework gloves from practically unprotected hands. 'No trouble! My lord Thompson, be so kind as to show the captain.'

Calmady turned his head. The Physician-magus, caught in midspeech, shut her mouth and leaned up against the inglenook wall in silence. Their cloaks shed, in blue and scarlet and orange silks and brocades the gentlemen-mercenaries crowded close. The boy pulled his torn lace cuffs into more splendid falls. The high folds of his cravat, soaked, subsided onto his azure-silk shoulders.

'Here!' he proclaimed.

Enthusiastically, Thompson and Arbella Lacey spilled the contents of four hessian sacks onto the kitchen floor. A dozen shirts, two patched doublets, odd pairs of hose, and innumerable sheets piled up. Calmady met the boy's pale blue eyes.

'Bevil . . .'

'You *said* we needed material to patch our uniforms with. We ambushed Captain Sforza's troop. We stole their laundry! It's perfect.' Doubt crossed his raw features. 'Someone's going to have to wash it first . . .'

Very still, Calmady looked down at the heap of dirty clothes.

'I have a message.' Bevil frowned with effort. 'From Captain Huizinga. He's holed up on the other side of the moor. He says would we mind returning the cow we stole from them. Their troop doesn't have any milk. He says he'll exchange her for two hens – but one of them isn't a good layer.'

Loud argument broke out: Gadsbury staggering to his feet to proclaim the value of the bargain, Hay contradicting; others on their knees, sorting through the clothes-pile. Pollexfen Calmady sat motionless.

'Captain.'

He turned his head and met the redheaded woman's gaze. Prepared to challenge at the merest hint of a smile, and (for all his exhaustion) to draw sword on a magus if this particular one should chance to laugh.

With equal parts gravity and courtesy, the woman said, 'I came down to bring you a message, messire Captain. The Lord-Architect invites you – all – to dinner.'

Desire stares out through the leafless February branches. Snow rapidly penetrates the thick copse.

Cut aside and trampled, barbed-wire coils. Fractured ice feathers down to lie on rusting black spikes. Beyond the forest's edge, noon darkens.

Fast filling up, the second mercenary patrol's tracks turn unmistakably towards the isolated hall.

The snow-front lowers the sky to the horizon. Cold stings her cheeks. Wind lifts the matt-black tendrils of Desire's hair. Her greatcoat billows over belted layers of skirts and doublets.

She carries a heavy dead branch, resting it against her shoulder, a two-handed grip ready to swing it in a crippling blow.

The blizzard drives hard across the heathland beyond the forest.

She staggers out, head down, at once ankle-deep in snow. Blasting wind robs her of breath.

Forced on, aware that she follows mercenary tracks, aware that there is only one place to which the tracks can lead; without shelter and without opportunity to reconnoitre, Desire plods towards the unknown hall.

'Well done,' the White Crow said softly.

Abiathar rested one hip on the arm of the White Crow's carved wooden chair, wiping her burn-scarred hands on her apron.

'Now if they weren't too exhausted and drink-besotten to realise, they'd see this is food fit only for pigs, which is after all what they are. Still, you call a dinner for fifteen extra at an hour's notice, and half-burned and half-raw is what you'll *get*.'

The White Crow grinned at the older woman.

The tattered silks and faded brocade of the gentlemen-mercenaries gleamed in the snow-light of noon. Lord Rule leaned back, the pale light shining on the rouge on his cheeks. The Margrave Linebaugh fingered a brown beauty-spot. Hands formally gloved, the company made elegant and drunken conversation.

Thick flakes sudded past outside the tall windows. A haze of smoke and the heat of drink and noise made the hall loud.

'They may prove friends of at least one of us . . .' Wincing at the ringing shouts, the White Crow added, 'Kitterage where he should be? And Hazelrigg?'

'Both with broadswords and muskets, ma'am.'

The White Crow leaned back in her chair, chin down on the lace ruffles of her shirt, the baby cradled in one arm. Around the four dining-tables hastily put together in a hollow square, Pollexfen Calmady and the gentlemen-mercenaries sat drinking. She eyed the Lord-Architect sardonically.

Abiathar shrugged. 'My cousin had soldiers billeted on the farm. Et the place bare. When they wasn't out stripping and robbing some honest man for the fun of it, that is. Roughneck rogues and drunkards. Of whatever quality.'

Watching her go, the White Crow shifted the shawl-wrapped baby to her other elbow, careful of the leather doublet's studs. Missing the weight of a swept-hilted rapier jabbing her hip.

'You're not very *fashionable* in the country, ma'am, are you? I see you don't even *paint* for dinner.'

The White Crow raised her head. The boy Bevil Calmady, in what she at first took to be watered (and instantly concluded was only water-*stained*) blue tabby-silk doublet and breeches, stood by the empty chair at her left.

She said, 'This isn't dinner, it's midday; and not by my choice.'

A spray of plumes buckled to his hatband fell forward, brushing his rouged cheeks. He fingered a beauty-spot which, like four others, had been pasted over a cluster of acne.

She searched her slashed doublet sleeves with one hand and held up a small linen square. 'True, we're very unfashionable. Have a kerchief. Your lipstick's smudged.'

The boy, midway through adjusting this, snapped his fob-mirror shut, suddenly distracted.

'You have a baby!'

He hooked a chair up with his heel and sat down, ignoring the growing revelry – drunkenness and relief from cold in about equal measures – of the other gentlemen-mercenaries. His pale blue eyes gleamed. He leaned forward, proffering a finger. Under the table, the White Crow's free hand loosened the dagger in her boot.

A hand no larger than a half-crown shut around the boy's finger. The orange-haired baby opened unfocused eyes of a shocking blue and dispiritedly announced, 'Yawp!'

Bevil's face glowed. He rested his arm on the chair so that the child's grip on his forefinger was unstrained. 'It likes me!'

'*Yawp!*'

'It's a she.' Calculating uses of trust, the White Crow added, 'Would you like to hold her?'

'*Could* I?'

Oblivious to implications or danger, the boy shook back lace falls at his wrist, and carefully cradled the baby against his shoulder. It vented a resonant burp. The White Crow stood, walking past the backs of chairs – fifteen or so men and women, in their thirties mostly, worn hard with long campaigning – and around the room.

'Your baby, ma'am?' Pollexfen Calmady called, raising a pewter mug.

'My daughter Jadis.' She nodded to the solemn eight-year-old, on his chair beside the Lord-Architect. 'And my son, Jared.'

' "Jared," ' Pollexfen Calmady said gravely, 'which in the Hebrew tongue is *rose*. I salute you, young man, as the emblem of your true Queen.'

Jared's small, stolid face froze. One serving-man banged a plate down in front of Lord Gadsbury. The White Crow winced at sudden tension. Apparently unaware of it – his gaze skidding across the servants as if they were human furniture – Calmady raised his mug again. He stood, elegantly massive in long curled wig and beauty-spots.

'I'll wager nobody present will fail me in this. The toast is, *the Queen and her Hangman!*'

Before the White Crow could speak, Abiathar shouted from the serving hatch: 'No one ever drank that toast in Roseveare. No one ever will. I'll give you a toast that isn't to that oyster-whore Queen Carola! The toast is, *the Lights and Perfections.*'

'No toasts.' White Crow took Pollexfen Calmady's mug and set it down on the linen cloth. She leaned against the table, on the far side of him from the Lord-Architect. 'Captain, you say you have business here?'

He shook his head, laughing, the curls of the periwig flying. 'Irony, madam. *Video meliora proboque, deteriora sequor:* I see the better way and approve it, but I follow the worse way. I drink still to her most Royal Majesty Carola – but, being gentleman-mercenary and commanded by pay, I bring the Protectorate's commission.'

With some satisfaction the White Crow leaned back against the edge of the table, weight on her wrists, and crossed her booted ankles. 'Now, see you, it was only a matter of time! I came home expecting trouble.'

'Madam—'

'It was only a matter of which faction got here first. This family's always had influence, and wealth, and I have knowledge of *magia: Someone* had to want to use that.'

Pollexfen Calmady put his hands on the chair-arms, buttoned-back cuffs and lace falling to hide his fists. 'Truthfully, madam, my commission isn't to you.'

'I – what?'

'Here's my man!' Pollexfen Calmady slapped his embroidered gauntlet across the Lord-Architect's shoulder. Casaubon took his nose out of a beer-mug, spilling brown liquid down his ruffled shirt, and looked up with an unassailably guileless amazement.

'Me?' He chuckled resonantly, caught the White Crow's eye, and stopped short.

The gentleman-mercenary continued with distaste. 'The damned bitch-General herself wants an architect. I go where I'm hired. Consequently, I'm hired to escort you to the Prince of Peace and Architecture, the most sovereign Protector of this realm – and I wish you joy of her – the great General Olivia.'

White Crow, slightly pink about the ears, looked back at Casaubon in time to see him steeple his fingers and remark: 'Ah! They must be having problems building the eye of the sun.'

Pollexfen Calmady turned and spat over his shoulder into the open fire. 'Without the blood royal, a pox-rotten mess they make of it! I saw the old bitch-General Olivia herself up on the foundation stones, chrism and sacrifice, *did* it work? No! Did she get away with a whole skin? *Just* barely. Plague take her!'

'Still,' he added, with some satisfaction, 'the temple's no further up than the lower walls, and not like to be, if tavern-rumour's true. What's built up by day is undermined by night, and they've taken to finding dead workmen there, too.'

'Murdered?' the White Crow guessed.

'No. Murder, madam, would be a matter for the Watch. *She* wants an architect.'

The door scraped open.

Plates scattered, swords ripped from sheaths. Abiathar, at the back of Bevil Calmady's chair, suddenly rested a sharp skewer in the hollow of the boy's ear, trapping him motionless with the baby in his arms. His startled gaze flicked to the double doors.

Edward Kitterage stumbled through, musket falling from under one long arm, his flaxen hair plastered across his face. On one arm and hip he lugged the unconscious body of a young woman. Snow crusted her sopping black hair. What skin showed under her bundled clothes was mottled blue and purple with cold.

The massive bulk of the Lord-Architect surged up, chair clattering over.

'Soup,' the fat man shouted. 'Hot wine! Abiathar! Quickly, woman!'

He caught and cradled the unconscious woman in his arms, resting her across the vast expanse of his chest and belly.

'Doing a round,' Kitterage grunted, wary gaze on the gentlemen-mercenaries. 'Found her out by the yard-entrance. Fell over her. She dead?'

'Not quite.' The White Crow touched fingers to the young woman's throat, skin chilled over invisible veins. A faint pulse of rose light remained where the White Crow touched, shaped in the whorls of a fingerprint.

With the swiftness of practice, she withdrew the bee-pin from her braids, pricked her index finger, and smearily traced a hierogylph across the young woman's brow. She smoothed back wet black hair.

Long lashes lay on clear-skinned cheeks, dotted with melting snow. Tears oozed from under one lid. Sharply delicate earlobes and nostrils were translucent white. She fingered the full lower lip down. A shiver of warm breath touched her skin.

'What has the same Signatures . . . ?' The White Crow mused aloud. 'Fireweed and gorse-flower, for the essence of the sun and warmth. Mandragora and moon-root for sleep. Blood for blood. Kitterage, I'll want you to make liver-broth. Put her . . .'

Her forehead wrinkled in concentration.

'Full moon, the Water-Carrier dominant, what ascendant . . . put her in the West High Chamber; I'll come to her there.'

The Lord-Architect wheeled and walked towards the stairs, carrying the tall young woman without effort. The White Crow stared after him.

'She's *stunning*.'

Spoken to the air, her words found an ear not far off. Pollexfen Calmady guffawed. 'Madam, you're jealous!'

An odd smile crossed her face.

'Not precisely,' the White Crow said.

CHAPTER 2

Pollexfen Calmady put down a card. '*Ten of Lances* . . . What ails your lady?'

'*Knight of Grails*. My trick. At the parting of roads that all Scholar-Soldiers come to. She has studied and become a healer,' the Lord-Architect Casaubon said, 'a Master-Physician. And she misses the blade, and hates herself.'

Pollexfen Calmady upended a pewter mug of beer and wiped his lips with a lace kerchief. He dealt again. 'All I can say, sir, is that your letter painted her in damned pastel colours!'

Casaubon said hastily, 'I didn't write to you.'

'So you didn't. I was forgetting.' He belched.

Icy wind screamed. Tall windows creaked open. Bess, Lady Winslow, standing by one, callused hands on the frame, kicked glass panels out so that the driving snow blew in. She leaned back to shout to Lord Rule, who tossed her another wine bottle.

Outside, the lords Thompson and Gadsbury pissed steaming yellow jets onto the terrace in competition, perilously close to Hay who, having wrestled Arbella Lacey to the flagstones, was putting snow down the tall woman's bodice and getting an ill-aimed knee between the legs for his trouble.

'*Dabit deus his quoque finem.*' Pollexfen Calmady rubbed the heel of his hand into his eye-socket. 'God will grant me an end even to *these* troubles!'

Bevis sat with one knee up in a chair, a cittern across his lap, picking out melancholy tunes. 'They're a fine troop, Father.'

'A fine troop of the destitute, I grant you!'

Cold yellow, the sky wept flakes that moved with the aerodynamics of feathers. Snow built up on terrace, balustrade, statues, and lawns. Eight inches and rising. Cold gales seared in the open window.

'*Close that!* Apologies.' Pollexfen Calmady kicked at the snow on the rug, sprawling in the chair before the roaring fire, thumbing through his cards.

The Lord-Architect's fat fingers prodded his cards with delicate concentration. He reached deep into the pocket of his sprigged velvet frock-coat, unearthed two rose-nobles, and wiped them on his sleeve. A trail of grease scummed the satin.

'I perceive,' he rumbled, 'that you still play for stakes vastly too high for your pocket.'

'I do. Let me see.' Pollexfen Calmady reached across, gripped the Lord-Architect's wrist, and turned it over. A small white scar crossed the flesh, an inch above the wrist's creases of flesh. 'Not gone yet, then? Blood brother still.'

Four o'clock light glinted in the mercenary captain's eyes. It silvered the waterfall-curls of his periwig, gleamed from brocade sleeves and breast and breeches. Something of the unnatural brilliant dark of daytime snow found an echo in those eyes.

'Madam White Crow.' He loosed Casaubon's wrist as the woman entered the long room.

'Our visitor's sleeping. Well, say you, are you persuaded to town yet?' She rested her arms along the Lord-Architect's shoulders, looking down over his stained satin lapels to his cards. 'It smells of collusion to me, I must say.'

'My *little* one . . .'

Pollexfen Calmady broke out in a great laugh. He threw his hand of cards down and grabbed the jug to refill his mug. 'There's for you, boy! The worst folly of a man is thinking he can *conceal* his folly. Do you confess to her now. The odds are in your favour, if I'm a judge.'

The Lord-Architect Casaubon spread fat-fingered hands, glancing over his cushioned shoulder at the redhaired woman. A slight pink coloured his earlobes. 'Well . . .'

The woman stepped back. Her thumb hooked over her breeches-belt. For some moments she stared at Pollexfen Calmady. 'This Protector of yours—'

'Not mine!'

'—must have architects of her own.'

'A few poor renegade-architects, perhaps. Geometry being considered in that court a Black Art.' Pollexfen Calmady snorted. 'Listen to me. "Renegade."'

An odd smile moved her mouth. He caught some quirk of humour that vanished before he could identify it. She said, 'Renegades have their own honour.'

'Madam, at a very respectable price.'

'Hmm. I suspect I would have known, even if you hadn't told me, that you were an old friend of his.' She wound a coil of the Lord-Architect's copper-red hair around her forefinger, tugging it sharply. 'How long since Casaubon last dragged you into this sort of foolery?'

The Lord-Architect said hollowly, '*He* inveigles *me*. Always has. All through university.'

'I remember the first day of your arrival at the Sun of Science.' Pollexfen Calmady regarded the fan of cards in his large fingers. 'Thin as a lath, in a filthy black doublet, on fire to show how much you knew of the Craft, and how much better than anyone else you could be at it.'

The Lord-Architect fetched up a belch from the recesses of his stomach.

'I *did* do it better. Pox rot you, I still do!'

'But not in the city you were born to?'

'I am allowing them to try the experiment of republicanism,' Casaubon said loftily. 'They'll come crawling back to me, any day now.'

'Ha!' the White Crow said.

'But you were right,' Pollexfen Calmady concluded softly, looking at his five-guinea hand. 'I did indeed gamble away my inheritance – estate, house, shares, and all.'

' "Thin as a lath," ' the White Crow echoed.

'We were younger then.' The gentleman-mercenary discarded the *Six of Grails*. 'And of more general service to the world, I doubt not; but forgive me, madam, would you have him any other way?'

'If pressed to an answer . . . no, I would not.'

The Lord-Architect pulled her onto his lap in an exuberant hug, played the *Seven of Swords*, and raised an eyebrow at her groan. 'Strategy. Forward planning!'

'My trick,' Pollexfen Calmady observed.

And night slides in across the curve of the world.

She sprawled across the workbench, asleep.

Air and darkness sang, struck. A warning of *magia* burned under her skin. Her arteries ran with sudden fire.

Hard metal bruised her hand: dagger ripped from its boot-sheath before she stood properly awake. Shaking her head to clear it, the White Crow staggered along the corridor from the herb-room.

The stairs and far hall shouted with drunken rout. A woman screeched a song. Dagger blades screeled, peeling strips from the panelling. One man hacked his heel to the beat of the song. Another – Lord Gadsbury? – vomited as she passed.

She took the narrow wooden steps two at a time. The wall banged her shoulder. Twisting the handle, she wrenched at the nursery door.

Locked. Pain in her wrist jarred her awake. She fumbled the key-chain from under her shirt and opened the door, eyes darting up and down the corridor.

Dim lamplight glared from the muzzle of a musket. The dark man, Hazelrigg, loosened his finger on the trigger at the sight of her. Beyond him, small bed and bassinet stood peacefully occupied.

'Madam?'

'*Whoreson stupid* – not you!' She hit her head with her hand, aghast; threw the key at him, and shouted, 'Don't open this door to anyone!' as she spun round and sprinted back down the corridor.

Magia wards fired her blood. Boot-heels hit stairs two at a time; she grabbed at her belt and again missed the presence of a sword.

Footsteps clattered up the stairs behind her.

Third floor: West High Chamber.

The door stood open.

Linen and blankets tumbled down onto the floorboards. A man's back hid half the bed. Thrown back in pillows, mouth loosely open, the young woman's head bounced up and down with the move-ment of the mattress.

Wig tipped sideways, showing his shaved head, and his breeches tangled around his calves, Pollexfen Calmady sprawled across the bed and the woman. His bare buttocks pumped. Pox-scarred skin shone yellow as old grease in the lamplight. One pale foot jutted from under the man's arm, trapped. Thrown wide, the young woman's other leg jounced and flopped.

Three floors below a fiddle pumped in gruesome counterpoint.

'*Leave her—*'

The bed's uneven leg knocked rhythmically against the floor-boards; the man grunting deep in his throat, oblivious.

He dug hard fingers into her left breast, her flesh swelling out pale under his kneading hand, and his nails raked red lines from her nipple to her ribs. The curled wig slipped: his mouth coming down hard on her right breast, chewing, biting; he worried at it, scarlet-faced; lifted a mouth dripping saliva and plunged it down upon hers, thrusting his tongue into her slack mouth. His hips jerked back: slammed forward, the back of her skull hitting the headboard.

The White Crow reversed her grip on the dagger to strike with the hilt; called up *magia* invocations from her sleep-sodden mind:

'*Tagla-mathon—*'

'Father!'

Something hit her elbow and knocked her against the door-jamb.

She glimpsed Bevil Calmady, eyes and mouth gaping. She pushed him aside. He skidded: another body barrelled past both of them. A whiff of familiar smells cut off her automatic reflex: she clamped her mouth shut on a *magia*-word.

'*Calmady!*' The Lord-Architect, flushed and his coat discarded, roared. His footsteps shook the floor. In two strides he crossed the room, grabbed Pollexfen Calmady by the collar of his coat and the back of his knee, digging fingers into muscle. He heaved, twisting: the man screaming at the awkward angle of withdrawal. Casaubon lifted the man bodily up from the bed and threw him. Eighteen stone of bone and muscle smashed a chair and hit the floor.

'*What—*'

Pollexfen Calmady screeched. He reared to his feet, grabbed the bed-hangings, slipped; and stumbled up again. His face burned purple, his eyes ran with water. Vomit stained the front of his brocade coat. He coughed a breath that stank of old wine and half-fermented beer.

'Wha's?—'S outrageous! 'S damnable! Gut me, I'll rip you!'

'Rapist!'

He slipped again, grabbing a bedpost. The curled wig slid down over his shoulders and fell to the floor. Thick stubble covered his shaven head, brilliant with drops of sweat.

'I did not—'

His shining eyes gained focus. One hand brushed at his ruffles. Tan breeches hobbled his ankles. His engorged penis rocked as he moved.

'She's willing, damn you! Never said a word. Never a protest, my life on it!'

The White Crow slammed her dagger down on the dresser and knelt up on the bed, straightening the young woman's body. Hands on the bloodied thighs, she glared up at Calmady.

'She's *drugged*, you whoreson bastard!'

The man's mouth opened. He stared.

'Yes, you pig-drunk shit! She's sick, she's drugged to make her sleep, to make her well! *How could you—*'

Bending to pull at his breeches, the man fell forward. He hit the floor face-down. The Lord-Architect drew back his foot and kicked Pollexfen Calmady over onto his back, the force of it lifting and throwing his rangy body a yard or more.

Abiathar blocked the door. She pushed the stunned Bevil aside, her head turned back, issuing orders to other servants to keep the gentlemen-mercenaries in the main hall. She gasped, seeing

Pollexfen Calmady. 'Blind drunk. As like to be fucking our old pig, or whatever he stumbled across, I reckon.'

'Drunk? Him? He's too capable of the act to be drunk!' Outrage made the White Crow breathless. *'Bastard!'*

Song echoed harshly up the hall and the corridor. The White Crow smoothed hair back from the young woman's unconscious face. 'I'll have to examine her. See what damage . . . Get that boy out of here!'

'I'll take him.' The Lord-Architect belched gently.

'Where the fuck were you?' she demanded.

'Dealing with fifteen others in a similar condition.' Sharp, if not sober, Casaubon's gaze took in the slumped man, the pale young woman, and the White Crow. 'You?'

'I went to the nursery first. I got here too late. I should have been here!'

He reached to put a comforting hand on her shoulder, but the White Crow sat down on the sick-bed, already bending over the sheet-covered form of the younger woman.

The sky is clear all the rest of the night, starshine on the new snow.

Towards morning, laden clouds gather.

'I remember nothing.'

The young woman put her hands down between her thighs, under the sheets. Pain stabbed at her face, muscles around her eyes contracting. Swollen flesh half-closed one eye; her lower lip puffy; and yellow bruises, just beginning to come out, marked all one side of her jaw, neck, collarbone, and breast. She shifted to one buttock, to the other; and leaned back awkwardly against the sloping pillows.

'But reason tells me, had you not drugged my sleep, I could have defended myself.'

'You're bruised. Something torn. Don't wipe off what you find down there,' the White Crow said, 'it's a salve I spent the early hours of this morning making. It should help.'

'Should it?'

The White Crow sat down on the edge of the bed. She took cold, slender hands in her own. 'Shock—'

'Was he diseased, this man?' Calm dark eyes fixed her. 'Am I carrying a child?'

'It'll be some days before I can perform the *magia* to know either. I can do that.'

The young woman took both hands back to smooth the hair away from her marked face. 'Yes. You're a Master-Physician, of the Invisible College. Valentine called White Crow, of Roseveare.'

Dark red brows indented. The White Crow stood. She folded her arms, hands cupping elbows. 'You – who are you?'

'My name is Desire-of-the-Lord Guillaime.'

'*Ah.*'

The black-haired young woman in the bed regarded her with self-possession. 'Are we secret?'

'Reasonably. Do I want,' the White Crow mused, 'to hear anything that has to be told to me in secrecy? No, I think I do not. I live a quiet, retired life here in the country. I'll hear nothing that disturbs it.'

Desire's black eyes moved under long lashes. The faintest slurring marked her speech, and her tongue licked out to probe her swollen lip. 'Not even a plan to fund the escape of Carola?'

White Crow blinked.

'This *is* Carola the Second? Her most Catholic Majesty? Her most indolent Majesty,' she added, and then shook her head in annoyance. 'I haven't seen the woman since I was twelve. And in any case, Desire-of-the-Lord, you don't have a name that I'd expect to find in the royal court.'

The younger woman leaned back, smoothing blankets down around her torso. Linen defined the shape of breasts and stomach. She gritted her teeth and grunted.

'No. I'm a good Protectorate woman, madam.'

'That I guessed.'

'And to be most honest, no one more wishes the escape of *Regina* Carola than the Protector. Her most Catholic Majesty is a liability. We'd sooner see her in exile.'

The White Crow stood. She rested both hands against the carved bedframe, and then took several paces one way, several paces back. The air chilled her skin. Snow-light shone up from the ground and in at the window, bleaching the plastered ceiling.

'This is the trouble, you see. Coming back after so long, belonging to no faction or party, being seen as—' She smiled, curiously, '—new blood. New fodder for the war.'

'This house has always stood for the Protectorate.'

'This house,' the White Crow emphasised, 'hasn't seen me since I was thirteen. We had *no* business coming back here; I knew what I was doing when I ran away to join the Scholar-Soldiers; I should never have *consented* to inherit! It's my inheritance. It isn't my concern.'

Desire shaded her eyes with her hand. She moved down in the

bed, painfully and awkwardly pulling sheets and rumpled blankets up about her shoulders.

'But you will do it.'

The White Crow turned. The unbruised curve of Desire's shoulders showed smooth, pale, marked with old scars of duty and church discipline. Knotted matt-black hair cushioned the young woman's head.

She reached down to pick at snarls in that soft, sweat-matted hair, flicking a glance at Desire's face.

'Will I?'

'Yes.' Black lashes swept down; back. 'Because I ask you. Because of what happened to me here.'

'That isn't something you use for blackmail!'

The White Crow's hand, still moving among the tangles of hair, felt hot moisture on the young woman's cheek. She stopped as if her muscles had locked.

'The Protector wants Valentine Roseveare.'

'Yes.'

The room's air is chill, snow-bright; the kind of morning in which to scrunch down under heavy blankets, in cloth-scented warmth and safety.

The White Crow said, 'I suppose I had better come to London.'

CHAPTER 3

Bevil Calmady's breath whitened the morning air. The young man put his heels into the big gelding's sides and manoeuvred down the snow-covered slope. The coach-and-six rattled down, scant yards away, its brakes squealing.

'*Hei!*'

He spurred past Gadsbury and Lacey without looking at them, coming up with the coach as the slope levelled out. Hooves threw up clots of snow and half-frozen mud.

The snow-covered heath and moorland stretched away, frighteningly clear under a pale blue sky. Against that sky the distant white hills shone; all their shadows blue and lilac. Leafless shrubs pricked the air. Bevil swallowed, cold drying his throat.

'Mistress Abiathar!' He leaned over, peering through the coach's horn-shutters.

The nurse huddled in blankets and a massive coat, the orange-haired baby almost smothered in its swaddling. Jared sat as stiff-backed as is possible for an eight-year-old in a jolting coach.

On the far seat, the black-haired young woman lay asleep. One heeled, black boot peeped out from under her six or seven layers of skirts. A thin coil of hair pasted to her cheek.

Abiathar's voice carried over the rattle of coach wheels, springs, team-harness, and the driver's cries. 'Let her sleep if she can. Don't you be bothering her.'

'I won't. I wouldn't.'

'I don't say *like father like son*, mark.'

His cheeks heated. Abruptly spurring the gelding, pulling its head round, he galloped away up the track. Almost a quarter-mile separated first and second coaches now, Abiathar's weighed down by the luggage and one mercenary guard on the roof.

Bess, Lady Winslow, pulled her mare aside as he passed. Her gloved hand went up as if she would have flourished her plumed hat in usual flamboyance. She arrested the gesture and rubbed awkwardly at her mouth. Cold stung tears, leaking from the corners of Bevil's eyes.

Strung out along the moorland road, point and guard, nearly twenty riders paced the coaches. The bright dots of satin and brocade startled the morning, scarlet and viridian against the muted browns of snow-pasted shrubs and low wooden fences.

'Be well enough if we reach London by Tuesday.'

Startled by a close voice, he rubbed the back of his gloved hand across his face and turned in the saddle.

The Master-Physician White Crow rode straight-backed, draped in a heavy leather cloak. She raised one hand to push her ermine-lined hood back from her face, and loosen the neck-clasp.

'Madam.' Bevil stood in the saddle and bowed. Chill air cut through the worn places in his silver-embroidered blue silk breeches. 'You think the snow will hold off until then?'

'Trust me.'

He stared uncomprehendingly, hearing an acidity in her voice and not knowing why. She shook the grey horse's reins, moving to pace him, to one side of the snow thrown up by the lead coach.

'You're wise not to choose to be rattled about inside one of those.' He looked up shyly from under fair lashes, frantic to steer the conversation. 'You must be more comfortable riding—'

'I am *not*. You try riding a horse in this condition, why don't you?'

Bevil Calmady hesitated, bemused by what he was not entirely certain was a rhetorical question.

The White Crow added, 'You don't happen to have a couple of kerchiefs I could borrow?'

Bevil hooked the reins over the saddle-horn and searched his pockets, finally extracting two darned silk kerchiefs. He passed them to her, watching as she tucked them down the front of her doublet.

'What are you doing?'

She took her hand out of her shirt and unkinked her elbow. 'Leaking, if it's any of your damn business.'

'Oh.' Face bright red, Bevil busied himself with the gelding's reins. The big horse skittered, one hoof skidding on a patch of ice. He recovered, spurring ahead.

'*Boy!*'

He found himself level with the lead coach's window. Inside, Pollexfen Calmady looked up from where he and the Lord-Architect Casaubon sat either side of a let-down card-table dealing *One-and-Twenty*, slammed the window-frame down, and leaned his head out.

'Is the bitch dead, or like to die? No? No! Then stop giving me those whey-faced looks!'

Confusion and anger choked Bevil's voice. He shook his head rapidly, fair hair flying.

'Well, damn you, then! For a puppy who won't own his own father!'

'*Who would?*' His voice broke, squeaked into childish registers.

'Can't man make a plain *mistake*? And what is she but some cast-off camp whore of Huizinga's or Sforza's? Gods! Sanctimonious boys—'

'We've missed the road, I think.' The White Crow's voice cut across the shouting. Bevil leaned forward in the saddle, seeing her ride at the coach's opposite window and snap her fingers for the Lord-Architect's attention.

The fat man, bundled to the chins in a fur-trimmed red velvet morning-robe, leaned his elbow on the window-frame and stared where she pointed. His copper-gold hair, scraped back and tied with a string of black velvet, shone with grease, and the swell of the robe over his belly was stained with old vestiges of egg and soup. He sniffed.

'You may be right, little one. Pull over ahead there, and I'll discover.'

Blind with a thundering pulse, Bevil Calmady rode ahead.

The sun, low in the winter sky, touched stonework with a paleness that hardly deserved to be called warmth. Cold air froze his wet eyelashes. He blinked. The burnt-out shell of a moorland church stood in a hollow, snow whitening walls and rubble. Shattered glass lined one pointed window. The weathercock still stood on the half-demolished spire.

He let the gelding pick a way down towards it, reins resting. The animal's body warmed his booted legs. The Lord-Architect plodded down through the ankle-deep snow, voluminous robe flying and padded arms waving for balance. 'Boy—'

Bevil Calmady gritted his teeth. 'Sir.'

One fat, gloved hand beckoned. He nudged the mount the few paces. The fat man's head was on a level with his knee, his breath clouding the air. It took Bevil a second to realise that the object held up to him was a metal flask.

'Try it, my boy. You look as though you need it.'

Abruptly, he grabbed the flask and took a deep swallow. A honey taste stayed on his lips 'Th—'

Tears leaked out of his eyes; he coughed, muffled it, coughed again, and finally wheezed air into his lungs and seared throat.

'—thank you. Sir. What is that?'

'A recipe of my own,' the big man said smugly. He lifted his face.

Cold blotched his cheeks and chin. Startlingly acute blue eyes fixed on Bevil. 'No reason why you shouldn't ride in the other coach. Abiathar always complains she could use help with the baby, and my little one there is thinking of other things now.'

Bevil followed his gaze to the White Crow. The woman sat her horse still, staring at the snow-covered hills. She stripped the glove from one hand and held up her fingers for the feel of the air to inform her.

'Will she trust me with the baby?'

'She did last night.'

'That was before.' The gelding nosed fruitlessly at snow-covered heather. 'Sir, if I hadn't seen it . . . It's a tavern or whorehouse joke, isn't it? A wench raped sleeping or unwilling. If I hadn't *seen* it. Oh god, how could he!'

Lithely, he kicked feet free of the stirrups and slid to the ground. The earth hit the soles of his boots, no give in it, and he staggered, for the first time aware that this is the winter ground that breaks bones.

'He's my *father*! I'm ashamed.'

The Lord-Architect Casaubon said nothing. He placed one heavy arm, with immense gentleness, around Bevil Calmady's shoulders. After a moment, Bevil nodded.

'Tell me, sir, how do you hope to find direction from this?'

A spatter of musket-fire rang out.

Mounted, spurring, all ingrained instinct; the gelding wallowing knee-deep in an unsuspected hollow. The top of the rise came on him before he realised. Bevil reined in, sword drawn. Far, far back – sounds carry over snow – puffs of flame briefly showed. Too far to smell the powder. A cluster of riders. He narrowed his eyes. One scout in saffron brocade waved a feathered hat: signalling *few and driven off*.

Beside the coach, where the team of six horses stamped and breathed plumes of white air, Captain Pollexfen Calmady raised his sword and brandished it once. A rider began to canter back from point. He looked up at the still-mounted Master-Physician.

'Yes, madam. Chessboard wars, as you say, between gentlemen-mercenaries. But do you prefer the reign of footpads and highway robbers or the conditions of civil war? I'd wager that you don't. *Ubi solitudinem faciunt pacem appellant*: they create a desolation and call it peace.'

The redhaired woman made no answer. She turned her head, looking past Bevil to the Lord-Architect, where he stood by the ruined church.

'Well? Are we in our way, or out of it?'

Bevil Calmady looked at the sun-yellowed stone. The Lord-Architect stood before the walls, arms crossed, the folds of his red velvet robe wet and white with snow. He sniffed, and with a sideways motion of the head wiped his nose on the black fur collar. A silver trail smeared. Casaubon straightened his massive shoulders and called up to the weathercock:

'Which way to London-town?'

Metal shrieked. The hammered brass eagle swung on its broken pole, creaking to face down the lefthand fork of the track. The bas-relief beak flashed back sunlight. It cried:

'East and south! Mark me, mark me! East and south from here!'

That day and night the skies remain cloudless, free of snow.

Two days' dirt engrained the whorls of her fingers.

The White Crow sat against a half-demolished brick wall, arms on knees, blinking at her snow-washed hands. The bonfire's blast seared at her face. Dawn froze her back. Above, a sky clear as water and early as sin birthed light.

'Sleep?'

She glanced over at Lady Arbella Lacey. The woman's nose showed in midst of rolled blankets and cloak, nothing else visible. The White Crow grinned. 'About an hour before midnight. Too cold after. You?'

'Madam, not a wink.'

An anonymous voice from another roll of blankets observed, 'Then you stay awake damn noisily, and snore while you do it!'

The White Crow rubbed her hands against her frozen cheeks.

The quietness and expanded senses that come with outdoor sleeping enveloped her, and all campaign reflexes – the ability to wait, and wait again, without impatience; to talk; to draw on inner resources; to think nothing, only to act – all filled her with a familiar ease. She stared through bitter air at the coach, the fire, the hobbled horses.

'—and then they both stopped in the hallway, in front of a suit of *armour*.'

The black-haired Lord Rule's voice rose. He gestured, one hand in its embroidered gauntlet pinning down Lord Gadsbury, where they both stood stamping their feet on the other side of the fire.

'Too drunk to know their own names, both of them, and Bess looked up at this thing, all six foot of it, full plate armour and helm, and *she* said—'

'—"I want to hear it talk before I fight it!"' the short man completed, grinning. 'Man, *they* were drunk? I was standing right next to you when that happened, and you too ratted to know it.'

'I admit I may have been a little inconvenienced.'

Rule adjusted his cocked hat, caught the White Crow's eye, and removed his hat again to bow, making much play with the plume. 'Madam: good morning.'

'Morning.' She nodded to both: Gadsbury a head shorter than the younger man; both in mud-marked lace and satin, wrapped around with thick woollen cloaks. An effort shifted her from the wall. Movement chilled her: she rubbed at her arms and stood.

Now the burnt-out cottage showed as little more than a floor plan: a few walls no more than waist-high, acting as shelter for the slumped forms of sleeping gentlemen-mercenaries and horses. Numb with cold, her feet knocking against broken bricks, she went aside to relieve herself. Empty moorland stretched away under haze and snow.

'Rule's ridiculous.' The tall redhead, Bess, fell into step beside her as they finished, and walked back through the deserted and burned herb-garden, lacing up her doublet. 'This is the man, mark you, I once heard in the thick of an artillery barrage, telling young Bevil he should please not sweat, since he'd be spoiling a five-hundred-pound suit of clothes!'

The White Crow chuckled. Aches shifted in her shoulders and back, shaken loose by walking. Anticipating later sleep in the coach, when the sun should be high and the day as warm as winter might make it, she wrapped her hands about her arms and nodded towards the fire, where the Marquis of Linebaugh and Bevil Calmady now stood.

'The hell with that: can he make coffee?'

Bess, Lady Winslow, looked down her prominent, frost-reddened nose at Lord Rule, where he squatted over a boiling can at the fire. 'Indifferent bad coffee, madam, and distinctly worse tea; but what would you? He was hardly born to this.'

Bevil Calmady tipped a shot of brandy into his tea mug and clinked it against Gadsbury's. 'The Queen and her Hangman.'

'Listen to the boy, will you? He thinks he's a soldier.' Gadsbury appealed to the cold morning. Arbella Lacey, rumpled and newly risen, chuckled. Gadsbury stabbed a blunt finger at her. 'You're no better. I remember *you* in your first battle – "*Oh*, sergeant, they're shooting at *us!*"'

The woman grinned. 'Yes, and what did you say? "*That's* all right, girl, they're the enemy. They're *allowed*!"'

'When I was a Scholar-Soldier—'

Light flashed. The White Crow broke off.

The green-painted coach stood with its window-curtains drawn, no sign of the Lord-Architect or Abiathar waking. Light flashed again beyond it. She walked rapidly across the frosted, exposed cottage floor, sliding into automatic concealment behind the coach. Her dirt-grained fingers' reached to her empty belt.

Hobbled, the older of the coach-horses stood mouthing in its feedbag. Jared sat astride, bareback, short legs jutting out horizontally. His small shoulders taut, and both cold-reddened hands clenched about the hilt, he held up a curved hanger.

The blade flashed pale light, wobbling, weighty.

'You cut thus, forward and down . . .' Pollexfen Calmady reached up, pointing. Dried mud marked the green woollen cloak about his broad shoulders, staining his curled periwig and the braid on his plumed hat. One gauntleted hand moved, mirroring the small boy's tentative lowering of the blade.

'Here.' He reached up and took the sword: a large man, bulky, ponderous. Her breath came short, anticipating the sudden metamorphosis; always there, always shocking: movement from the shoulder and so *quick* – wrist, arm, shoulder in sudden motion; coordination too swift to be recognised. The metal whipped in figure-eight arcs, bright against the dawn.

'Always paying attention to the main purpose of a cavalry stroke, which is,' he observed, 'not to cut off your horse's ears.'

Over Jared's surprised laugh, he added, 'Madam, good morning. I find talent but no enthusiasm here; still, *altissima quaeque flumina minimo sono labi*: the deepest rivers flow with the least sound.'

His voice blotted the others out.

'You—' Sudden cold bit her gut; forty-eight hours camaraderie vanishing with the return of memory. Shame tanged, a revulsion against speaking to the gentlemen-mercenaries, as if that could prove some collaboration in her. The White Crow walked towards the coach-horse, scenting old sweat and new perfume on Calmady's clothes. Reflexes kept her a step outside his immediate range.

He slotted hanger into scabbard with a click that echoed across the morning, and stood with gauntleted hands on hips. 'Do you think I'd harm a boy, and myself with my own son here?'

'Jarrie, tell Abiathar I'm on my way to feed your sister.'

'Yes, mama.' Swivelling his legs around with difficulty, the boy slid, dropped four feet to the ground, and walked towards the closed coach, tugging doggedly at his long coat to straighten it.

The morning quiet broke with noises. Voices called across the snowy, deserted landscape. One man coughed. Horse-tack clinked, being lifted onto mounts; Arbella Lacey hacked and spat. Meat sizzled on the fire and the smell filled the White Crow's mouth with saliva.

Impossible, now, to walk back to the companionable fire.

'Stay out of my sight. If you can't do that, don't speak. *Stay clear of me.*'

Urbane, the big man drew off one embroidered gauntlet, and wiped his mouth with the lace at his cuff. 'I apologise if you find your husband somewhat surly this morning. Throughout our long acquaintance it's been his desire to outdrink me; last night, as on many another occasion, I fear that he failed. My condolences.'

'*How he can drink with you—*'

'Madam, I've known him long and long.'

'He never spoke of you.'

'No . . .'

The light of very early morning, pale as water, found a reflection in Calmady's eyes. His lined face creased against brightness. The White Crow shivered, feeling every snow-covered wall, every frost-cracked tile of this burned-out and exposed kitchen, every mote of bitter air find its way into her bloodstream. Her hand moved absently in the lines of a *magia* sigil. Warmth glowed deep inside, where the shudders of sleeplessness and revulsion moved.

A sudden spurt of voices broke her concentration.

Cold rushed in, tingling at her fingers' ends, and she raised her head, looking away from Pollexfen Calmady.

'Mistress Guillaime!' Abjectly enthusiastic, Bevil Calmady, bright in azure satin against the trodden mud and snow, offered his hand to assist the young woman back up the steps of the coach.

The White Crow abruptly stepped away, putting yards between herself and the boy's father. She pulled her cloak over her doublet. Her knuckles tightened: white. Apology, appeal: all of this on her face before she could control her expression.

All gone unnoticed.

Clutching her oversize black coat about her thin body, laughing, Desire-of-the-Lord Guillaime tottered across the snow on borrowed, two-inch-heeled shoes a size too large. Cold reddened her cheeks and lips, made her dark eyes sparkle. She called something up to Abiathar, visible now at the coach-window, and put one bruised hand up to her sleek and curly black hair. Caught up on the crown of her narrow head, hairpins falling out, hair unravelled down; and she pushed at it and lost her grip on her coat, that swung wide. Layers of skirts flew.

A rough voice swore in a whisper. The White Crow recognised it minutes later as Pollexfen Calmady's. Bevil Calmady froze. The young woman's head whipped around.

Hollow-eyed, bruised, pinched with fear: she for one second faced him, long lashes soot against suddenly sallow-green skin. She stumbled clumsily up the steps and into the coach. The slamming door cut off a querulous, waking mutter from Baltazar Causaubon.

The White Crow walked on, past the horses. She stood staring into distance across the white moorland until the cold mottled her bare hands purple and blue, and her empty stomach growled.

A dry-mouthed thirst drove her back to the gentlemen-mercenaries around the fire.

Ten miles north of London the column shouldered a massive hill and the view of the London basin opened up: a thick green tide of forest washing up to the edges of the hills.

'There!' Bevil Calmady stabbed a pointing finger.

Riders plunged away towards woodland cover. The sun glinted from burgonet helms, breastplates, and the barrels of pistols. Maybe a dozen men. One rider lagging at the rear spurred viciously and uselessly at his straining horse.

'Oh, lord.' Gadsbury leaned and spat over his horse's shoulder. He chuckled. 'There's always one lackwit. Look at him – *Bevil*!'

'They're Protectorate men!'

Bevil spurred his horse raw. The downhill grassland jolted past him, cold wind whipping his eyes; and he struggled to ease the hilt of the sword in his hand, the guards bruising his knuckles as the blade slipped.

The other mount and rider spurred on.

Bevil swung the sword up, coming within bare distance; skidded his horse around in a turn that all but foundered it; cut a backstroke slash that hit nothing at all; and was away before the enemy rider could turn.

A sudden rush of sound. Bess and Gadsbury rode past him, pounding across the frost-slippery grass, yelling as high as baying hounds. He spun his horse back to follow them.

'Stand, you whoreson, *stand*!' A deep voice belled desperation. '*Hold the line!*'

Enough sense penetrated his wind-blasted brain to know that there was no line, no battle, nothing but a skirmish; himself way out in front, the riders near the woods about to turn, one lifting his arm . . .

The flat *crack!* of a pistol echoed across the morning.

Bess and Gadsbury reined in, deliberately and visibly leaving the pursuit. Across the hillside, the enemy force vanished.

'I—'

He turned in the saddle and the sky blackened.

The smell of pain dizzied him, a smell like cracked glass. He took his hands away from his face, unaware that he had covered it. Dark red blood ran across his skin. Cold stung his mashed lips and nose. He snuffled blood, staring.

'*That*,' Pollexfen Calmady shouted, 'is the wound you should have got to teach you skirmishing is no game. Never go in without support, *never* go in without orders: what do I have to *do*, boy?'

Bevil removed a patched handkerchief from his pocket and cupped it over his nose. Cold dried the blood on his gloves and bare wrists.

Muffled, he said, 'I'm sorry . . . Gadsbury, I'm sorry.'

'No harm done. Spirits,' the small man said gruffly, riding up; and Bess, Lady Winslow, added, 'High spirits, he'll lose that soon enough. Or at any rate, as soon as we do.'

'Then let him learn some devil-damned responsibility! Boy, you do the business attendant on this, and I'll check on your handling of it later.'

'Yes, Fa— Yes, Captain.'

Back in column, Bevil Calmady in turn rode beside each of the company's two sergeants, listing point-duty and necessary extra guard duties for the night.

In mid-speech he looked up to see the White Crow's eyes on him, the woman obviously listening; and no distaste in her expression, only memory and a kind of self-mocking hunger.

CHAPTER 4

The spiked heads on poles on Southwark bridge muttered their rote litanies of confession into the winter air.

White Crow glanced up at snow-crusted scalps and moving, blackened lips.

'The old place hasn't changed, I see.'

Snow clung to stanchions. Below, Thamys froze, cracking barges in the slow grip of ice. Iron-rimmed coach-wheels rumbled on the bridge, sudden sparks striking in the cold afternoon.

'It won't change. Not until we rid ourselves of the cause.' Mud crusted the hems of the young woman's skirts. Desire walked with her hands tucked up into her sleeves, grey coat billowing. The cold air reddened her cheeks, the marks on her face, at least, beginning to fade after three days. A sepia bruise darkened the lower lid of one eye.

Straight-backed, the White Crow leaned the reins against the dapple grey's neck, avoiding a sedan chair carried against the flow of traffic. The lead carrier muttered thanks, red-faced and sweating. The wigged Lady Justice in the chair made no acknowledgement.

'By cause, you mean the Qu—'

'I mean to speak nothing that would lead to my speaking in public.' A sharp jerk of her head, black hair flying, in the direction of the spiked poles.

'Still a danger?'

'Oh, yes.'

Saddle motion rocked her hips. The White Crow sat erect; momentarily touching the rein to the dapple-grey's neck and riding closer to the coach. Jared solemnly waved. She waved back. Cold froze her temples, but she did not pull her hood further down.

'You have a town-house,' Desire-of-the-Lord Guillaime said.

'My grandfather built a house in Roseveare Court, near the convent gardens. Twenty years' neglect is long enough to turn it to a slum, I don't doubt.'

'The General knew you'd come. She will have had it set in order.'

'Will she now. What does she *want* with him? Why don't you ride, for God's sake?' Exasperation rasped in the White Crow's voice; vanished. 'Unless you'd rather walk? It's as you will.'

Gentlemen-mercenaries rode by twos and threes, red-and-blue silk velvets stark against the snow and traffic. Lord Gadsbury and Sir John Hay shared a mount; Arbella Lacey rode Bevil Calmady's gelding – the boy riding in the second coach – and Captain Pollexfen Calmady reached across from the saddle to the first coach's window, taking the Lord-Architect's flask and drinking deep, and passing it to Arbella. Curses and laughter from the rest of the troop floated back down the bridge.

Bells rang out from the far bank's clustered streets.

'What did I tell you?' The White Crow shifted in the saddle, eyeing the horizon behind them. White cloud scarfed the hills. 'Safe until today. We shall have blizzards tonight.'

'That's not well. You may need to travel. For *Regina* Carola. And you must come to court – the Protector-General's court.'

'I haven't agreed to anything yet!'

'Tomorrow. And him, too: the renegade architect.'

The White Crow snuffled a small laugh. 'Casaubon, a renegade?'

'Madam, if he helps us build the eye of the sun, every royalist will call him renegade. I think with good reason.'

'You're an odd one, you.'

The young woman shrugged, moving shoulders and elbows in a gesture that managed to indicate crowded southern streets, ice-locked quays, solemn Tower, mineshafts, temples, and all.

'I know the town,' she said. 'It's a grave and gallant city.'

Tiny bells jingled on a white mule's harness. One of the child-priests of the sun rode down the centre of the bridge. The White Crow drew her mount aside, in the coach's wake, waiting until he passed.

The black-haired young woman rested a hand on the mount's stirrup. Ungloved, her flesh marbled blue and purple with cold. The White Crow watched her receive pain.

'Desire—'

'It is my discipline. Suffering mitigates.'

'I don't *believe*—!'

Dark eyes flicked up, the contact of gazes like a punch in the stomach. 'Sin is the flesh. Sin is the failure to defend. The failure to achieve.'

The White Crow glanced ahead at the lead coach. Casaubon's voice boomed, the higher registers of Arbella and Bess replying. She frowned. Between the ranks of poles lining the bridge, fragments of confessions drift down from dead withered lips:

'—*treason against her most Catholic Majesty Carola. Second of that name*—'

'—*the rack, and then drawn on a hurdle to this place*—'

'—*against the Protector, Olivia, this sin*—'

'—*pain*—'

'—*for crows to peck at, as a warning*—'

She snorted in black amusement.

'I'll do what you want.'

'Yes.' Desire-of-the-Lord Guillaime tucked her bare hand back into her armpit. 'I thought you would.'

'Tell me, is it me, or are you enjoying this?'

The young woman limped, heeled boots skidding on the bridge's trodden snow. The White Crow looked down at her unprotected bare head, tangled matt-black hair; reached down with one hand that she drew back with the movement hardly begun.

Desire lifted her face to the low afternoon sunlight. Cheeks red, eyes brilliant with cold. A transparent drop of moisture hung delicate at her nostril. For the first time that the White Crow could remember, her lips moved in a smile.

'Oh, yes.'

The White Crow rode silent all the way to Roseveare House.

'There's our old inn, *The Greene Lyon*,' Bess Winslow suggested, as cautiously as if she handled wild gorse. 'It's that or take Protectorate quarters.'

'You're quartermaster, do as you will.'

Pollexfen Calmady's voice rumbled, half-inaudible, his chin down in the lace at his throat.

Night blurred the fine edges of the winter afternoon. Roofs, weathercocks, towers, and gables all faded into sepia. Her horse's hooves crunched through the snow's ice-rime, grimy with coal dust. She glanced behind her at the company riding; bright plumes dimmed in a Protectorate street. They kept no perceptible distance between themselves and the older Calmady.

She said, 'You know I follow you.'

His head lifted. The creases of his face deepened as he smiled. He made a small sound in the back of his throat: amusement or cynicism or merely acknowledgement. '*The Greene Lyon*, then. And devil take the hindmost for a night's work – drinking!'

She looked at Gadsbury, close behind Calmady, and the other mercenaries. 'Count me in with you!'

Rising in the east, a piss-yellow moon stained the sky.

*

Sweat slicked her cheek.

Half asleep, she fumbled a fold of the sheet under her face and let it mop up the film of heat. Casaubon's flesh shifted under her, solidly warm.

She lay belly-down across the vast expanse of the Lord-Architect's hips, back, and shoulders; pillowed against the fat of his bolster-arms, her nose buried in the curly, short hair at the nape of his neck. Slightly rank flesh smelled warm in her nostrils. Rhythmic, untroubled breathing lifted her.

'. . . Mmrhhnn?'

Belly on back, sweat-glued to every contour of muscle under pillows of fat, she shifted one leg; her pubis resting on the cool flesh of his buttock, a foot trailing down to the bed. Heat and slick sweat woke her, and the frost-cold air that touched her unprotected ear outside the blanket.

Awkwardly, peeling skin from skin, she slid down into the folds of blankets tenting his body, and yelped at the touch of cold cloth.

'. . . *time* is 't?'

The White Crow hitched herself up against sloping pillows, grabbing at sheets to bundle round her bare shoulders. Brilliant, the morning light of heavy snowfall gleamed on every polished wood panel and candlestick of the room. Her breath huffed silver-grey. 'Wake up, rot you! It's late. General Olivia.'

'She can *wait*. So can t'other.'

The bedframe creaked loudly. The fat man, nose still buried in linen, reached one ham-hand up to grab blankets and rolled massively over onto his side; hunched down so that only a tuft of copper-red hair showed.

'Ei!' the White Crow hugged her bare breasts, left on the naked and blanket-denuded side of the bed.

'You should be *up*!' She hit the cloth-covered bulk, fist bouncing back from solidity. The Lord-Architect Casaubon rolled over onto his other side, in the bed that shifted on the floorboards and squeaked in protest, and rested his chins on his hand. Dark red lashes lifted. He beamed sleepily at her.

'I am,' he said, 'I am . . .'

Momentarily taken aback, she blinked and then grinned.

'Good.'

She ran her finger over the fullness of his lower lip, down his underlip to the deep swell of his chin. Soft against the pad of her finger: delicate flesh and moist breath.

Humour retreated, burned up by something more urgent in his eyes. His free hand slid across under the blankets and pulled her sprawling against his body. She dug fingers deep into his capacious flesh, wrestling, blind in the sweat and odour of desire; too urgent now to do anything but take.

The Lord-Architect Casaubon flicked open his court fan with a practised twist of the wrist. He eyed himself in his mirror over the black-painted, sequin-decorated sealskin, flirted an eyebrow, and gave a beam that the fan concealed.

'Perfect!' he announced. 'Ah. Little one . . .'

'Mmm?'

He turned from the full-length mirror. Outside the window, in Roseveare Court, a yellowing sky bled snow. Against this light, the Master-Physician White Crow bent to buckle the fifth chain-and-buckle on her left boot.

'Is that entirely wise?'

The woman straightened. She hooked a pair of thin iron chains from her belt, over her narrow black leather trousers, looping through the crotch and twisting to fasten them at her hip. Other chains tautened: at hip, knee, calf, and ankle. She put one hand to her cinnamon-coloured hair, braids fastened up with black-iron clips.

'Formal plain black. That's what you wear at the Protectorate court. Puritan black. I know these things, remember? I was born here.'

She laced the black leather bodice more tightly over her breasts, and tucked a black rose into their visible division. The bodice's straps cut into her bare arms. A studded collar circled her throat. A black-hilted dagger clinked, dangling from one thigh.

'And if the General should happen to *suspect* that I don't much like the puritan Protectorate – or being hauled out of Roseveare on business that isn't mine – or being emotionally blackmailed by her messenger Desire Guillaime – well, then: good!'

The Lord-Architect drew himself up to his full six-foot-five, weight back on one heeled shoe, black brocade coat swirling. He flicked the sealskin fan closed and secreted it away in an inside pocket. The immense turned-back cuffs of the coat snagged on the black-silk embroidery of his waistcoat and breeches.

'Sometimes, Master-Physician, you're just plain embarrassing company.'

'Ha!'

The White Crow slung a glove-soft leather cloak around her shoulders and pulled on black leather gauntlets. Her turn arrested partway: she stared herself up and down in Casaubon's mirror. 'I'm really going to go out on the streets like this, just to make a point about Olivia's self-styled puritans? No! Yes. I suppose I am. Let's go, before I lose whatever nerve I have left.'

Window-glass vibrated. A lump of decaying snow slid down. The Lord-Architect paced across creaking bare boards, opened the window, and gazed down into the snow-choked narrow street. Lamps burned in the row of booksellers' shop-windows along Roseveare Court. 'It's Guillaime.'

Her hand pushed his arm. He moved back. She leaned over the casement, looking down at the girl in her layers of skirts and coats. Snow settled and melted in black hair.

'I've called your carriage.' Snow distanced Desire-of-the-Lord's voice.

The Lord-Architect nodded ponderously. Beside him, White Crow lifted a hand in acknowledgement and pulled the window quickly closed.

'I'll have to find time to examine her today. She's healing well. Bodily. What's in her mind . . . *I don't know!* I suppose I can at least tell her if she has pox or a bastard.'

'Little one, don't be so bitter.'

'Oh, that's the strange thing. I'm not.'

The White Crow walked to the bassinet, lifting out the baby with automatic care. She nuzzled her face against it.

'Are you coming with us, then? Little Jadis? Coming to see what lunacy we're about to be roped into?'

'*Yawp!*'

The Lord-Architect Casaubon thoughtfully picked up two spare feeding bottles of milk, tucking them into one outside pocket, and slid a handful of rusks into the other. He licked crumbs from his gloved fingers. Milk oozed into the black cloth.

'Father!'

The Lord-Architect gazed around the small, panelled chamber. His gaze abruptly lowered. A beam spread over his face. Jared, in the doorway, and spruce in brown frock-coat and breeches, eyed his father with long-suffering patience.

'Father, why don't you let Abiathar carry those?'

Casaubon slowly squatted down on his haunches. Level with Jared's face, he met puzzled blue eyes.

'Abiathar is taking *you* to see the sights of the town. Won't that be nice?'

The eight-year-old clasped hands behind his back and frowned disapprovingly. 'I *would* like to go to the Stock Market, Father. And the 'Change, if I may.'

The Lord-Architect Casaubon raised his eyes. The woman shook her head, mouthing a sentence which he deciphered as *Nothing on my side of the family*. With some effort, he rose to his feet.

'Of course you may. Tell Abiathar that I said so.'

The door shut soundlessly behind Jared.

'No,' Casaubon said, '*I* don't know where he gets it from, either.'

'It's safer than taking him to court.'

The redhaired woman rested Jadis in the crook of her arm, swaddled in a woollen coat and her own cloak; walking towards the door. Chains jingled. She shot the Lord-Architect a speaking look. Casaubon shut his mouth. He followed her down narrow, winding flights of stairs. Snow-light shone yellow at casements and high clerestory windows. A tiny bell chimed, another, and two more: the clocks of Roseveare House striking ten in the morning, in anything but unison.

'At least one of those struck seventeen.' He reached past her in the narrow hall to open the door.

'I'm worried.'

'We can call in a clock-mender. In fact, I myself have some degree of talent in that respect—'

'*Not* about the clocks!'

'I know. I have also some degree of talent as regards the noble craft of architecture. Count on me to content this Protector-General.'

The door swung half-open and lodged. A wall of cold air hit him in the face. The Lord-Architect drew his foot back and kicked the door. The door banged open and back against the house wall. Congealed snow and ice spanged off the shopfronts across the street. A patch of snow slid off the opposite roof and fell six floors to pock the street beneath. The Lord-Architect blinked.

'*Cas*aubon . . .'

He slid gilt-and-sequined buttons into three-inch button-holes, fastening the black brocade frock-coat up to his chins. White flakes blew in and settled on his sleeves. He turned the coat-collar up.

'You'd better take this.' From the tail-pocket of the coat, he retrieved a metal flask and handed it to the cloaked woman, beaming hopefully. 'Pure alcohol. No smell on your breath! Keep you warm, though.'

He leaned out, looking towards the end of the street. Wrapped in coats, in snow deep enough to hide her heeled boots, Desire-of-the-Lord Guillaime stood by a closed carriage. Percherons in black drapes breathed plumes of steam into the cold air.

The Lord-Architect Casaubon, moving a step lower down,

clumsily wrapped his arms around White Crow and baby both. He kissed her.

'We shall be received separately at court, I take it. The Guillaime woman your sponsor. And Polly Calmady, mine.'

Towards mid-morning the falling snow obscured the upper storeys of the White Tower and the spire of St Peotyr's Chapel. Yellow cloud pressed low. Smoke whipped up and down from chimneys, fraying into the wind.

Shuddering against cold, Pollexfen Calmady stared through the whirling particles. Arbella Lacey and Calmady's son escorted the White Crow rapidly into the White Tower, towards warmth; the redhaired woman huddled about her baby.

The Lord-Architect stepped away from the carriage, heels crunching down the snow and ice. In his gloved hands he held the handle of an immense black umbrella. A few specks of snow blasted under the gabardine to cling to his unprotected hair and the shoulders of the black brocade frock-coat.

'She won't interview me out here, I trust?'

'Here comes the bitch-General now.'

Men and women, heads down, plunged from the shelter of the chapel. Snow crunched under heavy boots. Black cassocks and robes, torn at by the wind, flared open; black dresses scuffed up clinging wet sleet. A heavy figure stomped in the lead, the obscure morning light glinting from black steel breastplate and gauntlets; striding without pause across the grassy patch – hidden under a foot of virgin snow – of Tower Green.

Pollexfen Calmady called, 'Madam!'

The armoured woman lifted a hand in acknowledgement. She raised her head, looking up into the bite of the wind, eyes narrowed. 'The White Tower, if you please, Captain.'

He nodded, striding after the Protector-General, among the black-clad and silent men and women, clattering up the steps to the tower's entrance. The Lord-Architect walked unsteadily across the treacherous stones of the yard after him, at the arched doorway, folding his umbrella, shaking it vigorously over assembled Protectorate soldiers, and entering with a film of snow melting on his coat and head.

Pollexfen Calmady removed his plumed hat and shook out the curls of his periwig.

'Madam General—'

The Protector-General Olivia halted, a short distance into the crowded hall.

He glanced ahead, following her gaze. The Lord-Architect's wife stood, cloak now thrown back, holding the baby up under its arms, rubbing her cheek to the child's.

She carried her weight on the balls of her feet. Chains and belts jingled, slung on diagonals across her taut hips, encased in sober black leather. Her skin gleamed in the dark room: black rose wound into the fastenings of her tight bodice. Black-iron studs ringed her wrists; clipped up her spice-red hair.

Pollexfen Calmady surprised himself with laughter. 'A scandal to the view, and without infringing even *one* of the sumptuary laws – Madam White Crow, my congratulations.'

She raised innocent brows.

Olivia's weather-hardened voice cut across low gossip. 'You would be more comfortable in another room, madam; there are fires, and I would not have your child take cold. Captain Calmady, escort her.'

Pollexfen Calmady bowed, a movement calculatedly just too precise for the Protectorate court. 'Certainly, madam.'

His gaze followed the General for a moment: a small woman, brushing snow from her wool cloak, followed towards the guard-room-office by the Lord-Architect. The black-clothed court shifted out of the way of the fat man's oblivious progress.

'This way,' he said to the man's wife.

As he turned, he saw in snow-yellow light a young woman, black-haired and swathed in layers of skirts, who followed the Protector-General as far as the guardroom door.

The Protector unbuckled her gauntlets and held her hands out to the fire. She looked over her shoulder. Morning's subdued illumination touched her wispy hair, bulbous features, and eyes the colour of light. Her weathered complexion put her anywhere between forty and fifty: a woman not plain, but ugly.

'Master architect.'

He hooked his furled umbrella over one immense arm, and made a flourishing bow. 'Baltazar Casaubon.'

'And the woman with the child – your wife?' Without waiting for acknowledgement, the small woman went on: 'I cannot like her dress. And yet I like the humour of it.'

The fat man beamed. 'My thought exactly!'

'As to your task—'

She stepped to the scrubbed guardroom table and unrolled the first of a set of blueprints.

Spidered in thin lines, the skeleton of a temple rose over the city.

A great columned temple from which a white dome would rise, its topmost span open to the noon sun. The Lord-Architect reached down one fat finger and turned the paper slightly, aligning it to compass-points.

'The site was chosen for you, by necessity . . .' He squinted. The rolls of fat on his cheeks almost hid his chinablue eyes. 'And the time of construction, also?'

'I am given to understand dire portents if the building is not completed this summer two years on.'

'And you have what?'

'The foundations and some lower walls.'

'Nothing of the dome?'

'Nothing. What is built, collapses.'

He fumbled in an inside pocket and extracted a small steel rule. While bending over the plan and measuring scale, he murmured, 'How many other master-masons have you called in on this?'

'Two. One's dead, one is not dead yet – she being confined to Bedlam, and so like to die eventually. Does that dishearten you, master architect?'

Copper-gold eyebrows flicked up: he glanced at her and returned to the plans.

'Then I shall add dead workmen, to the number of five, all expert in their craft; more accidents than can be criminally accounted for; a site no man will approach after dusk; and there you have the truth of it.'

The Lord-Architect snapped the steel rule shut and tucked it back into his pocket. He straightened his back cautiously. 'And the eye of the sun has been building, what, three years?'

'All of that during period of the truce.'

'Under the Protectorate.'

'The worse for us if we confess a failure now. The godless monarch Carola will make much capital from it.' Olivia reached across, rolled up the plans, and presented them to him across her buff-coated arm, as one presents a sword. 'Suitable rewards, for success. Upon failure, follows – nothing but that I try again with another architect. Doubting, sir, that you will have survived, more than the first two, if you fail in this.'

'So *let* the Guillaime bitch complain.'

Arbella Lacey leaned back across the Florentine cannon in the Ordnance, one knee up, boot supported against its iron wheel. She picked under her black nails with a dagger.

'There's fourteen of us to swear an oath you never touched her, Captain. No, nor never even thought on it.'

'And the fifteenth?'

The big woman shrugged, her gaze dropping from his. Pollexfen Calmady smiled.

Down the ranked cannon, that stood displayed now in the vaulted halls, the gentlemen-mercenaries stood in groups: bright as oriels among the black dress of the Protectorate. Calmady looked for his son. A boy with curling fair hair to his shoulders, in silver lace and blue satin; the worst excesses of his dress curbed.

'Gadsbury has been tasking him over fashion, I perceive.' Pollexfen Calmady tugged his long scarlet coat straight. 'Well, will you wager with me on how large a bonus the bitch-General *won't* give us, for swift completion of her request?'

Muted sun shone in on the scrubbed floorboards, and on the whitewashed vaults of the ceiling. Outside the arrowslit windows, he glimpsed the snow-shrouded Bloody Tower, and flakes swirling to hide the heads above Traitors Gate. Loud footsteps broke his concentration.

'Master Calmady.'

'That is Captain Calmady, Master Humility, as I hope to give you cause to remember.'

'Sir.' Humility Talbot bowed a frozen inch. Black coat, hose, and stockings; not a silver buckle to his shoes, or a silver top to his cane. He sniffed, as if at some odour. 'He has accepted her commission – you may escort the Protector-General's architect home.'

Pollexfen Calmady whistled sharply, once, through his teeth. Arbella Lacey slid to the floor, lithely dangerous; Gadsbury and Lord Rule appeared out of the crowd. Heads turned.

Calmady let one hand fall to his sword-hanger, the weight of metal at his hip a reassurance and an enjoyment. Seeing the scandal in Humility Talbot's expression, he smiled the wider; swept his plumed hat off and made a low leg. Something in the cold air, the unornamented walls, or the isolation of the mercenary troop at this court of black daws, made a shiver walk the bones of his back.

'Talbot, my orders are given by the General herself. I would be obliged, sir, if you would take your rotten carcass out of the way while I receive them.'

The crop-haired man snorted, turned his back, and stalked off.

General Olivia closed the small room's door behind her as she entered. The redhaired woman looked up from the hearth-seat, where she sat by the fire, baby cradled in her lap. Olivia gazed for a moment.

'I see you don't carry a sword. I understood you to be a Scholar-Soldier.'

The woman put one foot up on the seat. Thin black-iron chains jingled; leather creaked. She grinned. Infectious: the skin around her eyes creased with warmth.

'Promoted Master-Physician, madam Protector. Does that make me useless for what you have in mind?'

'Not, I think you may regret to hear, necessarily.'

Olivia brushed wispy yellow-grey hair out of her eyes. She dropped her unbuckled back- and breastplate behind the door with a hefty clash of metal, crossed to the writing-desk, and slumped into the chair. Ignoring piled-up parchments requiring signature, she steepled her gnarled fingers and rested her chin on them. She studied the magus.

'You have a child.'

'I have two.'

'Nor that, neither, would not have prevented me calling on your assistance. You're Roseveare – how is it you like to be called now? Valentine? Or Crow, is it?'

'White Crow.'

'Mmm.'

Olivia laughed: a gruff, flat sound that surprised her in the snow-muffled air. A cold draught blew across her shins.

'Unsurprisingly, then, I would use the crow as my messenger bird. You know Carola.'

'I haven't seen the woman since—'

'Since your twelfth birthday. In the Banqueting Hall, the night of *The Masque of Death and Diamonds*.'

'Now how the hell did you know that?'

The woman reached down, picking the black rose out of her bodice and placing it on the bench beside her. Fire heated her skin to rose. Fingers unlacing the leather, she lifted the half-sleeping baby to her nipple. It sucked.

'Not that I suppose it matters. Your little girl – your messenger, Guillaime – told me, General. You want Carola in exile. Now, for one thing, the Invisible College doesn't get involved in civil revolt. For another, I hold no brief for the Queen *or* the Protectorate. And for a third . . .'

'Enough.'

Olivia slid down in the carved chair. Black hessian cloth galled her shoulders. She scratched at her nose, and then snapped her fingers. A servant entered silently with a tray of tea and sweet-meats.

'The Invisible College frequently interferes.' She waved the man away, and poured tea. The golden liquid steamed. 'I don't care about your loyalties, either. I have all the loyal people I can well cope with, Mistress magus. For once, I would deal with someone who understands plain dealing and advantage.'

She paused, testing the liquid's temperature with her finger against the side of the cup. The fire crackled. From outside, flat in the snow-filled air, came the clash of troops drilling in the bailey.

'I would be perfectly happy to go on fighting this civil revolt with mercenary troops. Why bleed my commonwealth to death? The false ruler Carola thinks differently. She'd rouse us all to fight. Well, we have this amnesty now, and the royalists know how badly they're placed: it's no secret. So, if funded, the Queen might flee into exile.'

'Funded?'

'After civil revolt, all of us are poor; but I have control of the town's funds, while I hold the town.'

Olivia sipped at the cup. Still too hot, the tea scalded her lips. She snorted, put it aside, and sat up. A rummage among the papers excavated a previously drawn-up commission. She tossed it to the redhaired woman.

'Roseveare doesn't have any money.'

'*Carola* doesn't know that. I'm a plain woman. I won't use subterfuge with you. Here is a draft for six thousand guineas. Take it to the Mint: the Master of the Mint will let you have coin. Take the coin to Carola, persuade her to take it on what pretext you will. Then go home to your estate. And stay untouched by the commonwealth's troubles.'

She watched the woman. A vagueness in the tawny eyes she put down to the nursing child; not deceived by it.

'Or else not?'

'Or else not?' Olivia confirmed. 'No penalties.'

'Anybody could do this. Why me?'

' "Anybody" did not meet the godless Queen Carola at *The Masque of Death and Diamonds*. Nor "anybody" has not been out of the commonwealth these twenty years, close on, and so is part of no faction.'

She swept the cup up and drained it at a gulp. Standing, she moved to the window. Specks of snow whirled black against the clouds. Faces, shapes, trees, demons, battles: all visible in that mutable white. From behind her, the husky voice said:

'I take it the Protectorate's grip on the capital isn't secure, but it's secure enough to lay hands on anyone *other* than Carola absconding with six thousand guineas?'

'I assure you.'

Warmth and movement at her buff-coated elbow: Olivia glanced sideways to find the woman beside her at the window. The baby, swaddled and up against a black-leather shoulder, burped. The Master-Physician Valentine Roseveare stared out through the leaded glass.

'If I can't persuade her?'

'No harm to you or yours. I'm not vindictive. If truth were told, I hold this as having one chance in five of success; enough to make it a worthy attempt. I would save future bloodshed, if I could.'

Creases crinkled around the woman's eyes. The faintest rose-pale illumination clung to her skin: a reflection from the child's red-orange hair. Olivia reached out and rubbed at the frost-patterns on the glass.

'Then you understand—'

Sudden laughter sounded by the hearth. She looked over her shoulder. An unsubstantial boy of perhaps ten, in an antique velvet suit, played with a rough-coated dog beside the fire. His ghostly elder, a brother some twelve or fourteen years old, looked down and laughed. The white-rose badges of Princes hung on chains around their spectral necks. The elder boy wore a circlet of gold around his brow.

'General—!'

'Holding court in the Tower has notable disadvantages. Take no notice. It's a common occurrence. Tell me if I have your agreement to this enterprise?'

Olivia took the woman's arm and turned her back to the window. Behind her, the laughter faded. Before it quite crossed the verge of hearing it became smothered: screaming began.

'I've seen women – *and* men – raped with knives. With broken bottles! Cut, butchered. Women raped by half a company, and then murdered. Male soldiers sodomised. The blood's hot after battles, so . . . *that's* rape.'

Pollexfen Calmady put his fists on his hips. Turned-back satin cuffs shone scarlet. He glared across the crowded audience hall, following the Lord-Architect Casaubon's gaze.

Bevil Calmady, with Gadsbury and the White Crow, stood waiting by the main door for the carriage.

'How can I ever be a boy again?' His breath clouded the air with a scent of alcohol. One puritan courtier drew back; he sneered.

'Too much happens to us, Baltazar. And we do too much, ourselves. Men have their peccadillos; if he's weak-stomached – man, what am I going to do! For a piece of woman-flesh to come between me and my son . . .'

He shook his head. The periwig's loose ringlets flew.

'If I were you,' Baltazar Casaubon said, 'I'd discover what he says now to your lieutenant Gadsbury.'

Pollexfen Calmady nodded. The icy air coming in with the continual opening and shutting of the doors breathed across his face, the skin fever-hot. The Tower's stone smelled dank. Hushed voices echoed between the whitewashed walls.

He stared wistfully up at the nearest arrow-slit window and the falling flakes.

'I was born on an estate of three hundred and sixty-five fountains dedicated to the moon . . . A place in the mountains. Bevil, also. He left too young to recall it. Gambled away. Some city bitch has it now.'

'Polly—'

The creases in his lined face deepened. His voice sounded harsh. 'I got myself into this one. No one had to do it for me. But, *fortuna imperatrix mundi*. I gambled away estate and wealth, tell me I'm not about to gamble away my boy.'

Two strides away he checked, turned, and added, 'Not a word to him. I tried to weep for it. My eyes are dry.'

He jostled a cassock-clad man aside and pushed between two crop-haired women, ignoring their pious curses. A neigh echoed from the yard beyond the White Tower's doors. Blue-grey light flooded in with a snarl of fine snow as the doors opened.

'Gadsbury, is he telling you what I conceive he is?' He caught the boy's blue-satin sleeve. 'Don't be a fool.'

'I'm leaving the company, Father.'

Air rushed into his lungs, only the bitter hurt of that to tell him that his breathing faltered. Pollexfen Calmady coughed. He looked down at the flagstones, seeing fine snow whisk about his boots. And raised his eyes to stare at the young man's pale, determined face.

'In Christ's name, why!'

A stir in the crowd made him step aside automatically; not until then registering that the Protector and her entourage were coming through.

'Why? All I've heard from you—' he dropped his voice to a rough whisper— 'since I took you from your mother's pap, all I've heard from you is *gentleman-mercenary*. Why alter your course now?'

The self-possessed young man met his eyes. In blue satin and ice-lace, as incongruous among these black courtiers as a jay; straight-backed and slender, one hand on the hilt of his sword.

'I'll join another company. Any other company.'

'Boy.' His face twisted.

The Lord-Architect's voice boomed as he passed through the door with White Crow; something about the carriage; and Pollexfen Calmady glanced up automatically.

Silhouetted against the blue outdoor light, a young woman stood with her bare hands tucked up into her armpits. Head bowed, boots neatly together; the topmost of her skirts a ragged black, and her topcoat grey. Without raising her head, she turned it; glittering eyes meeting his.

Pollexfen Calmady rested his hand on Bevil's shoulder. 'Madam Protector!'

The plain-faced woman slowed, fingers of her left hand busy buckling a gauntlet, her head cocked to hear another man read her a report as she walked. 'Captain Calmady? There is something more?'

Light from the slit-windows reflected from his eyes: a gaze with some manic glint of humour or despair, impossible to detect which.

'There is one more thing,' he said. 'There has, or there will be, a complaint of a rape laid against my name. Will you allow me to be tried and cleared of it?'

Bevil Calmady opened his mouth, shut it again.

The Protector squinted against the subdued lamps and snow-bright morning. 'Who lays the complaint?'

'Desire-of-the-Lord Guillaime is her name.'

Feet shuffled. He looked over his shoulder. Without a word, and as one, the men and women of the Protectorate court drew back, until a clear space of flagstones surrounded the black-haired young woman. She lifted her head. The light brought out the faded bruise under her eye.

Humility Talbot whispered, 'A soiled woman is the abomination of desolation spoken of by the prophet . . .'

'Desire-of-the-Lord, is it so?'

'Yes.'

Sullen, her low voice sounded clearly in the quiet.

'Then you're arrested, Captain Calmady, and your trial will follow.' The Protector briefly signalled, and did not wait to watch the helmeted guards move in to surround Calmady. Desire-of-the-Lord Guillaime hugged her arms more tightly about her body, standing alone.

'Father.'

Guards grabbed his shoulders. Pollexfen Calmady shrugged loose, nodded to Bevil, and walked with a jaunty step between the armed men, halting as he passed Arbella Lacey.

'Trooper.'

He dug in his pocket, slid a rattle of silver coin from his hand into hers.

'Take that down to Bankside. Get the best odds you can. I want to lay the heaviest wager possible that I'll be acquitted.'

CHAPTER 5

The White Crow straightened up from tucking a torn rag into the crack between wall and floorboard. She held her hand out for a moment, testing for cold draughts.

'That's one dangerous woman: Olivia. She looks like a farmer on her way to plough a field . . . and you agree to what she proposes without even *thinking* about it. Not that I'm well-placed against threats, with children.'

The Lord-Architect cocked an eyebrow.

'Oh, well enough, then; *we* aren't well-placed!' She pulled the nearest rug up to the clothes-chest, overlapping it, and sat back on her heels as Jared entered.

'Mama, Abiathar said it was too *time-consuming* to travel around town and see things. She let me visit the shops in the court, to buy whatever I wanted.' Jared, in stocking-feet and without his coat, manoeuvred armsful of papers carefully in and shut the door. 'I have *all* today's newspapers.'

'Ah.' The White Crow watched him trot across and settle in a deep armchair. 'Ah. Good. I suppose. Casaubon, they won't be building in this weather, will they?'

'Hardly.' The Lord-Architect inclined his head with ponderous grace.

She kicked the rug across to the hearth, and spread the bed-quilt over it. A last check between door and hearth, window and hearth; and she knelt down to take the baby from the bassinet.

'So you can look after these two while I go out.'

The orange-haired baby, unwound from swaddling wool clothes, stretched her limbs in crab-like movements, hitching herself face-down across the blanket in an approximation of a crawl.

The Lord-Architect Casaubon appeared miffed. 'The Protector-General won't take kindly to my delaying.'

'Nor me, either—'

'I must go to the site sometime today.'

'*Mama!*'

The White Crow, standing up, grunted as she received Jared's full weight in her midriff. The boy clung, his arms tightly round her waist.

'You're going away again!'

She met Casaubon's gaze across the room. Obscurely warmed, she scruffled Jared's neat blond hair. 'No I'm not, pudding. Promise.'

'You *are*.'

The White Crow bent from the knee, closed her arm across the boy's thighs, and with a grunt of effort hoisted him into her arms. She looked at his red face, level now with hers, and kissed his cheek.

'All I'm doing, pudding, is going somewhere perfectly respectable for the afternoon, if I can get through the streets.'

Her head cocked to one side, she suddenly grinned. The boy wriggled. As if recollecting his dignity, he slid to the floor and pulled his cut-down waistcoat straight. The White Crow squatted down on her haunches.

'Can we trust your papa to look after Jadis on his own, do you think?'

The small boy's gaze shifted to Casaubon. Before he could voice his obvious doubts, the White Crow concluded: 'How would you like to come with me on a visit to the Mint?'

Jared frowned seriously.

'I would like that very much, mama.' He hesitated. 'If you take me, then you won't look sus . . . suspicious, will you?'

The White Crow whistled, and looked across at Casaubon. The Lord-Architect's chins creased in a vastly amused beam.

'An infant after my own heart!'

She held out her hand, waited until Jared took it, and pulled him into a hug. 'But he's perfectly right.'

Desire-of-the-Lord Guillaime sat waiting for him in one of *The New-Founde Land Arms*'s high-backed cubicles. Sir Denzil Waldegrave, seating himself opposite her with customary insouciance, noted first something brittle about her body language, and then the traces of bruises on her face.

He put his ale mug down with care. 'One time, my little spy, you shall have to tell me why you do this.'

The young woman looked at him with dark, dancing eyes. She hugged her greatcoat around herself. Snow melted in her hair. 'Why? I suppose because it pleases me.'

Denzil Waldegrave sprawled back, fingering ringlets. 'No protestations of loyalties to myself, or to the Crown, or to the commonwealth? Merely, "it pleases me"?'

Something shifted in her face. She looked down at her cold-mottled hands, shrouded in fingerless leather gloves.

'You've said often that you know "my sort." My lord.'

Waldegrave shrugged. 'You might say I have a sympathy with you. A puritan girl for whom purity was too cold, and so she makes herself available to good Queen Carola's court, for sport or for advancement. Pardon my cynicism. I am a debatable case myself. No man – nor no woman neither – knows for sure who'll come out victor in this war.'

'I care not, either way.' Now her eyes did glow, but the humour had a new, bitter cast. 'I amuse myself. My lord.'

'Why, Desire, you're dangerous. Honest, and so therefore dangerous. A pretender, and so therefore dangerous. Joyful in a time of war, and so therefore dangerous.'

'Am I so?'

'You hide yourself from yourself, and are therefore dangerous – to yourself.' Denzil Waldegrave drained his ale mug. 'So: now. Without more delay. What word from that woman's court?'

'The sole news I have for my lord is this. She has her architect come to her from the provinces. He arrived yesterday. I'll tell you his name,' the girl said, 'and you can pay me your silver pennies later.'

The bulk of the building cut off the rising wind. Snow crunched, giving underfoot. The White Crow stamped her boots down into the settled mass. Jared, brown coat neatly buttoned, trotted in her tracks.

'Mama, sometimes I think father isn't very responsible.'

Her head went back. The White Crow gave a great bark of laughter. Jared stopped by the Royal Mint and Observatory's entrance and knocked the crushed snow off his boots. Cold flushed his cheeks red.

Snow covered the wide steps and the pillared portico. Squared Palladian roofs bore a weight of white. The glass of the observatory-dome glittered, each pane's snow thinning towards the centre, showing the light within.

'Mama?'

'I would say, don't underestimate your father, Jared – however, I suspect you're right. He *is* irresponsible. I've often said so myself.'

'Oh, Mama!'

The boy pushed his tricorne hat more squarely upon his head. He gazed up. The winged-dragon weathervane above the portico creaked around, bronze wings shrieking open, snow shaking down. It shrieked:

> *'Will you watch the skies?*
> *Debase the coinage of lies?*
> *New-mint a truth that we can know?*
> *Will you enter? Will you forego?'*

Jared lifted his hat politely. 'Enter, if you please.'

'Now.' The White Crow knelt. Cold soaked the knee of her breeches. 'Draw me the *magia*-sigil for finding your way back to Roseveare.'

He raised stubby fingers and drew, stolidly, upon the air. A faint flare lightened the snow: the White Crow quenched it with a gesture of her own.

'And the sigil for people not to notice you're there? Good. And to call me or your father, if you should need us? Yes . . . more after this fashion. Thus. Yes. Good, Jarrie.'

'I wish you wouldn't call me that, Mama.'

'You'll do.'

Straightening, her hand fell to her hip. Her gloved hand brushed her studded doublet, under the thick frieze coat that hung open; no sword-belt and no blade.

One of the pair of vast wooden doors creaked open. Golden light slanted into the dim daylight. A blast of heat hit the White Crow's face, bringing awareness of how cold numbed her skin. She rested three fingers on Jared's shoulder, steering him towards the door: a mother and her child, visiting tourist sights. A smile crinkled the skin around her eyes, deepening delicate lines.

'Yes?' A stout man peered out, loose brown satin robe falling open to show a fine linen shirt. A long brown periwig fell halfway down his chest and back. 'Madam?'

'White Crow, Master-Physician of the Invisible College. This is my son Jared. I'm told I can speak with the Master of the Mint, Master Isaac.'

The man stared from under heavy eyebrows. A wide mouth and large nose made his oval face seem crowded of feature. He plucked absently at one of the periwig's trailing curls. His gaze fell on Jared.

'Ah, I see. An *educational* visit. I am Master Isaac, madam. Come in, come in. Be *quiet*!'

The dragon weathervane cut off its chant in mid-shriek and pivoted north-north-east in a fit of pique. The White Crow grinned up at it. Boot-heels skidding in slush, she followed Jared through the entrance and into the warm corridors of the Royal Mint and Observatory. The door creaked shut behind them.

The boy stopped and stared around at the milling benches, the stone grinders, the cutters and clippers, and the baskets of coin that spilled across the floor. Workers glanced up at their entrance. Isaac signalled them to continue.

'Through this way, madam, if you please. We have a most interesting observation in progress.'

The metallic din faded as they passed a further door. The White Crow automatically trod softly, staring up in dim light at the brass barrels and adjustment-cogs and wheels of a great telescope. Frost chilled the air, the glass observation-dome cranked open a yard or two.

'This most recent comet may now be viewed in daylight.' Master Isaac bustled forward, a restraining hand on Jared's shoulder. 'As you may see, madam. Young man, a comet is a collection of rocks and visible gases that circle the sun; not, as has been in error supposed, a celestial influence—'

Turning to the small lens-piece let her hide a smile. Behind her, the boy gave a forty-five-year-old man's dry cough.

She peered into the lens. Whiteness swung and focused in a bright blue sky. Magnified, the white dot swelled to a clear image.

A snarling lion's mask shone against the sky.

Dust-hazed, distinct, and of a marble whiteness: a hollow lion-head. Unbearable highlights shone on wrinkled lips, nostrils, on the great rigid swathes of mane; the light of the sun reflectant in purple-blue, oxygen-starved space. Intense indigo sky showed through the hollow eye-holes.

'That's Sekhmet's Comet.'

Master Isaac's disembodied voice held surprise. 'You're well-informed.'

'After a fashion. It's not my specialist field.'

Sunlight, unhindered by air and dust, blazed from the point of one white-marble canine tooth. Pitting and scoring marked the stone pelt: the abrasions of aeons. Corroded dust starred the great stone mane, trailing in the Lion-comet's wake with invisibly slow ripples.

She stood back, blinking, to let Jared at the lens. Through the edges of the observation dome, the comet reduced itself to a chalk-white smear across a patch of blue sky.

'Rocks and gases?'

'Any *apparent* shape is coincidental, madam, I assure you.'

Her feet followed the man automatically, oblivious until she caught a door as it swung back and ushered Jared through in front of her into the milling room.

'I'll speak of the milling process itself in a moment, madam.' The grey-wigged man gestured with restrained excitement, his eyes bright. 'If I might prevail upon you for a moment, first, Master-Physician – this is something of my own. Young master Jared may find it intriguing.'

'Yes,' the woman said, 'he probably will.'

The Master of the Mint led them across to cupboards and benches, at the further side of the hall. He spoke loudly, over the noise of the machines, and the clink and snap of cut metal. On one of the benches, fashioned from steel, ball-bearings swung on the wires of an armillary sphere.

'That's interesting.' The White Crow, her voice carefully neutral, peered into the armillary sphere's interstices. 'This is unfinished.'

'No, madam. Complete.'

She touched a fingertip to the bands marking the degrees of ascension and declension. 'No engravings for which Sphere each world belongs to – Hermes, Aphrodite, Kronos, or the rest.'

'No, madam, and do you know why? Because it needs them not.' He straightened, hands clasped behind his back in a swirl of brown satin. 'You need nothing else, *nothing else* to account for the procession of worlds about the earth but the knowledge of gravitational forces! Look you, madam, you and that fool Astrologer-Royal doubtless say, with orthodoxy, that it is the planetary *numina*, the Intelligences of each Sphere, that propel the worlds in their orbits? That the *sphaera barbarica* and the paranatellons each have influence on our bodies and our fates?'

She nodded gravely.

'*Non astrum melius, sed ingenium melius*: it is not a better star which creates the genius, it is the loftier mind! The fixed stars, in their orbits a little beyond the orb of Saturn, and the sun and moon, follow a plain gravitational orbit about the earth. Nothing else but that moves them.'

He waved his hand triumphantly.

'I can prove my accuracy. Look, look here.' He pulled open a drawer stuffed with papers. Crabbed mathematical symbols covered every inch. 'The manuscript of my *Principia Mathematica* – which the Astrologer-Royal refuses to license for publication.'

She stood with her thumb hooked into her breeches belt. The long coat hung from her narrow shoulders, hem sweeping the parquet flooring. Her head turned, seeking the small boy who stood absorbed before another of the stamping-presses.

'You'd reduce the universe to a machine, Master Isaac, all springs and motion, unable to deviate, unable to change itself – and, by the by, the *earth* circles the sun.'

'My observations tell me otherwise, madam. I cannot comprehend why the Astrologer-Royal perceives the world differently.'

His shoulders slumped. Closing the drawer and tucking in a corner of the manuscript, he sighed.

'The universe is not animistic nor animate. Worlds do not turn because the Music of it pleases them. Weights and pulleys, madam. Wires and fulcrums. The universe can be accounted for solely on this principle.'

A flurry of snow beat against the far windows. Distant, through the glass, sounded the cry of the weathervane. The White Crow raised fingertips to the feathers growing soft at her temples, and the man's gaze went past her deliberately unfocused. One of his stubby fingers poked the air, delineating an example: 'If an apple falls from a tree it strikes the earth, it can never do anything else!'

Her fingers smelled of summer apples. 'I think it some while since you were in an orchard, Master Isaac.'

'I have my duties here,' he said regretfully, 'and thus haven't time for all the observations I need. I do a little practical alchemy, also, you understand, in the furnaces . . . The salary of Master is not great. Now General Olivia wants the coinage reissued, we having suffered so greatly from counterfeiters in the late civil revolt, that I have hardly an hour to myself. Upon my retirement, I shall complete the *Principia*.'

The White Crow reached into the breast of her coat. She held out a folded paper, sealed with heavy black wax.

He stared. 'That's the Protector-General's seal.'

'Jared, ask the gentleman at the far bench to explain the milling process to you.' She lowered her voice to the decibel-level of the Mint's machinery. 'Master Isaac, I didn't come to make your life easier. I came to bring the General's commission, which I like – about as much as you do. I have a carriage outside. Can your people bring it into the yards, please, and load the coin secretly as ballast?'

Cranes and gantries jutted, the tops of the tallest lost in falling snow. Snow pasted each stone, each rope, each beam; stark white against the yellow sky. Humility Talbot picked his way across a tarpaulin-shrouded stretch of earth, narrowly avoiding a ditch. His square-toed black shoes skidded. White damp-stains began to rime the worn leather uppers.

'This way, master architect.'

The Lord-Architect Casaubon clutched the handle of his black umbrella with gloved hands. Fat white flakes plopped against the taut cloth, sliding wetly down to merge with the snow covering the building site. He hunched his chins down into his buttoned-up frock-coat. 'You're damned close to the river.'

'We have the foundations sunk well enough,' Humility Talbot protested. 'The whole plan is aligned according to the sacred geometries of the site.'

Ponderously, the Lord-Architect folded his umbrella, shook it, handed it to Talbot to hold, and ducked under a low scaffolding platform. He pushed six inches of piled snow from the stone of the walls. It fell heavily and wetly into the dug pits of the piers and pylons. He tapped the stone.

'Master architect?'

'You're building the eye of the sun, rot it, not some village hall!'

The Lord-Architect Casaubon took one foot from an ice-starred mud slick; rubbed the upper of one of his shoes against his calf, smearing the black silk stockings; and cast another glance upwards. A lowering grey-yellow covered the vast site: stones, half-built walls, piles of uncut masonry, scaffolding, and gantries. Flakes of snow drifted down, black against the sky, white against the earth. A cold, damp wind cut through clothing.

'Where was your last trouble?'

'This way, sir.'

Humility bowed his cropped head. A snatch of wind threatened to remove his wide-brimmed hat, and he crammed it down more firmly. Two braziers burned to the north, half a street down towards the river, and men clustered around them, occasionally sparing a look and a curse. He led the fat man across laid-down planks, threading a way between barrows, casks, and temporary shelters; between two towering stone walls that would in time become a perpendicular door arch.

Unroofed, a vast circular building lay open to the winter sky.

No snow lay here. Rising walls, pillars, entrance-arches, pavements: all clear. Biscuit-coloured stone took the snow's light, transmuting it to warmth, glowing back with the heat of long summers.

'Rot you, at least you have *something* right.'

The Lord-Architect squatted down with slow and immense effort until he balanced on huge haunches. Without looking up, he snapped fat fingers at Humility Talbot. The Protectorate architect handed down the furled umbrella. Casaubon poked cautiously at the warm stone with the ferrule.

The gentle curve of the walls stretched away to either side, the nearest section already lined with fluted pillars. Paving ringed the interior: a warm yellow-brown stone, inset at every heptagonal junction with a star of gold or bronze.

Between the Lord-Architect's feet, an inset oval of silver gleamed in the paving.

Just a little further in, two more curved to pattern each other; then five, seven, seventeen, and more. Glass, backed with steel and silver; thick and curved and polished to mirror-brightness, stretching out in the same pattern all around the circular building: stone pavement becoming mirror.

Three yards further in to the centre of the roofless building, the patches merged to become a plain of mirror. It gleamed, catching all light into itself, light of dull clouds, hidden sun, falling ice-flakes; glowing with a burnished silver on the verge of becoming gold.

The Lord-Architect leaned forward, pressing the umbrella ferrule into the fretwork of pale stone. The steel, smooth as mercury, reflected his black brocade sleeve.

'We laid this first, to build around it. Geomancy left us no other choice,' Humility Talbot murmured. 'The smaller buildings around are planned to Golden Rectangles; this to a circle, and the whole thing in just line and proportion.'

The Lord-Architect planted the umbrella firmly and pushed himself upright. The umbrella's narwhal-bone ribs bent. 'The dome?'

'There we had problems before . . . this . . . began. Sir, you know how it is with master masons. They have their craft, and for building square, none better, but when it comes to the structural dynamics of a dome – the weight-bearing calculations, the necessity to lay curved stone, the placing of the ribs – they must and will learn to obey orders without my explaining every reason for it!'

'Any of 'em still working here with you?'

'Yes, sir, some.'

'Damn 'em for fools, then!'

Without waiting for guidance, the Lord-Architect began to pace around the pavement, staying back from the mirrored interior. Once he paused, squinting up to where the future dome would have masonry gaps to allow in the light of the sun: dawn and dusk's warm illuminations, noon's blaze.

'We prepared the ground! When there were accidents, we blessed the stones!' Humility Talbot waved his arms. 'The Protector herself came here with chrism to anoint the support armature of the dome! It made no difference, sir, the walls still crack and fall when we build higher than this, and workmen are still found dead – crushed under stones, or fallen from secure scaffolding, or – and there's this.'

Sound muffled: quiet enough now to hear the faint hiss of flakes melting as they fall to land on the eye of the sun. Quiet enough to hear the echoes of Humility Talbot's shouting, and his harsh breath.

The Lord-Architect placed fingertips against the inner surface of the wall. He stripped both black silk gloves off and rested his palms against the stone. A frown creased his broad forehead.

'I – ees*hou*!' The fat man blinked at the unexpected sneeze, stepped back, and wiped his nose on his sleeve. 'I find this place remarkably cold, Master Talbot.'

'I know. And I know that it should not be so: not the eye of the sun.' Almost humbly, Talbot touched the large man's arm. 'You will not say what the godless say in this town: that only the monarch could build this temple, and not we of the Protectorate?'

The Lord-Architect Casaubon stared intently at the blank wall. He frowned, the tip of his tongue protruding between his delicate lips.

'Master architect? Ecch!'

Humility Talbot's nostrils flared whitely. He stepped back, muffling an oath.

In the almost-heat of the temple's interior, a smell grew to prominence. Coppery, cold; a taste of metal in the back of the throat. Given a wind from the river, the stench of the Smithfield shambles might be drifting up. The snow fell in soft verticals, denying the possibility, intensifying the stink of blood.

'How can I build a dome?' Talbot's voice sounded thick with unshed tears. Plaintive, he wailed, 'The stones themselves are become an abomination!'

Thick redness bulged from between the impossibly tight masonry joins, liquefied, and ran down the sand-coloured walls in streaks. Blood poured, running from between the stones, dripping, spouting; until the great curving wall ran red from top to bottom, for the space of perhaps twenty yards either side of where they stood.

'As to th— *assshuu*!'

The Lord-Architect blew his nose between his fingers, wiped his hand down his coat, and looked at the spreading pool of blood as it crept across the paving towards his heeled shoes.

A yard short of the first inset mirrors, it ceased, rapidly coagulating to a brown scum.

'As to *that*,' the Lord-Architect Casaubon concluded, 'you have me, Master Talbot, whom you did not have before.'

Humility Talbot shivered. He tucked his hands into his sleeves, thin arms shuddering at the touch of cold flesh. 'That's all very well, sir, but what do you propose to do? I cannot return to the Protector with no reason for the temple's defilement!'

The fat man squinted bareheaded at the sky, from here fringed with the half-built walls of the eye of the sun. His gaze took the direct line that sunlight would take, when striking in through the dome's empty centre to the mirror-floor.

'Cheer up, man!' His ham-sized hand landed on Humility Talbot's shoulder. The impact staggered the smaller man. Guileless blue eyes gazed down. 'I need the hour of noon, and a sky clear enough to see the sun; *then* I'll do a heliomantic diagnosis for you. Here, on this very site! Tomorrow. Why not? Then we'll see. Tell your General Olivia to come.'

He beamed in satisfaction.

Humility Talbot opened his mouth, and thought better of it.

'All things are made known in their proper time,' he concluded weakly.

'Of course! Good man.' The Lord-Architect nodded in a congratulatory manner. 'Nothing to be done until tomorrow noon. I'm – *eeshuu*! – I'm returning to Roseveare House. Send a carriage for me there. Pray to the Universal Architect for an end to this poxrotten snow!'

Sometime in the early hours of the next morning the Lord-Architect Casaubon wakes, turning in the creaking bed with infinite caution, so as not to wake the woman beside him. The midnight feed was long, Jadis fractious.

He rises, treading delicately towards bassinet and bottle for the next feed. Fire's embers do not take the chill from the room. He bends ponderously over to poke the child in its belly with a fat, inkmarked finger.

'Coo,' he offers. 'Coo?'

Wrinkled red flesh moves. A tiny and baleful pair of blue eyes opens. The Lord-Architect's three-month-old daughter, in total silence, gives him a look of withering contempt. He bundles the child in his voluminous silk robe and feeds her.

'Ookums,' Casaubon tries, scooping the baby up against his vast shoulder, mildly reassured as she throws up a dribble of milk onto his lapel. 'Babba . . .'

The ginger-haired child closes her eyes in what appears to be long-suffering, patient resignation.

From the bed the White Crow mutters, asleep.

Casaubon, listening, hears amid her unintelligible speech the words *Guillaime* and *Desire*.

CHAPTER 6

The morning smelled of chill, of the brazier-fires of chestnut sellers further down Whitehall. The sedan chair thumped down into the snow outside the entrance to the Banqueting Hall. The White Crow caught up the hem of her dress with one hand, tossing a half-groat to the lead carrier with the other.

'I won't be long. Wait for me.' She nodded across the street. 'Be in *The New-Founde Land Arms*.'

Wind blew keen from a blue sky. Smoke rose from all the palace's cluttered chimncys. Sound carried across snow from the furthest yard. Tottering in heeled ankle boots and cursing yards of brocade skirt, she bundled her cloak about her and pushed her way through the crowds on the steps.

'Public audience!' a red-faced Protectorate sergeant snarled. 'Get to the back of the queue!'

The White Crow shook unfamiliar unbound hair back from her face. Men and women in rags crowded the lobby and the stairs leading up from it, forcing the main door open, their breath white on the air. She looked in wonder at scabbed faces, ulcerous hands and legs, cataracted eyes.

'God save her. The Queen and her Hangman!' A man sat, crutches under his arm, withered legs sprawling.

A mess of trodden slush made the tiled floor treacherous. She stared from the doorway, over their heads, and caught the eye of the courtier in peach satin who descended the stairs, scented kerchief held to his nose. His yellow periwig something disarranged, his rouge smeared; and with a woman clinging to his arm, her dove silk dress slipping to uncover a breast, recovered with giggles.

'Waldegrave . . . ?' She shrugged and called, 'Sir Denzil Waldegrave!'

The middle-aged man snapped his fingers. Two younger courtiers cleared a path between the queues of halt and sick. The White Crow opened her mouth to say *Master-Physician*, shut it again, and clacked across the tiles, skirt and cloak still held up out of the slush.

'Roseveare.' The man's round face beamed, under his golden wig.
He did not introduce his companion. 'Madam, the Roseveare family
face is unmistakable! You must be Mistress Valentine.'

'*You* used to visit my father. I remember you and – your brother,
was it? – at Roseveare, when I was very small. Sir Denzil, I need to
see her Majesty, Carola.'

He tapped his amber cane thoughtfully on the wet tiles, frowning
in concentration. A susurrus of voices came from the stairs and the
Banqueting Hall above.

'Today?'

'Now.' She shook back folds of the satin cloak and brocade dress;
the ice-blue and silver shining in the dim lobby. 'Are you a good
subject of the Queen, Sir Denzil?'

'Madam!'

'And easy to provoke, too.' She smiled. 'Well, I am more circum-
spect, but equally as good a subject, and I need to see Carola today.
How difficult will that be?'

Denzil Waldegrave's gaze travelled across the lobby. 'Most of
these will find themselves turned away. She tires. Come up with me
now, Mistress Valentine.'

He turned a satin-and-sashed back, walking languidly up the
turns of the stairs, his arm around the whore's waist; below the
shabby panelled walls and the pale patches where oil-paintings
might once have hung. The curls of his yellow wig bobbed to his
waist.

In sudden curiosity, the White Crow called, 'Do you know a
captain called Pollexfen Calmady?'

'That pirate?' Waldegrave shuddered. 'The man is nothing but a
footpad. A *mercenary*! Were any of the family left, they would
disown him; howbeit, he had the fortune to be left sole heir, before
he gambled the estate away. I hope you're not well-acquainted
with him, madam?'

Without waiting for an answer, the round-faced man gestured
the whore away, turned his head, and put his finger to his lips.

'These Protectorate guards, madam, are more for Queen Carola's
protection than her imprisonment, you must understand. There are
so many malcontents since civil revolt became amnesty.'

Four black-armoured musketmen lined the entrance to the
Banqueting Hall. The White Crow caught the gaze of their hard-
faced sergeant. She smoothed her brocade stomacher and busied
herself arranging the lace at her décolletage.

'—another Royalist bitch—'

Denzil Waldegrave's complexion reddened. The White Crow

smiled and rested her arm on his peach-satin sleeve. As if it were easy, she manoeuvred past the queueing sick and into the Hall.

Snow-light gleamed in from the long rows of windows onto the parquet flooring, bringing colour from the velvet and brocade hangings. She stared down the vast hall. Ushers with tall staves pushed the ragged men and women into line. Somewhere a baby cried. She caught the gaze of a boy with a bulbous growth at the side of his mouth, then the crowd hid him.

'Carola still touches for the Kings' Evil.' She marvelled.

'It behoves her, madam, to go cap in hand to the mob and perform whatever they ask.'

Surprised equally at shrewdness and bitterness, she glanced at Waldegrave.

'They *do* love her, madam. As they never did and never will love the soldier-whore Olivia. Come.'

Light from the great square-paned windows dazzled. She stumbled, treading on the hem of her brocade gown; her hands that plucked at it hot now, and moist. Above, in gem-colours obscured by the smoke of torch-lit banquets, the Reubens ceiling glowed. She lowered her head from images of planetary *numina* in all glory to the purple canopy of the throne, from which focal point alone they would appear in perfect perspective, and to the woman who lolled back in it, swarthy face grinning.

'Valentine? Mistress, you've long been absent from our court. We should be greatly angered with you.'

The White Crow curtsied unsteadily. The large woman in green silk and silver lace leaned forward under the throne's jewel-embroidered canopy. One of the courtiers in the lobby now stood at Carola's side, smugly informative. The White Crow wobbled upright, kicking a yard of skirt out of the way with her heel, and approached as the Queen indicated. 'Your Majesty.'

An old woman on her knees before the throne turned her head, showing an ulcerated mouth. Green-and-yellow pus made one cheek puffy. Rheumy eyes glared at the White Crow.

The swarthy Queen raised her voice.

'We will end what we have begun here, madam Valentine, before we speak with you. Nothing else becomes our majesty but to care for our people.'

'Even so, your Majesty.' Urbane, the White Crow bowed her head and retreated a step to stand beside Sir Denzil Waldegrave. He nodded fractionally in approval.

Footsteps and voices echoed down the oblong hall. Light fell on ragged cotton shirts and leather breeches, on thin and famine-worn faces.

The White Crow let her gaze travel around – rouged and beauty-marked men in red and gold silk watching an impromptu theatre performance at one window; an old woman in jade silks, a boy no older than Bevil dancing attendance on her; groups at tables gambling with cards and dice. Their groomed wigs askew, two men with rouged cheeks handled a young woman with the clean face of a whore. Ragged children ran through the crowded court, selling winter's delicacies: fried hedgepig, roast rook.

'Now, old grandmother.' Queen Carola reached out, sallow fingers touching the old woman's face. Spots of dried blood marked her bitten-down nails. The stench of unwashed linen drifted from the old woman, and a whiff of rot touched the chill air.

Carola wiped her hand hard across the old woman's mouth, smearing yellow pus. The kneeling woman swayed. Carola muttered, inaudible. She pushed her hand back. 'There.'

The old woman slowly dabbed the smeared pus away with her sleeve. Under it, her skin showed, wrinkled and spotted brown with age. Her searching fingers touched the ulcers that had edged her lips – dry, healing scars.

'Oh, lady, bless you!'

Carola sprawled back, nodding. 'Well, madam grandmother. It is well.'

'—all blessings on you—!'

'Help her, sir.' One languid hand gestured to a courtier, who took hold of the old woman's arm, helping her away. The Queen wiped her stained fingers on her rich silk breeches.

'We have need of refreshment. Our people will not grudge an hour?'

Raucous public reassurance echoed in the Banqueting Hall. Carola stood and picked up her long cane, snapping her fingers. Four or five spaniels in ruby-studded collars sprang up and tumbled about her feet as she walked towards the antechamber door.

'Valentine.'

'Your Majesty.'

'Waldegrave, see we are not disturbed.' The door clicked shut, cutting off sound.

The swarthy woman stopped facing the window, staring down at the morning and the frozen Thamys. Black curls fell to the small of her back, dark against the green silk of her coat and knee-breeches. She turned, one hand tugging the lace at her throat.

'How long is it since *The Masque of Death and Diamonds*?'

Black eyes glinted, humorously. She reached for the chocolate Nipples of Venus that stood on a plate on a side-table, cramming one into her mouth.

'Damnation, is it *twenty* years?'

'Close on, your Majesty.'

'And you had the temerity to leave our court. Or was it tact?'

The White Crow folded her cloak and put it over the back of a chair. This small, furniture-cluttered chamber boasted a fire, and she stretched out her hands to the heat.

'Tact.' She shrugged one bare, chilled shoulder. 'I've come to collect on the debt, your Majesty.'

'Indeed? You're not the only one to use the amnesty to attempt that.' The woman laughed, a resonant richness. 'We gave them the answer that we'll give you – although we give it to you with less excuse. It is none the less true. Despite all you see here, the royal treasury is *bare*. Bare as Olivia's heart.'

The last words came with lazy precision, as if presented on a stage. The White Crow cocked her head at the panelled walls, raising an eyebrow. The Queen crossed to a small door, flung it open, and jerked her head at the muscular dark boy sprawling on a bed in the room. He sulkily rose and walked towards the exit. Carola ran a hand over his tightly clothed buttocks as he passed.

'Now we're not overheard.'

The White Crow watched a reflection in the window, overlaying the frozen river and the north bank. A woman in a blue, lace-decorated gown, hair tumbling loose; nothing of the Scholar-Soldier or Master-Physician about her. 'The scars?'

The older woman pushed heavy ringlets away from her temples. The faintest white scars marked her skin. 'We remember. You were only a child. Your eyes so huge . . . you looked up from the pavane and cried *"Ware candle, your hair's afire!"* And muffled us in your gown when no one dared touch the royal person before she burned into disfigurement.'

'I remember.'

'We would have recognised you without spies to tell us.'

The White Crow stepped forward and took a wine-glass from another table. 'The Queen and her Hangman.'

She drank.

Wine tanged in her mouth, cold and numbing. Carola sprawled down on the couch, tossing wine-soaked biscuits to the spaniels. The White Crow walked unsteadily over and sat down on the same couch, in a swathe of brocade. *'Now—'*

The swarthy woman stared at her in glacial outrage.

'If you cannot show respect, we can ban you the commonwealth!'

'I am not used to monarchs. Nor to this land. It ought to have been my home and it never was.' The White Crow looked up with eyes clear as cold water. 'Listen to me while I collect on the debt you owe me. I have six thousand guineas. *Take it.* I have it; it's all I can do.'

'All? We expect more loyalty from one of the ancient houses.'

Half-humorous, half-despairing, her gaze met Carola's.

'When I left this was still one commonwealth. No civil revolt, no war . . . it didn't matter then if Roseveare's sympathies were puritan or Catholic. Your Majesty, for the sake of childhood, when just seeing the court in procession used to make my heart turn over with pride, I come to you with what little help I can give. And – because of what I've seen since, people leeched to death to keep your court in toys and luxuries – this is all the help I can or will ever give.'

The woman opened lazy eyes, looking up through black curls, and snapped, 'Stand *up*. Now. Yes.'

Unsteady, knees rubbery, the White Crow stood.

'There is a window through there.' One nail-bitten hand gestured towards the Banqueting Hall. 'One January day they built a scaffold outside it, and my father walked through, and they cut off his head upon a block. His own people! For whose government his nature was too mild, too gentle, too honest and civil. I saw Roseveare in the crowd! Saints became serpents, and doves became devils . . . Do you think I will take anything from traitors?'

The White Crow sighed. 'I was out of the commonwealth, then, your Majesty. Far from here. And that is not all the truth about your father.'

A spaniel whined. Carola rubbed its head absently. She leaned back, a large woman of some presence, staring out from under black brows. One heeled and buckled shoe tapped the carpet.

'If you owe me any debt, pay it by taking Roseveare's gift. My duty to your Majesty.' The White Crow's hands fisted. Her lungs a hot void, she drew shallow breath. 'As for what use you put it to – to raise troops, to corrupt whores, feast, found an art gallery, go into exile, put another bridge across the Thamys – *I don't care.*'

The White Crow stood motionless, aware of the faint voices beyond the door and the crackling of the fire. The purity of the morning sky burned beyond frost-patterned glass. She put the wine-glass down, releasing it from whitened fingers; and drew a deep breath. The scent of dogs and upholstery filled her nostrils.

Carola sighed. 'You have returned no honest soul, I think.'

'Honest enough. No monarchist.'

'Olivia's woman, then?'

'That neither.'

The White Crow picked up her flowing dress, hooked one foot behind the other, and sank into a curtsey. She backed to the door. As it opened, the black-ringleted woman's resonant voice sounded again:

'Roseveare, of *course* we'll take your money. Who'd be such a fool as to refuse six thousand guineas? But don't show your face in our court again. We consider we pay all debts, tolerating your outburst. We tell you where you stand now.'

The swarthy woman held up her bitten, ringed hand; thumb and forefinger a fraction apart.

'*This* close to Newgate prison.'

The sun hung high in the south. Blue-and-rose shadows clung to the curves of fallen snow. Olivia trod down the crispness. She raised her head, stopping abruptly amid the crowd of aides and captains.

'Is it noon yet?'

Dozens of soldiers crowded the trenches, half-built walls, masonry piles, and snow-shrouded gantries of the site. Sun glinted from mail, black armour, and faces reddened by the cold. Massed breath steamed up into the air. Talk quietened as she strode past.

'The bell in Ludgate struck quarter-to, madam General, no great while since.'

'Good Master Cord, find me the architect.'

Cord-of-Discipline Mercer floundered across a hollow, where snow had drifted in the night. The young man vanished into the crowd at the foot of the nearest crane. Olivia spared a glance up at counterweight and pulley and gantry, their iron-cuffed wood bright against a blue sky.

Her eyes narrowed.

'Tell Master Cord he may save his labour.' She pitched her voice to carry. '*Architect Casaubon!*'

The great wooden platform built for lifting masonry rocked in the freezing air. Chains and ropes groaned. The man inside raised one fat arm, signalling, and the crane pivoted slowly. Olivia gazed up at the vast figure of the Lord-Architect on the platform.

'Good day to you, madam!'

His booming voice rang out across the eye of the sun, succeeded by a whisper. Crammed in a corner of the platform, somewhat green, and in shadow, a crop-haired man stood with both hands locked about the wooden rail. 'Madam Protector . . .'

'Master Humility,' she acknowledged cheerfully. 'How are your consultations, master? What conclusion have you arrived at?'

She signalled. The platform lowered, settling on packed snow some ten yards outside the circular walls. She barely glanced at that sandstone-brightness, uncanny in the white landscape.

'I've shown Master Casaubon where we attempted to build the support armature for the dome. And over what area the destroyed beams were found.' Humility Talbot's white and gloveless hands gripped the rail. 'He advises, Protector, that no human foot be set upon the stone while this attempt is made to discover causes.'

'I see.'

She snapped her fingers. Humility Talbot scrambled from the basket, stumbling on solid earth and snow, red to the ears and panting. His eyes shifted wildly. Olivia cast an eye up at the crane.

'Mistress Patience, help me unbuckle this breastplate. Lend me your cloak, Master Talbot.'

Freed of weight, she swung the cloak about her shoulders, fastened the clasp, and swung over the rail and into the masonry platform. Icy wind blew, briefly, in her yellow-grey hair, moving the wispy curls across her eyes. She rubbed her nose with a leather-gauntleted hand.

'I understand that the sighting itself will be done from here? Very well, master architect. I accompany you.'

The Lord-Architect blinked at her from slightly red-rimmed eyes. He sniffed, cavernously; beaming; rolls of fat creasing his cheeks. 'Most welcome!'

Sun glittered here and there on the heads of crossbow-bolts, on basket-hilted swords, and long pikes. The planks jerked under her boots. She grinned, fiercely, the cold freezing her lips, and busied herself with wrapping her muffler more firmly about her neck as the platform lifted into the air.

'Now, sir, you are the safest you have ever been.' Amused, Olivia leaned her arms on the railing, staring down. 'Since I believe all these within my sight, at least, are loyal. And now we may speak together privately.'

Rising, the wooden scaffolding platform creaked alarmingly, seventy feet above the earth.

'Master architect?'

'A calculated strain.' The Lord-Architect waved his fat hand casually. 'High eno— *ee*shou!'

The plank platform twisted gently. The Lord-Architect Casaubon wiped his nose on his sleeve, leaving a wet silver trail across the black brocade. He squinted up at the noon sun. 'High enough.'

She raised a gloved hand, waving to the man, just visible, in the crane's cabin. The counterbalanced gantry swung with a gradual speed. The platform moved smoothly, earth sliding away beneath, replaced by stone, until it hung directly over the circular wall of the eye of the sun.

'Just so high will the golden sphere stand, that I will have placed on the dome.' Her warm breath moistened the wool muffler. She tugged it down, rubbing at her bulbous nose and cheeks, and stretched her shoulders; cold's rheumatism fading in the glory of height and clarity.

Below, the site spread out, the geometry of circles and rectangles plainly visible under the snow. Groups of workmen clustered around braziers and tool-huts, their pencil-shadows short and north-pointing. Beyond them the land sloped down through two streets to the river, an expanse of frozen white. General Olivia stared first across the Thamys at the far shore of Northbankside, and the distant hills of Middlesex and Rutland.

'An old city, master architect.'

She turned, facing south now, the noon sun almost warm on her skin. She laughed, small and gruff, dazzled. To east and south and west, snow-covered gambrel roofs, spires, crenellated towers, warehouses, palaces. Smoke threaded up from chimneys. A rook winged lazily northwards towards the river. Olivia gripped the rail in one hand, leaning out. Beyond the soldiers and masons, people crowded well-trodden paths about Smithfield and Spitalfields and the city-wall gates; riders and carriages coming in towards the markets, a bonfire burning down towards the convent garden.

'You would not know, from here, that all totters again on the edge of civil revolt. Amnesty is a fragile plant, easily blasted. I have said we puritans are the heirs of the pagan Romans, who by their Mithras foreshadowed our Lord. Is that true, master architect, do you think?'

'Oh, indubitably.' The Lord-Architect took out an off-white kerchief, brandishing it. He leaned over the side of the platform and waved expansively to the crowd below. 'Cooee!'

Faintly, a few answering catcalls drifted up. The large man beamed.

He swung his arm in a half-circle. Olivia ducked easily and came up again. His pudgy finger ticked off the panorama of Whitehall Palace, Observatory and Mint, the Guildhall; all the great façades lining frozen Thamys: 'Fantastic carapaces!'

'Sir?'

Stray wind blew his cropped copper-red hair across his forehead. He shoved clumsily at it with a half-gloved hand, eyes squinting against the brightness and void of air, and clapped her on the back.

'Buildings – our fantastic carapaces of the soul! Vitruvius writes that all habitations, laid out according to line and true proportion, reflect the lineaments of the universe itself . . .' His eyes opened wider, a startling bright blue; lost in a delight of theory. 'Like caddis-fly cases, cities *grow*.'

'Over many generations.' She stared down. 'This town has stood against war and famine, kept by plain men and women who suffered monarchy until it grew tyrannous. And who will not suffer it now. Yet I do wonder. I do wonder, master architect, whether the blood-royal that has nourished the buildings of this city be necessary still.'

Foundations and outlines of towers, nave, and courtyards rumpled the site's covering snow. She stared down. Directly beneath, across a void of chill air, naked stone shone. Warm, startlingly delicate white stone shown now by contrast with the snow to be biscuit-coloured. The foundation, piers, and pylons of the dome.

Baroque, fretted, bright as the noon sun itself, the inlaid mirror of the central hall shone.

'*Sol invictus!*' She crossed herself devoutly.

From here, the separate inlays formed a pattern: clusters of tiny particles that became larger, Baroque shapes that, seen from a proper perspective, formed feathered eyes, stylised wings, all facing inward to where inlaid steel and silver merged in one blaze of light.

'There!' Triumphant, she grabbed his coat-sleeve. 'Look you there, master architect!'

Hanging above a circle of mirror, pure as cold Western lakes, she stared down into reflection. A fringe of inward-leaning stone walls: perpendicular arches and half-windows. The underside of the minuscule plank-platform. Even the dots of their white faces. And held within that stone foil, lambent as sapphires – the azure winter sky.

The cold air smelled slaughterhouse-warm, rich suddenly with blood. Thinned oxygen whispered in her lungs.

Bulging up from beneath, coiling masses of guts pressed against the mirror. Flesh roiled. Bloody lights, torn muscle, ropes of entrails and bowel: blue and purple and red: all Smithfield's abattoirs, all the Thamys's shambles, all the battlefields of the civil revolt could not fill the Pit so disclosed. Demon faces formed and dissolved.

She coughed, wiping streaming eyes.

'Be certain I have not lacked, neither, for those who attribute disasters here either to ill-luck, or the Lord's will. It is otherwise.'

The stench abated.

'Demonic manifestations, eh? You should have called me in the sooner.' The Lord-Architect wrested one of the ornate rings from his fat fingers and sprang it open with a nail to disclose, as it unfolded, a miniature armillary sphere. He clicked the bevel of another ring, which lifted to show the spike of a miniature sundial; busying himself between the two for some moments.

'Noon in thirty heartbeats.'

Both rings clicked shut and were returned to their respective fingers. The fat man removed a notebook from his coat-tail pocket. His breath misted the air around his face. Drops of sweat slid down his face, runnelling over chins into a wilting lace cravat. He fumbled in the pockets of his tightly buttoned black frieze coat.

The Protector-General flattened herself back against the rail as he turned around, buffeted by elbow and buttock. 'I rely on you, sir. To tell me answers that, for all their expertise, my plain men do not dare tell me.'

The Lord-Architect extracted a pencil and held it up in brief triumph.

'Sir—'

'Rot it, be *quiet*, can't you? Heliomancy takes concentration.'

Amused, cold, dizzy with the exhilaration of height, she smiled and leaned back, her arms outstretched along the platform's rails. A smell of sand and earth clung to the wood.

The fat man looked south.

Following his gaze for the briefest second, her eyes filled with the sun's blazing whiteness. She muttered a curse. Green-and-purple images swum in her vision, blotting out the snow-covered cityscape below and the purity of blue sky.

'Master architect?'

'*Hurts*, rot it.'

Faint freckles stood out on his pale skin. The delicately carved lips thinned. His head lowered and she stared through blotched sight into blinded, dazzled blue eyes. One half-gloved hand fumbled pencil and notebook, and the fat man sketched, with quick and fine accuracy, the shapes of the images swimming behind eyelids.

'There!' He snapped the book shut, beaming. 'You're fortunate to have me, madam. Any other architect would take a week to draw up these configurations. Send a carriage for me and I'll bring the answers along tomorrow.'

*

The White Crow pulled the nursery door closed, listened in the
hall for a moment to Jared's quiet breathing, and plodded down-
stairs to the kitchens. An ache born of snow-walking burned in her
calves.

'And to think I sometimes wish I was back on the road.' The
White Crow grinned at Abiathar. 'The life of a Scholar-Soldier was
always better indoors; don't let me tell you any different!'

The older woman chuckled, handing over a mug of mulled wine.
The White Crow slumped in the kitchen chair, the warmth of ovens
blasting against her skin; sighed, and slid down so that she drank
from the mug at a dangerous angle, a few drops spilling onto her
shirt.

'The little one's asleep.'

'Good . . . did she take her bottle well?'

'Sweet as a nut.' Abiathar's tone chilled. 'How you can think of
risking yourself at the court, and that baby depending on you, *I*
don't know.'

Hanging hams, sausages; new loaves wrapped in cloth; jars of
preserves and heavy iron pans: all blurred in her sight with a
sudden rush of sleep. The White Crow blinked gritty eyes. 'If I
don't sort this out, it's flee the commonwealth, and Jared and the
baby with me. The which I would prefer to be a little older, before I
travel again.'

The White Crow looked over the rim of her pewter mug. Spices
and red wine stained her mouth. She licked her lips.

The older woman wiped her hands on a kitchen cloth. 'As if you
hadn't been fretting to travel since the day you came back to
Roseveare!'

'Me? No. I don't carry sword-and-pack now . . . Am I a disappointment to you all?'

Abiathar shrugged plump shoulders. 'Ask Hazelrigg or Kitterage
when they come in. Tell me the truth. How long before you leave us
again?'

'Roseveare ought to have a different heir. Jared would – no, he
wouldn't,' the White Crow concluded. 'He'd live here in town, and
be a merchant on the 'Change. At least I'm as confused by that boy
as Roseveare ever was by me.'

'And now we sit here with half a king's fortune in the coach-
house—'

'Oh, what?' The White Crow sat up. She banged the pewter mug
down on the scrubbed kitchen table. 'That's from my having
Kitterage drive the coach, I suppose? If he can't keep his mouth

shut outside the house we'll all have more trouble than we know what to do with . . .'

'Speaking of trouble.' Abiathar grunted. She reached up to the shelf over the range. 'There's a message left for you.'

The White Crow unfolded the scrap of paper.

Madam i hope this findes you in good health. I desire you will examine me as you promis'd you should, for dis-ease or else for whether i am carrying an unlawfull child. Yr servant in the Lord. Guillaime.

'Yes . . . I did promise her that.'

'Dirty soldier's whore!'

'Roseveare owes her!'

The White Crow stood, stretched, and walked out of the kitchen, rapidly climbing narrow stairs; three flights and then four, slowing as she reached the living rooms at the top of the house.

Deep voices resonated down the stairwell.

A sudden recognisable burst of laughter made her stop, frown, and walk on up more slowly. The door banged open as she reached for the handle.

'Dress, little one! Prepare! Tonight is the night of— *asshuu!*'

The Lord-Architect Casaubon searched in two pockets, and unearthed from his buttoned-back cuff an immense brown handkerchief. He wiped his nose.

'Of the Astrologers' Feast, yes.' The White Crow stood on her toes, attempting to see past the fat man and into the room. 'I have every intention of being there, given an hour to rest beforehand – *Cas*aubon!'

The Lord-Architect stepped out. She walked in. Just too early for lamps; light flickered from the hearth-fire and reflected up from the torches below in Roseveare Court. Lady Arbella Lacey, Gadsbury, Bevil Calmady, and the Margrave Linebaugh glanced up from their card-playing by the bright hearth.

'Ah.'

Dimness muted his scarlet brocade coat. The trailing white lace cravat stood out, that and his pale face under the darkness of the periwig's curls. The gentleman-mercenary captain Pollexfen Calmady sprawled in a winged armchair. His eyes flicked up to meet hers, with a brilliance either manic humour or ironic despair.

'Polly was arrested.' The Lord-Architect waved an airy hand. 'Who else could he come to for bail? I must shift my shirt before we go out—'

'*Bail?*'

The door clicked shut behind the Lord-Architect's large and rapidly departing back. The White Crow bit down on what she might have wished to shout after him. She crossed to the window and stared out.

Pollexfen Calmady's voice came ironically from the chair. 'Madam, I'm your lawful guest, it appears. Indeed, the courts say I may not now avoid your hospitality without being unlawful – at least until they try me.'

The White Crow breathed on the window-glass and rubbed a clearness, looking down at quiet fallen snow, trodden into a mire outside the bookshops, and the booksellers' doors thrown open and spilling yellow light.

Soundless, Pollexfen Calmady appeared by her side. His coat smelled faintly of scent and ordure. One of the wig's harsh curls scratched her cheek.

'Selling broadsheets,' he said thoughtfully, 'every hour of night and day, new ones.'

'Don't fear. You'll have your turn in the Newgate broadsheets.'

He turned, facing her in the dim room, drawing the skirts of his coat slightly back. Sword-hanger and blade both gone. He smiled crookedly. At the hearth, the card game continued.

'I appreciate that I am not a welcome guest. Nor, things standing as they do between myself and your husband, a guest that you can refuse.'

He shrugged.

'And the girl is your patient, Master-Physician; yes, all this I see clearly. But see you, I did no more harm to her than any sleeping husband who wakes to find himself in congress with his wife. If she have a child, I'll pay for it – if ever I have money. And if she needs a name I'll wed her, although truth to tell, there are those yet living who have had that privilege before her.'

The White Crow looked down at her hands. The faint luminosity of *magia* touched her skin, no brighter in this dim room than in full sunlight; pregnant with the possibilities of healing and destruction.

'*Excuse me.*'

She inclined her head curtly to Bevil and the rest, walking out. A few yards down the corridor she kicked a bedroom door open, walked in, shut it, and leaned back against the wood.

The Lord-Architect Casaubon stood with his shirt-sleeved arms over his head, fingers almost touching the plaster ceiling, his head muffled in the shirt's vast folds. Unbuttoned green silk breeches wrinkled massively across his buttocks and thighs. His elbows worked: muffled muttering succeeded by a ruffled crop of copper-gold hair emerging.

'Little one.'

Abrupt, he reached one fat finger to stroke her cheek. The White Crow absently pulled the drawstrings at his sleeve and tied the laces in a loose bow.

'The man is a rapist,' she said dangerously.

'He is one of my oldest friends.'

'Whom you haven't seen for – *how* long?'

The Lord-Architect shrugged magnificently. 'He came to me for help; could I refuse him?'

'You? Well, no, *you* . . .' The White Crow shook her head. 'But staying in this house?'

'Terms of bail,' Casaubon explained. 'And in any case, little one, he had a claim on my hospitality. Blackmail.'

'What?'

'If I hadn't conceded, he swore he'd tell you how I wrote to him last summer, and persuaded him to put my name to the Protectorate for the repair of the eye of the sun.'

'You *wrote*—'

The White Crow opened and shut her mouth several times. In the lamplight's yellow softness, she watched the Lord-Architect tucking in his shirt and buttoning his breeches up the sides, one hand reaching over his immense shoulder to grab the trailing ends of his braces.

'Yes. I can see that you wouldn't have wanted him to tell me that.'

'You'd be angry,' Casaubon explained, 'given that you don't know about it.'

The cinnamon-haired woman choked, and rubbed moisture out of the corner of her eye with her knuckle. She seized his wrist, that her two hands together could not reach around.

'I might have guessed. I might have *known*—'

He looked down at her over the swell of chins, chest, and shoulder. 'I believe I didn't quite catch that?'

'I said,' the White Crow observed, 'it's a good thing that he didn't tell me, and that I don't know!'

CHAPTER 7

The astrologer William Lilly plodded on from Eleanor's Cross in the dusk. White snow gleamed on the gables of the over-hanging houses. He trudged through slush trodden black, and over the yellow stains of chamber-pots emptied from upstairs windows.

A wolf howled.

He dug his chin into his collar, head down, hurrying for the arched entrance to St Martin's disused wine cellars. Torchlight and voices came up the steps: infallible signs of the Astrologers' Feast. He hacked snow from his boots on the worn brick steps.

A rough-coated body pushed past his legs.

'God's teeth, man!'

The wolf barged down the stairway, paws splaying, head low. Mange marked its grey-black pelt. William Lilly abandoned the entrance-way, slush and a searing cold wind blowing in, and followed. The wolf's muzzle swung to give him one glance with eyes as pale as ice. Scars and ribs could equally be seen under the thinning fur.

'Cannot you take a little more care?'

He came down off the last step. The arched brick vault danced with torchlight, shadows, and smoke. Immense barrels lined each side. At the far end, beyond an iron grating, the noise of the Feast's preparation echoed. Here nitre clung to the walls, and brickwork smelled of graves. The wolf whined, pawing at a heap of clothes.

Pale skin spread through its pelt.

Its bent limbs lengthened, straightened, grew. A faint cracking of bone echoed.

A shadow leaped upright on the wall.

The young man, his naked back to Lilly, and every knob of vertebrae standing sharply in relief, reached down and swung the bundle of clothes up. He thrust head and arms awkwardly through a black robe's neck and sleeves.

'Sir, I apologise.' He bowed as he turned, adjusting his white

falling-band and the belt of the robe. 'I beg your pardon – unseemly
– but my late arrival—'

William Lilly met the young priest's gaze: colourless as ice.
Underfoot, sawdust clogged with wetness; the pine-smell overlaying dankness and the perfume of oil-lamps. He bent and picked
up a black-covered book that had fallen from the bundle of clothes.
'Yours, sir, I think.'

'I thank you, yes.' A shy smile. 'It is the first time I will have
preached at the Astrologers' Feast. I'm to give the later sermon. The
text being Genesis 1:14, "Let there be lights in the firmament of the
heaven . . . and let them be for signs." '

'Then let me be first to bid you welcome. "*Non cogunt*: the stars do
not compel." ' Citing the Feast's watchword, William Lilly took the
arm of the young werewolf-priest and walked on into the crowded
cellars beyond.

'Master Lilly.'

The White Crow shrugged her shoulders, sitting back from the
piles of open books on the table. Muscles loosened and lost tension.
For a moment she stared into unfocused middle distance, not seeing
around her the powdered wigs, brocade coats and black robes, and
the ruddy faces of the assembly.

'Mistress White Crow.'

She smiled up at the thin man. 'Will you thank your compatriots
again for letting me use their library here?'

Voices burred. Above forty men and women stood talking in the
cellars; some here in the fire- and damp-proof library, more
through in further rooms lined with old casks and heated with iron
braziers. She unbuttoned her doublet, hot for the first time in days.

'May I help?'

'I'd be glad of it.' She pushed at the sprawl of papers on the long
bench and shifted a pile of emphemerides-tables. 'Geomancy isn't
my best line of work. And I'm not the architect in my family.'

'I perceived Master Casaubon was unwell.' The man smoothed
his black gown as he seated himself on the opposite side of the table.
His dark hair he wore long and natural. 'I can calculate you a
reading of any subject, event, or question within seven to ten
minutes.'

A large man in a curled grey wig and strawberry silk leaned over
his shoulder. 'What, Master Lilly? *Still* practising horary astrology?'

He raised his head, taking in the White Crow.

'Elias Ashmole, ma'am. Astrologer-Royal. This dunderhead still
thinks he can predict an answer based upon the astrological

moment of *asking the question*! Pure foolishness and delusion. If you have not the exact hour of a subject's birth, how may you predict anything?'

The White Crow leaned back and put one foot up on the bench, clasping her hands round her knee. She grinned.

'I'm by no means certain, masters, that prediction is possible in this uncertain world. The Invisible College has always denied it. Else where's free will? But it so happens that I need a reading of the Celestial Spheres, not for a person, but for a certain construction-site—'

Elias Ashmole held up a fleshy hand. 'No names. Madam, I beg you, no names. Our rules at these Feasts are, no oaths to be sworn, no toasts drunk to any faction, and *no* discussion of sympathies in the present civil disorder. How else could we continue to meet in harmony?'

'Well, yes, Elias, and I am certain she knows all of that, being a magus.' William Lilly chuckled. 'Nor I will not say that I do not recognise what is this date of construction you have here. But to the meat of the matter: what should the analysis discover?'

'Why such a sacred site is plagued with demonic manifestations.'

'Well now . . . I'll see what I can do.' His dark head bent over the papers. 'Pay me in kind: a Thamys salmon, or a hare; a sack of coal; something of that. No one is rich as the world stands now. Let me see . . .'

Ashmole tutted.

The White Crow settled back. Her shoulder bumped solidity. She raised her head, apologising; and a small and wispy-haired man blinked through half-spectacles at her.

'Madam Roseveare.' He smiled shyly. 'Could you spare me a little time, I wonder, for some speech about antiquities?'

'I beg your pardon?'

Unperturbed, the man gathered his moth-eaten robes about him and bowed.

'Your childhood recollections of Roseveare and this noble town of ours before the civil war. Such things are of great interest to me. I am writing a – no, I cannot call it a history, it is too brief. A collection of the lives of those whose names history should not forget. I wonder, madam, if you might speak to me. Even a child's memories may be useful.'

The White Crow smiled wryly. 'Yes, later, Master . . .'

'Aubrey. John Aubrey, madam.' He blinked and removed his spectacles, disclosing a young face surprisingly sharp and tenacious. 'Please remember that *I* spoke with you first. My friend Master

Evelyn has a diary that he is completing, on much inferior lines, and I wish my own work to see the printer or ever his should.'

'Yes . . .' The White Crow inclined her head. 'Excuse me, sir, please.'

The group of astrologers closed in around table and charts. She grunted, stretching, and walked down to the further table and slumped into the chair beside the Lord-Architect Casaubon.

'Having such a body of knowledge here it'd be criminal not to use it, *but*—! All this tolerance is beginning to get on my nerves. If I see one more royalist and puritan propagandist – beg pardon, "astrological pamphleteer" – breaking bread together . . . Here's Lilly drinking with Ashmole: you wouldn't think they'd been calling each other *the Commonwealth's Excrement* in a half-dozen broadsheets this month.'

Casaubon, head bent over plans, compasses, square, and rule, grunted.

'Oh . . . they may well keep in with each other, I suppose. They're going to need friends, whichever side wins. What have you got?'

Casaubon sniffed. 'I am not a superstitious man. I refuse to believe hocus-pocus about the necessity for "royal" blood! Patently obviously there is some fault in the proportions and patterns of the eye of the sun, that encourages disorder to manifest itself there. *Patently* obviously—'

He coughed cavernously. The White Crow looked at his flushed face above his unlaced shirt, noting beads of sweat that plastered his copper-red hair to his forehead.

'Except that I confess I cannot find it!'

She stood, pushing papers and books aside, and walked around him until she could lean on his shoulders, and put her arms about his neck. His fair skin burned. She rested her cheek against his, that sweat made warmly wet.

'I saw Carola touching for Kings' Evil today. It worked. She healed people. I saw.'

His vast chest rose and fell, the thickness of his breathing audible. The Lord-Architect frowned.

'Blood-royal? *Eee*shou!'

She stepped back. The Lord-Architect Casaubon squinted and felt the back of his head, apparently in some surprise that it was still there. He wiped his sleeve across his face. Phelgm trailed down onto the waistcoat that barely contained his belly.

'I— *shaaa*!'

The White Crow hauled a kerchief out of her breeches pocket and thrust it at him. He took it gratefully, wiping his reddened, streaming nose. He looked up through watery eyes.

'Rot it, I *almost* know!'

'I'll keep searching.' She walked over to the further shelves, elbowing between two arguing astrologers and an alchemist. Her finger traced bookspines, stopping at familiar bindings, and she hooked out a three-volume set of the *De Occulta Philosophica*, a second edition of *Ghâya*, the *Novum Organum*, and a much-thumbed *Picatrix*, and dumped them on the nearest unoccupied table.

Three minutes after she seated herself, a shadow crossed the lamplight.

'Damned ruffians! They nearly had my carriage over in Oxford Street.' A small man beat snow from his black coat. Breaking off in mid-movement, he leaned across the trestle-table and spoke quite naturally: 'There is a theosophist work you should read, Madam Valentine, if you haven't: *Under the Shadow of Bright Wings*—'

'—*In the Heart of the Womb*,' Valentine White Crow completed. She lowered her voice slightly. 'You're the first of the College I've met here, Master . . .'

'Harvey, William Harvey. Ashmole told me you were come. Your reputation goes before you.'

'And yours, sir. I know you for our foremost surgeon.'

William Harvey seized a chair and turned it about, and sat with his arms resting along the back, and his chin on his arms. She judged him in his thirties; a short, neat man with hair powdered and drawn back, and brilliant dark eyes.

'Overturned carriage?' she queried, closing a book and keeping her thumb in the place. 'Would that have to do with your medical research?'

He snorted with laughter without moving his chin from his arms, so that his shoulders jolted. 'It would. Damn me if I didn't take *four* sword-and-dagger men to Tyburn with me this time, thinking that's enough – and we cut the man down fairly, after many had come up to take the benefit of a hanged criminal's touch on head or breast – and had him shrouded and, as I thought, on the way to the Anatomy Hall. Halfway down Oxford Street I hear a cry. "*Reverence the dead!*" So we whip up the horses, and race a mob of two hundred . . .'

He lifted his head and spat on the sawdust floor.

'You'll be pleased to know I keep the Invisible College's name somewhat distanced from this, or else *you'd* find a Tyburn riot at your door.'

Conscious of the smooth movement of muscles under her skin as she stretched, feeling the blood's beat in her temples, the White Crow smiled ruefully. 'You understand their fears. To be dead and buried is one thing, to be cut up under arc-lights and studied . . .'

'How else can some ruffian make restitution for a crime? This whelp had all his friends there to see him turned off, and every one of 'em determined he should be of no more use afterwards but to be packed in clay and left to rot.'

Sir William Harvey spread thin, strong fingers; lamplight glinting from an onyx ring.

'I've tracked the blood's circulation, by examining where it passes through artery and vein. How else now can I examine different kinds of blood, without I have blood in profusion to do as I like with? Precious few will give it living; I have to make do with the dead.'

Letting go of the third volume of *De Occulta Philosophica*, the White Crow turned her wrist over so that the back of her hand rested on the table. Her left index finger stroked the skin, leaving a faint pale-rose illumination; all the sensations of the hard bench, echoing cellar, odours of cooking and parchment, cold air and men's sweat, intensified as she measured the subliminal drumming of a pulse.

'Madam Valentine?'

'Agrippa writes that the heart's blood is under the Sign of Helios; the blood of the extremities under—?'

'Technically, Thoth or Isis, according to ascendant.' Harvey leaned forward, one finger prodding the bench. 'Or, as it seems to me in my discoveries this last year, the constitution of blood is as individual as the constitution of your astrological nativity. The magus Agrippa hadn't my modern advantages. I've put blood to Chemicall analysis, finding in it, for each man or woman, a *unique* combination of such Elements as Paracelsus describes.'

'If that's true . . .'

Large hands cupped her shoulders from behind, the hot palms dampening the cloth of her doublet. Harvey's gaze lifted – and lifted again. She leaned back against the Lord-Architect's stomach, feeling him sway slightly, and blinked at the sudden strong odour of wintergreen and brandy.

'You heard?'

' "Blood-royal." The virtues of individual blood!' The Lord-Architect hit his fist into his other ham-sized hand, with a sound that echoed off the cellar's curved walls. Four or five people glanced round. He beamed at them.

'Casaubon?'

Overhanging the trestle-table, the Lord-Architect Casaubon held one hand up precariously and wiggled spread fingers.

'Pox rot it, it was there in front of me! You told me. *She bites her fingers.* Enough to cause blood to flow. And then touches for the Kings' Evil . . . And heals it, with whatever the virtue of her particular blood is. Amazing the woman isn't dead of some disease by now.'

The White Crow looked up over the swell of his black satin waistcoat, and the brandy-stained lace ruffles at his chins, and met the Lord-Architect's gaze. Sweat runnelled his face. She stood up, grabbed his sleeve, pushed him into her chair, and hitched herself up to sit on the table between Casaubon and the surgeon.

'I thought you were the one who didn't believe in the mystical virtues of the blood-royal?'

Both the Lord-Architect's elbows hit the table. The White Crow winced, feeling the vibration through buttock and hip. He leaned his chins on his fists. 'As to that – ask the Queen's Surgeon, here.'

She turned her head. Sir William Harvey's darkly brilliant eyes met hers.

'He is Queen's Surgeon, it's common College gossip.'

'Madam, how else can I get protection for my researches? General Olivia will have all bodies religiously buried, I can get no help there.'

The Lord-Architect coughed and blew his nose between his fingers. The White Crow gave him a look of utter disgust. He gestured at Harvey:

'Well, rot it! Am I right?'

'The royal family have always been able to touch for the Kings' Evil,' Sir William Harvey said. 'Because, passed down from generation to generation, they carry that disease themselves. Except that in them it's not fatal; and this ability to carry it harmlessly is what, I think, they pass on with their touch. You understand that the disease has lesions, sores, that allow such contact of vital spirits between her and her petitioners; so that even were there no apparent blood, she would still heal.'

He shrugged, finally.

'Of course, none of that royal line live much past forty, and most go soft-witted in the last year or so. If I were a man of science who did *not* value my head, I would tell Carola to adopt an heir. As it is, I praise the blood-royal for its noble healing qualities.'

'That's *it*. The newest Entered Apprentice could see it! "Mystical virtues" my arse. Where were my wits?' The Lord-Architect reached across and wrapped the White Crow's hands within his own. She winced at his grip. His booming voice dropped to a low rumble:

'This city has a perfectly respectable tradition of blood-consecration, and for centuries they've been feeding the earth – what? Diseased blood! Of all the whoreson, stupid, rat-arsed, pox-ridden idiocy! No wonder the place is subject to demonic infestation. It's a wonder they can stand one brick on another!'

CHAPTER 8

'I have probably heard as much as I should, unless this is College business.'

His chair scraped brickwork as Sir William Harvey stood. His bow was a bird-quick movement of the head. Still seated, the White Crow reached across and shook his hand: a thin and tenaciously strong grip.

'Thank you, sir.'

The Lord-Architect, holding his black brocade frock-coat open and burrowing in an inside front pocket, lifted his head long enough to say, 'My regards to young Janou, if you ever hear from any others of this pox-rotten College.'

'Sir: of course.'

She watched the small man's back as he threaded a way through the crowd that, almost by Brownian motion, began a drift towards the largest vault. White tablecloths and iron tableware shone, beyond the next arch. Smells of cooked pig, quail, roots, and gravy heated the air.

The Lord-Architect took out his hip-flask and lifted it to his lips.

'So you're to go to the Protector . . .' The White Crow hooked up one foot onto the table's edge, clasped her booted ankle, and rested her chin on her knee. 'And say: madam, you stand in need of Carola's blood-royal, because I see no way to banish these demonic manifestations but by use of this diseased blood. So you must agree to whatever terms the Queen may make, when she hears of it? No.'

Her finger stabbed the air.

'No . . . There'll be enough of her father's by-blows in the commonwealth that the Queen isn't the only one with such blood. Do you see Carola summoning up the energy or the courage to spill her blood on the eye of the sun? They'll search for some poor bastard of the last reign and use them.'

'No.' Casaubon coughed. 'Not at all that simple.'

'Why not?'

The Lord-Architect Casaubon sneezed and wiped his nose on the sopping lace-ruffles at his cuff.

'Go home.' She prodded his bolster-arm. He coughed again, resonantly; and she laid her hand across his forehead, brushing aside sweat-soaked hair. 'I'll come back in an hour and make a Chemicall Decoction. At least I know which of the planetary *numina* will cure influenza. Casaubon, will you listen to reason?'

'I don't want to leave you.' His breath touched her hand as she lowered her arm. Hot and moist. He coughed again, cheeks reddening.

'Will you go home in the carriage now, or shall I wheel you home in a cart later? I would sooner,' she said, changing from humour to seriousness in the space of a breath, 'have someone else in the house with Jared and the baby, apart from Kitterage. Will you go?'

'Of c— as*shuuu*!' The Lord-Architect stood up, swayed as he threw his muffler round his neck, and bent to plant a snot-wet kiss on the White Crow's hand. 'Of course I will, little one. You may trust me implicitly.'

'The trouble is,' the White Crow said morosely, wiping her hand on the back of her breeches, 'that I do.'

She watched his teetering bulk stagger away. The fat man ducked his head as he passed under the wine-vault's arches, knocking with his shoulder a cask that two men and a woman had to grab and replace. A last glimpse of copper-red hair and stained black brocade: she lost him in the crowd.

She turned, walking through into the main vault. Long tables lined the walls. Fires glowed in heavy braziers. It washed over her, the noise of more than forty men and women gathered talking, waiting to be called to table. She nodded acknowledgements; greetings.

'Valentine White Crow.'

Hot wire pulled itself tight from throat to gut.

She turned her head. Desire-of-the-Lord Guillaime stood with her gloveless hands outstretched to a brazier. A young woman, not tall; all her thin body bundled up in torn skirts, layers of shirts, a dark greatcoat a size too large. Snow clung to her black hair, melting. 'I was searching for you.'

'What do you want?'

'Is something the matter?'

The White Crow hugged her arms across her body. The doublet's studs chilled her hands. 'Possibly I'm coming down with the influenza. Well?'

The young woman's blue-mottled fingers moved to her coat, unfastening buttons slowly. She gave a slow smile. 'I would like something to drink.'

The White Crow reached out and took hold of the woman's elbow, the black cloth rough under her hand. Pressure steered Guillaime out of the crowd's main flow, into the space between two wine-casks taller than carriages. She brushed the young woman's frozen fingers away and unfastened the coat herself.

'There.'

She reached across, taking a pewter mug, and twisted the wine-cask's top to fill it. Claret glistened. The surface of the dark liquid shook. The White Crow steadied her hand and lifted it, drank a mouthful, and passed it over.

'Now.'

'Our friend sends me to make the arrangements for your "gift".'

The quiet, distinct voice carried no further than a yard. Using both hands, the young woman brought the pewter mug to her mouth and drank. She lifted her head. A red stain half-mooned the infinitesimally fine hairs above her upper lip. The White Crow noted the flush beginning to burn under the fine skin of her cheeks. Little trace of bruises now.

'I'll want more authority than just your word.'

Closed lips moved in a smile; all the warmth of that in eyes that lowered, flicked up again; challenging.

'You expect the royal Seal?'

The young woman bent and put the mug by her feet, a motion that carried her intense gaze across the assembled feasters. She plunged both hands into her greatcoat-pockets, standing with her weight back on one heel, the other hacking at the flagstones.

'I come with a password. *Newgate*. Will that serve?'

The White Crow pursed her lips and nodded slowly.

'Very well. What arrangements?'

'The coin's ballast in your carriage. Make her a gift of the carriage and horses. Many courtiers do more to gain favour. It won't draw suspicion. Nor it won't seem too easy to her.'

'Your Protector's a fool. Giving her money. It'll break the stalemate, there'll be real war—'

'She knows the godless woman better. So do I. I'm privy to her plans for escape.'

'You?'

Melted droplets of snow stood in the young woman's hair, she standing self-possessed with her hands stretched out to the brazier's red coals. The hems of her skirts were soaked knee-high with black slush. She shivered: a glimpse of flesh between coat-collar and muffler struck by draughts. Her upper lip curved, lifting.

'She'll give anything to be out of house-arrest at Whitehall. She plans to be across the Narrow Sea and in her cousin's court before you can say exiled monarch. And stay there drinking, and going with harlots, and dreaming of the return she'll never make . . .'

Teasing, acid, her tone flicked the White Crow's temper raw.

'Nothing but gossip, I see. But true enough, I don't doubt. Well? That's all. You can go. What else is there?'

The young woman leaned narrow shoulders back against the great cask's curving staves. 'You're a Master-Physician.'

'. . . The examination. Yes. Yes . . . Come to me tomorrow.'

Light glinted on brown leather and studs; on the tiny white pin-feathers at the White Crow's fair-skinned temples.

'Before noon. Abiathar will be out reprovisioning, but if you come to the front of the house, I'll let you in.'

Black lashes lifted. Eyes that seemed of no colour save brightness caught firelight.

A fiddle squeaked in the night air. William Lilly leaned forward into the cold wind, walking homeward; cloak bundled firmly around him. Snow slid cold and wet across his cheeks.

Ahead, a great bonfire blazed. Snow hissed, floating down from the darkness and falling, consumed, into the flames. Firelight leaped on the paving, on the crowds; sent men's shadows long into the colonnades and porticos of the convent garden.

'In truth, the skies being so obscured, I had forgot it.'

His boot-heels rang on the wet cobbles. He skidded in the slush, walking quickly to keep up with Sir William Harvey and the red-haired woman. The clock up on the portico chimed ten. A weathercock called '*All's-well!*' He tucked his mittened hands under his tightly bundled cloak.

'This new comet throws out all computations. It hangs in the Sign of the Archer now, about the hour of ten; moves towards the Greene Lyon.' Cold air dried his throat. He coughed. 'What charts I've drawn you, I can't guarantee.'

She turned and faced him, walking backwards for a few paces on the slick, frozen cobbles. The brown cloak swirled to briefly disclose boots, breeches, and the heavy studded brown leather doublet. No sword-belt, no blade. Beyond her, men and women danced and passed bottles; dogs barked. Torch- and firelight shone on her barleyrow Scholars' braids.

'I understand, Master Lilly. I had little hope of astral *magia* answering this, in any case. We need true geomancy.'

From the other side of her the small man growled, 'Sekhmet's Comet makes all unpredictable. And portends no great good to any.'

'As you say, Master Harvey. Now: my way parts with yours here—'

'*Surgeons!*'

Glass smashed.

Lilly stared down at the fan-shaped spray of fragments, each catching the light; sharp edges sinking into slush. High above, the weathervane's cry shifted: '*Beware!*'

He fumbled his coat open, the hilt of his sword cold even through kid-leather bindings. A voice in the crowd around the fire shrieked. 'Harvey! It's Butcher Harvey!'

The small man pulled up the collar of his black coat. His powdered hair slipped from its black-ribbon tie. 'Whoreson excremental rogues. About: we'll go by Henrietta Street.'

The redhaired woman nodded, walking back steadily and quickly beside the astrologer. Head down, her eyes glittered in the bonfire's light. He followed her up steps and under the portico's cover.

'Too late.'

A stone ricocheted from a pillar, skittering into the colonnade. A man swore. The crowd jerked: a living thing, all its chirascuro pieces of man, child, woman, and dog eddying suddenly like a flock of rooks.

'Their numbers are too great.' Lilly rested his rapier's point on the flagstones. 'Madam, if you can—'

Pain stabbed bitter on his tongue.

A hand under his arm dragged him up. Heat hammered his face. His back, snow-wet from falling down, froze, cloth clinging damply to his spine and calves. He grabbed for his dropped rapier. His hands knocked cold cobblestones.

'What . . . ?'

Her fingers touched the side of his head and he winced with the pain of the unseen wound. He looked stupidly down at his empty hand.

'Portending ill.'

White flakes floated slowly down from the darkness. Fire's orange and red seared against the blue dusk. Logs spat, burning. A rim of blue flame rippled down the planks of a cart, thrown on to make festival fire. A dozen men ran towards him.

'Whoreson bastards!' Harvey yelled, cudgel in one hand, rapier in the other, darting out between the pillars. Swords hit. Metal clanged, loud as any smithy, echoing back from stone. A cart swung up and over, crashing down: a woman launched herself off the top as it fell and struck a tall man between the shoulder-blades. Both fell, lost in the mêlée.

A bottle crashed against the wall beside him.

'A pox!' The redhaired woman picked splinters of glass off her sleeves.

'Madam Roseveare!'

Her face shone, blank with excitement. She moved from foot to foot, hands lightly clenched as if around the hilts of a sword and Florentine dagger. Her eyes fixed on the inexpert cut and parry of the brawl. She grinned and showed all her teeth.

'Oh, I wish—'

The woman abruptly spun round, slid down with her back to a pillar's shelter, and locked one hand in the other's grip. He stood dizzily above her. Shouts blasted his ears. A body knocked against him, jolting him: William Harvey slid to his knees, back in the pillar's shadow. Breathless, he grinned.

'Look out, they come. They mean to beat and kill me, I think.'

'Then don't assist them to it!' Lilly grabbed the small man's shoulder. Fear turned over cold in his stomach. 'Madam, what can you do?'

She looked up and he met her abstracted gaze: a little humorous, a little sad.

'I can wish I carried a sword, Master Lilly.'

Exasperated, he said, 'But you do not. Madam—'

'It isn't the ability to defend myself, or others, that I miss. Although there are times when a pistol or sword would be of more immediate service than *magia*. Yes.'

She smiled painfully.

'I miss fighting.'

Her eyes bright, she leaned forward, rocking just slightly, movements of muscles restrained. Unseen, someone shouted. A hard object hit the wall. A sudden rush of footsteps halted. Each noise made her eyes flick sideways, seeking.

A musket crashed, shot exploding across the dark sky in warning. Noise sang in his ears.

'Now that's enough.' The woman stood.

Sir William Harvey grunted and got to his feet. 'My apologies for this.'

The woman touched him lightly on the shoulder. She turned to face the convent-garden square. Snow fell on the rioting crowd, the speed and solidity of the flakes ignored.

She reached up and drew a long pin from her hair. Gold sparkled.

Without hesitation she held up her left hand, and thrust the pin through the centre of her palm. She dropped to one knee. Her bloodied fingers traced sigils in the frozen slush and on hard-trodden ice.

Silence.

The night darkened. Icy air breathed in his face. Lilly rubbed his eyes. 'Madam, well done!'

Thickening snow fell faster. A sharp crack echoed. He stepped back, thinking it a stone; another fell, and another.

Hailstones plummeted down.

The night skies opened. Within three heartbeats he could hear nothing but a million hailstones hiss and crack, splintering down on cobblestones; sky thickly grey over the convent-garden walls; the bonfires guttering to extinction. Splinters of ice shrapnelled the pillars.

In the open square men and women covered their heads with their hands, running abjectly for shelter.

Hailstones drummed. The woman hissed between her teeth, tugging the needle from her hand. The skin of her palm pulled up as the metal withdrew. Blood welled. She sat down hard in the slush, on the stone under the portico, legs sprawling; her face running with sweat.

Her voice, when it came, rasped with utter exhaustion:

'I was ten years a trained Scholar-Soldier. I was the best they had with a blade. Now I'm Master-Physician and no soldier . . . Don't think I never knew who I injured, or what it meant, or how much I risked. *I miss fighting.* I miss all the dangers of a duel. It was – it's like air and sunlight to me.'

A new morning chilled her. Olivia touched a gauntlet to the blood-marked stone and straightened. Soldiers crowded the construction-site behind her, pikes and crossbows ready under a cold and brilliant sky.

The workman's body lay already shrouded.

'And no answer from Master Casaubon?'

Humility Talbot shook his head.

'I'll have an answer today,' she said grimly, 'if I have to go for it myself.'

The Lord-Architect lifted one large, bare foot from the bowl of hot water, examined it morosely through the steam, and sneezed. His foot thumped down. Water flew across floorboards and bedroom rug.

'I am *perfectly* well!'

The woman sat back on her heels. She brushed at her now-wet shirt with a bandaged left hand. 'Of course you are. Or at least, you will be.'

Aromatic herbs floated in the steaming bowl. He sniffed. Under his vast nightdress, talismans on chains hung hot against his skin. As he watched, she unwrapped the rough bandage and squeezed a drop of blood from her palm into the water.

'Will that cure me?' he croaked hopefully.

'That and staying in bed for the next twenty-four hours.'

'I have no intention of going back to bed!' Casaubon paused; took out his handkerchief; blew a long, wet, trumpet-blast; and surveyed the result dismally.

'Except,' he finished weakly, 'possibly for the next twenty-four hours.'

The Queen and Sir Denzil Waldegrave stood at one window of the Whitehall Palace, looking down into the snow-choked yard. Carola cradled a bottle of Madeira. A team of four horses strained at the crack of a whip. The driver, a lanky fair-haired countryman, pulled the team up on treacherous ice. Washed, if not polished, the elderly coach shone in the morning light.

'Odds me, madam, a rare present.'

'More than you know.' The swarthy woman laughed, clinking bottle to windowpane, and pushing the window open. Freezing air cleared the fug of the night's marathon card-game. Waldegrave shuddered, pale.

'We will have you stow Roseveare's gift safely away. Very safely.' Carola hesitated. She pointed with one blue-silk-clad arm. 'Sir, who's that? With yonder little puritan girl.'

Below in the yard, the woman Guillaime entered under the arch and stopped dead. A gentleman-mercenary, one among many entering the Palace for the morning's audience, took off his tricorne hat and bowed. Brown curls glinted. The young woman straight-armed past him, skidding in the snow. His guffaw floated up to Carola.

'Captain Calmady, ma'am. A mercenary. An incurable violent man.' Denzil Waldegrave inclined his head as the man saluted the Queen. 'He raped the girl and must hang for it, since the woman Olivia has him under her arrest.'

She lifted the bottle to her lips and drank the dregs. A faint cheer drifted up from the crowd in the courtyard. She waved carelessly, turning from the window.

'The "Protector" is holding trial on one of our subjects?'

'A mercenary, your Majesty. And, the situation being how it is, it would hardly be politic to complain.'

She turned on him a face from which all humour and all laziness vanished.

'The Queen's writ still runs in this commonwealth, does it not? The Queen's justice is the fount of all justice?'

'Yes, madam, but—'

'Arrest Captain Calmady. Find witnesses and have him brought to trial. It may prove politic,' the swarthy woman considered, 'to have what Justice the woman Olivia approves of on the bench, but we will have no man tried but by the laws of this commonwealth, and they, after all revolts and confusions, remain *mine*.'

Desire walked to stand by the window.

The White Crow hesitated, closing the door. Noon's snow-reflected brightness shone in on the young woman's face, but called out no fire from the matt darkness of her hair. Each hand clasped an elbow. Her chin was sunk into the collar of her coat.

The door closed with a creak.

'I said I'd examine you, didn't I? Yes . . .'

The White Crow shivered, crossing to the fire and squatting down to place fresh coals. The scent of seacoal permeated the air. Frost-patterns starred the window-glass.

'I would know, if I carry a child? Or a disease?'

A quiet voice, low and resonant. The White Crow straightened. In some interest, she looked down at her fingers. They shook. She rubbed her hands together, a slight smile on her face; taking a brief glance around the room.

Books piled on window-seat, oaken chair, and floor. Bundles of herbs lay scattered across the big desk, together with half-incised talismans. She absently cleared the remnants of an amulet to one side, and tapped her finger to her lips, gaze moving along the meagre row of bottles on the shelf above the workbench.

'Sit down. The couch, there. Have you eaten today?'

'Nothing.'

'Good.'

Three bottle-necks between her fingers, the White Crow pulled the cork from a fourth with her teeth as she walked across the room. She held out the blue-white glass container.

'Do I drink it?' The young woman held the bottle, sinking to sit on the couch. White linen creased where she sat. The White Crow took the cork from between her teeth.

'Drink from one, spit in t'other. Then we'll wait. Trust me.'

'I already trusted you once.' Mocking, calculating: Desire's eyes shone. 'At Roseveare. You failed me.'

'You can't trade on that forever.'

'Can I not?'

'Oh, but *you* . . .' A wealth of tones in that word: speculation, resentment, admiration, envy. The White Crow rested her knee up on the couch, the bottles in her left hand clinking softly. Recalled, she held each up to the window-light in turn; shook each; and placed them one at a time on the floor.

'I'll have to examine you.'

The young woman lowered the bottle, frowning a little. A tongue-tip flicked out, clearing the last oily liquid from her lips. Noon leached colour from her pale, prominent cheekbones; shadowed her eyes with sepia and her lips with blue.

The White Crow leaned weight on her knee that rested on the couch. Close enough to breathe in all the scents of her – herb-comfrey, and the rankness of just-stale sweat – she watched Desire's fingers unknot the clasp of her coat.

Desire pulled her arms from the sleeves, awkward as a child.

A black, ragged doublet came next; buttoned at every second or third button. A grey shirt, clean but faded. Desire pulled her shoulders up, down; sliding the cloth free. Her hands dropped to her belt. She tugged loose the sash of a ragged, full skirt.

The White Crow slipped. Her knee skidded from the couch's linen cover. One hand, flying out for balance, knocked against the young woman's arm.

The air of the room tingled: hot with fire, cold with snow. Frozen condensation whorled the windowpane. A coal snapped in the grate. Her face burned. With hands now perfectly steady she reached out and unbuttoned the young woman's thin cotton shirt.

Black eyes glinted. One of the corners of her pale lips tugged up: as it might be Desire smiled.

The White Crow cupped her hands over the young woman's shoulders, every crease of the last white, sleeveless shirt pressing her palms. She slid her hands down around the small, heavy breasts; traced the sharpness of ribs; held her with one hand to each hip. Each impossible touch broke barriers between possibility and actuality.

Shaking, heightened; simultaneously aware and with a complete sense of unreality, she pulled the girl to her feet and tore at the buttons fastening her cobweb-thin shirt.

The young woman stood stiff, resistant.

'*Trust* me!' The White Crow reached out, knotting fists in the unbound masses of Desire's coarse black hair, pulling her head forward and kissing her fiercely.

One heel skidded on the floor: a bottle shattered.

The White Crow grabbed and fumbled her grip; ripped the sleeveless shirt, and lowered her mouth to lick at the sweat on the curve of Desire's shoulder. Smooth here, rough there with old scar-tissue: tasting of all sweetness, all sour discordancies of taste.

Breath hissed in her throat.

She sat back up onto one heel, staring the young woman in the face. Skin tingled. Silence sang, waiting for the shout that would break it.

The fire, the linen couch, the deserted floor of the house: all determined, all planned. To end here, with a face heavy-lidded, black and delicate lashes lowered. Feeding on itself now, the desire reified by its first act.

Deliberately moving the remaining bottles aside, she pushed the young woman's body back on the couch. Her hands dug to feel the heat of flesh across the slender back. She pushed her unbandaged hand under the waistband of the young woman's black skirt, sliding fingers across the soft flesh of her belly, fighting the resistance of cloth, fingers prodding between her thighs.

'I'm not—!'

An elbow hit her jaw and ear. Jarred, she shook her head to clear it.

'—not healed yet; it *hurts*—'

The White Crow recovered her free hand from under the solidity of flesh. She pulled at her own shirt, buttons flying. Some fierce grin fired her. She pulled the young woman's head to her breast, feeling the shiver of warm breath across her nipple; reached down and tugged her belt-buckle undone with a bandaged hand. Desire struggled.

'—*hurts!*'

A shrill whisper.

'I'll be careful. Trust me. Trust me.'

The White Crow forced her down, one arm now across Desire's collarbone, pinning her. A knee hit her shoulder. Her breeches slid down her hips, bare flesh shivering in the winter room.

'You're beautiful!'

Pressed bare breast to belly, sweat-slick, hand thrusting still between the young woman's legs, rubbing soft and damp hair; fingers probing hot, slick interior flesh. The White Crow caught her breath, dipped her head and bit roughly at warm flesh: at white-scarred arms and prominent ribs; mouthing saliva across small, heavy breasts.

The Protector-General Olivia lifted her gloved hand to knock on the door of Roseveare House. It swung open. She nodded briefly to the two black-mantled soldiers. They took up unobtrusive posts along the Court, cursing the deep snow. She stepped over the threshold.

Somewhere distantly upstairs, a bottle smashed.

She swung the door to and walked swiftly through the hall. One hand rested at the belt of her buff coat, on a pistol's butt. Stairs went up into gloom. She climbed, alert for further sound.

Silence.

Closed doors confronted her on the first floor. About to push one open at random, hand on the latch, she heard a creak from the bannisters of the landing above.

The Lord-Architect Casaubon leaned over, draped in the folds of a scarlet-and-gold nightgown, and with a tasselled nightcap on his head.

'No servants, master architect?'

The fat man wiped his eyes, fingering yellow sleep-grit from the corners. He stuck his finger in his mouth, sucked and removed it. 'Servants' day off, rot 'em. Valentine should answer the *magia* wards. I don't know what she can be thinking of. I, myself, am far too ill to leave my bed—'

'I need to know about the eye of the sun, Master Casaubon. Now. When I returned to the Tower this morning, I found your written report.'

'You'd better come up.'

He swirled yards of cloth about his arms, bundling himself up and raising the hem of the gown of his stockinged calves. Olivia chuckled. She took the stairs two at a time, following him into a bright room.

'However, I *was* working.' The Lord-Architect pried up the blankets on the immense four-poster bed and climbed back in.

Blueprints tipped across the blankets. Plans covered the bed, the floor; hung pinned to the bed's draperies, and crackled under the Lord-Architect as he leaned back against the pillows. He wiped his red nose.

Olivia cleared a space and seated herself on the foot of the bed. 'I want answers if you have them, educated guesses if you don't.'

'Guesses?' He unrolled a six-foot plan across his lap, pinning down the end with a jar of wintergreen ointment. 'I can guarantee you, the burglaries and thefts of St Sophia will drop by two-thirds

when you allow me to make alteration to the Rookery tenements.'
His fat finger prodded the paper. 'With these building alterations I
can guarantee a lessening in the crimes committed there.'

'The poor of this town don't need lessoning in crime.'

'Wittily said.'

Olivia stripped off her gloves. She pushed the wispy yellow-white
hair away from her face. 'The Rookeries are corrupt. Master
Casaubon, men are made of sin. I don't think you'll deny them the
desire to thieve by denying them one walkway to reach a window
by, or one more exit by which to flee. Now: the temple—'

'Pox rot you, they're not different! Structures compel—'

The man broke into a fit of coughing. The Protector steadied
herself on the bed, her feet not quite touching the floor. Heaped
blankets shook, covering the immense legs, stomach, and torso of
the man in the bed; he peering down at her red-faced, watery-eyed.

'Master Casaubon, the eye of the sun is builded according to
those proportions and rules that govern the universe; it has within
it an outer light to mirror man's Inner Light; it is a *temple*, and not a
slum!'

She stood up, pacing the room.

'Your report says that I need the blood-royal and that I can't use it
because it is diseased. *Why* can it not be used? What else is there?
Are the Rookeries your price for telling me?'

'The Rookeries slums are something you'll have me do if you
want to save your tenants from what *you'd* call opportunities to sin.
Death and furies!' He sat up in bed, a volcano-lava of sheets and
blankets spilling down. A smell of sweat and ointment breathed
across her.

'Master Casaubon: the eye of the sun!'

'This city's had its temples consecrated by the royal-bloodline for
how long? Centuries?' He nodded massive satisfaction. 'The
foundations of the earth have reached saturation point. Hereditary
– that blood carries a virus. By now it attracts as much demonic
power as it dispels.'

'Carola's blood feeds demons.' She tapped her gloves against her
bulbous chin. 'Consecrates ground – and attracts demons. And yet
the ground must be consecrated. I don't see the answer.'

'Blindingly simple.' The large man spread his hands. 'Build it in
another city.'

'What?'

'Your Carola.' He sniffed. 'The Sun Monarch herself couldn't
build a temple to the sun in this city! No matter how harmonic
the proportions, how much in conformity with the Universal

Architect's laws, you'll have an infestation of demons before the pox-rotted foundations are sunk. They've been taught to expect it.'

She stopped with one hand holding the bottom poster of the bed. 'I must build here. I must build in the capital.'

'Dammit, you can't!'

'Our Lord's light, and the light of reason, have to be manifest *here*.' Her hand closed hard on the carved wood. The edges bit into her fingers. 'We're the only legitimate protection against the godless woman's tyranny, master architect; and we can only prove ourselves legitimate in this ancient seat of government. I must be able to complete the building.'

'You may. Eventually. And have to call in a demolition expert inside a decade to get rid of the thing.'

'That dangerous?'

'I've seen corruptive architecture before.' The fat man leaned back against stacked pillows. The room's light altered, chilling to sepia; and she glanced at the window and saw, tiny and slow, black specks spiralling down against a yellow sky. Fire snapped in the grate. Somewhere in the depths of Roseveare House, a door slammed.

'You have a plain choice.' The Lord-Architect grunted, swinging his legs down and feeling with his feet for red-heeled slippers. 'Use some poor royal bastard's blood, build the place, and have it corrupt more of its worshippers than it heals. Or don't use it, and have the building collapse. Or, by the Great Architect's anus, build it in some other city!'

Olivia made a wry mouth.

'That's no choice at all. Obviously I cannot choose any of these actions – and yet – I must choose.'

The Lord-Architect plodded back up the stairs from seeing Olivia out. He paused at the door to the herb-room.

'Little one?'

The White Crow, visible thorugh the now-open door, sat up on the couch. The rucked-up sheet tangled her ankles. One elbow rested on her knee, and her forehead on her fist. Her shirt hung open, two buttonholes torn, and her unbuckled breeches slid down over her hips; brown cloth against fair, faintly-freckled skin. She looked up.

'Yes! All right? The answer is yes.'

The woman stood. The covering sheet slid from the couch to the dusty floorboards. She made to step over, holding up her breeches;

half-halted, and bent to pick up a bottle. She held it up to the light as she walked across to the bench, shook it, eyes narrowing.

'Veneral infection. Nothing too serious; I can make her an infusion to clear it up. I must let her know. *Casaubon—*'

She slammed the bottle down, turned.

The Lord-Architect walked across the creaking floorboards to her, and cupped her chin in large, strong fingers. His ink-stained thumb rubbed her jaw thoughtfully.

'Did you?'

She pulled away. '*Yes!*'

The Lord-Architect eased himself down into the large chair beside the hearth, sinking into voluminous night-robes. His gaze never shifted from her face. She, finished with buttoning herself and now buckling her belt, sat in the window-seat.

'I don't love her.'

The White Crow rested her chin on her wrists, staring down from the window-ledge as she talked. On the other side of chill glass, snow fell into Roseveare Court, and torches flared gold on the shoe-tracks and bookstalls and open bookshop doorways. Two black-mantled soldiers and a woman in a buff coat trampled the snow towards the main thoroughfare.

'I *hurt* her. She obsesses me. I can't tell you that she won't always do that.'

Casaubon sat still. His eyes narrowed very slightly.

'I can't give her up,' the White Crow added, 'and I'll die if I don't have you. I don't even pretend that that's fair.'

A tiny snap sounded in the room, in the silence that snow produces, muffling all other sound. The Lord-Architect looked down at the louse nipped between his thumb-nails, and smeared the body on his furred nightgown. Thighs spread, arms resting back on the arms of the chair that his body barely fitted, he looked up at the White Crow over a mountain of belly.

'I didn't win you for my beauty.' Pink coloured his creased cheeks. He looked at her sadly. 'I made you laugh. I make myself indispensable, because I can always make the melancholy Valentine laugh. But, of course, beginning so, you always see me so. I make you merry. There's an end to it.'

The White Crow lifted her head from her arms, and looked at him over her shoulder. 'You underestimate me. I know what you are. You're the man who pretends to be my solid rock and foundation, and proves ultimately as flighty and eccentric as – as anyone could wish. Did it never occur to you that I love you *because* you're an infuriating lunatic?'

The Lord-Architect cocked one dark-red eyebrow in her direction, paused for a calculated moment, and remarked, 'No. But I had hopes.'

'That's *exactly* – *that's* what I – you're the only man I know,' she said, 'who's smarter than I am, and that's something I won't tell you every day. But she . . .'

Casaubon rumbled. 'Did you really think I would be complaisant enough, or sufficiently insecure, to say that I would share you?'

'You may have to. For the moment, anyway.'

The Lord-Architect leaned back, to the creak of oakwood, and gave her his most childlike and innocent gaze. 'You may think so.'

She shifted to her feet in one easy movement, tugging her belt straight as she walked to the door and lifted her cloak from the door-hook. She swung the cloak, muffling herself to the ears, and then stopped with her hand on the jamb as she went out.

'Thank you,' she said, 'for not mentioning Jared and the baby.'

CHAPTER 9

Towards the middle of that same afternoon, with the snow easing and people once more on the streets, the Lady Arbella Lacey swaggered out of the little streets behind Eleanor's Cross. A keen wind cut at her nose, cheeks, and chin.

'Sir!' She caught the elbow of a man in frock-coat and plumed hat. 'Is there a hostelry hereabouts where an honest soldier can get a drink? And would you have a copper for a woman who's fought hard in the late wars?'

She let her shabby velvet cloak slip back and show the sword in its hanger at her side. Cold reddened her bare fingers. She sniffed and wiped her nose, mucus running from the keen air and from half a day's drinking.

'There. That's all.' The elderly man, somewhere between sullenness and good humour, pressed cold coins into her hand. 'My child went for a soldier, too; I'd not willingly see her comrades beg. And to your question – no, there is no inn hereabouts for honest soldiers, but there is *The New-Founde Land Arms* down yonder that will take a mercenary's coin.'

'The Bull bless you, sir!' Arbella Lacy grinned, breath huffing onto the cold air. 'Mercenaries, say you? Yonder there? I recognise the nags outside; you've found me my comrades and I bless you for it—'

'No more money Go.'

The man shuffled away. He leaned heavily on his ebony cane. Trooper Arbella Lacey amused herself for several steps with a parody of his walk, slipped, swore to herself, and plodded through the broken snow down towards the Whitehall Palace and the inn.

She stopped in the hostelry's porch to kick clogged snow from her boots. Some noise in the almost impassable road behind her made her turn, and narrow her streaming eyes as she stared back across Whitehall.

She spun to kick the inn's door open and rush inside.

*

A quarter of a mile away in the kitchens of Roseveare House, the White Crow cradled her sweat-damp baby in the crook of her arm. Exhausted, it whimpered; the whimper sawing up the scale towards a full-scale scream.

'Oh, shit.' She hefted the baby gently in both arms, glancing at Abiathar with red-rimmed eyes. 'You wouldn't think it had the energy, would you? Three solid hours . . . I'll see if I can feed her.'

'You'll feed her anger with your milk.'

'If I wanted blame I'd have stayed upstairs.' The White Crow unlaced her doublet without looking at the older woman, pulled the ties on her shirt, and offered the baby her nipple. The child refused, square-mouthed, beating with clenched fists.

'Here.' Abiathar reached down and lifted the child. Jadis fumbled uselessly at the woman's bodice for some moments, murmured indignation, and slid off into a half-doze. 'She knows your anger. It's in your touch.'

The White Crow ignored her own resentment and looked up at Abiathar. The older woman walked back and forth in front of the kitchen range, humming. Fire's shadows and winter afternoon light dappled the baby's bright hair.

'Did my husband say where he was going when he left?'

Abiathar shook her head. 'No word. I ast him if he wanted Kitterage and a hired coach, but he said no. Will he have gone to his old building site, then?'

She paused, looking down into the baby's face, and added, 'Won't be the first Roseveare to have married an odd man, you won't.'

'I'll leave her and Jared with you.'

Her face burned warmer than the kitchen stove could account for, feeling the country woman's gaze on her.

'For an hour or so. I'll walk over to the site and find him. I want . . .' She stood and stretched out her arms, feeling bones click and tendons stretch. 'I've done what *I* came to London to do. *He's* been to that site twice, and I don't know if he's any closer to an answer than when we came. I want to know how much longer we have to stay.'

Half a mile south of Roseveare, Shrine Paddifer leaned his elbows on the table in the St Sophia communal dining-room.

'The St Sophia commune has petitioned the Protector for aid against criminals.' He brushed his short grey hair out of his eyes. 'As we petitioned for the Queen's grace in the same matter, not so long since. All the blocks suffer the depredations of priggers, Abraham-men, footpads, and Tall Men. We tried our own vigilante patrols, to little effect.'

The very large man seated opposite coughed resonantly. 'The whole pox-rotten place invites 'em in! Provides walkways, blind corners, unlit passages; corridors where no one can see attacks; a dozen paths to flee by. The old proverb has it: *postern doors make thieves and whores.*'

The Lord-Architect Casaubon occupied all one side of the oak-panelled bench opposite, a broken meat-pie steaming on a dish before him. He waved an emphatic hand, meat and pastry held between large fingers.

'Madam Olivia will shortly be in need of—' Meat slipped, the Lord-Architect made a swift bite at it; grease rolled down his chin. '—much in need of a worthy building project. A public one. Rot it, if she cleans up St Sophia, she'll look sweet in the City's eyes! That's to your good, Master Paddifer. Take advantage of it.'

He sniffed, beaming, and wiped his nose on the back of one lace-ruffled cuff.

'You must excuse me. Haven't been well. No appetite.'

Shrine Paddifer eased as far back against the oak partition as possible, wiping at his spattered black shirt and undershirts. Raw wood, graffiti-hacked, caught threads in his clothing. Voices rang out loudly from the room's other tables, in their own cubicles; and a pair of children in layers of rags ran from the battered kitchen door to the far wall, sliding on slush-wet flagstones.

'You spoke of something attendant on this. A bargain?'

'A private bargain.'

The man scratched at his straggling cropped hair, smearing gravy and a fragment of mushroom in the copper-red strands. His lace collar untied, and buttons undone on his viridian waistcoat, the Lord-Architect leaned back with a contented sigh. Shrine Paddifer reached across and poured another cup of acorn-coffee.

'There was born and bred in St Sophia a young woman by the name of Guillaime.'

The faintest lift of tone implied a question. Shrine Paddifer, surprised, nodded. 'Yes. Down in the third tenement-block.'

The big man's hand slammed down on the table. 'Damnation, I knew it! Master Paddifer, I recognised her as a Rookery-bird by her dress.'

A smile spread across his face, creasing the rolls of fat around his blue eyes: immensely and innocently pleased with himself. Shrine Paddifer abandoned any idea of being insulted. He allowed himself an ironical smile.

'We give the Protector a number of her best people. What about Desire-of-the-Lord Guillaime, master architect? How is she part of the bargain for your services?'

Foosteps clumped across the floor above. A child cried. Two young men and a woman clattered down the narrow, winding stairs; threw the outer door open to afternoon's pale light as they ran into the yard. Shrine Paddifer eased himself out from behind the table and walked to close the door.

Behind him, the deep voice rumbled:

'I shall need to consult with the Sun of Science on the blueprints – that is, the Head of the Byzantine College. Young Mistress Guillaime seems very trustworthy. I want her to act as my messenger to Byzantium, while I remain here.'

The large man buried his nose in the cup of acorn-coffee. Shrine Paddifer returned to the table. Standing, his eyes were much on a level with the seated man's.

'She'll be honoured.'

'London can spare her for a few months. Travel broadens experience.' The Lord-Architect, as much as possible for a man of his size, hunched down in his green frieze coat. His eyes flicked up and remained on Shrine Paddifer's face: a steady and uncompromising gaze. 'That is my condition of employment.'

The afternoon light shone winter-brilliant. Desire-of-the-Lord Guillaime lay on her back.

'Put your feet in the stirrups. Now part your knees.'

The leather couch chilled her back and buttocks. She shifted awkwardly down. Her bare feet slid into wooden stirrups. Her threadbare shift only covered her breasts and belly, and she put one arm across her face, staring into the welcome dark of flesh.

'Be still.'

The immediate chill of grease made her startle. The muscles of her thighs tightened. Cold metal probed between her legs, pushing the walls of her vagina apart. She closed her hands into fists, never wincing. The speculum pushed deep inside, hurting. It halted, moved painfully to one side; moved again and drove deeper.

'Still!'

The Protectorate doctor's instrument snicked vaginal flesh as it withdrew.

'Dress. Wait outside.'

She shifted her cramped legs down. She fumbled on layers of skirts, belts, and buckles done up anyhow. An antiseptic scent choked her nostrils. The surgery door creaked as she pushed past it, and in the empty room beyond cupped both hands to her pubis and leaned her head against the cold window-glass. She made one sound, a sob or sharp intake of breath.

Under her hands, cloth warmed, slightly numbing the pain of flesh.

Silence muffled the St Sophia Rookery. White light blazed from beyond the window. Roofs, gables, all ice-fanged; all familiar. Known streets, trodden into slush and frozen again. Piled drifts of snow against tenement walls all burning with interior diamonds. A faint mist hazed Monmouth Street and the spire clock at the seven road's junction.

Desire-of-the-Lord Guillaime straightened. She brushed wet hair back from her forehead, and adjusted her belt-buckle, and pulled on fingerless leather gloves. She stared down at her discarded coat.

The surgery door opened.

'Master Hargrave?'

The priest-surgeon lifted his head, looking down at her; a tall man, white-haired, and with deep creases in his face. All his old warmth vanished, all consolation gone.

'I *am* ill? She would not tell me, she—'

'Ill? Yes, grievous sick!'

He made to turn, to go back into the surgery. She stepped forward. He caught the side of his white robe, jerking the hem away from her.

'Master Hargrave!'

'The Lord has visited justice on you. Your woman's parts, those parts that tempted the man of blood, are diseased. It is written that *a harlot shall rot in her pride.* Yes, you are sick.'

His nostrils widened slightly, whitening.

'You may not go to the Lord for many years. All that time you shall remain in sickness and sores. If the devil give you children, as it may be the man of blood has left his seed in your body, then the children of your body shall carry the disease. You shall become a stink and an abomination. And die, in the end, mad with your sin, the judgement come upon you.'

A snowball jarred the window. She tangled her fingers in her hair. Outside, a child shrieked, a dozen more ran, scuffing up snow. They would be making a slide in the old places, outside this surgery and at the Shaftesbury Avenue junction. A horse neighed: a carter swore. Apt enough to make her mouth tremble, a hymn sounded from the nearest of the Rookery's thirty-seven chapels.

'Is there *no* cure?'

He stared down at her: a young woman now, black hair disordered; a shirt buttoned crudely across her small breasts, and belted skirts hanging down to her heeled ankle boots. Her hands in fingerless gloves made fists.

'*Cure?*'

He bent, scooped up her coat, and threw it into her face. She stepped back, heels clattering.

'Cure! Why speak of cures? Your soul is irredeemably diseased. Desire-of-the-Lord, I knew your mother. The Lord rest her, she doesn't live to see this. I know your father and your grandmother, honest people, who live in the fear of the Lord: think, how will you shame them! No man can cure you of this sin.'

She leaned her back against the front door of the surgery.

Staring up into the sun, with no memory of leaving the place.

Away down the road, near one of the brick tenement entrances, a bundled-up girl of perhaps seven drilled a dozen like her: broomsticks for pikes, shovels for muskets; the smallest girl throwing snowballs; four eminently self-righteous boys singing a Protectorate marching hymn.

Her lips moved with ancient memory, mirroring the words.

'*Remember the crow is a carrion bird . . .*'

Valentine of Roseveare, called White Crow, stopped at the unlocatable murmur. She held her link-torch higher against the early winter dusk.

The site of the eye of the sun spread out around her, deserted.

'Who's there?' With the hand that did not hold the torch, she rubbed finger and thumb together. A rose-light glowed, gleamed with marsh-fire blues and greens. She lowered the flaming brand. The sweat on her right hand crackled, turned to ice.

'*. . . crow is . . . carrion bird . . .*'

The sky shone a dirty, darkening grey. A mist blurred the lines of cranes and gantries, scaffolding platforms and sighting-towers. No man nor woman moved on the site. She trudged forward to where the churned clay-and-slush gave way to sandstone pavement.

Mirror gleamed.

The White Crow held up her hand that flamed blue. The chill of the fire hurt. She stuck the link-torch into a gap between stacked masonry blocks and walked forward without it, her shadow jolting across the inlaid steel and silver of the dome-floor.

The knowledge that work such as could be done in this weather would have finished some two hours gone, and the lack of the Lord-Architect's presence; this and the grey evening might have accounted for the chill on her spirit. The White Crow showed teeth in a fierce smile.

'I know your kind,' she said softly, 'better than you know me. Show yourself.'

Feathers scratched at the underside of glass.

She walked forward on the pavement until she stood where the inset mirrors merged. In the dome to come, this would be the edge of prayer. And from the high opening, sunlight would stream down, illuminating the whole vast interior with a Light of eyes and feathers and angels' wings.

She squatted down on her haunches.

'. . . *a carrion bird* . . .'

Practised, she reached a pin from her hair and let blood from her left index finger. Two signs she traced on the sandstone paving. The third, a swift curve with complicated lettering, she wrote on the mirror surface itself.

Mist and ice ran away from the mirror as frost melts at noon.

The White Crow looked down into the clarity beneath.

'The crow is the bird that travels between the living and the dead,' she formally stated. 'If you have something to show: show. If you have something to tell: tell. But I hear with the ears of *magia*. Lies and trickery will not bite on me.'

Black feathers flicked at the underside of the mirror's thick glass. She wasted no time looking up into the London sky for them. A flight of black birds, beaks and talons glinting obsidian-bright; filling all the well of the mirror; and as the flock diminished—

She hovers above a field of bright grass. The white mists of artillery fire blot out horses as they gallop forward; she cannot hear the sound of the guns, but she can hear the caws of crows as the scavengers rob the bodies in the night after when – as always happens after day-long cannonfire – it rains. Rains on the cold, bloody dead.

She recognises uniforms: Protectorate and Royalist.

A coach on a deserted moor is halted, robbed; passengers bludgeoned and left for dead; she is too far from the vision to see, quite, who these people are.

Back alleys, sick beds, camps, sea wrecks; each tantalisingly closer. Almost close enough to see every face, every death.

'You are lying badly . . .'

Her voice is not as steady as she would wish. The White Crow sits for a while on her haunches while the link-torch burns down, watching faces. Because it *may* be a foreshadowing, it may be the warning that proves such fates avoidable, she watches faces, faces by the hundred, men and women in clothing familiar and unfamiliar; and in all those faces, watch as closely as she might, she sees no face at all that she knows.

A plume of white fire hung, still against night's blackness, drowning stars. Bevil Calmady swayed in the cleared middle of the square and stared up at the comet.

Motionless, frozen light.

As if speaking the words could ease him, he recited: ' "A sacrifice to Law's Majesty and an example to all malevolent men—" '

He staggered ankle-deep in new snow, sliding on the packed ice beneath; grabbed at his sword-hilt, and looked dizzily for Gadsbury, Lacey, Rule, Linebaugh: all gone into the comet-lit night.

'Boy!'

An oxyacetylene brightness illuminated the square and the frozen fountains. Ice ridged and rippled. Torches flared. Two linkmen preceded a sedan-chair down the treacherous road. One hauled out a cudgel, torch wavering in his free hand.

A head poked through the sedan-chair window.

'He's no footpad. Set down, set down!'

The carriers – four men, not two – set the chair down in the snow. Ice crunched as the Lord-Architect Casaubon pushed the door open and stepped out.

'What's the matter, boy? Answer. Is it the house?'

Bevil Calmady shook his head, conscious of reporting concisely. 'Not Roseveare.'

The wind cut under his plumed hat, bobbing one broken ostrich feather. An active, wet cold seared his chin, jaw, and ears. Under the comet's light the large man's hair shone black as shed blood. Bevil Calmady scented elderflower wine and warm breath.

Apologetic, devastated, he said, 'I know there's nothing to be done, sir. It's the Queen's justice. *Can* you help him? He claims you for his friend.'

'Damnation, slowly, boy. Slowly. Hold and then tell me.'

Sword-buckles and spurs chimed, clotted with ice. Bevil rubbed his gloved hand across his forehead, the kidskin cold and wet.

'His trial. My *father*. They held it this afternoon.'

'What, the Protector-General—'

'No, sir. The Queen's men took him.'

'The Qu . . .' The fat man squinted under the comet's brilliance, spun a coin to the lead carrier, and hooked his arm around Bevil's shoulder, steering him irresistibly along. 'Come to Roseveare. Tell me as you walk. What, rot it, they can't hold any trial, the man's on bail to my house!'

Shudders took Bevil's flesh, deep down inside his belly. The wind sheered through his wool cloak and silk doublet. He moved his shoulders out of the big man's grip.

'I knew nothing of it. Arbella and the company found me, about four of the clock, said, *"We've seen him taken under guard: quick!"* I followed. When we got to the Bailey, it was the Queen's Justice, John Whorewood, a notorious puritan.'

'Ah.' The Lord-Architect nodded.

'He had bunches of herbs on the bench, to ward off prison-stink!'

Tall gables in St Martin's Lane blocked the night sky. The comet's light glinted from glass and horn windows. The Lord-Architect's powerful legs thrust through snow, untramelled. His breath smoked on the air. 'Tried by a puritan judge, but in the Queen's court. Without witnesses?'

'Oh, yes.' Self-assured cynicism slipped. Bevil Calmady clenched his hands. 'They'd written depositions as if from the Guillaime bitch. Sir, have you ever heard a man . . . *"The sentence is that thou shalt return from hence to Newgate prison, and from thence to the place of execution at Tyburn, where thou shalt hang by the neck till the body be dead and in the Devil his hands, and the Lord his mercy on your soul."* '

Bevil stepped aside to avoid the corner of a standing cart, piled high with grit and shovels for the morning. Someone coughed at a high window. A feather of applause drifted from distant theatres.

'My father trained me to remember words.' Unacknowledged pain ripped in his stomach. 'He told us the bitch-General would never dare sentence him. Why should her Majesty want him hanged? I don't understand.'

He looked up at the older man, his back stiffening. 'Gadsbury says, *Queen's justice.* They drink to the Queen and her Hangman. Oh, would to God there was anything I could do!'

'How long has he?'

'Five days. Wednesday next.'

Late in empty streets, Bevil pushed heel and toe into ice to stay upright, his voice as slurred as a drunken man's. Feeling the knot finally cut that tied Gadsbury, Lacey, Winslow, himself: the dissolution of the company, gone with its captain. Or if re-tied, nothing the same.

And Pollexfen Calmady to die.

'What can I do, sir?'

The Lord-Architect Casaubon dug his chins down into his coat-collar, turning into Roseveare Court and the keen wind. 'Eat before you fall down. I'll take you to the kitchen.'

Bevil Calmady blinked water from his eyes. 'My father . . .'

'We'll— *Valentine?*'

Stunned with memories, a half-second passed before Bevil focused.

The woman sat on a step at the corner of the narrow street. Her cloak matted dark with melted snow. Red hair, damp-darkened, dripped ice-water onto fingers without sensation: she rested her face in her hands. Bare flesh, mottled by cold, shuddered.

The big man took three swift strides to reach her. His hands closed around her upper arms, lifting her; she twisted free and staggered off the steps into Roseveare Court. Cold blotched her face. Her tawny-red eyes fixed on Bevil.

'I have bad news,' rumbled the Lord-Architect. 'Polly Calmady. He's to hang.'

'H—?'

An aspirate too soft for speech.

'They re-arrested and tried him today. His boy here told me.'

'It's true.' Bevil's voice shook.

The woman giggled. Both hands clapped over her mouth, eyes bright. She snorted. She sprang back in a half-melted snowdrift, oblivious of cold; one hand out protectively: her bare flesh facing his suddenly drawn blade. 'No, that's . . . it's it's not . . .'

'*You laugh!*'

'No, you . . . I had no warning – but you can't say they lied . . .'

She wiped a bare wrist across eyes that brimmed, water suddenly running down her cheeks, her mouth twisting. Twice on an outbreath she struggled for speech: mewed. Beside Bevil, Casaubon's immense bulk stilled, his forehead creasing.

'*—she—*'

The woman shivered. Her jaw rattled. Through shudders, all but unintelligible, she managed to say: 'They just took her down when I got there.'

Bevil stared. Casaubon's outstretched hand sank back to his side.

'I found out from the Tower where . . . Desire Guillaime. I never thought of her *living* anywhere, you know that? I never thought. I had a talisman-cure for her illness, I thought I would go and talk with her on my way back, settle some things, I don't know.'

One of her barleyrow braids, unravelling, stroked her chin with wet tendrils of hair. Melted snow dripped from her cloak.

'They saw I was a Master-Physician so the old woman called me in. They'd taken her down and wrapped her in blankets and warmed bricks, but she was dead. In her room at St Sophia. She hanged herself. She left me—'

Her head went back. She laughed, breathless, great gouts of mist jerking out into the cold night; and the laughter echoing off wood-and-plaster shop fronts. Tears stood in her eyes.

Now her voice never wavered from its high, strained pitch:

'She left Valentine Roseveare a letter. I didn't own to it. When I left, the old woman *thanked* me.'

CHAPTER 10

Muffled church bells rang. Valentine White Crow scratched through tangled hair and caught up the trailing edge of her nightrobe. Bed's warmth clung. The bright-haired baby, half-asleep in the crook of her arm, nuzzled at her shoulder; and she put her free hand across the child's back, nudging the sixth-floor bedroom door open with her foot. The sounds of Casaubon's dressing came from the floor below.

For the first time in five days, she focused.

'About, are you?' A dark head appeared in the stairwell: Abiathar with a tray. 'This is late. Sorry. I've had a kitchen full of runagate mercenaries since five this morning.'

Snow-light spiked her puffy eyes. 'Mercenaries?'

'Wanting to talk to your husband.'

White Crow took the tray one-handed. A few rashers coiled on a tin plate, and a mug of half-warm tea slopped. Hunger suddenly growled in her gut.

'What day is it?'

'Wednesday.'

'I think I . . . slept a lot.' She hitched her elbow, offering the baby, and the black-haired woman came forward and cradled the child in her arms.

'Will you let me feed her now, then? I thought you were never going to let go of her.'

'I needed comfort. Jadis lets me talk to her. And doesn't say anything.' Both hands to the tray now, standing in the chill, bright hall; her feet cold on the floorboards. She strained her hearing. Far below, resonating up the stairwell, the sharp notes of a harpsichord sounded.

'*Wednesday?*'

The woman nodded curtly, vanishing down the stairs. 'A fine day for a hanging-match.'

Snow and harpsichord music: both sharp, alert.

She set the tray down inside the bedroom door, scratching at her breasts under her nightgown and smelling the frowstiness of five days a-bed. The merry music spiked behind her eyes.

Eating one-handed as she crossed and recrossed the room, the woman threw on long hose under knee-breeches, short knee-hose, two shirts against the cold, and the leather doublet over all. She finished the last of the tea standing, hooking one foot and then the other into shoes; banged the cup down on the tin tray, and took the stairs at a run going down.

Abiathar twisted her dyed-black hair around her fingers, pinning it back with polished bone pins. 'Is all set?'

'Ed Kitterage is back in the stables, with a musket. Damned if he don't freeze before this lot finish. I'll keep watch upstairs.' Hazelrigg spat on the sawdust floor. 'You'll watch here?'

Abiathar nodded. 'It's left to us to protect the children. She must always have been foolish. Why else would she have been thrown out of Roseveare to begin with?'

'Who knows what she'll do now? Wish I were back home.'

'You be careful with the little one, Thomas.'

The short dark man grunted. Jadis, in the crook of his arm, grabbed at the gloved fingers that he offered. Thomas Hazelrigg held out his hand for the feeding-bottle.

'She—'

A burst of loud laughter outside the kitchen parlour drowned out speech. Abiathar went to the door. A thin, curly-haired mercenary in pink satin leaned over the ground-floor bannisters. Slush and a searing-cold wind blew in from the front door.

'Have a jug of mulled wine sent up, while we wait on your master. Quick now, woman!'

'Sir.' She measured her tone just short of contempt.

'Half of 'em well drunken, and it's only nine of the clock.' Hazelrigg teased the bottle-teat around the child's lips until she fastened herself determinedly and began to suck. He eased back in the wing-armed kitchen chair. Glowing brown eyes met Abiathar's. He chuckled. 'Not one of 'em sober to watch their Captain hang!'

'Let him hang. He didn't kill her, but he might have, so let him hang.' The black-haired woman set wine to heat on the kitchen-range, that stank of sea-coal and pine kindling. 'Or they can hang *her*. They killed the girl between them. She'd have welcomed it any time these five days.'

The White Crow hit the last stair, swung round into the landing, and stopped. For thirty seconds she stood still, her expression blank.

Small noises of occupation came from behind the closed door. She raised her fist, rapped a sharp tattoo, and entered on the rumble of 'Come!'

'Hello.'

She walked forward. Blankets slumped from the bed to the rugs, showing where the fat man had risen. He sat silhouetted against the windows at the room's far end, head resting on one fist, staring down at the snow-covered yard and stables entrance. One brow raised as he registered her entrance.

'Breakfast!' She reached across his shoulder, filching a pork chop, and ripped off small bites of the meat, resting her back up against the window-shutter. Indistinctly, she said, 'You?'

'I'm not hungry.'

'The age of miracles!'

She threw the half-eaten chop back on the plate. A coal fire hissed in this bedroom's grate, whistling softly with the escape of gasses. Cold at her back, the leaded windows began to mist with the heat of her body. The White Crow chewed and wiped her wrist across her greasy mouth.

The Lord-Architect's chins rested on his plump hand, drowned in the lace-fall at his cuff. Waistcoat and breeches remained unbuttoned, his shirt-tail hanging into his lap. One garter fixed up a stocking, the other wrinkled about his ankles. He raised his eyes.

'I know. I'm sorry.' She swallowed the chewed lump of tough meat, wincing. 'I shut myself away from everybody, not just you.'

'Liar.'

The equable friendliness of his tone made her flinch. Turning, she rubbed a clear space in the window's frost, staring down at Kitterage as he led another gentleman-mercenary's horse into the stables.

'I forced her. As much as *he* did. I really did.' She wiped her fingers down her breeches. 'I'd sooner have slept and forgotten this day, I think. If it were over, I'd know what I felt.'

Her finger traced patterns on the glass: uncompleted sigils of power, of planetary *numina: Claviclulae* from ancient grimoires, and the Signatures of hedgerow herbs. The wet glass chilled her flesh. She expunged the patterns with the heel of her hand. His gaze prickled the hairs on the back of her neck.

'Is she buried yet?'

'St Giles Cripplegate. Here . . .'

Some apprehension twisted in her bowels. The White Crow put her hands in her pockets and turned, coming no closer to the seated man. He dug his plump hand into a waistcoat pocket and drew out a folded, stained sheet of paper.

'Here.'

'I don't want it.'

Hands on chair-arms, he pushed himself up lightly and quickly; blinking at her against the window's snow-light. One fat hand flourished impatiently in her face. 'Read it!'

'Who brought it here?'

A pause: she snatched the paper from his hand, crumpling it into a ball in her fist, and threw herself down into the opposite seat. She helped herself to acorn-coffee from the jug, drinking from Casaubon's cup, making a face at how cold and sour it tasted. 'Well?'

'The grandmother. Rot it, she could find *Roseveare* easily enough! If it eases you, she knows nothing to put Roseveare and a Master-Physician into her mind together.'

'No one knows. I'd almost rather they were making broadsheet ballads about it.'

Without opening her fist, the White Crow rested her mouth against her fingers. Tears thickened in her throat. She blinked rapidly. She dropped the crumpled ball of paper on the table, smoothing it down against the wood. A thin line in black ink superscribed it *Valentine of Roseveare*. She turned it over.

'The seal's broken – you've opened this!'

The Lord-Architect Casaubon hitched up black woollen breeches, abandoned the two top buttons as impossible, and shrugged his waistcoat across his mountainous stomach. He scratched through his copper-red hair. Blue eyes fixed on her.

'Of *course* I've read it. What do you think I am? Would I give it to you unread?'

'I never think, do I?'

She put her feet up on the table, booted ankles crossed. The crumpled paper rested in her lap. Outside, a lump of snow fell without warning from gutter to yard. Dawn dulled from acid-white to grey.

'Are you going to see him?' She snorted, shook her head. 'See you, I don't even know – have you seen him these five days?'

The Lord-Architect finished buttoning his waistcoat, head bent to the task, hair falling over his forehead. He straightened: not only a fat man, but a very large man also fat; blocking the window's light.

'If he doesn't hang for this, he'll hang for another rape. Or theft, or murder over a card-table. In two years or ten.' His voice rumbled. 'You'd have him hanged, not pardoned.'

She tilted her head against the chair's back. Snow-light gleamed in the ceiling's ornamental plaster strapwork. Winding patterns with no detectable cause or ending. She pulled a strand of white-streaked red hair to her mouth and sucked on it.

'He raped her. She's dead. Somebody ought to suffer for that. I . . . perhaps it should be me.'

'Read your damned letter. I'm leaving the house this half-hour.'

She touched the paper with a fingertip.

'What does it feel like, to write and be knowing all the time that you're going to kill yourself? Do you even believe it, do you think? These past five days I've expected her to walk in . . . and I *touched* her, I know how cold her body was.'

The Lord-Architect moved. The back of his hand rested against her cheek, and the White Crow leaned her head a little to that side, breathing in the scent of soap and new linen.

'I don't understand why she did it. I know it was my fault but I really, really, don't know why.'

A plump knuckle rapped her ear, too light to be a cuff. The White Crow took the letter up from her lap and flipped it open: thrice-folded, marked with fingerprints, torn down one edge, and the writing clear and uneven and without a blot:

Madam I understand now why you abused me the cause of it being my sickness which will be my death, so i will prevent by going first. I had begun to think of some affection from yr. self but now is much changed. You wd. not tell me my flesh is corrupted, is this your mark of affection?

Madam it was in my mind to pray you suffer as I do but the prayers of the corrupt in heart make no breach in heaven. I am become abomination. Or man or woman, they scent it out and come to me. If not before, then by this.

Guillaime

A coal popped in the grate. She moved her shoulders as one does unconsciously in sub-zero temperatures, tense against the shrinking of flesh.

'*What* sickness?'

She slammed the letter down on the table, springing up; standing over Casaubon where he sat on the bed, legs apart, fumbling between them on the floor for a stout shoe.

'Rot it, what sickness do you think? I went to the local priest-surgeon in St Sophia. Who else'd fill her head with damnation for the sake of a mild dose of pox?' The Lord-Architect sat up. Either exertion or anger reddened his face. 'He'd seen her two hours before she died. All righteous indignation and piety when I hammered his door down – *he* welcomed her death.'

The White Crow pressed a fist into her stomach, just under the arch of her ribs. Sweat chilled her. She snuffled a small laugh, shaking her head, blinking eyes rubbed sand-raw with weeping and now dry.

' *"I had begun to think of some affection from yourself"*.' Her fingers scrabbled across the oak, reaching to seize the letter from the table again. ' *"You would not tell me my flesh is corrupted"* – oh, sweet Jesus. Oh, lord.'

Tears spilled down her face. She pushed a wet hand across her cheek. The Lord-Architect bent his head, hooking on his shoe with one plump finger. She slumped down on the bed beside him and leaned against his solid arm and shoulder.

'You went there? Was it safe not to be jealous when she was dead?'

'Valentine!'

'The truth is always appalling. No – I don't do you justice. You meant to protect me, to find out the truth of this.'

She slowly folded the letter and put it in her doublet's inside pocket.

'Will you stop telling me what I did and didn't mean!' Casaubon trod his heel down into the buckled black shoe and stood. 'For my part I'd as soon she was alive and you with a chance to tire of her.'

'I didn't know she was so vulnerable.'

'Rot it, she's dead, there's an end to it.'

Roseveare House echoed to footsteps, calls. The clamour sounded louder from lower floors. the Lord-Architect reached up for his coat, laid it across the back of the chair, took two pistols from the pockets, and checked their priming before stowing them away again.

'Young Bevil will have me go to Whitehall again and plead a pardon.' He looked delicately at her. 'What will you do?'

'When does the man go to Tyburn?'

'Between two and three.'

'I'll meet you here before then.' She touched her doublet. Paper crackled. 'I have somewhere to go, first.'

The hired coach slowed and stopped. Jared leaned forward and peered between the blind and the window. A white world glowed: early morning.

'You wait here, Jarrie.'

The coach-door swung open. Wet, cold air blasted in. Jared drew his knees together and put his gloved hands on them. Plumes of white breath feathered away from him. He leaned back against the worn upholstery as his mother stepped down into the snow. His throat constricted.

The coach stood high enough for him to see over the wall of St Giles Cripplegate, into the churchyard. Heaps of tarpaulin-covered planks lay chalked with snow, the planks covering holes already dug before winter hardened the ground.

At the end of the row, raw earth stood proud of the snow in a long hump. Jared pulled the blind aside and stared down at the grave. His mother stood in the snow in front of it with her head down.

She squatted, suddenly, the folds of her leather cloak crumpling on the ground. One of her fists punched the earth's soft-looking new ridges. She lifted her knuckles to her mouth and sucked grazes.

Her footprints would be deep in the snow if she walked farther away from the coach.

He kicked rhythmically at the opposite seat. A splinter of wood sprang loose. He hooked the toe of his boot under it, worrying at it, sliding down in his seat until he lay almost flat. The cold air made his uncovered ears burn.

Deep footprints leading away, never returning.

The coach-door opened.

His mother swung herself lightly up, not bothering with the let-down steps. Her face shone red, shiny. Jared stood up as the coach jolted off and stumbled between her knees to put his arms around her neck. Cold air clung to her hair, smelling of ice and damp earth.

'Is that where the lady's dead?'

'*I'll watch him hang and be glad of it.*' Her voice buzzed beside his ear. She moved her head back. A moving strap of light, between blind and coach-window, striped her face and the shoulder of her cloak. His hands hurt where she gripped them.

'It wasn't *just* me, baby. It was him as well.'

Jared staggered as the coach cornered. He sat half on and half against her knee. 'I'm glad she's dead! She made you unhappy.'

'Jarrie, for the Lord's sake—!'

He reached up and touched the cinnamon-red braids, streaked with white; and let his fingers move to that most favourite familiar mystery, the tiny, soft pin-feathers clustered at her temples.

'I love you. I hate everybody who makes you sad.'

Skin around her eyes crinkled, as if the shifting sunlight blinded. 'My commendable son.'

'What's "commendable"?'

She hugged him hard, one arm about his shoulder. The coach jolted.

'If I had to go on a long journey, pudding, would you come with me?'

He leaned against her breast, kicking one foot against her boot. 'But will papa come?'

Still and silent for a heartbeat, she traced his cheek with her knuckle.

'You're going to have to wait in the coach again. I have one more place to visit before I take you home.'

Freezing damp breathed from the walls.

She walked swiftly down one side of Pit Ward. Wet straw rustled underfoot. Water running down from the high, barred windows congealed into ice. Men and women in worn clothes huddled in the straw. Coughs racked the air: prison-fever.

The cold struck up through the soles of her boots. One elbow on her purse, her hand near her dagger, the White Crow shoved through the crowd of prisoners and turnkeys. Steps ascended under a masonry arch to the Masters Ward.

The centre of each tread bowed, stone worn down a good five-fingers' depth.

She pressed a silver penny into the hand of a leather-coated guard, ducked under his halberd, and ran up the steps two at a time. The pile of papers under her arm slipped and she grabbed at it, showing her teeth in a fierce grin; paid another penny to the guard at the head of the stairs, and halted in the archway. She stretched one hand out to the iron-studded oak door for support.

Two or three dozen groups of ill-dressed men and women clustered in the hall. Light from half-hooped windows slanted down, barred, upon battered old tables at which prisoners and their visitors drank and played dice. A few tiny braziers glowed with coals. The raucous noise hesitated a second, summed up and ignored her. The White Crow narrowed her eyes.

A cold and acid pain seared in her stomach; her lungs struggled for air. The straw tangled her boots as she walked towards one window embrasure.

His scarlet frock-coat covered the granite, spread across the ledge under the window. He sat on it in a filthy shirt and breeches, leaning forward, the curls of his periwig crushed and stuck with straw; and all the strength of muscular arm and back engaged in stillness.

Pollexfen Calmady placed a greasy playing-card on top of a third, removed his hands with swift care. The card-tower trembled and stood. Five storeys high. She with one wrist-movement skimmed a handful of pamphlets into the cards, knocking all into the air. The man jumped to his feet. He stood barefoot, leg-irons around his ankles.

'*There.*'

The stone wall slammed against her shoulder-blades as she threw herself down to sit on the stone. She stared up. He slowly pulled up his coat and draped it around his shoulders. She bent and picked some pamphlets from the floor, flipping the Ace of Spades off a title page.

'*Captain Calmady's Last and Dying Speech, a Gallows Recantation.* And *The Ballad of a Gentleman-Murderer.* I like that. And more. There are hawkers selling dozens of titles outside the prison gate.'

Pollexfen Calmady sat down facing her at the far end of the window embrasure. His red-knuckled hand moved to separate the pamphlets. Chilblains whitened two of his fingers.

'*Confession at the Tyburn-Mare, or, The Ravisher Undone to Public View.*' Taunting, she let every syllable sound; mocking the gentleman-mercenaries' mannered tone. She reached up and tugged her cloak-tie open, struggling for breath. 'Do you like it, Captain Calmady? Will you say anything as good, do you think, before you dance on air?'

The big man shrugged his arms into his coat-sleeves. 'I suppose, as they say, I'll piss when I can't whistle. So it's seen: *plures crapula quam gladius*, drunkenness kills more than the sword.'

Morning sun fell on her cheek from the barred window. Almost warm. The stench of urine, excrement, smoke, and sour wine made her cough. She rubbed at the corner of one wet eye. The stone's cold sank into her back and thighs.

The White Crow stared.

Something loosened in her chest at the sight of him: the dirt-marked and ripped scarlet breeches and coat, and the battered periwig. His sword-belt hung, the hanger empty. The creases in his face deepened, by shadow or by starvation, and he snapped his fingers and looked aside, and took a tin jug from one of the ragged children running errands.

'I might have known Gadsbury or Lacey would pay to have you in the best Ward. Or is it my Casaubon's money?'

'Will you drink with me?'

She backhanded the jug, knuckles stinging. Brackish water splashed the straw. Her cloak slipped down. She lurched forward,

fisting both hands in the shirt and lace at his neck, fingers digging
into his flesh; knocked his head back against the wall and spat.

Spittle dripped down his eye, cheek, and lip.

'No, I will *not* drink with you. She's dead because of you.'

His brilliant dark eyes blinked. Not touching her, his hand moved
to feel the back of his head, the blow somewhat softened by his
long, curling wig. One foot on the floor and one on the stone
window-seat, she let the knowledge of his strength and her unused,
unhandy knife show on her face, and grinned, and in the middle of
it sat back heavily and caught her breath in the middle of a laugh.

'I know she's dead. I have learned to think on it, here.' He wiped
his sleeve across his face. 'No act of mine, but I look on this day as
my atonement for it.'

'*Atonement?*'

'You revile me rightly. I killed the girl as surely as if these two
hands hanged her. And your two hands.' The man's head lifted. 'As
surely as if you knotted the halter.'

Blood beat in her ears, and her heart's fibrillation shook her
breathless. She slowly stood up. The light glinted in his eyes, with
that manic brightness either humour or despair; subtly altered now.

'What can you keep from servants? One hears all from them.' His
shoulders moved under the torn coat. His skin glowed yellow,
waxy; and his teeth showed stained. Foul breath drifted across the
intervening space. 'Madam, whatever passed between you and her,
I am responsible. I am *glad* of this day. Now I would not have it
otherwise.'

'Oh, *surely.*'

She reached to touch his hand. Flesh, cold with stone-fever and
shock. She stepped back. A rat scuttled over her boots, and she
kicked it absently and instantly against the wall; its fragile skull
crushed.

'No doubt—' He got heavily to his feet, the striped sunlight
cruelly illuminating his ripped clothes and dirt. '—No doubt others
will visit me today, but I have this, now, to say to you.'

Pollexfen Calmady knelt, in wet straw and on cold stone, on both
knees.

'For any offence I may have done you or led you into, forgive
me.'

She stared, appalled. 'This is too serious for—'

And continued to stare, wordless. He lifted his head, meeting her
eyes.

'Valentine?'

Her feet moved her away, hands making small, unconscious

gestures of disassociation. 'You weren't so unconscious of your offence as you pretended, or else you couldn't have performed it!'

'You're not Guillaime, madam. It's you I ask.'

She looked down at her hands. They shook. She held them out, closing his scarred fingers in her palms; half-said a word, nodded, lifted her wrists so that he must stand, his hands still in her grasp.

'What did you ever do to her that I didn't do?' She let go, her hands clasping together. He looked down, his face dazzled. Her voice sharpened. 'Was yours an honest error? Mine wasn't. I knew she trusted a physician and I used that, and I didn't even *think* about not doing it.'

His hand lifted. She flinched. His fingers touched the pin-feathers at her temples, a touch as light as Jared's. She caught a sob in her throat and choked, stammered out, 'Damn you, I didn't know to tell her; I didn't know she'd go to some Protectorate fanatic; I didn't know she *believed*—'

She wiped her nose on her sleeve.

'Damn, you gave it her.'

He rested one fist back on his hip, unconsciously showing the rent lining of his long coat. The lines deepened in his face. He smiled a slow smile. 'Madam, you and I are, *ipso facto*, too alike for you ever to forgive me.'

'Alike?'

She took a breath, deep despite the stink of damp and excrement, held it, and let it out in a long sigh. Anger dissipated; she raked at it without result.

'That's true, of course. I've seen it for some while.'

He inclined his head. The periwig, dusty on one side, shone in the window's light. One chilblained finger stabbed the air at her. 'Will you hear me advise you somewhat? Purely for yourself, and because I will shortly have to speak truth about greater matters, and may as well begin to practise.'

She nodded silently.

'You use your *magia* less and less.'

The dislocation disorientated her. She grinned without humour. 'After this, I won't use it at all; I can't be a physician now!'

'You never could. This is not your husband telling tales, madam; I have eyes and ears – let me guess. You left the road and put up your sword, and since then have done less and less of the Noble Arts, until now you do almost nothing but doctor servants' influenzas and children's green-bone fractures.'

Precision and control informed him; she could only look.

'How do you know? And what's it to you?'

'I'm a dying man.' He spoke with undramatic sobriety. 'One of
the things I have thought of, these five days, is you. I know you as I
know myself. *Find yourself a war* – if you wait until spring, or
summer, the damned bitches will provide a civil war here between
'em, but you'd fare better fighting strangers. *Fight.* Aren't half the
Invisible College scholars and soldiers, as you were?'

'Oh, how can I?' She rubbed her hands over her face, fingers
rough against brows and hairline. 'I'm a Master-Physician, I heal
wounds, I don't make them. I *can't* do the *magia* that I used. Well
then: I can't.'

A ragged girl of seven or eight shoved between them. Pollexfen
Calmady leaned down and picked up the tin jug and tossed it to her.
The child ran off. He beat dirt off the fabric of his knee-breeches and
straightened.

'Admirable sentiments. Yes, and what I recommend is a worse
way. But answer me: is it in your nature? You do violence to
yourself, being what you try to be here. I say nothing in defence of
fighting, except that you'll sicken as long as you don't carry a blade
and use it. Oh, believe it, wars are pig-butchery and stink and no
honour; *I* know! Madam, I beg you ask yourself if you can do
anything *else.*'

'I don't – I'm not—'

A handbell clanged at the far end of the Ward. His head turned.

'I should be glad of your company now.'

'What is it?'

'The service for the condemned. I doubt my damned fool troopers
will be here until later. But this is appointed my day to die. I
welcome it.'

'Do you?'

'Were it vice versa, say, how would you stand?'

The White Crow looked away. Warders pushed through the
crowds of prisioners and visitors, sorting out candidates for the
service. The noise-level rose. She rescued her cloak from the straw
and put it about her shoulders, shivering.

'Will you do something for me, madam?'

With no hesitation she nodded.

'I have no more money. Everything in this rotten hell-hole must
be paid for, light and air included. Well,' Pollexfen Calmady said,
'Gadsbury and the rest have no money, either. Will you tell
Casaubon, either I must sell my dead body to the surgeons, or else
hang in rags. Tell him I won't hang without a clean shirt and
stockings to die in.'

A tall turnkey grabbed his arm and he shrugged her off, turning to follow nonetheless; shouting back over his shoulder: 'Will you tell him?'

'I . . . *yes.*'

She elbowed her way in his wake. A woman with a musket barged past; two black-jerkined halberd men at the far door jostled. She dropped a hand to her belt, found her purse gone; walking with numb legs until she knelt on the chapel's stone floor.

White granite gleamed.

The squat round pillars shone, dappled with yellow-and-gold from the stained-glass perpendicular windows. A dozen or so prisoners knelt and their warders with them. The child-priest Ordinary of Newgate strode up the aisle, black robe whisking into her face as he passed. The cold stone hurt her knees. She lifted her head.

Carved deep into the blank eastern wall, Square and Star shone with inlaid brass. In the centre the Circle blazed, polished by unwilling hands; enclosing the image of the Risen Sun. She drew the sign of Bull-horns on her breast, consciously resuscitating childhood practices.

Pollexfen Calmady and one other condemned man knelt at what at first seemed a low wooden table, set below the wall's bas-reliefs. Under his wig, his face showed white, calm, poised.

Abruptly a bell rang out, tolling harshly in Newgate's tiny chapel tower.

Split pine planks wept pungent scent into the air. She craned her head. The heads of new copper nails glinted in the open wooden coffin.

CHAPTER 11

J ared shivered after the long wait. His mother eased down in the coach-seat, digging into a concealed pocket. She counted a handful of pennies, half-pence, farthings, and extracted one remaining rose-noble.

'Give this to the coachman when he leaves you at Roseveare House.'

Jared folded his hand around the coin. The septagon's edges dug into his palm. 'What about you, Mama?'

'Looks like I'll have to walk.'

She flashed a smile that, from warm eyes and wry mouth, reached in and tugged his gut. He clung to her for a kiss.

'Don't worry! Tell your father I'll be back before noon. And I will be, pudding.'

The coach-door opened: shut. Tack jingled. The coach's wheels ratcheted on gravelled snow, skidding and then gripping. One of the leaders neighed. Jared jerked the blind and it rolled up.

Tiny between the grandeur of stone lions and frozen fountains, the woman walked fast, shoes skidding, towards Whitehall.

'What do you mean, she won't see me?' The White Crow glared at the elderly lady-in-waiting. 'She damned well *will* see—Denzil!'

Sir Denzil Waldegrave walked through the courtyard from the Banqueting Hall to Whitehall Palace's east wing. His amber cane poked delicately at the gritted cobbles. The wind moved the long, golden curls of his wig, and the azure ribbons at cuffs and cane.

'*Sir* Denzil.' She abandoned the woman and loped across the yard, pushing between Protectorate guards and royalist courtiers to lay a hand on the man's arm. 'I need to see Her Majesty.'

His leisurely stride never altered.

'Dammit!'

'Lady Roseveare—'

The mid-morning sun gleamed from the dyed-gold horse-hair

curls of his wig, and made his rouged cheeks into a clown's garish mask. From this, shrewd brown eyes surveyed her.

'—I can't conceive your business here. If it be for yourself, abandon hope. If for a friend, let your friend find some other advocate.' He paused to kick horse-dung from the heel of his court shoe, speaking in a measured undertone. 'The gratitude of monarchs is, never to forgive a favour. You have been of use. You have affronted her dignity. She has said that if she lays eyes on you again, she will send you to Newgate or the Tower. Be warned.'

The White Crow stared.

'Truly?'

'Send in to know as many times as you please. But expect her in due course to send out a sergeant-at-arms.' He extracted a watch from his waistcoat pocket, flipped up the silver lid, and in louder tones remarked, 'Five-and-twenty to eleven, an it please your ladyship.'

'This isn't for me.'

'Then, whoever's cause it is, your name will do them more harm than help. Madam, I beg you to excuse me.'

She slowed, elbowed by passers-by, staring after the man, buffeted aside. Sun glinted from the rows of windows. Ice hung jagged from gables, six-foot spears that could fall and impale a man. The cold wind sank bone-deep into her body.

The grave, not yet sunken, scars yesterday's snow. Frozen clods of its earth are rimed with white. No headstone. A pauper's grave.

Bevil Calmady absently fingers a hole in his blue silk waistcoat. His thick scarlet coat, hanging open, could wrap his thin torso two or three times. It is not his. He reaches up and removes his hat.

The broken plume annoys him; he snaps it off.

Whispering, 'I apologise for him,' he feels in his pocket for the crackling paper that, signed, will apprentice him to Captain Huizinga's surgeon (a Paracelsan of limited temper and great skill) for seven years. He adds, 'I apologise for them all.'

St Giles Cripplegate looms, cold black stone. The dragon-weathervane squeals, shifting to south-south-east, and cries in brazen tongues:

'*Eleven o'clock and all's well! Eleven o'clock and aaaak—*'

Bevil Calmady lowers his arm from a stoop and throw that is all one movement. The stone from Desire Guillaime's grave rebounds and rattles down the church tiles.

Sand melted old snow to the colour of excrement, a sick yellow on the cobblestones. Grit crunched under her boots.

The White Crow elbowed between groups of people crowding the bottom of the Charing Cross Road. Virgin white on the gables of shops, snow stood out against a sunny sky. Wind gusted coldly.

Her stomach growled with the smell of new-baked bread. She slowed under the white plaster and black-beamed overhang of the nearest shop.

A shape moved behind the irregular glass shop-window; pushing open the door to the street. The Lord-Architect tilted his head back, bit into a pastry, and caught sight of her.

'Valentine!'

A spray of crumbs dotted the slush and her cloak. She brushed herself off thoughtfully.

'I want—' She put a last fragment of pastry in her mouth, chewed, and raised her eyebrows. 'I need to talk to you.'

The wind blew tendrils of copper-red hair across his forehead. Cold reddened his faintly freckled face. A scarf muffled his chins; the green frieze coat's hem showed black with wet; snow and muck covered his large boots. Passers-by divided like a river to go into the road and around him.

'Any time these five days you could have talked to me.' The syrup pastry broke in his hand. He held up his large, dripping fingers and licked them.

'I know. I'm sorry.'

The Lord-Architect Casaubon probed with his tongue between ring and little finger, gave up on the last fragment, and brushed absently at the flakes of pastry around his lips and chin. His blue eyes glanced north towards the turn-off into Roseveare Court.

'Here.'

He pushed the shop-door open again, bowed to an elderly man leaving with arms full of loaves, and shifted himself sideways to climb crabwise up narrow stairs towards the first floor, not looking back to see if she followed.

At the head of the stairs, private coffee-rooms opened off the landing. She beat her hands against the warmth of returning circulation and walked into the front room. A fire burned in the hearth. Bottle-glass windows looked down into the crowded streets. The fat man sprawled across one complete side of the oak-panelled cubicle nearest the window.

'I hope you can buy me coffee.' She sat heavily on the opposite side. 'I don't have any money left. You know how much it costs in petty bribes in Newgate.'

His copper-red brow hooked up. 'You've spoken to him?'

'I've spoken to him.'

'And?'

A leather-aproned man put his head around the door. The Lord-Architect Casaubon listed rapidly: 'Coffee, dates, pork chop, steak; what sweetmeats you have; the coffee with cream if you have it fresh.'

'Sorry, master.' The man shrugged. 'Lot a custom on a hanging-day; always is. Take your coffee black, will you?'

'Black and without interruption.'

The White Crow sneaked a sight of the coin handed over: too large to be a rose-noble, more probably a sovereign. She leaned her chin on her hand, staring through distorting window-glass into the street.

The door clicked shut.

'And?'

'And – he has me forgetting that it was he who broke into a sick woman's room and raped her while she was unconscious. And forgetting that he gave her the pox when he fucked her. And that she died as a direct result of what he did.'

She sat back on the settle, burying her chin in the small ruffles at her neck.

'And forgetting that on campaign he wouldn't think twice about it. How many little girls has he fucked or killed, do you think, in forty years?'

'Fewer than you imagine.' Casaubon's voice rumbled. 'I won't call him innocent of what you say.'

'Innocent!'

Sickness roiled under her breastbone.

'And yet there's the reason why I forget. Because he does want to die. He's content. It makes me wonder what I should be?'

Casaubon snorted. His distorted reflection in the window scowled. She shrugged.

'How am I different from him? Shall I hang myself, all three? Wouldn't that make a tragedy for Master Kinsayder's theatre. Casaubon, what can I do?'

His tone came very drily. 'Little one, you can stop being ridiculous.'

She felt her cheeks heat. 'So I'm not about to hang myself. I won't say it doesn't have its temptations. I won't go to a man's hanging when I feel as guilty as he is.'

The fire's heat soaked through her damp breeches. She slid sideways on the padded seat and pulled off first one shoe and then the other, and massaged her sweat-dark hose. Exhaustion burned sweetly in her muscles. Brief sleep pulled at her eyelids. The door slammed open, the coffee-house owner carrying a tray; and she sat with her eyes shut and listened to his loading down the table. Hunger tipped into sudden revulsion with the smell of cooked meat.

She opened her eyes, poured out coffee into chipped china, and sipped at the too-hot liquid. The Lord-Architect prodded his heaped plate with a fork. With her free hand she reached across and snared his deep cuff.

'And you? What will you do?'

He brandished a fork dripping gravy from the chop.

'Rot the man, if *I* hadn't written, he'd be here in town still, and the Guillaime girl alive.'

'You're angry. And not just with me. Where did you go this morning?'

She felt down the cuff to his other hand, winding her fingers between his; resting their joined hands against her cheek. His voice, more vibration than sound, came quietly to her:

'To General Olivia. She claims no more say in the matter. Then I went to your Carola and she refused point-blank to see the General's renegade architect. The man was my friend. Guillaime never was, nor,' his blue eyes met hers, 'was ever likely to be.'

The White Crow frowned.

'Something else?' she asked.

He pulled his hand from hers. Her skin suddenly chilled, she tucked her fingers up into her armpit, in the warmth of cloak and doublet. He planted one plump finger on his steak and sawed at it with the blunt knife.

'I'm wondering—' he rested the knife, picked up the steak and bit it, and continued through a mouthful of fibres and gravy '—how you contrive to be so comprehensive a fool.'

'Me?'

'I will bear with you when you must come home to this commonwealth, it being your home; and I'll even bear with you when you fall for a pretty little face – and the idea that there's more brains than fanaticism behind it.'

He picked out a string of gristle from between his teeth and dropped it. It lodged in the wrinkles of his unbuttoned coat. He prodded the air in her direction with the fork.

'But when you go off into the sulks, and lock yourself away with that bawling brat of mine: *no*. When you claim to be the Invisible College's physician-magus and confine yourself to doctoring influenza and greenstick fractures: *no* – what did I say?'

Tears started in her eyes. The coffee burned her upper lip. She sniffed and took a deeper drink. 'Nothing.'

'I'll stand no more.'

He stuck a forefinger into his coffee-bowl, winced, drank it straight down and poured another, his cheeks reddening. She blinked. Sudden sunlight whitely illuminated the swell of his chest, the half-undone lace stock at his throat, and the delicate flesh of his throat, chins, and earlobes.

'I'm not your refuge to come home to when all else's exhausted!'

'No, I – yes,' the White Crow said. 'Yes, I did think . . . not to say *think*, but assume. Oh, damn you.'

He reached across and cupped her cheek with gravy-smeared fingers. 'Great Architect, but you're *white*.'

'Only in places.' Her voice wavered on the caustic tones. She sat back and smudged at her cheek with her sleeve. The sunlight brightened, leaching colour from the room; the crackle of the fire sounded loud in her ears. Breathing slowed: she leaned her head back against the oak headboard.

'You're not glad I'm back then?'

The large man stopped with a coffee bowl halfway to his mouth. He put it down as delicately as if the chipped china had been porcelain.

Without raising her head, his eyes lifted to hers. 'You might at least ask me whether I still want you.'

She smiled, mouth closed, a fold of interior skin nipped between canine and lower tooth, biting against tears. At last, and aiming for sardonic superiority, she said, 'I don't have to ask. I know. Which may be terrible, but is none the less true.'

The Lord-Architect Casaubon snorted.

One hand slammed down, palm flat on the table. Cutlery and cups jumped, spilled, rattled. His other hand grabbed her scholar's braids, pulling her up, half-standing over the wrecked table; he kissed her, and pushed gently. She hit the oak headboard partition between her shoulder-blades and sat down hard.

'Valentine. At least I've taught you one thing sufficiently well. Yes. *You know*. Now why did you ever forget it?'

Through the glass, the south-hanging sun warmed her cheek.

Fragile as ice, her composure started to return. She grinned, wiped her nose; and touched a finger to his. Sallow flesh against cherub-pink. She stared at his strong nail.

Grit-carts rumbled past in the street. Horses whickered.

'Did Jared tell you? I went to Whitehall Palace. Damn stupid thing to do; I ought to know *Regina* Carola by now.'

'If you'd stood witness, it couldn't have been in his defence.'

'I know that. You neither.'

She picked desultorily at the edge of a pastry, staring out of the window. Cold condensation webbed the edges of the glass. Wavering images of men and horses passed below. Shadows slanted northwards.

'It must be close on midday.' The Lord-Architect belched and got up from the alcove, scattering a handful of silver coin across his denuded plate.

She swivelled round and hurriedly pulled her boots on. 'Now what?'

Casaubon, standing by the table, held open his left-hand coat pocket and tipped the dish of dates into it; and slipped the remains of the pork chop into his righthand pocket. He picked up the last jam pastry and bit into it.

'As to that—'

Crossing to the door, he cracked his head against a low beam and winced.

'—I have something more to tell you.'

Outside, air dropped to freezing. The White Crow tugged on fur-lined leather gloves and stamped her feet. Gulls skimmed the roofs, skreeling north towards the river: flashes of white against the blue sky. Far down, past fountains and statues, the hundred chimneys of Whitehall Palace bled smoke into the midday haze.

The Lord-Architect, buttoning his coat, strode off up towards Roseveare Court. He spoke without looking at her and without slowing his pace.

'Did you know that Calmady raped the Guillaime woman twice?'

'*What?*'

'That first night that we got to town. I heard this about ten o'clock today, from Gadsbury and Bess Winslow. Rot it, the both of them are falling-down drunk; I think it's true.'

'What the—?'

Breath sawed in her throat. She grabbed his arm as he wheeled into the road and heaved him back from the path of a carriage. In a niche between a saddlery shop and a milliners she let go of his coat-sleeve, shoving him back against the beamed wall.

'What do you mean, he raped her twice?'

Plumes of white breath spiralled into the air. She moved from foot to cold foot, hugging herself, staring up at him. The fat man shook his head.

'The pair of whoreson bastards say he tracked her down to St Sophia, threatened to tell her priest-confessor she was nothing but the mercenary company's whore; then had the two of them hold her down while he stripped her and lay with her, so that they could swear on oath to her nakedness. Her whorish nakedness.'

She leaned forward against his chest, resting her forehead against the cold fabric of his coat. The rapid rise and fall of his breathing shook her. The weight of his arms around her shoulders pressed her to him, breath moistening the frieze cloth.

A sedan-chair carrier elbowed her, passing. She straightened.

'That first night?'

'I think so. This was two hours ago, Gadsbury so drunk he lay in his own piss and t'other no better; but yes, how else would they speak the truth?'

'Dear god. She couldn't tell me.' Dazed, she stared up into his face. 'He played young Bevil for a fool. Confessing and being arrested. He could *count* on her refusing to speak against him.'

'That's all one now.'

'Oh, sweet Christ!'

She reached up and linked her hands behind his neck. On her toes, breathing the cold wind, leaning up to kiss him on the corner of the mouth. 'Christ, what a thing for you to hear. I wish I'd been with you.'

He bent and rested his face in her neck, burrowing between ruff and braids; the warmth of his breath feathering her skin. She strained to encompass him in one embrace, slid back as he straightened up.

'What will you do?'

Casaubon shrugged massively. 'I don't know yet. I make a beginning and tell you.'

She linked her arm through his. The main bulk of the standing crowd left behind, she walked with him now between high brick frontages; the sun starring windows all down the road, hanging low in the southern sky and blinding her. Two horsemen spurred past. Clots of snow flew up, spattering her cloak.

'I . . .'

She stopped and stared back towards the square and Whitehall. 'He knows me almost as well as you do. Pollexfen Calmady.'

Casaubon cocked his head, mutely questioning.

'He said we were alike. Him and me. Alike.'

White haze blurred the far roofs. A keen wind blew up from the frozen Thamys. She hugged Casaubon's arm.

'Is that it? Do we just go home now?'

She frowned.

'And to Roseveare, in due course. Do we? If anything happens, it has to happen now: these next few hours.'

'Rot it, don't say *we* when you mean *I*.'

The White Crow winced. She narrowed her eyes against the winter sunlight, looking up at him.

She let go of his arm and stepped back, ankle-deep in slush at the roadside; pushing one thread of red hair back from her eyes. Voices called, chattered. Between hoofbeats and a distant sackbut, muffled church bells rang noon's thirteen chimes. The sun's warmth on her cheek felt a fragile thing.

She crossed her arms across her breast, gripping her upper arms. 'Will you . . .'

Not a smile: an upwelling of something too fierce and too joyous to be contained. She showed teeth. Her fingers dug deep into her biceps under the cloak. A deep breath: '. . . Will you trust me to do something, without my telling you?'

The Lord-Architect Casaubon raised his eyebrow, pained. 'I most certainly will not.'

'That's – fair.'

'Do what you want,' he said, 'and count me with you, but not without knowing what it is. Credit me with some sense, furies take it!'

'Rein me and spur me, will you?' She laughed. Astonished, feeling it shake her body. She swung on her heel and strode towards Roseveare Court's back alley entrance, his shadow leaping ahead as he paced beside her.

No shifting hooves sounded in the stables, the gentlemen-mercenaries' mounts gone. Sun glinted from frost and cobbles. Seeing Abiathar, she snapped her fingers: the click echoing off yard walls.

The black-haired woman held the kitchen door open. 'Shout next time. Kitterage might blow your head off. He's nervous.'

The White Crow laughed. '*He's* nervous.'

Abiathar and the Lord-Architect exchanged glances.

'Come with me. Both of you.' She threw down her cloak and took the stairs from the kitchen parlour two at a time, heard the woman's questioning tone cut off as the door swung to; and made it as far as the second-floor front room before they caught up. She crossed to the desk and unlocked the drawer.

Casaubon, no sign of exertion in his face, unbuttoned his coat as he came into the room. Sunlight and warmth: and the smell of polished wood long neglected. She thrust the sheaf of folded papers into his hand.

'I'll sign these, unless you tell me I shouldn't.'

In the far corner of the room an iron-banded long chest stood.

She squatted and tried the key in the lock, wrist exerting force against the rust-starred metal.

'Damn, I – there!' She lifted her head.

The Lord-Architect stood in the centre of the room, head bent, reading. He handed each paper as he finished it to Abiathar. The woman wiped her hands on her skirts. She frowned in concentration, reading.

The White Crow opened the wooden chest.

A covering cloth. Parchments, rough against her hands as autumn leaves, their inks faded into purples and sepias, but the sigils still clear and strong. Two or three untitled books. She stacked them reverently to one side on the floor. And under it all, a mass of buckles, chains, leather straps, and a scabbard.

'Deeds of property.' The Lord-Architect folded the last between two fingers and proffered it to Abiathar. She nodded acknowledgement.

'Abiathar, what say you?' The White Crow knelt up, buckling the wide leather belt around her waist, over her breeches-belt. Two riveted chains hung down: one short, one long. She clipped the one at her back to the lower scabbard-clip; the one at her side to the clip closest the hilt, and stood up.

And reached across with her left hand and drew the blade.

Oiled, cleaned, gleaming: no spot of rust. The razor edge of a live blade. She touched a fingertip to it, near the point. Burning as winter ice, a thin line of blood welled across the pad of her finger.

'It's as near as I can get to a collective.'

Abiathar cluckled sourly. 'Try and deed property to servants and they'll have you in Bedlam, not Newgate.'

The black-haired woman's eyes cleared. She tapped the papers thoughtfully against her other hand. 'I'll have to talk to Thomas and Edward. I suppose we may answer for those back at Roseveare? Now tell me if I have it right: you deed us power of attorney, and all other necessary powers—' She raised one script and read: '—for the maintenance of Roseveare Estate, its farms, properties, woods, and buildings; for as long as the Roseveare family remain absent.'

The sword's weight settled as the White Crow sheathed it, tapping at mid-thigh, hilt ready for her hand. She met Casaubon's gaze. Sober blue eyes watched, level.

'Absent for how long?' he asked.

'As long as you like.'

The slight stress on the penultimate word brought a curve to his delicately shaped mouth. He turned, took Abiathar's hand, and kissed it. 'Count on no short absence!'

'Oh, I guessed as much, my lord.'

The White Crow put both hands down to ease the sword-belt. At Casaubon's touch, she lifted her head. His finger caressed her cheek.

'You had this planned. Rot it, not because *I* want it?'

With a demure hilarity, she said, 'Not just because you want it. There are others concerned.'

'What about the children? Your son's no more than ten years from an age to inherit. And there's the child.' Abiathar frowned. 'I can promise you this, if either comes seeking Roseveare, they're as like to get a cold welcome as not.'

'As far as I'm concerned, I'm giving you the place. They'll know it. It's up to you to keep it.'

She snapped her fingers again, took the papers back and carried them to the desk, flipping open the inkwell and signing in scrawled quill-pen *Valentine Roseveare*.

'Now . . .'

Her boots clicked on the floorboards, pacing to the window. Roseveare Court's bookshops stood boarded up and left for the hanging-holiday. Snow choked all but a winding centre path. She squinted sideways, down between buildings towards the main road. Thoughts slotted into place, faster than words could follow.

'Bloody woman might have given the carriage back.'

The Lord-Architect spluttered with laughter. She turned.

'*Well*. She didn't need that. Unless she plans to travel in it when she goes into exile, I suppose . . . We won't be able to leave town anyway until the weather shifts. Love, will you act the difficult part?'

Casaubon folded massive arms. She went on:

'Take Jared and the baby. This place will get ransacked, but that's no harm; they won't assume servants know where we've gone.'

Abiathar, folding the signed documents, said, 'Where will you have gone?'

'I think . . .' She looked at the Lord-Architect, prompting.

'The Liberty of Northbankside. One of the rooming-houses there.' He stooped to kiss Abiathar's cheek as the older woman left the room. 'Rot it, it *is* the worse part. I'll do it provided I'm told all else. Now.'

'I . . . have to do something about Pollexfen Calmady. I've decided.'

'Oh, good.' The Lord-Architect beamed happily. 'At last.'

She made the sort of laughter that is really exasperation, one first clenched, swinging round to point with her other hand. The sword banged at her hip. 'Don't you even *care* if it's not moral – that it's the wrong thing to do?'

Casaubon continued to look at her, his immense body still, the sun catching his copper hair and fair skin. Visible in his face, finally, and visible to her: a ruthless benevolence.

The White Crow said, 'For you it isn't even a question, is it?'

He loomed over her; seized her under the arms and pulled her up into an embrace, her feet eighteen inches above the floor.

'You've made up your mind!' He kissed her enthusiastically.

In the face of that massive refusal of judgement, she sought interior certainties.

'So . . . it's the wrong decision, but it's mine, and I abide by the consequences.'

A single bell rang continuously, muffled, echoing down through Newgate's stone walls. Pollexfen Calmady rested his head back against the man's leather-aproned belly, stretching his throat and chin.

A razor feathered across his skin.

Prison ash-soap eased its passing. The last stubble scraped away, he sat up and dabbed at his face with dirty shirt-sleeves. Gadsbury raised a slurred cheer. Arbella and Rule supported the small man; the tall woman leaning in turn on Bess, Lady Winslow, and the Margrave. The company of gentlemen-mercenaries crowded close, shouldering strangers further off. All the Pit muttered and buzzed with talk.

'Sir.' Calmady rose and bowed to the man who shaved him.

'My pleasure, my master.'

'Now strike off the chains.'

Barred sunlight on the straw slanted north-east. Past two of the clock: the prison-yard outside a roar of gathering women and men and children. A shout went up at the rumble of wheels: the tumbril's arrival.

The brawny man acting as barber snapped his fingers. His hair and beard caught the light as he knelt, brass-blond; and he blinked slow, brandy-brown eyes. Two lads ran forward with mallet and chisel, a dozen younger brats at their heels. The man swept them back with a bare, muscular arm. He placed the chisel and raised the mallet.

Pollexfen Calmady, his back straight, looked down to his ankles. Iron chains coiled about his bare feet. The mallet lifted, fell. A rivet shot out, lost in filthy straw; one shackle sprang open. The reverberate echoes of the strike diminished in the vaulted hall.

Iron to anvil: smithy-noises. The second shackle fell loose.

'Again, sir, I thank you.'

He walked a few paces, barefoot, straw pricking the soles of his feet; light at heel for the first time in five days, and ridiculously, momentarily, light at heart.

The fair-haired hangman's assistant rose. A leather apron covered black breeches and boots. His open face squinted against a bar of sunlight. Pollexfen Calmady pointed at a small man hovering behind him.

'You – you've a damned surgeon's look to you!'

The small man's eyes travelled up and down Calmady's thick torso. 'Many a man has sold what he will shortly no longer need to purchase what he would not be without. I'll give you shillings enough to purchase clothes to be hanged in.'

Calmady locked eyes with the Margrave Linebaugh across the man's head.

'See I'm given honest *untouched* burial. If not, I swear you'll never ride without a dead man in the company!'

The Margrave lifted his arm slightly, weighed down with folded shirt, breeches, and coat. 'Your friend's servant brought money, Captain. And sends apologies that he dare not attend.'

Calmady snorted. 'Has Baltazar Casaubon sense enough to fear, now? That's a wonder!'

'You're a Queen's man, hanging; there'll be enough royalists there that the Protectorate's renegade architect might well fear for his skin.' Arbella Lacey held up polished white boots. 'He's done well by you, captain. As well as a man in his position could.'

He reached up between his shoulder-blades and pulled the stinking shirt over his head. He did not look around, nor look for missing faces. A hand held out a clean shirt, all lace and linen, that slid over his skin, covering dirt and prison-rash. He stripped breeches and stockings, received new, and turned as he finished the fastenings.

'My god, will you look at that?' Lord Rule carefully rearranged one of the black periwig's curls on his captain's brocade-coated shoulder. His gloved hand flicked across white- and silver-lace splendour. 'Flash. Very flash. We'll have no cause to be shamed, knowing you today.'

Pollexfen Calmady tugged boots on over white linen breeches and stockings. The silver-laced waistcoat buttoned a little tightly across his large chest. A momentary smile moved his lips at that constriction. He shrugged into the white brocade coat that Arbella held out, and put his fists on his hips, staring down the Ward: at men lying drunk or feverish against the walls, rats running across them; at a bare-breasted slut suckling a child; at the faces all drawn to follow him.

'I'm a magnetic north to them!' He trod his feet down in the new boots. Leather creaked. 'Because I'll shortly ride a horse foaled by an acorn. Let's not keep them waiting. Have you money about you?'

Sir John Hay shook his head. 'Not a farthing.'

'Furies. Attend. Gadsbury has my voice for captain.' He rested his arm across Arbella Lacey's shoulders as they walked, sparing a glance backward for the small dark man, staggering and supported between Linebaugh and Thompson. 'Tell him so when he's sober.'

The redheaded woman cuffed a prison brat aside. She rubbed the mud-stain left on her old kid glove. Brocade breeches and coat embroidered with silver plate and sequins flashed in the barred sunlight. From polished heeled boots to plumed broad-brimmed hat, the woman strode with a mercenary's brittle vanity.

'The company won't be the same. Do you remember Parry, at Aqua Sulis?' Reflective memory of the dead captain clear on her face. 'Damn, there was a shit-stupid man. *Attack through the sewers, men, we can take the town!* And us with a comfortable siege there to see us out the whole summer, if we nursed it along.'

'Not to mention petard mines in the sewer-system. I remember.'

His stride outdistanced her under the stone arch, exiting into the open, bitter-cold prison yard. He all but ran into a man coming in the other direction.

'Sir.' The man removed his plumed hat with some deliberation. Black hair straggled either side of a long, sallow face; his sharp chin made sharper by a small, pointed beard. Tan-and-cream brocade hung loosely on him as if his long coat had been made for a larger man.

'Phillip Nashe.' A cultured voice. He held out a strong-fingered hand. 'Queen's Hangman.'

Pollexfen Calmady, dry-handed, returned the grip. He took in the weather-worn face, the expression somewhere between shabbiness and pride; summing him up shortly. 'Captain Yates's – no, Captain Huizinga's troop?'

'Some four years since. I took orders Lammastide last.'

The priest-hangman drew a notepad from his waistcoat pocket and made notes with a charcoal-stick, glancing up, practised eye measuring height, weight, drop.

Cold air grazed Calmady's newly shaven chin. He rubbed one cheek.

The straggle-haired man smudged calculations with a dirty thumb, frowned and nodded. He indicated the cart and two yoked dray-horses by the gate. An elderly man in a white shirt already stood in the tumbril. 'I ride with you.'

Calmady walked beside Nashe toward the tumbril and the prison-gates. The swarthy man limped slightly.

'There are good deaths and bad deaths, we know that.' Pollexfen Calmady spoke quietly; businesslike. 'Shot in the stomach; thirst; half your face blown off by some sapper's mine; cancerous gangrene; well . . .'

Phillip Nashe's bearded chin jutted, indicating the scattering of black-coated men and women among the yard's crowds. 'Yes, and Tower Hill, your entrails and privates hacked out and burned, before the axe. That would have been Protectorate justice, Captain Calmady.'

Calmady's features twisted into a momentarily uncontrollable expression. His gloved hand pressed into the bottom of the new coat's pocket. A handful of metal circlets bruised his fingers. Relief, sudden and startling, sang in his blood.

'True enough, sir. Your business, now, is to tie a knot well, so matters expedite as quick as may be.'

The sovereigns slipped from his gloved fingers to the man's hand.

'You shall have a good knot. I shall have your coat and small-clothes too, or the compensation for that perquisite.' Nashe prodded the small heap of gold coins in his palm, and thrust them deep into his pocket. 'And Queen's Bounty. Sir, I'm obliged to ask what peace you've made, and how, and in what mind you're like to die.'

Shabby, dark-eyed, the priest's gaze by reason of his shorter stature fell below Calmady's face. Calmady shrugged.

'I'm caught between her Majesty and the bitch-General; a cause I've risked my life for, on either side. *Non sum qualis eram*: today I am a different man. It's a fine irony that I should be brought here to make my peace with God.'

Reverberate echoes from the cold masonry yard waked shivers between his shoulder-blades. Open, sunny skies blazed over the prison roofs. Wooden steps set at the back of the prison-cart sparkled, treacherous with frost. He halted.

'Captain. Here.'

He took a bottle from Lord Rule. His throat moved as he tilted his head back and drank, pale skin exposed to the winter sunlight. Another shiver walked the bones of his back.

Gadsbury's head lifted. '*Regina* Carola, damn her.'

'The Queen and her Hangman.' Rough brandy scoured his mouth. Pollexfen Calmady coughed. He pulled Gadsbury into a bear-hug, the stink of stale vomit and brandy hitting him in the face.

'Do you carry all your brains in your arse? Go broke on brandy now and how will you live out the winter?' He shook the small man roughly. 'Man, I remember you drinking! The night I lost the last of Calmady Estate on the turn of two cards. *Go for a soldier now*, you said, *or go be a thief*. We chose well enough.'

'You never would cheat at cards.'

'It brings me to this reckoning at the last.'

He squinted at the early afternoon sun, westering; turned his face briefly into the east wind. Brandy blurred vision. The wooden steps knocked his feet, swinging himself up into the cart. Phillip Nashe banged the tailgate up; the elderly man – *T* branded already on his forehead – vomited a small pool of liquid onto the straw on the jolting planks.

The tension of his shoulders against the cold loosened. He stretched his head up. Winter sun, warm now that the cart rumbled out of the prison gates and the wind, slanted across his face. A deep breath escaped him.

Deep, felt through belly and the pit of his bowels, the tumbril wheels scraped straw-covered cobbles. Iron wheel-rims struck sparks and children darted back. The constant noise of shouting filled his hollow chest, effervescent; so that he bowed to either side, with a conscious style, smiling as the puppets in the convent-garden booths smile.

Every tavern in Holborn, every inn and every gin-shop spilled their customers out into the slush-deep road. Men and women crowded around the slowly moving cart. He leaned down to clasp hands with a dozen, two dozen; lifted his hat to acknowledge cheers. Hundreds of bobbing heads dizzied him crowding the road ahead. He lifted his gaze to snowy roofs, to the street's windows, casements open despite the cold. Red-cheeked women cheered.

A yellow-haired girl leaned out to toss a bright object, fluttering down. He caught it from the air: a red rose, folded and cut from rosewater-coloured paper, bright against the winter white. He bowed, and removed his hat to fix the paper flower into the silver-lace band.

Winter cold bit his fingertips through his white gloves. The shadow of St Sophia's steeple momentarily fell cold on his face.

Children bundled in black rags ran along beside the cart. A stone rattled from the wood. He lifted his head. Every snow-ledged tenement window here stood jammed with black-clad men and women, white faces solemn, none shouting, none cheering.

Pollexfen Calmady took off his hat and held it to his breast, and bowed ceremoniously. Aware of how the skirts of his coat swung, flashing sunlight from silver trimming; how bright the paper rose gleamed against his bridal finery. He smiled as he straightened.

A sharp stone stung his hand. He did not flinch.

Bells clanged a muffled scale, tumbledown-notes: sound smashing the air, scattering up flocks of lean rooks and pigeons. The cart rumbled under the eaves of St Giles in the Fields. Deafened, he threw his head back and laughed into the sea-wild, shaking air.

The White Crow hung on, balancing on the coach's outside step, snow-wet air reddening her fingers. The sword-hilt jabbed her hip. Her tone provoked.

'It's *your* area of expertise, sir, after all. Didn't you publish *On the Circulation of the Blood*?'

Sir William Harvey peered out irritably between the blind and the window-frame of the coach. 'So must I have the Invisible College study a *magia* of the gallows?'

'Of course it's a *magia*. It's death without spilling blood.'

One heel on the outside step, the White Crow balanced leaning back against the coach's closed door, looking down across Tyburn field as she spoke. The horses plodded through the dividing crowds.

'This all patterns around blood . . .'

Her voice echoed flatly in her ears. Wind coursed the snowy fields. Makeshift booths crammed the paths, deserted now as people in their hundreds pressed down the slope towards the gallows platform. White copses gleamed in the distance. Men and women in bright, patched cloaks trod straw into the snow: fairground-rutted.

'I came home to Roseveare: that's family blood-ties. There's the eye of the sun's blood-sacrifice. Carola's diseased blood-royal. Spilled blood, the war. The demons. Hot blood: the acts of passion. And innocent blood.'

Her teasing tone vanished. She turned her head sideways to catch sight of the man's face.

'No . . . No. What it comes down to is what he did and what I did.'

Wind whipped at her braids. The coach stopped some ten yards from the gallows in a press of bodies. Horses snorted; the driver tied up the reins.

William Harvey put a white-gloved hand up to block his cheek from daylight. Disguising shadow moved across his features. He muttered acerbically, 'It's cost me six shillings for this coach, and a shilling each for men to help carry a body. Where's your giant – what's his name – Baltazar Casaubon?'

She rubbed at a full breast, cupping her hand over her doublet. 'With Jared and the baby.'

'You've left a man like that to protect your children? He looked nothing of a swordsman to me.'

'To tell you the truth, he *isn't* much good with a sword. He's not built for it. It's like asking him to play tennis with a knitting-needle. Now if we still had battle-axes . . .' She chuckled, breath huffing the bitter air. 'The times I've seen him in a fight, he's usually hit someone with the nearest blunt object. Last time it was a seven-foot, six-inch mahogany dining-table.'

'I see.' William Harvey blinked bead-black eyes.

'If I thought anyone could touch my baby I'd . . .'

'And Guillaime? The woman was something to you, you say. And you're trying to free her murderer?'

'I said once, *I hurt her*. Maybe this is to spite her. She dared to die. But I think . . .' The White Crow grinned fiercely. One hand hooked into the coach's door handle; she reached up for the iron grip to pull herself up to the roof. '. . . I *know* I've stopped caring why. I'll give you the signal. Be ready.'

Houses gave way to open fields. Mothers held up children for the touch of his hand.

Bobbing heads and backs stretched out in front of the cart. Tall, rickety galleries jutted up in the fields where two roads crossed: south to Edgware, west to Oxford. Pennants unfolded into the cold wind. He gripped the cart-rail. Bright-painted coaches, shabby in this amnesty season, crowded the flat ground by the scaffold; coachmen swearing as they sought to walk the horses against the cold, or else cover them in thick blankets.

His head jolted up. He stared across milling crowds: royalist colour and Protectorate black, focused on one face.

The woman sat on a level with him, on the roof of a stationary coach. Her booted feet dangled down. Tan hose, brown leather breeches and doublet, with the studs glinting silver in the afternoon sunlight; a cloak bundled up where she sat. One tan-sallow hand, uncovered, pushed at her cinnamon hair.

'I had her *twice*, you cunt!' He slammed his fist down on the cart-rail, voice booming. 'She'd be a better fuck dead than you would living!'

Cold or spite whitened Valentine Roseveare's face, drew it into a scrunched contraction of eyes and mouth. Her arms folded about her thin body. Stubborn, silent, she held herself aloof from the men and women who shrieked drunkenly around the coach and team of four. The horses stamped.

The note of wheels changed, from cobbles' hardness to snow, trodden to ice and covered with thrown-down bales of straw. He gripped the rail again as the cart lurched from side to side. The old man moaned, stinking of fear and excrement. Phillip Nashe murmured compassionate, inaudible words.

Tyburn's three-legged mare stood stark against sun and sky.

Stripped chestnut, knocked solidly together with iron nails – three upright posts, set at the points of a triangle, and three crossbars connecting them. The platform at the height of a man's head. Two old-and-rotted ends of rope hung down from the nearer crossbar, the ends cut and frayed and weathered.

The cart rocked, halted. Nashe leaped down, joined by his bearded assistant. Pollexfen Calmady stared up at the sky. Used to waiting, used to delays and substitutions; hearing finally the noise that four or five thousand men and women make. He lowered his gaze. Two more white hempen ropes dangled from the wood, each knotted into a noose.

He climbed down from the cart, planks chill against him, as Phillip Nashe hurried back across the straw-covered slush; and walked up the wooden steps to the platform. The elderly thief staggered behind, the hangman's arm under his, holding him up.

One trap swung to and fro, creaking, open.

The bearded assistant stepped back to haul it up. Pollexfen Calmady stared down from the platform at the front row of the crowd. Forty or so gentlemen-mercenaries of other companies reeled, drunken, at the elbows of his own troop. Lacey, Rule, Gadsbury, Linebaugh . . . one face missing. Piss-drunk; all their gear furbished up new for the spring campaign.

A harvest field of faces beyond; hundreds, perhaps thousands for this one of the year's eight hanging-days; some heads turned aside, talking; some chewing, shouting; vendors threading paths to sell hot chestnuts; young men and women clinging to the sides of makeshift stands; all taut, wild, anticipating.

'Listen to me, my children.'

He raised his voice, pitching it to carry beyond the company. Quiet spread. He jerked his head at the branded old man vomiting over Phillip Nashe's arm.

'I am brought here with another, who is to hang after me, and

you see what a sorry spectacle he is. Shortly I shall hang with him –
and then you shall see a pair of spectacles.'

Crowd-laughter hissed: breath whitening the air, rising in the
cold afternoon. His shoulders lifted, his spine straightening. Pollexfen Calmady: gruff-voiced, haranguing.

'We say, wedding and hanging go by destiny . . . Here am I
dressed in white, come to make a hanging-match with my bride.
Commonly a man is stiff after the wedding ceremony and certainly
this day I shall be stiff after mine.'

Two or three dozen men cheered among the laughter. Pollexfen
Calmady held up a gloved hand.

'You all know I hang for congress with a young woman, afterwards dead. She met the same death then that I meet now. And
since it is because of her that I die, you may truly say when you see
me: here hangs a man who died for love.'

Cold wind whipped his cheek, carrying their flood of sound to
ebb and to high-tide. Exhilarated, he planted his fists on his hips.

'I am brought here today to make a match. The bride has a
something wooden look to her. Her embraces commonly prove
fatal. Perhaps that is why the wedding-bells ring so dolefully
yonder. I've heard it said: gain a wife and lose a life. So all take
heed and love your single life while you have it.'

He swallowed. Cold air drying his throat, he reached a hand
down and took the bottle that Gadsbury tossed up; drank, acknowledged the raw, baying cheer with a lift of that bottle, and threw it
back.

Phillip Nashe stepped forward. 'You do them the honour of a
good ending. They only want to see you kick on air and turn black
now.'

'Let 'em wait one more minute.' He drew breath. The same pit-
stomach fear and excitement attendant on massacres after battles
shone on the faces below the platform. Raucous shouts assaulted
from all sides, prompts, suggestions; filling his sudden silence.

'I see the hangman hankers to his trade, to make me one flesh
with the cold clay, so I'll delay no longer. It is no groom's privilege
to come late to his own wedding, and I fear this bride will not
grant me that favour herself. But you may see, in plain view, the
wedding-ring provided, although I'll wager it's a close fit.'

Clotted humanity filled up the spaces between coaches and
stands, bare-headed or with hats pulled down against the cold,
men and women with breath steaming; forgetting now that they
carried bottles of spirit or hot pasties and chestnuts, mouths gaping,
all their eyes on him.

The noose, stark against the sky, danced at the edge of his vision. Phillip Nashe reached up. Calmady stretched out his arms.

'I am not come here to marry but to die. I come in this suit because, led into gross errors as I have been, this is the day that makes me white and clean. This is my soul's wedding day, wed with grace and justice and Judgement. And in the marriage bed I go to, I lie down with righteousness and I rise up with mercy. Of this, I have certain assurance!'

Hemp rope scratched his cheek, its stiff strands drawing blood from skin fragile in the bitter air. Arms clamped around his shoulders and biceps.

Phillip Nashe nodded, shooting a glance past his head to the assistant; his sallow hands stretching the noose with calm deliberation. Pollexfen Calmady jerked his head back.

'I'm not finished!'

The two men grabbed: he wrenched from side to side.

'No!'

The hangman's arms passed under his flailing arms. Strong-fingered hands locked across the back of his neck. His scalp stung suddenly cold, periwig knocked off and kicked down from the platform, trodden into the slush. He struggled, dragged bodily back from the Tyburn ladder. Jeers and stones and snow flew.

'No! Please!'

Wood slammed the side of his face. A long splinter jabbed his lip. He slumped against Nashe, stunned, pain a solid taste of copper in his mouth.

Tears leaked from his eyes. The wind from the north cut across the fields through white coat and shirt to shivering flesh; scalded his bare, shaved head.

'*No!*'

He shouted, bewildered, spittle flying; the two men gripping his body and dragging him back, heels hacking the frost-slippery planks. Bladder and bowel let go and he soiled himself.

'Please, I'm not ready! *Please, don't kill me!*'

Scarlet: scarlet at the edge of vision: a boy whose yellow curls fall to the shoulders of an over-large red coat, who wears an apprentice-surgeon's sash; standing whitefaced among a crowd on a knoll—

His eyes lock with the boy's. Bevil Calmady.

The White Crow hacked her heel twice on the coach roof: hollow impacts. She slid rapidly on heels, buttocks, and one hand; scabbarded sword clamped up under one arm; and let herself down

off the back of the coach and into the saddle of the hired brown
mare. Her gloved fingers fumbled the rein's cold straps.

She swore, hooked the second mount's reins over her saddle-
horn, and lay leather across the mare's neck. The mount plodded
sluggishly into the crowd. Men and women backed without looking, all their attention on the gallows-tree.

The beast's body rocked her: she clamped her knees tight. Over
heads, bare or wearing low-crowned and wide-brimmed hats, the
ragged plumes of the gentlemen-mercenaries bobbed. She felt in
her breeches' pocket, drew her arm back, and skimmed a pebble
accurately.

It struck her target. She dipped her hand. The cloak's hood fell
forward. She glanced back over her shoulder. The coach-blind
snicked up to disclose Sir William Harvey's powdered hair and
small face.

'*Surgeons!*'

Gadsbury's voice: hoarse with outrage and brandy. The mare
backed a pace, another pace; the crowd surged, one man swore, and
a child shrieked. Rule's shocked voice bellowed: 'Surgeons! Anato-
mists!'

Bright metal gleamed: rose, dropped. A flurry of screams and
shouting went up. People jerked back from the mercenaries.

She wrapped the spare mount's reins around her right hand,
backing the mare away. Arbella Lacey stumbled, threw an arm
across the Margrave Linebaugh's shoulder; both forcing through
the press towards Harvey's coach. The coach began to back. A high
voice screamed. One man, two, a dozen: all backing and pushing.

Level now with the gallows platform, she raised her eyes to
Tyburn's three beams: stark against the blue, hazed sky. The White
Crow leaned forward and took a long-barrelled pistol from the
saddle-holster. Bodies banged against her legs. The mare whickered.
The gunsight, soot-black, bobbed as she sighted along her arm:
fired.

Concussion deafened. Her arm and hand stung.

Chips of wood spanged off the back of the coach.

'Surgeons!'

'Bodystealers!'

She heaved on the mare's mouth. The horse swung, pressing
against the solid body of people, head tossing; hooves shifting
uneasily on slush and straw.

Crowd-pressure broke, one woman pushing past, a clear space,
men running; ten yards away the coach dipped over with a scream
of wood, one high wheel in a rut; whipshots from the carrier: the

team heaving free, clattering, the coach bouncing up; fifty, a hundred men and women running towards it.

'*Riot!*'

The White Crow raised her head. Frost-dark steps went up beside her. Her knee banged the edge of the wooden platform painfully. Silhouetted against the sky, two men held Calmady in a straining, solid grip. A hemp loop swung.

The elderly, branded man slipped down from the platform's far side; threw himself into the crowd, vanished.

'—*arrest in the Queen's na*—'

Screams and shouts deafened. Officers with staves spurred down towards William Harvey's coach, hard on its way to Oxford Street. She sat calmly in the frosty air; the taste of gunpowder sour on her lips. Women and men running in pursuit, arms flailing; stones curving across the bright sky; the smash of breaking wood, children squalling.

A short-haired girl of twelve screamed, pushed up against the platform steps. The White Crow locked eyes with her.

The child's mouth squared, screaming; tears ran down her dirty face.

'Help me!'

The White Crow dug heels into the mare's side, pushing the barrel-body against the mass of women and men; easing pressure on the trapped girl. 'Help for help. Give me your hand.'

'Help *meee*—'

'Your hand: *now*.'

Seconds or minutes? Bobbing heads hid the vanishing coach; staves rose and fell towards Oxford Street. In the open spaces men and women milled about, shouting. She jumped at another shot, stark across the afternoon cold.

The two men held Pollexfen Calmady bent over double. The blond-bearded man twisted both of Calmady's arms up behind his back; the dark, smaller man wrested the hemp rope over his shaved head; made a grab for the trap-lever.

Seconds. The White Crow grinned, fierce, riding it; riding the cessation of time that comes with action; all the time in the world now, if everything's done on the instant, and so—

Sir William Harvey and the decoy coach drawing off crowds, the riot well in progress, she leaned forward again to the open saddle bags. Paper rustled as she moved. A thin strip of parchment, inked over with hastily written sigils, wound around her wrist and thumb, pinned with a silver pin.

With that hand she drew out a greasy playing-card.

The winter sunlight gleamed on the oblong of pasteboard. Pale inks delineated the old image. A spear, whose iron tip bleeds stylised droplets of blood. Below the head, the dead wooden shaft sprouts a small green leaf. *Ace of Lances.*

'I would do this myself.'

She edged the mare between bodies and gallows-steps. The yellow-haired girl in layers of black rags bawled square-mouthed, deep shuddering breaths racking her with hysteria. The White Crow leaned down from the saddle, grabbed one of the hands that clamped across her face, and dug her fingers in hard.

'Ow!' The girl yelled.

'I would do this myself, but I'm going to need both hands later. Hold this. No: *hold it*. Trust me.'

A shaking, chilblained hand gripped the card.

The White Crow pressed the small hand against the side of the gallows-steps, the Ace of Lances flattened between the girl's palm and the wood. She reached behind to her left hip, drew her Italian stiletto, positioned it, and slammed the thin blade down between bone and tendon.

'*Aaahhhhh!*'

Screams ripped out of the child's throat. Her free hand lashed the horse's belly, clawed White Crow's boot. All around her eyes the skin showed fish-belly white. Shrieks split the air.

The White Crow put two fingers against the back of the child's hand, dabbling in the trickle of blood. She drew three short strokes on the wooden rail of the steps. She gripped the girl's wrist, took the stiletto out with one pull, and slammed the knife back to pin the blood-stained card to the wood.

A hard jerk shifted her in the saddle; she let go the child's wrist as the girl's teeth met in her hand; wrenched her gloved flesh away, swearing; and half-slipped, one foot losing a stirrup.

Screaming, sobbing, in shock, the child fell back into the churned slush under the wooden steps.

The White Crow sat back hard in the saddle. Her chilled foot found the stirrup, boot-toe knocking against the wooden framework of the steps. She shifted her sword and scabbard to lie across her lap. Wet straw, cordite, and urine: the air stank.

'Calmady!'

Bitter wind cut between her cloak-hood and ruff. The hood slipped down. She brought her left hand up to her teeth, tugging off the thick glove. The glove fell to the ground, the mare trampling it among discarded food, broken plumes, a lost shoe. The wind brought tears trickling from the corners of her eyes.

She leaned forward and spat. Saliva spattered the pinned card, trickling across the wet blood and the ink image. Bare-handed, she smudged the sigil's final line.

Wood creaked.

A scent drifted across her nostrils. All the muscles in her back relaxed. She sat easy in the saddle, the scent of cut grass in the wind.

The cold air shimmered.

A furnace-blast of heat hit. The mare's head lifted; the spare mount neighed and threw up its head, jerking the rein tied to the saddle-horn. Timber groaned, creaked, as ships do in deep waters, as woods do in a high wind.

The split, stripped chestnut darkened.

Green pinpoints ran the length of the step-rail, spread onto the platform, spread under the feet of Pollexfen Calmady and the Queen's Hangman and the hangman's assistant; green specks budding into knots of lime-colour, unfurling into tiny, pale-green leaves; sprouting, green nubs rising and lengthening, and the folded-down new leaves unfolding umbrella-upwards into the palmate sprays of chestnut foliage.

She plunged her arms across the edge of the platform into twigs. New wood scratched her skin, her face. The White Crow stood up in the stirrups; shouting, wordless, wild.

The blond-bearded assistant leapt back. His legs and feet lifted, no sooner touching the impossible leaves but he leaped up again; staggering back, mouth widely open, yelling; he fell from the back of the gallows platform. His body thudded down into straw.

'*Calmady, damn you!*'

The Queen's Hangman, arms above his head, wrestled white hemp rope down.

Fibres split, greening, twining; winding tendrils up against the hazed blue sky. Sweat and effort reddened the man's cheeks. The rope, unwoven, living grass, fell apart in his hands.

'Calmady! *Here!*'

The Queen's Hangman stood among sprouting twigs, all the platform a mass of five-fingered chestnut leaves. Each upright post twisted, new brown bark wrinkling across it; green shade dappled from the crossbeams, rustling with thick foliage. The hangman slowly began to strip off his tan-and-white long coat, standing in his shirt-sleeves.

The White Crow wiped sweat from her cheeks.

The mare whickered, lifting mobile lips and nostrils to scent at the new leaves. Its brown eyes rolled. The spare mount, a large-boned grey gelding, dipped and shook its head, uneasy. She unknotted the reins from the saddle-horn.

Swearing, his white coat catching and ripping on stout twigs, Pollexfen Calmady thrashed to the edge of the gallows platform.

The cold straps crumpled in her fist. She leaned up and threw the reins of the spare mount. He dropped to his knees among sprouting green leaves, big-knuckled hands scrabbling. Winter sun slanted among leaves. Silver lace and brocade blazed.

The curling wig gone, his shaved head exposed, Calmady's features stood out with brutal emphasis. Afternoon light shadowed deep creases around his nose and mouth. His ears jutted, prominent against his cropped scalp; muscles shifted across the breadth of his shoulders and back.

'Move!' She reined in, backing the mare.

Pollexfen Calmady lurched forward, belly-down across the gelding's saddle. He swung powerful legs up; his white breeches and coat now green-stained. Sweat trickled down his face. He panted. He reached across and ripped a chestnut switch from the new wood; buttocks firmly in the saddle, knees gripping; and slashed the gelding's haunches.

The White Crow wheeled, hacked heels into the mare's ribs, bowled two men over, galloping on uncertain ground, new icy wind slapping her face; all surprise, all speed, all instant flight.

CHAPTER 12

The gallows posts root.

Canopies of leaves lift from three new, rooted chestnut trees. The winter light through their leaves is pale, all the bright colours of green made into a fineness as of stained glass.

Staves thunk down across heads, shoulders, raised arms; sheriff's officers riding hard across the wake of the coach that now swings into the first houses and alleys off Oxford Street, the acerbic man clinging to the interior handgrips, swearing all the way.

A woman kneels, face stretched in a mask of pain, cradling a broken arm. Arbella Lacey squats down to help, ripping her brocade coat, that is smeared with slush and horse-dung, to use as an impromptu sling.

Two men carry a hurdle: on it, the trampled body of a third.

In the shadow of a platform become roots, a twelve-year-old girl curls up foetally, squalling; her mouth pressed to the back of her hand. Blood drips and soaks her black, torn coat.

A last breath of green warmth drifts over Tyburn fields.

'Did you enjoy it, the second time you had her, sober?'

Pollexfen Calmady eased in the saddle.

'Yes.'

'Were you sorry when she died?'

His face creased into an expression of contagious irony. 'When it seemed I should die to atone for it, I was repentant. Now that it seems I'll live, I find myself growing reconciled to the fact.'

'Ride.'

She said no other word for fifteen minutes. No noise but the beat of hooves on frozen ground, hard riding, and the whip of leafless branches to avoid: voices shouting, a distant shot.

'*Now*.'

She swung into cover in a copse at the edge of the Park. Dirty snow clung to trunks and twigs. Ahead, smoke breathed from chimneys. Her cheeks ached with the grin that, do what she would, stayed on her face.

'Leave the hired hacks to find their way back to the stables.'

She took Pollexfen Calmady's shoulder in her hand as he dismounted and came to peer out from cover.

'It'll be seen fast enough that snow keeps us from leaving town.' Her fingers dug into the white cloth of his coat. 'And so we must have turned back into town, which we have; and for the next I count on their thoughts running in an old track. Which is, that all criminals and fugitives take refuge in the stews of Northbankside, and to that there's but one way: the only bridge across Thamys, at Southwark.'

The big man blinked dazed eyes. 'They'll have set guards on the bridge by now and we're four miles away. Do we steal a boat—'

The White Crow turned her head so that her braids flew, cold hair stinging her cheeks. She shook him gently.

'All the Thamys is a bridge now! Ten minutes directly north of here, at Westminster, we can cross the ice and be in Northbankside, safely lost.'

The Protector looked up from her desk at Humility Talbot.

'We have six who claim bastardy by the godless woman's father.' Talbot folded his hands together against the Tower room's chill.

'Try their blood separately over the next six days. Omitting the sabbath, of course.' Olivia turned back to her papers. It became apparent that the man waited. She lifted bulbous, placid features.

'General.' Humility Talbot protested. 'You know my skill in architecture is scant. Too much knowledge of the Black Art of Geometry corrupts the soul. But even I can tell that a temple consecrated with bastard blood is no temple but an abomination!'

'A temple is a temple,' Olivia said tranquilly. 'I have no intention, neither, of letting the godless woman Carola use a failure of ours as steps to her own success. Do as I order.'

The last, said kindly, brought a flush to his pale cheeks.

'Take these as you go.' She held out a scroll of plans. Visible on one edge, neat inkwork lettered: ST SOPHIA REBUILDING PROJECT. 'They'll serve to kindle a fire in the outer room.'

Breath burned in her lungs, chest tight from exertion. The White Crow ran across herb-gardens, their surfaces nothing but lumpy snow; the paths' deep mud frozen and crackling under her boots. She leaped a fence to the embankment and ducked into a jetty's shelter.

Blue sky, fire-coloured to the west, spread out in a huge arc. Tall, tilted houses looked down on a slope that, in summer, would be stinking mud; the jutting piers and steps weed-shrouded. Now foot-tracked snow covered the banks and abandoned wherries of the Thamys.

Spars of wood and thrown bricks starred the ice that, ridged and rippled and deeper than the houses' height, gleamed black under the crusting snow. Voices rasped her nerves with their nearness.

Deliberately, she did not look back. Running the risk on the knife-edge, aware, alert; the White Crow smiled as Pollexfen Calmady plodded through knee-deep snow and into the jetty's shelter.

'Northbankside.'

Five hundred yards distant, across flat and exposed ice, the clustered tenements smudged the winter air with smoke. A little downriver the spires of Lambeth Palace jutted up. She cast a glance back over her shoulder. A mess of tiny alleys ran down from Westminster to the river houses here.

'It was as well, perhaps, to dress in white.' She slid the leather cloak from her shoulders, reversing it to show the undyed wool lining. 'You—'

Almost forgotten: who stands beside her. Almost forgotten, almost taken to be one of the Scholar-Soldiers who, in other days, shared other escapes. The shock of seeing his creased, sweating face made her head sing.

The gentleman-mercenary looked up at the sky.

She snarled. 'Damn, there used not to be sentries at Westminster but I don't know now: *move!*'

The winter sun shone on his shaved head, skin blotched red and blue with cold. He took three strides down onto the embankment, staring across the frozen river. Hurriedly she swung the cloak about her shoulders and followed.

His shoulder struck her a glancing blow.

She swore, staggered ankle-deep in fresh snow; grabbed to steady herself, and fell straddling a broken oar, frozen into the mud.

The big man sprawled on his knees, his head bowed. '*Have mercy upon me, O God, according to they loving-kindness: according unto the multitude of thy tender mercies blot out my transgressions.*'

His bass voice boomed, resonant.

'Oh, Lord.' The White Crow wrenched her knee and leg out of the snow, shivering, and slipped down beside him. 'Now's a fine time to think of the Hanging Psalm. *Captain!*'

Metal scraped scabbard.

A glimpse of blue cloth against blackened timbers: the tall soldier in redingote and plumed hat strode out of one alley. Cavalry boots crunched slush. His long sabre sliced sunlight. She in that one instant caught his eyes, bright with cold, registering the kneeling man all in white. The soldier opened his mouth, beard rimed with frozen breath.

'Hold! I arrest you in the Queen's name!'

She appeared to stumble, rising from beside the kneeling man; drew her sword a fraction of a moment after the soldier raised his; stepped forward to engage and threw the handful of gathered ice into his eyes. She parried his thrust away one-handed, metal showering sparks; bashed his blade down; recovered a two-handed grip on her hilt and chopped an axe-blow up at his throat.

Explosive: hot, salt-wet liquid splashed her face and breast and shirt. She dripped red. His body's weight pulled her forward. She braced, tugging the blade back, wrist jarred by contact with jaw and skull-bones. He slumped awkwardly on the frozen bank, head fallen back. Pierced jugular spouted rhythmically, dying to a dribble.

Hot wetness chilled. She coughed, choking on the butcher's-shop stink. She pulled her doublet and shirt away from her body, wiped hopelessly at her breeches.

Blood dried taut on her skin.

She knelt and cleaned her blade on the dead man's lace ruffles. His body cooled.

Snow, melted in her hands, ran red. She rinsed her face. The chill cut bone-deep. She wiped her boots with handfuls of snow, dabbed at stained shirt and abandoned the idea; and straightened to face the cold wind and the bright sun.

More distant voices: urgent.

She stooped again and went through the soldier's pockets. Empty. A farthing lurked in the last, among fluff; she held it for a second and then threw it down to sparkle, bronze, on his chest.

His wig tipped back off his head into the snow; disclosing a young face, a scalp furred with baby-fine stubble.

Every muscle shaking, she turned. Pollexfen Calmady stood, barely risen to his feet. Blood soaked into the slush-ridged embankment. She guided the tip of her blade to the sheath with her other hand and snicked it home.

'*Deliver me from blood-guiltiness, O God, thou God of my salvation—*'
Light moved on his face between his nose and cheek. The tear ran down and dropped. Calmady bent and picked up the dead soldier's

sabre. He shouldered past the White Crow, boots skidding as he crabbed down the river bank to the ice.

'I had as soon he'd lived. It was too sudden and I too unsure.'

Her words lost themselves flatly in stinging cold air. She snatched up her cloak, bundled it over her reddened clothes; scrambling for the Thamys ice with the sound of other sentries' calls echoing behind.

'Why should we run, go into exile?' The swarthy woman smiled. 'Will you not fight for us if we stay?'

More soberly than one might have expected, Sir Denzil Waldegrave said, 'Men will fight for your Majesty. Not win – the rebellious forces are too strong. But not entirely lose either. Bloody battles if you stay, madam.'

'Would you have us abandon our father's kingdom?'

Carola laughed, lazily, and rolled over among silk sheets and ruffled the boy's hair. Denzil avoided his son's eyes, glimpsing that young man's nakedness under the cloth.

'We have it in mind to hold a masque.'

He frowned. 'Excellent device, your Majesty, had we but the money.'

'A masque . . . upon Thamys, we think, the while it remains frozen. We will have the ice carven into fantastic shapes, and ways to bring fires out into midriver without danger – to moor balloons, perhaps, and suspend fires from them? And then to feast there, we think, a week and more; and then to hold the masque with such costumes, jewels, paint, and musicianry as was never seen before . . . The scenery itself carved from ice! Commission young poets to write it.'

Sir Denzil Waldegrave lifted his comfit-box and selected a sweetmeat. He stared past the swarthy woman, through the window, towards the sun on the frozen river.

'As your Majesty desires. I . . . forgive me, these poets, cooks, bakers, mechanics; all will demand hard coin. There's no more credit to be had in this city. I tried for that when it came to refurbishing the ordnance for this spring.'

Regina Carola chuckled deep in her throat.

'We have the money. What, man, don't look so amazed. We are this land's monarch, and some are loyal still . . . We have six thousand guineas. We will devise this masque ourselves. Now hurry! And it shall be called – yes – *The Masque of the Contention between Abstinence and Desire.*'

*

Walls of frozen snow bashed her shoulders as she stumbled down the narrow, lumpy corridor. The sky made a pale ribbon above her head. Deep trenches crisscrossed the Thamys: footpaths worn down and buttressed up through the snow that, where untouched, lay the height of a man on top of the river's black ice.

The edge of the inside-out cloak hood rasped her cheek. The White Crow scratched at her face with fingers whose nails were rimmed brown-red. The cold numbed hands, face, feet. Rounded ice betrayed her steps. She staggered, shoulders tense.

Pollexfen Calmady's breath echoed in the trench behind her. She spared one glance to see that he kept his head down. The brief sight showed her no glimpse of the far-distant bank, invisible above the ice-trenches. She must assume soldiers outdistanced and North-bankside scant yards ahead.

'Here!'

The trench shallowed, opening up ahead of her. Late sun, pure and clear as honey, shone on the backs of tenement houses. Practised, her eye picked out the safe path to them, the path in cover – from concealing trench to pier to walled river bank, where frost-damaged masonry sprawled in collapse.

'Even if they can cross, that's useless to them. This place is a maze! But wait.'

She moved up a few yards, crouching in the shelter of the shallow trench, the trodden-down snow giving under her. A glance behind showed Westminster distant and deserted. For a moment no cold seeped through. Her breath feathered the air. A breathing, warm body shouldered down beside her. She gazed up, taking him in from slush-blackened boots to disarranged shirt. His lace cravat had burst open and now trailed down his half-unbuttoned coat, his chest heaving. A mutual campaigners' conspiracy ignored the stink of shit.

She stared with nothing to say, almost shy: the man momentarily become again a stranger.

'I conceive it possible we'll fight now.' Captain Pollexfen Calmady handled the dead cavalryman's sabre. 'No?'

'No.'

'Why not?'

'Not because of Desire Guillaime. And not because of Casaubon. And not even because I've got two children and know your feelings for Bevil and his for you. And not because of fear.'

'That last I credit. The first I don't apprehend.'

She hacked one heel at the river's dirty, thick ice. Cold gnawed at her feet and fingers and earlobes, reddened her cheeks, fired all her blood.

Away across the white expanse behind them a tiny flame flared. Seconds after, the shot's echo sounded. Speculative fire. She drew the reversed cloak about her, the undyed wool lining merging into the colours of snow. Half-dry and half-damp shirt cloth crackled.

'Once I had to nurse a sick man in a little room. He died. Everything outside that room seemed to fade away. We were insulated, away from the rest of life.' She shrugged. 'What goes on inside that room is pure, if you like, but it has very little to do with our decisions outside it. Being born and dying are the givens. They're what happens, that's all.'

Now she smiled.

'I would be a liar *now* if I pretended that I cared for Desire Guillaime any more than you do. I have my guilt. Killing you – that would just be rank hypocrisy.'

The man brushed snow from his white-dirty sleeves as one might flick away thread or ash.

'You don't know that you could kill me. I would gamble, myself. You see, I have no regrets.'

She broke cover, loping towards the shelter of the pier. No shouts. His footsteps and breathing sounded at her back. She picked her way cautiously up the icy river steps and into the cover of a dockside wall, among timbered houses.

Here voices sounded from behind closed doors, the noise of song, drinking, eating; pigs in their pens grunting for scarce scraps, and the tarred bodies of malefactors hung in chains chanting their confessions. Four or five alleys led away into Northbankside's stews. And Casaubon and Jared and the baby where?

She turned her head.

'Nor I—'

Only an empty river bank: Pollexfen Calmady gone.

The thirty-year-old woman scratched at her aching, full breasts, irritated by the dried blood. She stared into empty air.

Downriver.

Into a hazed white void, edged with the city. Frozen water. Whitehall's distant spires. The ragged scaffolding of the eye of the sun. And, furthest, the forest of bare masts at the docks, pointing towards the sea.

The open sea.

The last of the afternoon sun cut a bright line across chimney-stacks and snow-covered roofs. She shrugged her cloak off and reversed it to its proper side, drew her blade to carry loosely in her left hand, and walked at random into the frozen alleyways. Her steps, slow at first, quickened. Before she had gone a hundred yards she began to sing under her breath.

SHORT BIBLIOGRAPHY

ACKERMAN, James S., *Palladio* (Penguin, 1966).

ANDERSON, William, *The Rise of the Gothic* (Hutchinson, 1985).

BARTON, Anne, *Ben Jonson, Dramatist* (Cambridge University Press, 1984).

BUDGE, Wallis, *Egyptian Magic* (Kegan Paul, Trench, Trübner, 1899).

DAVIES, Natalie Zemon, *Society and Culture in Early Modern France*, Polity Press edn (1975).

EVANS, E. P., *The Criminal Prosecution and Capital Punishment of Animals* (William Heinemann, 1906).

FRENCH, John, *John Dee* (Routledge & Kegan Paul, 1972).

GARSTIN, E. J. Langford (ed.), *The Rosicrucian Secrets: Dr John Dee* (Aquarian Press, 1985).

HONOUR, Hugh, *Neo-Classicism* (Penguin, 1977).

HORNE, Alexander, *King Soloman's Temple in the Masonic Tradition* (Aquarian Press, 1972).

McINTOSH, Christopher, *The Rosicrucians*.

——, *The Rosy Cross Unveiled* (Aquarian Press, 1980).

McNEIL, William H., *Plagues and Peoples* (Penguin, 1976).

MUMFORD, Lewis, *The City in History* (Penguin, 1961).

SCOTT, Walter, *Hermetica*, Vol. 1 (Boston, Mass.: Shambala, 1985).

SEZNEC, Jean, *The Survival of the Pagan Gods* (Princeton, NJ: Princeton University Press, 1940).

SHEARMAN, John, *Mannerism* (Penguin, 1967).

STRONG, Roy, *The Renaissance Garden in England* (Thames & Hudson, 1979).

VITRUVIUS, *The Ten Books on Architecture*, trans. Morris Hicky Morgan (New York: Dover Publications, 1914).

YATES, Frances, *Giordano Bruno and the Hermetic Tradition* (Routledge & Kegan Paul, 1964).

——, *The Occult Philosophy in the Elizabethan Age* (Routledge & Kegan Paul, 1979).

——, *The Rosicrucian Enlightenment* (Routledge & Kegan Paul, 1972).

——, *Theatre of the World* (Routledge & Kegan Paul, 1969).